COMMANDING FLAME AND SHIELD

REVISED SECOND EDITION

GRAYSHELL RISING

S.J. BARNETT

COMMANDING FLAME AND SHIELD

AUTHOR'S NOTE

"A truly great library contains something in it to offend everyone."
- *Jo Goodwin*

This book is intended for adult audiences and is <u>not</u> suitable for readers under 18 years of age.

THIS BOOK HAS BEEN REVISED FROM ITS ORIGINAL EDITION, AND WILL NOT SYNC WITH THE AUDIOBOOK

As of today (9/27/24), the first edition of my debut novel (this beautiful book) has received over 540 reviews, and all I can say, from the bottom of my heart, is thank you.

Thank you to my incredible readers, who poured life into me and fell in love with this world, in its rawest form. Who overlooked the simple mistakes of a baby author with limited resources and fell in love with the characters and premise.

That first edition was self-edited with a friend, and I can honestly say I never anticipated the love you all would shower it in.

In the nearly two years since I first published *CFAS*, I have grown leaps and bounds as a writer and finally assembled a professional team worth their salt. It was with that in mind that we decided to revise—*cutting nearly* **seven thousand** *words* from the original manuscript—and polish her up to the best of our ability *while preserving the plot* and core columns of the story.

As the sequel is already published, and books 3-5 are well under way, it was **mostly** a deep dive on technicalities, but *a couple of original scenes were cut* and/or combined for the sake of pacing, but I feel like this baby will shine all the more for it.

Grayshell came to me in a dream in 2009, and in the more than decade since, the visions of this world poured out and solidified into life and color, and I'm so grateful they're finally on paper. Much of the original manuscript was first drafted when I was in high school and then gathered dust until I brought it to life in 2020-2021.

The characters in the **first** book are predominately—*though not exclusively*—Christian, and while they're incredibly flawed people who love and make mistakes like the rest of us, they make a valiant effort to fight for that paradigm while other characters, the world, and their circumstances challenge their faith. Religious themes are naturally interwoven in their world (they are half angels fighting demonic forces, after all).

If you have religious trauma, know that we do too, but this piece of them was so integral it had to stay. I know how deeply those wounds can go and did my best not to allow my own history with church hurt to overshadow the adventure of their world. When Alvara and the crew first came to me as strongly-rooted Christians, I was more than a little curious as to where their story would go. As a writer, I'm a firm believer that it is my job to be their vessel and not their dictator, so I ran with it.

That being said, throughout the *Grayshell* series, **we will also meet 'hierarchies' that <u>don't share</u>** this set of beliefs and come with all of their own flavor, spirituality, traditions, and natural conflicts. If indulging in a wide variety of beliefs, character psyches, and thought processes isn't something you're comfortable with, this series might not be for you.

If, however, your mind is open to watch this wild world, I am pleased to introduce you to the *Grayshell Rising* series.

Xoxo-SJB

YOUR MENTAL HEALTH MATTERS.

This book contains content that may not be suitable for all readers, including, but not limited to: blood, gore, and death, gratuitous violence, torture, explicit sexual thoughts and scenes, reincarnation, alcohol use, mention of drug use, vampirism, soul groups, fantastical romanticization of the nephilim, psychic activity, elemental magic, decapitation, implied suicide, death of a loved one, mention of rape, hostage situation, panic attacks, demonic ceremony, possession and exorcism, resurrection, extensive religious and spiritual themes, prayers, and christian traditions, anti-religious rhetoric and discussion, eternal mates, and an abundance of foul language...

If any of the listed elements may negatively impact your mental health, thank you for considering Commanding Flame and Shield, and deciding instead to honor your own well being.

This one is for my mama bird.
You made me promise to dance, even if I was breaking. To get up...just one.
More. Time. Ten years after you earned your wings, I'm doing the damn
thing.
Loving you always.
Until we meet again.

ONE
LOST SOUL
ALVARA

My temples ached as I scoured the broad room, searching for his scent, energy, or anything that could lead us to him. But with all its musty aromas, this cluttered shop was full of distractions and secrets—just not the ones we sought.

Dust glittered in a ray of sunlight that sliced through the gloom, but my attention caught on to something beyond it. The piano's honey-colored wood showed blatant age, and the worn keys looked so loved that they might break under my touch.

I walked to the corner where it sat, a smile on my face before my fingers even connected with its weathered surface. My favorite part of my clairvoyant existence was my gift to read history within objects.

I pulled my long hair back into a bun at the nape of my neck and took a cleansing breath.

The instant I caressed the intricate Victorian design engraved on the instrument's side, my eyes were forced closed, and they plunged me into the piece's demanding energy, witnessing flashes of its story.

Dozens of balls, pirouetting figures vanishing into smoke on either side...A grandmother's foyer, where her children and grandchildren gathered to watch, enamored, as her wrinkled hands flew across the black and white keys...Young children—her grandbabies perhaps, now grown a few years—learning to play at the side of a woman bearing a striking resemblance to the grandmother, minus a few decades.

Eyes open once more, I slowly stepped around the corner of the piano, hands sliding onto the keys.

Ahh.

There it was. Thousands, perhaps millions of melodies broke free in my mind, and I slowed them down, rewinding and fast-forwarding until the tunes were intelligible enough to pull apart and truly appreciate.

"Can I help you, ma'am?" asked a voice with a hint of impatience.

The intrusion abruptly and rudely snapped me from my reverie, forcing me to yank my hand away from the tantalizing energy.

Sometimes, it was easy to lose track of time as I danced through visions and histories. Humans were sensitive to people holding too still for any prolonged period, assuming we were suffering a stroke or panic attack rather than simply observing. We had to make a continuous effort to *move* for them.

I immediately tucked my fists into my sweater pocket. "No," I snapped, my tone sharper than intended.

The woman visibly recoiled, expression affronted as she blinked up at me. I didn't have to pry into her mind to feel the insults scrolling through it.

She was shorter than most mortal females, leaving me staring down into flat brown eyes. Her blonde hair was tied back, silver pieces weaving through a braid, and a few stragglers hanging down around her heart-shaped face.

I tucked a loose strand of hair behind my ear and forced my most winning smile to make an appearance. Softly, I added, "*Thank you.* No, thank you, just looking."

She warmed slightly, though her eyes were still less than trusting as she mumbled, "Okay, let us know if you have any questions," and wandered off.

Questions.

Why, yes, ma'am, how on earth did an antique piece—surely a once prized family heirloom—land in this rathole, gathering dust and oil and what appear to be a small child's jam-covered handprints?

I peered around the cluttered thrift store. My companions were on task, and there were no thoughts of urgency among them. A little probing couldn't hurt.

My fingers dropped onto the piano again, searching through the many decades of stories it yearned to tell me. I refined my question and focused on it, asking persistently.

As I had guessed, the last member of the bloodline had no sentimental attachment to the beauty—and with a small flat in the city, she could never warrant keeping such a grand instrument. Besides, she didn't even know how to play.

I sighed. Mortals had no appreciation for history. Too stuck in the here and—

My breath hitched in my throat. *There.*

Like a burst of lightning through a looming storm, just a flash of an image. An image of *him*. That handsome face, tan fingers gently gliding across the keys, drawing out a melancholic melody. The warm light fell across his eyes as they lifted into a piercing ray of sunshine, illuminating them to reveal that striking shade of emerald green that held my attention captive.

Nothing new, and nothing of particular gravity, but the man was inexplicably mesmerizing, and my mind held onto the latest vision the piano had given, that beautiful, sun-kissed face, relaxing as he played.

I opened my eyes, blew out a long breath, and surveyed the scene. Aren had his hands on garments, but his eyes were locked on mine.

Enjoying yourself?

Yes, thanks for asking. I winked at him.

Aren's mental voice was as crystal clear to me as his physically embodied one. It was always the most predominant sound among the constant bedlam around us—my anchor in the chaos.

He grinned back at me now, then shot an intimidating smile at the cashier, who was eyeing him, before returning to his mock perusals.

Oh, for fuck's sake, Lana griped. *Can the two of you stay focused for half an hour?*

No. Why would we do that? Aren smirked without moving his eyes from the drab clothing in front of him.

There wasn't an item in the store any of us would wear of our own accord, even without the constraint of sizes. Most of us were lanky and tall, save for Aren. Aren was a mountain of a man, his muscles wrapped over bones like stone chiseled by a master sculptor. Spectacular, even for our kind. His pieces were almost always made specifically for him.

His angled features and eternally stubbled jaw were the first things I'd seen when I woke up after my ascension, disoriented and petrified. He was my sire, the one who'd first sensed me out there alone and came to free me.

Just as I would be to this mysterious, green-eyed man, Lord willing.

I'm hungry. Lana whined internally. *It's been days since we've had even a scrap of food. Let's get up and go.*

At this, there was unanimous agreement. Nobody had picked up the scent of a fresh trail, not even Fae. The one we had followed vanished on the sidewalk outside, and the lingering fragrance of our quarry's skin on the worn books in this shop was *days* old. He didn't seem to have stayed long, either. The books and piano were the only pieces that had noticed him; everything else had remained oblivious to the man who'd come searching for something on these dusty shelves.

Another dead end.

Slowly, led by Ansel and Lana, we made our way for the doors.

Well, most of us. Alec lingered with his arms wrapped around Fae's waist, resting his chin on her shoulder as they studied the old relics.

Finally, most of us reunited with our partner before exiting hand in hand, like genuine couples would, Aren ducking to fit under the doorway.

Useless. This entire escapade was useless. We were no closer to locating the missing soul, and my patience was growing thin as the storm brewed beneath our feet.

We needed him. Them. *All* of them, to ascend. And we needed that *now*.

Outside, the alley reeked of booze and piss, and I wrinkled my nose.

Foul creatures, humans. Disrespectful. Ungrateful. Slaves to their own fall. Half the time, it felt a waste to dedicate our lives to stewarding after the beings so determined to damn themselves.

We were stones in the riverbed, unmoving, unchanging, and stuck as time passed by. Too damned for Heaven, too perfect for Hell...and so we sat here in purgatory, doing our best to look after the self-sabotaging beings. To usher them toward the potential He saw in them.

I shook my head, cursing the fruitless use of time that was this calling.

Aren's lips turned up in amusement at my thoughts. Lana shot me a sideways glare, though she couldn't bring herself to argue. But Alec, ever mankind's defender, ground his teeth together, and I could feel his eyes on my back without needing to read him.

That's what happens when you eavesdrop. You hear shit you don't want to, I shot at them internally, drawing the chuckle that had been brimming on Aren's breath.

I knew as well as they did; we didn't have a choice but to listen. It was what it was. Still, despite all our years together, it was annoying.

Without further delay, we formed our circle, backs to one another, each sensing both this world and the next. Fingers intertwined at our sides, our minds connected to ensure we would make the jump safely. When we were all satisfied with the energy field before us, we closed our eyes, and then in the space of a breath, and with a familiar twist and swell of energy, we left just as quickly as we'd come.

Grayshell's forever blinding light assaulted my eyes, and I blinked away the tears that sprang up every time we came home. A faint glimmer of voices lingered in the air, like a distant echo of the choir, hauntingly beautiful. The dazzling white walls seemed to ring with the vibrations, more sound than a solid surface.

The seemingly infinite vertical stretch of windows, blinding stone walls, and airy, white floor bounced the omnipresent sunlight onto every object in the hall. Its stretching, weathered, dark wood tables were empty today, and our party was evidently the first to return.

I closed my eyes and sensed for trouble, but it seemed all was well with our brothers and sisters. The breath escaped my lungs in a whoosh, my hand massaging my neck as though I could ease the air back in. Chest heaving, pulse hammering against my skull, I resigned to the agonizing reality that we were too tired to return but too frustrated to rest. We were blessed with protection today, with everyone home in one piece, but that was all we had come home with. Nothing new. Just another shard of a vision, like shattered glass, where an image should be. No blood. No answers. No leads. Not even a name. Tomorrow would mark our third *month of* trying to track this one evasive soul.

Failure was not an option. Not this time. While logic couldn't justify the way my throat was closing or the slick sweat on my palms, something buried deep within was intrinsically screaming that I couldn't survive the permanence of that loss. Not again.

With a frustrated, booted kick, I overturned one of the long tables so it flipped and hit the ground with a deafening clatter. A growl rose from my throat as my panic grew.

Ansel eyed me warily before summoning the object back into position with a flick of his hand. Never one for emotional outbursts, his somber gaze drilled into me, full of concern and disapproval.

As we all were, Ansel was beautiful, a marble statue of symmetrical features across unearthly, pale skin. His full, fair lips contrasted with a perfectly manicured black beard and slick hair that waved like sand across dunes. Piercing slate-colored irises bored into mine beneath dark, impeccable brows and flawless, long lashes.

"Pull it together, Alvara. He will not elude us forever. Don't lose faith." He shook his head reassuringly, running a hand through his hair.

I massaged my temples as Alec shifted forward and Aren walked to my side. He wrapped his immense hands around my biceps to pull me into him. Grounding myself in the familiar steady rhythm of his heart and warm, comforting scent, I fought the stinging in my eyes.

Have faith, echoed the thoughts of my family, each of them feeling the agony threatening to break through the bones in my chest.

It wasn't every day we were called to awaken one of our kind; some never received such a summons. And the weight of it, the responsibility of finding a lost soul before the enemy could...it was crushing. Knowing that a spirit weighed in the balance—not a life, not a vessel, but the soul itself.

"Take a moment to pray for what you need." Aren tucked a strand of hair behind my ear, and the group echoed their prior sentiment.

Together, we inhaled deeply. Each of my five soulmates surrounded me, resting their powerful hands on my body, reaching down into my energy. Mercifully, I could feel Alec's gift wash through me like an emotional anesthetic, forcing my pulse to steady, the pounding in my mind to cease, and the tearing in my ribs to calm.

I shook my head, clearing the cloud of panic they reached past. *Faith,* I echoed weakly.

Aren leaned back to nod at me as a gentle, unwavering smile crept into his eyes.

WARM, shimmering light reverberated off every edge within the temple—the ornate paintings across the ceiling, the gold emblazoned over so many edges of the room, of paintings, of frames, of the metal trim in the stained-glass windows and scattered over altars. It danced across every color in the vast, domed space and warmed the air.

We abandoned our camouflage, trading combat boots for sandals and denim for spirit armor. Lacing the gladiator ribbons up my legs, I was grateful my fingers were no longer shaking. Together, we stood and walked toward the altar. We humbly and hungrily approached the marble steps in unison and lowered to our knees to pray.

I inhaled the familiar aroma of incense and bowed further into my meditation, trying to silence my racing mind and keep my heart level. I anchored myself in the stone's chill beneath my legs and the song that hovered in the air.

Beyond the blessed connection to our source, the silence in the temple's heart was a luxury rarely granted anywhere else, especially for me. Each soul was created with its own gifts, and mine was a far-reaching clairvoyance that often left me deeply overwhelmed as I attempted to discern meaning from the babble.

But there, in the glittering temple, the ability to just be...myself. Just *my* thoughts and emotions for a moment. That was priceless, like the first gasp of air after being held underwater for too long.

And I was just as desperate for answers that evening as I would have been if I'd fought my way free of being drowned. I needed to address my fears and countless questions.

It felt like I spent hours listing gratitudes, requesting wisdom, begging for guidance—in spite of myself—and asking for protection for the lost soul. I was asking for protection for the man whose face had haunted my dreams, no doubt plagued by the shadows nipping at his heels.

Some days, divine energy moved through me like water breaks from a dam: direct, overwhelming, and unarguable.

Some days, there was only its absence.

That hopeless afternoon was mostly the latter, and my resulting distress made it hard to quiet my mind long enough to tap into what was rightfully mine. The connection I was born to wield.

I continued to push thoughts and fears aside, stuffing memories of past failures back into the dark prisons they belonged in.

I could not, would not, fail a *soul*.

Just as I prepared to rise, to take my blessing and leave, resigned to the silence, I was given a single word to cling to like a life raft.

His name.

And the moment I received it, a vision came in like a tsunami.

My heart descended into my gut.

I rose to my feet, spinning to Aren, eyes widening with fear.

We're too late.

TWO
JUST A DREAM
AUGUST

The thing about music is that while it can be taught, it can also be intrinsic. Like oxygen in our lungs or water passing over our lips, music is built and bred from within, flowing like lifeblood whenever its vessel is sliced open.

It had always been that way for me. Since childhood, my mother often told me I was born with music in my bones, and she did all she could in order to ensure I understood how to set it free.

The late sun warmed my skin through the large panes of glass, illuminating the loft in an orange haze. I kept my eyes closed as my fingers worked their way across the piano keys. I enjoyed leaning into the warmth more than witnessing its bright reflection off the glossy black instrument in front of me.

There would be other melodies dancing with this one—under and over, an entire composition braiding together in my mind. I felt her energy behind me, a smile creeping onto my face before I felt the touch of her fingers chilled by the glass they'd cradled only moments before. She gingerly stroked the back of my neck, careful not to be too distracting, and then gently ran her fingers into the short curls she loved so much. I kept it this length for her, unable to disappoint those sweet sapphire eyes by cutting it shorter.

Layla inched around to join me on the bench, and I scooted over to make room without breaking the melody. I opened my eyes to drink her in. The red satin of her nightdress clung to her curves, mercilessly peaking across her breasts, thin straps set precariously on the edge of her shoulders. She slowly lowered her hand onto my back, eyes closing as she breathed in the song. Cascading golden waves of hair were determined to wrap around her shoulder.

Finishing my new song, I transitioned into her favorite, and her smile broadened.

The summer had been long and chaotic in its best moments, and I was regretful that businesses had dominated my time, leaving her to her own devices more often than not. Her patience for me was endless, and for that, I was grateful. She had her own hobbies, and work kept her busy most days, but her hours weren't nearly as long as my own. And then there were the dreams that had kept me staring at our city most nights. Nightmares that, even now, made my blood turn cold as I remembered the sight of them. The otherworldly demons that plagued my mind.

Between sunrise meetings and terror keeping me from my mattress to scowl out at the city, Layla must have grown tired of cold sheets and lonely evenings. But somehow, through God's grace, here she sat, thin lips stained red, brushing along my arm in thanks for *her* song. She inched them up over my shoulder, desire building in my core as she traced my collar, teeth teasing my neck before she whispered in my ear.

"Come to bed, my love."

I nodded slowly, leaning my face to hers as she pressed her lips into mine, burning with desire and demand. The melody came to an abrupt halt as I turned towards her, pulling her against me as longing grew urgent.

"August," it hissed, eyes like hot coals piercing my soul. The creature was as black as the gap between stars, its webbed hands dripping with foul-smelling liquid. "Where are you, half-breed?" The thing demanded in a breath. Its razor teeth coated in what looked like blood.

I didn't answer—couldn't answer as the air trapped in my chest. Not that I would have wanted to tell that creature anything, even if I could regulate my damned breathing. I looked around the alley, finding only trash against the large dumpster and an abandoned box home—nothing to defend myself with outside of my own hands. As it advanced, the creature shuddered forward, crab-like in its movement and baring fangs, which I was now certain dripped with blood.

Other horrors emerged from the shadows of the buildings—all different shapes and sizes, all dark as night, darting in and out of the black along the walls. I felt my body shudder as I turned to run—swearing at my helpless, unarmed state. Of course, I was fucking barefoot.

Muscles firing obediently, I sprinted from the alley, nearly being sideswiped by a taxicab as I darted into the street. I risked a glance back over my shoulder to see the creature who had spoken had swollen into a gargantuan shadow in the alley, long fangs bared in anger, as the rest of the shadows flew from the lane, blending effortlessly into the blackness under the cars racing across the street, hiding from the streams of lights above them.

Skidding to a halt after a long leap over one of the stretching silhouettes onto the sidewalk, I threw my arms out to repel my body from the brick wall, ignoring the scrape of grime and gravel below my naked feet and the ache of my hands as small beads of blood sprang forward on the skin.

Unsure of where else to go, my feet led me towards home. Could monsters be killed with bullets? Knives? I hadn't a clue. But I didn't know what else to try. I bypassed the elevator at the front of the building, noting the absence of the reception team and security guards. The stairs burned through my legs as I raced them, painfully aware of the terror building in my body as I forced my muscles to keep leaping up the flights of stairs.

You will not die. You will not die.

I burst through the front door, turning for our room where we kept the pistols, but staggered to an abrupt halt. Layla.

Long tendrils of hair eerily dancing in the air, Layla was suspended above the ground as though by magic. Her eyes unseeing as their empty pupils stared straight at me. Through me. Past me? Her face was horrifyingly slack, a small trickle of blood escaping her lips. An animal scream ripped from my chest as I lunged for her.

Just in time for the shadow creature to emerge—somehow concealed behind her limp body—and run a blade through her heart. The scream being torn from my throat turned barbaric, my body running cold as I lunged at the thing, energy swelling in my chest in a frantic cry of panic. I threw up my hands, and an enormous light blinded me as the room filled with white—a twisted howl of pain coming from the creature as someone or something rammed into me, throwing me to the ground. I pushed myself up, back to my feet, frantic, only to come face to face with emerald eyes, ringed with gold—wide with panic, grief-stricken tears raining down a perfect, intensely pale face. The woman's high cheekbones were glittering with tears. Long brunette waves framed either side of her face, caked in dark, viscous liquid, blood splattered along the side of her neck.

"I'm sorry." Her voice was breathy, as though she had just run up the stairs after me. In any other circumstance, I would have been spellbound by her radiance. She stood, wearing white linen beneath ancient silver armor that could have been metal but moved like leather. Her torso was draped in a silver chain—a bandolier—with sheathed daggers on either hip. An antique leather archer's glove on her hand. Her body was long and lean. A warrior. Too perfect. Tall enough to wrap her defined arms around Layla, freeing her from whatever horrifying magic bound her. She lifted her as though her body weighed nothing at all and set my fiancé on the floor in front of me. She gently closed those haunted, unseeing eyes. I hadn't realized I had fallen to *my knees until I felt the blood pooling on them as it poured from Layla onto the glossy concrete floor.*

"I'm so sorry," the ethereal woman whispered, eyes distant. I couldn't fully tell if she was speaking to me, Layla, or herself.

The light in the room faded, and I could make out the shapes of others like her in the corners, hands extended eerily in front of them. Their undeniable, energetic presence was as demanding as the sea upon the shorefront. As my vision returned, I realized they all were very much alike, tall and serene looking, eyes staring unseeingly forward, as Layla's had been.

The screams assaulted my ears before I realized they were my own. "Help her!!" I demanded, fury seething like fire in my lungs. I repeated the phrase, reaching down and scooping her to me, her blood soaking my bare skin.

"Aren," the woman called over her shoulder, too calmly, in her metallic voice. A man circled around at the sound of his name. He had at least eighteen inches on me—and I am no mouse of a man. He nodded solemnly, eyes darting warily to mine. As though he didn't trust me. He bowed his head, holding out his enormous arms as if to ask my permission.

"Help her!" I begged again. He nodded once and scooped her out of my arms like a child lifts a doll, her bloody body limp, cradled against his broad chest.

The woman looked at me, eyes narrowing intently. "Where are you, August?!"

The demand sent a shock through me, and I held my breath, looking from her to the mountain of a man walking away with Layla, her blonde hair tinged with crimson. Was this a rouse? Was she a siren, damnably perfect, come to retrieve the information the monster had failed to claim?

"Help her," I repeated, desperation in my voice. "Please, I love her."

The woman nodded, glancing once more over her shoulder towards the man called Aren before bringing her eyes back to me.

"Where are you?!" she repeated, voice anguished. "We cannot save you if we cannot find you. Where are you?!"

I stared back at those piercing green eyes, shivering as shock set in. I shook my head, scared this was a trick.

"Where are you?!?" She set her slender hands, calloused and speckled in thin, white scars, on my arms and stared into my soul. "August?!?"

That clear, ethereal voice rang in my mind. My name reverberated around the inside of my skull in that bell-like tone that had ripped from her throat as the world fell away.

August?!?

The torment in her voice was enough to run goosebumps down my spine as my eyes flew open. I threw my body upright, dinner rising in my throat as I turned to vomit onto the floor. Flipping over, eyes scouring the early morning blue of our room, I found Layla sprawled out on the side of the bed, her bare skin a warm caramel color, even in this early light. I pulled the stray curls off her cheeks, soaking in the steady rise and fall of her chest.

Just a dream. Just a dream. Just a dream. Another horrible, too-vivid dream. And, as always, I was immensely inadequate.

Out of panic, I led them right to her. Brought the monsters to our door. Too slow and too weak to save either of us. I ran my shaky hands down the length of her back, and she hummed appreciatively, stirring into my touch in her sleep. My fingers lingered on the spot of her spine where the monster's blade would've pierced. Skin smooth as ever, I forced my lungs to inhale before slipping from the bed. I cleaned my mess as quietly as possible and snuck, yet again, from the room.

By the time she rose, my skin stung with sweat. I couldn't really get myself to look at her—that horrifying image still ingrained into my vision. With each breath, I forced another pushup, relishing in the shake of my arms and aching spasm in my core. *You will be strong. You will be strong.*

I had used the mantra through the years, refusing any alternative. But it seemed my subconscious felt it was not enough. That was the repeated warning these cursed visions brought—never enough.

"AUGUST?"

I turned automatically to the sound of my name. Sam's gruff, familiar voice intruded on my reverie as I stared out at the city through the vast glass walls of the Goodfellow building. The city was soaked in orange light, smoke, and smog mixed into a soup that saturated our air. Summer struggles. Perhaps it would be better if I scooped Layla up and we left this mess. Escaped. While we could. But how could I explain spontaneously uprooting our entire life to her in a way that wouldn't sound completely insane?

"August?" He said again. I couldn't help but hear the echo of my name in my mind, but it was the woman from the dream that I heard between my ears. The vision of her too-perfect face, those piercing eyes set above such defined cheekbones, with skin so pale it was nearly translucent over them. Sam snapped his fingers in front of my eyes, a mixture of irritation and amusement on my best friends' faces as he demanded my presence.

"Sorry?"

The board room laughed in unison, some forced and others sincere. I looked around the table, shaking my head. I forced a smile onto my face, clearing my throat and straightening my tie.

"Are we moving forward with the mid-west expansion?" My brother eyed me warily, a furrow between his dark brows. James was two years younger than me and definitely not used to seeing me falter. His slick navy suit was fitted, shoes polished, and hair meticulously gelled into place, omitting one curl across his forehead. Prepared. Present. What his leader should be.

"I'm sorry, gentlemen, my mind is stuck on other matters."

"If you laid eyes on his fiancé, you wouldn't wonder what those other matters were." Sam winked, a cheeky grin on his face as he ran his hand through his short blonde hair. He smoothly began sliding his files into his briefcase. The men around the table chuckled and began following his lead to end the meeting. I forced myself to do the same.

"Oh, leave her out of it," I grumbled, unable to completely wipe the smile out of my response. "I'll review your projections, gentlemen, and give you a response by end of day."

"I'll see he sticks to that," James mused, reaching across the table to shake hands with the CEO we'd spent the last few months negotiating with. I stood and did the same. Twice our age, Theodore Allen was a regal man with silver hair and skin showing his exhaustion. He looked less than amused at my hesitation. I sent all my positive energy towards him, and if I didn't know better, I'd say the muscles in his jaw relaxed slightly before he turned his attention back to my brother.

James and the man exchanged formal pleasantries as the room emptied out before he walked him to the door, closing it gently behind him. Then he turned on his heel to face me, eyes skeptical.

"Bro. What the fuck was that?"

I shook my head, falling back into my seat and pinching the bridge of my nose. "Sorry, James, my head isn't in the game today."

"I see that," Sam chuckled. He came around to lean against the table by my side. "Still not sleeping?"

"Not at all."

"Tell Layla to give you a break already." James laughed.

"It's not her." I shook my head.

"Well, take an Ambien or something tonight. Do you realize what we have riding on this? What's the hang-up?"

"Do you think we should move forward?" I asked matter-of-factly. I stared at him, watching his calculating eyes as he chewed over the question. James gave a slow, steady nod, and I turned to Sam, who mirrored the motion.

"Their numbers are solid, the market research supports it, and projections look to be conservative. It's a good expansion." Sam patted me on the shoulder. "I think it's a home run, August. Really. And the buy-out is a drop in the bucket as far as our acquisition budget goes for the year."

I nodded, having read the proposals a dozen times before ever meeting with their team in person. Everything had felt good, and nothing in my analytical or intuitive mind said otherwise.

"Give the green light then," I said with a nod to James. "This is your baby, little brother. Bring it home."

James gave one curt nod, patted me on the back, and turned for the door. "Get some rest, August. You look like shit."

Sam stretched out his hand, and I took it as he smiled. "Congratulations, man."

"Thanks."

"You and Layla out bouldering again?" He asked as I pulled my hand back.

"No, not recently. Thinking about heading out this weekend. Why? You wanna join?"

He shrugged and nodded to my hand. "Eh, I figured that's how you scraped up your palms. You're not exactly a DIY kind of guy."

Sweat dripped down my back, a vice clamping around my lungs as I looked down and noticed thin scrapes across my skin, already healed enough not to sting but still rough to the touch. I ran my fingers over the narrow scabs. The hard ache of ricocheting off the wall crept back into my memory. But it had only been a dream. She was fine. *We* were fine.

"Must've hit something in the gym," I said, partially to Sam and partially to my heart, pounding like a war drum against my ribs.

Just a dream.

THREE
SUMMONING
ALVARA

Smoke settled in the valley, thick as morning fog on the icy fields in December, turning the sun a faint orange and filling the humans' lungs with heavy ache. The undesirable effect of summer fires was a frequent plight here—where they had nestled their city in a deep bowl between pine-covered mountain tops. Yellow light angered the mind, leaving a throbbing in our foreheads and temples despite our increased endurance.

August. We were hunting August, in August. His green eyes were so piercing they nearly matched my own. No coincidence in that, I was sure. Almost inhuman. If he truly was just a braid, he was a strong one.

I had burned the look on his face as we scooped up his moribund Layla into my retinas. The terror in his eyes danced with the unmistakable shadow of intense guilt.

We nearly missed the huge pulse of energy that meant one of our own was in danger—arrived only a few breaths before the exact second when her paralyzed soul would have abandoned that broken, bloodied, heartbreakingly beautiful body...and we could not have covered up the mess of our mistakes. The direct effect of our inability to track our calling.

We were finally close—I'd been able to smell this polluted air through the veil—and I could faintly sense the vibration of his mind. But he was still so distant. Still unreadable. Impossible to trace more than a few feet at a time.

A shield? I shook my head. Impossible. Or nearly so. Shields were the holy grail in a hierarchy arsenal. A two-carat blue diamond in a sea of quarter-carat amethyst. We hadn't encountered a shield in over a century.

And he was here, in our ranks, ready to be deployed. The odds of another one incarnating *here*, now...slim to none.

Braids rarely made it so long unnoticed, and as we began tracking his energy bursts, we realized why. There was something different about this one. Something behind him called to me—a soul I'd entangled with in one life or another, I was sure.

I had never personally been given a soul in any of my incarnations. And while I could see the thoughts of my sire and friends, I couldn't fully embody the emotion behind their memories. Had no way of knowing if the responsibility sat on them, the weight of an unforgiving tide that pulled them under. No idea if the intensity of my obligation to this man was to be expected. No idea what challenges they had overcome to find their own souls.

Did Aren feel this way when he sought me?

I had never been so desperate in the countless assists I had offered to my comrades—always a tool that was easy to deploy. Never failing to allow my energy to weave with the one we sought. Despite the ongoing silence from the city, I walked down the street, unyielding to the stream of people moving opposite me. My hand was outstretched, bare skin gliding down the sides of the buildings, wiping through endless grit and dust, and seeing only the continual pulse of the city. No sign of him came into view, no matter how many filthy structures I read along the way.

It was infuriating to not be able to get a read on a mark. If I couldn't do it, there were few, if any, in the hierarchy that could. Regardless, I appreciated their presence here today, scattered through the thronged streets. Because I was failing. And I could not fail. Not now.

Alvara.

I turned in the direction Lana was calling from. The image of two men in fitted, extravagant suits was vivid in her mind.

They smell like the Braid.

She pushed her energy all around where the men stood, but there was no other trace of him. The faint hint of his scent on their clothes suggested they'd been with him not long before. I shoved off the wall I'd been leaning on, gloving my exposed hand in the same motion, Aren mimicking the movement in unison a block away. We had been partnered for so long that there was not much we didn't do as one being, and this was no different. Aren's hulking form stepped from an alley, the crowd on the sidewalk parting like the great sea to make room for him as he turned towards Lana's pulse. They kept a distant berth from our kind, unsure of why the hair on the back of their necks prickled or their hearts raced when they saw us. Shaking confusion from their minds, it became hard to recall the strange face they'd seen only moments ago. A million myths crossed their collective consciousness. Unperturbed by their eyes on him, Aren's energy was steady, heartbeat matching the confidence in his bright aura as he waded through the crowd of humans.

The conviction in him calmed my racing heart, and I forced myself to inhale through my nose. My hand absently rose to rub the pulsing amulet on my chest, the pink calcite serving as the best guard between me and the countless minds around me. Today required focus and some semblance of peace, which was always impossible for me to achieve when enveloped in the city.

I saw the girls right as they saw the men we were seeking. Fae and Lana moved in beautiful synchronicity—their connection easily renewed after their ascensions. Their souls had danced through many lives, always together, always sisters, or mother and daughter. The men they had eyes on were handsome, too, just like August. Dapper in their luxurious business attire, they reeked of wealth and ambition. There was no malice in either heart. Fae inhaled deeply, and the rest of us soaked in their smell. Both faintly connected to him. But one. One of them smelled *like* him and looked so similar it was glaringly obvious they were family.

The younger of the two donned dark brunette curls, one straggler laying loose across his forehead. His dark blue suit was pinstriped and fitted closely to his lean form. Armani, if my eyes served me well. Dark, thick brows lined his serious, expectant eyes. For a moment, I debated pulling the amulet from my neck to get a read on their minds, but a quick, nearly imperceptible shake of Aren's head kept me focused. He stood in line at a food truck smelling thickly of spices and simmering sauce, but I knew the motion was for me, not the vendor.

Stay focused, Ally. Stay focused. My coven's nickname for me made me smile despite myself, and I nodded.

As I watched the younger man's motions, I grew certain this was a relative of August. The hold of his broad shoulders, his torso's triangular shape, and his strong stance hinted at powerful legs for a mortal. He was fully immersed in their conversation, gesticulating passionately to his friend as they dressed their tacos with a heavy squeeze of lime juice and a generous amount of hot sauce. A laugh broke free, and the furrow finally left his forehead. *Brother*, I decided.

Fae, her shiny, straight platinum hair swaying at the edge of her belt, danced forward, eyes glittering. She gave me a sideways grin and applied a soft pink gloss to her perfect, full lips. She was the smallest of us—still five ten—and the most human in stature, somehow possessing feminine curves most of us were lacking. Her head came up just below the younger man's eyes.

No ring. Her singsong voice rang out to us. *My turn!*

She didn't bother to conceal her smile as she gracefully made her way towards them. Aphaea was the oldest of us, not in this life but in all of them. And she remembered most of her cycles with intense clarity. Practiced. While I might be the most overwhelmingly adept reader, Aphaea was the tracker. She could trace sound, smell, and aura better than any of our kind I'd met in this life. Her long, toned hourglass form and preternatural grace made her even more mesmerizing to the human males.

She literally cracked her knuckles and popped her neck before running her hands through that flawless hair. I chuckled and rolled my eyes, unable to block out the others' amusement any more than my own. Alec's snigger was prominent above the crowd, always egging her on.

Without hesitation, she strode up to the two gentlemen. While I could easily focus and hear the conversation, I allowed my attention to wander.

Aphaea needed no babysitters.

I gave them one last glance as heat rushed to the young one's cheeks, and his friend chuckled. No. She certainly did not need a chaperone.

I inhaled deeply, aware of all the scents overwhelming us here. Aren was guiltlessly indulging in a gyro—his favorite city food. And I couldn't begrudge him such a simple pleasure. Despite the grim circumstance we had intervened in last night, we had never been closer since the braid had been assigned. And the resounding confidence in the group, all so sanguine on this smoky afternoon, brought a lightness to my chest. Voluntarily feeding on their optimism. We would do this. We would free him. August would ascend, and we could begin his training. He would ascend, and my heart could stop racing for the first time since I was called to him.

Fae was running her finger down the arm of the man's suit now, and with a toss of her hair, the heat returned to his cheeks.

Ridiculous. Lana snickered. And for the briefest flash of a second, Fae threw a glare her direction, husky blue eyes flashing a warning, before returning a gooney smile to the men in front of her. Harlequin romance novel flirtations.

Despite their constant chorus of movements, mirroring petite stature and platinum blonde locks, Lana and her "sister" couldn't have been more different. Pragmatic, strategic, and oftentimes ruthless, Lana was the hunter. The final outcome, allowing for Fae's skills to reap their reward.

Ansel rose from the bench he patiently sat on and strode towards her with the prowess of a predator. Just as lethal as Lana when he chose to be, but not as callous as his mate. Ansel liked to follow our lead, loyal to Aren's command, more than the whim of his emotions.

He wrapped an arm around the small of Lana's back, pulling her to him, and slowly pressed his lips to hers. His free hand tangled in a strand of her silvery hair.

"Patience, my love," he breathed. She resisted his hold for a moment before leaning into the kiss and relaxing her tight fists against his chest.

Where Lana was all fury and passion, impulsive action, and vigor, always the sword and dagger...Ansel was calculated and subtle. He and the sisters came together in each life without fail. Sometimes, they ascended together. They spent other lives searching for each other, only to be devastated by headstones. Reckless and broken until they were granted death. But upon successful ascension, they were always inseparable. Alec had joined them two ascensions ago. A hidden soul, and so intensely powerful. I never ceased to be amazed as I watched the dynamic between the group.

I'm walking James back to work. Fae's voice was innately feminine, even as she announced her swift victory.

Good work, Fae. Aren and I thought in unison. Alec's pride was inescapable, without needing to see him concealed in the crowd.

<hr>

FAE LEANED against a steel and glass skyscraper, her smug smile still radiant on her delicate features. Her frilly blush dress and strappy sandals stood in ridiculous contrast to the uniform most of us wore—long denim jeans, simple T-shirts, and combat boot-adorned feet. But she knew her role and wore it well, unashamed to be the irresistible lure at the end of our line.

"Are you ready to perform a summoning?" She took two graceful strides forward and tossed her hair over a shoulder.

"Hell, yes." I smiled back. We took our time finding our places around the building. Aren, Fae, and I took the front, under the overhang, shielded from the sun. That was where we assumed he was most likely to appear. He was palpable here, and while the others still could not find his mind either, his scent was everywhere—on the food cart pedaling hot dogs, all over the front step of the building, the metal door handle, even the column nearest the entrance. As though he lingered there often. I could have taken a moment to read the spaces, but there was no time. And no point, as the evidence was plenty sufficient for full understanding.

Once our sentries surrounded the building, I smiled, reaching for Aren's mind. We connected. And then we linked to the rest—our usual partners and the rest of the hierarchy. The energy was electric and immensely powerful, and my stomach flipped as though I'd missed a step coming downstairs as months of searching culminated in this moment.

Mind sharp, heart steady, muscles wound tight, I inhaled as deeply as I could. Alec cast his protective circle. No one would notice us here, lingering at all exit points of the building. With a breath, he expanded it, and I inhaled too. I freed the amulet from my neck, dropping it to my feet and breathing into the rush of power that wound in my chest, grateful Alec held the continued reprieve of voices. His shield was like a powerful spiritual Novocain, blocking the strain and ache that usually accompanied a place like this; my focus grew intensely acute.

August? With one last steady breath of smoky city air, I called for him and set my hands into the cool steel column of the building, feeling as though they might melt below my fingers as I leaned into their vibration. Alec increased his hold on my nerves, numbing them and upping his shield for me. Increasing my focus.

I closed my eyes. And we began.

FOUR
CRAWLERS
AUGUST

The faucet flicked on automatically, a flood of warm water wrapping around my hands. I surveyed the scrapes, unable to suppress the acid in my throat. Fearing that my lunch would make a reappearance, I willed myself to keep it down.

Just a dream. Just a dream. Just a dream.

I shook my head and splashed the warm water on my face. Blotting it with a white hand towel, I looked up into the mirror. For the briefest flash, my green eyes were surrounded by her face instead—the pale woman from the dream. But her surreal features faded away, and I realized her eyes were not that different from my own. Just. *More.* More intense, more depth, more amber around her irises where there was only hazel in mine.

Something stirred in my chest with the effort of recalling her face. A tickle ran down my arms like a finger lightly traced down my spine. My mind drifted to the way the weapons draped across her torso. Her body was too lean and too defined to be real. The ruby and emerald encrusted daggers in the leather sheaths upon her hips.

A vivid dream. A vivid dream about a warrior from another world. One too many Spartan movies in my teenage years.

I tossed the soft towel into the laundry bin and unrolled my sleeves, straightening my cuff links before turning towards the door. A quick survey in the full-length mirror on the wall told me that James was right. Exhaustion had worn dark circles under my eyes, and my skin looked flat. It wouldn't take a brother to spot that I was not at my best. Maybe the stomach flu had at last taken a vengeance. And...hallucinations?

I re-buttoned my suit jacket, and for a split second, she was there in my reflection again.

Jesus. I needed to sleep.

As I went to reach for the handle, her voice rang in my mind, clear as day but less frantic than it had been in the dream.

August?

I startled, shaking my head, flying out of the bathroom, and rubbing my temples.

And then it was like she was everywhere. The building seemed to buzz with electricity, like I was standing in a lightning storm, and her voice was singing my name out above the din. A siren on the corporate sea.

Panic rose in my chest like a vice tightening. Everyone else stayed attentive to what they were doing—working, conversing, laughing, cleaning up spilled coffee. The volatile buzz in the building seemed to grow louder, and my tie felt so tight against my suddenly sensitive skin that I furiously pulled it loose as sweat dripped down my back again, and my blood pounded like a war drum in my ears.

This is what a heart attack feels like.

You're not dying, August. Your heart is fine. Her voice filled my ears. I sputtered, and two of the women from the office looked at me, concerned. I put a hand to my chest and waved them away, trying to reassure them. *Better than fine, from the sound of it, you fit, son of a bitch.*

She sounded...happy? Happy? Was that right? Relieved, perhaps. Her words didn't match her playful tone, and I realized I was evaluating the voice like a person. I had to stop. Had to stop this madness. Exhausted. Just exhausted.

The buzzing grew, a million angry bees humming in the walls, vibrating my feet, fingers tingling as though they'd been asleep, and the blood was returning. Painful needles pricked along my skin. I fought the shout building in my chest and made a beeline for my office, too fast to not draw attention to myself. Panic attack in full swing, the nausea swelled again.

Step. Step. Step.

August. Listen to me. You're going to be okay. The bell of a voice rang in my head, as clear as if she spoke in front of me. No one else turned. No one else noticed.

August. If you can hear me, say my name—I'm Alvara.

Alvara? The thought danced in my mind for a moment, familiar despite its alien intrusion into my consciousness. Like I'd said it a thousand times, it danced in my memory like a lucid dream. Familiar, as my tongue silently formed the word.

Yes. Now. Listen to me. You are okay. You're not mad—we are real. We are here. How are your hands?

The hollow place in my chest where my heart once belonged dropped into my stomach, and I closed the door to my office. *This isn't real. Not real. It can't be real.* The scrapes on my palms seemed to throb in response.

I would find a doctor. Medicine. Something.

August. Don't leave me, don't do that to me. I just found you.

Found me?! I echoed, slamming my back into the door and sliding down onto the floor. *This isn't real. You're not real. You're a dream. I'm tired. Too tired.*

August, listen to me. You're not safe here. Please, just say my name. Say my name out loud. August—

My fists flattened against my ears, and the pressure in my head forced my eyes shut, trying to push the alien voice out of my mind. It seemed to work because it was silent for a moment over the noise of the office. I took a steadying breath, fully acknowledging there was a high probability this was a damned psychotic break.

What was it called? Schizophrenia? That was it. Schizophrenia.

The vibration was picking up strength, buzzing through my bones. My eyes found my favorite picture of Layla and me in Hawaii—the glass rattling against the simple silver frame. My entire desk shook, and I looked at the glass wall of the office.

Now, they were noticing. Nervous glances were exchanged between co-workers as the building trembled, the ceiling fan rocked from side to side, and cheap artwork rattled against the nails that held the frames. It was an earthquake. I had been sensing an earthquake. People do that, right?

August!!! Her voice was near a cry, desperate and high-pitched. The lights flickered above me. Some acid trip fucking earthquake. *Listen to me, dammit. They will feel this. They will come for you. I cannot protect you if I don't know where you are. Please don't run. Please.* Alvara pleaded inside my mind. And for some reason, I wanted her. Here. Wanted to see her elegant face again. Wanted to trust her. Wanted her voice. Something buried deep inside of me was being called to the surface as she said my name. Like a childhood memory being ignited by the sound.

August! Fresh alarm was in her voice, sending a chill down my body. *They're here. August. Say my name. For the love of God, say my—*

The tremor in the building ceased just as suddenly as her voice vanished. The office took a collective breath, nervous laughter broke out, and rushed footsteps thudded through the floorboards. Shadows darted back and forth by my window of a wall as they all relished in the excitement.

But I didn't feel relief at the end of the shaking. My heart was still in my stomach, and a sinking feeling crept up my neck, leaving the hairs on end.

"That was crazy!"

"Earthquake?!?"

"I guess—not a very big one!"

The chatter morphed into one big collective voice as I forced air into my lungs. Again and again.

I crawled to my desk to chug the glass of water there, then pushed myself to my feet and hurried to the window to survey the city below. And then...everything in me bristled, and I turned towards the door, which had been cracked open. An icy chill wrapped its tendrils around my neck and arms. Although I could see nothing, I was not alone. And this didn't feel like the damned siren scouring my mind.

This was different. This was suffocating emptiness—a deep, bone-freezing *lack*. Head pounding, I tried to inhale. While the sun shone all around me, darkness seemed to be all there was—all there would ever be.

I slammed my fists to my temples again.

Wake up. Wake up. Wake up.

And then...I was on the street across from my building, cars racing by, horns blaring, the collective voices of thousands of rushing people, and a sudden roar in my ears as my heartbeat assaulted them from the inside. My suit and dress shoes still adorned my sweat-slicked body—*better than barefoot.* I blinked a few times, resolved to orient myself—and to do so quickly.

What in the fuck is going on?

Where could I go? Not home—not with that horrifying image of Layla suspended in my mind. Not back to the office—where that desperate darkness sucked the air from my lungs, a demonic vacuum forcibly attached to my throat. I strained a shaky breath, attempting to clear the confusion.

Someone was screaming. In my mind, or in the world, I hadn't a clue. The sinking feeling in my gut was deepening.

I couldn't put together how I had gotten out of the vacuum—out of the building. But there were the front doors. The bustling food vendors cooked their fare like all was well in Ivy Springs. My eyes were inexplicably drawn to a slight woman in a blush dress and platinum hair so long it brushed the curve of her lower back. Her eyes were closed, face and palms turned to the sky—like the sentinels in the dream. She was just as odd and striking as the woman in the vision...Alvara.

Alvara.

I jammed my eyes closed, willing my body to wake up. Barely more than a whisper, I demanded my lips breathe her name, "Alvara."

And there, as though by magic, she stood when I opened my eyes. No longer clad in warrior's shields, she wore a simple black t-shirt, dark faded denim jeans with holes in their knees, and tightly-laced combat boots around her feet. She was standing by the woman in blush, who smiled coyly in sharp contrast to Alvara's serious gaze, which was now locked directly on me.

In an instant, she was across the street. I'd never seen her cross—a glitch in the dream. But she was directly in front of me, eyes scrupulous, the corner of her too-perfect, full lips quirked to one side, as those fierce emerald irises bored into mine. She was my height, frame long and lean. Alvara ran an exquisite hand over her brow, wiping small beads of sweat away from her glowing, fair skin.

"August," she sighed aloud, "thank God."

The woman in blush danced across the road, weaving through traffic like the cars were bodies in a ballroom. Effortless. Everything about her was effortless. She was just as beautiful as Alvara, just a few inches shorter and fuller in shape.

More...graceful. Less warrior-like.

She extended me a delicate, pallid hand before saying, "Hello, August. We've been searching for you for a while. Thanks for *finally* answering. I'm Aphaea. Friends call me Fae."

I looked to Alvara, hesitant. And then saw them. Saw them everywhere. Tall and ghostly pale, they were weaving through the crowd towards us. Maybe a dozen of them. A giant of a man with a familiar face and hulking form was crossing the street now, a cocky smirk twisting his lips. The cat that ate the canary. Was I the prize?

Aren, I remembered. The man who helped Layla. If he was a *man* at all. Upon further inspection, they were only men and women at first glance. Everything about them was otherworldly. Alien. Something of legend. *Vampires?* No. Not *dark*.

Alvara's expression softened, and she gave me a gentle nod of encouragement.

I reached for Aphaea's outstretched hand and gave it a tentative shake. "August Porter, ma'am."

She smiled, obviously meaning to reassure me. Instead of releasing me, she pulled me into her body, linking our arms and intertwining our fingers as though to take a stroll together. She was slightly chilled, as though the day had begun with frost on the grass. My heart sunk, confused, as she leaned her body into mine—as though we were the oldest and dearest of friends—as though I had forgotten her name.

Unwilling to drop Alvara's focused gaze, I forced myself to look at Aren as he arrived, bearing a gold necklace with a large, pink, polished stone dangling from it—he gingerly placed it around Alvara's neck, and she seemed to melt, closing her eyes, brow relaxing, and inhaling at his touch. My stomach clenched in a territorial frustration.

"They're close, Al," Aphaea said in a hushed tone, her voice still unbearably feminine despite its urgency. "It's time to go." She turned her doll-like face to me, grimacing. "Sorry about this."

The world abruptly fell out from under my feet, a swirl of color and a crescendo of manic noise, and then it all went black.

FIVE
SIRE
ALVARA

August slept soundly, his steady pulse and even breathing the only things keeping me from jabbing him in the ribs to startle him awake. I'd been just as motionless, sitting on the floor, with my back against the wall, watching the steady rise and fall of his chest. There was something about him that was inexplicably captivating. My obsession not lessening now that he was safely in Grayshell—unable to shake the memory of the unabashed crawlers that had flooded into his building, hunting for him, surrounding us. They'd gotten too close. Even now, their darkness was thick on his skin. Inexplicably, they had managed to breach his office despite our presence there, perhaps already in waiting. They had gotten quite bold in Ivy Springs—we'd allowed them to go for too long, unresisted. That would inevitably change now that we knew of their numbers.

I bowed my head back to my knees, closing my eyes, still pleading with my heart to slow and steady. As I'd soaked up his energy, it quickly became apparent that August was much more than we'd known. His energy, even in sleep, was immense. The power came from him in waves, like heat off the desert, radiating from his core as his ascension unleashed all of that bottled-up potential. I wanted so badly to reach out and touch him. Set my hand over his heart and listen to all that he was. All that he would be. But that kind of intrusion needed consent—his memories and the very depths of his mind were his for the keeping. This was no braid. No fragmented soul wound into a mortal. This was...more.

Could he be a full half-blood?

Anxiety gripped me, and yet, we had not failed. He was safe. But nothing in my body felt like we were victorious. The others were in the lounge and gathered in the hall, celebrating another successful acquisition and promise of a new ally. But my intuition told me the fight hadn't even begun. As though a wall of a storm darkened on the horizon, and I was on alert, just waiting to be swallowed by rain, wind, and sea.

Hey stranger, come eat. Drink something. I looked up and saw Aren leaning against the doorframe, a playful smile on his lips. Even Aren couldn't understand the sinking in my stomach. He also felt the sleeping man's intense, energetic draw, but none of the conflict I sensed in my core. This was a "W" in his column—and he even got to vanquish a few crawlers threatening his mark. So, it had been a "fun win" at that.

I'm fine. I insisted for the hundredth time.

Come on, Ally. He's been through enough. He doesn't need to wake up to your scrutiny. Give the man a moment to breathe when he wakes.

Alone. In a different dimension. I'm not sure if that's better.

Al. It's been days. His vitals are steady—he's moving through ascension. Let him rest.

It wasn't a request anymore—a command from our Commander. I sighed and acquiesced, rising from my perch and joining him in the hallway, where Lana waited with some smutty romance novel wedged between her arm and chest, its spine cracked and worn from frequent use.

"I'll take over as guard, Alvara. He won't be alone when he wakes."

I pressed my hand into the wall again, confirming that the vision had not moved. Not only would he not be alone—he wouldn't be with Lana. Aren and I were both present when he would wake in most of the threads. I closed my eyes, wound the visions into a karmic ball, and pulled them out one at a time. There were very few visions of him waking without me here.

I sighed. No matter how many times I checked, it still felt wrong to walk from the room, but his consciousness was potentially days away. And I needed my strength.

The lounge was my favorite part of Grayshell, next only to the safe harbor that was the nearly silent temple. Not illuminated in the blinding, omnipresent light, it was the only place my mind and eyes felt like they could actually relax. The windows were successfully blocked out, usually draped in dense red fabric curtains Fae had found in an Indian street market a literal lifetime ago. Pleasant grey paint coated the walls—the soft color of the morning on an overcast day on the North Washington coast, and it felt as mellow as the mist that habitually hung in the air there. Fae's collection of leafy-green, potted plants, and trees only enhanced the effect.

In lieu of the white hardwood floors, Alec and I painted ours black and then gradually cloaked it in a myriad of eclectic rugs we had collected from our adventures in the world. The black, gold, and red Persians were my favorite, with their hand-woven designs and plush padding.

A towering dark wood bookshelf was built into the wall above, full to the brim of countless leather-bound volumes of history and healing. It encompassed a bouquet of my favorite scents—perpetually burning incense, musty parchment, leather, tea, and freshly brewed coffee. A few of our favorite indulgences from the human world.

While we didn't *need* food, the way a human would daily, it was the fastest way to ensure our strength remained where we needed it, and there was always a lingering comfort in food and drink. Perhaps a long-engrained habit from before our ascensions. The opposite side of the room housed our kitchen, responsible for the perpetual smell of warm drinks. Black cabinets were mounted by stained butcher block counters that Aren and Ansel had painstakingly hand-crafted themselves rather than manipulating energy, which would have been much less sloppy. Ansel insisted it would have been a great deal less satisfying as well, muttering something about working with his hands. A deep copper farmhouse sink had been added a few years back, and long matching pendants hung above the island, which we used more for strategizing than we did for family meals.

Fae and Alec were tangled together on a large, tufted leather sofa that faced the great hearth in the center of the room, fire blazing. They often wrapped so tightly around each other that it took a moment to discern which limbs belonged to which person. That afternoon, they were lying together; Alec braced against her weight, his hands holding the book she read to him mind-to-mind, indulging in some sort of literary escape.

But the story failed to hold his attention with his mate curved so tightly into his body, and Alec trailed kisses down her neck, nipping at her shoulder. Fae playfully shrugged away from him, eyes on the words, but Alec didn't relent, his need for her all but screaming down our mental connection. The duo had an intensely physical relationship, and while it was usually endearing, it could also be nauseatingly painful with the lack of privacy. Like right now, as he ran his teeth over her skin, arousal pressing into the soft curve of her ass.

My eyes widened in time with Aren's. "Woah there, big guy," I scoffed, "for the love of God, lock it up."

Alec snickered. "Oh, loosen up, Ally." He did his best to shield their more intimate moments, but anytime his guard was down, or his mind drifted to her without shielding, we'd all attempt to close our connection or take a walk into the temple for silence. "You just need to get some action."

Ansel slowed his piano playing just long enough to grant me a two-fingered salute right as Aren choked on a laugh. I elbowed him between the ribs, scowling over at Ansel's subtle smirk. "Hey!" I barked indignantly.

"What?" Aren chuckled, raising his hands in mock surrender. "He's not wrong."

Human decades went by before Aren and I both gave up on our mates ever making an appearance in this existence. Aren was centuries older than me, and while the loneliness was inevitable, we had cheerily resigned ourselves to our quippy, sire-offspring dynamic as our care for each other grew. Soul mates weren't always *mates*, so much as an intricate soul group bound together just the same. Companions, like magnets, are drawn to each other from one life to the next. While Aren had stood in place, I'd always circled back to him over time.

"Tell you what, Ar, I'll go get some once you do."

The heavy door clicked shut behind us, and I followed Aren to the stove as he gave a resigned shrug.

"Don't get too bent outta shape, Ally," Ansel grumbled under his breath, fingers still flying. "This is Alec we're talking about. Would've been over real quick."

Aren barked a laugh as he grabbed two steel mesh tea balls, tossing back, "Honestly. Two minutes, *max*. Right Fae?" He filled them with his favorite assortment of herbs and poured us both mugs. Ansel began to play a notch louder, bringing a smile to Aren's face as he slid our drinks around to the barstools that lined the island.

"Oh, now fuck off you two. Babe," Alec nipped at Fae's ear, squeezing her hips between his thighs. "Gonna help me out here?"

"Not a chance," she drawled nonchalantly, turning the page as though she couldn't be bothered and earning a chorus of laughter from the three of us.

I took the stool Aren pulled out for me, mindlessly dunking my tea strainer as he walked behind me to pick a game.

Mancala—an old favorite. He set it down on the wood counter in front of me, a laid-back smirk on his face, as he placed the marbles in their spaces. It was as though nothing of significance had occurred this week. And I found myself relaxing into his calm, soaking up the confidence he always exuded. Aren had a way of setting the tone of any room he was in, his energy so demanding that it was hard not to blend into it.

We played half a dozen rounds before Fae and Alec peeled themselves apart and walked out of the room, hand in hand, to relieve Lana of her guard duties. She appeared a moment later, the novel still clung tightly to her chest and a gooney smile on her face as she made a beeline for Ansel, still at the piano, to smother him in kisses. He chuckled, closing his eyes and leaning into her touch as his fingers effortlessly continued their tune. I glanced amusedly at Aren, who grinned and made his next methodic move.

And then the world seemed to fade, colors losing their vibrancy and noises withering away like someone had shoved cotton into my ears. The music was almost silent before Ansel's fingers slowed and ceased playing as he leaned into the vision.

Running, sprinting, breathless. Long scarlet hair and blue eyes set in a fair, heart-shaped face. A park, not two blocks from where we had found James earlier today. And it was swarming with crawlers. It was a distress call from someone in the hierarchy who had lost their calling—another braid.

We all bolted into the temple to retrieve human clothes and our weapons, carefully dipping each of our blades and arrows in holy water before placing them in sheaths and quivers. In unison, our group swiftly made it to the hall to move into formation. A breath later, we jumped.

Untethered from the weight of my first calling, it felt like flying. My legs were free to sprint at full throttle, my feet quietly thudding down the street, and I all but took to the air under the streetlights. I skidded to a halt as we came to a large brick wall, gravel screeching out from under my boots as I lowered into a squat, slamming my hand into the pavement to ground myself there. No longer distracted by my missing calling, I reached deep into the energy of the asphalt to search for this one. Closing my eyes, a full smile split my face as I sorted through the last few minutes of the timeline. A laugh escaped as I saw her—red hair like fire in her wake, crawlers on her heels.

Only moments ago, heading east back into the park. It had only taken seconds to get a read on her.

I could feel the anticipation as Lana and Ansel bounced on their feet before returning into a sprint. Aren skid to a halt by my side. He might be our muscle, but me? I was our speed.

Ansel was gaining ground out ahead of Lana, who gritted her teeth in frustration, lengthening her strides. They could smell her now, the scent left behind on branches she'd run through on her way into the dark park— shadows looming eerily everywhere. Where was she going? Why pull into the city and then back into the shadowed park?

Ansel sent a huge wave of energy out and could feel her in his grasp. Her terror was palpable even from here. I leaned into my run, ignoring the stitch in my side, eager for an uncomplicated acquisition.

It had been too long.

Even as Ansel inhaled, I could tell they were close.

Crawlers, his voice was clear, but a growl rose in his chest, and Lana picked up her pace to catch him just as shadows began to move under the trees, spindly limbs inching towards them.

Ansel unsheathed his blade, and Lana keenly yanked throwing knives from both hips simultaneously, crossing her arms for the briefest flash. She made her first throw—a nearly imperceptible flick of her wrist—as one of the shadows materialized into a blood dripping, toothy smile. It struck true to her mark, and the crawler shrieked in agony, vessel hissing as it burned from within. Her second throw hit home too, striking the crawler in the throat before it could so much as utter the slightest growl.

Ansel had already sliced two, grinning as they burned, eyes glowing like the last of the coals as the fire within them died out.

Save some fun for us, Aren laughed aloud.

Move your asses, Lana countered sharply.

Just then, there was a huge flash of light not far ahead of them, the creatures of the shadows screeching as it reached them. My eyes widened.

The braid! It was a unanimous thought as we all sprinted in the direction of our ascending soul. Ansel and Lana must have each destroyed a dozen crawlers, moving so fast not even demons could compete with their skills. Lower-level demons were fun to kill, if I was honest with myself. These ones just scuttled about the shadows, easy to burn with a blessed blade. But they were just clearing the path for Aren and me to make it to the girl without opposition. They couldn't have been more on the mark, because as I rounded the corner on the paved path, I saw her.

Suspended in the air, her red curls flying everywhere on the wind around her, the girl's eyes glowed a vibrant blue, light escaping from her entire being, hands clutching her throat. I drew my bow, inhaling to steady myself as I nocked my arrow. An average-sized man stood in front of her, wearing jeans and a hoodie, and I could sense the demon stuffed within the body. An innocent man in the wrong place at the wrong time turned into a meat suit. His hand was extended, telekinetically pinning the braid to an invisible wall. It was throwing false promises of freedom and power—the usual demon bullshit—and its words came to an abrupt halt as my first arrow pierced its hand, dropping the woman to the ground.

It whirled on us as Aren reached it, immediately palming the man's face as he roared, "Impius Vincendum!"

Energy pulsed from my heart through my limbs as the body collapsed in a heap on the ground, black energy steaming away from him as the demon was forced back into its true form. With a sharp twang, I released my second blessed arrow, and as it met its mark, the demon exploded into sparks, and the heaviness in the park vanished with him, frantic crawlers making their escape through the shadows as rapidly as they could manage, with Ansel and Lana on their tails.

Aren let out a howl of victory, and I could feel Lana chuckle despite herself as she cut down two more crawlers. She was our steadiest hunter but still felt the shaky high in her body like the rest of us. Aren winked at me before dropping down to feel the pulse of the man crumpled at his feet. His heart was still so steady he couldn't have been possessed for long. Minutes, if that. He held one large hand out over the wound in the man's palm, and after a moment of blinding white light, the flesh there was flawless. I gave him a nod as he scooped the man up and vanished.

With triumphant joy radiating from every cell in my body, I walked to the young woman on the ground, who was staring, stunned, at her hands, still faintly glowing blue.

"Hello." I smiled. "I'm Alvara. What's your name?"

She stared at me, stupefied, before stammering, "E-Em-Emilia."

I grinned at her. "I know you're scared, Emilia. We're here to help you. You can make that stop by wishing it so." I nodded to her glowing fingers. The glow slowly vanished as she focused. "You're in for a long night of questions and answers, I'm afraid. Shall we start with a drink?"

She eyed me warily before nodding slowly and reaching up to accept my outstretched hands.

I COULDN'T KEEP the smile from my face as I walked through Grayshell's hallways. I hadn't lost my touch. Not even a little—I was created to vanquish demons and liberate our kind from their chains. It was just August that had thrown me for a loop. He had to be a shield—there was no other way around it. *Un-freaking believable.* At least Alec would have company. I thought about that for a moment as I slid my glove from my right hand, grounding myself in the brilliant stone walls, which curiously told me that he would finally wake soon. By early morning, by the looks of it. Just enough time to get some food and a long overdue reprieve to rest.

I had sent Lana and Ansel out into the city to check on Layla, who would undoubtedly be in a flurry of panic about August. They couldn't reveal anything to her, but at least we could cast more protection around their loft, and they could scour the building for crawlers. While we didn't have to physically be there to check on her, it made me feel better knowing they were taking the extra step of precaution for August's sake.

I hadn't had anyone to worry about me when I vanished from my "life ." I winced, thinking of the agony of grief, and spoke a quick prayer for the beautiful woman August planned to wed. Their connection was written over every piece of furniture, every wall of their grand loft in the city. Whatever August did in that immense glass building, he did it very well. I thought for a moment about the place the green-eyed man called home. The tall ceilings, glass wall framing an incredible view of the skyscrapers surrounding it, exposed brick, and extraordinary, modern furnishings and finishes. That concrete and steel fireplace, though, was impressive. Especially so as I thought about his age. I guessed maybe thirty years to his name in this life. Nothing in his energy screamed generational wealth. Humble. Tenacious. Resilient. Something about him and his brother... seemed gritty. Like they had climbed that mountain together. Stone by stone.

The common room was deserted when I arrived. I walked to the stove and started water for tea before turning to the fridge, pulling out my pre-portioned chicken and greens and setting them on the counter. As the door to the fridge closed, I swiped the bottle of wine out of the door and popped the cork with a quick energetic pull. I set its chilled neck right against my lips, sucking down a long swig of Rosé before setting the bottle back on the counter. After I'd forced down the last of my vegetables, I snagged a dark chocolate from a crystal bowl, popped it in my mouth, and walked over to the hearth, the last of the flames flickering feebly in its heart. They warmed my skin, which I hadn't realized was still chilled until that moment. With a long yawn, I slid a pillow and blanket from the couch, placed the long, soft fabric around my shoulders, and laid down against the warmth of the floor in front of the fireplace. The flickering of the embers swiftly captivated my mind, silencing the voices and the noise of Grayshell around me.

It took all the energy I had left to do one final search of the energy in the halls—reassured that all was well in our home and family.

The moment my head hit the pillow, I found sleep.

Footsteps intruded on my dreamless reprieve, and I blearily blinked the haze from my eyes as my fingers automatically found their way to the blade at my side. I yawned and peered into the darkness. The unmistakable silhouette of Aren in the doorway returned the breath to my lungs, and I brought my hand back to the pillow, allowing my eyes to slide shut again.

"I remember being exhausted when I was called to you."

I reluctantly opened one eye to peer at him through the gloom. "You do?" My voice came out dry and drowsy.

He nodded, face serious. "Yeah. I just. I couldn't wrap my head around the weight of being bound to *you*. The weight of..."

"Being responsible for the fate of a *soul*?"

He nodded, eyes softening.

"You did good, kid. That was not an easy first call."

"Thanks." I smiled at him softly before allowing my eyes to slide shut again.

"Love you, Al. Proud of you."
"Love you, too. Thanks."

I didn't feel Aren lift me onto the couch or tuck me in with a great fur blanket, so I started, cocooned and a bit sweaty when I awoke there. With a quick roll, I was facing the roaring fire he must have stoked for us. Aren had taken my place on the floor, unmoving, face lit by dancing flashes and simultaneously marred by their shadow. The energy was stirring impatiently in my chest, and I blinked the sleep away, rising to brew us coffee. We were close. So close. I could feel the anticipation reverberating through the halls, buzzing in through the bottoms of my feet. I poured three steaming mugs of coffee, taking one to Aren and setting it at the foot of the fireplace.
"Aren."
"Mmm."
"Aren!" I nudged him gently, whisper-yelling at my Commander, who slowly peeled one eye open to look at me. I didn't have to see my face to know the grin stretched cheek to cheek was comical enough to make him open that other eye, mouth quirking. "It's time."

SIX
ASCENDED
AUGUST

The scent of coffee crept into my consciousness, and I smiled, pulling the blankets tighter against me and stretching out my hand, searching for Layla. As I started to stir, I felt a deep ache in my muscles, as though I'd run a marathon. My joints yearned to pop, and my pulse pounded away in my ears. The worst headache of my life set in right as I heard her gently call my name.

"August," she cooed.

Only. That wasn't Layla. My heart started pounding, reality wrapping its cruel fingers around my windpipe, and I flew upright, facing Alvara—alive, real, and more radiant than I even remembered, sitting on the edge of my bed. Everything about her seemed to release light—not like she glowed or anything crazy; she just seemed to *emit* lightness. Her long form was somehow slender and simultaneously powerful. Like a majestic warrior of lore. An Elf from *Lord of The Rings*. Only, she wore normal clothes today—the same form-fitting black t-shirt and fitted jeans clung to her subtle curves. Even in those worn jeans, her muscles were obvious. The warrior held her head high, her shoulders back, and her body open to the world. She had a blade in the case on her hip, and her feet were bare—toes painted a glittering pink that seemed far too childlike for the warrior goddess. Her piercing eyes were kind and full of warmth, and she was smiling. Smiling *at me*.

"Alvara?"

She nodded, and I saw the big man in the doorway shift slightly, arms crossed, pointedly watching me as though ready to come to her defense.

Not like I'd stand a chance. He wore a tight t-shirt today, and I was intensely aware that the man's arms were as large around as Alvara's defined legs.

"Aren?"

I swore his mouth quirked up just a bit as he, too, nodded. Sky-blue eyes sat below a strong brow that gave way to curved cheekbones and a stubbled, angled jaw. Beyond the brawn, there was strength in the set of Aren's features.

Her voice was clear, like a bell in the air. "Good morning, August. I know you have a lot of questions. We have much to discuss. But for now, you need to drink and eat—you've been out for a while. Ascension takes work, my friend, and by the looks of it, you did a great deal of it." Alvara's alluring smile broadened. Something deep in my chest stirred. An inexplicable desire to reach out and wrap my arms around her, to feel her hard body in my hands, rushed over me. I could vividly imagine her lips would be soft and sweet.

Fuck, what is wrong with you? Layla is waiting for you at home.

I snapped my mind back to the moment when she shifted her weight in front of me and shook my head to clear it. There was just something about that warrior-princess vibe and her clearly having saved my life from whatever those things were that came for the power they believed was buried in me—a long-abandoned fantasy.

I nodded slowly, swinging my legs over the edge of the bed before accepting the cup of coffee in her outstretched hand.

"Where am I?"

"Grayshell." She grinned like I should have known what the hell that meant. "Our home. Your home, should you choose it." She gently shrugged her shoulders.

"Layla!?" My panic choked the question, but she nodded again.

"She's fine. She's okay. She's anxious about you, of course, but we have a team on guard, and they've cast a ring of protection around her home. Your home, I suppose."

"Cast? Like a spell?"

"Of sorts. Humans call them that."

"Like...magic? Are you a witch?"

"I've certainly burned for that accusation before." Her brow furrowed, but her eyes still looked amused. "But no. Not in the black hat, chanting naked in the woods kind of way. I, um. I manipulate energy. We do. I mean, you can too."

"I can—"

"Move energy. Yes. However, we don't know to what extent. You're just coming through your ascension."

"Ascension?"

"Your rise, August. Your rise into your true power. What you were created for." Her words took me back to the dream—the memory?—of the monster that attacked us.

"Who—who are you? What are you?"

"I am Alvara, sixth ascension, in the third coven of the hierarchy of Grayshell. *You* are the seventh."

"What the fuck does that mean?" I looked to Aren for clarification, but the brute's face was curled with amusement, and he pinched the bridge of his nose, shaking his head. There was so much knowing there when his mirthful expression again found me. I wasn't the only one bemused by her explosion.

She choked on a laugh before saying, "Our ancestors were the Rephaim, August. Some of us are braids, although most choose life on Earth. All part angels. Part human. Angels are too immense to hold a human form for long, so they send pieces of themselves to earth, embedded in chosen souls, called braids. We assumed you were a braid—a fragmented angel spirit within a human vessel. But I..." quickly, she looked over her shoulder to Aren before she finished her sentence, "...saw that you're *more*. I don't know for sure, but I *believe* you are truly *our* equal." She pointed to Aren, then tapped her chest, eyes glittering with anticipation.

"A true half-breed, incarnated in this time for a specific purpose," Aren boomed from the doorway. He strode forward to stand by her side.

Images of giants—of demons—crept into my mind, and I felt myself recoil.

"Like...like the Nephilim?"

Her eyes grew serious, and her voice was softer as she said, "At one point. Yes. We are the closest living relatives—the remnants—of the Nephilim. The Rephaim. Men of Renown." She wrinkled her nose as she said the last phrase, then watched me as though she expected I was about to break.

Nephilim. This tall, inhumanly beautiful creature believes I am half-angel. I'm so far from an angel; it's nauseating.

I felt that way too. And thank you. Her lips didn't move except to smirk, but that clear, mesmerizing voice rang through my head.

I felt my eyes widen in shock, and I stared at her, unblinking, nearly missing the tiny flush in her cheeks. Then, the memory of the internal chaos at the office flooded back into me, muscles immediately shaky with adrenaline. She had led me...led me to her—from inside my mind.

"We are connected, August. All our kind are connected to their hierarchy—their soul groups and mates—after our ascension. Trust me when I say there are no secrets in Grayshell. It's handy at times—like when I needed help to save you."

"Save?"

"Yes." She nodded gravely. "Save. Those crawlers—demons—were doing all they could to sink their teeth into you. Literally, I'm afraid. Crawlers work for Lucifer. And he wants you on his side, too."

"Lucifer?"

"Yes. *The* Lucifer. Did I stutter?" She chuckled with a playful grin, snapping her fingers at me. "Do *try* to keep up, August. Satan, the enemy, pick a name; it's all the same. He wants anyone with power to align with him."

"Like me?"

"Like you."

I ran a hand through my hair and forced a breath, grateful my stomach was empty, as my heart had just fallen through it.

"How long was I asleep?"

"Nearly four days in human time."

"Four days?!"

"Yes."

"Layla. Layla must be—"

"Anxious. Yes. I am sorry about that. We will make sure you can get word to her."

"Word to her?! I have to go home!" I stood abruptly, sloshing coffee down my front, suddenly very aware of my bare chest and lack of pants. Only my briefs remained. And everything seemed...different. The ground was wrong—*am I taller?!*

"I understand your panic, August. But you cannot go home. Not quite yet. And yes, you're taller." She didn't bother to hide her smile now. She looked quite pleased with whatever changes she could see in me.

Anger flared in my chest. "Like hell, I can't."

"You are free to do as you please. But—listen to me—it's not safe. Not yet. You're much too strong and simultaneously much too weak to leave Grayshell. You don't understand your angelic powers—and let me tell you, they are here." She pointed at my chest as though she could see something emanating there that I could not. "You could hurt her without meaning to or reveal yourself to a stranger. There are too many things that could go horribly wrong. And if the crawlers feel your energy, they will come for you *both.*"

"Hold up," Aren cut in. "You already have too much to process and much more to come. Give the man a break, Ally." Aren revealed a folded pair of jeans and a simple t-shirt and set them on the bed behind me.

Alvara—Ally—bit her bottom lip before sighing and asking, "Let me warm that for you?" She nodded at my cup, and I held it out, not in the mood to eat or drink anything. She held her slender fingers above my coffee and swirled them around. The dark liquid mirrored her motion, sloshing around the rim of my mug before it started to steam.

"Take a moment. Breathe. Drink your coffee and get dressed. I'll be waiting for you in the hallway. Whenever you're ready."

With the room to myself, I took a moment to get my wits about me. Everything in the room was dazzlingly bright. The floor, while solid beneath my feet, seemed iridescent. A compact mist that had gained enough mass to hold me upright. I took a desperate sip of coffee, mind clamoring for anything with a sense of normalcy, and was relieved that it was a hearty dark roast. The taste and feel were both familiar in my mouth, as was the slight sting of the burn to my tongue. With a steadying breath, I stepped toward the vanity, pausing in front of a floor-length mirror framed in gold curves.

I was taller. Inches taller. Not only that, but my muscles seemed larger and more defined. My eyes raked over the reflection as I turned my limbs this way and that, attempting to reconcile the longer, stronger-looking frame to the body that I knew. My perpetually tanned skin seemed pallid compared to what it had been only days ago. Not as pale as my new companions, but certainly not the sun-soaked bronze I'd grown used to, spending all my spare time outside as I did.

Part angel. Part human...We are the closest living relatives—the remnants—of the Nephilim...Angels are too immense to hold a human form for long, so they send pieces of themselves to earth in chosen souls...

Our conversation rang in my head, which had grown light. I set the coffee down on the sink and retreated to the edge of the bed to sit. To try to breathe through the dizziness. *Nephilim.* Were we some kind of demons? The Nephilim were depicted as evil—the result of sin. And while I had certainly grown ambitious in James' and my mission to change our family tree, I had never fallen into a pattern of...of evil. I couldn't be...*evil.* Flawed, lustful, and too quick to anger, perhaps.

Alvara had said that the devil was after our power. But she made it sound as though we weren't his for the taking. So many questions ran through my mind, and I had to work to keep my heart from racing as the blood roared in my ears.

Slowly, I got dressed in the clothes Aren had set out for me on the bed. Their simplicity felt alien after years in a suit and tie or athletic wear without time for much else. Everything felt terrifyingly foreign, so I picked up my mug and headed for the door.

SEVEN

A BEAUTIFUL ASCENSION

ALVARA

August's ascension was impressive, even having seen more than a handful in my lifetime here. His body had gone from recreational athlete to fierce predator. His eyes had grown so much clearer, and I could imagine his vision was sharper through those emerald windows to his soul. The veil, quite literally, had lifted. His energy seemed to grow stronger as I waited outside his door, although maybe that was my own excitement.

No. It wasn't in my head. Couldn't be. His power was palpable. Just as palpable as the arrival of a ghost in your room or a mountain lion in the woods. Every instinct in my body was poised to react to whatever this man had in his arsenal. But I didn't feel threatened. There wasn't an inkling of darkness in his growing vibrations. He was light, embodied. Strength personified.

Good.

I knew that much. And my concern that Lucifer would sink his claws into him faded quickly. It would take a great deal of agony to dim that soul. I shivered and shook that fear out of my body. August would be guarded from that now. I was certain the hierarchy would hold up their walls for him, as they always did for those being trained.

His energy shifted as I heard his footsteps come to the door. He hesitated, then stepped out into the hallway, head held high. He swallowed his nerves and met my gaze, quick to return my tentative smile.

"Let's get you something to eat."

He nodded obediently.

THE CREASE between his brows never disappeared as he compliantly sat in the hall to eat, eyes occasionally surveying our surroundings. I did my best to shield his thoughts and focus on the plates full of hash and biscuits as he served himself his third helping. Ascension was exhausting. And even watching his post-rise meal, I chuckled, remembering the gnawing hole in my stomach when I woke and shared a very similar silent meal with Aren. When finally satisfied, August slid his plate forward, chugged the water by his hand, and set it down with a heavy thud.

His eyes were immediately piercing into mine.

"What now?"

"Now, you get all of your questions answered."

Aren arrived then, three glasses of orange juice in his enormous hands. With a curt nod to August, he said, "Hello, friend. Shall we start from the top?"

The very concept that angels took human form long enough to love or seduce human women is hard to wrap your mind around, and August stayed quiet as Aren and I took turns sharing our favorite pieces of our history. The debate was between angels who fell being the predecessors of our existence and divine angels somehow staying blessed. Aren shared his belief that while our ancestors may have fallen from Heaven, that didn't make them evil to their core—he believed their lust simply got the best of them.

"The tricky part is that all we've learned is that time passes differently for us than it does for mortals. The theory, in fact, is that time does not exist for angels. Within an instant of creation, they are blessed with the divinity of Heaven or cast down to hell or purgatory, depending on their loyalty to God at that precise moment." He ran a hand over his sandy hair before continuing. "And if time doesn't exist as we know it, they don't have a chance for redemption. But here's the kicker. We're not *full* angels. And while we can manipulate pieces of time to an extent, while Grayshell exists in its own time, we still exist *within* time. This means that our minds and souls change, and we learn. When Christ came to sacrifice himself for humankind, that included the human pieces in *us*. But since we carry the lineage of the fallen...we cannot fully ascend to Heaven. But we are not evil, and because we serve His will, we cannot be sentenced to an eternity in the lake of fire."

Aren laced his fingers, leaning forward conspiratorially. "We obviously have no way to confirm or contradict our theory. But it's the only thing that makes sense. We are stuck here...in purgatory of sorts while we do the bidding of the light. We are strong enough to vanquish veritable demons, yet human enough to relate to their impulses and damnation." Aren chuckled at the end of his lengthy explanation. "I've known enough mortal women to not judge our forefathers too harshly."

August looked at us, eyes bewildered, brow furrowed.

"The Nephilim are supposed to be giants?" He finally asked.

Both Aren and I nodded. I took that question.

"We're not exactly *small* people. Aphaea is the smallest in our coven and she is tall for a human woman. We believe that we may have gotten smaller each generation as they bred us into humanity. Or perhaps as we reincarnate, we come in a form that allows us to blend into our surroundings."

August was quiet for a long while, taking a sip of the coffee. Aphaea had brought us each a cup when the orange juice was dry.

"If...Nephilim are real, as demons clearly are; what about the rest of the supernatural world? Vampires? Witches?" The question was hesitant.

"I'm afraid that we explain a great deal of the legends you know. There are rare souls among us who can manipulate energy to such an extent they take on new forms. Like...shapeshifters. The darkness associated with most of your legends comes from dark souls and demons." Aren looked at me, expression grim.

"If we were created through angels that didn't turn from God but fell due to lust or true love...we believe there were others created from *truly* fallen angels. Demons among men. And they—they embody the evil we know as folklore. Their blood sacrifices. Their goal of immortality and power. We've found demonic entities drinking human blood and performing rituals that explain a lot of what an onlooker would call witchcraft or vampirism. Literally stealing a life force before destroying the vessel. Whether there is hope for the souls spawned from the demons...we don't know."

"But we're pale enough to be taken as sunless creatures," Aren added with a chuckle and a shrug of his shoulders.

"Why *are* you so pale?"

"We live here for the most part, and there's not much in the way of sun. We also heal significantly faster than humans do. Tans are, well, damage to otherwise fair-skinned vessels. We heal so quickly after our ascensions, we aren't really able to retain the benefits." I tracked August's gaze as he studied one of our earth wielders, her dark complexion radiant with the same glow that left my porcelain pallor nearly translucent. Her smooth mahogany skin was meticulously—*inhumanly*—unblemished. "The only scars you'll see among souls are those we chose to preserve in testament to earning them."

"Damn." August sat back, crossing his arms and nodding appreciatively. He looked around the grand hall, eyes skipping from one side to the other, taking in the vast space. Slowly, he emptied his mug and placed it down in front of him, turning so the handle was parallel to the edge of the table. We granted him his silence for a few minutes—ascension was a lot to take in when you *weren't* a half-breed. Braids had the easier go of it—anointed with a specific mission and able to mostly return to the life they knew. Still life-changing, but not in the way finding out you're half angel, built and ordained to defend humanity through battling demonic forces does. After a long while, he took a deep breath, eyes locking with mine again; the grief there was obvious.

"So...you keep saying we incarnated, or reincarnated...?" I nodded, hoping to encourage him. "So, my parents—my siblings?"

"Are still your Earth Family, August. Their love gave your soul a new vessel to use when your last was broken and raised you to be a man worth saving. I didn't sense divinity in James, although he is a good man."

He nodded in agreement, a little crinkle appearing between his brows again.

"How long ago—I mean, when was I here—there—before?"

"We don't know yet. That would take a past-life regression, a reading, a trigger, or a life-and-death scenario to dig up. And I'd strongly recommend you avoid the latter." I gave him a wink, and he smirked a bit, his sweet smile crooked and endearing.

"Here I thought all that past life stuff was bogus."

"Most of us did in our human years."

"So, I'm not...human?"

"Not entirely. I mean, our angelic sides are stronger and become the real us when we ascend, as you just did."

"Which is why you said not to go home?"

"Yes. Most of our powers are divine—they are designed to do good. But the same light that heals the body can also burn the skin. As we can if we don't understand how to anchor our energy. Panic, for instance, tends to draw unexpected energetic reactions. There was a soul who literally blew a hole in her apartment wall out of anger when her husband wouldn't believe what she was saying. Sharing the truth with mortals, it—it doesn't usually end well. Humans will do almost anything to pretend only the known exists." I hoped he could see the sympathy in my expression.

His eyes looked glossy and pained.

"Layla."

I nodded.

"Can I tell Layla?"

"That's your choice. But I've never seen it go over well. Just be prepared for that."

I could feel his anguish twist as the punch of reality set in. Everything in me wanted to reach out and take his hand, which was limply lying on the table by his coffee cup. His energy, so confused and desperate, was drawing me in like a moth to a flame, and it took all my willpower to resist touching those outstretched fingers.

He must have a choice. I chanted silently in my mind.

I realized I had not used enough willpower to keep the shields in my mind up when his serious and intense eyes snapped up to mine. He slowly reached forward to take my hand, and I slid it away under the table.

"Must have a *choice* in what?"

I felt the blood warm my cheeks, and I looked at my hands.

"I'm a reader, August. I—uh—I don't just manipulate energy. I interpret it. All of it. Past, present, and future. You're a shield of some kind, so you're probably a little trickier than most. But even the strongest shield in the hierarchy melts like butter when I touch his mind—Alec and I have made a bit of a game out of him trying to protect secrets and then me finding them anyway. Like a messed up, clairvoyant hide and seek," I laughed as Alec turned at the sound of his name and shot us a wink.

"So, when you say I'd need a reading to know my past life...you mean, *you?*"

I nodded again, doing my best to hide the nerves from my face.

"Did you—I mean, have you—"

"No!" I blurted, shaking my head vehemently. "No, I do my best not to read someone unless they've invited me to do so. I mean—our kind. I do my best not to read our kind."

He took a deep, steadying breath.

"So, that's what you meant. I have a choice in being *read.* So, how does that work?"

I held out my hands, willing them to steady despite my nerves. "It just takes a touch. The longer we touch, the more I can see."

He confidently reached out towards me, and butterflies flipped in my stomach at the idea of reading *him,* even as I slid my own hands back under the table.

"August," I warned him. "I see *everything.* There are no hidden places—your darkest and fondest memories, your pain, pleasure, intimate moments. All of it. They're all there. I can't pick and choose the first time I read someone. The reading kind of has a life of its own."

He let out a sigh and securely crossed his arms, surveying me with the caution that was more than deserved. I swear he smirked when he noticed the flush in my cheeks. Naturally, the attention intensified the heat in them. Even my palms felt cold and clammy, and I nervously wiped them on my jeans.

"And once I've read someone, those memories are as much a part of me as they are of them. Which means I can share them with someone, too." I closed my eyes, dropping my mental blocks and drifting through memories until I stumbled on Alec meeting Aphaea for the first time. I focused in on her energy to him—how alluring she was. Her long hair was brunette in that life, softly swirled into a pompadour bun. The enormous, floppy burgundy hat upon her head matched her elaborate dress adorned in black lace and ribbons. The smell of roses was thick in the air as he held his hat to his chest, lowered into a polite bow, and accepted her outstretched hand. The instant they touched, his shield dropped, and he wanted all of her. All her energy, all her baggage, all her strength. He sensed her power, her predatory grace hidden behind layers of silk and lace, and was drawn to it.

I opened my eyes to find his, wide and fascinated, trained on me intently.

"Wild," he breathed again. I laughed and gave him another nod, my head feeling absurdly awkward for being attached to my neck with all that bobbing.

"It's more intense if I touch you to show you. You would nearly feel the air on Alec's skin. But that requires also being read."

"Damn." The smile was there in his voice and eyes before it touched his handsome mouth. A slow laugh was exchanged between us, and the air once again felt charged with an intensity that made my head spin. I pulled a pair of gloves from my pockets and slid them onto my hands, smiling as his eyes studied the movement.

THE FAMILIAR SOUND of knocking an arrow filled my muscles with anticipation, and I drew back, took my quick, steadying breath, and released. August's eyes were wide as I met my mark, and when the next arrow split the first, he laughed out loud.

"Damn! Can you teach me to do that?"

"I'm not sure you could handle it yet." I winked back at him. "And you, my friend, will remember how to do this if you've done it in a past life, which I suspect you have." I tapped my outstretched bow against his brawny chest.

"Oh, I bet I can handle more than you know. I don't mind getting my hands dirty."

My mouth popped open, and my gaze flicked to his hands, beautifully tanned and outlined with bulging veins and tendons that made my mouth dry. Was that *insinuation* in his tone? Couldn't be, could it? Eyes narrowed, I lifted my chin and shot back, "Prove it."

"Challenge accepted." His voice stayed level, but I would have sworn pink crept up his neck into his cheeks.

"I guess we'll see what's in there, Mr. Porter." My fingers tapped the side of my head as I grinned.

We walked across the hall, tables pushed to the sides of the room and a grand white abyss stretching down to our targets. They were lined up in front of the Grayshell crest on the wall—great fanned angel wings, with a sword in place of the spine—and I noticed him study it before turning his attention to the bows, quivers, and countless arrows laid out on the table. August grabbed one up, and I followed him back to the starting line. He stood for a moment, feet all wrong, and took his first shot. Lucky to have landed on the target, he winced and looked back at me.

"Awfully bold words for a *rookie*."

He shrugged playfully. "I'm more of a gun guy."

"We'll get to that later." I offered what I hoped was a reassuring smile and jerked my head over toward the display of supplies. "Come back to the table for a moment."

He stood in front of the countless weapons splayed across the grand wood table and ran a hand through his hair.

"I'm regretting skipping that station at camp." He shot me a cheeky grin, and despite my better judgment, I returned it. Being with August was easy. Effortless. I didn't bother reading the rooms or any objects because being present with this soul was intoxicating. His energy was light, optimism radiated from his core, and there was a determination in his eyes and the set of his stubble-shadowed jaw.

His tour had felt like talking to an old friend, and the onslaught of questions never felt tiring, as it had when I had helped others train their braids and recruits. It was fun to be in his presence—he felt young and somehow unjaded despite a soul pulsing with so much strength that I knew he couldn't be new.

His Earth life was good—raised in middle-class, blue-collar America, his parents were still happily married. He and James had a younger sister, Freya, who had surprised their parents when the boys were eleven and twelve. Her arrival kept them together during a tumultuous patch, and as she grew, their love reconnected.

August was the first in his family line to earn a degree. He quickly moved up the ranks at his corporate job until he walked away and started his own financial firm. While Aren would've been enthralled by the depth of details he shared about his work, finance had never been an arena I was particularly interested in. Therefore, I had a very limited understanding. I preferred to use my visions to accurately stake my investments rather than actually study what made them tick. Not necessarily moral to use my gifts to fund my adventures, but neither was the stock market.

Over the years, he, James, and his best friend, Sam, had built quite an empire for themselves. Once the firm was flush, they'd started investing in properties, primarily low-income housing and vacation rentals. He was coming up on thirty and already had accumulated more wealth than most humans can wrap their minds around. If it were a normal mortal length, he could've walked away from everything and never worked another day in his life. And I couldn't help but feel this deep-seated pride for the gorgeous man pouring his entire story out to me. He worked hard—endless hours of midnight oil. And that was something I could admire above almost any other trait. He would be a sharp asset here. Or at least, that's what I told myself when I realized I was prying too far into his personal life.

The sound of him tossing an arrow back on the table brought me back into the moment, and I grinned.

"Take a moment. Breathe. Deeply. In through your nose and out through your mouth. Again. Close your eyes. Ask them which one belongs to you."

He slid one eye open, smirking at that last statement. I elbowed him in the ribs, and he laughed before closing them again.

"Ask them which one belongs to you; let your hands hover along them and see which one speaks to you."

He ran his fingers across the table and came to hover over a long bow.

"Pick it up—feel the weight of it."

He moved swiftly and obediently, holding the bow away from himself before drawing the string. It was nearly his height, and something about the way he drew it, focus etched on his face, made the hair on the back of my neck stand up. I nodded. He closed his eyes and pulled an arrow from the accompanying pile—sleek, all black except for the navy blue fletching. He felt it, turned it between his fingers, and returned it to the table. Slowly, he let his hand drift over the assortment of tools, and his fingers stopped on a traditional wood one. He examined it in much the same manner as the first before looking at me, eyes narrowing suspiciously.

"It feels...familiar."

I smiled and gave him another approving bob of my head. My hair was still on end in the static charge of our energy, and goosebumps popped up along my skin as I stepped back and watched him correct his stance and take aim. Hot damn, that bow looked good on him.

The sharp twang of the release was ended by the quick, definitive thud of the arrow in the bullseye. He turned to me, deep v between his brows, eyes disproportionately serious, and something else. Fearful?

"Alvara," he nearly whispered, voice husky. My name on his lips wound my stomach into a sudden, unfamiliar knot. "I remember."

EIGHT

ALEC

AUGUST

The sharp brine of blood on the air overpowered the rank smell of sweat, sea, and steel. Everything in me ached, my heart booming against the inside of my ribs. Exhaustion heavy in my limbs, I cursed the weight of the armor on my body as the mud squelched below it. My fingers traced the edge of the bow, and I lifted my eyes to the rain...

"Alvara," her name barely escaped my lips; something about the attentive way her eyes found mine made the feel of her name in my mouth significant. Weighted. I forced my eyes closed, pushing into the images flooding my mind. "I remember...I remember it—the battle. Agincourt. We —we crossed the channel. I was an archer. A soldier. It's as if the bow *told* me. I remember. The weight of it in my hands was so...familiar," I stared down at the longbow—the *English* longbow. I had been an English soldier, and we had taken Agincourt.

When I opened my eyes, Alvara's cheeks glittered with tears; her hand was on her chest as though she couldn't breathe.

"Are you okay?!"

Tears streaked her face, but she laughed, sounding as sweet as chimes in the air. Seeing that smile on her was so intoxicating I had to force myself to return to the moment. *I was a soldier.*

"Alvara?"

She inhaled sharply and smiled at me again, shrugging her shoulders. "Proud, I guess," she said uncertainly. "That's great work, August. The first trigger is a really significant moment. Did you say Agincourt?"

"Yes—we came over the channel. I-I remember it, Alvara. I remember it so vividly like it was just yesterday."

A great booming laugh broke the air between us, and I turned to see Aren entering the hall. While immensely intimidating, he only seemed head and shoulders taller than me now.

"Agincourt!? You were in that shit show? Damn, brother—that was quite the standoff." He turned his eyes to Alvara. "Your calling was in the Hundred Years War, love. Judging by the trigger, I assume he served King Henry the Fifth. We'll swap battle stories soon, friend. This is great progress for one day. Unfortunately, for now, I require your sire."

In a mind-to-mind exchange, Alvara let me know someone would be along for me and told me to stay put with my bow. I loosed a handful of arrows before a woman's familiar, trilling voice broke the air.

"An Englishman, then?

I turned to find Aphaea walking my way, her gait somewhere between a saunter and a waltz.

"Evidently so."

"It never gets less strange, remembering lives long past. Just so you know."

Her ever-present shadow—the man called Alec—followed behind her. He had silent confidence to his stride—the broad hold of his shoulders, the subtle, always present smirk on his face. But the gentleness in his light brown eyes somehow disarmed me. He didn't feel like a threat. Which, of course, made me wonder if that was intentional. He was, after all, *the shield*. Alvara said he was the strongest shield in the hierarchy. While I didn't know the numbers behind the claim, I knew it meant I should respect whatever skills he had, hiding in that inevitably misleading exterior.

He ran his calloused hand through his shaggy, light reddish-brown hair. He wore it longer than the rest of them, and it came down below his jawline. Slowly, eyeing me, he grabbed a bow.

"You are a strong one," he chuckled. "I thought Alvara was pulling my leg. But this. This should make things more...interesting. I'm Alec."

I nodded, already aware.

"I remember. I'm August Porter."

He leaned back, assessing my frame before his light eyes found their way back to my face, still analytical. "I've been assigned to begin your training, August. Alvara wanted you to rest, but Aren thought you'd be up to start. How you feeling?"

"Fine. Let's roll." It would do me no good to show any of them weakness. As it was, I was still full from breakfast and had more energy reverberating in my body than I could contain. While my mind was weary with information, I wanted to prove I had control of these new abilities. I wanted to prove I could go home and tell Layla I was okay. Whether I was demonstrating that to them or to myself, I hadn't decided.

TRAINING WITH ALEC WAS...INVIGORATING. He didn't hold back the way Alvara seemed to. Instead, he seemed to like pushing my limits—he was constantly evaluating how I moved and rebounded when I fell. It seemed he was administering an unspoken test of my abilities. He was just slightly smaller than my new 'ascended' frame, and our capabilities were often even. This new body was just as fast, just as agile as his.

With a broad, amused grin, he raised his hand for a high five as we finished our run. I obliged quickly. I liked Alec, despite myself—in spite of some intrinsic knowing that his threat was more than he let on. As our hands met, an image flashed in my mind of a man in armor on horseback, frame squared to our attackers.

His smile faltered, and his eyes looked distant for a moment before he turned his dubious gaze back to me.

"Carlyle?" His voice was serious and not really a question.

The name sent me into a vicious whirlpool of color and sound—countless images of a life I immediately knew to be a long-lost memory. Countless memories of battle, of hunger, the smell of horses and steel. The cry of the dying. The figure of a woman—my woman—slipping into a steaming spring surrounded by trees, only her long hair concealing her bare back. A moor draped in fog. Countless ships. So much blood. And a young man, bow slung around his scarred shoulder, mischievous smile always on his face, even in the direst of circumstances. His name laid heavy in my mouth. As the visions faded, I found myself queasy, as though I had been on the tilt-a-whirl for one too many rounds.

"Robert?" I retorted.

Alec's eyes widened frantically, like a man coming up from the depth of the sea for air.

"Brother!" he bellowed, throwing his arms around my shoulders. I held him tight, eyes burning as the reality set in.

"Jesus Christ, it's been a hot minute." He shook his head.

"Holy shit—Agincourt?" I asked.

"Among many. Christ, I never thought I'd see you again. I knew there was something about you. Bloody hell." He shook his head again as though to clear it. "No wonder you were so damn hard to kill. The way they followed you despite your rank—you were their shield then, too. Damn. Did any of your scars come through this round?"

"Scars?"

Alec turned his head to the side, pulling the neck of his t-shirt down to reveal a long, thin birthmark along the line of his shoulder. I could see the end of it peeking out of the hem of his short sleeve across his bicep. Exactly where his scar had been. A blade, meeting its mark, slicing through his muscle. I had covered him as he retreated to the medics.

"Holy Shit! I don't know. Of course, I've never known to look." As the words came from my mouth, I thought of all my birthmarks. Alec reached for my arm, grabbing it at the elbow and turning it towards me, tapping on a line of freckles along the bone there.

"I remember that one." He chuckled before tapping my chest. "Any birthmarks above your heart?"

I eyed him curiously, thinking of the dark pattern that had always been there.

"That's how they killed you, mate. At least in that life."

I shook my head and took a steadying breath. This was bound to be a wild ride.

More memories made their way into my mind as Alec and I sparred. The man called Robert was in most of them. Hunting trips. Nights full of ale and chasing women. Endless marches. Miserable, eternal nights standing guard through pouring rain and sleet. And countless—literally countless—fights, brawls and battles. I'd only made it as far as Agincourt before I'd been stabbed by a French soldier after the battle, exhausted and guard down in victory. I managed to slice down the man behind the blade, and then the world went black as night. Despite much encouragement and incessant coaxing and coaching from Alec, I couldn't jump into the next life.

"Ahh—you'll get it," he growled as he kicked my legs out from under me. I landed hard and winced as the fall rippled through my body. I deflected his next move quickly, rolling to avoid his attack. As the memories returned, I recalled his advances, his fighting style, and how he moved his body. He was my dear friend in that life, and we had survived too many violent encounters to count, side by side. The memories spilled through my muscles—a new body remembering lessons from lives long past, much to my amazement. The motions flew through my limbs as though I'd done them a million times. I supposed I probably had. Just not in this life.

Eventually, he had me in a chokehold, and I tapped out, aware he was more practiced in this body than I was. He was quick to his feet and turned, reaching out a hand to help me to my own.

"You're remembering quickly. I don't know who you've been in your ascended lives. But if Carlyle was any indication, a fearsome being is all I can foresee now." Alec slammed his fist to his chest, bowing his head the slightest bit before allowing that trademark smile I knew so well to slip back onto his face. He handed me a water bottle, and I gulped it down obediently. "And we share a gift beyond battle now," he tapped his scarred fingers to his temple and gave me a wink.

We were shields. Both physical defenders in past lives and, from what I'd been told, mental as well. Alec's shield, it seemed, included emotions to some extent. His ever-easy-going demeanor was achieved through some greater control.

"How do I use it?"

"In time. It'll all come in time."

"You had to have been assigned because of your ability."

"In part. Alvara and Aren both have a good sense for souls that connect deeper, though. She can't always explain it, but she usually has some semblance of intuition of who has been in a soul group. Hell of a mentor you've got there."

"She seems it. Can you tell me about her? She hasn't exactly been... forthcoming. Beyond talking about Grayshell."

He smiled. Playful and familiar, he teased, "Inquiring about another woman, old friend?"

I laughed. It seemed I had not been the kind of fellow to take a wife until the end of that life—there were only a few memories of the woman I felt tied to before the blackness.

"I just mean. You all seem to have a deep respect for her. Is she...your leader?"

"Of sorts," Alec shrugged. "Aren is Commander. She's Aren's calling. His second. And she's got an immense amount of power in that mind of hers. Spooky, honestly. She's skilled in *most* things. Her clairvoyance is parallel to none—the visions she casts are scary accurate. And even without a vision, her intuition is very rarely wrong. If you tell her I said this, I'll kick your ass, but she's probably the most lethal of us when it comes to combat."

"The *most* lethal. Really?" I snorted. She was all kinds of intriguing, ungodly beautiful, but she didn't seem *lethal*. That ethereal voice lingered in my ears, mesmerizing eyes imprinted on my vision.

"Aren doesn't count—he's a legend for a reason. And I'd wager...she's second only to Ansel *if* she's *really* tired." He flashed a pearly grin that dripped in a cocktail of arrogance and endless stories. "That kind of power, wielded in such a disciplined way...it earns respect."

I felt more than heard someone approaching behind us and turned to see The Commander himself. He leaned a casual shoulder into the door frame, his hands sliding into his pockets. "How do I put this nicely..." Aren chuckled. "Our Ally...has a natural inclination for violence."

I about spit my water out my nose as he laughed.

"Don't get me wrong, she's pretty easy-tempered; it's just...when she's done, she's *done*. Like...It takes a *lot* to get her going. But there's no slowing that train down once it's gotten up to speed."

"I certainly wouldn't cross her," Alec laughed before chugging the rest of his own bottle. Something unspoken passed between the men, and they reached their hands out for each other. The moment they grasped each other's forearm, their eyes went hazy. The fog only lasted a matter of seconds before Aren nodded in approval.

"Nice work, gentlemen. Eat. Drink. Alec, show him how to be a shield."

"What was that?" I asked when Aren had gone.

"My shields are almost always up. It takes a decent...err...distraction to drop them." Aphaea appeared in the doorway, walking to his side as though on cue. She snaked her arms around his bicep, rising on her tiptoes to kiss his cheek.

"Sometimes it's easier to share my mind if we touch, and Aren and I can communicate quickly that way. Alvara and I have the opposite challenge. While she must work to clear her mind, to lend us privacy...I have to work to invite them in. I suspect you'll be much the same. It's what made you so hard for her to find."

"The dreams—"

"Were real. You were tapping into the spiritual plane. She was trying to reach you there. How long do you remember them?"

"It feels like a lifetime. She popped up in them for some time before they got more...desperate."

He nodded, expression grim. "I don't know if you realize how close you were to being swiped by crawlers."

My skin prickled into goosebumps, hair on end. "The demons."

"Yes. Very much real. And very strong on that dimension."

"Layla. I dreamt they killed Layla."

He grimaced. "That wasn't a dream either, I'm afraid. Alvara got the vision at the last possible moment."

"How was it the spiritual plane if they could have killed her?"

"We are souls in bodies, August. Not bodies with souls. If they destroyed her soul, she would never have woken from that sleep. Human doctors label them as heart attacks or strokes. But it was spiritual warfare."

"My hands?"

He smiled, but his eyes fought the gesture, still grim. "Some of our minds have stronger holds on our bodies than others. Your spirit is immense. Intimidating, if I'm honest. It's why I believe you survived as long as you did through endless wars. Who knows what you've gone through in other cycles. Did you ever hear about a schizophrenic dying when they hallucinate a shooter?"

I had, in fact, heard of those unexplained occasions. I inclined my head.

"Our minds are powerful tools and quite obedient to the experience of the soul."

Alec's wisdom had accumulated tenfold since the life in which I called him Robert. He was coming up on his hundred-and-thirtieth birthday in this life. Their mortality hinged upon being murdered or committing suicide—otherwise, no injury or disease was a threat. *My* immortality. That was a staggering realization.

We ate a lunch of herb-encrusted roast turkey and mashed potatoes—one of my favorite meals. Comfort food. It tasted eerily close to the way my mother would make it for Thanksgiving. I couldn't help but suspect Alvara somehow knew that minute detail and made it appear on the table for us that day. Her energy was undeniably nurturing towards me. Being sent out on a mission with Lana and Ansel, whom I'd met only briefly, didn't seem enough of a deterrent to keep her from looking after me.

Ansel and his mate were the first members who didn't seem overly concerned with welcoming me. His steely eyes surveyed me like a threat, which, oddly, was his job, I supposed. When Alvara turned to motion to his mate, the sharp-eyed blonde sauntered forward.

"August, meet Alana."

Alana's eyes rolled so far back in her sockets that I thought they'd vanish there. She huffed a breath as she accepted my outstretched hand. "Only my mother was allowed to call me that. And as she's been worm food for over three centuries, It's *Lana* to you."

"Alright," I chuckled, and her eyes brightened. "Nice to meet you, Lana—never Alana." And then they were gone, off to retrieve a braid.

Mental sparring was far more strenuous than physical sparring. We were in the coven's lounge—the room dark, except for the dwindling fire under the great carved mantle. The decor was eclectic—in stark contrast to the uniform white that was Grayshell. Alec told me each piece had a story—a collected item from those in the coven. The kitchen gave the room a homey feel, and we settled in around the island.

Sitting across the counter from Alec, I practiced dropping and raising my shield. It took immense energy to let him in, his voice finally ringing in my ears while his lips remained motionless. Alec promised to keep his shield down as we practiced so I could hone the skill of telepathic communication with another Nephilim in our coven.

Alvara seems to break through when the rest of you don't. Is that because she's my sire?

Maybe. But Alvara has yet to meet a mind she cannot master. Perhaps you were her calling *because she could crack you when others wouldn't.*

Perhaps. Is it normal to feel...attached to your sire?

Yes. There had been no hesitation in his response. *Sire and calling are assigned intentionally. God doesn't make mistakes. They are almost always in a soul group. Like a spiritual family who cycle through together.*

Why don't I remember her? If we're in a soul group?

Patience, mate. Memories come back over time. You're already making killer headway. If she's in your soul, you'll remember each other. Unfortunately, contact helps.

And she won't touch me?

Not unless you're ready for her to know everything.

Everything?

Everything. For her to see past lives, you'll have to hang on long enough for her to filter through this one. She can't...sort memories. She sees them all.

That's...

Uncomfortable? A nearly perfect vision of Layla's charming face popped into his mind.

With the metallic finality of a prison cell slamming shut, my mind closed in on itself — shield back in place.

"Good instinct." He smiled. "You protect those you love. That's admirable, August. An excellent trait to have on this team."

My head was pounding, and I bowed it into my hands, rubbing my temples.

"We can be done," Alec said, more a question than a statement.

I shook my head. "I just need a break."

"Aye-aye. Whiskey?"

"Angels drink?"

"Hah! I'm no angel." He flashed a cocky grin. "Just the descendent of a rogue one." Alec winked, then snapped before pointing a pair of cheesy finger guns in my direction.

I chuckled. "Hit me, then." Relief washed over me as Alec pulled two small crystal glasses from the cabinets and poured us each a dram. We drank together, and he began to pour again when the glasses were back on the counter.

"Slàinte!" He smiled before downing his.

"A Celt, too?"

"More than once." He grinned. "I'm excited to hear your stories, mate. I wonder if we've cycled together beyond Agincourt."

"Wouldn't we remember?"

"Eh—it's hit and miss. Human memories take triggers. I don't think we've ascended together, though. We usually remember those lives when we wake up."

I shook my head, "I don't remember ascending."

He cocked his head to the side. "That's...intriguing. Maybe you shield yourself—ha!" He laughed.

"Can you do that?"

"I dunno, man."

We practiced our shields again, and then Alec taught me how to open certain memories or thoughts to be read on contact. It was exhausting work. But there was a part of me that felt triumphant. Evidently, most souls had to be trained at length to shield their minds. To keep prying souls and phantom hands from getting any information they didn't wish for them to. As a shield, the role was different. Alec and I inherently had shields in place. It was part of who we were. As I grew stronger, I would be able to expand my shield to the team or demand it retreat within me. Those were the skills Alec would teach me. A small, human corner of my mind flinched from that notion...but somehow...that just felt...right.

The clock chimed midnight before we took another break. The warmth of the whiskey and glow of the fire had long since extinguished. My mind was drained, but my body was still energized, buzzing with the excitement of the day—the reunion with an old friend...a *very* old friend.

"Alright," Alec gave me an approving smile and poured us another round without so much as shifting his legs from their lazy sprawl over the bar stool between us. "This part is more important than the rest. It's critical that when we need to, we can communicate to the entire team. You've mastered letting me in. You need to master dropping them completely. So, the team can reach you when they need you."

"So...push it farther out?"

"Yes. For me, I visualize an actual bubble around me. It helps me to push the boundaries to let others in. For some, they collapse the shield within themselves. Just play with it."

I took a deep breath and closed my eyes, resting my head in my hands. I visualized the bubble around me and exhaled slowly, envisioning it expanding. Slowly, Alec's ever-calm consciousness entered mine. And then I could feel Aphaea, her thoughts on a book somewhere in her quarters. Aren, in his rooms as well, mind intent on a map on his desk with dozens of names scattered across it. He was watching his keep. His legion, as it were.

Then there were more voices—an overwhelming amount of them—thinking, planning, laughing, and loving. I allowed my eyes to open and made no effort to hide the wonder I was feeling, eliciting that broad grin from Alec. He gave me a thumbs-up.

Good work. Keep going.

I closed my eyes, and the voices became a roar in my mind. I could feel my pulse quicken and knew that Alec could hear it, as I could hear his steady one across the island.

Slow them down. Break them apart.

How?!

Push August. Force them apart.

Focusing in, slowly but surely, the voices began to separate into coherent thoughts. With a start, I realized I was hearing...prayers, wishes, and cries for help.

I...I hear...prayers?

Excellent! Can you make any out?

Right as I tried to dissect the voices, a sharp pain formed in the center of my forehead. I closed my eyes tighter as though I could push it away. But a hot steel blade was being forced into my skull, and I grunted in pain, doubling over.

"August?! Pull back, dude! Pull it back."

I tried. I tried to pull the boundary back, but it wasn't moving fast enough to cut the excruciating pain. Hot steel. Piercing my mind. A bruising ache radiated down to my temples, violent tendrils wrapping around my spine. My neck was going to break. Bones were going to shatter. Mind would go liquid.

Make it stop—

I cried out, unable to contain the agony as it ripped from my chest. Suddenly, I was vomiting, but the release did nothing to stop the burning. My mind was on fire. Splintering into a thousand pieces. A vase dropped off a balcony.

Alec touched his fingers to the base of my neck, and an eerie numbness inched out from the place he pressed. The tingling trickled through my body—that returning circulation sensation creeping through my skin. He was lending me his shield. Like the numbing shot they gave before filling a cavity. The pain slowly began to ease, but the pressure in my mind was pounding against my skull, inescapable. Heart thudding frantically, I tried to draw in my own shield, and then I saw the most horrifying image that had ever entered my mind. Alvara. Drenched strands of hair sticking to her bleeding face, which was twisted in agony—she was tossed to the ground and wrapped her arms around her torso to hold her waist, as though binding her insides together. Her lips were already bruising from whatever impact caused the blood to pour from her mouth. There was a deep gash across her shoulder, and her arm was saturated scarlet. A man's voice was screaming her name, and I realized Ansel was not far from her, but his blade was clashing with a giant of a man in a billowing cloak whose eyes were black as night. He was defending Lana's limp body lying on the grass.

Ansel threw his weight against his blade and, in a desperate cry, bellowed, "Aren!!!"

Suddenly, my shield snapped closed. A guillotine, beheading, the nightmare emblazoned on the back of my eyes. Ringing in my ears.

Alec jerked his hand away from my neck as running footsteps echoed down the hallway.

"Alvara?" His voice was a whisper, soaked in disbelief.

"That wasn't a dream?" I forced out the question, knowing the horror of the answer in my frantic heart. Ice had replaced the blood in my veins. My voice was husky, and the strain of the burn slowly eased from my head.

"No. I don't think so." Alec's face had gone wan, his eyes wide.

Aren and Aphaea both came skittering around the corner, horror etched across their perfect faces, a deafening alarm screaming through the halls of Grayshell now. I could feel them before I could hear them. Countless boots thundering on the marble floors.

"Ally?!" Aren roared as he turned the corner, Aphaea looking fierce on his heel.

"New York," Alec responded.

"Now!" The Commander boomed, and Alec and Aphaea sped to his side. Others, so many flawless faces I didn't know, all crumpled with grief, many with closed or unseeing eyes as they muttered prayers, gathered robotically in the hallway. Their hands immediately outstretched to connect with the shoulders nearest them.

"The Men of Renown have our own." Aren bellowed over the crowd. His canine teeth elongated into predatory fangs. The chill that ran through the crowd was palpable and shuddered down my spine, too. "As children of the King, they will fall on our swords before they can be taken. As will we."

"As will we!" the gathering echoed. The warriors had all drawn fangs, rage seething in their eyes, and they slammed their fists against their chest in terrifying unison. Suddenly, they were all clothed in the unearthly white linen and the light leather and armor I'd first seen them in, weapons sheathed at their sides.

My stomach turned in agonizing circles, vise constricting my chest, and sweat was dripping down my back. Alvara. She needed me. And although I couldn't understand why the depth of my attachment was what it was, *I* needed *her*. Some deep-buried intuition said I had to go. Had to go with the group of celestial warriors. Had to fight for her. To bring her home...home to me. I couldn't explain how it felt like the air would leave my lungs if I failed. The way I knew without a doubt it would shatter me.

"August. Stay put." Aren's thunderous order filled my feet with leaden ice as though I had no choice but to concede to his order.

"Like Hell!" I barked back, blinking at my audacity. But the icy hold on my legs thawed, and I looked down as a gust of wind replaced my own clothes with armor that matched Alec's. There was a sword at my side and a long bow in my hand. I could feel the quiver pressed against my back. My bewilderment only lasted a moment. And then the Commander eyed me, a quiet fury burning in his gaze. The fire seemed to fade as he assessed my materialized weapons. The briefest flicker of surprise flashed across his face. His chest rose and fell once, eyes shifting to Alec by my side. And then he nodded.

Hang on, kid. Aren's voice echoed in my skull.

I reached forward, and the moment my hand met Alec's shoulder, the world swirled into white and warm brown, and the ground fell out from under me again.

NINE

FLIGHT

AUGUST

In the time it took me to blink my eyes, we had landed on hard ground, and the air was chilled and charged with a summer storm. The wind whipped the air around us, heavy with the smell of sweat and steel. The suddenly familiar cacophony of conflict filled my ears.

I opened my eyes and staggered backward. The giants in dark cloaks were all our height or taller. Their features were hard and angular, skin so pale it was nearly grey, and their eyes were woven with shadows. They roared in their effort, and I saw their teeth were all razor-pointed fangs. Their skin was ashy gray, in stark comparison to the luminous pale of the white-clothed warriors. Our group exploded—bright shrapnel flying into the dark clearing in the park, engaging immediately with the opponent. Steel on steel and shouts of effort echoed into the night.

I spotted Aphaea's white hair as she dove into the fray with seemingly no regard for her own skin. She flung her throwing knives into the throats of two of the giants, and they staggered back, gurgling as their wounds hissed and sizzled, steam erupting from their necks as they collapsed to the ground. In three swift motions, she dove through the mess of cloaks, slicing them down as she went—their throats slit as they fell to their knees. Her speed was astounding. With another flick of her wrists, two knives found two spines of giants looming over a huddled mass in the grass. And then she dove to the ground. I started towards her, and then Ansel stepped into view, a veritable wall with eyes promising death. Aphaea scooped her arms under Lana's limp form and vanished into the night.

With his attention free, Ansel's lips snarled over lethal bared teeth as he slaughtered more of his assailants in a haunting dance of muscle and metal.

A sudden burning stab sliced across my torso, and my hands flew to my ribs. They came up dry, and I knew in my heart it was Alvara. I turned on my heel, somehow sensing where she would be in the melee. She was surrounded, skin glistening with blood and sweat, one arm wrapped tightly around a wound in her torso, rivulets of blood pouring through her delicate fingers and down her exposed abdomen. Somehow still fiercely menacing, she swung her sword in a tight circle. A small woman with black hair cowered behind my sire, her face bruised and smeared with red. For the briefest moment, Alvara's eyes met mine. The momentary shock was replaced with desperate understanding.

Save the braid, she demanded, right as a clap of thunder released the sky's fury, rain pelting my skin. I dove into the chaos, drawn to Aren's wake as he sliced down The Renown. Also, heeding her call for aid. He was the only one that seemed to be a match for their size, and he was a flurry of great swinging fists—daggers slicing across their throats and chests—and striking swords, leaving heaps of bloody giant to either side of his path. He marched with a single-minded focus toward his calling, not slowing to ensure their demise. With a cry, the behemoth closest to her disarmed Alvara, and she fell to the ground, scampering to right herself, an animalistic hiss escaping through her bared fangs. But she wasn't fast enough, and the monster fell on top of her, fist slamming into her delicate face with the momentum of his descent. Agony rippled through me as though I was absorbing her pain.

Before I could process my movements, I had released an arrow, and it went flying into his spine. He fell on top of her as another dove, colossal hands wrapping around her neck. I screamed her name as her free hand wrapped around the fingers closing on her windpipe. Something stirred inside my chest as I let another arrow fly. While it flew sweetly, too, the monster only roared at the pain and tightened his hold on her. Her ivory fingers were dyed a dark red, and they grappled across the ground.

My head was spinning. Everything was a blur of dark and light, and Aren was engaged with three of the giants, outrage roaring from him. I slid through the mud, slicing the back of a giant's knees and rising in a tight spin as another fell on my sword. It was *memory* guiding the whirl of blades. The chaos was too tightly wound to wield my bow. I cried out in disgust as my eyes found one of the monsters with its razor teeth embedded in the neck of a thrashing Grayshellian. My sword met his skull with a sickening, meaty thud, and the soul dropped to her knees, clutching the bloody bite at her neck. She nodded at me once and vanished, leaving only darkness in her wake.

August—Alvara's internal voice was weak, and I could feel her eyes on me. A barbaric cry ripped from my throat, alien energy surging through my veins as a blinding pain tore through my skull. Blood filled my mouth, and I spat it on the ground below me, tongue tracing the sharp point of my own drawn canines. Instinctively, I threw my arms towards her and saw sparks cross the gap between us. The sound of a bomb erupting burst into the clearing, and the giants suffocating and battering Alvara were thrown into the air, projected several yards away from her. I was instantly aware of the countless eyes on me now.

Run, August! Run, dammit! Alec.

I dove forward, rolling to avoid the swinging arm of one monster, only to leap over the kick of another. Over the tumult, I could hear Alvara coughing, spluttering, gasping for air as she rolled to her side. She held her head in her hands, screaming the most blood-curdling sob I'd ever heard, goosebumps erupting down my arms, and white-hot pressure building in my head again. She squirmed and writhed in apparent agony. Without fully understanding what I was doing, I threw my energy toward her, envisioning the shield swelling out to cover her. A moment later, she stilled, gasping for air, blinking the pain out of her eyes. She rolled onto her belly, eyes finding me in my mad dash towards her. We locked gazes, and her desperation nearly undid me.

Steeling my resolve, I cut down more of the Renown, unwilling to stop to process what was happening. *Just get to her. Get to Alvara.*

She staggered to her feet right as something hard and heavy smashed into the back of my head, knocking me to the ground. The shield collapsed back into my mind. I rolled and dove onto my feet, lurching to steady myself as my vision blurred. The creature advanced, sadistic smile across the sharp features of his ashy face. Soulless eyes full of pleasure. His sick grin was all teeth, and he swung his giant arm—steel sword flashing through the air. I barely had the reflex to block his assault. Again and again, his heavy arm swung, and it took all the strength my body possessed to press back against him.

His eyes flashed with anger, and before I had time to deflect, his other arm jabbed forward, the blade slicing through the thin skin on my ribs. Feet staggering, my hold faltered. Fear stabbed my racing heart as I fell to my knees. But I had to stand. Had to rise. Because Alvara. Was. Screaming.

You will not fall. Not here. Not now. Get. Up. I demanded of my shaking body.

Die a different day. Aren's voice ordered into my mind. Although if it was to me, or the cadre, or to himself, I wasn't sure. But the magic obedience demanded that I stand. My sword rose ahead of me, swinging with a rage that echoed in the minds of all our kind. With one irate burst of steel and deep-buried hatred, I put down the giant between me and Alvara.

She was crumpled, hands pressing into her temples, agony rippling through her scream. I fell to her side, horrified at the amount of blood pooling around her, at the desperate, piercing cry tearing from her. It was her head that she cradled in her bloody hands. The way her body writhed in unseen agony. I knelt next to her, hands fluttering uselessly over her broken form. She was supposed to be indestructible. This couldn't happen. Not now. Not to her.

Aren!? Alec?! Anyone?!

Sand or sea! Something too vast for her mind. They knew her. Wash her clean. Water, August—call forth clean water!

What?!

Alec's bold energy planted the image of pulling water from the ground with magic. The image made me panic. I couldn't—didn't know how.

Suddenly, Alec was standing by my side, eyes hard with focus, blood dripping from his brow, and Ansel guarding his six in a mad duel with two monsters, masterfully parrying their attacks. Though he had been engaged with the giants the longest, he didn't even seem winded, arms still steady. Lethal, as he drove his sword into the heart of one before pulling it to cut the throat of the other. Only the bead of sweat on his brow revealed the effort. Behind them, it seemed Aren had taken on six himself.

Alec inhaled deeply, planting his feet in the Earth, and reached his fingers downward with an energy I couldn't explain. As he exhaled, beads of water rose from the ground, spiraling around his outstretched hands. He brought his arms upwards over his head, and the droplets merged into an enormous stream of water. *Clay cleanses and grounds the energy.* That was all the explanation we had time for.

Alec swung his arms forward, an invisible axe slicing through the air. The water poured over Alvara in waves so heavy I panicked she'd drown, but slowly, her body stilled. The wind kicked up viciously, and I knew that was my friend too—drying Alvara, perhaps.

"Shield her!" was all he said to me. He released his magic flow of water and air, scooped up the trembling black-haired girl behind Alvara, and vanished. He reappeared alone only a moment later and threw himself back into the skirmish. Ansel took his place between us and the clash of bodies and steel. The metallic smell of blood and reek of sweat overwhelmed me. The cries of the injured engulfed all my senses.

I knelt by her side, took a breath, and focused on expanding my shield. As it enveloped her, her body went limp, shoulders collapsing in on themselves, head falling into the mud to her side.

"How do we get her out of here?!" I barked at Ansel.

"I need a cloak!" He roared into the void, sword slashing violently, tearing blood from our enemies. "She can't handle a read right now! Find something to wrap her in!" He bellowed over his shoulder.

I felt them before I saw them. The eerie chill reached up into my bones. The shadows seemed to slither and stretch. *Crawlers.* That's what she'd called them.

Frantically searching for a cloak, blanket, anything—panic wrapped around my throat as the demons snaked through the compact crowd towards us. I started to tear my own shirt from my sweat and blood-soaked body, but a spark of golden light caught my eyes.

I looked down at Alvara as gold electricity danced between her fingers, and an adrenaline chill shook down my body with inexplicable *knowing.* Slowly, she opened those piercing green eyes. The gold encircling her irises seemed to glow, the same electric color as the sparks on her fingers. She pushed her torso off the ground, lethal eyes surveying the chaos of twisting bodies of swirling airy white and heavy black fabrics.

She snarled, lips pulling back over bared teeth. "Enough!" she growled. Outrage flashed across her haunting features. She wiped the blood from her mouth as she bowed onto her hands.

"I said enough!" Her voice was magically amplified to echo out over the clash. Her irises glowed gold as the sparks popped and sizzled on her fingertips, tendrils dancing out into the ground around her hands.

Without explanation, I turned to the group, throwing my shield out as far as I could push it, envisioning a web of protection around our kind, and screamed in my mind, *Fly, dammit!*

I just knew that we could. Knew what she was about to do.

And we all leaped into the air as though they had to heed my command. As her kin safely left the ground, Alvara slammed her hands further into the Earth, which bent under her fury. The electricity surged through her, the ground erupting into an explosion of crackling, gold lightning. Everything in contact with the Earth was scattered into the air—rocks, branches, dirt, and grass flying under our feet. The crawlers and Men of Renown were tossed into the void, electricity sending their bodies and shadows into quivering seizures. I saw the eyes of those closest roll into the back of their sockets. And with an enormous crash, they collapsed, sparks still surging through them.

Our comrades gracefully landed, gliding in a unified movement towards Alvara, white shirts and cloaks billowing out in the wind behind them eerily. Some slowed to scoop up injured. Or dead? I didn't know. We all moved towards her as she leaned back on her haunches, her shoulders curled in with exhaustion.

My Queen. The thought was a shielded whisper.

Only Aren stepped towards Alvara, unstilted, eyes pained as he assessed her. His white linen shirt was torn and stained with blood. Aren's eyes narrowed as he looked at me with distrust. I took a step back from his glower and looked back to Alvara. Her gaze also trained on my face, a mixture of shock and pride in her eyes. Slowly, her irises lost their haunting glow, returning to her unmistakable emerald.

"August, I—"

She collapsed forward, eyes sliding shut. I fell to catch her but got shoved sideways, out of reach. Sparks of anger ignited on my own fingers, and I looked up to see Aren, who slid under Alvara's limp form easily, cradling her to his blood-soaked chest.

His wary eyes returned to my face, voice a menacing growl when he spoke, "Who are you, August Porter?"

TEN
ANOINTED
ALVARA

It was a long swim out of the black. When I awoke, I kept my eyes closed, my mind doing an inventory of the damage. Everything ached, and my head felt as though it had split in two, pain radiating down my spine. We healed fast after ascension, but the agonizing flash of fire under my left ribs reminded me they had lanced me through on a demon blade. Or two. I couldn't discern whose weapon had gone where. Or why they cared about a damn braid enough to risk a full-scale battle in central park. It all came flashing back in startling, vivid, painful images. Lana being smashed in the back of the head and falling into a heap at Ansel's feet.

I pushed my energy out and found them both quickly, sipping on tea in the common room. Relief washed over me, and I took a deep, painful breath. My attention quickly diverted to a familiar energy, pulsing in the air to my side, and the familiar faint scent of something sweet, leather-bound books and spring rain.

Did I...summon lightning?

Aren inhaled sharply. "Jesus Christ, Alvara. Scared me to death."

I forced my eyes to open, ignoring the way they burned from the sand chucked into them. The swelling was already reduced enough to see him clearly. His bloodshot eyes were ringed with exhaustion, the surrounding skin nearly purple. The gashes on his face and chest had already healed, leaving behind only thin white lines, which would reduce to nearly nothing within a day.

"Sorry," I mumbled, sitting up and wincing as pain shot through my ribs. I blinked into the brilliance of Grayshell.

He shook his head, a familiar smirk stretching across his face. "And yes. It was fucking badass. But where the hell did that come from?"

"I don't know, honestly. I was just. So angry. And August was in danger —he shouldn't have been there. But he was—was fighting alongside us, fighting for me..."

Aren shifted uneasily in his seat, the chair creaking beneath him as he leaned forward to brace his forearms on his knees. I snapped my eyes back to his face as he ran a nervous hand across his short, sandy hair.

"What?" I demanded.

"August, err..."

"Is he?!" The panic burned through me like a thousand demon blades, my heart hammering in my chest, terror devouring my mind. And Aren...his mental shield was a wall, impenetrable in my exhaustion. I would rather be impaled by the giant with the poison sword than lose August.

"He's fine, Ally. He's upstairs, under Alec and Ansel's guard."

The word clanged through me. "Under *guard*. Why?!"

"Ally. He's... He's different."

"And?"

"Ally he...he commanded the coven to *fly*. And we were forced to obey. The entire legion flew, Ally. Like—"

"Angels."

He nodded.

"Damn," the word came out in a whisper, and I stared down the familiar ice-blue eyes of my sire. "But that means he's..."

"Either an old Commander, one of Lucifer's Commanders, or—"

"Archangel blood," we said simultaneously.

"How?"

Aren shook his head, eyes heavy. "I mean, before, he threw sparks at you, and you sent off a shockwave like a bomb. And then you..."

I winced. "Conjured lightning."

"Yeah. That."

"Damn," I said again, rubbing my aching head and then pinching the bridge of my nose. *Think, Ally, think.*

"Don't think too hard," Alec rounded the corner into the infirmary, cocking his brow and smirking playfully. "Wouldn't want to get yourself hurt. Well. You know, *again*." He tousled his tawny hair and grinned at me. "That was pretty badass, Ally. Guess you *can* teach an old dog new tricks."

I couldn't help but laugh as Aren glared at him but said nothing. Alec's clothes were virtually unscathed—a small splatter of blood at the hem of his shirt and belt, the only sign he was even in the battle. Damn shield.

"Aren, I've come to request the release of my charge." He unceremoniously collapsed into the chair beside Aren, leaning back and kicking his feet onto the bed. "August is no harm to us—he's in *my* soul group. We fought together for England."

"Agincourt."

"Yes. I knew him well in that incarnation. Owed him my life many times over. And he has been nothing but obedient and vulnerable during training. He opened his mind, Aren. All of it, to me—there was no shield left. I'm not Ally, but I saw nothing there to ward against. He—" Alec eyed me quickly, amber eyes glistening like pools of whiskey. He seemed to change what he was going to say, and I didn't have the strength to pry into his vaulted mind. "He cares for Ally. Deeply. I'd bet every dollar in my wallet that they're soul group. It was karmic devotion to *her* that charged his command."

Aren opened his mouth to argue, "Only Commanders—"

"Can take charge of the hierarchy. I know. He doesn't remember his past ascensions. He might have been King once." Aren had never been willing to claim such a title, so he infinitely stayed The Commander.

"I've been in this coven for nearly seventeen hundred years, Alec—you think I wouldn't recognize a past Commander?"

"I don't know. But he doesn't recognize *us*. Only a Commander, or Archangel blood, can perform the feat he managed. Riddle me that," Alec winked.

"*Any* Commander, Alec."

"I know." The tension was palpable between them, leaving me wishing I had something witty to say to slice it open.

"Listen, you're my Commander, Aren. I will obey your lead and trust your instinct. But I do want you to know. I trust him. With my *soul*. I do not believe the devil has snuck a wolf within Grayshell." Alec planted his boots on the floor, slapping a hand on Aren's shoulder. "But if the human Carlyle could survive all he did and garner the respect and following that he acquired...an ascended one will be...*astounding*. I won't argue. I'll take my leave. Your move, Commander." Alec rose and stepped forward, laying a hand on my chest across throbbing collar bones. He took a breath, his hand glowed white with his unscathed life force, and I felt the pressure in my chest release, bruising easing palpably. "Rest, Ally. The world will still need saving tomorrow."

His spiritual Novocain poured over me, and I let it pull me back under the veil.

I awoke to the aroma of olive oil and the familiar damp trace of anointment across my forehead. Sage and wildflowers lingered on my skin, bringing a smile to my face. They called in the best healer for this mess.

"Saraya?"

Her silky hands were instantly on my head, cool and unmistakable, washing over me like a mountain spring.

A voice like music, she hummed back, "Hello, sweet Alvara. It's been too long."

I opened my eyes, grateful the stinging had subsided and soaked in her familiar face. Saraya was in a far-off coven within the hierarchy, so our paths didn't cross often. But she was the best healer any of us had ever seen. Unnecessary. But I appreciated the gesture. Aren would, of course, pull out all the stops for me. Her hair was bright as flame, cascading red spiral curls tucked into a neat plait down her back. Saraya was nearly as old as Aren— the second longest lifeline in the hierarchy. She would be the next Commander if the succession followed tradition. A thought I couldn't even grant energy, as the idea of living without Aren was unfathomable.

Deep brown eyes peered down at me like pools of melted chocolate.

"Any better, sweet girl?"

I inhaled deeply, noticing the ease in my ribs and spine, the lightness of my head. I nodded, smiling up at my old friend. "Thank you for coming down."

"Anything for you, sweet girl. Besides, who could pass up a chance to heal the lightning bearer?"

I winced, wrinkling my nose. "Good Lord, I pray that doesn't stick."

She laughed, the sound light and welcome. "I'm not sure how you can get rid of that particular moniker. It sounds incredible, Ally. I've never heard anything like it before. And I'm no spring chicken." She winked and took a seat on the edge of the bed, crossing one leg over the other.

"I still don't know how I did it."

"Does it really matter? What matters is you did it. And the entire hierarchy is indebted to you. The Men of Renown caught us off guard, my dear." Saraya gazed off into the distance, sensing something unspoken. "What do you think drew that power forth?"

"I don't know for sure, but I think it had to do with protecting August."

"Your warrior calling." Warrior calling. August dove head first into battle alongside Nephilim with centuries under their sheaths. He crashed right up against our true giant cousins with no hesitation and cut them down in his path towards me. Had thrown his shield over me—that skill took Alec nearly a decade to perfect, and August had guarded me within a day of waking. My breath had grown shallow as I walked through it in my mind, and I inhaled deeply.

"Evidently so."

"Have you read him yet?"

"No. It's his choice, Saraya. You know that."

She shrugged, closing her eyes as if to say, 'what's it matter'. Reaching forward, Saraya pressed her palm to the pulse point in my wrist, and a wave of our missed months flooded through my mind. She truly was amazing at what she did.

I grinned at her. "You have no secrets, sister. He had a life. A wife—"

"I saw no ring on the handsome man I kicked out of here not twenty minutes ago."

"Okay. A soon-to-be wife," I laughed. "A business."

"We all had lives, sweet girl. We all ascended to our greater calling. Have you asked him?"

"I didn't really have the time. I'd only just told him about my abilities when Westerlund called for help with the wave of braids in New York, and, well, you know what waited there. Marcus and his brothers were already spread too thin, and I was so distracted by August that I didn't see it coming."

"It's safer for all of us if you know him. *See* him."

I shook my head, and she laughed.

"His choice, I know!" She threw her delicate hands up in surrender.

"So...he was here?"

"Yep, sent him away to eat something just a few moments before you woke up. He left muttering epithets." She raised her brows, the corner of her lip twitching. "He cares for you, Ally."

So, Aren let him go—trusted Alec's judgment...my judgment. That, at least, was something. "That seems to be the consensus. Sire-offspring bonds are intense, as you know."

She smiled but narrowed her eyes. "If you say so."

"I would've hovered around Aren, even in the beginning."

"As you say, sweet girl."

She didn't remotely agree with me, but she brushed the hair out of my face with her cool fingers and turned around to a small metal trolly on wheels, plucking up a cotton ball, dipping it in clear liquid, and swiping a wet washcloth. Saraya turned her gaze back to me, and dabbed the cloth across my cheekbone, which still stung, and then moved her attention to my ribs which only ached now. She ran the damp cotton over both wounds, and leaned back, smiling.

"You were always stubborn. Resilient. It comes in handy when something should've *killed* you." A wry smile crossed her beautiful face but didn't touch her eyes.

I shrugged, not necessarily agreeing but not arguing either. "Super healing," I said with a wink, trying to brush it off.

"Super healing doesn't count with cursed swords and daggers, dear. Honestly, at this point, the healers are going to make you a frequent flyer card."

I rolled my eyes. "It's not that bad."

"You're on a first-name basis with the entire wing."

"I'm their second in command; it's in the job description."

"Not if you only know them because they constantly keep you on just this side of death, darling."

"Hey," I winced as I sat up, scooting against the headboard. "Somebody's gotta take the hit."

"Doesn't have to be you every time," she said softly, brow furrowing with concern.

"You know better than to bet against me, Sar."

"You have an entire coven to lean on, Alvara."

"Like hell will I let any of them get hurt on my watch. I can't go through that again. I won't survive it twice." I yanked at the back of my tight neck, exhaling harshly. "That shit sticks with you; this, on the other hand," I motioned vaguely to my body, "will heal within a day."

Saraya blew out an exasperated breath, cradling my cheek in her palm before patting it twice. "Perhaps. I just don't want to see you call a play you can't come back from. As it is, you're lucky that calling of yours had the vision when he did."

That brought me up short, and my gaze flew back to hers. "August? August had the vision?"

"At the same time, Aren heard Ansel call for aid. But August...August is why we knew what we were up against and just how many of us were needed."

"We thought he was a shield—not clairvoyant." I thought for a moment about August and couldn't remember any sign of a gift like mine. But then again, his mind was always tightly sealed shut and took a good amount of effort to pry into. The way he moved through the battle—as though he'd done it a thousand times, on Aren's six. He certainly didn't fight like a white-collar man. He fought like...me. Like he could anticipate their moves before they got there. I closed my eyes, trying to picture his face and remember how he looked in his angelic armor. He was beautiful, now that I wasn't trying not to die. And as they did in the dreams, those bold green eyes lanced into my soul. I ached to see his face. To study him. To read him.

Saraya's sigh brought me back to the infirmary. "Whoever you caught for us, he's not born to be an underling. And the way I heard he commanded the troops. I've never heard of anything like it."

"Aren either."

She shook her head. "Be careful, Alvara. Until you've truly seen his mind, be vigilant."

I bobbed my head obediently. "I don't sense danger in him." Her eyebrows shot up, so I quickly added, "Danger for *us*, Saraya."

She smirked. "I was going to say. A dozen kills in his first fight, casting shields, commanding armies—doesn't exactly sound docile."

"Alec says they fought together—it would have been centuries ago—as humans."

She nodded thoughtfully, pushing a loose spring of vibrant red hair behind her ear. She pressed a relaxed fist against her mouth as she chewed over some train of thought on the subject before outstretching her arm, palm facing the sky, fingers limp.

"Can you?"

"Show you?"

"I want to see the lightning bearer in action." Smirking, she stretched her hands towards mine. I took a deep breath and reached for her, grasping her arm firmly at the elbow, our forearms connecting down their length. I opened the gates.

After a long moment, she pulled her arm away from mine, eyes looking just as puzzled as before.

"There are legends. Legends of a chosen one—"

I rolled my eyes, and she cut off her thought, smirking.

"I know, but hear me out. A Nephilim, who is *also* braid, a god-ordained Commander that cycles through when he or she is needed."

"Impossible. Aren—"

"Is an unprecedented leader. A gift. Truly. But he's not the first exceptional Commander. And he won't be the last."

I flinched away from her words. Somehow, in my mind, Aren was the final King of the hierarchy. The final Commander.

"We only grow stronger the longer we live. If he hasn't fallen in over sixteen hundred years—"

"It would take a great opponent to bring him down. No doubt. But there has never been a Commander that hasn't fallen on a sword."

"There has never been a soul that survived as long as he has."

She shrugged, conceding to that point.

"As legend has it, the ordained Commander—the King of our kind—will only appear when his wisdom and blade are absolutely necessary. And his word would hold more weight than the reigning Commanders."

"Which would mean..."

"A storm is brewing, Ally. We've all sensed it. All feel the urgency to listen to our callings and acquire them quickly. All sensed the value of training, praying, and seeking guidance. Trouble. It feels like trouble."

I thought about the countless panic attacks in the months we tried to find August. The way my heart was racing indefinitely. The way I felt like I could not fail a single braid. Couldn't give even one up. The pressing sensation that we needed all of them to ascend, with no time to waste. She wasn't wrong. There was trouble vibrating in the very air surrounding the earth, an evil buried in its core.

"I've seen no visions of a King. Of a grand finale. Of an imminent war between dark and light." I had seen a white horseman. Heard a reverberating bass voice growling threats. Neither of which seemed particularly connected to August.

"The war has *always been*, Ally. Think about it. The humans are always entangled with the enemy, constantly wrestling with his tricks. But the demons I've encountered have been...bolder. They're not hiding anymore."

"No. They're not. But I haven't seen any of what you're describing. How could I miss something monumental like that?"

"You're the closest thing we have to an omniscient mind, but being close doesn't make you so. Even Alvara, second in command of Grayshell's armies and the greatest reader of our time, is part human. Even you are fallible, my sweet girl."

I took another breath, grounding myself. Forcing my focus away from her perfect face, I eyed the grand walls of the infirmary, stared at the luminous mist that was our ceiling, the omnipresent glow of white everything, and breathed in Saraya's comforting scent of olive oil, sage, and something sweet and floral. I didn't want to think of myself as fallible. I'd yet to miss a vision that could affect the hierarchy. From the moment Aren led me to ascension, I had been the guardian of these halls. The watchdog. The last line of defense between us and the evil that lurked all around us. Our little dimension and the souls that lived within it had not been attacked since I had joined them. And I took an immense amount of pride in that. Close calls? Yes. But never a downright mistake.

...Until yesterday. Until I was so preoccupied with my calling that I didn't see us attacked by The Men of Renown. The fallen Nephilim of legend and lore. The enemy's army against us. I shook my head, infuriated.

The periphery of my consciousness detected a kind, anxious energy making its way here. No thoughts encapsulated in the vibrations. My heart sped, and I smiled.

August. We're about to have company.

I'll take my leave. She smiled sweetly, moved the clattering metal trolly to the head of the bed so it would be out of the way, and left the room.

ELEVEN
LIGHTNING BEARER
ALVARA

Only seconds after she'd vanished from view, I heard Saraya scolding August in the hallway. Relief trickled through me when he insisted he'd eaten as she'd ordered and informed her unless she wanted to drag his dead weight away, that he was staying put. A laugh escaped her lips, and I could picture her charming smile as she walked away. Little did August know a soul Saraya's age could easily scoop him up like a petulant child and whisk him to wherever she wanted him to be.

I had just taken a sip of water when he walked around the corner, handsome face stretched into a beaming smile.

"Good. You're awake! Your hair kind of resembles a straw bale, but it's cute. Very human of you."

I about shot water out my nose. Coughing and spluttering on what had gone down the wrong pipe, laughter erupted between us. "I'm sorry, did I wake up in some teenage vampire book?!"

Heart hammering in my chest, I sat up and ran my hands through my hair, pushing it to part to the left, where I preferred it, and pulling the long ends around to the side, attempting to straighten the mess.

He shrugged. "They were super popular in high school, and the girls there liked them. Some of them were cute."

"*You* read them?" I asked, incredulous.

"Don't judge me."

"I won't," I smirked. It was like sitting with an old friend again. If I closed my eyes, I could forget everything racing through my mind, everything Saraya said, and soak his energy up. There was no doubt that we shared a past life or two. "I read them too. But I read most things the humans like. It helps me...relate to them a bit more."

"I find that hard to imagine. You're...well...the lightning bearer."

"Oh God, not you, too." I closed my eyes, feigning pain.

"It's got a good ring to it."

"No, it doesn't." I shook my head.

He chuckled, and I opened my eyes to survey his handsome face, his strong jaw, the shadow of stubble having deepened since we sat together last. His wavy hair was looser without the gel I'd grown accustomed to, but I liked it better that way. And those eyes. Mercy, those eyes. They were hauntingly familiar, and the longer I held his gaze, the more something in me swelled and settled into knowing. Knowing him—he was soul group, no doubt. Although Alec and I had no known tangled lives before he found Fae, there was a huge gap between this incarnation and Agincourt, so the possibilities were endless. He held my gaze for a long moment, and the humor and lightheartedness slowly drained away.

"Alvara." His voice was husky, and the sound of my name on his lips made my stomach squirm uncomfortably, like a sudden drop of an elevator or ride at a county fair. He cleared his throat and ran his hands through his thick curls. "Why didn't you call for backup sooner?"

I scoffed, "Because this isn't *Reno 9-1-1*."

He rolled his eyes and glared at me, but the slightest quirk pulled at his mouth.

"Ally I...I don't know how to explain it, but I can't lose you." A sudden wave of anger rolled off him, and I met his gaze again. "What the fuck were you thinking?"

"Excuse me?!" I sat up straighter, narrowing my eyes at the accusatory tone.

"How could you be so reckless? Barreling into a mob that size alone?"

"I wasn't alone."

"Okay, barreling into a legion, outnumbered ten to one?"

Ten to one. I weighed the truth of his words for a moment, grinding my teeth at the accuracy of the assessment. Keeping my tone flat, I said, "We've beaten worse odds."

"Not without a strategy. Or so I'm told."

"We strategized."

"Without preparation. Alec says you've never missed a conflict before. He says you always have the vision first and wind the timeline around like a spool of thread until you see your victory."

"Apt description."

"You had no vision. No proofed strategy. How could you have been so foolish?"

Scowling, I rocketed off the bed, wincing as the movement pulled on my injuries. August rose suddenly, staring at me unflinchingly as I barked, "What's your problem, kid? There wasn't *time*," I ground out the last word. "We had the braid, and they wanted her. We had to fight. Simple as that."

He yanked his fingers through tangled locks as his feet began to pace, voice guttural as he said, "You could've come home."

"Oh, don't lecture me, rookie." Tone condescending, I glared at him, lengthening my spine as August spun back towards me, prowling forward. "We couldn't jump home with a celestial enemy so close and nothing to keep them from stowing away." I took a step backward as he stalked towards me, the hard set of his jaw and sharp gaze sending my heart sprinting. Throwing my shoulders back with a painful tug, I continued, "Grayshell has never been breached in *my lifetime*, and I will keep it that way."

"How long is your lifetime?" He snapped, tone haughty as he closed the gap, yanking on my tightly chained temper.

I crossed my arms defensively as my back hit the wall. "Three hundred and twenty years, *Rookie*. You've got forty-eight hours and—"

"How old is Aren?" His stabbing gaze was pointed as he cut in, leaning a forearm on the wall above my head, caging me between him, the wall, and the bed. "The *Commander* said you should have sent for aid." He quirked his head in silent demand, pinning me in place with his gaze, embers of power lighting the irises as the air thickened.

"Fine. I underestimated the Renown. Happy?" The audacity of this newborn soul. Did he know who the fuck he was talking to? I raised my chin defiantly, heart racing at his intense proximity. "Not that I owe you a damn explanation, but I didn't know their numbers at first, and they're not normally so organized—it *should* have been easy." August was towering over me, a muscle in his jaw feathering, his heat and temper tangible, raising goosebumps across my skin.

He scoffed, swallow audible as his Adam's apple bobbed. August flexed his fingers before he jammed his hand into a front pocket. But when his livid emeralds snapped back to mine, they captured my breath with the depth of the fear concealed there.

"Look. I'm sorry if you got freaked out. But this is *what I do*. Yeah, it was a close call, and I'm the first to admit it was unexpected, which I'm not used to. I was..." I swallowed thickly, realizing he'd shifted closer still, his breath hot against my face. For a heartbeat, my eyes lingered on his full lips before I snapped them back to his. Finally, with a shake of my head, I huffed, "Distracted."

"By?"

"You." The clipped answer was just as pointed as his questions and seemed to cut him short. He blinked. I took a long breath to dispel the tension settling in my chest. He looked at me for a long moment before sighing and pushing off the wall. The sudden space between us steadied my breathing, and August palmed his jaw as he surveyed me.

"Why? Why did *I* make you miss something so critical?"

"I don't know." I was determined to keep it honest. "You're my first calling. I suppose that warrants some degree of hyper-fixation. Seeing you're trained, taught, and cared for, adjusting to your new world. I didn't intend to throw you into the deep end."

He shifted his weight from one foot to the other, expression vaguely disappointed as he looked at his feet. Anger still came off him in palpable waves, leaving salt and acid in the air.

"August?" I finally prompted after a long moment, tension building instead of dispersing as I'd hoped.

"It felt...it felt like I was being lanced with a hot iron. Like I would split in two. I can't describe it. The thought of losing you was—" he shook his head, brown hair shifting frantically as if to sweep his mind clear. With a heavy sigh, he collapsed onto the edge of the bed, bracing his elbows on his knees. I stayed rooted against the wall, my arms crossed. "Agonizing. And... familiar. In the way Alec's smile was familiar before I knew we'd cycled together. Like...I lost you...*failed* you before. Like you were sacrificing yourself again."

"Again...you think we've incarnated together? I died for someone?" I mean, that would track. There wasn't a soul in the hierarchy unworthy of falling on a blade for. There was no fear of death for me, as we didn't truly lose our lives. Not really. We just... cycled our way back through, usually stronger, collecting skills and gifts as we went. And Aren would find me again; I knew it in my soul.

He bobbed his head once and ran his long fingers through his hair again. I stared momentarily at that one nervous tick, betraying how deeply his emotions affected him, and wondered what those shiny strands would feel like against my skin.

"I can't explain it. I couldn't in the moment, either. But. You've been out for hours, and I've had time to think it all over, to analyze the way everything played out. I didn't have a word for the pain I felt. But it was grief, Alvara. *Grief.*" He let out a long breath, eyes on his hands clasped between wide knees.

"I'm sorry," I finally whispered. "Sorry you felt that."

"Not sorry you about took yourself away from—from us." He turned his face up to look at me. This was personal. An old hurt we'd have to face sooner rather than later.

I shook my head, gently coming to sit on the bed beside him as I softened my voice. "It's just one cycle, August. If I have to come back through to keep a soul safe in its mission, so be it."

The anger rolled off him again, the intensity of it flashing in his eyes, and sparks jumped between his fingers. The reaction caught his attention, too, and the heat settled instantly. He stared at his hands.

"Nice trick." I flashed him my most effective smile.

"It's gold, like yours."

"August," I chuckled, "I don't conjure lighting."

His dark brow furrowed, and he cocked his head to the side. "Bullshit, you don't. You killed all those Renown with it."

"Well. I hadn't ever conjured lighting *before*. Not until yesterday when you..."

"You think I gave you the lighting?!" He chortled a panicked laugh.

"I mean. I don't know how else to explain it. You were there for the first time—kind of a badass, by the way—you threw energy at me. Something sparked across the air like static, and I was able to shove them from us with a burst of energy I didn't have left to give. And then, the next time you were scared..."

"You were the lightning bearer."

I nodded.

"That doesn't make sense. I got the sparks from you. Not the other way around."

"August. I've been battling demons and Renown for nearly three centuries, and not once have I channeled electricity. You show up. And I explode with a wave of it I can't explain? You got another theory?"

He shook his head and finally broke that penetrating gaze. He stared up at the misty, evasive ceiling for a long moment before his voice came out, hushed and husky again.

"I...I knew what you were going to do before you did it. That's why I yelled for them to fly."

"Why you commanded them to fly," I corrected.

"I didn't know I could do that, either."

"You're an infant, August. We have no idea what you're capable of at this point. But they were forced to obey. You made them fly."

"Apparently, we don't do that?"

I shook my head. "Only true angels fly. We can jump from one point to another, as they can. But only angels actually...levitate off the ground in a controlled manner. Or at least, only angels *have* been able to fly. Evidently, you knew something the rest of us didn't."

A gentle, crooked smile broke free of his indignation.

"I mean. That's kind of cool."

"Big first day, kid."

August rolled his eyes. "Why do you and Aren insist on calling me that?"

"Because you're a child." I laughed, and he shook his head.

"I guess when your mentor is a millennium old," he said with a shrug, "that really does make me a newborn."

"Correct."

We both laughed, and I was grateful to feel the tension leave the space between us. He sat still for a moment, eyes closed, breath deepening. I couldn't help but notice how beautiful he was. His muscles held more weight than most of us—he was broad, like Aren, whereas many of us grew lean. He had new thin lines on his hands, and callouses had already healed where his sword and bow had worn them the day before. Ascension had worked well.

"Alvara," he said my name slowly, this time like he was rolling marbles across his tongue. "Can we...know if we've cycled together, without—"

"A reading?"

He nodded.

I shook my head slowly, lips pressed together.

"I don't understand a lot of what I feel in this place. But. It seems... urgent. To know. Like I'm drowning. And answers will feel like...air."

"I know that feeling." I breathed deeply. I had to force the motion because I was also drowning. Drowning in the steady pulse of his heart and the strength of his energy. In the need to feel his mind. To feel his skin beneath my fingers. He was right. Everything about August felt familiar and alien all at once. But a reading was an intimate thing. Not everyone in the coven had opened themselves up to my mind that way.

He inched towards me, but I leaned back, turning my back to the headboard. Like drawing up a shield, I forced myself to picture the petite young woman dressed in red, her gold hair in curls down her back, denim-blue eyes too large for her pretty face, and red, painted-on, kewpie doll lips.

His chin quivered just a touch, and he nodded.

"Yeah. There's that." There wasn't a great deal of affection in his tone. A begrudging, protective edge on his voice.

We sighed at the same time and then exchanged familiar smiles.

"You love her."

He eyed me deliberately and then nodded once. "Yeah. I did—do. Being here. In this place. It's as though she's...a memory. I don't understand. When I try to imagine her, it's like a shadow of Layla in real life. Everything feels. Wrong."

I remembered what it was like when the veil lifted for me. After ascension, my memories of my human life—the friends I had left, the distant memory of family—seemed to fog. As I recalled past lives and started training under Aren, they quickly swirled away into the mist. They were no easier to grasp than catching steam with your hands. Only triggers pulled the memories into clarity—only memories I needed for survival.

All that remained real was here in Grayshell—Aren, the others, and our endless hours of training. I could only remember a few ascensions from my past cycles—each of them starting with the agony of grief, as though I had lost someone dear to me before being saved, always by the soul we call Aren. He was my guardian, always waiting for the familiar pull of his calling to reach maturity, prepared to pluck me away from the mortals like a ripe grape falling off the vine. Always alone. Always aching for someone whose face and name I couldn't place when I woke.

I was born to be a spirit warrior. Not a mortal. And my mind seemed to shake off the memory of humanity like a terrible cold. Each ascended body was different, but it was always the same mountain of protection waiting for me to wake, and each wave of recollection came faster and harder, knocking the air from my lungs. But my training built upon the layer of mastery from the last round, and I grew sharper, faster, and more in control of my capabilities each life. This was my longest life so far—usually, if I was lucky enough to make it to ascension in the first place, I'd make it a century or so.

Aren had been quite anxious as we rounded my one hundredth 'birth' day by his side, and his nerves weren't really still for another fifty years. Finally, he relinquished his controlling hold on my whereabouts and released me into the role of second in command.

Aren was the longest lifeline recorded. The only fitting mentor for a soul like me, which I supposed, was why God continually sent him back for me, round after round. I couldn't recall a life before him. The fog was an impenetrable wall of white, like the gleaming ceiling of Grayshell. It called to me from time to time, and I tried to force my consciousness into it, only to rebound back into the here and now. Frustrated, flustered, and mystified, I eventually gave up on retrieving anything before Aren. He had little in the way of inclination as to what was hiding in the depths of my soul. His past ascensions didn't seem to include 'his little shadow' as he referred to me now. The mist seemed tantalizing as I looked over August's expectant face.

"Alvara?" He said, amused, and I knew from his tone it wasn't the first time he'd said my name.

"Yeah?"

He chuckled. "What did those monsters do to you yesterday? That crippled you so badly? I kind of had it in my head that you were invincible."

"Definitely not. They must have learned who I am. Did Aren tell you what I can do?"

"I've heard bits and pieces from Alec, mostly. Aren seems...protective.

Alec said they knew your powers and hit you with sand or sea? Is that a parable?"

I inhaled. "Unfortunately not. So, you know I'm a reader. I read objects, too. Their memories. The older an object, the more memories it holds. Water holds memory. Everything does, but the immensity of the sea is too vast for my mind to comprehend. All those memories have settled in one enormous space and collided. It's like it...sends my mind into...overdrive. If that makes sense?"

August nodded solemnly.

"There's too much input for me to unwind or separate them. You said it felt like you were being sliced in two—that's what it feels like when I'm hit with sand or sea. Like I'm being ripped into pieces. The sound. God, the fucking sound. It's like a million screaming voices, a million radios blasting static, all at once. Clay helps me absorb the chaos and cleanse it. That's the closest description for it."

I rubbed my temples, my head was throbbing, just explaining it to him. August's low chuckle caught my attention.

"What?" I asked.

"That's where I hold tension, too."

TWELVE
KING CALLOWAY

ALVARA

August left only to fetch refreshments and entertainment from the lounge. He brought in the *Mancala* board for me and a tray of colorful fruits and cheeses. We played a handful of rounds before Saraya came by with tea and tinctures, making happy noises of approval as she lifted my shirt to check the progress of my wounds. August respectfully faced away, anxiously tapping his fingers on the side of his arms as she examined me. I laughed at the thoughtfulness. Modesty was not a luxury often afforded to soldiers. The wounds would be clear by morning at this rate, and we could get me out of the limelight and back into training August. His training felt so urgent, and his presence almost made me anxious. He should've been with Alec or Aren, learning the ropes, triggering memories, and stepping into his power. But the idea of him being away also gave me anxiety—a cruel, vicious cycle between the two, playing tug-of-war with my heart.

He told me stories of his childhood, revealing more nerdy pastimes as we adventured into adolescence.

"Who was your favorite character?" I demanded when he brought up standing in line at midnight premiers for the *Harry Potter* books. If I'd known that simple question would dissolve into three hours of geeking out over the plot and premise of his favorite childhood books, I might have snuck away to the bathroom first. But watching the man smile was like basking in sunlight, and every chuckle and anecdote served as a balm to my soul.

His dad was a *Star Trek* fan, so naturally, we had to lament the endless hours of space trivia. His mom liked to garden, so he'd spent a fair amount of time with his hands in the soil, and there was something about it that felt like home to him after all his years in the city, surrounded by metal and asphalt.

Finally, he told me stories of James and his sister Freya, whom he hadn't discussed much. The age gap was a bit of an impediment in their relationship, but he had an intense protective energy whenever he spoke of her. She was seventeen, and the fact that she was popular like he had been and already dating vexed him immensely.

"Teenage boys suck," he said with a roll of his eyes. "I sound like such a *dad*, but they've only got one God damned thing on their mind, and Freya is...cursed with beauty, in my opinion. I've always been afraid it would make her an easy target. She's spunky and, lucky for me, *loves* martial arts, but I'm still afraid I'm going to have to kill some asshole someday."

"She's lucky to have you. You can still picture her face?"

He nodded.

"Good. I think that means you're in a soul group—if they're vivid to you now, you should keep them." Relief flashed across his features.

"So, if I can't remember Layla clearly..." He trailed off, but his question was clear. I shook my head apologetically. August's eyes went hazy as his ribs seemed to compress. Before his gaze could refocus, his thoughts began to pour out of him. "I know I should be sad, but...I feel...*numb*." His brows dipped low, pinching together as he scrubbed at his jaw. "What does that say about me?"

August meant it when he said he loved Layla, as he all but hurled her into Aren's waiting arms. The struggle to reconcile what he knew with this new reality was evident within those stormy emeralds as it raged inside him. My heart ached in sympathy, dragging me into a moment of hesitant silence before I could compose an answer to the question that pained him.

"I don't know if there's a *should be* when it comes to handling ascension. Everyone is a little different. Fae has the oldest memories among us and retains her human lives as clearly as her ascended ones. She's a walking history book, in that way." My lungs sucked in a long, pointed breath. "Your concern for how this impacts Layla when you had no say in anything happening to you says everything about what kind of man you are, August. Don't question your heart because the world flipped on its axis."

He huffed, face looking distressed.

"Tell me more about James," I prompted, needing to distract him from the ache permeating every inch of air between us. August's eyes snapped up to mine, still hollow and haunted, even as he feigned what was clearly meant to be a reassuring smile. I could tell he knew what I was doing, but he didn't seem to mind.

We told stories for a while after that, banter easy and lighthearted, back to being effortless. He asked me about my lives, and I shared what I could remember. As my earth family had died before my ascension, I didn't have a whole lot to share in that department.

"I'm sorry," he said, eyes intense.

"Don't be. It was so long ago. Lifetimes—literally."

He nodded obediently and asked me about Aren, the giant. I snorted and shared everything I could think of about my only inevitable companion with him. Somehow, he had leisurely sprawled across the foot of my bed before the afternoon was over, sitting precariously close to my legs for a man who had not given consent to my mind searching through his own. I was careful to keep the blanket draped between us, but the ease with which he seemed to rest there was unique.

Ansel was much more careful to keep a wide berth from any of my skin —even in the thick of things last night, careful not to overwhelm me by scooping me out of harm's way when he knew I couldn't handle a new reading on an immortal. Ansel had always been made for battle, with acute observational skills. Early in this lifetime, he'd put together that my gifts had manifested before I ascended.

Between stories and his uncanny ability to read people's faces, perhaps an intrinsic knowing he couldn't explain, Ansel had put the pieces in order until he realized I'd been reading in my mortal years. He realized my energy could be down to the dregs, and my mind would still deep dive on a read when I didn't have it in me. Involuntary with contact of skin. He'd interrogated me about it once when he realized the depth of that gift. When my mortal life was ending, I had bitten an attacker and, without the strength of ascension, read every detail of his life, mind, and past. From then on, he'd been the most cautious of my companions, handing me gloves or cloaking my skin after a strenuous battle. A good General in his past lives, Ansel told me he had an uncanny ability to know what his soldiers needed and when. It seemed to translate to protecting my mind as much as my body. And so, he kept his distance.

However, as the evening wore on, mellow darkness creeping into the room, August slowly began setting his hands on my legs over the covers, gesticulating as he told stories and sharing random tidbits of knowledge from his time on earth. I didn't pull away from him as I ought to. It was comforting, having him there, like a favorite TV show playing in the background or a book I'd already read a few times.

Desperation finally overruled my intrigue, so I excused myself to go to the bathroom. Relief washed over me when my movements weren't met with stabs of discomfort. When I came back, I was immensely disappointed to find the room empty. My sadness lasted only seconds though, because he came into the room behind me with a broad grin, two cups of steaming tea in his hands, and a book tucked under his arm. Upon seeing him, the smile that stretched across my face was beyond my control.

"Saraya told me this book might be helpful for you," he said quietly, as though lulling a child to sleep.

August draped a blanket over his shoulder, creatively covering his arm and neck, and climbed into bed next to me. We sat against the headboard; book splayed open on our laps as we looked through the pages. It was the legend of The Great Commander—the King of Kings. *That sly little sneak.* Planting awfully big seeds in his mind. But the history—the legend—of The Great Commander's soul was fascinating. Without fully thinking through the gesture, I rested my head on his covered shoulder, listening to his husky voice as he read me the legend of King Calloway—a Nephilim warrior, braided with an angel—possessing both the strength of human form and pure spirit of his angel counterpart. This spirit was our only true Commander, a leader so strong all must follow. I closed my eyes to let them rest as I listened, and the moment I did, I drifted back into the darkness.

THIRTEEN

HONEY

AUGUST

She smelled like honey, sage, cinnamon, and summer—somehow, she emitted the scent of sunshine. I hadn't even realized that was a fragrance until her now-loose curls pressed against my face, an all-encompassing warmth radiating into my heart. Breathing her in, I did my best to ignore the stirring her scent elicited from my body—the images it brought to my mind.

I'd wrapped her in a little blanket cocoon, avoiding her skin despite the pestering drive to do the opposite. Once the blanket was safely between us, I would softly stroke her arms when she stirred, and she would quickly settle back into sleep, breathing steady, deepening with her rest. As though my touch—my presence—soothed her. When Alvara tucked her knees up and curled into me, the fabric shifted, wrapping tightly around her chest and accentuating the slight swells of her breasts as she sighed sleepily. I closed my eyes, smacking my head against the wall behind us before glaring at the ceiling. *Great. Now I'm jealous of a fucking blanket.* A wave of guilt washed an icy reminder down my spine. *She almost died, asshole. You're here because she's hurt, for Christ's sake. You have a fiancé likely in a manic tailspin, and you're pining after your new superior. Lock it the fuck up.*

Alvara let out another breathy little sigh as she shifted, and I forced myself to think of absolutely anything else. It had to be well into the morning, and Lord only knew what we'd be facing tomorrow. With that reality in mind, I slowly released every bit of air from my lungs, closing my eyes and leaning into the wall, ignoring the pinch in my shoulder, courtesy of supporting her lean frame for so long. She'd more than earned my discomfort. I relished in the feel of her weight against this new body, and my fists tightened on the blanket until the strain highlighted my knuckles like my body instinctively adjusted to protect her—shield her—from the world, she was clearly so determined to defend.

Sleep claimed me more than once before exhaustion finally settled into my bones. My dreams were full of mixed-up snippets of light. Like a movie reel playing too fast to catch the details of the story. Laughter, slow dances, an open meadow, an icy plunge into white water rapids. And slow, soft kisses, smelling like honey.

I startled awake to the sound of footsteps, a familiar feel to the mellow energy in the room as Alec tapped softly on the door frame and entered. Ansel leaned into it behind him, arms crossed over his chest, omnipresent concern carved on his face. Alec's gift had a way of setting the tone in the surrounding space, setting me at ease even in the presence of the old general, as Aren called him, and I pondered that for a moment, wondering if I would possess the same ability.

Alec shook his head, grin rueful, and ran a battle-worn hand through his shaggy hair.

"Dangerous game you're playing, August."

"I don't know what you're talking about," I retorted too quickly.

Something vaguely resembling a smirk tugged at the corners of Ansel's lips as silver eyes flicked to Alec, whose face split in amusement. "Oblivious," Alec's eyes darted back to me, "or stupid?"

"Excuse me?" I straightened as both men turned to survey me, anger and embarrassment heating my cheeks. Probably my cue to unwind my hold on Alvara, but the idea of leaving her unprotected...

Ansel nudged Alec with a shoulder. "Come on, man, give the kid a break; he's still adjusting. He'll learn."

"Uh...thanks?" I quirked my head, unsure if his tone would leave me relieved or insulted.

"You've got this Rookie." Ansel turned towards the hall, sliding cash from his pocket and palming it to Alec without even an attempt at subtlety. He lowered his voice enough to sound sneaky without achieving it, "Put me down for stupid." He shot an arrogant smirk over his shoulder, chuckling as I scowled at him before he vanished into the hallway, and I slipped my arm out from under Alvara.

"What's your problem?" I snapped as my blood began to boil. "There's no game," I insisted. "I think I was sent here to protect her."

Alec snorted. "Of course you do."

"I mean it. The strongest clairvoyant in the hierarchy is called to a shield. You think that's coincidental?" I fumbled to keep Alvara propped up while stretching for the pillows she'd knocked onto the floor.

"There are no coincidences. You'll learn that quickly. Only fate, a volatile mistress." He shook his head again, shrugging his shoulders as I successfully managed to prop her on the pillows without waking her. "We're just fucking with you, mate. Come on... There's work to do."

"YOUR SHOW of strength was astounding yesterday," Alec applauded.

Jesus. Was that only yesterday? Once Alvara and I cooled our sparking tempers, being with her came as naturally as drawing breath, and I couldn't fully explain it. I'd never fought with Layla like that—not with any woman who'd waltzed into and out of my life before her—never experienced the kind of anger that brewed in my blood in the hours after Alvara put herself in harm's way.

Fuck, even our argument felt familiar. The tension between us electrified my skin, making me want to lean down and taste her before slowly peeling that tiny gray tank and matching pair of sweats off her tight body. Made me want to *show* her what she did to me with my lips, tongue, and teeth.

Like our flesh could speak the language, our words couldn't.

The very thoughts had been treacherous and treasonous, and I'd loathed myself for them, resorting to pacing like a man unhinged. I could never do that to Layla. She deserved so much more.

It wasn't until Alvara seemed to internalize what that loss would do to me that the boiling in my veins ceased enough to see reason.

It was Alec, no shock, to yank my wandering thoughts back into the present. I had no idea how many of his words I'd missed.

"August, focus. What you did took me *years* to master. Let's make sure it's not just beginner's luck."

I smirked. "If that's the case, shouldn't they pair me with someone who can keep up?"

Alec's amber eyes flicked to me, something predatory slithering beneath his amusement a heartbeat before I found myself groaning on my back, ache slamming through my breathless ribcage, staring up at the Grayshell wings and blade, where they were painted on the ceiling. Vaguely, I remembered his hand slamming into my chest and foot yanking my leg out from under me, but he'd moved at such an impossible speed that it felt surreal.

Alec's shaggy hair and satisfied smirk crept into view as the oxygen returned to my lungs.

"Oh," he winked, "I think I can handle it." He stretched out a hand, and I glared at it for a heartbeat before accepting help to my feet. "Ally has visions. I have my shield and my speed." Alec turned and continued as though he hadn't just laid me on my ass. "Today, we need to practice jumping."

I hopped once on my feet, and he rolled his eyes, grumbling something about being a smart ass. *Only for you, old friend.*

"Jumping is crucial. Until yesterday, no one could fly. So that should be interesting to watch play out. Regardless, it's the fastest form of transportation and the only reliable way in and out of Grayshell."

"As in, to jump from one place to another."

"Yes. All we are is energy, August. We're not actually solid matter. You must release that expectation in your mind and accept energy can materialize wherever it may choose. The crucial part of jumping is that an energy burst that powerful can be used by anyone nearby. So, you must scour both where you are and where you're going for anything predatory."

"Stowaways."

He quirked a bit, smirking, and then nodded. "Yeah. They can tag along on your heels if you're not careful. Or bait you with trouble and wait for when you arrive. If we jump into chaos, it's best to be prepared like yesterday."

Alec walked me through the process of moving my energy from one place in the room to another, which came fairly easily, to my surprise. We then moved from one *room* to another after he'd altered the wards to allow it. Grayshell only allowed jumps into the hall so that should there ever be a breach, they might contain it. We then moved from one floor to another once I'd mastered the allotted rooms. And eventually, to the grand hall, full of all its distractions, and back. He almost seemed disappointed the clamor of the hall didn't slow me down. But it was second nature, like a reflex, the moment I'd done it once. Leaving the bedroom, I popped back into the hallway he was waiting in, only for him to lunge at me—I parried, throwing up my arms to block his advance, but I staggered backward, and he swept my legs out from under me. Again. I rolled to the side, lunging to my feet, anger pulsing. But his shit-eating grin stopped me in my tracks.

"Asshole."

"Number one rule—don't get cocky."

We followed my wild hunch to go to the lounge, something in my gut telling me that's where I should be. Alec was a big proponent of following intuition. As were Aren and Alvara, according to him. They believed that the sixth sense was scarcely wrong.

The only dark room in all of Grayshell, the lounge, had already become my favorite place. We stepped into the dim, cozy space, the strain of the light leaving my eyes immediately. The smell of honey, sage, and summer hit me, and I looked around expectantly. The sight of her in another tight tank top, leaning casually against the island, dark hair curling down to the small of her back, left my heart brimming with warmth and beating in an uneven rhythm. She seemed to be studying a map sprawled across the counter.

Alec snickered at me and then strode forward to take Aphaea in his arms, pulling her away from the counter. He nuzzled into her neck. The envy of his ability to touch her. To press his lips against her bare skin. To wrap his arms around her slight waist. It was overwhelming. I craved the contact. A pang of guilt twisted my gut as I realized it wasn't Layla's touch I was yearning for; I had no business wanting anything from a stranger.

Alvara turned her face to me; it was like I'd known her all my life. Her eyes were my anchor. Steadying a bucking boat in heaving seas. The only woman in the world. Like any ties I'd had before had been carefully pruned away. Unwanted branches, meticulously plucked from a shrub.

She beamed at me and crossed the small room. For a moment, I thought she was going to grab my hand, and then she shoved her own into her jean pockets.

"I saw you learned to jump today," she said proudly, chin lifting.

"Saw—"

She tapped her fingers to her temple and winked at me.

"Oh. Right. Err—you look good." I shuffled my feet. Did I just *shuffle my feet*? "I mean—you look like you're feeling better."

"Christ," Alec muttered as I felt his eyes on us, "at least I don't have to worry about Fae with that level of game."

I shot him a glare as Ansel and Aren chuckled, and Alvara suppressed a smirk, keeping her eyes on me. She smiled softly and said, "Much. Thanks."

"Yeah. I'm glad. So, what's on the schedule this afternoon? Another daring rescue?"

She snorted. "Not so far. No promises, though. Would you like to go outside with me?"

I'd heard nothing about the grounds at Grayshell, and my curiosity peaked. "Sure—I haven't seen anything but the walls of the castle since the battle."

"Real air will be lovely."

"Real air?"

"I thought we'd head to Colorado for some practice."

"Oh." Earth. Back to Earth. Back to real life. To the human dimension. I could do that. Couldn't I?

"Oh?" She kicked her boot against the floor. Did she sense my trepidation? "Personally, I'm ready to feel clay and fresh air."

It sounded nice. I agreed, and she walked me through the complexities of a jump between dimensions. Alec and Fae joined us and then took her hands on either side—both having nothing to hide from her eternally prying mind. I grabbed Alec's free hand and felt the way the energy bent and flexed around my mind. Felt the clarity of the mountain we were beaming ourselves to. And together, we jumped.

After all my practice with Alec, the ground collided firmly below my feet. Cool air whipped around my face, smelling of pine and earth. I noted the way my body felt; all my senses dramatically enhanced after ascension. Suddenly, I was intensely aware of the pressure of an oncoming storm in the air, the feel of the moisture on my skin, and most acutely, how strongly the world smelled of grass, dirt, sap, and pine. There was a vibration to everything, and I wasn't sure how I had missed something so glaring for my entire life. I took a long moment to sense the energy in the ground, as Alec had taught me.

Just as we had felt when we probed ahead of us, the peak was clear of life—outside of the towering pines, covered in climbing moss, an endless variety of berry bushes, and the abundance of insects crawling and flying around. I slapped a mosquito that landed on my arm and chuckled at the simple feeling of normalcy. Grayshell had no form of life outside of the souls inside it. And I hadn't realized the absence of other beings had felt so strange until they were back.

Bows slung over our shoulders, we followed Alvara's long stride as she led us further into the mountains.

FOURTEEN
THE CABIN
ALVARA

Tucked discreetly away, deep in the towering granite peaks of the Rocky Mountains, sat my favorite safe house. The cabin was so isolated that it could only be reached on foot, or in our case, through a jump, making it one of the safest places to rest our minds, renew our spirits, and train a recruit as talented as August. Surrounded by treacherous terrain, thick woods, and a blanket of wildflowers, the log cabin subtly rose out of the vast blur of green and stone. With a river rock fireplace and foundation, it looked like a piece of history, perfectly preserved. The front porch still held four idyllic white rocking chairs, a red, southwestern rug tucked below them. Everything about it warmed me, a Norman Rockwell painting amongst a life lived in shadow and nightmares.

I glanced at August as we stepped into the tiny clearing around the house, watching this reaction as he took in the sun-soaked green field, speckled with yellow, purple, and orange wildflowers. He took in the meadow, the cozy cabin, the picturesque log front porch, and he turned to smile at me.

"Just felt like a little getaway, did you?" He grinned.

"Of sorts," I admitted. "This place is so peaceful." He hummed in agreement, climbing the last fifty yards towards the house.

Alec and Fae had sauntered ahead of us, hands tightly interwoven between them, laughter carrying on the mellow breeze back to us. The three of us raised our free hands, and I closed my eyes as we approached, feeling the air and searching for energy that didn't belong. In his usual lightning-fast motion, Alec pulled the key from his pants pocket and opened the front door with a long creak.

In stark contrast to the walls of Grayshell, the safe house was left as expected. The log walls were a blur of wood and mortar, light streaming through the aged windows, dancing across the dust in the air above a rustic collection of leather furniture, and patterned, sage, and burgundy wool rugs lined the floor. There was a new heavily textured cream one with diamonds —Fae, inevitably, had picked it up somewhere. The lingering scent of fire smoke greeted us like a wall at the threshold, and I soaked in its cozy aroma. Alec casually slung his bag and bow down on the tan leather sofa, and Fae followed suit before he could pull her curvy hips against his own. They exchanged a long kiss and then told us they were going to nap, disappearing into one of the guest rooms in the back. Alec's shield rose so high and strong that it cast an invisible wall between us that I was convinced would physically deflect me as well, and I rolled my eyes.

August wandered around the cozy room, eyes trailing from one framed image to the next as he walked slowly and deliberately. The pictures were all of the members of the coven, all from different decades. It would look like we frequented themed photo studios everywhere we went, or perhaps we were simply a quirky group of Halloween enthusiasts, should a mortal ever stumble on our hiding place. August liked bouldering, hunting, and fishing, and I had thought this place would feel so much more like home to him. Hugged by stone and forest, it should feel more familiar than Grayshell. Although, he didn't seem to mind our little hidden dimension much. The natural unease faded quickly for him, and he had taken to most of the skills as seamlessly as climbing back onto a bicycle after a long season of snow. He hadn't mentioned a desire to return to the human dimension, but I knew it was overdue. There were obligations to resolve here, and I wasn't sure how he would approach them. The matter of his business, his family, and his poor fiancé, who I knew would be so scared, confused, and inevitably angry with his disappearing act. I tried not to think about Layla much, as I could only imagine what she was feeling. The letters August had written were concise and provided little in the way of answers outside of a mysterious business trip and his well-being.

Layla was beautiful, I'd give her that. But a possessive edge seemed to carve into my mind when I thought of August. Protective, perhaps, of the calling I'd hunted for over so many exhausting months. Tracking a soul whose mind is guarded was not my easiest feat. Layla felt like the only real threat of losing him to the world again. He belonged in our world now, or at least that's what I told myself. He wouldn't fit in hers any longer—his power was immense and palpable, and it was only a matter of time before someone or some*thing* came to take it for themselves or strike him down if unprotected. Beyond that, she would age, want a family, grow old...die. And August would remain exactly as he was—strong, courageous, caring, and forever twenty-nine. But I couldn't help but wonder...would she be the first? The first mortal to believe the impossible words gushed out by a desperate, pleading partner? He said his memories were distant in Grayshell, but here...in her world, with Layla standing before him...It would be different. My stomach squirmed uneasily, and I told myself it was out of nervousness for August. For the inevitable conversation and ensuing confrontation, he'd never asked for. For the innocent girl whose whole future was just tossed upside down. But there was a stirring in my core, saying there was more to the anxiety than that.

What if he chose to return to her? To renounce his place in Grayshell, to deny his mission as a Nephilim soul? To abandon...me?

I watched August's face as he studied the portraits on the wall, evidently fascinated with each image. He lingered on a colorful painting that was the consuming chaos of a battlefield during the Revolutionary War, and I wondered if he spotted the likeness to Aren in the face of one of the rebel medics. We did our best to stay out of human history—but would involve ourselves where we believed good could come of it, most often as healers. I did my best to keep my wall up—much easier to do in a place so quiet. I quite enjoyed his bright presence, and it brought the same kind of relief into my body as a jug of cool water, condensation dripping down the frosted sides after a trudge through the late summer desert.

The idea of him turning his back on all he'd learned in his days with us and returning to life as he knew it...left my mouth dry and my mind just as panicked as if I was crossing the sands of the Sahara.

Breathe, Alvara. If history had taught me anything, it was that we were far more resilient than we ever believed ourselves to be. We would move on and turn our cheeks to the absence of a soul built for our group. Continue fighting for what was right, good, and light, always. But there was a cruel rock in my stomach when he finally spoke, snapping my attention to the painting in front of him.

"Is this...is this Notre Dame?"

I looked up and smiled. "Yes. Aren painted that many years ago. Why?"

"It tugs on my memory a bit. Like I should know it."

"It would make sense. If I remember correctly, it would have been erected before the timeline you share with Alec. I think you would have been a three-day ride from Paris. Less, I suppose, on an excellent horse or if you could change mounts."

He nodded slowly, lips pressed together, and eyes narrowed as he studied the grand arches Aren had captured so perfectly with his brush strokes.

"What is this place?" He gestured now to the room around us.

"One of our safe houses."

His eyebrows hiked a bit, "Safer than Grayshell?"

"Nothing is safer than Grayshell. The angelic wards are strong, so our safe houses go largely unnoticed by mortals, and it would take one hell of a demon to make it past our defenses. But sometimes we need somewhere safe to go on Earth. Either to stay close to a mission or somewhere safe to bring a braid or an ally. To train a rookie..." I winked.

He grinned and nodded as though that made perfect sense.

"This is Aren's home, technically. His safe space. It's my favorite one, though. We each have them—easier to keep a cover if we have somewhere to take people if we're on a mission. Can't exactly go babbling about half-breed angels to everyone we save."

"Braids?"

"Yes, or sometimes we clash with dark forces who have corrupted humans, and there are mortals that serve God, too. They need somewhere safe to go when they've been targeted."

"Makes sense."

"Come on." I tugged on his fingers with my gloved hand. "Let's study the King of the Nephilim." We crossed the welcoming room to the blonde log table in the dining room, and I swung my pack down, unzipping the back compartment and sliding out the *Book of Legends*, setting it with a significant thud on the table.

AUGUST SILENTLY KNOCKED HIS BOW, and I watched with pride as he aimed, released, and his deer collapsed to the forest floor. The hunt and the kill were both nearly effortless to him. He'd already been a skilled hunter in his human life, but reuniting with his bow and warrior self had enhanced his abilities beyond my imagination. While I could shoot the shadow off a horsefly, August was impressive—easily as skilled as Ansel or me when it came to the weapons he could remember. I anticipated he'd take to those he'd forgotten just as well.

He made quick work of the deer with Alec's swift help, and they had our freezer full before the afternoon sun could settle onto treetop stilts. The aroma of seasoned, cooking venison filled the cabin and made my mouth water. I didn't often eat as much as I had in the last few days, but healing from the injuries inflicted by demonic steel had been strenuous, and I wasn't complaining. Fae proudly brought her salad to the table, and Alec, with sleeves still rolled up and scarred arms already washed clean, wrapped himself around her belly and kissed down her neck. Their love for each other was proof enough to me that God still loved us and wanted us to be happy. Sometimes, for a flash of a moment, I could forget they were both lethal enough to single-handedly bring down an entire battalion. I smiled as she tossed her head back in laughter and reached around to wrap her fingers into his hair. Feeling his gaze on me, I turned to see August, that bright grin across his face, and the intensity in his eyes flushed blood into my cheeks before I could jerk my head away and return my eyes to the book on the table.

It hadn't yielded much in the way of actual information about this soul Saraya so incessantly believed was August. Only confirming the source of the legends she had shared with me. The story of the mighty warrior, returning only when God knew how badly we needed his strength leading our forces and fighting amongst them.

Bellies thoroughly stuffed with savory venison and Fae's garden salad, we moved into the tiny living room to share more of our stories with August. I slumped down into an oversized armchair, yawning and tracing the new scar across my ribs through the thin plaid shirt I'd swiped from the closet in Grayshell. Alec played the acoustic guitar for some time before handing it off to August, whose big hands expertly plucked the tune from the strings. Fae and I harmonized for a while, singing angelic melodies more than actual lyrics. Eventually, I sprawled across the loveseat, propping my arm across the back, and just soaked in the sight of them. An early night chill had set into my bones, and I was growing sleepy, a yawn building up before I could speak.

"Alright, Sparky, start us a fire." Alec lifted his chin towards the open hearth, grinning at August.

He shook his head, but his expression was playful. "Yeeeah, I don't think it works like that."

"Of course it does." I cut in. "You telling me those fingers are scared of a little heat?"

Piercing emeralds flicked to me, only a beat before they darkened, those full lips twisting to one side in a cocky smirk that made the little divot in his chin appear. The two had me swallowing my words as said fingers ceased the methodic plucking of strings.

August arched a playful brow and, tone dripping insinuation, said, "Not in my experience." He set the guitar aside, gaze roaming down the length of my legs, where they were stretched out on the couch, before leisurely climbing back to my face. It was only then that I realized my lips had parted in surprise, and I snapped them closed, fighting to swallow as my stomach and thighs both clenched. My mouth dried out, words vanishing just as quickly.

It was Alec clearing his throat that finally severed the spell his words had over me. "Ummmm, anyways. Let's see what 'cha got, rookie. Light it up."

August rose from his place on the floor, leaving the guitar in a stand. "Life and death situations only, I'm afraid." He sat on the couch beside the fireplace, where Alec and Fae were curled up.

"We all manipulate elements to some extent," Alec encouraged.

"Like the water to wash off Alvara?"

"Exactly."

"Most of us are telekinetic. Although some move objects *on* the air, rather than their own energetic pull," Fae added in, tucking a long strand of hair back behind her ear. I tried to listen to what she was saying—I *really* did—but I couldn't stop thinking about August's hands and what they would feel like against my skin. What those string-calloused fingers, honed from years climbing slick rocks and boulders, might do to a woman, and then my mind wandered to *those sparks...*

It was the searing pressure of his gaze on my profile that snapped my attention from the flames and the wildly inappropriate string of fantasies. I caught August smothering the cocky smile from the edges of his mouth—as though he knew exactly what I'd been thinking about—before he bowed his head and then returned his still-amused gaze to a lecturing Fae.

"...Almost all of us can play with wind, earth, water, and fire, but you might take to one more naturally than the others."

"Alvara likes earth, wind, and fire," Alec added, and I shrugged, unable to deny that. A slow smirk crossed August's expression.

"Like...the band."

I snorted. "That's my *Boogie Wonderland.*"

August chuckled, but his eyes narrowed, and he ran his hand through thick, unruly curls, nervous. "But you didn't kill the Renown with fire. You electrocuted them. Is electricity an element?"

"Apparently. Honestly, August, we still don't know exactly how that happened the other day. But I know it has to do with you."

"And your desire to save Alvara," Alec added helpfully. "You got all sparky again when Aren knocked you away from her. We were all a little freaked that you'd like...fry him for stepping in or something."

August's eyes widened, looking dubious. He brought his hand to his stubbled chin and then asked, "So, to conjure it on purpose, I would just need to *think* it into existence?"

"Essentially." The two men looked at each other meaningfully. The trust between them had grown exponentially since they rekindled past life memories. August bobbed his head thoughtfully, still rubbing his jaw. "You think it, *feel* it into existence. Yes. That's a better description."

As if on cue, the three of us flung open our fingers to reveal small flames hovering above our palms, dancing in the creeping remnants of sunlight through the windows. He looked mystified and mimicked our motion, laughing when nothing happened. We all put our flames out.

"Like Alec said, you have to *feel* it. Feel the warmth of it; imagine the glow of it above your hand." I did my best to be encouraging. Manipulating the elements was always the hardest learning curve. Violence came naturally to humans—an essential piece of survival, and so it flowed through us like rapids down the river-bend.

"And try not to burn down The Commander's house," he said cynically. We all laughed, energy intensifying as his nerves did.

I held my other hand in the air for a moment and breathed deeply, summoning the limited moisture from the air, and a small pool of water began to flow from the open window behind me, spiraling into a dancing stream above my hand.

"Don't worry, I'll put it out." I winked before sending the water back outside. No point in mopping the floor tonight. He shook his head, not seeming to make any effort to hide the astonishment on his face. "I'm not the best with water," I conceded. It had always been a point of frustration for me. "That title goes to Alec."

Alec mock bowed to an imaginary round of applause, drawing giggles from Fae as she kissed his cheek. She tangled her fingers in his tawny hair, twirling strands around before releasing one and finding another.

"Alana and I prefer Earth, but it's a bit messier to demonstrate," Fae conceded, resting her cheek on Alec's firm shoulder.

"I'll take your word for it," August said. *Feel it into existence. Feel it into existence.*

I smiled at his internal chant. He tried again, but nothing happened.

Alec winked at me, and my gaze flicked to him. *Give him a word.*

I nodded and turned back to August. "Sometimes it helps to push power through an incantation. Latin seems to work best for me; it's probably something about my past lives. But there might be something that works better for you. English or French. Try it and say the word flame."

"Flame," he said confidently, flipping his palm open. Yet again, nothing happened.

"Elemental work was hard, even for the very best of us, August. Take your time here," I assured him, not entirely sure we had time to take before he'd need every skill I could give him. "Try Ignus."

"Ignus!" he said, tone demanding now. A tiny spark sizzled off his fingertips.

"Better!" I encouraged. He tried again, but with nothing to show for it, slumped back on the couch, looking defeated.

I felt the energy shift before I saw anything, and the way Alec's hand flew to his dagger got my heart racing. I saw the vision from a perspective that was not my own but rather looking back at me. It was too late, crystal clear, and solidified, with no threads to pull on.

Oh, shit.

Frustration grew in my chest. Learning new things had always been frustrating for me. Learning new things I was not naturally good at? Not worth the time. Needing a skillset I didn't possess, surrounded by superhuman celestial beings who all did it without effort? *Absolutely* infuriating.

A sudden vibration pulsed through the air, and I pulled myself from my pool of self-pity to realize the energy had shifted. Alvara's eyes were wide, and Aphaea's were no calmer. She released her hold around Alec's neck right as his hand drew his blade from its scabbard. I jumped to my feet and turned over my shoulder to the closed door, only to hear a clatter of wood and both women scream.

When I turned around, Alec had already cleared the room and had Alvara's back pinned to his chest. Her loveseat and the short coffee table had both been overturned. She was up on her tiptoes, scrambling for her balance. Against her throat was Alec's dagger, his expression mirthless.

"Come on, August," he hissed through clenched teeth. "Show us what you are!"

My stomach was in my chest. Heart frantic. Sweat dripping. I looked frantically from her wide eyes to Alec's cold and calculating ones. Right as I started to tell myself he wouldn't actually hurt her, he pressed the knife further into her skin and pulled her off her feet. She held her breath, hands clamoring for a hold on his arm. I wanted to scream, to roar at him, but my voice froze in my throat.

"Alec!! Stop this! What the fuck are you doing?!" Fae cried out, hands shaking as she drew her blade. What she would do with it…

"Come on, August. What will it be?" He flicked his eyes to the fireplace and back to me.

"What the fuck are you doing?!" I finally yelled. "Drop the blade. This isn't fucking funny."

"Do you see me laughing?" He pulled Alvara tighter to his chest, and she clung to his arm, trying to lift her weight, the blade right against her artery; her voice croaked out only his name.

"Stop it! Stop this!" Fae screamed again. Her hands trembled around her blade. No better ideas than I had, apparently.

"What *are* you!?" He demanded again, eyes beating into mine.

That was why we were here. He didn't believe me after all. Aren must have ordered him to get more information. Which I didn't even have to give him in the first place.

"You wouldn't dare!" I roared back at him.

"Aren would feed you to the Renown! Alec! What are you doing?!" Fae sobbed. Alec turned his head to the side, evaluating me, a sly smile on his face as he pressed the blade somehow tighter against her skin.

"She's due for a new cycle. She'll come back," he growled and turned his dagger. Small crimson droplets slid onto the steel as Alvara let out a tiny sob, and something in my chest exploded. Suddenly, there was fire everywhere.

Alvara

GOD DAMMIT, *Alec!* I growled at him internally, a small involuntary noise escaping my lips as his blade bit through the tender flesh on my neck. *Asshole!*

The energy shifted so dramatically that the air flew around me, the supernatural wind blowing my hair out of my face. I pulled Alec's hand away from me, and he dropped me to the floor. When I turned my face, August exploded. I froze as flames erupted down his arms, a ball of fire surrounding his entire body, manic tendrils flowing from his fingers, licking at the surrounding floor, and eyes glowing a vibrant green. His lips pulled back in a visceral snarl, and a growl ripped from his chest.

"August!" I shouted, lunging forward. I threw up a shield of energy and rushed for him. Alec and Fae summoned water as fast as they could, drawing it forth from the surrounding mountains. His luminescent eyes found mine, and the flames vanished as he wrapped his arms around me, scooping me off the ground and tucking me protectively behind him before the flames licked down his arm again. The briefest strobe of memory had slipped through my mind, not clear like a vision but hazy like a long-forgotten dream. There was no time.

My heart was already thrumming like a manic hummingbird, and I thought my stomach had jumped into my throat. Feet firmly planted, I calmed my voice as best as I could. "August, I'm okay!"

Alec stood, eyes wide and amused, water spiraling between his hands over his head in an eternally mesmerizing dance. "Well..." He smirked. "*That* was unexpected."

"I'll show you unexpected, motherfucker," August growled.

Fae threw herself between them, hands protectively outstretched in front of Alec. "That was *not* funny." She shot an angry glance back at her mate. "But it *worked*, August!"

"August! I'm okay!! Alec has a *sick* sense of humor," I spat. "But I'm okay! He would never actually hurt me," I insisted, ignoring the sting across my neck. I threw my hands out to rest against his back, and his muscles all tensed as another quick strobe flashed in my mind. I yanked my hands off him. Visions dulled through the clothing or not, I didn't intend to read him.

He shot a glance over his shoulder, eyes frantically surveying my face, before turning back to Alec. There was pain there, a swirl of undeniable grief.

"What. The. Fuck?" He growled at him, but he moved his arm like he was snapping a whip, extinguishing the flames from his flesh in an instant.

A nervous giggle tore from Fae. She buried her face in her hands and shook her head. Alec had always been gutsy, but something about August had made it more so. She'd had the same split-second heads-up I had when the idea crossed his mind. But Alec wasn't exactly indecisive. He always listened to his intuition. And without hesitation, he had listened to the instinct that said August would only react if he felt a genuine threat. A dozen memories raced through his mind now, all extraordinary heroics for the soldiers in their garrison and the women August loved.

Fae collapsed back onto the couch, a relieved sigh escaping her lips.

"*Fae*," Alec scolded, glaring at her over pursed lips. "You know I would never."

"Had me fooled," August snapped before she could respond, his voice still guttural.

"It worked, didn't it?" Alec insisted. With a smirk, he added, "Just like I knew it would. You're a pyro. Just like Ally. I've sensed it for days."

The impulse was as quick as Alec's had been, so I didn't have time to react to August's either. His fist collided square with Alec's face with a sickening smack. "Pull a stunt like that again, and I'll turn you into a fucking lightning rod."

Alec staggered backward, rubbing his jaw, eyes watering, before he let the smirk climb back up his cheeks, completely unapologetic. "You're a natural guardian, August. Your abilities will only awaken if something you love is threatened."

"Go to hell." August threw his hand towards the fireplace, and a massive fire erupted in the hearth, consuming the stack of wood there and licking at the stone edges. He was to the door in an instant and threw it open with a bang as it smacked into the log wall before he vanished into the night. I winced and then stared at the roaring fire with butterflies flipping in my stomach. He was incredible. He radiated power in all he did, and his fierce need to protect his own was staggering.

"You know," I said, glaring at Alec, "I didn't bother to *read* the cabin, and I never had a warning of you attacking me while on vacation."

"Don't let your guard down, sis." He winked and swallowed what I assumed was a mouthful of blood by the smell in the air. "You're getting rusty, Alvara. Too comfortable. Now, are you going after him, or am I?"

"I'll get him." I walked to the door and then shot a smile back at Alec. "You're an asshole, you know that? You've spent too much time with Ansel."

He shrugged. "At least I'm an effective asshole."

Well. I couldn't argue with that. Alec was still a soldier through and through, and as long as the outcome justified the means and nobody was seriously hurt in the process, his lines could be a little fuzzy. He wasn't actually prone to violence—ironically, the most peaceful among us. But he knew August in the most intimate way out of the group of us, and I was trying to trust him.

August's chest was still heaving in ragged rises and falls when I met him at the edge of the incline. His arms were tightly crossed, and I couldn't help but notice the stance emphasized the carve of his biceps. He had already been beautiful, and I couldn't help but admire him now. The tendons across his forearms were livid, and the vein in his temple bulged.

"August, I'm so sorry, that was—"

"Fucked up. Royally fucked up."

"Yes. Alec was impulsive and inconsiderate and—" I reached my hand for him, and my mind was overtaken by an image of August pressing his lips to me, hard and urgent. His arms wrapped around me, and there wasn't an inch of his mind left unexplored. I yanked my hands back and crossed my arms snuggly over my chest. He noticed the moment of hesitation and correction and narrowed his eyes. A past life, perhaps. It didn't feel like a vision.

We remained quiet, not feeling a need to fill the void for a long while. Cautiously, his breathing slowed, and I could hear his heart rate gradually steady, and I knew mine did the same.

"I've watched you die before."

Shock shuddered through me, and I shook my head, my shoulders raised.

"Not a question, Ally." He pinned me with a smoldering glare that tightened my throat, his chest still rising and falling with lingering adrenaline. "We've done this...many times, you and I."

"I, I only remember a few of my lives," I spluttered, tucking my hair behind an ear.

"But you can't honestly tell me I'm wrong."

I wet my lips, muscles working to swallow. "I remember nothing before Aren. It's totally possible, August. You're familiar to me too," I admitted, taking a cleansing breath, allowing my eyes to wander out at the glittering constellations for a moment. "We probably have. I don't know. But I—I have had a few short visions. And, at least, the most recent one would indicate you are correct."

"You touched me tonight—or I touched you, rather. At least at first. Did you..."

I shook my head slowly. "We're both protected by long sleeves tonight, thankfully."

He nodded before running his fingers through his hair again.

"I think I'm ready, though, Alvara. I don't want to hide anything from you."

"I'll want you to be *very* certain of that first."

"I know. Just know, if you got more than you're letting on—" August emptied his lungs in exasperation before finishing, "I trust you, Alvara."

My poor heart was hammering all over again, and my mouth withered with drought and lack. I needed a glass of water or something spiritual to quench that urge building in my chest. I lowered myself to sit on the ground, leaning back on spiked pine needles and cool, damp earth. August joined me, huffing a bit as he settled again.

"I don't think that I'm...like you, exactly. But. I think I get visions, too. Or memories. You said you burned for being a witch?"

I nodded solemnly. It was one of my earliest memories—a witness to a telekinetic rescue, then demanding my death for witchcraft. Because even holy deeds done through unsanctioned means warranted condemnation. Better to let the innocent die. I certainly wasn't strong enough to fully ascend, but I had somehow tapped into my power, and my body burned for it. *Burned* for daring to save someone in a way that defied science as they knew it.

"I was there. I don't know how to describe it."

"It's hard to wrap our minds around past lives and memories. Past scars and traumas, August. But Alec seemed to know that would trigger your power."

His full lips pressed into a fine line, and he stared up at the sky again. The night was crisp with mountain air, and no clouds blocked our view of the Heavens in the clearing. The only light snuck through the curtains of the cabin in a thin slit, pouring across the tall meadow grass. It weaved in glimmering patterns through the long blades.

"I know Alec's approach wasn't...orthodox. But our true strength—both spiritually and physically—it's all just beyond your discomfort, August. I'd be full of shit if I told you it would be a pleasant transition into mastering what you are now." My eyes found his in the darkness, whites glistening in the full moon's glow. "We have to let go of who we believe we are to step into who we're destined to be. Your powers will only trigger when you feel a legitimate threat. It will be a..." I tried to think of a delicate way to put it, as to avoid bristling his already threadbare nerves, "journey. To say the least."

He turned his face back to the treetops and constellations above us. With a deep, cleansing breath, I dropped my mental walls, inviting him into the two visions that appeared between the chaos.

The first—while short—had been a man I knew to be August, flying without wings, fire roaring from his hands in a terrifying dive into battle.

Thoughts of Layla settled like lead in my heart, but August looked at me expectantly, and there was no hiding this from him. The second image was the kiss. Warm and urgent souls erupting and merging into one, no secrets between us...and smelling of the mountains in summer.

His eyes widened as he looked at me.

"Layla?"

Head shaking, I gave an apologetic shrug of my shoulders. "It was too fast for me to be sure, but I *believe* it was past."

The frustrated v formed between his brows, and he turned to assess the forest, his heart rapid. The wind caressed my skin, whistling quietly through the trees, and their stretching silhouettes slowly swayed against the shimmering stars.

"Fucking Alec. A volatile mistress, indeed." He rubbed his jaw as I blinked at him.

"What?" I asked over a nervous laugh.

"Nothing," he chuckled darkly, dragging his lower lip between his teeth as his face fell, palm running over his hair.

"You lost me," I admitted.

"Just...something Alec said. Doesn't matter." A secretive smile curved his full lips, and I tracked the movement, forcing my eyes up only when August said, "I don't know what this is, Ally. I can't make sense of it. But I need to let her go. She won't fit in this world...or at least...I don't see how." His words made my heart quicken inexplicably, and I demanded it slow, knowing he could hear it. "None of this bullshit is what she signed up for. I can't let her get hurt, and they used her once. She's...she's too good for me. For this."

I blew out a long breath, allowing my eyes to take in the look of him and soak up the familiar pulse of this soul so clearly tied to me. He was like a novel I'd read too many times over too many lives. Leather-bound and beautiful but worn with love and sunlight, parchment torn and repaired, dogeared, with notes in the margins. A smell I liked to breathe in on chilly autumn days, wrapped in a chunky braided blanket, sipping tea in the window seat of the cabin by the fire. He smelled like fire. Like mountains and sunlight, and everything good and pure.

I stayed silent, granting him space, not wanting to influence his decision but also wanting passionately to affirm his choices. I yearned to crack open the familiar cover and allow his stories to pour forward. Yearned to reach one hand to his still-flushed cheek and stroke it down his beautiful features. His pull was immense, as though everything I'd survived in the last three hundred years had led me to this exact point.

Guilt washed over me, and I curled onto my knees, rubbing my temples. Layla. He should have gone home to Layla that day after work. He shouldn't have had to be saved and scooped out of his world.

It's not your fault. He had turned to stare at me, expression soft but undoubtedly pained. *It's not any of your fault. It just...is what it is.*

How could he take everything so well? All my years of spiritual teaching rang in my head, and I still found more strength and resilience in those bottomless green eyes than in every lesson emblazoned on my ironclad memory.

Maybe I should have let them think I died.

The thought startled me, and my eyes flew back to his. Even that thought—of him dying—rattled my insides like a pebble in a blender.

"August," I breathed, unable to keep the admonishment from my tone as I shook my head. "They *love you*. Don't put them through that. Their lives are so incredibly short and devastatingly fragile. They'll be lost to you long before you're ready, no matter how many decades you have them. I want you to hold them as long as you can."

He nodded thoughtfully. "We don't get an afterlife? The way they do?"

"If we do, none of us have earned it yet. I don't think the sins of our ancestors have lifted."

"Hardly seems fair."

"It's not. But we make the most of it." I watched as he processed the events of the evening and then smiled at him again. "Finding long-lost friends is kind of fun, though."

He smirked at me, eyes finally looking playful. "Is that what we are? Long-lost *friends?*"

Heat rushed my face, leaving me grateful for the blanket of darkness. I shrugged and said, "I'd like to think so. Eternity is a long time to wait for someone you're lukewarm about. I mean...you about burned Aren's cabin down to defend me."

He laughed and pointed out, "You know, for someone who is supposed to *see all,* you're a bit blind."

I wrinkled my nose before the laugh bubbled up my throat. "Oh, piss off Rookie." With a shove and a roll of my eyes, I added, "What do you expect when I'm sandwiched between *two* powerful shields?"

"I didn't think that would be your thing." A panty-melting grin spread across his face, and he knocked into me with his shoulder. "For the record, I don't intend to share."

Eyes flying wide, jaw popping open, my reaction earned every ounce of his ensuing satisfied cackle. I elbowed him hard, but he only laughed louder, the sound infectious as he clutched his side.

"Oh. You're trouble," I breathed out, still gaping at him.

"But you knew that from the beginning." His sly smirk was cute and cocky, laced with playfulness. With a wink, August said, "You think I'm powerful?"

I choked on my amusement. He couldn't truly be so oblivious to have missed all the things he'd accomplished in a few short days, could he?

"In all seriousness?" He nodded, and I flashed him a broad smile. "Possibly the best I've seen. Aren and Alec say so, too. And that was before your temper tantrum in there."

"Damn," was all he uttered, fingers running across the stubble along his jaw. The breeze again carried that evening chill across my skin, filling our lungs with the scent of pine and fire.

"Most people take more time to figure out their powers—months or years, not days."

"Do most people reincarnate with old friends?"

"Most of the time, we recognize at least a soul or two. You got lucky, really, with Alec. His intuition is amazing."

He snorted. "Is he accustomed to threatening our family to prove a point?"

For a moment, I evaluated the wording of his question. *Our family.* We were a soul family in a bizarre celestial way.

"No, that's more Ansel's style. Aren, even, if he needs to push someone into their strength. Something about you...well—something about the energy of the world right now—it makes us anxious. Everything feels urgent. Like trouble is around the corner, and we're out of time. None of our seers have cast a vision to explain it. He's probably as anxious as I am."

"Great," he said flippantly. I laughed and laid back on the ground. The stars were my favorite part of being on Earth, or at least, they were one of them. August sighed, and I could feel the heat of his gaze on my profile. "What about you? Was I lucky to get you?"

I scratched my head for a moment before finally whispering, "I hope so."

SIXTEEN
TRAINING
ALVARA

The ground rattled beneath my feet, pine needles shuddering across the dirt as a chasm split before us. Up soared a shard of broken earth, a great sheet of stone, mud, grass, and moss rising in front of us like a wall. I turned my head and narrowed my eyes before twisting my hands and punching one forward with all the energy I could muster. The attack soared, an invisible torpedo, and the wall burst apart, showering us in mud and grime. Fragments of rock flew past my face, soil caking in my hair and splattering my skin.

Before the dirt was even cleared, a wave of water poured down, and I threw up an energetic shield, grunting with the effort of holding it as the force slid my bare feet into the warm, wet muck that smooshed between my toes. I twisted, shouting with the force of my parry, and the water flew into the woods behind us, flooding the forest floor with a small wave. Trees dripping, I narrowed my focus and sucked in a breath that moved my target with it. I pulled a large fallen log up and over my head before tossing it across the clearing towards Alec. He threw his arms up and redirected its momentum telekinetically, tossing it back to the ground with an impact that was so jarring that it jolted through the earth. I felt the wind start to draw out from the ground, and a low whistle sounded like a distant train barreling towards me.

I felt the smirk on my face. *Oh no you don't, sucker. Wind is mine.*

Pulling in a breath, I closed my eyes, throwing my arms out towards the ground and spreading my fingers as wide as I could, pulling my power up from the earth's core. With a shout and a clap of my hands, the wind rushed forward in a barreling wall, and Alec was thrown flat onto his back. I could feel it knock the breath from him, and stepped forward, grinning at the twisted smirk on his face. I shook my head and telekinetically pinned him to the ground until he relented, giving two solid taps to the earth below him.

When I released him, he immediately leaped to his feet, breathless laughter crossing the clearing to us. Fae gave me a round of golf clap, and August joined in. I could feel his grin before I even turned around. Everything about August was energetically palpable as if I should be able to reach out and touch his enthusiasm or scoop a handful of joy from the air.

Our endless demonstrations, trainings and sparring matches had filled the week following Alec's gutsy fire stunt, and his energy had returned to unabashed fascination. *Magic*, he called it. It was the easiest way to explain what we could do in all reality. But I picked up on enough of August's thoughts to know his smug grin was mostly from watching Alec get his ass kicked time and time again by the same woman he'd pretended to threaten only days before. He didn't seem to mind that he would also get schooled any time we went toe to toe. To be fair, he liked me too much to burst into flame or turn me into a kabob with his sizzling personality. He was learning quickly and would be lethal the moment he needed to be.

Days stretched into weeks, and our evenings were spent laughing, reading, playing games, and telling stories around the fire while taking turns on the guitar. Listening to August sing was as deep of a spiritual experience as I'd had in a few centuries. His voice was electric—just like his gift—and I'd found myself lulled to sleep more than once, listening to his quiet serenade to the fire as it flickered into coals.

It was the kind of peace that only came once or twice a century and not something I took for granted for even a moment.

The fire was nearing its end one evening, Fae contentedly dreaming on Alec's chest. Nervous, we'd wake them with our chatter, August and I had escaped out onto the front lawn. The evenings had grown longer since we'd been up in our hideaway, and I realized with a jolt that it was September.

The restfulness on the mountain had lulled me into a fireside haze of complacency...and something else. Contentedness?

But now it was time for us to move on, to get back into the grind of a battle so much larger than us, and for August to face the music he'd never asked for. He needed to do right by Layla, his family, and his company.

After a long pause of silence, August, all smiles, caught my eye. "So...what now?"

"Now? Now, we need to bring you back to civilization. We'll create trails for you to follow, and you can practice the hunt."

"Sounds like fun?" It was a question, his tone hesitant.

"It is, I promise. You'll do fine, August."

He nodded, silent for a long minute. "Am I safe to go home?"

I knew the question was long overdue, but my heart sank despite myself. I forced a smile across my face and gave him one quick nod of approval.

"Home," he whispered. "Why does it feel like I don't even know what that means anymore?"

"Your people are your home, August. And yours need you."

"Aren't you my people?"

"Yes. But so are they—your family deserves an explanation. Have you thought of what you're going to tell them?"

"Yes, and no. Yes, I've thought about it. Endlessly. But I don't know what to say. I've never lied to them—any of them. I'm not sure how to continue that dynamic now."

I chewed on my lip before suggesting, "Save lies for when they're absolutely necessary, and share truths whenever you can, as often as you can."

"I just don't know...how much they would believe, even if I wanted to share it."

"That's the hard part, I'm afraid."

The two of us had become frequent companions to the stars, most of our evenings ending beneath their shimmering blanket, pouring our hearts out. That night was no different. We sat elbow to elbow on the ground, contemplating his training, his mission, and how he could return home to Ivy Springs after a long, vaguely justified, mostly unexplained month of absence.

"Perhaps I'll tell them I bought an inn, and I'm leading bouldering trips in Colorado," he finally quipped. August was lying by my side, hands laced behind his head in the tall grass. He hadn't taken his eyes off the Milky Way for quite some time, but he glanced at me nervously.

"Wouldn't Layla just come with you?"

"Maybe. If she hasn't assumed the worst in me by now."

"Impossible."

"But she has a life in Ivy Springs. A business, friends, and family. Uprooting everything...it just doesn't make sense. Not even for a boyfriend having a mid-life crisis."

I snorted. "Maybe a third-life crisis?"

"Maybe." August's endearing, lopsided grin appeared for a moment. And then his face soured, a little stress v appearing between his eyes. "Let's talk about...anything else. Are you excited about going home? To Grayshell?"

I shrugged. "I like it here."

"Because of the quiet?"

"Yes, mostly. Between you, Alec, and the mountains—this is the first peace I've had in centuries. I wish I could just stay here forever."

"Nobody wants to hide out *forever*."

Oh, how I wished we could just stay here, hidden from the world, surrounded by nature and music. Laughing our nights away with Alec and Fae. But cabin or no cabin, the storm was coming for us all. There was no staying.

"Certainly not if we want to stand a chance against whatever storm they have brewing. We can feel them coming. Can't you?"

He pursed his full lips and then nodded. "Like...anxiety...deep in my chest. It feels like war." I hadn't been sure if he was interpreting the pulse beneath our feet as we were, but, trained or untrained, August didn't miss much.

"But does it have to be *you* to take all this on?

A humorless chuckle slipped between my lips before I could stop it. "Somebody's gotta do it. Generally, my gifts are a great tool in the arsenal. You might not have gotten to see that," I smiled ruefully. "But I would dishonor them if they were anything less than top priority."

"Jesus, Ally, you've served them for *centuries*. I think they'd understand if you decided to live for you for a few years. Even Christ took a day to rest every now and then. Why not stay here for a while, renew your spirit?"

I chuckled and turned onto my side to look at him, and he did the same. My hands were beginning to feel the chill of the September evening in the ground below us, shivers rolling through my frame. He inched closer, his knees centimeters from my own. Our hands nearly touched, and he tossed his flannel blanket over my wool one, and then I freed a hand and summoned a flame for warmth. August's expression was intent, with a hint of sadness under all that strength as he studied my face.

"I'd be lying if I said I hadn't thought about it." I twirled the fire between my fingers, turning my palm so he could see how it snaked around me like a ribbon, but his attention was back on my face in a heartbeat. "But I have this dream. It just...runs on a loop. And I can't shake it. It's always the same..." The flame flickered as my sorrow nipped at my heart, even after all this time. "And every time, I save him. *Every time*, like a consolation vision, it shows me that if I had just been...better, stronger, trained like I am now, I would have saved him—them." August hovered his fingers over the flame, shifting them incrementally and prompting the fire to split into two dancing ribbons.

"It's just a dream, Ally. You can't actually save them all."

"And *that*...is a lesson I won't learn twice."

"You're not a God."

"I'm as close as it gets down here." I cleared my throat. "Besides, if I didn't fight to defend them, who would? Where would that have left you and Layla if I wasn't guarding the coven?"

"Don't get me wrong. What you all do is extraordinary. But beyond *endless* battle, you deserve to live a *life*. We all do."

You deserve to live a life. The words hung heavy as a chain around my neck. For centuries, I had only existed to avenge and protect—the coven, humanity, braids, and souls—until they could do so themselves.

He stared at me, fierce and unyielding. The air felt thick on my skin like I could carve a piece out of it with the dagger tucked in my boot. My heart quickened as his eyes searched for something in my own, and for a moment, I just breathed in August's scent, tangled with wood smoke and pine, his musk growing more familiar to me than my own.

"I gave up the right to do more than survive and protect when I answered the call of the sword." My voice was softer than intended, flame extinguishing. "I am indebted to Aren in more ways than I can count. Indebted to the hierarchy for their sacrifice."

"Did Aren tell you that?"

"Of course not. Aren would never begrudge me leaving. But...where would I go?" I shrugged. "Hang up my sword, trade my guns for Saturday morning farmers markets?"

"Come on, Ally. I *see* you. The real you, with your shield down. I love that you're a badass, but I think it's bullshit you act like that's all you are. And while you might be close, you're not a god. You can't carry the world on your shoulders."

He surveyed me for a moment, and my breath hitched as I pushed the emotion back down where it belonged. I was a soldier—a divine soldier, forged of wind and fire, destined to destroy demons, and that's all I knew. The wind kicked up around us as the panic grew in my chest. Icy chains wrapped around my throat as I tried to remember anything before battle. Anything before the sword...and came up blank.

"If you say so, August. You must remember different lives than me."

Each memory August had shared of his known past life was of battle, the celebrations of victory, or pained nights in pubs trying to drink away his losses. Unless he was cleverer than I knew and had hidden his memories, that's all there was. That was the downfall of humanity.

"Walk with me?" I asked after a good stretch of time. He silently rose to his feet, dusting off the strands of grass and pine needles from his clothes. Pulling the end of his sleeve around his hand, August reached down to help me up, and I tentatively accepted his kindness.

Gravel and pine ground beneath our boots as we wandered down the path deeper into the woods. The stream not far from us gurgled a mountain melody into the night. We wandered, exhaustion not yet nipping at our minds. August often looked up at the sky, eyes tracing the silhouettes of the trees and the glimmer of constellations before looking back at me. Gradually, my stomach began feeling unsettled, butterflies blooming there.

"You said you were alone when Aren found you?" He finally asked.

"Yes."

"How old were you?"

"Nearly twenty-five."

He was quiet for a moment, and the tension in the air thickened with expectation.

"Did you ever have someone? Like Layla? I can't bring myself to be okay leaving her there after all this time. I just thought...if you understood..."

I shook my head slowly. "Not since ascension."

"Before?

"Yes," I admitted softly. "We were attacked by a group of men. They were going to..." My throat was tight, a heaviness settling over me as I remembered the terror in my muscles. "They wanted *me*. He managed to get free and then fought for us. And they...*stabbed—*" My voice cracked with an ancient ache, and I cleared my throat, staring at my feet. "He kept fighting, but they just kept coming...until he couldn't stand...and I—"

When my breath hitched, he set his hand on my lower back as he finished my sentence. "And you ascended."

I nodded. "They were already dead or dying when Aren got there. It was too fast, though. If I'd understood my powers, I would've taken my time before sending them to face their judgment. Aren has always reassured me that sending them to face the gatekeeper was the best thing I could've done." Fuck, had I ever shared this part of my story with anyone other than Aren? I cleared my throat, sucking in a long breath before I could continue.

"I was crying out for help, still holding onto him, when Aren jumped into the alley. Flesh traders. That's what he told me was the most likely scenario—and no man controls another in such a barbaric way without first entangling with something demonic. They were drawn to me like the crawlers were with you."

His lips pressed tight, eyes tortured. "Aren couldn't heal him?"

"No," I whispered. "His soul had already detached. And Aren had pried himself from the depths of battle. He was wounded and just beginning to heal, and certainly didn't have the energy to perform that kind of healing, even if there'd been time...Michael wouldn't have survived the jump to Grayshell."

Something ahead of us pulled into my consciousness, but I ignored it. A passing fox or deer, most likely.

"He was called Michael?"

I smiled and gave him a gentle nod.

"Michael is most of what I remember from my human life. My family had already been murdered when we met. We were kids, really. Fifteen." August motioned towards the forest floor, and I stepped over the gnarled root that snagged his attention. "He held me through my grief, and I guess he's all that's worth remembering. We were together for ten years before they took him..." I cleared my throat, working to keep my voice from betraying me. "I can't ask you to give up Layla for this life. If you love her, August, keep her as long as you can. If she'll let you...keep her close."

"Watch her grow old, alone. Watch her die, *alone*. Send her to an afterlife I'll never join. That's no life for either of us, is it?"

I pursed my lips and shook my head timidly. I needed to make sure he understood every complicated facet of the mess he'd unwillingly inherited.

"There's something else you should know, August."

"That sounds bad."

"Not bad. But it complicates your scenario a bit."

"Oh, good. It wasn't, you know...complicated already." He chuckled anxiously and ran his hand over his hair again.

"Fuck, this is awkward."

August raised his eyebrows, but he seemed to know what was coming because he suddenly narrowed his eyes and then wrinkled his nose disapprovingly. I huffed.

"God intended the marriage covenant to start at consummation."

"I'm afraid you're a bit late for *the talk*, coach."

I laughed. "Now that you've awakened, the dimension your soul is on will *hold* you to any contracts you make now, in a way your human body didn't. Ascended souls are entangled, not just for life—but for the afterlife, too. When we truly mate, we bond in such a way that our souls re-circulate together."

"So, Fae—"

"Had not known a man in any ascended lives before she found Alec. They've fallen and risen together both times since."

"Damn. I mean, that's kind of cool though. Takes the sting out of the loss a bit, knowing they'll come back?"

"I wouldn't know."

August winced.

"It does seem to bring them some comfort. Except for the fact that they basically throw themselves into impossible scenarios to re-circulate with their mate's timeline." The horrifying image of Alec diving into a battlefield of Renown he'd known he could never come out of slammed into me. Fae had already fallen. August's eyes widened.

"So, you—Aren?"

I shook my head slowly. "Neither of us has found the soul we're bound to. And so, we wait."

"For centuries?" His tone was dubious.

"For a millennium, evidently."

His eyes grew wide, but there was respect there, too. "Damn. I can't imagine."

"I mean, Aren has dated—Christ, have you *seen* the man?—But he learned about soul-entanglement the hard way and takes eternity very seriously after over sixteen centuries. Can't blame him."

"No. I guess not. But damn."

"Layla—" I hesitated.

"Would be alone. In her afterlife."

"Her soul would wait for her partner for eternity."

Silence hung, heavy as the impending death between us. Finally, August's eyes found mine again.

"Can you see her?" He tapped his temple.

"If you stop shielding me, I can look for her."

"Her future, I mean?"

I nodded, embarrassed I hadn't yet dared to look—I selfishly didn't want to know if he would choose her. "Pull in your shield."

He closed his eyes, and as I felt his energy draw back into his core, the hair on the back of my neck stood up, goosebumps erupting down my arms.

"August, something—"

His eyes flew open, and he nearly pressed a finger to my lips before catching himself. The reek of wet fur and decaying grass hit me right as the world turned heavy and predatory. August's energy expanded, as though he could shield me from this. *Maybe he could.*

He shook his head in warning, eyes peering into the darkness with unmatched urgency as he stepped in front of me.

Then, the night before us stood up, shadow towering more than a foot above and nearly twice as wide as August between us. And in a heart-wrenching moment of terror, I realized he was staring down a bear. Before I could fully process what I was seeing, the great creature released a rumble that rattled my ribcage; August spun and dove toward me. We collided with shocking force as his arms wrapped securely around me, and we toppled to the ground. The energy swelled, and the twist of light through my closed eyelids was chaos before we slammed into the hardwood floor.

I blinked. The log ceiling of the cabin stared back at me, August bracing himself, arms under my head and back protectively. His body was pressed down firmly into mine, and I could feel every inch of him as his chest heaved. Slowly, cautiously, he raised his arms to survey me.

Those piercing eyes were so round the whites were everywhere, scraping frantically over my body. Then his alarm changed to amusement, and we both huffed out our breaths. Laughter exploded between us, relieved, raw, and still a bit panicked. He bowed his head to rest it on my shoulder, his face so close to mine I could feel his warmth. His body shook with his laughter, and I could feel his breath, balmy against my neck, sending new goosebumps across my skin.

As the laughter slowly faded between us, he rose to peel himself away. August was straddling my torso, sending a wave of heat chasing away the adrenaline, when his face changed from mirth to a wince of embarrassment. The energy of our now-awoken companions hit me before Alec cleared his throat.

"Did I miss something?" He questioned groggily.

We both erupted into chuckles again, and August slowly shifted himself off my waist and rose to his feet, sliding his sleeves down so he could help me up.

"Well, there was a bear," August started.

"And August jumped us here to escape," I finished. Mirroring shit-eating grins permanently etched on our faces, August reached up, thumb tucked in his sleeve, to wipe dirt from my cheek, freezing my ribs in place.

"*August*, jumped you here?" The surprise underlying Alec's question made my grin broaden, and I realized August's had done the same. Alec and Fae were staring at us over the back of the leather sofa, faces bemused with a hint of skepticism. I nodded proudly and examined my new companion carefully before finally speaking.

"It's time to take him home."

SEVENTEEN

TRACKING

ALVARA

Walking between Alec and August, the city was eerily silent. Occasional prayers still pressed onto my consciousness, but the usual assault of voices was absent, mercifully extinguished by the shields on either side of me and the amulet around my neck. Anxiety had gradually wound a tight fist in the center of my stomach, and I wasn't sure if it was my own or if I was just feeling August's nerves as his mind raveled and unraveled hollow words he knew would bring Layla no comfort.

Despite the inevitable heartache of the evening, August was learning quickly. Fae had ventured out ahead in the city, giving us about a twenty-minute gap to close, and we were leaving it entirely up to August. Every few moments, he would pause, inhale, open his palms to the ground to sense the energy, and decisively choose our next direction. He wasn't as in tune as Fae and, compared to the gifts I had in my arsenal, would seem sluggish if we were in a pinch. But before the timer could sound, he found his mark, and I felt myself release the anticipatory breath I'd trapped in my lungs. Aside from the continuing struggle to wield Earth's energy as a weapon, his arsenal of tools was looking more and more encouraging for whichever path he chose.

Reunited, we walked towards the center of town for a bite to eat at one of August's favorite restaurants when a familiar pull called to me on the air. I paused, closing my eyes. Histories whispered my name. I beamed at August and slunk down an alleyway, giggling as Alec and Fae guffawed. The store was a magnificent collection of books, antiques, and artifacts, and I gingerly unclipped my necklace and placed it in my pocket before walking through the many dusty aisles. My fingers dragged across each object in their path, and I absorbed each story piece by piece. Swirling images, scents, and sounds absorbed me, and my heartbeat accelerated the smallest amount as my mind soaked up everything. There was nothing of note, per se, but I loved them just the same.

"Is that not overwhelming?" August's voice was inches from my ear when he spoke, and I jumped despite his familiar tone. A nervous laugh escaped my lips.

"It can be," I admitted. "But when I have the energy, it's one of my favorite parts of my gifts. Being able to read all the history in places like this. It's fun to see the stories."

He grinned. "Will you show me one day?"

"Yes." It was a promise. Because I knew I wouldn't be able to resist August's touch much longer. He stared at me with that endearing, crooked grin, and beyond the pull to know what his skin felt like beneath my fingers, I knew there was a part of him that wanted to know our own history, too. I could feel it buried between our souls, and it was beginning to drive me mad. He seemed to sense the significance in the vow and ran his now-calloused fingers over his growing beard.

"You like reading old stories."

"Not all of them. Ghosts and trauma can be jarring. The feelings are too visceral. But places full of items that carry history without spirits are my favorite." I slid my hand over a stack of books that had once belonged to a Harvard professor and laughed aloud.

"This one, for example, recorded an affair between a Harvard professor and the dean's wife."

August laughed. "Naughty," he teased and then gestured toward my outstretched hand. "That never seems to get less weird," he noted.

And it never will. Alec added internally. I laughed.

"My Aunt Estelle is a bit of...a collector. I think you'd love her house—you'd go crazy for all the antiques." The briefest vision of a grand Victorian house, the color of April sunshine, flashed in his mind. It was burrowed among corn fields, and the interior was brimming with every kind of collector's item she could get her hands on.

"Will you show me one day?" I smiled, repeating his words back to him.

"Yes." His was a promise, too. And for a lingering moment, our eyes locked again. My cheeks ran warm, and I pulled my gaze away, closing my eyes to soak up a few more stories before we got to the real mission of the day. But his promise, and my own, seemed to hang in the air like ripe fruit begging to be plucked from their branches. My stomach hovered closer to my heart than it should have, and anticipation swelled in my chest.

We parted ways at the entrance of his condominium building. Until he'd said it that way, I hadn't realized the building we'd rescued them from was one of his many real estate acquisitions. Of all the subjects we had spoken about endlessly in the mountains, the amount of wealth he had built for himself wasn't one of them. He never mentioned money, instead telling me about the excitement of work and the variety of businesses he owned, and listed countless employees—by name—that he'd raised up and trained until they started their own companies. August loved little more than becoming their patron and watching his people win.

He spoke of his pride at Sam and James being on board and having his back, as well as the countless ideas for new ventures he had written in a notebook for the future. I was painfully aware that future would no longer come to pass, at least not as he had believed it would.

"August!" Layla cries, throwing her arms around my neck and burying her face in my chest...

I jammed my eyes closed, and my hand flew out to find Alec's. He grimaced at the pang of sadness that radiated from me to him, and his eyes, warm pools of whiskey in the September sun, turned to me. They were as pained as mine felt, and he shook out his tawny hair before gingerly telling Fae it was time to go.

YOUR GREATEST STRENGTH IS LOVE. That was what the tag on my teabag said, and I flipped the little square of paper between my fingers. Steam swirled in little halos above my cup, and I breathed in the smell of honey and herbs. Seeing those words as I lifted our mugs from the bar to bring them to the table was a strange stab to the gut. An ironic message, sent from someone with a sense of humor, I was certain. The same culprit is also undeniably responsible for the voices of Ray LaMontagne and Sierra Ferrell singing "I Was Born To Love You" over the shop speakers.

We had jumped far enough across the city that August's thoughts wouldn't demand my attention and tucked into a cozy little shop painted in countless colors. While clutter poured from every surface, all the items were new, made as gifts to sell with their refreshments, so the only stories I had to hear were those of the human patrons chattering around their tables. Tearing my attention from the tea tag, I studied the collage of empty golden picture frames on the walls, in bright contrast to the mulberry paint and heavy burgundy tapestries hanging over floor-to-ceiling windows. The air was thick with steam and espresso, and the merged babble of a dozen voices, their internal echoes audible only to me.

Alec and Fae were each reading books, their backs pressed together on the long, converted church pew piled in soft, velvet cushions the color of eggplant. Fae had kicked off her shoes, and her bare feet were crossed on the cushions. She enjoyed the feeling of velvet on her skin, and she caressed it with her free hand, rubbing patterns in the malleable surface and then wiping them away again. Her mate's focus was intent on the literature in his hand. He frequently shared that the best part of our unaging existence was he could live a thousand years and never read all the books committed to paper. Determined as I was to lean into his steady calm, impatience was furling and unfurling in my chest. It had been just over an hour since we'd abandoned August to his heart-wrenching task, and I couldn't shake the feeling of their reunion from my bones.

My stomach twisted painfully at the thought of them touching in that way, with all I knew of his soul. And yet, I had no right to be protective or jealous. He was hers. I had no claim to him, and neither did the coven—his free will was all there was between them. And I had given him all there was to know.

I let out an exasperated huff, and Alec eyed me, tense beneath a facade of calm.

He's fine. It's just my nerves.

He dropped his gaze back to his book, nuzzling into Fae a bit more than before. Alec was a gift in my life—more than he possibly knew—and I was grateful for the friendship he offered to August, even if it had taken weeks to earn forgiveness for his brash method of teaching. He was so steady and slow to anger that his display of theatrics in the cabin was the most dramatic, rash action I'd ever seen him take. The way he guarded our coven and his unyielding dedication to his bride forever cemented our love for him. I believed August loved in very much the same way, and somehow, a knowing settled over me that he would come back to us. What felt like an eternity of silence fell over our little group, and I allowed my mind to wander.

When the last afternoon shift change swapped the little brunette barista for a six-foot man, my nerves bristled, and I looked around for whatever energy had pulled on my mind. I was hit with the familiar scent of sage and pine, and the energy grew in my chest. Suddenly, body moving of its own accord, I was standing, tea abandoned on the table between us. Because August was watching us through the cafe doors, eyes red rimmed and glistening, and he wiped his nose.

I had never felt his energy in defeat before, and it completely undid me. He was anguished, and it felt like he might shatter right there on the sidewalk. I closed the gap between us in long, urgent strides, threw open the shop door with a loud clang against the bell, and wrapped him in a bearhug. With my hands safely tucked in my sleeves, I set one on the back of his neck and the other wrapped around his broad back, pulling him close to me. He tentatively returned the embrace, paying acute attention to where he placed his hands at the small of my back. He leaned his head forward as if to bury himself in my hair, and his hesitation broke through me like a kick to the gut. It wasn't fair. It wasn't fair that I couldn't comfort him as he needed me to. We held onto each other for a moment, and then I leaned back, ignoring the feel of him wrapped around me, to stare into those bottomless eyes. Words were evading me, so I mentally told him I was sorry, and he nodded and released his hold.

A cleansing breath whooshed into my lungs, and my attention turned to the army bag he had dropped on the sidewalk when he'd seen my intention to collide with him.

"It would've been easier if she hated me."

"I don't know if that's possible."

He gave me a begrudging chuckle and a half-hearted shrug. "Still. It would've been easier if she yelled. Or screamed. Or threw me out. She's too good for me."

I vehemently disagreed but kept my opinions to myself. It would do no good to voice them while he bathed in grief and an undeserving sense of betrayal. August had reassured Layla that she had no need to leave the condo—the beautiful, modern home they'd made for themselves. It was hers, indefinitely, and he had no need for her to pay rent as the leases on the building turned a hefty profit, and he wouldn't feel it one way or the other. A gift of condolence. A heavy tear rolled down his cheek into his beard, and he held out his hand. There, in his palm, was his grandmother's wedding ring he had proposed with. His fingers trembled, and I pulled my sweatshirt down over my skin before wrapping his hands up in my own, closing his fist around his ring, needing to stop his shaking.

"She'll be okay, August. I mean it."

He nodded, slowly bringing his glossy eyes back to mine. Unblinking, he stared me down with an intensity that burned into my core.

"Will you check for me? Did I do the right thing?"

I pulled my hands back from his and swallowed hard. My mind cast into Layla's future, sorting through hundreds. Many suitors danced on the horizon, some with familiar faces I recoiled from—I wasn't so sure he'd want to know about the men she could turn to. Some visions were cut short, but those threads were murky at best, leading me to believe she would make choices that led her down one of the longer lifelines.

"There are too many paths right now, August. Losing you is like a big knot. There are literally hundreds of threads erupting away. We have to let her emotions settle and let her make some choices, and the paths will narrow and solidify. There are other variables at play too—"

"She won't be alone, will she?" His voice was gruff and pained.

My heart sank at how close a few of the men were in the timeline. It seemed that sweet Layla would seek solace in the arms of someone she knew.

I only shook my head, reassuring him. I couldn't judge her, not for filling a gap in her heart like the one August just inevitably left. But I was certain she would be okay. She just had to choose her paths wisely, and the threads with new love interests all stretched out before her.

Alec and Fae had come out to stand with us, and August gave them a curt nod hello. Finally, he turned to me, took a heaving breath, and said, "Let's go home."

EIGHTEEN
BRIMSTONE
AUGUST

Guilt had been my constant companion in the weeks since we'd left Layla in Ivy Springs. She'd been so kind. Too kind, really. And I couldn't wrap my head around her grace. Or how I'd stepped all over her beautiful soul and abandoned her. Abandoned her to a world more broken than she could even know. But she was safer with me gone—without angels and demons battling in her life. I had done the right thing.

At least, that's what everyone told me. Aren had reassured me as often as Alec had, although Alvara had said it only once. She seemed to feel my guilt and the pain around the subject, and she turned deep into herself as we returned to Grayshell. Although there hadn't been much time for them to trouble themselves with my broken heart.

Just before we'd made our jump home, Alvara had cocked her head to the side, her beautiful features twisted with confusion. The light and joy I'd grown used to in her eyes guttered. She pursed her lips, turned her gaze to me, and quietly said, "Something is wrong."

Without further explanation, she'd hooked her arm in mine, and we jumped anyway.

When we arrived, chaos and a desperate panic greeted us. Trepidation saturated the air and swept down my spine when my feet hit the ground. The great hall was a cacophony of voices, hundreds of souls buzzing about the room. There was no lingering scent of food or hum of music. I'd never been there without someone offering me a morsel of something irresistible.

Most of them wore spirit armor, and the electric charge of war was thick in the air. Two colossal men who wore their wavy hair at their shoulders, sections twisted out of their faces and pinned back with gold, came rushing forward the moment we landed. They held spears in one hand, bows slung across their backs, and each had a sword sheathed at their side. I studied them as they approached us and realized they embodied the Greek soldiers of ancient times. If I hadn't known Aren was the oldest among them, I would have guessed he had scooped them right out of the battle of Troy. In formal greeting, both quickly slammed a fist across their heart, kissed it and extended it to Ally. A salute of sorts.

Head and shoulders above me and half again as wide, the soldiers were Aren's size, if not more substantial. The blonde man spoke first, not hesitating to reach out and take Alvara's hand to turn her in the direction they were rushing.

"Alvara, thank God. We need you in armor yesterday."

Her eyes grew wide and frantic the moment he touched her skin, and her voice came out haggard and breathless. "Take me to him. Now."

"Already on our way," the dark-haired one boomed.

Two of our kind were missing. Both were from another coven in the hierarchy. And while they were only supposed to report in that morning, there wasn't a soul in Grayshell that could reach their minds. Even as the rookie, my blood went cold as they explained the details on our hurried walk to Aren.

The men burst into the war room, but Ally hesitated on the threshold, eyes on her feet as her chest rose and fell faster with each draw.

"Ally?" I lowered my head, trying to catch her gaze. Her full lips were parted slightly, eyes far away, as though she could look through the stones to the dimension below. She raised a trembling hand to rub at her furrowed brow, shaking her head. She breathed something that sounded a lot like *I can't see them.* "What?"

She blew out a hard breath, straightening her spine and dropping her fingers to the knife at her hip as her eyes flicked to mine. That lethal power danced like embers within them, running goosebumps down my spine. "I should've been here," she breathed in disbelief.

"Ally, don't do that—this isn't your fault." The words rushed out as I watched her slender shoulders pull back in defiance.

"Yes. It fucking is." She clenched her jaw, squeezing the bridge of her nose between her thumb and forefinger.

"Al?" Aren's voice carried from the room beyond. "Westerlunds are on the line—coming in hot with allies from New York."

When her eyes opened, they'd gone stone cold, and she dragged down a breath, gave me a curt nod that seemed more dismissal than direction, and turned to face The Commander.

Being earthbound, guarded by Alec and I, had left her detached from the others. Aren had admitted it had left a hole in their defenses, but he would never have blamed her. *Couldn't* when he knew better than anyone the burden of her gift. But in Ally's eyes, every single soul in Grayshell was hers to protect.

I'd never met the lost souls, but Sebastian was a skilled healer and Skyler—Ally called her Sky—was a master at potions and poultices. Both were from Saraya's coven. The healer had not returned to Grayshell since they'd vanished, determined to track down her people herself. Over the next weeks, she checked in telepathically about twice a day to update the hierarchy on what she'd learned, but even Saraya's trails went cold. We joined in the search when Alvara left the war room, popping back and forth between Chicago and Grayshell like manic inter-dimensional popcorn kernels. But I could tell Alvara expected the very worst. Mission after mission revealed no more information on the missing souls.

Previously, I'd been the only mark she'd ever struggled to locate, and if she could not hear Sebastian and Sky, more than likely, there were no longer minds to find.

Beyond Layla, I felt the constant burden of guilt weighing her down. It had been my training that had required her absence, my shield that kept her oblivious when they cried out for help.

"Stop blaming yourself, mate. There's no point. We can't change it," Alec reassured me as we sparred one afternoon. "If they're there to find, Alvara will find them."

His confidence did nothing to put my mind at rest.

"YOU SAID this bar is a hangout for demons?" I couldn't hide the skepticism in my voice. A hangout. For demons. At a bar, blasting *Rebel In The F.D.G* by W.A.S.P. so loudly the air and asphalt vibrated with it. This world got stranger and stranger.

Ally managed a forced smirk at my tone, but Aren shot me a sideways glance. His telltale sense of humor seemed to have vanished with the missing souls.

We entered the bar, filled with cigarette smoke and the glow of red neon light. The smell of nacho cheese and spilled beer was heavy on the night air. As we entered, the entire place went silent, save for the music, and the patrons stilled to stone. Dozens of dark eyes, all ringed with exhaustion, were on our group. We wore human attire, but I could tell from Ally's quick survey, the rapid ebb and swell of her power, and the unabashed snarl across her lips that there were no humans here to cover for.

The place erupted into chaos as Ally, Alec, Ansel, and Lana dove into the room. Rather than drawing swords, each pulled out a Glock. Each silver bullet met its mark as though without effort, and the bodies sizzled into puddles of black, steaming, viscous fluid on the floor. It took them only seconds to vanquish two or three dozen of them. The creatures didn't even have time to react.

A lone demon stood on the far side of the room, tucked behind the bar with a glass and towel still in his hand. His head was cocked sideways, and pale lips curled back over his teeth, eyes black as asphalt. There were no whites around its eyes, and it did not seem to fear the warriors' guns, now trained on him. They formed a half circle, cornering him as Aren advanced.

"Where are they!?"

"Who?" The black-eyed man retorted slyly. As I studied him, I realized his skin was paper thin, like a corpse that had already sat for too much time. The energy pulsing from him was icy cold, like the crawlers. I listened intently and realized what the others must have noticed the moment they entered. He had no heartbeat. The host had long since left its vessel.

And he knew something.

In one swift motion, Aren launched himself over the bar and pinned the man to the wall with his forearm.

"Where are they?!" He roared again, this time inches from the demon's cold face.

"Something wicked this way comes," the thing spat.

"No shit," Alec snarled.

Alvara stepped forward, her head inclined to the side, more animal than human. A soft smile turned the corner of those sensuous lips. The confidence in the demon spilled away, leaving its onyx eyes darting between us. I could feel the surge of power that grew in her chest before it lashed for the now trembling demon. Could feel her phantom hands pry into its mind as she honed in. Those emerald eyes were a pair of trained daggers, focus unwavering. An annoyed sigh. There was more than what the demon currently feared revealing. More she needed from him. She stepped forward to press her hand to its head. Her eyes went fuzzy and far away for a moment. When she stepped back, she nodded at Aren and held an image of a tall, black-cloaked figure in her mind with a crown of thorns, paper-thin skin stretched over skeletal hands, a gaunt skull, and eyes that were all pupils.

"Fuck," Aren growled the word through gritted teeth. He heaved a great breath. "Second hierarchy."

The demon smirked and then started to laugh, the sound sick and distorted over his crushed windpipe. Despite the information that would likely be his death sentence, that taunt returned to his eyes.

"Too late, half-blood."

And with his final jeer, Aren snapped its neck. An effortless twist of his arm. Aren slashed his blessed blade through the mist as the shadow lifted from the body. It crackled like electricity and vanished into smoke.

For all their jokes and wagers, the coven moved with unparalleled precision, their executions swift, reminding me that at their core, they were as much a cadre as they were family. Ally could have destroyed entire flocks of demons alone, and Lana and Ansel were nearly as lethal. Aren was like a God among them. Never a scratch. Never a sliced piece of clothing or blood on his skin. Half the time, the demons would surrender to their fate when they laid their eyes on him. I gathered that he was known among them. After sixteen hundred years, it would be hard for them to miss the hulking warrior who offered only swift justice.

But our dozens of missions brought us nothing. Only more vanquished demons and the repeated image of the second hierarchy monster with a crown of thorns and skeletal face and the ice it seemed to put through all our veins.

As the days passed without any new answers, determination reached into my soul. As did a peculiar knowing. Without fully understanding why, I approached Ally in the common area. Her energy was frantic. It infected anyone within a good fifty-foot radius. Which is why the common area had been nearly deserted for weeks since we returned to the news. She was bent over the island, studying a mess of maps and pins, brow furrowed. Her long hair was pulled into a braid that had grown loose, and dark tendrils reached down around her cheeks. I didn't think she'd slept in days and knew she hadn't eaten. Aren sat in the armchair closest to her, unyielding stone, eyes firmly closed. Only the steady rise and fall of his chest revealed that he was alive.

Neither reacted as I came into the room, like perturbed statues carved out of snowy granite. I watched her for a moment. Her pupils had grown to dominate her eyes in the low light of the lounge, and it gave her focus an eerie lethality I was growing used to. It would be worth a great deal of caution to never be on the wrong side of the fire burning in her soul. Vigilantly, I closed the gap and stood beside her. Her body gave off a manic static, like being elbow to elbow with a thundercloud.

"Ally, I can't explain it, but I think we need to search the hospital again." Her eyes darted to me and then back to the map, where red pins marked the places we had scoured. Each hospital in Chicago had been searched by teams of trained hunters, and no one had felt a thread. But something in my gut said we needed to be there. Now. Me. Alvara. Fae. Her lips parted as she read my mind, and I felt her push around my subconscious for a moment before she turned her face to the side.

"Aphaea," her hushed call rang like the final gong in a summons to battle. The air seemed to charge with the same finality I'd felt from her. Electric and unyielding. The energy around her swelled, and Fae and Alec appeared by her side, eyes immediately focused on her intently. Without a word or palpable thought, they each reached out to firmly grip her shoulder. Aren rose, face stoic, and did the same. She turned to me, eyes lethal, and held out a hand gloved in leather.

"Take us there."

I didn't even have a name for the hospital. But I focused on the room in my mind, and we flew through space until the energy stopped twisting, and our boots landed with a clap on white tile floors.

The room was empty, as I'd somehow known it would be. Phantom sirens rang in my mind, ears buzzing with dozens of voices, words, and diagnoses I didn't understand, and I realized Ally had removed her pendant in the same motion of her landing. Her walls were down. And her mind was louder than usual as she sorted through all the chaos around us. We'd arrived in the basement, in some sort of storage room, and the sounds of the hospital seemed to reverberate down to her there. She pressed her hands into the wall as though she was bracing to move it back a few feet.

Fae stood by her side and inhaled as deeply as she could, finding no trace of our comrades.

But Ally didn't move as she sorted through the thousands of voices, and a chill climbed up my spine. She could sense...something. Something that wasn't right.

"The demon?" Aren's booming voice sliced above the babble with a fierce finality to it. Ally closed her eyes, and a low growl rumbled in her chest.

Yes. He's here. Many demons. Strong ones.

She held the image of the tall, cloaked figure with its signature crown of thorns in her mind. Its eyes, which were still all pupils, had grown somehow darker. And he was *here*. She could *feel* him.

"Fuck," Aren growled.

Ally gave a slow, ominous nod.

"We should call the others," Aren said, his words heavy with a weight that set the hair on my skin on end.

"Call. But we cannot wait. There is no time," her words escaped in a rush of breath. The image in her mind was horrifying.

Blood. So much blood. A girl with dark eyes, wide cheekbones, and black hair was slain or sleeping at the feet of a giant, drenched in still more blood. She lay in a pool of the dark liquid, her face a ghastly pallor. The giant stared unseeingly forward, eyes as black as the demons'. He was ghostly pale and too perfect. One of ours.

Sebastian! Even in her mind, his name was a sob. Lost to us. That was what she saw in the possessed man. We lost him. He had to be for the thing to invade his body. I shook my head, not as convinced. But I'd never witnessed an exorcism, so I didn't know what it entailed. And I was sure beyond a doubt she had witnessed many. The giant envisioned in her mind snarled quietly.

As though he still heard her call.

"Where?" Aren thundered, his knuckles white, hand wrapped around his quickly unsheathed dagger. With a jolt, I realized I'd never seen him physically reveal that an emotion had overrun his discipline. Ally breathed in a deep, jagged inhale. The icy smell of metal and chemicals filled our minds, and Fae seemed to recoil.

"The morgue," she whispered.

"Fuck," Alec said in the same tone the Commander had, and he rolled his sleeves up. He and Fae both drew long knives from their belts. The hilts were jeweled with emeralds the color of Ally's eyes, a Celtic pattern emblazoned under the stones. Alec dropped his shield, and the world grew immensely louder. Aren sent a blast to the others—The Commander delivering a Hail Mary summons that I knew in my gut would be too late. We moved for the door, and Aren threw it open, so furious that it flew off its hinges. He cast it onto the floor, unflinching, and we ran down the abandoned hallway. The walls reeked of rotten eggs, and the lights had dimmed low with an ominous flicker. With horror in my stomach, I read the word on Fae's mind.

Brimstone.

She looked like she would be sick. Whether from the stench or the anxiety pulsing through the group of us, I wasn't sure. But my mind lingered on the word she'd thought.

Like fire and brimstone. Is this creature straight from the gates of Hell?

Yes. Aren answered internally. I winced.

We ran in unison, our footsteps thundering off the walls of the endless, deserted hallway. Demons could sense us, as we could sense them, so there was no point in keeping quiet. Ally and Aren simultaneously summoned telekinetic shields, their hands raised eerily in front of them as they spun their heads from one side to the other. I kept my eyes glued straight ahead of us.

"Sebastian!" Aren roared, thunderous voice echoing in a battle summons. Adrenaline coursed through my veins, shaky breaths, and tensing muscles preparing for the fight I knew I would not avoid. I drew my blade as the buzz of the flickering lights grew, and the air ran cold.

The shadow rang with a long hiss, like snakes hidden along the walls.

"Do you have a name for the demon?" Aren muttered to Ally, and she shook her head, lips pressed together. "Damn...Sebastian!" He roared again as ice crept up the walls like stretching spiderwebs. The lights crackled and popped as frost ran over them, and then, with a deafening crack, they all extinguished. We were enveloped in blackness, and my heart pounded a pleading drum of escape against my ribs.

"August," Ally hissed. "Give us some light."

"Right," I rushed before igniting a ball of fire above my palm. Ally turned back to me, eyed the flame, and then waved her own hand to do the same. She cast the flame out ahead of us, and I threw mine, too. Together, we illuminated the hallway in the flickering light of fire. My heart sank.

Standing at the end of the hallway, unmoving, stood Sebastian. He wore his angelic uniform of white pants but was missing his breastplate, and the entire cloth had been dyed deep red, his chest streaked with it. We slowly advanced, each of us searching the doorways we passed for an attacker. The stench of brimstone filled my lungs, and the nausea Fae had fought off hit me with ferocity. I nearly doubled over, but staggered and held my ground.

Sebastian's sacred dagger was still sheathed at his side, long bloody fingers dripping a trail on the ground below him. As we closed the gap, precariously close to him now, Aren spoke, his voice low and commanding.

"Bash! You're stronger than this!"

"Bash is gone!" Its voice trembled the ground.

"Bullshit. Bash!" Aren rumbled, "Bash, *be* stronger than this."

The man staggered forward, eyes rolling to the back of his head, and the baritone voice crept into my mind, exhausted and defeated. *"Sky is dead. I—"*

The demon was back in a fraction of an instant, and I felt the outrage and anger of my family burning in my veins. We fanned out, blocking the hallway, each holding our own shields. I stayed close to Fae, concealing her between Alec and me. She seemed so fragile compared to our larger frames.

"Bash!" Aren demanded, and the ground shook, power coming off him. "Revertere ad nos!" It was a command. The kind we *had* to follow. Sebastian's body began trembling, seizing. Aren threw his hand out, and the others did the same. To my astonishment, my own hands were in front of me, heeding The Commander, and the hallway exploded in light. I realized, with shock, that they were sending him their strength. *We* were sending Bash *our light.*

The demon roared in pain or panic and lunged forward. But Ally was faster. She met his advance, throwing out her free hand to pin his seizing body telekinetically to the wall behind him. Her jaw was clenched, and fire burned in her eyes. The thing was vastly overpowered, but I couldn't shake the feeling of trouble creeping through my bones.

Sebastian's body was convulsing as we surged more light through it, and Aren roared, "Redeo ad lucem!"

The thing cried again, jaw hyperextending, a nightmare from a zombie game. Its black eyes were frantic as it looked for an out.

"The half-breed burns with me!" It bellowed before screaming out in pain as Ally surged forward, her light filling the entire hallway. She twisted her hand into a fist and turned it, twisting a dagger that wasn't there, and the thing screamed in agony. With a flick of her wrist, it fell to the ground, and she slammed her body down on top of it, smashing her palm onto Bash's sweaty forehead.

"Impius Vincendum!" She screamed, and the light exploded out of Bash's eyes and between his lips. A dark cloud escaped his open mouth, and in a quick motion, she was on her feet, throwing her dagger into the mist, and it crackled like a hot kettle before vanishing.

"Bash!" Fae cried, diving forward. She scooped her arms under his armpits and dragged him to the wall, where she propped him upright. She gently wiped the blood away from the corner of his mouth and felt for a pulse.

It's faint and slow.

She placed her hand on his chest, and more light enveloped him. Her voice came out in sobs, "Come on, dammit! Don't you die on me, Bash. Don't you even think about it!"

Bash remained limp, and Fae grew more frantic in her attempts to heal him.

But Aren and Ally were circling back, and I stayed glued to her side, pulling my attention from Fae and the fading Sebastian.

The threat wasn't gone yet. They were still on high alert.

"Still no name?" Aren said under his breath, and she shook her head again. In their minds, I realized they could summon the demon if they had a name. A desperate cry ripped through the air, and we saw Fae frantically powering Bash's fading heart, her desperation palpable. Alec knelt at her side, placing his hands on either side of Sebastian's bloodied face, and he breathed out light, trying to heal his mind as she made an effort to revive the body. Alvara gasped, and I turned to her as she folded over her knees, clutching her temples. She sobbed as she pressed there, and agony rippled through my own head. Dark talons began to claw at my mind, and I locked my shield up, expanding it to cover Alvara and the others. She released her hold on her mind and gasped for air.

The meaty sound of a blade running through muscle and bone ran chills down my spine.

I turned around as Alvara's blood-curdling scream rang out Aren's name. She dove forward to catch his colossal frame as he fell to his knees, eyes wide in shock, hands grasping at the blood-soaked blade sticking from his chest as it smoothly pulled back out.

Looming behind them was the stuff of nightmares. A cloaked skeletal figure with obsidian saucer-sized eyes.

The cloaked and crowned demon.

NINETEEN
BURN
ALVARA

"Aren!!" The scream tore from me, and I lunged for him. My head still recoiled from the attack as though the creature had taken a mallet to it. The weight of Aren's frame brought us both to the ground as the sword slid backward out of his body.

"No!!" The scream was unified among us. No. It couldn't be. In three hundred years, I had never seen Aren struck, let alone lanced. *Impaled.* I summoned my strength, looped my hands under Aren's great, muscled arms, and pulled him away from the towering demon as it raised its blade to strike again. My Commander was nearly silent, releasing only a small grunt as I heaved him out of the way, his eyes staring down in shock at the rapid crimson blooming across his white shirt.

The others all rushed forward towards the demon in the cloak. His eyes were void of soul, and his lips pulled back to reveal razor-sharp points to rows of teeth, all stained red with blood. I pried into his mind, my head burning in agony as I slammed the attack towards him. He had drained Sky dry to steal her life force. To take her power. I recoiled from my hold as Alec collided with the creature, only to be thrown to the ground like a rag doll.

Aren wordlessly clawed at his chest, and my attention turned back to him, his hot blood pooling against my lap. I tore his shirt apart, and my eyes burned—the flesh the blade had pierced was now charred. Poison.

"Saraya!!!!" I screamed. "Saraya!!!"

She appeared in a moment, a mess of red hair fanned out around her shoulders, and her eyes instantly filled with tears. "No!" she cried, shock thickly lacing her voice. She dove for the ground by my side, pulling Aren's great body forward onto her chest, light erupting from her hands and heart to spin long glowing cords around his body, binding them together. Her glistening chocolate eyes found mine. "Grayshell," she whispered.

I nodded and released my hold on him, frantically shoving his weight off my legs so I could stand. "I'll cover you!"

The others were all between us and the demon, shields held high. Only August's horrified eyes met mine as he glanced over his shoulder. "Hold the shield!" I demanded, and power surged around him like a forcefield, knocking the demon back a few steps and sizzling through the shadows. The shield began to crackle with August's electric charge, and I turned back to Saraya and commanded, "Go!"

They vanished.

My eyes lingered for a moment on the smeared pool of blood where Aren had been, my heart tearing through my chest, pounding with frantic desperation to follow. But the demon was advancing, and August had revealed his strength, painting an enormous target on his back. August seemed to know my fear because he turned his attention back to the demon king as it moved forward, its shield sparking against August's and shaking violently as it collided with the wall of energy our team had conjured.

I forced my way between Fae and August and cast my shield, knocking the thing backward. Stepping between my family and the threat, I let my anger course through my veins, pouring into my fingers. Alec believed my temper was a weakness, but Aren had always told me my strength was planted there.

Aren.

Deep sickness twisted in my stomach, and furious energy poured out of me.

A snarl tore from my lips, and my teeth bared as I pushed forward. An eerie green glow burst across the demon's face, casting darker shadows under its eyes. My soul was surging. August stepped forward by my side, eyes also glowing a vibrant green. His nerves had been replaced with a vibrating rage, and the demon narrowed its onyx eyes.

Slowly, straining against our energy, the thing looked from August to me and back again, inclining its head slightly to the side. "Impossible," he growled. Terror unmistakably filled its dark eyes. The word gnawed at my core as I surveyed him. Frustration rose in my chest as I futilely fought to reach back into its mind. Then August was there in mine.

I'll hold your shield! Go! Move!

My eyes blinked, and then his strength surged through me, my muscles bracing for an explosion.

I released my shield, and August's took its place, electricity crackling through the air, sparking like tiny bursts of lightning. The demon shot a panicked glance at August and roared the word, this time like an epithet, "IMPOSSIBLE!"

I stepped forward, feet heavy, as they pushed through the demon's barrier. Throwing my hands up, a wall of fire erupted between us. Stronger than I'd ever cast, my outrage like kerosene, I cocked my head to the side before snarling and advancing again.

The flames grew, encircling the entire hallway. Raging oranges and reds, even flashes of blue, the wall of fire seared the demon's fingertips, and it hissed as it shoved back against the crackling force field.

The ground trembled, and long vines of earth, twisted and braided tree roots burst through the tile floor and spun around the demons' legs, binding him to the spot. *Alec.*

Earth continued to break through the floor, whipping and snapping against the beast as it yanked free from the roots. They quickly replaced themselves, as relentless as their wielder. My canines elongated as the growl tore from me, strength surging.

His shield cracked beneath the force of August's, splintering like webs through glass. I reached my hands forward to attack, but two blades *thunked* into his chest like an axe to a tree, and it staggered back, eyes widening again. *Fae.*

The thing faltered. Black blood sizzled around the hilts before its shield fell completely. August dropped his, swung his arms forward, and grabbed the hilt of Fae's knives before roaring, "Burn!"

The demon went up in flames, batting frantically at itself as it screamed in pain. It collapsed into a heap on the ground, and I bombarded it with a wave of water before stepping on its throat.

"Why did you take them? Who are you?"

"Impossible," it croaked again.

"Why did you take them?!" I screamed.

"He'll come for you, he'll retaliate, he'll—"

The lifeless eyes rolled back in his head, and the demon's words cut off under the weight of my boot. "Let them come," I snarled back, rage seething in my chest.

Then he melted into steaming fluid beneath my foot, and I recoiled, flinging the demon guts off my boot against the wall. I turned to find August's eyes nearly back to their normal shade of green and grounded myself within them. He looked as desperate as I felt, and bone-chilling anguish bubbled up in my chest.

My voice came out in a desperate sob, "Aren!"

With a series of small pops and cracks, the others began to appear, lining the hallway with their energy. Too little, too late.

"We'll clean up!" Aphaea's voice quivered, and her hands trembled, but she met my gaze, her eyes resolved. "Go!"

TWENTY

STORM

AUGUST

Alvara stepped forward the moment our feet hit the floor. She threw her bow to the table beside her without breaking her long, urgent strides. The chaos around us was exponentially louder than it had been when we'd arrived the day Sebastian and Sky had gone missing.

Some were weeping. Men were hollering. Thundering footsteps echoed in the hallway beyond the gathering room. Someone swore. People were shouting above us in the infirmary, where Alvara had been healed only a month ago. There was the loud crash of something metal being tossed aside.

Saraya's voice could be heard over the tumult as she barked orders to those around her. She was upstairs, too, and her voice echoed through the stairwell.

The encounter with the demon had lasted only minutes, but I couldn't unsee that blade piercing Aren's chest. Or the way Alvara's entire body had glowed with rage under the flames that erupted down her arms, her eyes a fluorescent green. So much had happened in a few ticks of the clock.

She rounded the corner one pace ahead of me, and as spectating eyes found her fierce expression and blood-soaked clothes, the onlookers silenced and parted to make way. Those in varying armor bowed their heads, bringing a fist across their heart and then to their lips before extending their fists or outstretched weapons to her—that salute I'd seen only one other time.

Only the healers still whisked about, in and out of the infirmary, rushing for supplies and to fetch the souls Saraya needed.

I felt the tug on my mind just before their voices lifted to the heavens, reverberating off the walls in raw unity.

"Our Father, Who art in Heaven..." My mind buzzed with the prayer enveloping us, but my heart grew cold as we followed the long, splotchy trail of smeared crimson down the center of the hallway.

"...Glorious Archangel St. Raphael, great prince of the Heavenly court..."

The congregation of voices continued their prayer, the hall lined with unmoving statues, except for those nervously shifting out of our pathway. Alvara's lips moved over the memorized prayer, but her eyes were unblinking, trained on the infirmary doors. She threw them open and strode into the room of sprinting healers. Their hands were busy, and they buzzed between carts full of tinctures and bottles and the bed where Aren had been laid, his pale skin somehow turning flat and grey, body concealed by the wall of healers.

"...Because you are the medicine of God, we humbly pray you to heal the many infirmities of his soul and the injuries that afflict his body. Glory be to the Father..."

The healers, brows furrowed in concentration, whispered the prayer under their breath, inaudible under the chorus of warriors calling out behind us. Aren opened his eyes, a twist between a smile and a grimace pulling at the corner of his lips when his eyes found Ally crossing the room.

The others? His mental voice was quiet and reserved but clear. The fear in his eyes was the only giveaway to the direness of the situation.

Safe. She played a quick recap of the chaos in the hospital in her mind as she rounded the end of the bed and fell to her knees.

Badass, kid. He managed an exhausted chuckle but winced, reaching a crimson hand towards his wound, his bicep flexing beneath letters more scar than a tattoo, only to be slapped by a focused Saraya. Her flaming hair had been thrown back into a messy bun at the nape of her neck, blood clumping pieces together. Her face was streaked in red, and focus hardened her brown eyes. Aren smirked, somehow still capable of amusement, and pulled his hand away, allowing his head to fall to the bed below him. He turned his face back to us and narrowed his eyes.

Impossible. What did it mean by that?

Arrogant shit, didn't think he could be defeated? I don't know.

There's more to it than that. It had to do with August.

Alvara nodded and then slowly shook her head. *I don't know. Rest, Aren. All we need you to do is heal. Do you hear me?*

He nodded slowly and relaxed his head deeper into the pillow. His eyes closed, and he seemed to work to keep his breath steady as the prayer continued.

Ansel and Lana were suddenly standing beside us, and Lana raised a trembling hand to her mouth, shaking her head. Denying what her eyes were telling her, a healer with blood smeared up to his elbows turned for another vial of something. Ansel wrapped his arms around Lana, pulling her to him. His silver eyes were grave as he assessed the laceration and pools of blood the Commander had spilled. He locked eyes with me, questions of the encounter flooding in his open mind.

"St. Raphael, of the glorious seven who stand before the throne...." I heard Fae's chiming voice join the choir of prayer. And then she stood beside Lana, her arm wrapping around her sister's waist and pulling their frames together.

"Heal or cure the victim of attack. And guide our steps when doubtful of our ways..."

All of Grayshell rang in an eerie silence for a moment. Then, the prayer began again somewhere below us, gathering momentum as the rows of onlookers raised their voices for the second time.

Saraya's eyes glistened as she prepared a poultice. She fought back her tears, drawing air in through her nose in desperation. As she removed the thin sheet of fabric and lifted the gauze that had been held to Aren's chest, I staggered back. Helpless.

The wound had already fouled. It sliced right through the inked cross over his heart, oozing a sick yellow pus. The edges were raised in a livid blister as though burned by fire. Spiderwebs of black reached away from his heart, through his veins, clear into his arms. Webs of raised black coursing down his muscled biceps. Ansel let out a sharp huff of air as the panic swelled in the room. Alec arrived and fell to his knees by Alvara. His blood-spattered face was drenched in tears, and he bowed his head onto the bed by Aren's great leg. Saraya rushed to apply the sloppy black poultice.

The surreality of the moment struck all at once, as my mind grappled with the image of the unyielding giant lying broken in an infirmary bed. This could not be. There was never a scratch, not a movement missed. Sixteen hundred years old.

Alvara sobbed as though her mind had been fighting with the same realization, "I'm so sorry!" The floodgates had opened at the sight of the wound, and her face glistened in her agony. "I failed. I missed it. I missed him. I'm so sorry!"

Ally, this is not your fault. Don't you do that. Aren shook his head incrementally and grunted as he lifted his bloody hand to tuck her dark hair behind her ear. She leaned her face into his crimson-soaked palm, tears pouring in a steady stream, leaving streaks down the drying red on his hand and arm. Her lips quivered, and she looked fragile for the first time since I'd met her. More vulnerable than when she had been in that very bed herself.

"Sixteen hundred years and a few decades..." He sucked a rasping breath. "Damn impressive run." Aren's mouth quirked, and then he winced.

"Don't you dare!" Alvara's words were a command, and his body seemed to tense as she spat them.

She is becoming the Commander.

A vice closed around my ribs as I watched from the sideline. Sparks popped between my fingers, charged for a conflict my power couldn't solve. Alvara threw her hands out over him, her palms glowing with white-hot light above the wound. A cry of effort escaped her lips, and she narrowed her eyes in focus. The spiderwebs receded back up his arms towards the wound, but it quickly zapped her energy.

She shook her head in panic and forced out another few bursts before her hands began shaking. Alec gently pushed her aside and repeated the motion until his life force diminished, too. Someone brought her water, which she gulped down in seconds. The webs had retreated significantly, and the team each took turns lending him their strength until the creeping lines were contained to his chest.

I stepped forward to do the same, but Saraya reached her hands out and shook her head. "Not yet. We have not trained you to heal. You could burn him."

My eyes stung in frustration, but I pulled my hand back. Aren's frosty eyes locked on mine, and they softened a bit. *Thanks for watching her back.*

Always, Commander.

He grinned softly and then rested his eyes again. But Alvara's gaze was a dagger on me, and when our eyes met, hers widened. Fear? No. Something else. She was *determined.*

"August," her voice sounded in a steely command that locked my resolve. I was to her side in a few strides, the team shifting out of the way nervously. She felt like a bomb, posed to explode and take us all with her.

"*Heal or cure the victim of attack...*" The echoing prayer finished again, and without hesitation, they sang out the first words for the third time. The hallway vibrated with potent anticipation, and I could feel the warmth of their energy flow now.

"Anything," I whispered. I knelt beside her.

"Heal him."

I leaned back, staring at her in disbelief. "I...I don't—"

"August. Heal him." Her eyes were desperate as they raked over my face and my body. "I've *seen* it, August. It's the only way." She pressed her hand across Aren's chest and jammed her eyes shut. Aren grunted in pain as she pressed into him, light glowing faintly below her fingertips. And then I saw it. As vivid in her mind as the room before us, she could see my hands hovering over him, next to hers, and the demon poison rushing from his veins in a violent swirl as it pulled up into the air in small, glistening beads. Saraya would collect it in a vial.

"You're The Healer, August. Now, heal him!" Somehow, I knew her words were true and turned from her gaze.

Saraya's eyes were wild as she studied Alvara's face. Her hands remained protective between Aren and me. Their gaze locked for a moment; Saraya just as fierce as Ally.

I felt Alvara's anger bubbling to the surface in my own chest.

"Stand down, soldier," Alvara barked at her friend. Saraya didn't change her protective stance. "Move," Alvara demanded through gritted teeth.

"Ally—I—he could."

"I said, move."

"Ally, I can't turn a—"

There was no time. Ally's outrage burst from her chest in a wave of static electricity, knocking every healer and onlooker to the ground. It took one quick glance to realize her energy had not touched anyone who believed her. That trusted her instinct. She stared down at Saraya's defiant expression as she started to rise, and Ally stood obstinate and outraged. Wind began to tear through the room in a torrent, assaulting her face with whips of her hair. She cocked her head at her old friend, who shouted something inaudible through the lashing current.

I felt her courage, anger, dread, and finally, absolute certainty rise in my chest. Suddenly, her emotions were mine. And it wasn't her prying into my mind. It was a deep, organic reaction within my bones and soul. I felt the power surge between us as the air picked up speed, a tornado building strength in the room. Only Aren's bed and our team stood in the eye of the storm. Saraya fought to get to her feet, pushing a shield against the force of the air. Alvara threw her hand forward, pinning Saraya to the floor telekinetically.

You'll kill him, don't you see?!? Alvara's voice rang in our minds, and I watched as the eyes around me all went hazy. Only Alvara's, now unblinking and trained on mine, were clear. And I realized she was filling their minds with her visions. All of them. And then my world vanished too, only the floor remaining planted under my feet.

I watched in horror as she unraveled the future thread by thread so that all the healers could see. One by one, we watched their failed attempts to draw the infection and save The Commander. Again and again and again, we watched him die. Again and again, we watched his most loyal souls throw themselves to his body to sacrifice their life force. One by one, we watched Grayshell fall to an onslaught of demon attacks. Watched the four horsemen freed from Hell and take the mortal world into the Apocalypse. We needed Aren to stand a chance. They needed me.

One short, glimmering thread. Foggy at best. That's all she had. And she shoved the vision into our minds like an uppercut to the gut, knocking the wind from our lungs with the force—me. Me, healing Aren. Me, commanding our armies.

When the vision stopped, I shook my head to clear it. *Ally is very rarely wrong.* Aren's words rang in my mind, and I lunged forward to wrap my arms around her waist. I pulled her away from the bed. Her anger was so powerful that I wasn't sure if she could see they had surrendered to her will. The wind came to a violent stop as she submitted to my arms wrapped around her.

With hands hovering over their blades, Lana and Ansel placed themselves between their seer and the healers, livid gazes surveying their faces.

The Great Commander. The unified prayer had ceased in Ally's storm and had been replaced with chilling quiet. The thought echoed down the hallway as all their minds turned to *me.*

"Ally," I whispered as she panted with the effort, "I believe you." She went still in my arms, chest heaving. I turned to Aren, whose eyes were wide in shock. He slowly nodded at me.

I trust Ally. So, I trust you. He turned his head in my direction. "Do your best, Commander Porter."

TWENTY-ONE
STITCHES
AUGUST

Those two words reverberated through every bone in my body, and I felt their strength swell in my chest as the power they held was unlocked. I released my hold on Alvara, and she spun to face me, her skin stained with blood, tears, and desperation. Her eyes met mine and stilled.

"Together," she commanded. I nodded. "Saraya, get the holy water and a vial for the toxin."

Saraya's eyes were cautious, but she heeded her second in command, Ansel and Lana shifting like furious sentinels. When the supplies were in hand, Ally turned to me. The poison was already webbing back down through Aren's veins in an aggressive counterattack. His broad shoulders were covered in its dark spindles. There was no time.

Ally stared at my eyes, and something in her soul told me we were one in this battle, one in this life.

"I'll say go." She focused her gaze on Aren. "Give him something to bite down on. This is going to fucking hurt."

He nodded and turned his face as a healer brought him a bit of leather.

Alvara closed her eyes, gripped Aren's hand, and stretched her other arm out over his body again, only inches from his skin. *You hang onto me. Do you understand?* His fingers tightened around her hand in answer. When she opened her lids, her eyes glowed a frightening green. Like before. In the hospital. Her light began to radiate down towards the wound. The tremble started in her fingers and inched its way up into her arm, straining from the exertion of what she pulled from him. She slowly rotated her splayed open hand, everything in her trembling as the web of poison was pulled back into the wound, and her eyes went all foggy.

"Now!" she cried. I threw my hand out over his chest, and our life forces entangled in a dancing spiral, braiding together before swelling until the light blinded the room. I closed my eyes but didn't dare yield. I felt the swell of toxic, icy energy move towards my hand. Deeply buried survival instincts screamed to pull away, to escape the threat, only pushing me to lean in harder. Aren let out a shout of pain, and Saraya cried out that we were killing him.

"Keep going!" Alvara countered, screaming the words. "Jesus. Stay with me, Ar." I opened my eyes to see her staring at Aren's chest through the glow as his head limply fell back. Dark beads of demonic poison had been pulled into the tornado of our energy, spinning around our entangled life force. Saraya carefully scooped them into the vial, holding her hand steady as she cried out, her flesh burned under the ray of light.

"*Fuck!* Come on!" Alvara held an image of the skin being stitched in her mind, and Alec dove forward, using his gift for speed to lace the wound up with expert hands. She released her energy, and her body swayed precariously. I made to react but couldn't get my legs to move. Alec wrapped his arms around her as she collapsed into him. Somewhere, my subconscious knew Ansel had abandoned his post and was watching me intently from a foot away.

And then the world went black.

TWENTY-TWO
TEQUILA
AUGUST

The Grayshell Nephilim honored their fallen soldiers as the ancient Norse honored their kings. They took solace in knowing their souls would return to new, uninjured vessels when the time was right. However, their knowledge of demons possessing the dead made transporting the bodies to Grayshell impossible; burning them was essential. As The Great Commander, I was expected to assist Aren in preparing our fallen soldiers and placing them in their boats. With Aren still healing, Alvara and I took on most of the work. She bathed and dressed Sky, while Alec, Aren, and I prepared Sebastian's body—cleaning his wounds, washing his hair, and slipping him into the telltale white spirit armor.

Night fell, and we placed our final gifts in the greenery surrounding them on the small canoes. Some brought flowers, others stones or energetically charged crystals, and still others brought coins and treasures. Photos littered the bottoms of their canoes, and Fae carefully placed their blades on their chests, crossing their arms over them. A procession of goodbyes lasted over an hour, each warrior kneeling at the edge of the sea to pray over the departed souls.

"Until we meet again." Over and over, the farewell was spoken aloud and internally. But here, the goodbye meant something very different than it had among humans. As Nephilim, we would likely meet again—in this life or the next.

Saraya, the leader of their coven, gave the eulogy. I didn't know the fallen healers, but grief still gnawed at my chest. Alvara's pain and guilt seemed to radiate through me. Our hands, tightly intertwined through leather gloves, clung together as the boats were pushed off to sea by their coven.

As two of the hierarchy's best archers, we joined the others, knocked our arrows, lit their flames, and, on Aren's command, loosed them into the boats. A chill ran down my arms as the flames grew around the bodies. An impossible memory tugged at the corner of my mind.

We waited until the canoes were fully engulfed before members began the jump home. Alvara remained rooted to the spot, her face glittering in the moonlight. I gently wiped the tears from her cheeks, the dampness permeating the gloves.

I was why she had been late. Why she hadn't heard them in time. Likely why she had missed the demon coming through the shadows after Aren. I had not wanted to voice my suspicion until I was certain. Until it was too late. My instincts in this existence seemed much sharper; I needed to learn to trust them. Studying Alvara's grief-twisted features, I resolved to do just that. *Trust your gut.*

I wanted to strip the gloves from my hands and soak her fallen tears into my skin. She deserved so much more than what I was giving her—deserved to be touched and soothed without reservation. My fingers flexed, hands buzzing with the need to be that source of comfort—to feel what she felt like against them.

Sensing my trepidation, she turned to me, her glistening eyes fierce as ever. Our gazes locked for a long moment before she briefly looked at my lips, then closed her eyes and leaned into my gloved hand. The tears came faster then, and I wasn't sure if I was helping or hurting. But nothing felt more important than showing her she wasn't alone—that she didn't need to hide from me. And somehow, I knew in my gut, I needed to stop hiding from her, too.

THE HALL WAS quiet in the weeks following our loss. Alvara was quiet, too. She had turned inward, and there seemed to be some aftermath to her outburst—the damage of the storm in its wake. It wasn't until the approach of Samhain that low chatter began to return to the halls. It wasn't anticipation, as it was among our mortal counterparts, but apprehension.

"The veil is thinner, which means we need to return to Ivy Springs and increase the protection on your family," Alvara said one evening as the Day of the Dead drew closer. I nodded, not fully understanding.

"So, all the Hallows Eve, Halloween, Day of the Dead stuff—"

"Is founded in truth. They don't fully understand our world, but they aren't stupid. The veil is thinner, leaving mortals more vulnerable, spirits more restless, and demons more ambitious to cross the lines of dimensions. Grayshell is even vulnerable this time of year."

Not liking the sound of that, I stayed close on her heels. We didn't fully understand what being The Great Commander entailed. I still wasn't sure if I believed all the lore surrounding the position. Ansel and Lana had glumly told me it couldn't be possible, as a first hierarchy demon had shredded The Great Commander's soul in two. Alec insisted God could heal all things and would have used The Great Commander's fall for glory.

I didn't feel like a *great* anything. Certainly not a Commander of God's army between worlds. Certainly not wiser or stronger than Aren in his nearly seventeen hundred years of wisdom and practice.

We agreed to return to earth a few days before October thirty-first to place stronger wardings on my family's homes and for me to visit Sam and James. I'd given them the same mid-life crisis excuse for my absence that I'd given Layla for our breakup. Fat chance James would tolerate that for long.

Aren, still healing from that damned cursed blade, would stay behind and call us home at the first sign of trouble.

***

SERVERS BUSTLED between chattering tables and the kitchen. The pretty blonde hostess hurriedly whisked menus from their stand and directed people to their tables. Spices and cooking meat lingered in the air, and countless voices buzzed in a cacophony of stories, orders, children laughing, and babies crying. The yellow ceiling gave way to orange walls covered in art and lime green trim. Decorative painted porcelain plates were mounted high on the walls, above paintings and plastic fruit. There was a lot to take in, and I wondered what this place felt like through Alvara's eyes.

I sensed her gaze on me—intense and smoldering.

"Still no more visions?" I asked, slicing my fork through the steaming tamale. My mouth watered. Good God, I missed real Mexican food. She shook her head glumly, returning her gaze to her plate, and took a bite of her street taco, drenched in lime and hot sauce, just like James. Despite myself, I was grateful to be on solid earth. And more grateful that she was making time for me to see my family.

While our positions at Grayshell were all-consuming, the quiet hours still left time for me to miss them. Despite myself.

Alec cleared his throat, trying to cut the tension. "Tequila shots, anyone?"

"Lord, yes," Fae sighed, relieved.

I laughed. "That would be nice."

Alvara remained silent, her perfect lips pressed tight together. She took another bite of her taco.

Alec flagged down the server, a small brunette with salsa spilled on her uniform, and ordered a round for the table. An idea to see Alvara smile slowly brewed in my mind. I chewed it over as much as I chewed my food for the next thirty minutes and then smiled at her. She hadn't allowed herself any kind of fun in weeks. My growing suspicion was that she was punishing herself for either the death of her friends or for missing the demon's attack on Aren. The walls she'd placed around her abilities and the stones she kept on her body were effective guards of her mind, so I couldn't be certain. Either way, she was not omniscient. She'd told me as much herself. It was foolish to carry so much of the burden on her conscience.

When the tequila arrived, Alec set one of the shots in front of Alvara with a slosh.

"It's been a while since you drank with me, Al," he chided. She shot him a sweet smile, but it didn't touch her eyes.

"You've never drank with me," I pointed out, and she narrowed her eyes. Her full lips quirked.

"I guess that's true." She lifted her glass to ours, said, "Cheers," and together, we drank.

Several rounds later, the numbness had set into my muscles, and Alvara and Alec began exchanging stories as they had around the fire in Colorado. Their banter eased my breath, and I relaxed into my booth a bit.

Her eyes locked on mine as she finished her story. "So, I stare at Alec for a minute and finally ask if that's blood on his hands. He says '*no?*' And I don't know why, but it struck me so funny I couldn't stop laughing. I mean, it's not really a great question to answer with a question."

Alec rolled his eyes. "I still say it was a fair response. It was freaking dark out."

"You hit him. With your *knife!*"

"I'm pretty sure the term you're looking for is '*stabbed,*'" I added, rubbing my temples. Alvara choked on her gulp of margarita, coughing through her laugh.

God. Seeing her smile—really smile, with the way her eyes wrinkled and her nose crinkled with true humor—made my heart swell. The vice that clamped around my chest when Aren was attacked finally seemed to loosen. I focused on how radiant she was—the way her eyes glittered in the lamp light, her dark hair falling in long waves, and the animated way she moved her hands as she told her stories. The tight muscles beneath the delicate fabric she wore. I was so used to seeing her in t-shirts that the cursed sundress, draped off her shoulders, had become a distraction a few shots back.

Thin and light blue, it clung to her slight curves, accentuating the arch of her small breasts and revealing most of the pale skin on her shoulders. Fuck, I wanted to taste her. Trace her defined collarbone with my tongue until it met the long column of her neck, then graze my teeth along the sensitive skin there. *Goddamn sundress.* I would've assumed it was one of Fae's, except Alvara was a head taller, and the dress fit her like a glove. This was her own piece, no doubt tucked away for an occasion like Fae begging to go out and do something fun on our trip to the mortal dimension. I would have to thank her for that someday.

Alvara had begrudgingly agreed, and the girls had vanished to get ready together. I hadn't fully soaked in how radiant she was until I watched her there, in the low lamp light. She tossed her hair over her shoulder and shot me a wink as Alec told some past-life adventure I'd shared with him. My chest warmed, and I grinned back at her, no doubt looking like a drunken fool. She was laughing about something he said when she snatched a chip piled with queso and jalapeños from the nacho plate, popped it in her mouth, and sucked the cheese off her long fingers before licking her lips. Jesus Christ.

I shifted, uncomfortable with the intensifying desire pulsing in my veins and fighting the need to adjust myself. I wanted to wrap her in my arms, feel her pressed against my body, to finally know what her smooth skin felt like under my hands. What those lips might feel like under my own. And that tongue...

"I'm going to the bathroom, don't go anywhere," I told no one in particular. I needed to put some space between us. She nodded and continued her conversation with Alec. But her eyes stayed locked on mine as I left for the men's room. She didn't drop her gaze until I rounded the corner, out of sight.

I washed my hands and splashed my face. One too many shots of tequila. But my intuition told me there was more to it than that. There had always been more. Alvara was amazing—powerful, dangerous, demanding, a defender. She was a warrior. Captivating. Tantalizing. Always just out of reach.

But I didn't want just any woman. I wanted her. The world spun a little, and I forced a breath. My legs suddenly refused to do my bidding. Another splash of water, and my focus seemed to solidify again.

I wanted the badass, demon-slaying queen sitting back in my booth. The vanquisher of darkness. The defender of Grayshell. The second in command. The key to unlocking my own power.

Somehow, I knew that to be true. My strength lay within Alvara. And something told me that hers lay in me. We were...kismet. That was the word for it. Not even an angel could argue with fate. Her words of covenants and contracts weighed heavy in my heart. And yet, they didn't change the draw I had to her—the draw I'd always had and just wasn't ready to admit to myself.

I steeled my resolve and made my way back to the table, my jelly legs barely obeying my commands to walk. Step, step, step.

And then I saw her.

Did she know? Did she know that her smile completely undid me?

I sat down in the booth across from her and took another breath, willing my mind to clear of the chaos inside. Aren was not yet at full power. Bash and Sky had only been dead for a few weeks. It was too soon—too soon to put anything else on her plate. Selfish, really. But I could do everything in my power to keep her smiling. And I would. Even if that meant just having her back. But fuck, if I didn't want to earn her for myself.

As I watched Alvara tuck a strand of hair behind her ear, flashing her full-throttle smile, I knew that I would love her either way.

"I have a gift for you," I finally said as my plans solidified, grateful the words weren't slurred together. Her bright eyes widened, brows raising, and she pointed at her chest. I winked. "It's about damn time we made good on those promises."

TWENTY-THREE
ESTELLE
ALVARA

Aunt Estelle's home was a life-size Victorian dollhouse, nestled among cornfields on all sides, except for the front, which faced a two-lane dirt road. Its white front porch wrapped around sunny yellow walls, adorned with rocking chairs and a softly swaying porch swing that creaked in the wind. I'd forgotten about the promises we'd made during our first trip to the mountains. They had been washed away by chaos and grief, overshadowed by the frantic search for Bash and Sky, the panic to heal Aren and keep him safe while he recovered, the funerals, the endless research, and the hunt for the mystery demon seeking retribution.

But August hadn't forgotten.

I jumped down from his Jeep and followed him across the expansive, perfectly manicured lawn. My mouth fell open as I took in the enormous fountain in the front yard. A naked man and woman were intertwined, their cores covered by a tangled sheet. Her exposed breast pointed to the sky, while her long arm arched over her head into her flowing hair. The man's arm wrapped around her waist, and water poured from the tips of her fingers back into the pool. Apollo and Daphne, perhaps.

August strode ahead, hopping up the steps to open the door for me. A shy smile tugged at his handsome face. He had promised to bring me here weeks ago, but I never imagined it would actually happen.

I stepped inside tentatively and was greeted by a grand staircase. The energy was magnetic, charged with the countless antiques overflowing from every surface within the white walls. To the left of the sunny entryway was an octagonal sitting room, brimming with artifacts of every kind. Floral-patterned Victorian settees and sofas rested upon a dark rug. Above the room, a large tapestry hung on the wall, depicting a somewhat comical scene of children playing by a lake with a small goat.

I hadn't realized I was beaming until August's satisfied smile caught my attention. His eyes were fixed on me, as if trying to read my very soul. Every object in the home seemed to have a story, begging to be read, understood, and cherished. I wanted to touch them all—every sun-browned scrap of lace, every bustier, book, lamp, and armchair.

"August, I—" My voice caught in my throat. I blinked several times, my eyes stinging with the beauty of the place. He grinned shyly and looked at his feet before sighing and meeting my gaze.

"You like it?" He bit his lip before seeming to realize what he was doing, his expression softening back into a smile.

"I love it—I, I don't know—"

"I know. Take your time. We have all day."

Standing there, in his aunt's house, thinking of our time in the mountains, and the fact that he had kept his word, left me speechless. He seemed to sense my inner turmoil, smirking knowingly and giving me a reassuring nod. He crossed the room with easy strides, settled onto the settee, and spread his arms across the back of it, leaning back as if to show me he was content to stay a while.

I moved towards a grandfather clock, its brassy hands frozen at six-oh-five. I breathed in the oak and absorbed the scent of lamp oil and parchment—stirring up memories of my own before reaching out to begin reading.

As we made our way through the house, August's interest in the stories —and in my gift to see them—seemed to grow. Long since abandoning his relaxed sprawl on the couch, he stayed close to my side, his hand often finding its way to the small of my back as he guided me through the old house. By the time we paused to drink the cold glasses of sweet tea August had brought out, the sun cast hard shadows on the ground, indicating high noon.

August ran his hand over his short beard as I told him the names of the family that had first owned a Greek bust atop a bookcase as old as our country. His eyes pierced mine, as if he could see to the very depth of my soul, setting a wave of butterflies loose in my stomach. He shook his head in awe.

"Damn. You're amazing, Ally."

Blood rushed to my cheeks, and my eyes fell to the antique runner beneath my feet. It would take several days—maybe a week—to read everything in the dollhouse walls.

"Thanks," I finally said, once my cheeks had cooled. His grin brought the flush back, though, and I laughed, tossing my hair over my shoulder to braid it as a distraction.

Ever a magnet, I found myself leaning against August repeatedly as we toured the house. Like slow-motion bumper cars, we continually bumped into each other until our shoulders nudged us apart again. He laughed when it happened for what must have been the dozenth time in the narrow hallway upstairs. The walls were plastered in pastel floral wallpaper that seemed to dance as August ran his fingers through his long curls, inching closer to me. He straightened his posture, his lips so close that I felt the heat of his breath on my cheek as he chuckled. The feel of him so near made my stomach flutter in an unsettling yet desired sensation.

"Sorry, again," he muttered. "My mom always told me I'm magnetic. Could never walk a straight line next to her."

I grinned. August's past was fascinating to me, but the evident intent in his eyes made my breath catch. Slowly turning my back against the wall, our eyes locked, and August turned his body towards mine. Heart hammering in my chest, my hands grew clammy, and I wiped them on either side of my sundress. The open neckline, leading to sheer, off-the-shoulder sleeves, felt intensely vulnerable with the yearning that had built up in me over the afternoon. And with the way his eyes roamed over me now. He placed his hand against the wall, his muscled arm a brace between us, and gently twisted a strand of my hair. He spun it between his fingers, thoughtful and focused, and my breath quickened. Warmth flooded through me as he said my name.

"Ally... I know you have so much on your plate, but I—"

The sudden bang of a door being thrown open and the yip of small dogs erupted in the downstairs foyer. August recoiled from me, a blush coloring his cheeks. I drew a heavy breath and smiled as his eyes searched my face.

"August?" An old woman's voice warbled with excitement.

"Up here, Auntie!" he shouted back.

"By George, you're really here!" she croaked. August ran his fingers through his hair again with an exasperated huff, but his eyes were smiling as a smirk played on his lips. Two eager Yorkies bounded down the hallway, yipping excitedly. Their entire bodies wagged with anticipation for some affection. He scooped them both up and offered me one. The little brown dog turned, trying to lick my face, drawing a laugh from my lips.

"That's Mindy; she prefers other girls." He chuckled, our laughter mingling.

"Okay." The word came out all wrong. My voice was breathy, but his smile broadened as I spoke. It had been a long time since I'd felt this out of control. "Hi, Mindy!" A small scratch behind the ear had Mindy's tail wagging furiously. I forced in the deepest breath I could.

"Who's with you?" Estelle's voice was closer.

"I brought a friend, Auntie. She's a collector too." His voice was a smile as he said it. Aunt Estelle came around the corner, and I recognized her from some of the pictures downstairs. She had been absolutely beautiful in her youth, but there was something hypnotizing about her in maturity. Her silver hair fell in kinky waves on either side of her face, and a pair of pink half-moon spectacles sat on her nose, in front of Yale-blue eyes framed by deep laugh lines. She surveyed me intently through them.

"Alvara, meet Aunt Estelle. Auntie, meet Alvara." August motioned between us, and I extended my hand.

"Nice to meet you." I smiled as she accepted the gesture. I saw her life unroll in my mind—fast, beautiful, and tragic. A rollercoaster of the highest highs and lowest lows. Estelle's late husband had been a dream of a man, tragically killed by a drunk driver some years ago.

"Dear Lord, boy! Get your girl a sweater. She's freezing."

"Oh, I'm fine!" I laughed. Her voice cut the visions short, but I released her hand gratefully.

"Nonsense. You're cold as ice."

August rolled his eyes, his smirk still wide as he stared at me with that depth-of-my-soul surveying gaze. Estelle narrowed her eyes at him accusingly.

"Don't you roll your eyes at me, boy. I'm old, not blind. So," she turned her attention to me, "you're the broad that scooped him off the face of the planet."

He did as he was told, stripping off the hoodie tied around his waist and wrapping it around my shoulders. Involuntarily, my breathing hitched as he set it against my skin, the world growing hazy with memories of football games, Layla stealing it to dodge the rain, laughter around bonfires, bouldering with Sam and James—and these long days with me...

I waved my hand in front of me defensively, shaking my head, just as August chortled and said, "Oh Estelle, it's not like that, and you know it." But his eyes remained fixed on me, a knowing amusement tugging at the corner of his lips as he perceived the visions passing through me—the stories hidden beneath that seemingly innocuous hoodie.

Estelle raised her eyebrows suggestively and lowered her spectacles down the bridge of her nose to scrutinize me. Unabashedly, she examined me from top to bottom, leaving me with a curious sense of vulnerability. I longed for my black t-shirt and high-top jeans but gratefully wrapped August's sweater around my bare shoulders.

"Why not?" she demanded. "A tall drink of water like you—there must be a reason I was uninvited to a wedding I'd been eagerly anticipating for years."

My face flushed, and I looked to August for help, guilt washing over me. She wasn't entirely wrong, but she wasn't completely right either. I didn't choose August; he simply was who he was.

"I've lost weight! And I bought a dress for the occasion. You owe me an explanation, young man."

"I'll pay you back for the dress."

She clucked her tongue. "Oh, it's not about the damn dress."

August's explanation was succinct, essentially summarizing with, "We've just grown to be very different people."

Estelle guffawed but seemed satisfied. She uncrossed her arms and, with a demand for me to "put some meat on my bones," led us to the living room, which was open to the kitchen. She gestured for us to sit on a large purple sofa that immediately flooded my mind with memories. August grinned, aware of the sensation running through me as my eyes fluttered. I could feel his gaze as I processed its history and heard the rhythmic click-clacking of Estelle's steps into her cozy kitchen.

"Earl Grey?" she asked, putting the kettle on for tea.

We both nodded, and as she turned to fetch the bags, August shot me an internal, apologetic look.

I smiled and shook my head. This was the most entertainment I'd had in several very long weeks.

I FIDDLED with the radio knob as the Jeep bounced down the washboard dirt road. Most stations were playing country, and while I could enjoy them in the right mood, today was not that day.

"Picky about your music?" August finally asked.

"Sometimes," I admitted. He navigated the road with familiar ease, his eyes frequently darting back to me. On those long, empty roads, he couldn't seem to wipe the grin from his face. My gaze lingered on his handsome features: his strong, bearded jawline, defined cheekbones, full lips, and those incredibly sharp green eyes beneath thick brows and dark lashes. Every time he caught me studying him, my cheeks flushed, and I made an effort to look at the fields and farms we were passing.

"What kind do you like? I might remember a station."

"I'm kind of in the mood for seventies or eighties. Hair bands were a lot of fun."

"A fan of the classics?" His heart-melting smile returned. I laughed.

"They're only classics to a spring chicken like you."

"Spring chicken?" He raised his brows. "What does that make you?"

"A history book, I suppose."

"Well, that's not very fun."

"Sorry to disappoint you. I'm not all that creative."

"Somehow I doubt that... Try eighty-nine point five."

"Will they have my *classics*?"

"They should." He forced his gaze back to the road but kept glancing back at me every few seconds. I swapped the channel and laughed as *Highway to Hell* by AC/DC came on.

"A little generic, but it'll work."

"Angels like *Highway to Hell*?" Mirth thickened his tone.

"I'm no angel," I reminded him with a wink. Amusement played on his lips as he shook his head.

"Alright, *rebel*, put that on." He gestured at the hoodie still draped around my shoulders. I complied, curious as more visions sparked, and he pressed a button that retracted the top. The wind immediately swept my hair away from my face, and I turned to the sun as the shadow crept past me.

He turned up the music, and I raised my hands to feel the wind. Chuckling under his breath, August slid on a pair of sunglasses and leaned into the accelerator, finally paying full attention to the road. This gave me a few moments to admire his handsome face again. Not for the first time, I studied the nearly imperceptible crook in the bridge of his otherwise straight nose—a frisbee, he'd told Aren and me during training, thrown by an overly enthusiastic James when he was ten.

Bobbing his head, he started singing the words, and I threw my head back in laughter, stretching my right arm out the window to feel the sun on my hand. Fae wasn't wrong. It was one of the last beautiful days of the season here, and August's fleece hoodie provided just enough warmth. His voice, as stunning as his face, was smooth and low. I'd heard him sing with a guitar in the cabin, but it was different out here. With no one else watching and the sun on his face, he belted out the lyrics with brazen confidence. He was better than he thought he was.

A joyful noise escaped me when Queen's *Bohemian Rhapsody* came on next. August shook his head in disbelief as I joined him in singing both parts of the song, laughing when one of us reached for a note we shouldn't have. By the halfway mark, we were both animatedly gesticulating, and laughter consumed us. I reveled in the sound, the ease of sitting next to him in his Rubicon, combined with the immense trust in his hands on the wheel, leaving me optimistic for the first time since we'd hidden in the cabin.

We left the singing to the professionals for the rest of the drive, enjoying effortless, wordless companionship. Our journey ended too quickly as we entered the city, reminding me that we were here with work to do. August was meeting with James and Sam to catch up and review matters. He'd always intended to step away from running their company together, though it had ended more abruptly than he'd anticipated.

"Eh. Life is full of unexpected twists and turns. You never know where the road will take you, so you might as well enjoy the ride."

"Very apt description, given the afternoon you gave me."

That entrancing smile was back. "It was intentionally chosen. Do you have things you can do in the meantime?"

"Layla never saw me. I'll place stronger protection over the loft. Alec and Fae are planning to join me at some point. We'll inevitably grab tea, and Alec can't come to this dimension without buying new books. There's plenty."

"Okay. And we'll meet up afterward to place new wards over James' and my parents' homes?"

"Perfect."

"Perfect," he echoed. "This might be overboard, but can we guard Samuel too?"

"Not overboard, August. Anyone you care for. Anyone who could be linked to your scent. Of course, we'll protect Sam."

He let out a breath I hadn't noticed he was holding. "Good. Thanks."

I smiled as reassuringly as I could manage.

"You're all welcome to stay at my house tonight. Alec mentioned there was work to be done in the morning?"

I hesitated, not due to a lack of curiosity about August's real estate, but because Bash and Sky's empty eyes were still fresh in my mind, along with the image of them sailing away on flaming boats, destined for a watery grave. My heart sped up against my ribs. He noticed and narrowed his eyes.

"It wasn't your fault, Ally. You have to let it go. If you feel better going back to Grayshell, we can. I just... I like the time with you here. It feels like we're really getting to know each other."

I forced my breathing to regulate and pulled up a blanket of calm from my center before letting a small smile play at the corners of my lips. "And getting to know each other is important?"

"Incredibly." His response was unwavering, so I decided to press.

"Why?"

"Because *you* are important to me, Ally. Because I want to get to know you. You are destined to be in my life, aren't you? Karmic companions. Isn't that what you call them?"

I nodded softly, my heart back to its thunderous sprint in my ribcage again.

"You're important to me too, August. Just... shields down tonight, okay?"

"I'll do my best." He winked, sending my heart skittering even faster. There was a weight to the motion, an insinuation in the way he leaned towards me. His smile broadened as he felt my heart racing. I focused and realized his was nearly matching the pace.

"Then yes, August Porter. I would love to see your home."

"It's one of my favorites," he said with a shrug. "We called it the lake house."

I realized the "we" he referred to was most likely him and Layla, and I pushed away the thought. The sinking feeling it brought in my stomach was most unwelcome.

I cleared my throat. "One of?"

"Yes. *One of* my favorites." For the first time, his expression hinted at arrogance. Confidence oozed from his body; his eyes unwavering as they locked with mine. While his sweet, humble nature was endearing, there was something incredibly appealing about the certainty he radiated. He had worked hard for all he had, and if anyone deserved to be proud of their accomplishments, it was August.

We were in the city now, and the flickering shadows of buildings across the Jeep brought that October chill to the air. He closed the top and maneuvered into a parking space just vacated by a soccer mom van with a stick figure family in the back window. I turned to survey his expression and noticed a peculiar seriousness in his eyes and the set of his full lips. He put the Jeep in park and turned towards me, intensity emanating from him.

"Okay. I have a favor to ask of you now."

"Oh? Do you?" I asked skeptically.

"I'm serious, Ally." He really meant it. His jaw was set tightly, and he locked his eyes on mine with unmistakable protectiveness. I raised my eyebrows.

"I can't shake the feeling that if I let you out of my sight, something awful will happen, and I won't be able to help you. I know you're a badass, and no human could touch you. But my imagination has gotten... larger these last months. So please be careful. Will you summon Alec and Fae before you do any demon warding or hunting or anything?"

I narrowed my eyes at him. I'd taken care of myself for centuries before he was even born.

Sensing my retort, he reached out, pinched a strand of my hair between his fingers, twirled it around his index, and then released it gently. "For me?"

"Well, since you asked so kindly, I suppose I may be inclined to acquiesce to your request."

"Thank you, my lady." He bowed with a flourish, mocking my

formality. "But really, Ally. Thank you. I mean it. Nothing stupid tonight, okay?"

"Sheesh, *Mom.* Nothing stupid." I raised my hands in mock surrender and blinked pointedly. He smirked, and I returned the playful expression before jumping out of the car. The street was bustling but not packed like it had been the day we found him. I melted into the crowd, making my way to Alec's favorite bookstore. August's eyes pressed into the back of my head until I reached the door and turned to give him one last smile and wave before he drove away.

Nothing stupid, I echoed back to him.

TWENTY-FOUR
THE PUB
ALVARA

I ignored two distinct readings of satanic work to keep my promise to August, and Alec seemed to think it was hilarious that such a ridiculous deal had been struck.

"He cares for you," he offered with a grin as he walked hand in hand with Fae down the dark road toward Layla's condo. The streetlights cast harsh shadows across their faces and the sidewalk below. The city had come to life as the sun set, with people buzzing in and out of bars and clubs in costumes, the festivities starting even before Halloween.

"Evidently so." That goony smile stretched across my face, despite every muscle fighting to suppress it.

"Could it be that after all these long years, Miss Alvara has feelings for someone?" Fae teased. We passed another porch adorned with towering steps covered in pumpkins of every color. I eyed them, partially envious of the simplicity of ignorance.

"Perhaps," I admitted, crossing my arms around my ribs.

"You hear their heartbeats around each other, don't you? Frantic little hummingbirds. You two are karmically entangled, aren't you?" Alec narrowed his eyes.

"How would I have entangled with him, but not with you?"

"August and I only have one known life together. It's quite possible your timelines just didn't overlap that go-around."

"Perhaps," I conceded again.

"If only any of us were as good at reading as you are, I'd love to tell you that history." Fae winked and then fell back in step with her mate.

"You and me both," I sighed.

"So," she pressed, "are you going to read him? Tonight? In his fancy lake house?"

"It is long overdue," Alec added ruefully.

"I suppose that's true. He's been fairly guarded—understanding, but guarded. I wanted him to be sure... you know, because of Layla."

"Yes. But he chose this life over Layla. He chose you."

"He didn't choose *me*," I corrected. August had been protecting Layla from our world, from the demons he would wage war with for the rest of his life. Protecting her from the life of aging and dying alone next to a perfectly preserved statue of the man she fell in love with. A sickening twist of grief and desire burrowed into my stomach. "Let's get something to eat. My blood sugar is low."

Alec raised his eyebrows. "We don't get low blood sugar."

"You know what I mean. I need something to eat."

THE SERVER WAS AN AVERAGE-LOOKING, stocky man in his twenties, dressed in black from head to toe. His blonde hair was cropped short, and light blue eyes sat in a round, fair-skinned face kissed with freckles. Perhaps he would have been handsome if August's striking features weren't emblazoned on the back of my eyelids. He was quick and kind, taking our orders within moments of our arrival, which filled my heart —and stomach—with gratitude. Returning with our drinks and a basket of bread, he flashed a grin at me, and I realized that yes, he would have been handsome under other circumstances.

I grabbed a piece of rye bread from the wicker basket, dipped it in my square of butter, and popped it in my mouth. They trained their eyes on me, but I ignored them, feigning focus on my roll. Their energy was thick in the air, an entertaining twist of amusement, curiosity, and concern. When my hand was empty, I reluctantly looked up to meet their prying eyes.

"Awfully fascinated with the way oats cling to black bread, aren't we?" Alec quipped, shrugging off his jean jacket.

I shrugged, unapologetic.

"You know, I've been in his mind too. I've seen it all. And you know what I know about him? August—Carlyle—in all his cycles has loved his woman. To the death." Alec leaned forward, pinning me with a pointed stare. "If you're his mate in this life, he will give you everything he has, and then some."

I swallowed the lump in my throat, trying to shake off the unease that idea stirred. But he was right. August would give anything for those he loved. He would sacrifice himself for those around him, and while I loved that loyalty, it terrified me too. Our work wasn't exactly safe, and the thought of something happening to him made me sick...

Quickly tearing off another piece of bread, I searched for the butter, but the pad had been snatched off the table. Fae dangled the metallic wrapper from her fingers tauntingly, and I snatched it back telekinetically. No one else was around in our little corner booth.

I proceeded to butter my bread as Alec continued.

"His soul was always restless. Always searching. Women always love August, and August always loves them. And then there's always one who steals him, mind, body, and soul. He'd watch the world burn if it meant keeping her safe."

"Is there a *point* to this regression lesson?" The idea of August's hands on anyone else suddenly made my skin crawl. An image of Layla burned in my mind, and I realized with a pang that much of my unease with her was likely an inappropriately acquired jealousy.

"My point, dear Second, is to be careful."

I snapped my eyes up to him, and even Fae pressed her lips together.

"You haven't read him. You don't know what he's capable of. He might be The Healer in your heart, but I believe the vision is true. He is The Great Commander. Legions of souls, far beyond the hierarchy, will bow to him, if we are right. Light... and dark. We need him for the war to come. If he loves you like I think he does—or will—he could be your undoing, Ally. All your walls, all your rules, all your discipline... it doesn't stand a chance. He will give his all for you. And you will do the same. He has sacrificed entire armies to protect those he loves. Don't think he wouldn't do it in this life too. Just... be careful with his heart. Be careful with yours."

I stared back at him, awestruck. Alec wasn't one for drama or prophecy, but his intuition was spot on. As I looked into his amber eyes, I could see the memories surfacing there. The man he'd known, and the men he'd seen when he and August had delved into his subconscious, were men of immense power. The passion in that soul could lead him to greatness or to a devastating fall that rivaled the mortals.

"Ally," Alec's tone was warning. "I didn't see a single life where he... survived for long. Every journey I saw in his soul was short. It's clear to everyone that the two of you fit together like..." he searched for the right words. "Jigsaw pieces. But maybe, prepare yourself for the worst case. You've been through enough."

An icy chill ran down my spine. I cast my mind forward for what felt like the thousandth time, but August's threads were still too numerous to count. Too many undecided things hung in the future for me to know where his path led or which threads to pull on. Nausea rose in my chest, and I swallowed it back.

"That being said, his love—the way he loves—and the way he looks at you, respects you... I want that for you, Al. I really do."

My voice was quiet when it finally rose in my throat. "Thanks for having my back. It could be different this time. I've never survived to see my hundredth birthday before this cycle. And look at me, nearly four times that."

A gentle smile played on his lips, and he turned to Fae, pressing his lips into her platinum hair. *I want* that *for you too.*

LAYLA'S APARTMENT was silent when we arrived, the atmosphere serene and warm. Her mind was calm with sleep, and I felt my heart settle, knowing she was okay. August's scent and energetic signature were still faintly detectable in the building and the hallway leading to their door. The low vibration of crawlers lingered in the shadows, but they didn't seem to have returned since we'd taken him away. Perhaps I could reach Layla through a dream, though human minds are more challenging to access than ours.

The three of us raised our hands in unison, spoke St. Michael's prayer for protection, and cast an energetic circle around the unit. Another one was cast to guard the building, as August's presence was pervasive. It would have to suffice for now.

As we left the front lobby, a sense of unease conflicted with my previous certainty, and I paused for a moment.

Alec turned, cocking his head to the side. *"You feel something?"*

I closed my eyes, breathing in the energy around us. *I thought* I sensed something, but it was fleeting.

"We've placed the best protections. Do you need to read her?"

I slowly shook my head. It felt too intrusive to pry into Layla when August had worked so hard to protect her all these months. It would be disrespectful to his explicit wishes.

I think we're okay. I just... can't shake the feeling that *I'm missing something.*

Anything more we can do, outside of posting guards?

I shook my head. "No. Grayshell wouldn't be able to spare guards with Samhain right around the corner. Her threads are still too numerous to sort, just like August's. Until decisions are made, Layla will remain in a pool of uncertainty."

We continued down the sidewalk, Alec and Fae wrapping their arms around each other. The first hint of fall was in the air, and I breathed in its familiar scent. Despite the countless autumns I'd experienced, the crisp leaves, warmth of squash, and spice of the season were always a welcome change.

We were passing a bar that smelled mostly of beer, and the patrons inside were singing an Irish shanty that caught my attention. A radiant energy reverberated off the building, drawing me in. We slowed to listen, feeling their excitement as a woman dressed as a provocative bunny and a man dressed as Caesar began a surprisingly accurate Irish dance, much to the onlookers' delight. The crowd clapped to the beat, fueling the dancers' energy. The bar was dark, its walls nearly black, with bronze and hardwood accents. The well-worn wooden floor, the color of warm amber, flowed beneath the dancers' quick feet. The crowd around them danced and gyrated, entirely out of sync with the rapid rhythm, but their intoxicated minds didn't care.

My heart quickened, and a warmth spread in my chest as I sensed his presence before I saw him. He must have sensed me too, as I lingered just outside the bustling entrance. Or perhaps he saw me first. August was weaving through the crowd of laughing patrons, and gyrating bodies. His eyes were locked on me. Sam and James followed in his wake, Sam beaming with a child-like smile, and James looking a bit uneasy. They appeared so young compared to the ascended August at their center, and I grinned at his confident stance. My feet had moved me into the bar without my acknowledgment, and I returned his enthusiastic grin.

August flowed around me with the grace of water around a bend and rested his hand on the small of my back. He leaned forward to close the gap between us and his guests, raising his voice to be heard over the singing.

"You must have felt us talking about you! Alvara, this is my best friend Sam, and my little brother, James!"

Sam's cheeky grin broadened as he offered his hand, but James eyed me like he was assessing a rattlesnake.

How much do they know? I asked mind-to-mind.

Everything.

I raised my eyebrows in question, and August shrugged.

I've never been a great liar, and I didn't want anything more between us.

They know about my powers?

Was that supposed to be a secret?

I suppose not. Do they believe you?

They seem to.

Shrugging in acknowledgment, I accepted Sam's outstretched hand. His life swirled in circles around my mind, fast and brief. Younger than August, his life had been turbulent. Loyal to the death, he loved his best friend—the man who had pushed him through school and given him a place in his company, equipping him to grow and thrive in the corporate world. His heart was honest—a shallow pool of crystal water on a sunny day.

I pulled my hand back, feeling the smile in my cheeks as I locked onto his dark denim eyes. He scratched his head through short blonde hair, a nervous grin on his face.

"See anything I should know about?"

I pursed my lips in a tight smile and shook my head. "Nice to finally meet you, Samuel."

"It's Sam."

"Then nice to meet you, Sam." Shifting out of the way, I motioned to our companions. "This is my brother, of sorts, Alec, and his wife, Aphaea."

Sam reached his hand forward to shake with Alec, whose palm engulfed his. Even through the amulet, I could see Sam's complete fascination with Alec as he shook his hand. He had been the kind of child that obsessed over the paranormal, so in a bizarre way, this was an affirmation of all his childhood fantasies—like he had been waiting for a supernatural being to enter his life and shake it up a bit.

"Call me Fae." She danced forward, and his cheeks flushed. He eyed Alec apologetically, shaking his head as if to rid himself of the influence of the siren that had just presented herself to him.

James, however... while his heart was essentially good, at this moment he reeked of guilt. He stared at his feet during the introductions with Sam, thoroughly piquing my interest with his inability to meet my gaze. Additionally, he was diligently picturing a mountain lake. Clever.

I studied him a moment before slowly reaching out my hand. He stared for a beat, then eyed August warily before looking back to me. Shame pulled his eyebrows together in the center. To avoid being rude, he took it. His skin was rougher than Sam's—a woodsman, like August—but his mind was even more so. He focused on their childhood and their adventures, but it only took a fraction of a second to see through his flimsy human guard to a beautiful woman, golden with a love of the sun, lying naked on his bed. Her curves were small but appealing. His outstretched hand brushed golden hair off her slight shoulder as she turned to face him, her smile tentative.

I yanked my hand away, and our eyes snapped to each other. The scowl on my face was probably harsher than intended, but there was no point in hiding the emotion that crawled up my skin. I spun through the visions immediately ahead of us—winding and unwinding the different threads—and realized without a doubt that the best chance for a peaceful resolution was an immediate confrontation. *Well, shit.*

"How long?" My voice was steel, cutting through the room's noise. August's eyes were wide on me, and I wasn't sure how much he'd caught through my amulet and Alec's shield.

James looked at his feet. "Not before... if that's what you're asking."

"Maybe not in a physical way," I corrected, and he looked up at me, horrified.

"Y-years," he stammered. "But I swear, never before—"

Sam shuffled out of the circle, moving to stand at August's back, his expression glum.

August, eyes wary, stared at me for a minute before glancing back at his brother.

"No," his tone was disbelieving, and he took a step back, shaking his head. He glanced between us. "No. You wouldn't..."

James gathered his courage, puffing out his chest and meeting his brother's gaze.

"Layla?!" August demanded, his voice a mix of rage and shock.

James' eyes fell to his feet before he could meet August's again. "Never before, August. I swear."

"Layla?!" August demanded again.

"She came to *me*, and I know it doesn't justify it, but you just... vanished. She was hurting, and I was angry, and one drink turned into three, and—"

"And you were just bringing her comfort? Am I right?" August's glare was fierce, the same warrior glare that had helped me bring down the coven of Renown. The lights above us flickered. I eyed them nervously, wondering if I could counter the fluctuation of rage coming off him. But as they calmed, I realized Alec must have been doing so.

"No," James countered. The admission seemed to stop August in his tracks, and suddenly everything around us felt louder. The lights evened for the time being, and he jammed his eyes shut, concentrating on not blowing the place up, I hoped.

"I—I love her, August. I have for *years*, but I buried it because she was always your girl. Your... There was no point in ever saying anything." He shook his head. "I would never have touched her if you hadn't left her. You have to believe that."

August's desperate gaze found mine, and I nodded. He was telling the truth. No wonder he'd looked at me like a viper as we came in. James had anticipated this moment and was bracing for it.

"He could have rejected my touch, August. He didn't have to let it be known. He was going to tell you when he summoned the courage. Weren't you, James?" I narrowed my eyes at him once August's gaze had turned away. The young man gave a slow nod.

. . .

AUGUST HUFFED and ran his fingers through his hair. He paced in a tight circle for a moment, trapped with nowhere to escape. After a heaving breath, he turned back to James. His voice was cold but steady when he spoke.

"You fucking take care of her, James. Don't hurt her." His voice was a warning, but he stretched out his hand.

James' eyes glistened, and he nodded, accepting the shake. But August pulled him in for a hug and patted his back.

August shook his head as they separated, his eyes a bit wild.

"Damn. Strangest year ever. I need a fucking drink. Anybody else?"

My mind grappled with what had just happened and how quickly August had deescalated. James, too, looked as though he was in a bit of shock. But Sam stepped forward, his lean body slicing through the space between us, and walked with August to the bar to order drinks. They returned only a moment later with a tray of shots, and we each took one.

Sam lifted his glass in the air and said, "To new beginnings."

We murmured our assent and drank.

Our little crew dominated one of the back booths for most of the evening, sharing appetizers and ordering rounds of drinks like old friends. James loosened up, the relief evident in his scent, his relaxed face, and the amount of space he took up in the booth. August had remained pensive for a while but soon started sharing stories with Sam. We laughed at ridiculous childhood memories. The three of them had been inseparable all their lives until August's ascension. My heart ached for the absence they must have left in his.

If he'd been hurting, he hadn't said anything. Always there for what needed to be done. Always there for what *I* needed. My face flushed as I watched him, and I shook my head before grabbing another potato skin covered in melted cheese and bacon.

August and Sam made their way to the bar to order more food. The inseparable lovebirds were dancing out on the floor with all the costumed humans, and James' eyes landed on me.

"So," he said quietly, "how long?"

"Excuse me?"

He smiled dryly and then threw my words back at me again, "How long?" He raised his dark brows, his expression startlingly similar to August's. He nodded towards his brother across the floor, leaning against the bar.

"Nothing's happened but—"

"You want it to."

"Yes," I admitted. I had demanded abrupt honesty from James, so it seemed only fair to give him the same level of transparency.

"You haven't told him yet?"

"Not in so many words. Things are... complicated..."

"I don't think so. I think we make things complicated."

"You're bold for a mortal, aren't you?" I sighed. "Sex is... complicated. For our kind. Which makes love complicated."

"That whole eternal-bond thing?"

I narrowed my eyes. "You boys covered a lot of ground while we were apart."

"Sam and I didn't really get much of a chance to cut in. August isn't one for tall tales, so we assumed if he needed to unload something, he meant it. He also isn't one to abandon an empire he built without a good fucking reason." James narrowed his eyes at me before asking, "So? Am I right?"

I smirked at his curiosity. Mortals rarely believed what they were told, so I'd never had to sit and answer questions for one before.

"Yes. We take courting very seriously. Soul entanglement is fairly intense."

"Don't you think he ought to know... if you want to... *entangle* yourselves?" He smirked slyly, enjoying my shift in discomfort. I supposed it was a justified retaliation, so I smiled at him and shrugged.

"I think... on some level, he already does. He must. There was a draw from the beginning, and it just intensified when he freed Layla." James' eyes flitted to his hands for a moment, still nervous about my judgment. "There's something about him that's just... familiar. Like coming home when you've been gone for a long time. Does that make sense?"

He nodded. "For him too... If it means anything, *warrior queen*," he grinned around the words August had evidently used to describe me, "he never looked like that when he talked about Layla. Through every story he told us today, you were at the center of it."

My stomach hovered precariously close to my heart. James' gaze went past me, and curiosity danced in his eyes. He narrowed them. "Although watch yourself, you might have competition."

I turned around to find August standing still as a statue in the center of the dance floor, talking to a woman wearing a long cloak. The club music had long replaced the shanty that had initially caught my attention. I smirked, and then James spoke again, his voice softer and revealing the nerves he carefully concealed.

"Did you know he would forgive me for Layla? Earlier?"

I turned and smiled at him as a big sister might. "There were a few outcomes. It was your best chance at a quick reconciliation. I'm sorry I didn't have a kinder way to warn you."

The corner of his lip quirked. "It needed to be done. He doesn't hate me, so that's something."

"It's a big something," I agreed. "Are we good?"

"We will be... when you grow a pair and tell August how you feel."

I shot him a glare. James was familiar too, though he smelled entirely human. Perhaps it was just his link to August. But I smiled and nodded. "That's fair. I'll send you a note when we can be friends then."

"Oh, I'm sure I'll know. He won't be able to keep that one quiet for long." He nodded behind me and took a sip of his whiskey.

I turned to find a grinning August, a gold mask now covering the upper half of his face, holding the cloak he'd evidently bribed off the woman on the dance floor. In his other hand, he had a masquerade mask embellished with crystals and feathers and a pair of black gloves. He held them out in offering, and I raised my eyebrows. An image of me wearing them popped into his head, and I cocked my head to the side.

"Dance with me?"

The pieced-together costume played through his mind—a cloak and gloves to cover my hands and arms so nobody would touch me. The mask simply fit the theme of the evening. I laughed out loud, and he nodded encouragingly.

"August, the last place I would ever willingly be is a dance floor."

He shot me a cocky smirk and jerked his head towards the crowd expectantly.

"August, I don't dance."

"Luckily for you, I do. And you've never liked crowds because you've never had me." He tapped his temple with the mask. He wasn't wrong. I'd never been able to dance with a shield before. James reached across the table to pat my shoulder and push me up. Little did he know he could push with all the human strength he had and never move someone like me.

Butterflies fluttered in my stomach as I stood to accept the gifts from August's outstretched hands. I placed the black mask over my eyes, slid the silk gloves onto my fingers, and August wrapped the cloak around my shoulders, smoothly sliding my arms into its long sleeves. They were a bit shorter than intended, but between the gloves and the heavy draping fabric, it served its purpose.

He took my now-gloved hand in his and led me away from our dark corner. My head didn't stop shaking, mind swimming in denial and a bit of peculiar, awakened human fear as I followed him into the crowd. Their energy was pulsating, but between the stones and August, my mind was only assaulted by the normal noises outside it.

August spun me in a wide circle, turning me to face him. He beamed when our eyes locked, and he pulled me up against his body, making my heart hitch. His eyes narrowed for a moment, and he dropped my hands to raise the hood over my head. Then, and only then, did he lean down to press his cheek against my shielded temple. He had thought of everything.

His hands found their way to my low back, pulling me tighter to his hips, and I looped my arms around his neck. I wanted to take the gloves off, to feel his skin against my own, to drop the hood and feel his scruffy face, to breathe him in.

August's fingers squeezed into the back of my hips as if he couldn't get enough of me either. The world slowly vanished, and it was just us there, holding onto each other in an empty sea of muffled music. He spun me in circles and pulled me from one side of the floor to the other, leading my steps. I followed his incremental pulls and pushes, and if I didn't know better, would have thought Aren had taught me to dance at some point. But it was all August—his precision, his control, his ease that led me.

I melted into him, soaking up his energy, seeping into his movements. The way he smelled, the way his hands roamed my body as if I were something priceless—gripping my ribs, my waist. My heart thundered, mind spinning as heat pooled low in my belly. August made me feel delicate. Feminine. Like I could just let him take care of me, even if just for this moment.

If we weren't bowed together, his eyes were always on me, unwavering. We spun in a tight circle, faster and faster until I couldn't contain the shriek of laughter that spilled from my lips. When he pulled me to him again, I could feel his desire, his erection firm against me. Heat rushed through my core, burning in my legs as my thighs clenched together. My breath came hard and fast, and relief washed over me when he put a bit of distance between us, his hands going slack where they rested on my hips, his subtle smile telling me he knew exactly what he was doing to me. August made me feel... way too much, and yet—not enough. I craved to let go... to give in to him.

When the music changed back to a slow song, he smiled, a bit out of breath, and asked if I wanted a drink. If I was wise, I'd keep that space between us and regain some semblance of self-control. But liquid courage, combined with the aching need filling my body, made wisdom sound like a euphemism for wasting time.

So instead, I fisted the fabric of his t-shirt, pulling him back until our bodies collided. "The drink can wait," the words whooshed out, my voice breathless as need drowned me.

His eyes darkened, nostrils flaring as his fingers tightened on my waist, swallowing me in his hot palms. "Fuck, Ally," August growled in my ear, digging his fingers into my back, thumbs sinking into my abs. "I'm really trying to be a gentleman. But keep looking at me like that—I won't be able to control myself much longer." August reached up to slide my hood down before wrapping his strong arms around my back. He took a deep breath into my hair—my heart hammering ruthlessly in my throat as I inhaled him too, soaking up his familiar musk.

August reached down to grab my hand, running his fingers over the silk, and stepping back as he brought it to his face. He leaned into it for a moment before breathlessly saying, "You are so damn beautiful, Alvara. I've always thought it, but I don't think I ever said it. At least, not to you." His lips quirked, and he continued before I could say anything. "I'll get you a drink."

August curled my hand around his own and raised it to his lips. He pressed them against the black silk over my knuckles, then released me into the crowd.

TWENTY-FIVE

SARAH

ALVARA

There was no hint that the lake house belonged to some wealthy city slicker. August was something of a closet millionaire. His shoes were basic, his watch from Target, and his home was humble—a small white cottage nestled in a broad circle of towering aspens, clinging to the sharp decline of the beach. His hideaway had one cozy bedroom, a loft he used as an office, and a pullout sofa.

A welcoming white kitchen featured a gray granite island, the only place to eat. An espresso pod machine sat on the L-shaped counter, with a simple glass bowl holding the little aluminum pods beside it. Only the stove hinted at extravagance—a fancy stainless steel, eight-burner gas range with two ovens. Curiosity burned as I wondered if he knew how to use it. The interior was cozy and rustic, with sage green, warm yellow, and wood accents composing the color palette.

Alec and Fae had excused themselves to bed, claiming they'd danced the night away and that we all had an early morning ahead. They reminded us of the urgency to return home and guard the gate between dimensions before Samhain. But it was their words outside the bar that replayed in my mind.

"So," Alec said with a smirk as we walked just out of earshot, giving August a moment for goodbyes with the boys. "What stage are we in?"

My brows pinched together in confusion. "Wardings, dummy. Then to the lake house."

He snorted, Fae mirroring his amused expression as she clung to his arm, our steps slow as we lingered on the street corner.

"Yes, Ally," he said, his tone dripping with condescension, "I'm well acquainted with our agenda. I meant in the mission to acquire *August Porter*."

"Alec," I scolded, glaring back at his mischievous amber eyes.

"*Ally*," he drawled, mimicking my tone. "Seriously. What's the plan? The entire bar watched you two eye-fuck each other all night. I half-expected you'd just burn his clothes off."

Fae burst into unapologetic laughter, burying her face in his bicep.

"No plan, asshole." I lengthened my stride, but they mirrored the motion.

"Ahh," Alec breathed, turning down to Fae with mock-surprise etched across his features. "Good. Denial. Next phase—*acceptance*," he hissed dramatically. When he caught my glare, he just chuckled. "Seriously though, Ally. Either you have your way with him, or I will."

"And on that note—not just so you can get laid," Fae interjected, earning another snort from her mate. "I mean, it's long overdue, don't get me wrong. But we need to know everything we can about what he is— what's coming for him."

"Plus, if you can wake up those memories, he won't need as much instruction. As it stands, Aren and Ansel are planning a more aggressive method if he doesn't wake up soon. You're still his sire, even if you start hooking up—his training comes first. You owe him this."

You owe him this. Those words looped in my mind as I watched August reach for earth-toned mugs from the open shelving, intending to pour us cups of tea. I tried to shake the nerves of anticipation that had settled in my stomach. The alcohol had worn off as we guarded Sam and James, but the tension between us had yet to dwindle.

We were both in pajamas—August in loose gray sweats and a simple white t-shirt that hugged his muscles tighter than I would have liked. His hair fell in messy waves across his forehead, and I had to exert considerable effort to stop thinking about how it would feel between my fingers. The desire between us seemed to have taken on a life of its own, and I was desperately trying to control a flame that had gone wildly off course.

A jazzy instrumental track he loved played from the stereo system in the back corner. While it faintly resembled Miles Davis, I couldn't quite place the artist. Jazz had never been my forte, but August hummed along with the melody, and his familiar voice had me entranced.

His smile was soft as he handed me my mug of chamomile tea and then nodded to the corner, where a small piano stood against the window, in the spot where a dining table would normally be. I padded across the soft rug, pulling down at the hem of my shorts, suddenly wishing I'd opted for pants.

August set his cup on an end table beside the piano, sat down, and used voice command to silence his stereo. He then began to play. A rush of memories and sensations hit me so quickly that I couldn't tell if they were past or future, and I stared at him, mesmerized, as his broad hands moved fluidly across the keys. The melody felt as optimistic as August was, light and content like a music box tune. His eyes were closed as he felt his way through the song, which ended on a light, promising note.

I smiled at him when he opened his eyes. "You know, I can't wait to hear you in another century or two."

"Damn. I never thought about that. Getting to learn across consecutive lifetimes. That's kind of amazing," he said, closing his eyes again as he leaned into his instrument. I pressed my warm mug to my lips and breathed in the sweet aroma of the tea, soaking in his wordless serenade. Finally, as his song moved toward another soft, sweet close, I gathered my courage.

"August?"

"Hmmm?"

"Can I read you?" I said it with more certainty than I felt. He stopped playing and turned to look at me, his eyes piercing mine for a long moment before tracing my lips and taking in the rest of me. He looked back up, amusement playing at the corners of his lips.

"Why now?"

"Because I see you. But I need to know you." I looked down at my hands, nerves burrowing into my belly. "To know what our story is, if my intuition is correct that there is one. I would really love to get inside of you."

He raised his eyebrows, amusement returning to his mouth. "That's what he said."

"Oh jeez, you know what I mean," I scolded, rolling my eyes. But then I laughed and shook my head.

"*Sure* you want to get to know me?" We locked gazes for a long time, unwavering. Finally, I nodded. Our faces were only inches apart, sitting side by side on the piano bench. "And this is important to you?" His tone was quiet but playful.

"Incredibly." I didn't hesitate.

"Yes, Ally...you can read me." My heart hitched in my chest, and my breathing quickened. Finally, after all this time and anticipation, he would be mine to understand, to read, to feel...to have?

There was a certainty in my gut that there were answers in his mind I could never find without a reading. Answers a trigger would never properly reveal, as they hadn't over the last months of his nearly constant companionship. And then he smiled at me, almost undoing my resolve, until he spoke.

"Hang on though—if we're getting inside each other, we should set the mood." He winked at me, and my mouth fell open. But then he walked to the fridge and pulled out an expensive-looking bottle of chilled Moscato. I laughed, shaking my head.

"You're ridiculous."

"I've never had anyone dig through all the shadows of my subconscious before. Or tell me about my many past lives. Is it wrong that I'm a tad nervous?"

"I suppose not."

He poured us both glasses of wine, and I downed mine in three straight gulps. August's eyes widened in amusement as I set the glass back down on the counter with a soft clink. He refilled my glass, more generously this time, and slid it across the counter to me with a soft scrape.

"Afraid of what you'll find in there?" He mused, tapping his temple. When I only smirked and eyed my cup, he filled the silence. "You know, I tended bar in college. They knew me for August-sized pours. Of pretty much everything. I didn't go through a huge party phase, but I've never exactly played anything small, either." He took a slow sip and then ran his fingers through his hair.

"So...uh...how does this work?" He asked when we'd both finished our second pour.

"You *want* to know your past lives?"

He nodded. "I mean, I don't remember many—and we dredged up most of those through Alec's meditations—so I guess this would be the easiest way to dig them up. The Great Commander, and all that nonsense?"

I took a deep breath. Or two. Steadying myself as the wine's warmth crept into my mind, making my neck tingle. "If we're going for a full regression, it can take some time. The last time The Great Commander ascended was hundreds of years before Aren woke. There were two Commanders between them."

"So, we might be in for a long night?"

"Maybe. Maybe not. Sometimes it all rushes out at once, and sometimes I have to do some digging. If we share many lives, it can take *days*, so why don't we get somewhere comfy, so it's not hard to sit for a while if I dive all the way back to the beginning? I think that's our best bet for really understanding."

"I know this is going to sound wimpy, but will it hurt?"

I laughed softly. "No more than reading my mind does. If something is really buried in there, you might end up with a headache, but I'm sure you've already thought of that." I traced my finger around the rim of my glass, delighting in the crystal's melodic hum. The feel of it always amazed me, and once again, I marveled at August.

"Good enough for me." He stood, the air between us crackling with static as though he were barely containing his electric field. Anticipation tightened in my chest, and my fingers hummed as I rose to join him on a luxurious Italian leather couch, tufted with bronze pins. He moved the pillows aside, muttering something about an interior designer, and sat down. I settled next to him, heart racing and mind buzzing with the wine. I crossed my legs and faced him.

"It helps if I can see your eyes. But it's not necessary."

He mirrored my position, turning so we were face-to-face. I should've poured another glass; my nerves were electric, buzzing in my mind, and my body was enveloped in a wave of warmth.

"Ally," his voice was warm, "I trust you."

I nodded, taking a few deep breaths.

You can do this, Ally. Focus.

I yanked the hair tie from my wrist and gathered my unruly hair into a messy bun, tucking the loose strands behind my ears.

"Oh shit, she's getting serious." His smirk was childishly defiant. I rolled my eyes.

"Shush you. I'm... nervous. I'm not usually nervous?"

"Too much wine?"

"Maybe."

"We can wait."

"I don't think I can, actually." I let out a breathy laugh, more fitting for a schoolgirl than a second in command. "You've been driving me crazy. Like a puzzle just dying to be solved."

"I'm a puzzle?"

"The *only* members of the coven who haven't opened their minds to me are Ansel and Lana. Most of the hierarchy has let me in by now—many rely on it."

"You like that. Being needed. Being trusted."

"Of course," I shrugged. "Don't you?"

"Of course," he echoed. Then he wiggled his arms, as if trying to shake off his nerves, and let out a long sigh. "Okay. Let's do this, yeah?"

"Yeah," I agreed.

He placed his hands, palms open, on his knees, and I reached forward.

But as I neared, the world vanished.

I was plunged into the icy, flickering gray of a hospital corridor, the stench of brimstone so overpowering it made my head spin. I blinked, disoriented. I was running, sprinting toward the end of the hallway, crying out for help. It was going to catch me. Please, God help me. St. Michael, the Archangel, defend us in battle—

I snapped back, nausea swelling in my throat, tears streaming down my cheeks. August's face was inches from mine, his lips pressed together, eyes wide.

"Alvara?!"

"Alec! Aphaea!! We have to go! Now!" *Aren! We're in trouble. Someone is in trouble. In the hospital. The corridor.*

Fuck. His mental voice was foggy, as though he'd been sleeping too. *The one where—*

The very same. Wake the others. I might need them.

Done. They'll be on your tail. Ally I—

Don't, Aren. It's not worth the risk. Prepare the healers, just in case.

On it.

Thank you.

Be safe, kid.

I replayed the vision in my mind as the others woke, and August's eyes remained locked on me, horror etched on his perfect features. We hastily donned our clothes, clumsily buttoning jeans and pulling on t-shirts. Telekinetically, we summoned our blessed weapons, each of us armed to the hilt. The clock struck midnight, and I swore under my breath. It was the damned witching hour. On Devil's Night. *Fuck me.*

August's eyes conveyed a mix of anger and fear. "Alvara, we should wait for the others. We need backup. That demon got the best of us, and if it was working *for* someone—"

"Backup?" I laughed, though it came out strangled, my unease bubbling angrily in my chest. I forced it down. "August, have you considered that *I* am the backup? Who does the entire hierarchy call when they need help? Me. This is what I do."

August scowled, sensing an argument brewing, so I added, "Really. I've got this. Someone just *prayed* for *help*. We have to go. *We've* got this."

His eyes betrayed the terror in his bones, but he swallowed hard and nodded curtly as he drew his sword. "Okay. Let's get this motherfucker."

THE HOSPITAL FELT EVEN eerier the second time, remembering the last time we'd trudged through the endless hallway. The lights weren't flickering, but they were still dim, casting unsettling shadows. Ice was thankfully absent from the walls, but the energetic chill—some kind of demonic warding to keep people from wandering down there—was thick enough to slice with our blades.

August led the way, his fire hovering a few feet ahead, adding extra light to the hall. If there was any fear left in him, he had buried it deep.

Our pace quickened as urgency spiked between us, our feet thundering in a full sprint as we reached the end of the hall. Death's presence was thick, almost tangible.

I wasn't sure if it was the memory of Aren being impaled or the current spirit driving us forward. It was a combination for me, and a glance at the others showed the same. August halted abruptly where Sebastian had stood weeks before. Fae and I stepped forward, raising our hands to sense the energy.

"This way," we said simultaneously, turning left into the darkest part of the corridor. Despite centuries of practice, every instinct in my body screamed to run in the opposite direction, to protect myself. We approached the door, and the tangy scent of blood hit my nose. I risked a glance over my shoulder; the others smelled it too.

Please let this be a blood bank.

I knew the thought was futile, but I sent it out anyway. I just wanted one damned night to relax with August. Was that too much to ask?

Evidently so.

As I opened the door, smears of blood trailed away from the doorway. A metal table lay overturned, items scattered across the floor. My stomach churned, and I regretted that bottle of Moscato. Demon shit never got easier.

Electricity crackled between August's fingers as alarm spread through the group. His arms flickered with it. The room's energy was vile, weighty, and as sinister as the demon that had attacked Aren, if not more so. Death's icy tendrils crept into our mouths and lungs. The lingering taste was of someone like us—sweet, like summer—and my heart thundered. A braid. The blood smelled like a braid.

I spun, frantic, my eyes scanning the darkness as I ignited the lights. The fluorescent glow was blinding, making my eyes ache, but it illuminated the room enough to reveal the horrors within. Fae let out a shriek, burying her face in Alec's chest. He wrapped his arms around her, his eyes darting between the overturned body and the blood-soaked floor.

The braid is dead. The message was meant for Aren. *This is ten kinds of fucked up.*

The energy around us surged, and Ansel and Lana burst around the corner, swords drawn. They hesitated only a moment before joining us.

"Do we need more?" Ansel asked, eyes wary as Lana took in the scene behind us. I shook my head slowly, unsure myself. But I pushed my energy into every corner and found no living or undead beings, only the fragmented trace of the soul, in shock from the desecration of her body.

"I think they're gone."

"What the fuck?" August's pallor was ghostly, as though he might vomit. He scooped the young woman's body into his arms, cradling her gently. "Ansel!" he snapped, telekinetically righting the stainless-steel exam table. We were in the morgue.

A message pulsed through the air, and I looked up at August. "Her name was Sarah. I can still feel her. She's in soul shock."

Ansel lunged forward, drawing his dagger. "She belonged to Saraya?" His question was tinged with recognition as he pressed his hand against her neck wound.

Ansel sliced through the rope binding her feet, and the weight of the woman fell into August's arms. He carefully laid her on the table, his brow furrowed with concern.

August's voice, just above a growl, came out hoarse. "Her body isn't even cold. This *just* happened. How far gone can they be for us to still save them? She's kind. Can't you *feel* that? She deserves more than this."

"They all do. Only moments, not really much time at all once the heart stops," Ansel shook his head. "Besides, August, her throat was slit. We'd need to heal both to save her, and we're out of time."

A low growl rumbled in August's chest, and his words came through gritted teeth. "So do it."

In unison, we rolled back our sleeves and moved forward. Hands levitating above her body, we closed our eyes and summoned the life force back into her soul. Blood trickled backwards, like water defying gravity, glittering in the air as it flowed back into her veins. When enough had returned, August placed his hand over her neck with determined resolve, closing his eyes.

The room illuminated with a light brighter than Grayshell, and a deep vibration filled the air. I stared, astonished, between August's hands on her neck and Alec's awestruck expression beside me. We channeled all our light into her.

"More," August's voice was guttural. "Give her more!" There was a knowing in his energy, as if he'd seen this before. I poured my energy into the effort, drawing from the depths of my soul. We recited our prayers through Raphael, each word magnifying the energy that surged between us. Without warning, August pulled his hand away, revealing only a fine scar. He abruptly pushed us aside telekinetically. My boots skidded against the tile, and I threw out my arms to steady myself, head spinning with exhaustion and alcohol.

Eyes wide, we exchanged confused glances as August slammed his hand onto her chest with enough force to break her ribs. He growled, "Fuck!"

I lunged forward, but Alec grabbed my wrist. I nearly burned his fingers off in my outrage, but his shocked expression conveyed the explanation.

August was channeling his lightning into her heart—a supernatural, breathing defibrillator.

Suddenly, Sarah sprang upright, and we all jumped back, raising shields. A scream tore from her throat as August cut off his electric charge. His eyes filled with grief as he met her frantic gaze.

"You're okay! You're okay. We've got you."

Her eyes brimmed with tears, and I stared at her in disbelief. Over the years, I had witnessed many miraculous healings, been on both ends of incredible gifts of a second chance. But never had I seen the dead brought back to life through a soul's hands.

Daughter, your faith has made you well; go in peace, and be healed of your disease. The passage whispered in the far corner of my mind. An overwhelming chill enveloped me as I stared at August in disbelief. Aren always said we were destined to perform the miracles of Christ—that humanity could, if enlightened. But I'd never seen it come to pass.

August wrapped Sarah in an embrace, and she collapsed into his chest, sobbing. There was an uncanny familiarity to their connection.

I don't know how, but I know her. His pained eyes were only for me as he thought it.

When Sarah's breath finally steadied, she pulled away and looked between August and me, her voice cutting through the air with steel.

"I never thought I'd see you again, Commander."

TWENTY-SIX

BOUND

AUGUST

"You know me?" My voice sounded much more authoritative than I felt.

Sarah gave a tentative nod, glancing warily at Alvara, who looked like the Goddess she was, armed to the teeth, green eyes glowing, and hands marked by battle scars.

"I know you both. You were there when the hierarchy fell."

Alvara and I locked eyes.

"The hierarchy stands," Alvara's voice cut through the air like ice. "It has always stood."

"It stands now. But no, my lady, it has not always stood. There was a great battle, many lifetimes ago. I witnessed its fall. As it is poised to do now."

Alvara narrowed her eyes and extended her hand. "Show me."

"I cannot."

"What do you mean?"

"The memories are... bound. You are welcome to try, my lady. But you will not succeed."

"Memories can only be bound—"

"By an archangel," Sarah finished. "Or by Lucifer, or the Lord himself. Yes. But I fear they don't want us prying too deeply into the past of light and dark."

"How do you know all of this?"

"How does anyone know what they know?"

"Something triggered you."

Sarah nodded slowly, her eyes traveling between the two of us before they narrowed, like *she* was skeptical of *us*. "I don't... I don't understand—"

Sarah was cut short by Fae's sharp voice. "Ally. What is this?"

Aphaea and the others stood, staring at the mess of bloody symbols on the cement wall—like an upside-down goalpost, littered with X's and O's. Ally turned her head to the side, eyes narrowing with focus. She stepped forward, hand outstretched to read the bloody mess.

Sarah's small voice sliced through the air again. "It's the sigil of Raphael."

"Inverted. She's right." Ally turned to me, eyes wide with terror. "August, they're attacking our healers. An inverted sigil—August, it binds the power behind the symbol. They're not just attacking healers; they're *binding* them. They're attempting to bind Saint Raphael himself."

"Can an archangel be bound?"

Tears filled her fierce eyes. "I don't know. But they certainly seem to think so."

"We need to get to Aren." It was all I was sure of. "Can Sarah come with us to Grayshell?"

Alvara narrowed her eyes, her full lips pressed into a fine line. She walked to the wall, placing her hands in the blood. Her eyes fluttered shut as she focused on the night's events. I caught glimpses of the memories stored there. The demon that killed Sarah was nearly identical to the one that had run Aren through. Whatever they were, they served the same cause. Watching Sarah defend herself was worse than finding her dead. The way she fought with everything she had—it wasn't enough. Alvara's eyes weren't any calmer when she turned to us and went straight to Sarah. She grabbed Sarah's wrist, her red fingers pressing against the pulse point and intertwining with her other hand in an intimate embrace. Sarah didn't resist, meeting Alvara's intense gaze. She understood Ally's gift.

Her eyes fluttered again, then she stepped back, her expression calm.

"She's not possessed. And we've thoroughly botched whatever sacrifice it meant to achieve tonight. It's best she remains hidden and protected. If it's her will, she can come to Grayshell."

Ally used her powers to turn on all the faucets in the room. With a grunt of effort, she pulled the water from the lines into a cascading current, spinning above her, and hurled it at the sigil on the wall.

MAGIC. There was no other word for what the residents of Grayshell could do. Every soul gathered in the hall in their spirit armor. There were more weapons than souls within those grand walls, and they raised their pale hands to the sky in unison before chanting a long string of Latin words I hadn't learned yet. Not only did the ground and walls tremble, but the sound shifted. Normally, the melody of voices reverberated off the walls in a constant chorus of noise. But as they lowered their hands, it felt as though the castle had submerged into a pool of water, and everything was muffled—like firing a gun too close, with the shock and ringing in my ears.

Alvara explained that they sealed the gateway on nights when the dimensions overlapped.

It was all hands on deck. That was Aren's ringing command. If Hell wanted our healers, they'd have to go through all of us first. He'd sent messages to the other hierarchies, requesting their Commanders follow the same protocol. No soul was permitted to remain on earth through Samhain's thin veil. Even braids were summoned home. Not everyone would answer the call, but I couldn't fault him for trying. Alvara and the other seers were to be in a meditative state, on watch.

"If we're all bound here, who defends Earth?"

She shook her head. "There aren't enough of us to guard the light world and the mortal world. For tonight, the mess is up to God and his angels. They're on their own."

"Demons can't reach Heaven?" It was only partially a question.

She shook her head. "No. Nothing evil can enter Heaven—*they're* safe."

We turned and walked from the hall together. I wanted desperately to reach out and grab her hand, but our chance for an in-depth reading seemed to have vanished. Overwhelming Alvara was not the goal.

"An Archangel bound Sarah?"

Her eyes narrowed as she stared at me for a moment. "She believes so."

"What did you see?"

"Not as much as I hoped. Her memories just... cut off."

"Like yours?"

Expression grim, she gave me a nod. "And yours."

"But Sarah believes she remembers beyond what you can see."

"That's what concerns me."

A haunting choir began to sing in the hall, and the wave of energy sent chills down my arms as a thought solidified.

"Satan was an angel once?"

Her steps slowed, and she side-eyed me. "Yes, Lucifer... you don't think..."

"The devil himself bound our memories? I don't know. But can you think of another explanation? We're between worlds, aren't we? As vulnerable to him as we are to any of the others."

She rubbed her temples, stress evident between her brows. After several long paces, she looked up at me and shrugged. "I don't know."

"Must be a new sensation for you."

"You know, I'm getting used to it." Her lips quirked. "But yes. It is."

Aren poured eight mugs of tea and slid them across the island.

"CAN you tell us everything you know about the great battle of light and dark?" Alvara's voice was urgent.

"Which one?" Aren raised his eyebrows, a smirk on his face.

"Funny, Aren."

"The one I *wasn't* alive for? I know as much as any of you. Demons infiltrated the hierarchies of the Light. Our bodies are vulnerable when we're earth-bound too. They opened the gateway and waged a war like nothing ever known. The mortals were plagued and faced famine. But we... we were ravaged by the servants of the underworld. There was no rest. It wasn't until the angels beat back the horsemen of the apocalypse that things turned in our favor. But not without unspeakable losses." Aren nodded at me.

"Legend has it that The Great Commander led our warriors through an assault on the underworld. He joined St. Michael in a great attack on Hell itself, taking the fight to Satan and Abaddon before they could regroup. But Abaddon—"

"Tore The Commander's soul in two," Alvara finished the story, her somber eyes shifting from me to Aren and back.

"Evidently, Abaddon wasn't as powerful as we were led to believe. The Great Commander is said to be a warrior so fearsome it's hard to look upon him when he rises. He only returns during the gravest of battles. And he must survive the human world long enough to ascend. He led us to victory in the battle of light and dark, but not without sacrificing himself. A soul split in two..." Aren shook his head. "I never knew what to make of that. But martyrs are supposed to move on to Heaven. They're not supposed to come back. His sacrifice saved us all—gave us the advantage long enough to throw the horsemen back where they belonged and seal the gates to Hell. I always believed that The Great Commander was at peace... If August is, in fact, *The* Commander, then Ally's dark visions hold true. The gates are about to open again."

TWENTY-SEVEN
WITCHING HOUR
ALVARA

August placed his hand on the small of my back, a silent reassurance that I wasn't alone.

"We will not be afraid. We will not bow down. If God is with you, who can be against you? Steel yourselves and lean into your faith. If we are to remain in the in-between for this battle, we will see... everything." Aren drank the last of his tea, wrinkling his nose. "Anyone want something stronger?"

I did. I wanted to drown the rush of fear that had crept into my body, the suffocating ice that reached into the depths of my soul. The sound of a horn reverberated in my mind.

"Shouldn't God's army stay sober at this point?" I mused.

Aren smirked. "Even Jesus drank wine. You don't suppose we're more anointed than he was?"

"Were we going to drink *wine?*"

He pulled a bottle of red off the counter, swiping our tea bags out of the line of empty mugs. Each of us was poured a few ounces of his favorite merlot, and I drank, grateful for the warmth that spread through my chest, melting the winter of horror that had wrapped its icy fingers around my heart. I was about to ask him about Sarah's memories, about mine, and August's, but Aren's gaze was fixed on me.

"I'm sorry. I don't have more answers, kid. Before my lifeline, I'm afraid."

I nodded, my mind spinning and heart pounding. I noticed August's eyes studying my face, flitting between my eyes to my mouth, and then down the line of my body. There was a hunger in his gaze that resonated deep within me. His touch, his hand on my back, and the powerful energy emanating from him threatened to unravel all the discipline I had built over hundreds of years. It felt as if he were my home, not just the walls surrounding us. As I searched his face, my breathing steadied, anchoring myself in him and his scent.

One of the younger seers, Morganite, entered the common room, her blonde locks tied into a braid down her back. Her frame was slight, not as muscular as the rest of us.

"Alvara, there's a bit of a disturbance I don't understand. I thought you might make sense of it."

"It's probably just Samhain. Witching hour is approaching, and the energy gets ten kinds of twisted."

I nodded to Aren, my eyes lingering on August for a moment before I followed Morganite out of the room, reluctant to leave him behind. It felt like leaving a part of myself. We headed into the hall, where the gate remained sealed. The seers had gathered at the bright space near the tables by the door. Their eyes found mine, desperate, their lips pressed tight.

"It's... fluctuating. But we don't understand it. It's not like anything is trying to get in, but like..."

I felt the intense pull of the energy from the door, its strength undeniable. "Like it wants us to come out."

The others nodded. I took a cleansing breath, trying to clear my head, and stepped forward. The energy was magnetic, eerie—otherworldly but not demonic. Earthbound? But mortal humans shouldn't be able to reach us here. August appeared by my side, and I looked at him, raising my eyebrows.

"I heard my name."

My brows furrowed. "Nobody called your name. We haven't really said much for that matter." I narrowed my eyes, replaying the last minute while studying the door. August's attention was fixed on the space where the door should be, his eyes distant.

"They're... calling to me?"

Chills ran down my arms as I turned to him. "They?"

"I don't know who, but I just... know. Like I knew the demons were in the hospital. I don't understand it."

A great huff escaped my lungs as I studied the energy coming from the portal. It was nearly midnight, the time when the energy crossover would be most potent. Slowly, I raised my hands to press into the energy and was pulled into a swirl of broken visions.

A world on fire. Bodies in mass graves. Grief-stricken news anchors. Crushing white walls. The Horsemen running through New York City with a legion of dark spirits on their sides. Masked demons taunting us. A skeleton of a city in ashes. Endless eyes. Layla. James. All that was visible of their terrified faces, was their eyes, as though they peaked through a small crack. A bloody Aren fighting an enormous jaguar. And then, in slow motion, a winged horse and a warrior with a raised sword.

The warrior was August.

I pulled my hands back. The visions made no sense. Were they parables? I turned, desperate to touch August's face, to show him all that had been shown to me.

But his eyes were wide, and I knew he'd seen them too, as they raced through my mind.

MASS WAS EVEN MORE PACKED than usual with the braids all being called home. I stood in the back, wedged between the wall and a tall gold fountain, not wanting to accidentally rub shoulders against someone who might not want their mind pried into. Under the circumstances, we could use a spiritual reminder of who we were. The priest's message focused heavily on the war between Kingdoms, the eternal struggle we were all a part of, protecting mortal souls from the enemy's lies. Lies that could easily deceive us as well. The enemy that brought deceit, fear, and death. The enemy that led us away from Faith.

A message pressed heavy on my heart as the service concluded. Each step across the tile floor to the exit seemed to echo in my ribs.

Give the battle back to me. Let me fight it.

I made straight for Aren and extended my hand to read his face. He stopped mid-sentence, turning from his companions, who gave us space upon seeing me, and locked eyes with me. I pressed my fingers gently against his temple. The light shone briefly, and he blinked, puzzled.

"*Are we... supposed to stand down?*"

"*It would seem so.*"

TWENTY-EIGHT
ALL SAINTS' DAY
AUGUST

Alvara's long, dark hair fell in curls down her back. On one side, she had braided several thin rows away from her face, fastening them with small gold rings. Full waves framed the other side. A dress the color of sea foam draped over her fair shoulders, reaching the floor and making her lean frame look impossibly elongated. The blue gradually darkened until it resembled the depths of the ocean at her feet. Were it not for the tall silk gloves sliding over her hands to the elbow, she might have been Helen of Troy—damnably perfect and swiftly becoming my deepest weakness. Those gloves were all that reminded me of exactly who and what she was. My heart hammered against my chest as I took her in.

She was radiant. Breathtaking. An enchanted queen.

As if sensing the change in my heartbeat, her eyes found mine amidst the chaos, a coy smile playing in the depths of her emerald irises. Another warrior woman ascended the stairs, pausing to grasp Alvara's hand. They exchanged smiles, words, and laughter. The sight of her joy made my chest swell, and I followed the pull towards her. Someone slammed into my elbow, snapping me out of my daze. I realized I had frozen in the center of the hall, mesmerized. The world around me buzzed with activity, bodies weaving around me like a rock in a river. I took a deep breath and dove into the flow of people moving towards the hall.

She met me in front of the grand doors, and her smile was genuine as her eyes surveyed me from top to bottom. The evaluation felt intensely intimate. But her smile was warm, and her chiming voice greeted me.

"Well, hello, Stranger. You clean up well."

My stomach flopped like a pancake. I looked down at the light linen outfit Aren had left for me and decided then and there that I'd be acquiring it in every color.

"Thanks. You look absolutely breathtaking."

That heart-wrenching grin broadened, and color rushed to her cheeks.

I hadn't realized I'd reached out an arm until her smile changed to a polite nod, and she wrapped her gloved arm around mine. God, I wanted to feel her skin against mine. To trace her innumerable scars with my fingers. Together, we joined the crowd of souls hurrying into the hall. As we neared the great archway entrance, the smell of rosemary, cooking meat, bread, cinnamon, and citrus overwhelmed me.

After Aren led the prayer, we were served a mouthwatering course of herb-encrusted roast beef and artisan bread. The crunchy golden crust was covered in rosemary, salt, and what I believed to be sage. Small potatoes, tossed with garlic and onion, adorned the edge of the dish. The taste was so rich that the best meals from my human life now felt like sand on my tongue. I'd dined in Ivy Springs' finest restaurants with colleagues and Layla, and I'd experienced nothing so exquisite. When everyone had finished, glasses drained of wine, and conversation resumed, Aren clapped his hands. The scraps vanished from our plates, quickly replaced by towers of baked goods. What looked like oddly shaped scones, glazed and dotted with raisins, appeared in front of me. My mouth watered, and I reached forward without hesitation.

"Soul Cakes," Alvara smiled at me, offering a thoughtful explanation. She was always pleased when I was happy. "And Catalan Almond Sweets," she added, levitating a small ball of something covered in cocoa powder onto my plate.

In my thirty years on Earth, I'd only seen feasts like the Grayshell celebration in movies, and I shook my head in disbelief. The distended satisfaction of my stuffed stomach and the lingering taste of the sugary orange and cinnamon soul cake were happy reminders that the lavish feast was indeed real life. As was the beaming goddess sitting to my left.

When I pressed for an explanation about all of Grayshell standing down instead of returning Earthside to reconcile the damage, Alvara told me to follow her to her rooms in the tower. Before my heart could falter, she added that Alec, Fae, and Aren were already committed to joining. She knew that Ansel and Lana would follow us up the hardwood steps as well.

Hand in hand, she led me up the incandescent stairs. Even after months of walking Grayshell's halls, the world still felt surreal to me. The nearly omnipresent glow of every surface had grown less blinding as my eyes acclimated, but it remained no more normal to my still-human perception.

We climbed for what felt like an eternity. Many floors above the infirmary, the chatter of the hall had long since faded.

When we finally exited the spiraling stairs onto a landing, my eyes widened. The hallway stretched the same looming length as the floors below, but great wooden double doors lined its bright walls. Their curved tops peaked, and wrought iron hinges stretched across them with the ancientness of a medieval castle.

"This is the Commanders' hallway. As second, I stay to his right." She indicated the most substantial set of doors, then led me to the slightly smaller doors beside them. When she approached, she reached down into the neckline of her dress. My mouth fell open as her long fingers slipped between her tight breasts, sending my heart sprinting and my balls aching.

Fuck. I wanted to graze my fingers over those soft ivory swells, wanted to feel them fit in the palm of my hand. They'd be perfect. I already knew it. When her fingers emerged, she held a miniature Scottish dirk, and I laughed. Great. I was jealous of a fucking knife.

"You know, I was wondering where you would hide your blades in that dress."

Alvara chuckled, giving me a playful wink, her full lips twisted into a smirk, but said nothing. Instead, she slid the glove from her opposite hand and pressed the blade to her forearm. Small beads of blood sprang up along the tip. I stood there, unwilling to admit my discomfort watching her slice through her perfect skin. She brought the tip of the blade to the metal lock in the door and smeared the red droplets across the keyhole. Long, pale fingers rested against the lock, and she flicked her wrist. With a reverberating click, the lock released, and Alvara pressed into the door.

Her rooms were dark and moody, like the common room. The grey stone walls resembled those of a historical castle. Most of the room reminded me of the quarters of royals long since dead. A four-poster bed draped in heavy deep red curtains sat to one side, its blankets looking barely used. I knew from experience that Alvara only needed to rest every few days if she wasn't in battle. Her mind and duties kept her alert most nights. I could understand how legends of vampires had come to be, now that I'd been in the company of immortals for some time.

Books were piled in corners and towered on tables. Even her vanity held a stack of them. Great maps layered the desk on the far side of the room, near the gargantuan stone fireplace. Artifacts and art from every age hung on the walls. I smirked as my eyes found volume after volume stuck in every nook and cranny. They lined the floor under most of the furniture, stacked on the mantle, and piled on the top of a grand armoire. The actual bookshelves on the opposite side of the room from the fire were packed to the brim, with books squeezed between the tops and shelves above them.

Three hundred years of research and literature. A sudden curiosity about Aren's space brewed in my mind.

Alvara excused herself, telling me to make myself at home, before vanishing behind another thick wood door. I collapsed into a dark chair by the fire. When she returned, she had changed into her favorite pair of grey sweats, her signature fitted black t-shirt, and her hair had been spun into a messy bun on top of her head. Only a few loose curls remained around her face. For a moment, I found myself visually tracing the long lines of her exposed neck and collarbones. But I quickly stuffed the sensation that stirred away and returned my eyes to the pile of books towering on the small table between my oversized purple armchair and the next. One of the books on the pile closest to me must have been what we'd come for because she reached out her delicate porcelain fingers to pluck it from the top. But my eyes focused on her smooth forearm.

Quickly, I reached forward, catching myself only an inch from her exposed skin.

"You healed that quickly?"

"It only takes a few minutes for us if we weren't hit with cursed weapons. Or demonically poisoned, in Aren's case."

"I guess...I guess I hadn't seen a normal angel injury heal before. Without, you know, one of you overseeing it."

"Nephilim," Alvara corrected with a smirk. "I'm not an angel. Although I suspect they heal even faster than we do."

"Why don't we see them?"

"Angels?"

"Yes. Why don't we...you know. *See* them. Why aren't they *here*? Why don't they come to us on Earth?"

"Strictly speaking, *we* are forbidden. We're not supposed to exist. For a long while, we believed that the Archangels and angels who serve them were supposed to execute us if they found us. But then...well, Aren, I, and a few other seers began receiving orders from Michael himself. More among us began to have visions and dreams of the angels giving us instructions or leading us to what we needed to survive and win in battle. We are devoted servants. Aren and I both believe they have seen our dedication and allow us to continue existing."

"What about the Renown?"

"We don't know, to be honest. They're difficult for us to kill. I'm not sure if angels find them challenging as well, but I can't imagine anything would be hard for them, aside from demons of equal power. We don't understand why they keep breeding or why the angels don't eradicate them from the face of the Earth."

"Can angels...die?"

"We believe so. But since none of us have ever spoken to one directly, we're not certain."

We fell silent as we caught the scent of our companions on the air, moments before we heard them lumbering down the long hallway. The heightened senses still felt surreal. They whispered among themselves, and this time, Alvara telekinetically opened the door. The rest of the coven entered the cozy room, their emotions mixed. Aren seemed unaffected by the questions hanging in the air, while Alec wore his usual amused expression. Ansel and Lana, ever vigilant after Aren's injury, remained battle-ready, their faces taut with anxiety.

Wordlessly, they gathered around our small table. Aren carried over two large armchairs, one in each hand as if they were mere props. Ansel retrieved a third. Alec, having taken a turn as he entered the room, closed one of Ally's armoire doors, an antique bottle of brandy in hand, a mischievous grin on his face. The liquid's color, reminiscent of the eyes flashing back at us over his grin, sloshed in the half-full bottle.

"You know, I loathe when you hold out on me."

"Your lack of observational skills does not equate to me holding out on you." Alvara didn't lift her gaze from the book in her lap as she spoke. Alec snorted, and Fae grinned. As Alec took a step, he pulled the cork out with his teeth and shot it across the room toward Alvara with a pop. She caught the cork one-handed, tossing it onto the table beside her, the corners of her lips quirking slightly.

Fae pulled over an oversized beanbag chair I had overlooked, and Alec took a long swig from the bottle before sprawling out on it like a cat playing with its mate. Fae grinned and joined him, curling her back against his chest as he wrapped around her, trailing kisses down her shoulder before settling into the beanbag.

Alvara remained focused on her book as Aren brought over mugs of warmed water. Once we were each sipping chamomile tea, he cleared his throat to break the silence.

"So, we don't know much more than any of you do. Ally was instructed to leave the battle to God, so we stood down through Samhain. Obviously, there were no attacks on Grayshell. But we haven't yet surveyed the mortal world. Our seers have been...quiet."

"Too quiet." Ansel's gravelly voice cut through the silence. "Don't you find it odd?"

"A little," Aren admitted. "We've all sensed the storm beneath our feet, but we don't know why or what exactly is coming. And as you said, our seers have gone silent simultaneously. It's as if their connection has been..."

"Snuffed out," Alvara finished pointedly. "It feels as though our connection has been snuffed out. As if we're not meant to know. Do you think the humans are being punished?" Her gaze was dark, fixed intently on Aren. He pursed his lips, leaning his colossal frame forward to rest his arms on his knees. For a moment, his comical size distracted me as he dwarfed the chair beneath him. Then he exhaled slowly.

"I don't believe our God would forsake His children. He wouldn't abandon them."

"Are you sure? Doesn't it feel like Evil has stopped hiding? Each time we leave Grayshell, it feels more prominent—demons in the eyes of politicians, reading their news. Crawlers roaming the shadows in broad *daylight*—attacking our souls at high noon. My visions have repeatedly shown signs of a coming famine and war. And...crushing walls. I can't stop thinking about it." She closed the book in her lap and locked her eyes on Aren. He turned his face to the fire, mulling over their shared experiences.

Silence hung like a suffocating fog. Lana looked as if she might chew through her lip, and if Ansel could wield fire like my sire, there would have been an eruption on the rug he stared daggers at. After a long pause, Aren took a heaving breath and met his second's gaze.

"It's not what He ever intended for them. Their free will damns them daily. They have turned from God, not the other way around. It's their own will, their selfishness, their deceit. We can pray, and I believe we can intervene where we're able—to guide them and protect them. But that's as far as our arsenal goes."

The small stress line appeared between Alvara's dark brows as she stared into the fire, her anger and distress palpable as she wiped her palms across her lap. After an eternity of heavy silence, Aren tilted his head towards her.

"Speak, soldier."

"Why do we bother? After all this time, why do we continue to bother with them? They've made this mess—why do we keep trying to clean it up? They don't deserve the Grace they're given."

"Careful, Ally, you sound like our uncle." Alec's tone was serious, though a smile played at his lips.

"Uncle?" I interrupted, intrigued.

"Lucifer led the fallen angels. In theory, our ancestors. We are as much his kin as God's. Just as flawed. Just as selfish," Alec said matter-of-factly, his calm impenetrable.

"I've never hesitated to defend them with my body, mind, or soul, have I?" Alvara crossed her arms, chin raised defiantly. But her eyes glistened, betraying her true feelings. I knew her gifts allowed her to feel more deeply than the rest of us. Only I could possibly be more in tune, given how recently I had been mortal. I could feel her pain radiating, her mind racing through memories of their plight. I wanted to reach out, but I forced my hands to remain gripping the armchair.

"And we know you will continue to, even though you question the calling. Which is what makes you who you are, Ally. You question His plans, but you still act in faith. You hurt, and ache, and don't understand, yet you serve humanity with everything you have despite it." For a moment, she locked eyes with Aren, then pursed her lips and turned back to the fire.

"So, for the rest of time, we will continue to fall on blades defending creatures too broken to defend themselves."

"Until Christ Himself calls them home."

"What about us?" I interrupted. "What happens to us when the humans go home?"

"As half-humans, we pray that includes us. But we don't actually know." Aren's face showed no sign of distress. His open posture suggested an acceptance of the unknown. For the first time, I saw the years behind his pale blue eyes—millennia of wisdom surfacing. His usual playful demeanor made him seem younger, but his honesty etched the years over his pensive gaze.

Another long, weighted pause.

"Does the order to stand down have to do with him?" Ansel jerked his head in my direction, and all eyes turned to Aren again.

"My intuition says that August is here to prepare us for the battle to come. We are to awaken him. Perhaps we are conserving our energy and resources in the meantime."

One by one, all eyes fell on me. I shook my head. "I don't understand any of this."

"That leads us to believe Sarah is right about the block in your memories. We should prioritize triggering that until it's cleared," Aren said.

"What better way to destroy the greatest spiritual weapon our kind ever had than by hiding his potential from himself?" Ansel's low drawl grated on my nerves. His eyes remained fixed on me, brow furrowed in frustration. I shook my head, not feeling like a weapon. Certainly not like a bloody Commander.

"It's quite brilliant, really. It's what the demons do to the humans— whisper lies long enough and often enough until evil and apathy become all that remains." Aren's eyes narrowed on me. "August, if you're ready, we can start pushing you to trigger. Unfortunately, dire circumstances usually bring the most vivid memories."

"Like Alec attacking Alvara." Fae wrinkled her nose, wincing at the memory. "It's not exactly...pleasant."

Alec grinned and shrugged. "He can handle it. He handled the Renown that night in the park."

Ansel threw him a side eye, and Aren, contemplative but still smiling, huffed. "Let's not rely on beginner's luck."

"He can handle it," Alec repeated.

I stared down my old friend, wondering if he was a little twisted in the head. But the confidence in his eyes reassured me, despite the mischievous smirk on his face.

A deep breath later, I muttered, "Whatever it takes, I guess."

Aren mirrored Alec's mischief but then let a genuine smile creep onto his face as he locked eyes with me. "We start tomorrow."

Everything in my body recoiled from the anxiety of that statement. I felt entirely human, immersed in my panic. But I forced myself to look at Alvara, searching for reassurance. Her expression was dark, still focused on the fire. Treacherous shadows danced in her eyes. Slowly, as if entranced by the flames, she turned to us, the crease between her brows still etched deep. "Something feels... wrong. Something feels..." She shook her head as though trying to shake away the thoughts like water off a dog before she finally finished her sentence. "Off..."

Six serious pairs of eyes turned to her. She shook her head, her gaze growing distant and uncertain. I realized she was searching for answers to the unease in her heart. Her eyes flickered closed, a grimace twisting her features as the vision overtook her. The shadow seeped into my bones, and as each beating heart in the room quickened, I knew they felt it too.

"Ally?" Aren's voice was cut off as she raised her hand to stop him, her eyes looking through us into the other world she accessed.

"Something... has changed..." Her voice was distant, breathy. "Battle. It doesn't... make... sense." Suddenly, her vision splintered back to the present, and her eyes snapped to mine. "August? Why would you..."

A vision forced itself into my mind. From the collective intake of breath, I assumed the others were experiencing it too. *A blood-soaked battlefield strewn with slain Renown, broken bodies of shadow demons, and souls alike. Smoldering woods. And me, walking hesitantly forward, alone. Alvara cried out somewhere behind me, her voice guttural and grief-stricken. I approached an enormous man of Renown. Alvara noted that his face would have been as attractive as our kind if it weren't twisted with cruelty. And I held out my hands to be bound.*

"He... he gave himself up?" Alec's eyes burned with anger, brows furrowed with betrayal as he looked to me for an explanation. I only shrugged my bewilderment, and he stared back at Alvara.

"Why... why would you...?" Alvara's voice trailed off as she searched for answers. There was a swirl of visions; she seemed to rewind and fast-forward them like a tape in a VCR. Weighing them. Some were of the battle; others were of a clash with the towering man. Flames shaped like great wings. Four crushing white walls. Powers being slashed away. A bass voice—the kind that rumbles in your ribcage—repeating *one and the same...*

Her breath hitched violently, the air rushing from my own lungs. She doubled over in her chair, clutching her ribs. *The man placed manacles around my wrists, let out a dead cackle, and abruptly shot his giant hand forward, clutching my neck. Slowly, he lifted me off the ground.*

"He's called Adrastos, I think. That's all I've managed to make sense of. The shielding... I can't..." Alvara drifted away for a long string of heartbeats, her voice floating with her. Alec, brow furrowed to match the deep scowl on Ansel's face, stared into the fire and sipped his tea. They gave her a decent stretch of time before anyone broke the severe, pregnant silence.

"Why? Why would he go to them? Turn himself over?" Aphaea's voice was a whisper.

Alvara's eyes turned to mine, grief evident. But confusion also swam in her glossy irises. "I—I don't know. I can't see it. Whatever they draw him out with... they haven't decided what to use yet. But every thread I see... whatever they find, it works. August, they know who you are."

"I forbid it," Aren boomed. His voice was the only steady one among us. "If August is what we believe him to be, there's nothing that would justify the sacrifice."

"No," Alvara agreed. "There's not."

My head swam. Blood pounded. Dread rose in my gut like bile.

"With all due respect," my voice came out like gravel—strained and forced. "I'm not exactly some Keanu Reeves character. I'm not worth more than any of you. Less, really—"

"Name one prophesied leader—fictional or otherwise—that believed they were the chosen one, dumbass." Alec grinned, and his mate mirrored the expression. "Good reference, by the way. I like him."

"Epic is more like it," Aren smirked. "It's been a while since we had a *Matrix* marathon."

"So, say I am. Say I am The Great Commander. Wouldn't I be obligated to sacrifice myself for anyone in the hierarchy? Wouldn't I have to—"

"No!" The coven shouted in unison, and I snapped my mouth closed.

"The Commander is said to lead us into and through the greatest battle in our history. August, we need you here for that." Alvara's eyes were smoldering, and for a moment, it was as though the flames she wielded danced in the gold ring within them. Consuming me. Engulfing my very soul as she stared me down. Despite myself, I wanted the flames to devour every inch of me, blazing through every mortal weakness and freeing the man she saw in me. She seemed to understand the gravity of her strength, because the embers in her eyes faded, and I faded right along with them.

I bowed my head in submission to my sire. "Your move, My Queen."

Alec and Aren's snickers cut off abruptly as Alvara jutted out of her chair with inhuman speed. Her movement caused the roaring fire in the hearth to flicker, and the book that had rested in her lap clattered to the floor with a loud thud. She narrowed her eyes at me, the embers reigniting within her. When she spoke, her voice was breathy with a semblance of panic.

"Why did you call me that?"

"It's the only way I can think of you."

"Since when?"

"I don't know. Since we battled The Renown."

"Ally?" Aren's voice was a rumbling warning, and he cocked his head to the side, cautiously curious. "Did you just trigger?"

"Yes. But I... I don't understand it *again*." She slammed her palm into her forehead, jamming her eyes closed. She uttered a colorful string of profanities under her breath, and I couldn't help the amusement that inevitably played on my face. "You called me your *Queen*. Why does that sound... right? I can't see. I can't see the trigger. It's... cloudy. But it's there, dammit. Why did that hit my heart like... ugh!" She groaned and yanked the tie from her bun, freeing her long locks in a wave. "Nobody has ever called me that here."

"Certainly not," Alec snorted.

"But it resonated," she said, eyes still locked on me.

"Because you are a Queen. Because you're worthy of man's loyalty." My tone was matter-of-fact, and Alec's cocky smile made me want to sock him.

"You would have a past life ruling over mortals, wouldn't you?" Lana sneered from the corner. Something about her was familiar, but her sharp eyes did nothing to earn my trust. Like a fox, she was clever and attentive. Her mate looked mildly amused but shrugged in agreement, methodically rotating his slender cigarette tin between his fingers.

"Not that I remember."

"Doesn't mean as much as it used to, does it, though?" Fae's voice was soft, gentle, accepting. "If you really were bound, it would make sense. Technically, we need to work on unbinding you both."

"Tomorrow." Aren grinned at her, and her breathing slowed. She huffed before returning to her chair.

"Normal people feel this confused all the bloody time?" Alvara spat the question at her sire. Alec and Ansel both laughed.

"Annoying, isn't it?" Alec raised his light eyebrows.

"Even more annoying when you're surrounded by immense clairvoyance." Ansel's dark face cracked into the first genuine smile I'd seen in a while. He seemed to relish Alvara's struggle, and it grated on my nerves. I gritted my teeth in frustration but forced a breath.

We spent the rest of the night discussing battle strategies, debating potential traps for the Renown on Earth and the crawlers invading the mortal world in broad daylight. Aren remained quiet, his expression eternally inquisitive, save for the questions he had for Alvara regarding her visions and the mysterious Adrastos. As it only seemed to aggravate her, he relented and left Alec, Lana, and Ansel to bounce ideas off one another. But Alvara simply stared into the fire, her inhuman stillness settling into her muscled limbs. My eyes couldn't pry away from her; I studied her, watching the way she breathed, the shadows that played on her eyes as she fell in and out of focus. She wasn't about to let the snippets of visions she'd gathered fade away.

It was only when Aren's resonant voice called her name that she finally pulled herself from her reverie. There was a politician on the East Coast of the United States with a demon in his eyes that Fae and Alvara wanted to go after. Alvara broke her focus long enough to tell them she didn't fully trust either proposed plan of attack and that she'd think it over. The fire claimed her mind again, and I watched as her eyes glazed, a sinking feeling settling in my gut as the shadows danced across her skin.

TWENTY-NINE
TRIAL BY FIRE
AUGUST

Alvara woke me before the blue light of dawn could fill my room. Her dark hair was braided back into a low bun, and her serious eyes threw clothes across my bed. Training. Without another word, she spun on her heel and left, the energy of her departure crackling like a brewing storm. She had risen long before the sun, sent Earthside to retrieve an ascending soul.

Dressed, shoes laced, and hair brushed, I entered the hallway where she waited. Impatience emanated from her, and she turned to look at me with an expression devoid of the warmth I'd grown to love. My mouth went dry, words evaporating, so I simply followed.

It was the first time I'd stepped outside in the Middle Realm. Surrounding the castle lay a courtyard and a garden, a luminescent imitation of the world below. Too bright. Like a cloudless day with a vodka hangover. The colors were lighter, almost iridescent, but the ground was solid beneath our feet as we ran. And ran and ran and ran. My lungs felt like they were on fire, and my muscles screamed as cramps demanded rest. We stopped only once my stomach had rejected the meager breakfast I'd forced down in my room.

Alvara handed me water to rinse my mouth. To her credit, she didn't look shocked or disgusted as I wiped the vomit from my lips. She summoned a small wave of water to wash the bile into the grass.

"You need to practice your endurance," she said flatly. She inhaled deeply through her nose, her hands braced on her hips. Slowly, she exhaled through parted lips. "If you're to stand any chance against the Renown."

I wanted to protest, but as she spoke in full sentences and my lungs were only good for rasping in breaths, I chose to nod instead. Alvara's breathing remained controlled and steady.

"Most of survival comes down to one thing and one thing only. Discipline. You're a good soldier—and have been before—so somewhere in you, you already know that." A measured breath. "But this body has not been pushed as your others have. It has not been trained. It has not survived trials. So, we need to give it—"

"Trial by fire?" My panting had slowed somewhat. Amusement flickered across her beautiful face. I studied the shape of her parted lips, watched the way she wrapped them around her words.

"In a manner of speaking, yes. The others will be taking over portions of your training. It seems I have a bit of a...blind spot for you. We'll train you as we've trained the others. Aren will see to it that if we can't change your fate..." She hesitated, her throat bobbing. A deep breath. "You will at least stand a chance of coming back to us. Of surviving whatever hellhole you put yourself in." The bitterness in her voice revealed the fear that the vision had wrought. Bitterness at me, for turning myself in, in a future scenario that might or might not come to pass. She rubbed her slender hand across the back of her neck, staring at her feet.

And so, it continued for the following weeks. She trained me physically, while Alec worked on my shield and elemental skills. Over and over, I'd hurl up breakfast, and she'd hand me water. There were only three mornings she had been called away for, and Alec or Ansel would run with me instead. For the most part, Alvara returned to Earth for her missions after we trained, but I found myself missing my painfully beautiful drill sergeant whenever she was gone.

Coffee in hand, sitting across from Alec as he smirked over his own mug, I cursed her perpetual absence—or rather, my inability to trigger my memories or watch her back. When I glanced toward the portal corner for what must have been the fifth time that morning, Alec ran his tongue over his teeth, an arrogant smirk carving his features as he flicked his attention to me.

"Expecting someone, Rookie?"

"Piss off."

Satisfaction dripped from him as his coffee absorbed his amusement. "She's fine—it's Alvara. She's always fine."

"Until she's not."

"Happens less than you'd expect."

As if on cue, the energy shifted, and Ally materialized by the portal, her hair swept back into a smooth ponytail, braids keeping the sides tight to her head. She flashed a broad smile as the room's attention landed on her, both hands resting on the shoulders of two men—blatant athletes, both looking confused as fuck. She gave them a gentle shove forward as she strode between them, her attention on Aren, who rose, grinning.

"That's two more before my coffee," she said sweetly. "Surprised you boys even bothered getting out of bed this morning," she added with a wink back at our table. Aren stifled a laugh, stepping forward to introduce himself to the newcomers. When Alvara turned to the room—most of whom had the decency to pretend they were no longer watching—she made a beeline for Ansel, whose eyes had narrowed.

By the time she reached us, he had a rolled-up twenty in his hand, and she snatched it before collapsing into the chair beside Alec, who leaned over with a bill of his own, tucking it in the strap of her tank top. Fae and Lana both snorted into their mugs as Alvara leaned back and balanced in her chair. For a flash, her smile radiated toward me, but as I met her striking gaze, her emerald eyes hardened. She diverted her attention to the mug on the table.

Once her coffee was drained, Alvara cleared her throat and turned to Fae and Lana beside me, as though I didn't exist. "Ladies, I've got another soul in Montana. You down for a hunt?" The girls wordlessly set down their coffees and rose in smooth, synchronized motion before flanking Ally as she headed back into the portal.

A throat cleared. "What the fuck did you *do*, Rookie?" Ansel growled, his wide eyes glued to where the girls had just vanished.

"Nothing," I muttered, abandoning my breakfast and leaning back.

"*Yet*," Alec corrected, glaring pointedly at me.

"Yeah," I sighed, rubbing at the ache in my temples between a thumb and forefinger. "*Yet*, I guess."

Ansel released a slow sigh, rubbing his jaw quizzically. Aren whistled, catching his attention and bringing him to his feet in the same breath.

"Hang in there, kid. She'll come around." He rounded the end of our table and shocked the living hell out of me when he squeezed my shoulder. "Once she figures out how to save you."

The days went by, and the ice queen remained. Running and weight training, yoga and stretching, calisthenics and swordplay—Alvara hit me with endless drills that left no room for conversation, until one morning, I managed to finish the run without puking. I saw the change in her eyes.

Alvara began our usual cooldown walk back around the broad courtyard, and I realized with a bit of shock that the hard surface beneath our feet was composed of iridescent cobblestones. I'd never bothered to notice what the ground was made of.

Lungs screaming in protest, my breaths slowed, in through my nose and out through my mouth. Slowly, everything steadied, save for my shaking muscles. A phantom breeze licked at my skin, cooling the sweat, and I wondered if Ally was bending the air to cool me off. Regardless, it filled me with gratitude. We walked silently for a moment, my heart aching for the ease and chemistry we'd had before that goddamned vision.

Fuck it, this was ridiculous. Before I could confront the distance she'd wedged between us after Halloween, Alvara whirled on me, hand on the door handle.

"Aren and Ansel will begin training you for combat, although you will spar with each of us to get exposed to different fighting styles. The Renown will fight much more fluidly than the humans you remember—more like us. So, it's good to learn how to anticipate their movements."

Alvara pursed her lips, the shadows from the looming list of unknowns still playing in her eyes. "Good luck today." She chewed on her bottom lip, and I couldn't help but track the movement. "Aren does not pull punches. You'll want to dodge his blows. He's big, but he doesn't tire easily. Don't be fooled by his healing time—he will still give me a run for my money. Study Ansel's movements, but know he rarely dodges the same way twice. If you detect any pattern, seize it. It will thrill him but also push you. He's a good fighter. Alec and Aren will continue with much of your elemental practice. I will...observe. And see if we can change your threads."

She opened the great wooden door to the castle and motioned for me to enter.

"Alvara?"

Her piercing eyes drilled into mine.

"Thank you." I bowed my head. Her lips were a tight line, but the edges quirked, and she returned the nod.

"Kick some ass, Mr. Porter."

THIRTY
PLAY
AUGUST

The ground struck hard and fast, my face slamming into it with a painful crack. Pain engulfed me as I gasped for any available air. He was already advancing, and my screaming muscles fought against the earth. Tremors were unavoidable. My feet staggered beneath my weight as the next blow landed. Once again, I found myself sprawled on the ground, staring up at the endless stretch of white abyss, gasping and spluttering for air.

"Get up!" The Commander's voice was a harsh mix of barked command and mocking amusement. My head throbbed, my ribs ached, as I struggled to force air back into my lungs. Finally, choking, I managed to inhale. One, two, three desperate breaths. "Come on, kid, you'd be dead already," Aren growled. Obediently, I forced myself to my feet and raised my guard.

"Advance!" he bellowed, his broad shoulders pulled back, arms relaxed at his sides, his predator's gaze locked on my struggling form.

I did. But before my punch had fully extended, the great man parried and struck. The blow brought stars to my eyes, the world dimming as my ears rang. Damn, he could kill me with one bloody strike.

"Move, August! Move your feet!" Alvara's voice cut through, her gaze still trained on me like a prowling lion, pacing the edge of the ring. She was still cheering for me.

Aren swung again, and I dropped to my knees to avoid the blow, whipping my leg out to sweep his feet. But he anticipated the move and dodged it effortlessly, then planted his foot in my chest. I couldn't rise. Couldn't breathe.

"They'll strike you down before you catch your breath, Mr. Porter." Aren lifted his foot off me and barked, "Stand, dammit!"

I rose, only for the Commander to slam me back to the earth. Something cracked, and distantly, I could feel Alec and Alvara wincing.

"Dead. Now, stand!" he commanded, the scarred, nearly translucent letters on his bicep stretching with the movement.

Fuck. Everything hurt. My head, my back, my throbbing hands. I pushed against the earth, only for a kick to the ribs to send me sprawling back to the ground. Air. I needed air. I needed a moment to catch my breath.

He was trying to make me trigger—trying to force my mind, my soul, to *remember* what I was. I wished *it would fucking hurry*. Panting, I scanned the room for anything. Anything to buy time. Anything to defend myself with.

"Stand."

The command didn't change. Obediently, I summoned the wobbling strength from that well in my chest. I threw a shield out with one hand and used the other to lift my battered body to its feet. Gasping, I steadied myself and raised my guard. Aren grinned, all teeth and vicious amusement.

"You've got more than that in you, August Porter. Show me," he snarled.

A quick nod, and he hooked. I dodged, anticipating the right thrust, and sprang away. Two strikes to his ribs, and he staggered a foot away from me, a genuine smile spreading across his face. Staying on my toes, I advanced. He dodged my first fist, but when I spun into a kick, my foot met his chest, and he staggered a step. A booming laugh echoed through the room. Then I was on my back again, staring up at the damned empty ceiling. His large hand was around my throat, his knee crushing into my chest.

"Too slow, Mr. Porter!" The Commander's voice boomed, thick with taunting amusement.

"Fuck!" I swore as he released me and I wiped the blood and sweat from my brow with the back of my arm.

"Take five." He extended a hand to help me up.

Once upright, I wiped my face with my hands. Holy shit. I remembered all my mortal hand-to-hand combat training. But there was no competing with the ancient power in Aren's bones. He wasn't even using his immortal gifts—just brute strength and wits. And I didn't stand a shot in hell.

Alvara, chin high and shoulders back, was still pacing at the edge of the mat, her eyes on me, willing me to perform, to learn, to survive. She grabbed a water bottle and a small black rag from the windowsill and tossed the towel to me as I approached.

"Aren is the best of us. Not just here. Anywhere. It wouldn't make a lick of fucking sense if you could keep up." She took the towel from my hand. "You have to learn to pace yourself—pace your suffering."

Alvara was insane, I realized. Actually insane. But I nodded, fighting back a wince as she pressed the dark towel to my split brow. She held up the water bottle next, and I gulped it down in a few long swallows. Sweat stung across my burning skin, aggravating the cuts that had opened during our spar. Alec had been watching quietly, sprawled across a pair of chairs in the corner, his gaze locked with mine, lips pursed, thinking deeply. I couldn't help but wonder how Alec fared in the ring with the Commander.

"When you are outmatched and outweighed," Alvara continued, "as you will be with the Renown, leverage becomes your greatest asset. Knock them off their center of gravity. Your own weight is your salvation or your undoing. Discipline of that weight is everything. Use your energy wisely."

Aren was already back at the center of the mat, cracking his knuckles and neck, his great grizzly grin widening. He had barely broken a sweat as he beat the daylights out of me. Crazy. They were all crazy. I turned to face the madman in the center of the ring. He shook his head and flashed his canines, waving me away like a fly that had bothered him for too long.

"Alvara!" he boomed. Aren's grin broadened, mirth dancing in his light blue eyes. His arms spread wide, revealing how deep a disadvantage we were all at with his wingspan. How far he could reach and how bloody strong those hits were. The Commander's thickly muscled frame was a patchwork of jagged and brutal scars, making me shudder at the thought of what had caused them on an ascended soul of his power. A slight disruption through the intricately inked cross on his chest was all that remained from his run-in with the second hierarchy demon. Not for the first time, I eyed the lone scar below his right eye—a narrow line—and wondered who or what had been strong enough to strike him there. "Come play!"

I turned to find Alvara's expression now comically twisted. Her eyes narrowed, muscles tight with playful accusation. She pursed her lips, and a thunderous laugh rang through the hall. Then Aren *clucked* like a damn chicken, taunting her as if she were a child at the playground. Alvara's pursed lips twisted into a knowing smile. Eyes still slits, she shook her head, her smirk bright and playful. She leveled him with a glare, but her eyes were full of amusement.

"Winner takes the New York politician."

"Oooh-oooh-oooh! Playing for stakes, are we?" Another ringing laugh. Alvara granted him a single, unblinking nod. "Loser gets the demons in Ivy Springs," Aren added.

I bristled at the mention of my home, but Alvara grinned, the expression feline. She sighed, the movement long and exaggerated, as if humoring a small child after a long day.

Alvara's fingers swept through her hair as she spun her long silky locks into a bun atop her head. She popped her neck and rolled it from side to side to stretch before cracking her knuckles. The intensity of her gaze on Aren, like a lion watching her prey, would have been menacing despite her beauty if it weren't for the victorious laughter echoing in the ring. My heart faltered as she pulled her loose t-shirt over her head, revealing a slender, chiseled abdomen beneath. Even her smooth belly was speckled with scars. She tossed the shirt aside, wearing a tight sports bra and high-waisted leggings from our morning run as she strode into the ring, head held high. The outfit left very little to the imagination.

Realizing I was gawking, I pulled my attention back to the men in the room, mouth dry. Alec smirked at me. Aren, thankfully, seemed oblivious to my lapse in control. Did she have to be so damnably tempting? I peeled my tongue from the cotton of my mouth and wandered to Alec's side as the lioness began to circle the bear. Alec kicked his feet off the chair they'd rested on and leaned forward onto his forearms. I sensed that he thought something to Alvara, but it was only for her, shielded from the rest of us. She flicked her eyes to him and gave him a quick wink before turning back to Aren.

Alvara continued her prowling, that feline focus mesmerizing. She would not be the first to throw a fist. Aren laughed again and closed the gap, slow and steady. Without warning, he lunged at her, but she dropped her weight low and thrust a powerful blow to his chest, forcing his weight across her body. She returned to her prowl as he righted himself. In an instant, he swung his great hand, and she jerked out of the way, dropping low to swipe at his leg. But he evaded her advance too. Long minutes ticked by, their level of skill mind-boggling. A mesmerizing and excruciating sequence of movements unfolded, so disciplined they seemed choreographed as they dodged and wove together. She moved like lightning, and Aren's hulking form did nothing to slow him down. They swung, struck, parried, and escaped each would-be blow—a swift dance to a rhythm only they could hear.

Then, breaking the pattern, she lunged forward, but his palm thrust out, connecting with her jaw. She staggered back a step, hissing, but still ducked his next blow. As he stepped away, she spat a mouthful of blood to the side of the mat, narrowing her eyes in focus. Another victorious laugh came from her sire.

He swung forward, but she wrapped her hands around his arm, pulling him towards her and jerking her knee into his ribs. He grunted from the impact, the air crashing out of him. Alvara tossed Aren's arm aside and raised her forearm to strike his face—one, two, three breakneck blows— before he had her arm in his great hands. She threw her weight forward, against his grasp, just as she raised her other elbow towards his throat. Between the two, he dropped her arm while blocking the second.

They staggered apart, fierce smiles playing between them. Aren raised a hand to his lips, wiping blood from his mouth.

"One for one," Alec muttered under his breath, amusement lacing the words.

A low, breathless laugh and an accusing smirk broke from Aren. Alvara returned the smile, but her eyes remained fixed on her opponent. I realized then, with a twist in my stomach, that she was truly formidable if she could last this long on her feet against The Commander. Her draw to serve and protect was more palpable than ever. Not that she needed any help in that ring.

Aren kicked, and she deflected. He swung his great arm, and she twisted into a grab, tossing him past her. Aren staggered but caught his balance in an instant. Next, she advanced, using her elbow again in her lunge, but he was ready this time. He grabbed her arm and yanked her with such force that she fell to her knees. She rolled and was on her feet in an instant. Alvara sprinted the three swift strides forward, throwing herself around his body like a pole, spinning upside down to lock her legs around his neck and toss him forward with her momentum. Aren's body toppled, and my eyes widened as she straddled him.

The victory was short-lived as he flipped her onto her back. She landed hard, and I felt the impact shudder through my ribs—a memory, or perhaps sympathy, I wasn't sure. But then he was on her, his massive form straddling her hips. She threw her arms forward, but Aren was faster, pinning her hands by her head. She tried to twist away, but his weight crushed her to the mat. My stomach twisted in silent rage, seeing him loom over her as if to claim her. A warning growl rumbled in my chest of its own volition.

In an instant of blur and a roar, she bucked her hips against him, her strong legs shoving his weight over his wrists, while simultaneously yanking her hands down to her sides, turning her face from the impact of his body as he face-planted. Another blur of motion followed as she elbowed his braced arm, feet still planted, and threw her weight to the side. They rolled. Then Alvara was on top of him, lunging forward. I heard, more than saw, the hiss of the blade sliding out of its sheath, and then it was pressed against his neck.

A wry smile twisted her lips, and my own heart hammered with her victory. Aren narrowed his eyes for a moment, then the grin broadened.

"Pinned ya," Alvara said, her tone childish and mocking. She pulled the blade from his neck, and he boomed with laughter, rolling with it.

Once he caught his breath, Aren said, "Good form."

"I thought you'd like that." In a graceful move, she rose, palm outstretched to help Aren to his feet. He accepted her hand.

"You know, I didn't come armed. I think that's cheating."

"You laid no ground rules."

"Fine. Rematch tomorrow. No weapons."

"If you want to get your ass kicked two days in a row and get pinned by my *teeth*, that's fine by me." She licked along the front of her drawn canines.

A breathless chuckle escaped him. "Don't get cocky now. Best two out of three?"

"Hell no. I get New York. You get Ivy Springs."

"Come on!"

"Don't be a sore loser."

"You brought a knife."

"I *always* have a knife."

"A little unfair."

"Don't blame me because you came without a weapon. Proper preparation prevents poor performance."

Aren tousled her hair, messing it out of the bun, and she shrieked and giggled. "Asshole!"

The sound of her laughter was a warm fire on a snowy night. She elbowed him in the ribs, and he boomed again as she freed her hair from the bun, the elastic snapping. The bear returned his grin to me, finally looking satisfied, and waved me into the ring.

"Alright, August. Again!"

Alvara sauntered over to her collection of belongings, pulling the black t-shirt over her head and shaking out her hair. I dragged my eyes from her bruising face, tracing the soft curve of her swollen, bloody lips. With a breath, I turned back to the Commander. His already healing mouth twisted into an eager grin. I thought for a moment about the way Alvara spun their momentum—the way she used his substantial weight against him, never taking him on directly.

Well. Here goes nothing.

ALVARA HEALED my cuts and bruises as Alec healed Aren's. She had already stitched her own mouth back together with her magic and was happily crooning taunts to Aren about their coming rematch. Close enough to feel the warmth from her fingers, I focused on my breathing. I held it steady, but her warm scent saturated the air, stirring something in my chest.

Her fingers wiggled back and forth, tapping on invisible keys, and the cuts and scrapes healed shut. Bruises lifted. Something in the closeness of her filled me with warmth, my mouth going a little dry. Her eyes never left the wounds she sealed, her focus unwavering even under Aren's taunts.

"How did you..." I trailed off, not entirely sure I wanted to know the answer. Not sure if I wanted to know why her *inclination for violence,* as Aren had called it so long ago, had been so necessary after her ascension. But she read it on me—either my face or my mind. A soft smile tugged at her mouth, but her eyes held shadows I sometimes caught within them.

"After...the end of my mortal life, I was so angry—livid, I suppose, because that anger kept me from dropping into the darkness—that I had been helpless. That he died protecting me, and I had been...so...so helpless. I decided never again." She shrugged, as though the tale was self-explanatory. I tried not to think too hard about the fact that she almost never said Michael's name, though he was still so much a part of her.

Alvara pulled her long hair up into a bun as she continued, "Aren was... gentle with me. His need to protect his calling was so strong. But he treated me like I was made of glass, and it only fueled my anger. I didn't *want* to be fragile—stay so exposed—so eventually, I convinced him to train me as he trained the others. So I might never again be at the mercy of a man. The anger may have fueled me, but training with Aren...focused me. Helped, somehow. Until fighting became as much a part of me as breathing. Until my outlet became...who I am." Alvara paused, a soft smile on her lips. Aren was watching us from the corner of the room, his lips pulled to the side with amusement and a bit of pride glimmering in those pale eyes.

"When she says *convinced* me to train her, she means provoked me until I *wanted* to beat the shit out of her." He moved closer, taking a swig from his glass of water.

Alvara's eyes flashed with that fire, the challenge of it. That soft smile turned into a full-fledged grin. For a moment, she looked like the wildfire she preferred to wield. "He didn't," she clarified. "Though I would have deserved it, if I'm honest. I was...itching for a fight." Aren snorted across the room as he unwrapped his hands. She rolled her eyes and continued. "I was so weak that we had to begin with the very basics. You have a leg up, having already been active, remembering some bits of your past life skills. For me, it was a process. So many planks and pull-ups, I was convinced he must loathe me."

"But she'd do them," Aren added. "Grumbling, but obedient. She wanted it enough that the pain, the blood, the vomit...it didn't slow her down."

Alvara gave an apologetic little shrug, as though I might be offended by the details. After I'd hurled my own guts up time and again over those grueling weeks, a reality that still made me flush when I thought of it.

"Most of us can't wield like you do. Not at first. So, Aren taught me to control my gifts—fire, especially—before we began sparring or training with weapons."

"I enjoy not being Commander brulé," Aren said, as though it needed explaining.

Alvara finished with the last scrape, my skin smooth without so much as a trace of purple, and pulled back. "There," she said, straightening her shoulders. She locked eyes with me, her cheeks filled with warmth. "Much better. Do you feel anything else?"

I shook my head, not about to tell her what other feelings were brewing in my body as she stood inches from my face, her breath warm against my cheek. She smiled sweetly and jerked her head towards the door.

Warm aromas of garlic and roasting meat had slowly filled the hallways, and my mouth watered. The week had been long—painful and exhausting. Alvara had not exaggerated when she said Aren didn't pull punches. But I had learned a bit about anticipating the Commander's strikes and redirecting his momentum. Alec and Alvara insisted that fighting Aren was as close as I could get to fighting the Renown. His sheer size, brute force, and relentlessness were a decent sample of their capacity for dealing pain.

Ansel, it seemed, would give me a better taste of defending against demons. I'd snorted at that, grateful there was no liquid to shoot out my nose, and thankful he wasn't there to see my reaction. I wanted to like Ansel and his sharp-eyed mate. I really did, but there was something weighted and evasive about him I couldn't quite put my finger on.

THIRTY-ONE
BULLETS AND BALLS
AUGUST

Dawn had not yet warmed the glass, and the hall gradually filled with souls seeking breakfast when Alvara strode in, a young man in tow. Victorious and unscathed, she marched forward with Fae unharmed beside her.

I grinned as she passed, delivering the recruit directly to Aren. Pausing at our table, she braced an arm on the edge, snatched Alec's coffee, and took a gulp.

"Oh, boys, just keep looking pretty; I've got it handled." She flashed me a radiant smile, setting Alec's mostly drained cup in front of him before continuing with her mission. She let me know that the boys would be training me today since she would return for another soul with Fae.

Aren turned his head, his hand coming up to cover his mouth in an attempt to hide his smile. Mischief sparkled in his eyes as he zeroed in on Ansel, whose lips twitched. Aren ducked as Alec smirked, shaking his head and sipping his coffee.

"Okay," I said, my brows pinching together. "What am I missing?"

Alec flicked his eyes up, amusement breaking his facade as he took another drink, his gaze on Ally and Fae as they strapped on weapons. "Wait for it."

Scowling, I leaned back, looking from Aren to Ansel and then back to Alec without explanation. The moment Alvara and Fae vanished, Aren loomed over our table with a mischievous grin.

"Brody!" he called down the long table. Ambroise—one of the blonde Greek brothers—leaned back in his chair, cocking his head. "The boys still in Denver?"

"Yeah."

"Pity. What day is it?"

Blonde brows furrowed, Brody blinked twice before realization dawned, and his face broke into a mile-wide grin. The feet of his chair slammed into the stone as he stood with a laugh. "Happy Sunday!"

"Happy Sunday?" I questioned, glaring at Alec and beginning to resent being on the outside of whatever joke I was missing.

"Happy fucking Sunday." Alec and Ansel both rose to their feet, even the old general's face cracked into a grin.

Aren beamed at me. "We're playing hooky, Rookie."

Jersey already in place and blue cap on backward, Aren had his boots propped up on the edge of his desk, tossing a baseball in the air as the guys continued their trash talk and yanked on shirts and hoodies.

"No fucking way. I've got fifty on the Bears taking the Packers with a two-and-a-half-point spread," Alec said, popping out of his hoodie, wild grin in place as he grabbed his denim jacket. Aren chuckled from his perch as Ansel choked on a laugh.

"Oh, you sound real confident in your boys there, dipshit." Ansel spat. "Fifty on the Packers. Thirteen-and-a-half-point spread."

I observed from the sidelines, still shirtless after our run—so Alec could, in good faith, tell Ally we trained—as they both slapped cash on Aren's desk. Brody tossed me a blue and orange jersey, and I stared at it for a beat, smirking.

"What if I like Green Bay?"

Brody snorted, shaking his head. "You want *Alvara*, and you're seriously asking me that?" When I glared, he just barked a great laugh.

"Nah, nah, nah, leave him alone. He's got good taste," Ansel countered.

"Well, I agree, but Ally won't."

Aren caught his ball and turned my direction, his smirk dripping with confidence. "Brody's right, man. Trust me." With a roll of my eyes, I slipped the slick jersey on. Aren planted his boots on the floor, rising to his full height and swiping a dark blue hat off his shelf before hooking it over my head. "You're a Bears man now, kid."

It turned out, in addition to betting on sparring matches, calling counts, and demons dispatched, the coven had a fanatic love of all things sports. From summer baseball rounds to the Super Bowl, they bet on anything and everything they could get their hands on. I flipped the cap around backward, grinning.

"Alright," I narrowed my eyes on Ansel, who mirrored the motion. "Ally's a Chicago girl. So, I've got fifty on the Bears, thirteen-and-a-half-point spread." They erupted in a chorus of jeers and cheers until my cheeks ached from smiling. Aren slapped me on the back as he led us out the doors and back to the hall.

Teams neck-and-neck, Ansel and Aren braced their elbows on the bar on either side of me. Where Ansel's fingers seemed to have permanently laced together, Aren liked to talk with his hands, gesticulating as he explained the ins and outs of using my shield.

"Anybody trained that wields energy like we do can—and will—break through a shield with a consistent attack, like a blade, or even hand-to-hand combat." He knocked on the polished wood bar counter. "But a bullet—unless you're bone dry in the power department—those fuckers will just bounce right off." His eyes flicked back down to the field just as a server came into the suite, swapping one of the empty metal trays for a full one before silently slipping back into the hall.

"That's why we all wear our shields the entire time we're earthbound," Ansel explained, his eyes locked on the field as a white-and-green uniform sprinted down the edge. His posture straightened as a blue jersey collided with the man with a crack audible over the speakers, both players flying out of bounds and earning a wince from Brody. "*Christ*," Ansel growled, rubbing his temples as Aren leaped to his feet, hands in the air.

"Fuck, yeah!" Aren and Alec high-fived as the crowd roared, while Brody swiped his beer off the light wood counter.

"Anyways," Ansel continued as the commentator updated the stadium. "We like being proficient in a myriad of weapons because they're helpful in different situations. Your work in the gun range has been great—really—and while demons in human bodies will drop with a bullet, you've got to kill the spirit too. Blessed blades, holy water, take your pick. The only surefire way to end them in their true form is—"

"*Rip his head off!*" Alec roared, hands flying up to his mouth as though he could be heard through the glass down on the field.

Ansel snorted and shrugged. "What he said, but in a literal sense."

"You *decapitate* them?" I blinked, peeling the label off my bottle.

"Only way to take 'em down. And even then," he shrugged a shoulder, "I've seen some weird shit." He drained what was left of his beer, setting it on the counter with a soft thud before swapping it for the bronze cigarette case he'd set aside earlier.

Aren settled back into his stool with a sigh, returning his attention to the conversation. "The most crucial part of the process is burning the bastards after the fact. Collect all the pieces and throw them in the fire. Don't leave anything for them to reanimate."

"*Reanimate?*"

"Think zombie apocalypse—ARE YOU FUCKING *BLIND*, REF?!"

Aren slammed his fist on the bar as Ansel rocketed out of his stool, chest-bumping Brody in the same motion. "Dammit," Aren growled. "I need a snack." He rose, turning around my stool for the buffet arranged by stadium caterers, which no doubt cost more than my first car. With his broad frame removed from view, I smirked at Alec as he scowled at the field.

Hands laced behind his head, bouncing his chair back and forth with his toes against the wall, Alec mumbled, "Intentional grounding, my ass."

"Anyways," Ansel said again, running his thumb over the cross carved into the metal. "Aside from that, you really just have to learn how to dispatch different kinds of demons. Crawlers are easy—kinda fun, honestly—tormentors get a little trickier, and once you're up in the blood wolf category, it gets...gory."

"Eh," Alec grunted, his glower still trained on the game. "Only if you let it. Tell you what, kid, if you ever get a chance to watch Aren snap their necks clean off, do it. It's fuckin' wild."

"Or your Alvara," Brody cut in. "She has us all beat. Just incinerates them. Lights 'em up like the Fourth of July. No mess left."

"True," Alec acquiesced. "Couple of scorch marks. Easy enough."

Ansel elbowed me in the ribs, a subtle quirk to the corner of his mouth as he surveyed me. "*Your* Alvara. How's that going, by the way?"

"Seemed a little less ice queen this morning. Has she forgiven you for sacrificing yourself yet?" Alec glanced my way, and I returned my focus to peeling the sticker off my bottle.

"Seeing as I still don't know why the fuck I would ever do that, I don't know."

"Ally's been through enough." Ansel stated, turning his attention out the glass window. "She doesn't need to let her heart get sliced wide open again."

"I wouldn't—"

"A good 'ol boy like you? Of course you would. For her. For an innocent. Don't play villain, August, you're too obvious for that." He fiddled with his case, popping it open and closed with muffled clicks. "Besides, if you convince her to let you back in and break her heart, I'm going to have to—"

"Fucking take him out!!" Brody bellowed right as Alec roared.

"Go, baby, go!!"

Ansel turned a glare my direction, the threat clear. I snorted. "I have no intention of hurting her, Ansel."

"You better have no intentions shy of worshipping the ground she walks on," Aren growled, sitting down with two plates piled high with food. One was stacked with fruit and cheeses, the other with what looked like fancy sausages. He held them out, and I swiped a link and took a bite. My confusion at the flavor and texture must have been obvious because Aren chuckled. "Plant-based, for Fae. But I'm still not so sure about 'em."

"What about you, Rookie? Great Commander aside, should we be sure about you?" Ansel's question drew four sets of eyes off the field and onto my face, and I sucked down a breath. In all our days running and training, I'd only learned a bit about Ansel. In all his lives, he'd been a soldier—dealing pain and death his specialty—and in every single incarnation...he *loved* Lana. It was his harsh eyes, fixed on my face and hard as stone, that I stared down as the question settled between us.

THIRTY-TWO

PIZZA

ALVARA

August's training was advancing at his ever-impressive pace, but none of his teachers had managed to provoke another trigger. No amount of stress, strain, exhaustion, or pain seemed capable of drawing those distant memories back to the surface. Whatever had been hidden in the recesses of his consciousness was expertly concealed, buried beneath inconsequential moments and fleeting flashes of his existence. The precision with which whoever had bound him—whoever had bound *us*—had done so was unnerving. The very idea of a being with such magnitude of power made the muscles in my back bristle and my hair stand on end.

In my centuries of clairvoyance, I had mastered many things, including the ability to alter brief moments of mortal memory. But erasing an *immortal* mind entirely from existence? The thought alone was enough to make my soul shudder. The notion that such a being existed at all, and that August might have been their unwilling victim, was disconcerting.

Not even *my* gifts could penetrate memories bound by divinity. Despite my numerous visions, I could see with certainty that they would not alter August's future. He still ended up on the battlefield. One morning, August had asked me, as I delivered two wide-eyed callings before Aren and Saraya, why a reading wasn't the answer to all of this. To be honest, only a small part of the answer was rooted in the knowledge that I couldn't break through an archangel binding. The rest was that my workload, combined with training August and the influx of new souls, had me beyond exhausted. Never in all my years, or Aren's, had we faced so many callings for Grayshell or so many rescues of souls and mortals alike. Earthside families needed our protection in the form of wardings and my role as their personal celestial guardian. For the first time in centuries, I was spending more time on soil than on iridescent cobblestones. Beyond our missions, Aren had me meditating, keeping my inner eye open to visions whenever I could spare a moment to sit and breathe.

Reading *The Great Commander*—a soul to which I was bound in at least one past life, our memories interwoven by some greater power—would be like deciphering a myriad of patchwork. It would involve gingerly plucking out false threads to reveal the true ones. A nightmare of woven clues and false positives to scrutinize slowly, which could take days or even weeks, depending on the depth of the history. *If* I was even powerful enough to dissect them at all. As it was, I scarcely had time for the food Aren insisted I consume or the sleep he demanded be prioritized, much less sit for a week studying a soul of such unspeakable complexity.

And yet, as I unlaced my combat boots with slowly healing fingers, I found myself wondering if we should have shelved everything else and prioritized him—prioritized replenishing my strength and diving deep into the past with August. As if in answer, Aren summoned me to fetch yet another soul awakening Earthside. He, Lana, and Ansel were up to their elbows—literally—in demon guts after another healer had been attacked. We were drastically short on trackers and readers. With a sigh, I re-laced my shoes, rose on aching legs, and left once again to retrieve our newest brother.

As our little team returned repeatedly with new souls in tow and everyone uninjured, August seemed to grasp from the start how unique his situation was. The callings were coming in unprecedented, colossal waves, arriving two, three, or even four at a time. This reinforced our theory that whatever was on the horizon would require God-sized miracles to overcome. Miracles like a twelve-day ascension that had our team spread thin and demonic attacks on our healers demanding reinforcements. New York was falling prey to a series of attacks, and we could no longer ignore the situation with Senator Jones at the center.

My visions had nearly run dry—like hitting the bottom of a well in drought. Whatever was coming would require all hands on deck. Yet, August remained our training priority, at least in the arena.

August rarely allowed his eyes to stray from the courtyard path ahead of us, his chin parallel to the ground, shoulders back, and arms swinging with the motion. He had been intensely focused over the past few weeks, working to better himself and become what we needed him to be. The effort was evident in the rippling muscles down his back, his chiseled abs growing into defined ovals, and the steady growth in his arms and legs.

Being Grayshell-bound for so long could make for a weary mind and soul, so it was with that in mind that I finally spoke as we slowed to a walk. Sweat dripped down every inch of my skin, pooling between my breasts and sliding down my back. With relief, I noticed he was also drenched.

"We've sent a few sentinels to New York to investigate the politician and missing healers. A few have been in and out of Ivy Springs to monitor the crawler situation and ensure it doesn't escalate."

He nodded appreciatively as he gulped down air. "Any good intel?" he panted.

"Not much from Ivy Springs. It seems calmer now that you're not there to be hunted. New York... New York is a shit show."

He grinned that beautiful, crooked smile, his emerald eyes sparking. "Isn't it always?"

"You've got me there." I blew out a long breath.

With a slow swipe of his arm, August wiped the sweat from his brow and chuckled. "So, what do we have on this guy?"

"He's been on the list for a while. Suspected of everything: affiliations with the mob, sex trafficking. His policies are barbaric. But his eyes went physically dark a few months ago, and his power grabs are worsening. The sentinels who've gotten closest say they can smell demonic energy on him. But supposedly his vibrations aren't possessed, just influenced. We'll see."

He gave me an approving nod. "Why is it always politicians?"

"Power. That's really all it is. Demons want power, and politicians have it. Simple as that."

"Are they all—"

"Oh, God, no. There are genuine leaders, too."

"Far and few between, I suppose."

"You could say that," I conceded without further explanation. August was intuitive and had been Earth-bound more recently than I had. He would be well aware of the evils lurking there, eager to enslave as many lives as possible.

We took a few paces to catch our breath, the sound of the breeze hissing through leaves and the soft thud of our feet on the winding, iridescent cobblestone paths the only sounds. The silence of Grayshell had always been a blessing, with only the distant mental chatter of souls thinking through their day tugging at the edge of my mind. It was easy to avoid opening my thoughts, even to them, with August at my side.

"Sentinels?" His half-formed question broke my reverie.

"Hmm?"

"You sent sentinels?"

"We have them everywhere."

"Couldn't you... you know... just read the situation?"

I giggled. "Like I said, Aren oversells my abilities. I can't just... read any situation. The visions aren't summoned. They just hit. We don't fully understand how it works—what triggers and what doesn't. People I know, people I love—sometimes I can focus on them and the visions flood in. But full readings require contact."

"What if you went? Instead of the sentinels?"

"To New York? Assuming there's no shield in his circle, I could read his current thoughts."

"So..."

"Why do we send sentinels?" He huffed a laugh and shrugged his broad shoulders. I laughed too and added, "I can't be everywhere, can I?"

"I'm actually relieved that you can acknowledge that."

I rolled my eyes, but it didn't stop the blood from rushing to my cheeks.

"What if... what if someone in the coven decided to go? To investigate? Would you see it then?"

"Aren and I have experimented with that. Sometimes I can pick it up. But their resolve has to be concrete enough to trigger the threads. It can't be a game. It has to be an actual plan, which is hard if you're not *planning* to do what you're deciding to do."

"I've always enjoyed New York," August flashed a mischievous smile, his eyes sparkling. My own narrowed in response, and I felt amusement tugging at my lips. "Lived there for a few years, back in college. Had a condo for a while before moving everything west. I even remember my favorite pizza from this tiny hole-in-the-wall pizzeria tucked in a daylight basement office. It was barely big enough for a kitchen and a couple of tables." August smiled with unabashed fondness as he continued, "They drenched the slices in olive oil—each piece was too big to fit in your hand, so you had to fold it. The first time I took Freya, she tried to blot the oil off with a napkin, thinking it was grease from the cheese." His handsome face glowed with the memory.

"She sounds adorable."

His chuckle made my cheeks ache. "Oh, she's a pain in my ass. But yeah, she is."

"Aren't all sisters?"

"Touché."

"Dammit. Now I'm hungry." My stomach growled in response. Had I eaten in days? "You'll have to take me sometime."

"Oh, we'll go... sooner than you think." August winked, and I sighed, narrowing my eyes.

"It wouldn't hurt to try," I admitted. "Senator Martin Jones is our target."

"Holy shit, really?" His eyes widened.

I laughed. "Yes. Do you know him?" A half dozen images of galas and dinners flashed through August's mind, and he raised his brows as he nodded. He'd always seemed kind to August, but August knew it was the weight of his wallet, not his merit as a man, that caught the politician's interest. "Excellent," I mused. "That will help. Plan your trip to learn more about your old acquaintance—where you'll stay, how you'll arrange a meeting with him, and who will accompany you. Plan it in detail."

He nodded and closed his eyes as mine fluttered shut. Flickers of light and city scenes began tugging at my mind, and my breathing deepened. The images started small and hazy around the edges but gradually solidified, like watching water turn to ice.

A busy tarmac. A man named Jerald holding a sign that read "Porter," followed by a sleek, shimmering black town car. Giorgio's pizza—God, it was delicious. A snort of laughter escaped me as I realized August was bringing me with him. *Our usual group—Alec, Aphaea, and I—folding the oil-drenched slices into manageable pieces and laughing as we stood around a too-small bar-style table shoved into a shadowed corner.* Laughter filled that vision, and my chest warmed, knowing he would take the time to show me the things he loved.

Giorgio's dissolved like sugar in water, and I was suddenly standing in a gold gown that shimmered and clung to each line of my body. What in the hell kind of push-up bra did that to my breasts? The click-clack of high heels echoed off the marble floor, so polished it was slick. The aroma of chicken, garlic, and sickly-sweet champagne thickened the air. August was by my side, our group dispersing to explore further. He placed a hand gently at the small of my back, and I clung to the clutch between my fingers to keep my arm away from his barely exposed wrist below the cuff of his suit.

Then he was there, introducing me directly to the target. Senator Jones extended a middle-aged hand, smooth and pampered, which I took, plunging me into a reading that was too fast and furious to make sense of without direct contact.

When my eyes opened, I found August smiling, his eyes glinting with amusement. He had seen everything in my mind.

"You were saying?" A cocky grin lifted his mouth, and his eyes sparkled.

I sighed, amazed and my mind swirling. "How did you..."

"I just... had a feeling that you could see my path clearer. I knew if it was *me* deciding, you'd be able to do it."

"How?"

"I dunno. Maybe we've worked together before?"

I nodded, a mix of assent and bewilderment. His thoughts shifted over the visions that had played out before us.

"You couldn't see the reading in the vision?"

I pursed my lips and shook my head. "Not enough of it. It was too fast without actual contact. We could try again?"

"At your service," August's voice wrapped around the smile stretching across his handsome face as he flourished a bow. My heart sang at the sincerity there. He meant it.

Aren's light blue eyes stared out at the gardens, his large frame curled inward as he rested his elbows on his knees. His lips were tight as he contemplated what we had laid out before him—what the visions had revealed. He ran a calloused hand over his lightly stubbled jaw.

"You're sure about this? About his possession?"

A quick nod from both August and me. Aren chewed on the inside of his cheek, his usual humor replaced by protective, overbearing contemplation. After a long moment of silence, he bobbed his head, and his stern features softened.

"Ally, do you feel confident taking this on?"

"I do."

"How many do you need?"

"Just the usual cadre."

That signature smirk returned to his face, and his eyes flitted across the garden to the castle, as if he could see through the stones to the people within.

"What about Brody and his brothers?"

"I don't believe we'll need them, but your will is mine."

The mischief returned to his grin as he brought his eyes back to me. "You know they'll be angry for years if I don't let them accompany you into Marcus' territory." There was an unspoken rivalry between Brody and his two brothers—whom August affectionately referred to as The Greek Brothers—and the Westerlund brothers in Chicago. But New York was technically their territory. We'd only sent Bash and Sky because they were needed in that damn hospital for specialty procedures.

I mirrored his amusement, allowing it to show on my face. "All the better if I get bragging rights for a decade or two."

Aren huffed a laugh. "You know I would come with you if it weren't for all this bullshit? I've got to stay focused."

"Of course, Aren. It's a simple mission. Nothing we can't handle. And we don't need Brody." I rolled my eyes.

"I suppose Marcus and Damien will be more welcoming if it's just you anyway. Jason is always happy to work with you." His smile was full of humor as his mind thumbed through all our interactions. Jason had always made his interest in me apparent, much to my chagrin and Aren's eternal amusement.

"As for August, we'll need to protect his identity should anything go sideways. You will go in two groups—August and you, Alec and Fae with the Westerlund coven. You two can scout, and Alec and Fae can act."

Bowing my head in approval, I gave a quick, "Yes, Sir."

That bearish grin spread across his face, and Aren flicked his eyes to August.

"You. Guard her back, you understand me? We'll do our best to shield your reputation from the reality of what you are. But if shit hits the fan, *you guard her back.*"

August's expression flickered from offense to amusement. "Always."

That certainty settled in my bones, and I knew it was true. He would give all he had for me, just as I would for him. This could work—would work.

"I'll send word to the Westerlunds that you're coming. Go get what you need."

THIRTY-THREE
WESTERLUNDS
ALVARA

"You mountain dwellers always loved to make an entrance." That ancient British bass voice rumbled behind us within a second of our feet meeting the slick concrete floor. The enormous glass wall in front of us stared out at the city lights, nearly as bright as day. I turned on my heel and heard the soft thud of luggage hitting the floor as our coven dropped their bags. In my periphery, I saw August's hand rest on the dagger at his hip as he settled and took in the man before us.

Nearly Aren's size, Marcus towered over me, hands braced on his hips in mock disapproval, his bulging, tattooed muscles straining against his white t-shirt. His dark curls were cropped shorter than when I last saw him. The contrast between his deep amber complexion and electric azure eyes made him even more mesmerizing as he surveyed our little group. His gaze landed on me before that bright smile stretched across the broad planes of his face.

"Alvara, it's good to see you, sister." He closed the gap, and we wrapped each other in a tight hug. His hard muscles felt like embracing a warm stone. He stepped back and offered me his hand in a gesture of brotherhood. Accepting it, my eyes fluttered closed as he shared the last few years with me, like strobe flashes of lightning.

"You have been busy." I smiled, letting the taunt settle into my tone.

"Don't let him fool you; he's been sitting on his ass." Alec teased as he strode forward to wrap his arms around our Eastern cousin.

"If he'd been busy, we wouldn't need to be here, now, would we?" Aphaea chided as she strolled up behind her mate. Three rumbling laughs filled the living room as Damien and Jason spirited into the space from opposite hallways, their steps silent despite their colossal frames. The round of embraces continued, and then Marcus jerked his chin toward August.

"Who's your friend?"

"Gentlemen, I'm excited to introduce you to August Porter. August is my first calling." Jason and Damien both raised their eyebrows—I snorted and shook my head, earning three sets of narrowed eyes. Marcus was the first to offer a formal greeting, extending his muscled, scar-flecked hand to shake August's.

"Marcus Westerlund, at your service."

August gave a nod of thanks, then reached for Damien, who promptly introduced himself. His smooth accent matched his brother's.

"Which leaves Jason, if I'm correct?" August and the third brother clasped hands, and I realized this was August's first impression of another coven—another hierarchy Commander, and his second and third. Frankly, it was probably the easiest introduction between all the Commanders. The other clans were... different. These brothers led much like Aren, Ansel, and I did. Which, I supposed, was why the friendly rivalry had formed between the guardians among us.

Damien and Jason both shared their eldest brother's chiseled frame, though they lacked his towering height. The twins stood level with Alec and August, but the resemblance between them was uncanny, down to the way they moved their lithe bodies like the great predators they were. Their curly locks were just a bit longer than their leader's, with a bit of sun-bleaching towards the ends. In particular, their otherworldly azure eyes made their connection undeniable. Westerlund eyes, as Aren referred to them. Present in each of their children like a signature of the bloodline. Siblings bearing ascending souls weren't all that uncommon, but it was still always a bit jolting to see them together.

Another telltale sign of the brothers was their ability to shift physical forms. Only a handful of souls were shifters, and most of those were assigned to the far north. It took an immense understanding of your body and how to manipulate the energy of your cells to transform into another shape, let alone possess their biological strengths.

The Westerlunds were over five centuries old and had only been shifting for the last of those. Aren had always been deeply disappointed that he hadn't mastered that gift in all his years. In all our encounters, I'd never been able to see them complete their shift or the great predatory animals they took the form of. Rumors had circled of lions, jaguars, or cheetahs, but the brothers would neither confirm nor deny any of the stories.

Our cousins to the northwest took the form of great, terrifying wolves.

The stuff of nightmares, they rose as tall as most mortal men when they shifted, their great jaws as powerful as any sword.

August's wide eyes caught my attention, and I realized I'd left my thoughts open as I ruminated over the legends. The brothers all shared toothy grins as I centered my gaze back on them. They enjoyed my frustration of not knowing, taking pride in the legend of their other forms. Jason met my eyes with amusement, his mind thick with hope that his shift could be enough intrigue to buy us time together. He didn't balk as I smirked, a mirthless smile. We stared each other down for a moment, mirroring smiles and taunting humor. I made sure Jason was the first to blink.

Marcus, energy heavily amused, led us to the yellow, mid-century modern sectionals and bohemian tufts in front of the electric fireplace, which flickered with a welcoming light.

"So. You're going after Jones." There was no question in Marcus' voice as he sat down on the couch between Damien and Alec. He leaned forward with lethal grace, bracing himself on his knees just as Aren so often did. Jason leaned against a thick iron column behind the gathering area, arms crossed, observing from a distance. "His armada is dangerous, Ally. We've been observing them for decades. Even in youth, he posed a threat."

"We know." I held my chin high, staring down those stunning blue eyes. "We're prepared."

"You've got a plan."

"Yes. August has an in for us."

The Commander flicked his eyes to August, looking him up and down. "The rookie?"

"The rookie," August grinned, his tone haughty, "has been introduced on more than one occasion."

"So, you keep sleazy company?" Jason interjected, earning a quick glare from his Commander.

August smirked. "Unfortunately, it's an occupational hazard when you attend galas and fundraisers of any caliber."

"August and his brothers built a bit of an empire for themselves," I explained. "And as such, found themselves invited to all kinds of events. With all kinds of company."

"Martin and I share an alma mater—many decades apart, of course."

"So, college alumni gala?"

"Or a scholarship gala. I don't know which for sure, but we've seen it."

"*We've?*" Marcus raised his eyebrows, and August gave a soft jerk of his head my way. "We've?" Marcus echoed again.

"August figured out he can make decisions and allow me to see the outcome before making his next move. The telepathy allows him to see what I see and adjust as needed."

"Like Aren did to bolster the wars?"

"Similarly. Only more thought out. Aren and I worked in unison *while* we acted. August was prompting the visions to plan our advance, not cover our asses as we went."

"Aren was never one for sitting on his hands to plan." Marcus smirked.

"More action than preparation-oriented," Damien offered, and his twin nodded. August bristled.

"Well, he's three times your senior, so his plans are obviously not too shabby," August said, nearly gritting his teeth. A strange mixture of pride and bewilderment flowed into my veins. Alec and Marcus mirrored the smirk that stretched across my face.

"We mean no insult, brother. Aren is the greatest among us. But let's be real. The man is not known for his analysis as much as for trusting his gut instinct."

"His intuition—especially after siring *her*—par none," Jason added. August's shoulders relaxed a bit, but his expression didn't soften.

Alec released a pointed sigh. "So. We'll all be attending a stuffy gala that August can get us tables at. And then...?"

"Ally can get a read on Jones. See the depth of the deception. Her visions show us performing an exorcism down every thread. The question is whether his loyalties lie with the dark prince or the light," August explained.

Jason's eyes flicked to me, his dark brows arched as he thought, *Ally?*

I just rolled my eyes. *Most of the hierarchy calls me by Aren's pet name these days.*

Can I call you Ally?

My friends do.

Are we friends?

I pressed my lips into a tight smile. *I certainly hope so.*

Jason gave me a soft grin, and I could have sworn his cheeks warmed a bit. He uncrossed his arms and stuffed his hands in his jean pockets, eyes on the floor. When his gaze again landed on mine, he glanced between August and me, a soft, resigned expression carving into his features.

Aphaea's voice trilled, "I think an excuse to dress up sounds absolutely lovely." I tuned into my companions' thoughts and realized they'd been lamenting a sting at a black-tie event. She was always on the glass-half-full side, and for that, I was eternally grateful.

"I'm sure you all clean up beautifully," I added. Alec snorted and flicked his eyes to me.

"So," Marcus said suddenly, shifting the tone from jovial to inquisitive as he turned his gaze on August. "Mr. Porter. We've heard whispers from the west that Alvara's calling is the prophesied Great Commander." *Whispers from the west*—hah. If I hadn't been so miffed they'd gone without me, I would've laughed at the absurdity of Brody dropping by after their boys' day to spill the tea. "I assume, given your sire and the power rolling off you, that's you?"

August shrugged, locking eyes with me as he replied, "That's what they say."

"Bloody hell," Damien muttered under his breath.

"But you haven't triggered anything?"

"We believe that our memories have been... bound," I interjected.

"We?"

"Yes. We. A healer we rescued says we were both present in a past life that neither of us remembers. The fall of Grayshell was bound in her memories, and it took seeing us for it to resurface... but we didn't trigger each other. It's a bit of a mess, to be honest."

"You've seen the attacks on healers in your region too?" Marcus' face grew solemn, his brows knitting together with a fierce intensity.

"Yes," August answered.

"Both souls, braids, and mortals alike."

"Same here," Marcus said, scowling.

"Why, is the question of the hour," Alec interjected.

"The coming attack will be... pathogenic, perhaps?" Marcus rubbed a calloused hand across his smooth jaw.

"That's our only assumption." Alec nodded.

"Any connection to Jones?" August asked Marcus.

"Not that we've observed, but we haven't been looking for connections either. Time will tell. But all of this is why you're here, I assume?" Marcus gestured toward August.

"Aren believes so. Believes it's all connected."

"I think he's right."

The entire group nodded solemnly in unison.

"So. How has training progressed?"

"Well. August is a natural," I said, flashing him a smile. We ran through August's months with us, detailing everything from his command for the hierarchy to fly to his resuscitation of Sarah. The trio gradually regarded him with more and more reverence. When Marcus asked about any other elemental gifts, August drew up his shield, expanding it around our group and silencing the mental connections. The brothers leaned in, brows raised. Marcus straightened as the silence enveloped his mind, and I swallowed a laugh.

"And he's the strongest damn shield I've ever seen—no offense, Alec."

"None taken," Alec laughed, raising his hands in surrender. "The lightning bearer has earned that title."

"I'm really not that special. They oversell it, I swear." August shook his head, and Marcus' smirk turned into pure amusement. "So, what are your gifts?"

"Well, we're not lightning bearers by any means." Damien huffed a laugh.

"But, as Alvara was contemplating earlier, we're shifters," Jason explained.

"As in... shape-shifters."

"The very same."

"Wicked cool. What do you become?"

"Wouldn't you like to know." Jason quipped. "Tell you what, kid, come on by on the full moon and see for yourself."

Marcus snorted just as Damien groaned, "Oh, *here* we go."

"What?" Jason shrugged, eyes widening with feigned innocence. "Pup here is just curious."

"Ignore him," Marcus said, pinching his nose between his thumb and forefinger. "We all do."

"Worth a try," August shrugged, shooting me a smile, remembering my own curiosity. Marcus rose from his place on the couch and walked to the office, intending to grab a whiteboard. August pressed for more information. "Do you have more than one form or..."

"So far, we have one avatar, but we're young as far as shifters go. So, who knows."

"Still—damn cool."

"Yeah, it is," Jason hummed happily. "But lemme tell you, feathers are a bitch to keep clean."

"Well, now that we're all acquainted." Marcus cut in, shaking his head as he shot a glare in Jason's direction. "How about The Great Commander outlines this strategy for us?" He returned and set the whiteboard down on the coffee table between us, handing the marker to August. He took it, smiled at me, and then began.

WE SPENT most of the evening huddled over the whiteboard, strategizing our approach for the gala—August had discovered it was an alumnus gala fundraising for the new art building, only three days away. He'd already donated a sum large enough to make mortal men squirm, in exchange for three tables at the black-tie event.

August's breathing came hot and heavy, sweat dripping down his face as he did pushup after pushup on the bedroom floor we were sharing. I'd finished my set and was gulping down water as he finished his. We'd already completed a full circuit, and this was the last stretch, so I allowed myself a few swigs of water. After wiping sweat from his brow, August reached for the bottle and I tossed it to him, drinking deeply and panting when he lifted it from his lips.

"Thanks."

My responding smile seemed to be all he needed. I considered suggesting we go into the city to find formal attire for the gala, but a vision flashed through my mind, and I decided against it. I bit back the words, a smile tugging at my lips, which I quickly subdued.

August narrowed his eyes at me. "What?"

"Nothing. I'm just... proud of you. That's all."

That endearing crooked smile stretched across his face, a dimple popping into existence on his freshly shaven chin. "Well, thanks then."

The blood rushed to my cheeks, and I didn't bother to suppress it as he stretched in long, disciplined movements. I had been so busy over the last few weeks that I'd forgotten how breathtaking he was up close.

"You can shower first if you'd like."

"Thank you, I'll be quick."

He nodded and strode across the room to our open bags, beginning to rummage through his belongings. I followed in his wake, grabbing fresh undergarments and my favorite silk pajamas.

The bathroom was simple and elegant. Smoky gray walls met a white tile floor, and a black metal lattice shower wall stood out. Stepping up to a white vanity with black counters, I flipped on the warm water and pulled out my tiny toiletry bag to retrieve my often-neglected skincare. I jumped in and out of the shower as quickly as possible, while still taking care to shave and wash my hair.

Hurrying out the door, I signaled for August to take his turn, and he vanished behind me. The door clicked softly as it closed. My bookmark fell open to the page I'd left off, and I settled in with my novel. Fiction had always been a favorite pastime in the human world.

August padded out of the bathroom wearing only sweatpants, revealing each and every chiseled muscle he'd further defined through those long weeks of training. My core tightened as I took in the dark hair trailing from his sweatpants to his chest, fingers tingling with the urge to touch him. I tucked the blankets up a little higher against my slip, trying to suppress the response that stirred.

He had no business looking that good. None.

Wordlessly, he crossed the room, tossing his dirty clothes atop his bag.

The way he moved, with dark, damp curls sticking to his forehead and emerald eyes shadowed by the night, sent my heart racing to match my shallow breathing. That fresh sage scent hit me like a jolt of adrenaline, leaving me feeling painfully vulnerable in my silky nightgown. I'd forgotten why I'd leapt at every calling, every mission, every nest of demons, just so I wouldn't have to sit here salivating over the man I couldn't allow myself to want. No matter how I maneuvered the pieces, the vision remained the same, and surviving that twice was... impossible. But damn it, the man had me twisted up, my body demanding to feel him, and—*for fucks sake, Ally, stop thinking about licking his obliques. Jesus.*

August hoisted an armful of heavy blankets from an armoire and began to make a bed on the floor. He flicked off the light, leaving only the glow of the city to illuminate our room. Our eyes met as I sat upright in the bed.

"Oh, you don't have to sleep on the floor. I don't mind the couch." He eyed the loveseat skeptically. "Somehow, I didn't note the sleeping situation when we cast this vision." My cheeks burned, and he smiled as if he knew exactly why I was babbling like an incoherent teenager.

"How dare you." He rolled his eyes. "I'm fine. I really don't mind." He plunked down on his makeshift floor bed with comical finality and then raised one arm in the air. An aching grin stretched across my face as I tossed him a pillow. He caught it, thanked me quickly, and settled in.

A beat later, August muttered, "Fuck, it's really hard."

Choking on a laugh, my face scorching, I said, "Pleeeease tell me you're talking about the pillow."

"Oh," August chuckled quietly. "That too."

"Jesus," I laughed nervously, grinning as I tucked deeper under my sheets, his amusement settling in my chest. I tossed another pillow his way, but he hadn't expected it, and it landed smack on his face. I snorted a guilty laugh as he chuckled, the sound warm and comforting.

"Goodnight, Miss Alvara."

My face couldn't seem to remember how to do anything except smile as I thought about the man lying on the floor below my feet. It took a bit of effort, but I finally managed to respond.

"Goodnight, August Porter."

THIRTY-FOUR
SUN'S UP
AUGUST

Those damn silk pajamas would be my undoing. I knew it the moment she stepped out of the bathroom, scrunching a towel through her long, wet hair. Alvara gave a quick nod for me to take my shower, then zipped across the room toward the solitary queen-sized bed. I moved with the same urgency into the bathroom she'd vacated, the door clicking shut behind me.

Even the scalding shower did nothing to erase the image of that black lace trim edging the silk gown—the way it clung to her curves, her breasts tight beneath the fabric, nipples hard with cold. The lace plunged between them, framing porcelain skin that left nothing to the imagination. My heart thundered feverishly, and it took a frigid jolt of the coldest water to finally douse the reaction she had sparked... over several agonizing, disciplined minutes. Desire was a cruel mistress.

Dried and dressed, I kept my eyes glued to my feet as I entered the too-small room. We needed distance—perhaps a football field would let my breath settle. Or a canyon.

Marcus had shown me where the spare blankets were, and I grabbed them from the wooden dresser, hastily throwing together a bed on the floor. She protested, murmuring something about her clothes, which I adamantly tried not to think about. I turned down her absurd offer to sleep on the loveseat—it was much too small, even for her—and bid her goodnight.

Several heartbeats later, she whispered, "Goodnight, August Porter."

Every time her voice said my name, it was music to my soul. My heart raced again, and I drew in deep, steadying breaths. In through my nose. Out through my mouth.

After what could have been hours or mere eternal minutes, she spoke. Her voice was soft as the silk clinging to her, though her senses were sharp enough to know I wasn't asleep.

"August?"

"Hmmm?"

"What do you miss the most?"

The question came out of left field. I hesitated for a breath. "About... being human?"

"Mmm-hmm."

"Damn. I haven't really... let myself think about it." A dozen things churned through my mind as her emotions shifted—nerves, maybe guilt. Not that it was her fault.

For a moment, I craved the simplicity of mortal life. The ease of day-to-day challenges. But primarily, it was the faces of my family. And then there was Freya. "My friends and family, I suppose. But mostly, I miss Freya."

"Your baby sister."

"Yeah. She's way younger than James and me, but she's so full of life. A complete pain in the ass—stubborn, full of shit, irreverent in all the best ways. Somehow sensitive but untamed, but so caring for the people she loves. Loyal to a fault. She was always nurturing, wise beyond her years. If I could have one thing back... it would be her."

Sorrow washed through the room like a river. Whether it was hers or mine, I wasn't entirely sure. Perhaps a mix of both. We sat in silence for several long breaths.

"Irreverent?" She chuckled. "After the discipline twins before her?"

I huffed a laugh, swallowing the growing ache in my chest. "Yeah, she didn't exactly take after us. But I loved it—when it was directed at people who deserved it."

"Tell me a story?"

I closed my eyes, dropped my mental shield, and let her in. Her breath caught as the walls fell, and the phantom touch of her mind entwined with mine. It must've been strange, not knowing everything about someone she cared for. She hadn't asked again since the night we rescued Sarah, and I wasn't sure how to remind her that my offer still stood. So instead, I opened the memories I wanted her to see.

Freya at age two, with a mix of green and blue eyes, her auburn curls tight around her cherub face, demanding and directing James and me in her broken little language...

Freya, her hair now to her shoulders, her round face still youthful. She wore a moss-green dress that matched her eyes and a red backpack. I wiped a tear from her cheek, held her hand, and walked her across the blacktop to her first day of kindergarten...

The lawnmower's roar came to an abrupt halt as I swore. Ten-year-old Freya fell to her knees in the grass, tears streaking her face as she scooped the bloody toad into her hands.

"August! How could you?"

"I—I'm sorry! I didn't see him!"

"He barely had a chance to live!"

"Freya! I swear, I didn't see him!"

"Murderer!" she spat, sprinting for the house.

She wrapped the toad in toilet paper like a mummy, placed him in her jeweled keepsake box, and buried him in the backyard, exactly where he'd leapt in front of the mower. She made us all attend Jimmy's funeral under threat of eternal grudges...

Fourteen-year-old Freya, long and lanky, hair in a frizzy plait, climbing through her bedroom window. She froze mid-step when she saw me waiting.

"Well, look what the cat dragged in," she purred, feigning indifference.

"Funny. I was about to say the same."

"I've known you to be many things, big brother, but never a prowler. What are you doing here?"

"Catching a liar while our parents are sleeping. What are you doing?"

"Having a little fun. Nothing you wouldn't have done."

"I never climbed into a two-story window to avoid our parents."

"Nothing you wouldn't have done if you had the balls to." She smirked. I shook my head.

"Best be careful, Freya Porter. You're looking for trouble you can't get out of."

"I can handle myself."

I closed the distance and pinned her to the mattress with my forearm. She glared at me in defiance.

"No. You bloody well can't."

"Fine," she hissed through gritted teeth. "Then teach me."

"Enable you to continue this nonsense? No, thank you." I released my hold on her, and we sat up together, neither of us willing to blink first.

"They're suffocating me, August. Christ, you have to remember how they are."

"They're parents, Freya. Their job is to keep you alive. Let them do it. Please." I ground out the last word. She narrowed her sharp eyes.

"Then talk to them, please." Her tone turned mocking. I shook my head but couldn't help the smile that crept onto my face. We both broke our gaze and sighed together.

"Sleepovers, at least. I don't drink or anything. I just... I want to see my friends."

"I'll try to talk them into sleepovers, but I'm telling them about tonight too. So, expect some consequences."

"You're the worst," she groaned, dramatically collapsing back onto the bed. But she grinned up at me knowingly.

"Oh, I know."

I never did tell them about her sneaking out...

The sterile smell of sanitizer filled the air, machines beeping loudly down the hallway. Her long hair was pulled over her right shoulder, cheekbones shimmering with salty tears.

"It's going to be okay, Freya. It will be okay." I meant the words, but there was a hollowness in my voice.

She looked up, red-rimmed eyes empty and solemn. Her lips pressed together in a tight line. Freya blinked, then gave a slow, nearly imperceptible shake of her head—a motion that said simply, No. It will not.

She held our mother's weight through the entire funeral, keeping her upright as she wept over the coffin. Our dad stood in stunned silence by their side, fingers intertwined with his wife's. Freya never left her, except to fetch water or ask the servers to bring Mama food...

The Jeep door slammed behind her, and I raced off the camp road.

"Do I wanna know?"

"Took care of it."

I snatched her chin, turning her head to inspect the split across her cheekbone. "Fuck. That's gonna scar, you know."

Hazel eyes flashed with satisfaction. I turned my focus back to the highway, fighting my own amusement.

Not bothering to hide her grin, she whispered, "I left him something to remember me by, too..."

Freya, as she is now, with auburn hair cropped just below her jawline in a straight sheet, a cocky grin on her face as she leaned onto the table in front of the college-aged boy she was serving. The boy laughed at whatever she'd said, and I shook my head. A broad smile stretched across my face. Somehow sensing me, her eyes flitted away from her table and landed on mine. Only the briefest flash of surprise, and then she abandoned her order book and sprinted for me.

"You're home!" she cried, hurling herself around my neck. I wrapped my arms around her tiny frame, holding her as tight as I could...

Her singing in the car, belting out with that disproportionate alto voice of hers to a song on the radio...

She sprinted out of the Jeep and into the lake house, her last words ringing in my ears. "I have a surprise! I knew you wouldn't mind!" I followed her, brows raised in skeptical caution. Freya stood in the now professionally decorated living room, arms raised in victory.

"Ta-da!!!" she beamed. "This place has been your getaway for so long. It was time you made it feel like a refuge instead of a cave." Freya danced over and wrapped her hands around my middle, laying her face against my chest as I took in all the beautiful décor. She was amazing. "You're welcome!" she sang, pulling her face away from my chest...

"There are too many to pick from, if I'm honest." I smiled despite the burning in my eyes. My Freya.

"She's wonderful, August. Just like you said. A spitfire and a blessing. Your Freya."

"My Freya," I echoed. "She was so much younger than me, she felt like *my* Freya. My responsibility. James was too caught up in his own life—his popularity—to give her much time. So, we spent a lot of time just the two of us. She was there for everything. My first heartbreak. My first drive in my first car. Her little voice always gave advice that was much too old for her." I shook my head as if to clear the memories.

Although I couldn't see her, I could feel her smile in the air. There was a long moment of silence before I asked, "You don't remember your family?"

"Not much. It was just... so long ago. Aren has been my family so much longer than they were. They were all taken from me. Michael was the best thing that happened to me before Aren in this life. And he was taken, too." She sighed. "I don't share for pity. But I do want you to relish them while you can. Soak them up, August. Mortal lives are so short."

I nodded, my stomach twisting at the mere thought of outliving my family. Outliving Freya.

"I hope I get to meet her," Alvara's words were tentative, as though she didn't know if I'd want her to.

"I would love that. Sometime soon, perhaps?"

"I would love that."

A KNOCK at the front door startled me awake. Before the sleep had cleared from my eyes, I had leapt from the bed and was down the stairs. Marcus arrived, eyes sharper than mine felt. He opened the door, revealing a delivery girl in the hallway. She held a tall stack of garment bags. The young woman stepped back in surprise. She was maybe twenty, slightly built but curvy. Pretty in a girl-next-door kind of way. Her eyes darted between Marcus and me, and she flushed as both of us stood there in nothing but sweatpants. I flashed a grin, as did Marcus.

"Good morning," she said, voice breathy. "I have a delivery for August Porter."

"That's me. Thank you very much." I stepped forward, arms out. She set the stack of bags in my hands, clearly relieved to be rid of the weight. I signed her form and turned back to the living room. Marcus hovered behind me, peering over my shoulder as I unzipped bag after bag until the white fabric gave way to glittering gold.

"Excellent," I muttered. The gown emerged, and I tossed the bag aside. It was exactly as it had appeared in Alvara's vision. For a moment, I wondered if I would have selected it if I hadn't already seen it in her vision. Perhaps. It was stunning—form-fitting and shimmery, the thin fabric would caress every curve of her body. I had the designer build sheaths into the bodice for her blades, with two thick garter belts to hold the others. I scooped it into my arms and leapt up the concrete stairs two at a time.

As silently as possible, I slipped into our room and hung the gown on the coat rack in front of the bed, so she would see it when she woke. Alvara slept soundly, her breathing deep and even. She felt safe here. Safe enough to really rest, surrounded by her cadre and the Westerlund brothers.

When I came back down, Marcus flashed an impish grin, thick with knowing.

"Subtle, mate." He smirked as his brothers came into the room. Damien, bleary-eyed, made straight for the coffeemaker.

"We're all about to train. You want to join?"

"Absolutely. Let me grab Alec. He'll chew me out if I don't wake him first."

"Fair enough." Marcus chuckled, jerking his head toward his brothers. "They're the same way."

Alec was harder to rouse than usual. When he finally peeled his eyes open, he glared at me.

"It's early," he grumbled.

Fae opened one eye, shooting me a glare as grumpy as her mate's. Then she pulled the comforter over her face and rolled back over, cocooning herself tightly.

"Sun's up! Time to train."

"I just got back."

"From where?" I demanded.

He groaned, sitting up and rubbing the sleep from his eyes. "We had a calling."

"Last night?"

"Yeah. Here in Chicago. Late last night—shit, early this morning? I don't even remember. Alvara didn't wake you when she got dressed?"

One look at my stunned expression told him everything. "It was no big deal. Easy peasy—demons vanquished, soul dropped with Aren—we were back before sunrise. Ally might be tired, though. She kinda... runs the show, you know."

I snorted in acknowledgment. "Are there usually so many? Callings, I mean?"

Alec's lips twisted into a grimace as he shook his head. Then, without warning, he hopped out of bed and smacked his hands against his cheeks twice. "Alright. Sun's up. I'm up. Let's hit it."

THE TANG of blood and salt ricocheted through the air. My skin ached from exertion, stinging with sweat. That metallic taste lingered on my tongue as I wiped my sore mouth on my damp arm. I lifted my gaze to Marcus, who paced the edge of the ring, his eyes never wavering. Alvara had to be right—the men must take feline form when they shifted. They moved like great predators.

He snapped forward, and I parried, tearing him past me. The Commander stumbled but quickly regained his balance. Alvara's method of using their brute size against them was my favorite defense. Fighting the Westerlund brothers wasn't much different from fighting Aren. The biggest distinction was their speed, which suppressed my own Commander's. But in all honesty, Aren's strength was unmatched. It only took a few rounds of sparring to adjust to their nimble movements. We were evenly matched— none of us remained dominant for more than a round or two before our opponents found a weakness to exploit.

This was my third round with Marcus—the tiebreaker. I'd bested him in the first round, and his skin was still stitching back together under his eye. He'd taken the second, and my jaw throbbed as a reminder. But Marcus was nursing something on his left side, and I'd watched enough of his swings to solidify a plan. I mimicked his movements, parrying the way he did. After a few more missed swings, I let him make contact. One, two painful blows to my side. On the third, I twisted with his momentum, hurling us both to the ground. Marcus took the full brunt of the impact with an "oof."

I didn't bother hiding my smile as I pinned him down, anchoring my full weight on his chest. My hand held to his throat, as if it gripped a blade. His husky blue eyes widened for a moment before a grin spread across his face. The challenge in his expression reminded me so much of Aren that I nearly laughed. I jumped to my feet and extended a hand to pull the Eastern Commander up.

Both panting, Marcus shook his head once he found his feet.

"You fight like Alvara," he said breathlessly.

"Are you saying I fight like a girl?"

Marcus scoffed. "I'm saying you fight like the *Angel of Death*. Woman or not. Take the compliment."

"*Angel of Death?*" I snorted.

He flashed a taunting grin. "That's what the other hierarchies call her. Alvara's a bit of a legend. She's the second most powerful warrior most souls have ever seen. The first being—"

"Aren."

"Aren," he echoed with a nod.

We crossed to the towels he'd left draped over the back of his couch. We'd shoved all the furniture against the far wall after our run through the city. Mats now covered the concrete floor. Wiping our brows, we took the water bottles from our brothers. Once Alec handed me mine, he and Jason stepped onto the mats.

"You know, she beats him about half the time they spar."

"He picked his second well."

"He did."

"The girl's only coming into her *third* century. If your hierarchy continues to guard her like they have, she'll be unstoppable by his age." He spoke as if Alvara were a mere child. Given that he was nearly twice her age, I supposed it felt that way to him.

"No doubt. I got... lucky, being her calling."

"There's no luck."

"You don't believe in coincidences?"

"Not even a little bit. There's a plan to all of this. We just haven't seen it yet." He took a long swig from his water bottle. "She was—is—his prize. Of all Aren's accomplishments, she's his proudest. Don't tell her I said that, though. It'll go straight to her head."

"She seems pretty grounded. I'm not worried."

"She's too grounded. On second thought, a little ego might serve her well." Marcus smirked.

"She knows her limits."

"She limits herself," he countered. "If you can't feel the power locked up in her, you're blind, brother." He raised his eyebrows. "That kind of power... I don't envy her. The weight of it. The responsibility. Maybe that's why she keeps it buried. Can't you feel it?"

Memories of the summer flooded my mind. The way she fought, prayed, meditated—her power always just an extension of herself. A phantom limb, always reaching, stretching. The way she clung to Alec and me to quiet the world. His words settled deep, resonating in my core.

I met Marcus' gaze, and he grinned as I took another drink of water.

"You're her mate."

I nearly choked, gulping down the swig and clearing my throat. "Excuse me?"

A deep chuckle. "You and Alvara—you're her mate."

I shook my head. "We haven't—"

"It doesn't have to be consummated to be real. Your souls are intertwined, deeply. Don't bother denying it." He jerked his chin toward the men on the mat. "Jason has a gift beyond shifting—he sees souls, auras. The two of you are braided together. His pride is a little more intact, seeing you both like this. Eases the sting of centuries of rejection from the one girl he wanted and couldn't have."

We both stared at Alec and Jason sparring on the floor, their movements fluid, each dodging and striking blows in equal measure. A long silence stretched between us, and my mind drifted. The blur of their fight faded into memories—of her, of us, and the compulsive pull she'd had on me ever since those damn nightmares, which weren't nightmares at all.

Marcus' lips curled into a knowing smile. "She calls to you, like the wind calls a bird to fly. My mate... she was *magnetic*. I would've been anything she needed: friend, mentor, protector. That she accepted me as a lover, a husband... was more than I could have dreamed."

A beat of silence passed as he stared at the fight with unfocused eyes. "She hasn't read you yet." Still not a question. I shook my head.

"You're as much a clairvoyant as Alvara?"

He smirked, his eyes flicking toward me as he crossed his massive arms. "Not quite... but close." Marcus rubbed a hand across his jaw. "I don't unravel threads of the future like she does. But I can dive deep into the minds around me, like her. You didn't bother shielding yourself today."

"Didn't want anyone to think we had something to hide."

"I appreciate the open book. Newcomers are... always a little unnerving, until they prove themselves."

"Aren's the same way."

"I learned it somewhere."

I laughed, but then my companion's mental chatter caught my attention from upstairs. Alvara opened her eyes, saw her gown, and her conscious shields snapped up. My stomach twisted, hoping she loved it as much as I did. My mind filled with memories of her vision, and that familiar stirring clenched my gut again. Marcus grinned at me, and without a word, we moved into the kitchen to brew coffee for the girls.

Alec finally pinned Jason, and they both rose, cackling like a couple of hyenas.

"*Son of a bitch*! How often do you train?" Jason lamented. Alec flashed him a cocky grin. "Best out of five! Come on!"

"Don't be a sore loser," Damien smirked, pushing off the wall where he'd been watching. "I'm up next."

Jason ran a hand over his hair and shook his head. "Aren's army, I swear to God. You're all machines."

Marcus rolled his eyes and pressed the start button on the coffee pot.

"Grayshell has always been known for its warriors. Not exactly a shocking realization," Marcus muttered, shaking his head as he moved to the fridge. He pulled out toast, eggs, yogurt, and a basket of fresh fruit, setting them on the island—a silent offering. "I don't know why they're still surprised their half-assed training doesn't hold up."

"Who's our Goddamned Commander?" Jason threw an orange at his brother, and Marcus caught it absentmindedly.

"Who won't listen to a *command* to save his life," Marcus muttered. Jason cursed under his breath and sat down at the bar counter with a huff. He snatched a second orange, peeling it in one ongoing spiral. *The things you learned when you were immortal, I supposed.*

"You all have a Middle Realm home too, don't you?" My question brought two sets of vibrant blue eyes to my face.

Marcus' smile turned wry. "Yes, Rookie, we have a Middle Realm too."

"Does it have a name? Aren only refers to your hierarchy by your surname."

"Westerlund is the name of our home now. It takes on the title of its Commander, and changes as leadership does. But with the three of us in senior ranks, it'll probably stay Westerlund for quite a while yet."

"Has it always been Grayshell? Aren said the fall happened before his timeline." I'd never considered that the realms might change with their leader, or that the home we retreated to would change at all when the Commander did.

"Grayshell has always been Grayshell. Not all hierarchies operate the same way. We all have our... differences." He jerked his chin, and I snapped my eyes up to find Alvara descending the stairs, her deep brown hair in a tidy braid over one shoulder. She viewed Alec and Damien, now sparring on the mats, with obvious amusement. Then her eyes found mine, and she seemed to glow as she smiled. My mind threw up shields in a desperate attempt to hide my physical reaction.

Marcus set a mug of steaming coffee in front of me, and I scooped it up as my feet settled beneath me. When we met in the middle, I handed her the cup, and she brought it straight to her lips, inhaling deeply as the smell wafted her way.

"Thank you, August," she said, her full lips still curved upward.

"Of course."

"And thank you for the gown. It's perfect."

I beamed despite myself. "Good. It was no big deal."

"It is a big deal," Alvara countered softly, a blush warming her pale cheeks. "You're always so... thoughtful."

She meant it, and I felt my own face flush. Every instinct screamed at me to deflect or redirect, but instead, I said, "I'm glad you think so."

"Know so." She gave a soft laugh and looked down at her mug. Those long fingers tucked a strand of hair behind her ear. Slowly, she lifted her eyes back to mine, the intensity of her gaze stopping my breath. She pressed the mug to her lips and took a long sip, giving a quiet groan. "Damn, that's a good cup of coffee."

That sound. Her soft lips. They consumed me for a moment, and it took all my self-control not to take her mouth against my own right there in the kitchen. I wanted to hear what other sounds I could draw from her. To feel whether her lips would be delicate or demanding, yielding or urgent against mine. Her heart was racing, and I knew she could hear mine echoing the same rhythm. Neither of us dropped our mental shields.

After another agonizing few heartbeats, she turned her attention to the basket of food on the island.

"Oh, good! I'm famished," she sighed, crossing the room. I followed in her wake.

"Good morning!" Marcus smiled at her as he set a pack of bagels and a tub of cream cheese on the island alongside the rest of the food. "I assume your appetite hasn't changed?"

Alvara gave a breathy laugh and surveyed her options. "No, I can't say it has."

"Must be exhausting, saving the world all the time," Jason chuckled from his barstool, now pulling apart slices of orange. I stuffed down the territorial growl that rose in my chest.

"Oh, whatever," Alvara rolled her eyes, her tone amused. She slid a plate over and grabbed a bagel, splitting it apart with her fingers. "Thank you," she nodded to Marcus, who slid the tub of cream cheese toward her. She took the butter knife balanced on the lid and slowly spread the cream cheese across the bagel. Two bites in, she looked up at us again.

"So," she said, her tone steady, "I had an interesting vision when I woke up today."

All three of us snapped our attention to her. She took a slow, deliberate bite.

Marcus gave a dry, knowing smile. "You know."

She grinned. "You could have just asked."

"But where's the fun in that?"

"What?" I demanded, and she turned that amused smile on me.

"The Westerlunds could use our assistance disbanding a group of demons."

There was a clamor of grunts and a loud thud. Damien swore, and Alec choked out a breathless laugh. I didn't have to look to know Alec had been victorious again.

"Just another... Wednesday morning, then?" Alec panted, hands braced on his hips as he strode to the counter. "So... what are we dealing with?"

A cruel hint of a smile stretched across Alvara's perfect face as she tilted her head slightly. Her piercing emerald eyes flicked from Marcus back to Alec.

"Vampires."

THIRTY-FIVE

VAMPIRES

AUGUST

"I thought you said vampires weren't real." The words tumbled out of my mouth before I could stop them. She turned that fierce gaze on me.

"They're not. Not in the way you think of them. The unfortunate truth is that most paranormal tales and folklore can be traced to our kind. There are demons steering Renown bodies, feeding on life force, sometimes draining mortals of their blood until they're nothing but husks."

"Like over-dried fruit," Alec said dryly. "Only Alvara could get excited about encountering that particular kind of tormentor." He bared his fangs and ran his tongue along their sharp tips, illustrating how our dark cousins achieved such horrors.

"Tormentors are second-hierarchy demons, aren't they?" I tugged at the memories from our lessons.

"Some of the worst. Like the one that stabbed Aren."

"Great," I said matter-of-factly, setting my mug down with a clunk.

"You've already seen our plan," Marcus stated in that eerie, all-knowing way of his.

"I have," Alvara said softly, sipping her coffee with the nonchalance of someone discussing the weather.

"And?" Jason demanded, impatience dripping from his voice. Again, I suppressed the urge to growl at him, my territorial instincts flaring dangerously close to the surface.

"I've made some improvements." She flicked her hand, and a flame danced between her fingers.

Marcus grinned, all predator. "Excellent."

The moment the vision struck, Alvara read the apartment, the memories lingering in its walls, the discussions that had taken place. She had even snatched up a pair of Damien's combat boots from the upstairs hallway landing—boots he would've worn for an encounter with tormentors. The vampire Renown. She could see where they nested, laid traps for drunk prey that would willingly follow, and began setting her own plan in motion.

When she emerged from our room, she wore a tight black battle suit, concealing more weapons than I could count. Her favorite blades were hidden in skintight sheaths, while two double-stack Glocks pressed against her back and stomach. Her long hair had been braided into an intricate pattern, forming a high ponytail, a cascade of voluminous curls flowing down her back. Her makeup, black and dramatic, was applied with precision, more war paint than cosmetics. The black shadow around her eyes made her emerald gaze hauntingly bold, terrifyingly so. The demons might run with just one look at this celestial assassin.

That was what she'd become. Death in boots. Her preternatural grace as she descended the stairs sent a chill down my spine. That otherworldly lethality in her stride. The fluidity with which she accepted a leather coat from Alec and slid into it—a movement so smooth, it was almost a dance.

"There will be twelve Renown in the den tonight. They're guarded by two sentinels—crawlers in skin suits. I can't tell if the mortals are still there. If they are, we free them. If not, we dispose of them quietly. Our target is the nest itself. Damien has dibs on the leader, who'll be... tricky to deal with. But if Grayshell takes the basement, the three of you will win."

Fae appeared by her side, her footsteps nearly silent. Her style was as dramatic as Alvara's, with a matching leather bodysuit and biker jacket hugging her fuller frame. Platinum hair was braided back, and her face was painted in the same dark makeup.

All the men wore thick denim, white T-shirts, and fitted leather jackets, their weapons concealed beneath.

The sun had long since set. Only the orange pendant lights above the island and the electric fireplace lit the apartment. Alvara took her place between Alec and me, cracking her neck and popping her fingers. She flashed a feline grin at Marcus, who returned it.

"Just like old times," she sighed. A heartbeat later, we made the jump.

THE WOMEN LED THE FORMATION, the five of us flanking them like bodyguards. Shields down, buried deep, ensuring we stayed on the line tonight. Alvara's slim hips swayed in her leather boots, and I soaked in the way her body moved, the swagger she and Fae adopted for their roles.

Alvara had fully embraced her moniker, *the Angel of Death*. Her confidence was staggering—like a royal among common men.

Alec's focus weighed on me as he muttered, "Need help with that?"

Brows furrowed, I glanced around, dread coursing through me when I came up empty. Risking a glance at him, I caught the devilish smirk twisting his lips.

"With what?"

"That drool on your chin, rookie. Here, just a smidge." He lifted a hand as if to wipe my face. I scowled as Jason and Marcus choked back their laughter. Their amusement cracked my irritation, and I rolled my eyes, turning my focus back to her.

"Oh, fuck off." There was no bite to my tone, and Alec's satisfied snort was the only answer before the shadows guttered.

The bar they led us to glowed under a flickering yellow downlight, as if the building itself knew what was inside. "Sabotage" by The Beastie Boys blared over the speakers. A long line of choppers fenced off the road from the crowd of people waiting to get in. Staring at phones, making out, dragging on cigarettes, the line snaked around the building. The mental and vocal chatter flowed like a river, but Alvara didn't so much as glance their way. My heart began to gallop, quickening as Alvara's did, ever so slightly.

"Alec," she said, his name a command. He set his hand gently between her shoulder blades, his shield rippling down her body in a wave. Her heartbeat steadied. I stared at him in question, and he flashed a cocky, crooked grin. Repeating the motion, he sent a pulse of magic down my spine, calming the terror clawing at my insides. The rest of the group held steady. Alvara and I synchronized, our adrenaline spiking at the same moment, as though our bodies recoiled from the same scent. The very vortex of energy around the building seemed to settle, dropping like a weight into my stomach.

Alvara walked past the line of people, causing a wave of protests. A sweaty middle-aged man snarled something vile, and Fae shot him a literal wink in return. Of course, that only riled him further. Alvara didn't even glance his way. The Westerlund brothers behind us merely crossed their arms, and the man fell silent. A bouncer stood at the door, a man built entirely of sharp angles in a too-tight shirt. Alvara made straight for him.

"There's a line, ma'am," he said gruffly, but when she draped herself onto his counter, his heart began to race like a freed stallion.

"Hello, handsome." Fae sauntered up beside her, extending her hand. He reached for it instinctively. "I'm Kayla. This is Elizabeth."

And then it happened. When he took Fae's hand and then Ally's, a huge pulse of energy shot through the air, drawing me forward. Normally, Alvara's reading was subtle, but this was something else. A wave of energy rolled from her chest as her clairvoyant power struck forward, weaving into the bouncer's mind like a spider spinning its web. Fae's voice was so soft, even I strained to hear her words, though I was only feet away.

"We're here *for* Siren, and you're going to be a good man and let us in, aren't you?" He nodded, his eyes vacant of recognition as he spoke his agreement. Fae patted his cheek, flashing a radiant smile as she tossed her platinum hair over her shoulder.

"Good boy. You're not going to tell anyone we were here, either." The bouncer shook his head. "Thank you, handsome." Alvara released his hand, and Fae stroked his cheek in a flirtatious, familiar way.

"See you tomorrow, Colin!" she called over her shoulder as we all entered the club. Her voice, loud enough for the crowd outside to hear, carried a sweet familiarity. It took a great deal of restraint not to run and catch up with her as she slid her black gloves up over her elbows. Taking two strong strides forward, I grabbed Ally's leather-covered wrist, giving it a quick tug. She flicked her eyes toward me, a playful, coy smile already forming on her face.

"What the hell was that?" I asked.

"When you master your clairvoyance, you can project your will too. You'll learn in time, Rookie." She winked, smoothly pulling her wrist from my grip and returning to her bold stride, fully immersed in her role—her job. She was walking in a skin she called Elizabeth. A strong sense hit me that this Elizabeth was best left alone. This was a lesson too, one I was meant to watch, not question. Not yet. So, I took my place beside Alec, whose amusement radiated as he followed in his mate's wake. Behind us, the Westerlund brothers split off. *I'm Insane* by Ratt blasted through the club, loud enough to make my skull ring.

I've got the East door, Marcus' mental voice rumbled just like his real one.

West secure, Jason confirmed. *Handful of crawlers—you won't miss much.*

At the bar in the front. Eyes on the owner, Damien added, already in position.

The energy in the crowd made my head swim—dark and heavy, twisting toward the back of the bar. Toward the very stairwell we were heading for. I quickly marked each exit, door, and window, just as Alec and Aren had drilled into me for months. I knew Alvara's visions were thorough, but always confirm. Always cover your ass. That was protocol.

Alvara moved through the crowd as smoothly as water, swift and fluid. The roaring music echoed through the floor, vibrating up my legs and into my chest. Strobe lights flickered over writhing bodies, and the salt of sweat mingled with the stench of something...other...drifting from the dance floor.

That'd be the drugs, mate, Marcus' amusement thickened in my mind. *Nasty, aren't they?*

Repulsion churned through me. No words formed as I followed Alvara and Fae across the club. Alec clasped my shoulder in a brotherly embrace, and the unease in my gut settled.

Teach me how to do that, I shot back.

He chuckled out loud, releasing his hold on me. *I will.*

Alvara led us down a stairway, her ponytail bouncing with each step. Though the basement room was abandoned, it was full of smoke and reeked of bone-deep dread, permeating every inch of the building. She paused, sliding a glove from her hand, shoulders held tall. Pressing her palm to the wall, she closed her eyes, a soft smile playing on her lips before she jerked her chin forward and slid her other glove off.

Alvara strode down the shadowed hallway, turning right when it forked. Awful, icy air filled the narrow passage, reeking of decay. It felt like pushing against an invisible forcefield as we moved on. Energy pooled in the upper corner of the far wall, and my eyes blinked against the gloom as my heart froze.

The great, webbed blackness arched from one wall to the ceiling and down to the next—a dark, soul-sucking presence, pulsing with steady power. Steady with...sleep. I felt it in my core, but still glanced at Alvara. She nodded.

Sleeping tormentor. I need Grayshell with me, Marcus.

Already on it.

Alvara placed her hands against the wall, her thoughts playing out as she studied where our target had vanished. Still, she sent the thought to the group to ensure none had missed it.

Third door on the left.

We crept down the hallway, careful to avoid rousing the tormentor in the corner. Vampires, crawlers, webbed beasts suspended in the air—I wasn't sure I wanted to know what they were capable of. The stench of adrenaline and sweat clogged my nose, and I fell in line behind Alec with urgent ferocity.

Fresh fear—sharp, unyielding. We could save this person. Whoever it was, they didn't want to be here. Beyond the partygoers upstairs, something evil lurked. *Close.* Too close.

Alec paused at the third door just long enough for us both to take a deep breath. Alvara's eyes fluttered shut as she ran through her vision of what we would find. Where we needed to be. Energy pulsed off Alec, so feral I half-expected him to kick the door down. But when he obediently tried the handle, I was caught off guard. That Hollywood entrance wasn't our style.

The door was locked, but Alec turned the cheap brass knob, and I heard the soft click of the mechanism. As the music upstairs shifted to "I Don't Need Love" by Sammy Hagar, he tossed the door open silently and surveyed the room.

We moved in, quiet as shadows. I forced myself not to hold my breath. The first of the Renown had his fangs buried in his mark, a girl whose eyes were wide with terror. He pinned her against the couch, her tiny arms above her head. His massive body dwarfed hers. The color had drained from her face, her cheeks already hollow.

Sick.

I'd never felt anything like the wave of despair radiating from her. Her exhausted, purple-rimmed eyes flicked toward us, widening slightly. Before she could even react, Alec had his knife buried in the monster's neck, slitting his throat before any alarm could be raised. Rotten blood spurted across the girl's horrified face. The monster turned, enraged and shocked, only to collapse to his knees, giant hands pawing at his gushing throat. Alec sneered and kicked him to the floor with a soft thud. He looked at me, jerking his head as a reminder to stay close to Alvara and Fae.

Fae, following her nose to confirm Alvara's vision, magicked her way into the locked bathroom. If the images in her mind hadn't told me she was successful, the heavy thud of two bodies hitting the floor would have. Anger pulsed off her like a freight train, shaking the air.

Too late.

Goddammit, Alvara growled.

You knew we would be, Al, Fae reminded her, shifting into position.

We had to fucking try. Alvara's curse was low, filthy, and threatening. Now she wanted a fight. I'd seen the aftermath of a Renown battle before, and I wasn't eager to witness another.

Focus on who's left. We've got the first floor, Marcus commanded. The moment he spoke, Ally was moving.

I stayed glued to her heels as she flowed down the hallway, her dark ponytail billowing on a phantom breeze. Horror and awe washed over me as I realized it was *her* breeze—her anger—and the only warning the next room would have before she snuffed them out like candles. She flashed me a wicked grin, raised her booted foot, and kicked the door in.

THIRTY-SIX
FOREPLAY
AUGUST

The woman's unseeing brown eyes stared right through me, as if I were nothing but a phantom. Perhaps that's what we were to them, in that form, under that spell. Yet she sat, unmoving, as I washed the blood from her neck and face. Fae drew water from the sink, wrapping it in rivulets around the woman's matted blonde hair, cleaning it as I healed the bite wounds on her sun-kissed neck.

"Cameras are clear," Damien informed us as we finished. I rose to wash my hands while Fae dried the woman's hair. The sudden tang of rancid blood wafted into the air as Alvara dispatched another tormentor she'd found lurking in a closet, her lip curled in a snarl as she dropped its flaming corpse to the ground. Her flames were a contained force—like Brody had said—incinerating the bodies we left in our wake.

She whirled on her heel, chest heaving, black and red blood slipping down her pale hands and dripping onto the tile. It was Fae's victim—now healed and clean—who whimpered in her hypnotized state, catching Alvara's attention. Emeralds snapped between me and the woman.

"Fuck," she muttered, taking a heaving breath and wiping her palms on her shirt as she closed the distance. Alvara was the one who instructed the victims on what they would remember and wiped away what we didn't want them to know—namely, *us*. They had already turned the bodies to ashes, the cameras were erased, and the memories of onlookers altered by the Westerlund Commander. Slowly, Alvara crumpled to her knees, her jaw locking as her hands cupped the woman's tiny, trembling ones. With a maternal touch that shocked me after all she'd just done, she wiped the tears streaming down the woman's face. Emeralds locked onto those deep brown eyes as Alvara's voice cracked when she said, "I'm so sorry."

In that enchanting, melodic tone I'd first heard in my dreams, Alvara told the woman the story she would remember and what she would do. I looked away, unsure if getting into someone's mind like that was kinder than the harsh reality.

The reality of being kidnapped, tortured, and fed on by demons? Alec pressed. His living mark had already wandered—a bit dazed—back through the crowd of dancers upstairs, toward her car on the curb a block away. Jason and Damien ensured her safe arrival home with wards around her vehicle.

Well...when you say it that way.

A snort from the other room was the only response.

Once the scene was clean, we sneaked out a back door. Jason had disabled the alarm while Marcus disposed of the suspended tormentor in its true form in the hallway.

It had taken only seconds. Under a minute from the moment her boot smashed the door in, Alvara became a phantom on the wind. The literal wind, as she unleashed a surge of anger, transforming it into a smaller version of the tornado she'd spun when Aren was wounded. She had learned how to harness it, wrapping protective circles around the victims as they fled. Before anyone could scream, I raised my shield as instructed, and Alvara had three Renown telekinetically pinned against the wall in a heartbeat. In the next, two of them crumpled to the floor, their thick necks broken at unnatural angles.

The third remained pinned against the wall, blood beading across the surface of his face as small cuts appeared—her wind tearing across his flesh. He clawed at his throat as the air was sucked from his lungs, and she stared at him with the predator's finality that would freeze hell itself. My mouth went dry—and it wasn't from the storm. Or from the two surviving women who made a desperate dash to accept my outstretched arms.

"Where are the rest?" she demanded, her voice steady through the roar of the wind I had contained to our room. I pulled both women around the corner, passing them off to an awaiting Fae and Alec, and rushed back to Alvara's six.

The monster sneered, inclining his head to the side, pure feline. She tore more air from his lungs, and his eyes widened as his body failed to fight the force pinning him there. As though he attempted to summon a shield, but couldn't. He made to speak but had no air to do so. Without warning, the storm ceased, and she dropped him into a heap on the floor.

The monster tried a second and third time to open his mouth, but it failed again. He gasped for breath, the stench of him thick in the air as he worked to suck any trace of it into his lungs. She lowered onto her haunches, bowing her head to look into his eyes as he clawed onto hands and knees.

"Where are the others?" she demanded, her tone soft, unruffled.

A low chuckle escaped him as he wiped blood from his nose. "Why don't you *read me* and find out?" His voice was barely audible as he panted, but still defiant. Then he spat rancid blood toward Alvara, who—of course—had seen that coming and blocked it with a shield.

"So, we're acquainted? Not the best way to greet an old friend."

"Alvara of Grayshell," the man rasped, "is no friend of mine."

"Well, I would certainly say not." Alec stepped into the room, washing his hands with a glowing ball of summoned water. "She would never sully herself with the likes of you."

Alvara's lips curved upward, and with a flourish and contraction of her long fingers, she began sucking the air back out of the beast's lungs. His eyes widened, and Alec laughed—a sound that was humorless and cold.

"I would tell the lady what she wants to know, if I were you," Alec stated flatly, bored. He carved the blood from under his nails with a silver blade. "This is her idea of foreplay, and I assure you, you don't want to see how that ends."

The monster raised his onyx eyes to survey his captors, his gaze hesitating when it fell on me. He sneered again, blood soaking his rotting teeth. Those dark eyes twisted with ire. Fighting against the restraints, he raised one shaking hand and pointed at me.

"He will... come for you... Commander. He will claim you."

Despite the warning in her vision, I could tell hearing those words aloud turned Alvara's stomach as much as it did mine. It was just a flicker of shadow in her eyes before her mask was back in place.

"I'm bored of this," Alec drawled. "Doom and gloom, my master will find you, yada-yada. Let's skip past that bit. Give us something useful, or I'm inclined to tell her to be rid of you."

"A name might be helpful," Fae sauntered forward, her hands dripping with dark, rancid blood. She had enjoyed her last kills, just like Alvara—their revenge for mortal women who couldn't defend themselves.

"We do not speak it," he rasped.

"Well then, I suppose we'll let Alvara do this her way." Alec swaggered forward, kneeling beside Alvara. They exchanged a cruel smirk. "She does love to put on a good show." The monster's black eyes filled with dread—real, true terror—before he was thrown back against the wall in a great, icy gust of wind. Alec took over the shield, and Alvara flicked her fingers open to reveal a dancing flame. She allowed it to lick forward with the snap of a whip, but it didn't touch him. The monster cowered but didn't yield.

She sighed. "I'm bored too. And I'm afraid we have plans after this, so let's move along?" Alvara stared into those unyielding eyes, sighed once more, and strode forward. She pressed her bare hands to either side of his face. Her lids fluttered as she absorbed the information we needed, and when the visions stopped, she blinked once, deliberately.

"Since I know you won't dare take a message to your leader, I'll send one of my own." The beast's black eyes widened, his expression desperate. "Don't worry, though. Adrastos will meet you in Hell soon." There was a flash of heightened fear at the sound of his master's name, drawn unwillingly from his mind, and then, with an inhumanly quick twist of her hands, he was dead on the floor.

Once we'd cleared a block on foot, led by Marcus and his hulking brothers, they turned to face us. Alvara turned back to us as well, seeking Fae's eyes.

A soft smile played on her lips as she said, "We're going to need an outfit change for the next part."

We watched the new information solidify into light, color, and structure in her mind. Her plan came together as she pulled on each thread. Marcus' brows furrowed, his lips a tight line.

"We're going after Lorenzo's?" His question rumbled steady, but there was a flicker of fear in his energy.

"Yes. We're *clearing* out Lorenzo's."

"I didn't intend to throw you directly into the hub, Ally. Aren would have my head on a pike."

"Aren will have to dredge you up from the afterlife if you attempt to do this without me." She meant it, and Damien scowled. "As for retribution for taking me with you... He'd have to catch you first," she winked, her mental shield snapping up fast as a whip. The hint of teasing was sincere in her voice now, all traces of acted swagger gone. Marcus narrowed his eyes, turning his face slightly away from her, his shield snapping up just as quickly. The brothers did the same.

"You know." His voice was wry, mirth glinting in his eyes.

"Yes. I do. And I have to say, it's splendid you boys lasted so long." She didn't bother to hide the taunting tone or the sparkle in her gaze, like a baby sister teasing her big brothers. Jason and Damien both narrowed their eyes. The former swore under his breath and let his gaze settle on his feet. The latter rubbed a scarred hand over his brow.

She knew their other form. I realized it at the same time Alec and Fae did. Alec started, eyes widening.

"Tell me. Tell me, tell me, tell me!" Alec rose on his toes like a child. I smirked.

Alvara shared my reaction but reached a bare hand toward the Westerlunds. "There are two threads that will require your... furry friends to make an appearance. And three that don't. If we can execute one of those three, then nobody else needs to be the wiser. But you need to see the triggers now, so you're prepared... and I don't die."

Jason snapped his eyes up from the ground, shock slithering across his features as he soaked in her steady expression. She wasn't exaggerating. The cost of not shifting could be her life. Marcus and Damien exchanged wary glances, and as one, reached forward to grab her arm so she could project the paths for them to examine.

As one, they nodded obediently when they released their hold on her. Marcus lifted his chin in defiance before he spoke.

"No harm will come to you, Alvara."

The black lace dress hugged every curve of my body, a slit up the leg cutting clear to my mid-thigh. I shifted my weight, testing the fabric to ensure it allowed enough movement. The fur-lined boots and the matching coat set on the bed would more than compensate for the winter chill. Marcus had insisted that Eloise, his mate, wouldn't mind this one being sacrificed to our cause—a preliminary thank-you for not allowing him to fall on the field, as he inevitably would in our absence. His intuition had told him as much, without the ability to cast visions and dissect them choice by choice. That was why he'd needed our help, why he hadn't proceeded without us, patiently waiting to see what would bring our paths together.

Jaw flexing, Marcus shook his head, hesitation clinging to every ounce of his aura. "Aren would never forgive me if anything happened to you." His bright eyes flicked from me to Alec, who rested his arms around Fae's waist, then to August. "A member of Grayshell would be bad enough. But risking half of his deadly seven..." Marcus shook his head again, that muscle feathering in agitation.

"Not to mention The Great Commander," Jason interjected, knocking a shoulder into August.

"Marcus, we can do this—*you* can do this—you have my word." I'd played verbal *Jenga* for the better part of an hour, but my words did nothing to ease the idea of taking four of Aren's prized warriors right into the heart of an insidious nest. "Nine out of ten threads end with everyone standing. If we abandon you, none of them do. But you know that."

"Fuck," he growled, pacing, his eyes flicking up to his brothers, seeking some form of reassurance.

Damien obliged, shrugging. "You know we'll have her back. Let Ally take the lead for once. Aren listens to her. For someone who admires him so much, maybe you should take a hint." I smiled softly, suppressing a chuckle, just as Jason draped an arm around August's shoulders.

"Besides," he flashed that mile-wide smile, "I've just been dying to sharpen my claws. What fun is a secret if there's no one else to keep it?"

"Fine," Marcus growled. "But so help me God, if you let them get to her—"

"There will be hell to pay," Alec cut in. "Yes, they know. Let's move this along."

Three shimmering threads positioned August and Alec right where I'd need them, and those were the threads I projected for the coven to view and memorize.

"Alvara, this isn't what we came here for." August reminded me for the millionth time, straightening the deep merlot tie over his white button-up shirt. In the corner, Marcus' old record player quietly hummed the vocals of Ella Fitzgerald and Louis Armstrong singing, *They Can't Take That Away From Me.*

"And if we withhold our help, Marcus will fall at the hands of the Renown." I stated flatly. August groaned, the sound desperate. "Marcus has a wife—a mate—and two children to return to. I will not turn my back on him. And neither would you. Your power is strong enough to turn the entire evening around, if you let yourself." He flicked his green eyes to me, and I knew he would find no trace of fear in my own, that he would scent the same confidence from me as his nostrils flared. "Remember. This is what I do, August."

It was true. I had stared down death more times than I could count, and my team had more than earned my trust. With August by my side, and the Westerlunds on high alert, ready to pounce at any of the triggers I'd shown them, we would all be fine.

August pursed his lips, unease still shining in his eyes. "I don't like this."

"I know. But this is who I am. Who *we* are. In three hundred years, you won't think anything of throwing me out like bait on a hook." I flashed him a wink, but he flinched. I softened my expression, my voice along with it. "August, I have complete faith in you. In Alec and Aphaea. In Marcus and his brothers. If a temporary risk is the price for saving my brother's life, it is no price to pay."

He nodded, but obedience, not confidence, shone in those emerald irises. For now, obedience would do. The visions assaulted my mind again, the thread where August was responsible for saving my life solidifying into a more concrete picture. I smiled up at him.

"See? Sixty-forty, you keep me alive yourself."

He glared at me. "Not helping, Ally."

"It's helping me." I snorted a laugh, and despite himself, August grinned. That beautiful, sincere smile I found myself living for more and more with each passing day.

LORENZO'S FINE Italian Dining was a stunning restaurant; the tan stucco walls gave the entire room a warmth that was enhanced by the abundance of vibrant dark reds and the fact that every metal surface shimmered gold. Black tablecloths covered the dining surfaces between each velvety merlot booth. I marked the easiest exits—both doors and windows—and confirmed the numbers to match the visions. An old habit that refused to fade.

August's hand against the small of my back was a tether to this world as I honed in on my own battlefield calm. The energy of our group was palpable, and I felt the eyes on us from behind the open kitchen wall. The operatic Italian music seemed to grow quiet, at least muted within my own mind as it slowed down and grew cold. Again and again, I walked myself through the thread that had grown most vivid, the others watching it play out in my mind.

I sat at the armchair at the head of the table, not missing the perceived authority it conferred to its occupant. Watching the vision on that chilly street corner, Marcus grinned when he saw me take it, reminding me internally that symbols have power. This was my mission—take it. So, I kept my chin high and shoulders broad as my hands settled on the arms of the chair. The smell of garlic and pasta overpowered the presence we knew to be in the building. Any other time, I would have allowed the growl in my stomach to steer me toward food before this strike. But as a man in a black suit, with eyes as dark as obsidian, sneered at me as he walked toward us, I knew our plan would unfold as quickly as we'd thought.

The demon's energy was palpable, dark and warped within the skin suit. I flashed a grin back at the man as he moved our way, knowing it was all teeth, and that my power would be vivid in my eyes. Public assaults were never my favorite venture, as there was too much potential collateral, but the plan accounted for that too. Fae, graceful as ever, walked toward the back of the restaurant to the hallway that held the bathroom. The possessed man eyed her warily, no doubt sensing exactly what we were without needing to be any nearer. The way he surveyed her—black eyes a dark contrast to his pale skin and honey hair—told me he was indeed the head of this nest and would know where we could find Adrastos.

The energy of the building spun into an eddy, tight and heavy at its center as the demon lost control of his glamour. The mortals around us pressed hands to their full stomachs, as though sensing something that reminded them of nausea. I kept my eyes on the possessed man, unwavering, power poking and prodding for any sign that the host remained. As the cyclone tightened its dark pull toward the back of the building, I sensed the others beginning to approach, intending to kick us out of the restaurant. With a smooth rise to my feet, napkin in hand, I blotted at my lipstick, giving Aphaea her cue.

Screaming ensued.

For a heartbeat, the puppet froze, glancing back over his shoulder. But when Aphaea's distant, shrill, panicked voice shrieked, "Fire!!!" The resulting chaos was perfect, and I flashed a taunting grin at our adversary. He advanced.

Our table stood as the others began their panicked dash for the exits, each of us locking our eyes on our targets as they emerged from the kitchen and stairs to the basement, where our true aim and greatest challenge lay hidden. Fae repeated her panicked scream, and the guests began to sprint, knocking over glasses of wine that lapped against the hardwood floor and ripping the tablecloths as they fled. The metallic clatter of silver and the shatter of porcelain and glass became a cacophony within the room. Like granite statues, we held our ground in the center of the restaurant, hands flexing as we dove into our power to draw out our most lethal blows. The crowd parted around our long table like a river around an island, flowing out into the open air beyond us without noticing our lethal stillness.

And then they struck.

A whip of darkness lashed out at me first, and I deflected it with a flick of my wrist. The others braced shields to absorb the lethal whips of power.

Voice calm, unmoved, I demanded, "Where is Adrastos?" The name of nightmares, confirmed after all this time. The puppet recoiled from the question, and I smiled at him, summoning all the sweetness I had left. "We'd like a word."

"Bitch," was the only insult the puppet could muster. I laughed, and the sound was echoed by my comrades.

"Very original." Alec smirked, now facing the oncoming dozen attackers. That fiery swagger burned in his tawny eyes as he turned them on me. "Didn't tell us we'd have a wordsmith on our hands, Al."

Fae snorted as she strode back across the room, ignoring the two sentinels closing in on her position. They wouldn't get a chance to touch her, and she knew it. The puppet glared at me and unleashed a string of vulgar insults. I wrinkled my nose, allowing disgust to twist my features as I gathered my power into my hands, bound together at my chest.

"Language, boys," I hissed quietly. With that, I flung my hands out in a great wingbeat; power exploded from my chest, and the possessed bodies flew with it, bones crunching against the stone and stucco walls with lethal finality. I snapped my fingers, and the empty corpses ignited into roaring flames. Only the leader remained, staggering, snarling low and guttural, just as I'd anticipated. I flashed him a toothy grin, and our dance began.

The others all sprinted for stairwells or jumped out of the room to their designated positions downstairs, and I kept my eyes trained on the demon. Only Alec remained by my side, his steady heartbeat an anchor as I lashed out.

I pitched my arms forward with all the force they had—one, two, three whips of fire cracked toward him. The demon deflected the first two, but the third struck with a branding wound to his shoulder. Dark blood blossomed through his white button-up, and he hissed with pain, quickly slipping his arms free of the black suit jacket, which crumpled on the floor.

Thoughts swirling with hatred, pain, and malice, the demon stalked forward, dark power summoning to his outstretched fingers. He hesitated for only a second when I flashed him a cocky wink, mimicking Alec's irreverence, and then threw up an enormous shield, shoving it forward. He barely leaned into the impact, unfazed, and Alec added his own barrier. Together, we pressed forward, and the demon set his hands against the wall, which sizzled and cracked against his flesh as he leaned into it, a snarl on his lips, shoes screeching across the hard floor as they were forced forward. Chaos erupted below us, and only the visions, along with centuries of training, kept my feet rooted to the ground beneath them.

At once, Alec and I released our shields, and the puppet stumbled forward. A sickening roar erupted in the basement, and I knew the tormentor beasts had been released. My stomach twisted. The timing had to be so exact to work. So, so exact. I hissed, and we both bared our teeth at the demon. I threw up one more shield to no avail and gave up on the telekinetic attacks.

Alec, recognizing where we were in the timeline and who we faced, pulled on his water-wielding abilities as flames erupted down my arms. Fear flashed across those onyx eyes before he schooled his expression back into a sneer. The tang of blood and adrenaline filled the air. I knew that scent. That fear.

August.

Before I could process what it meant, a wave of black energy pulsed forward, pushing us back a step. Alec held a shield against the darkness, but he roared in pain that was not his own, the bond to his mate tugging on him like a noose. He bellowed, and we moved in unison. Alec threw his rope of water toward the demon's feet, while fire roared from me in a wall. As the demon whirled to avoid the flames, he was pulled on the current of raging water, feet sliding out from under him. The instant he hit the floor, I conjured wind and flame into a fiery tornado. The puppet had just risen to his feet when the firestorm wrapped around him. Too much energy drained to make a jump. Still pulsing my power toward him, I sprinted for the stairwell, ignoring the shriek of agony as the demon was burned alive. I shook off the familiar smell of charred flesh.

We took the stairs three at a time, madly dashing for our friends and coven as the screaming demon was snuffed out. My power happily returned to the well in my chest as we rounded the corner onto the last landing. But that reunion was brief, as icy terror filled the air, chilled and palpable, as we skidded to a stop on the long landing.

My heart plummeted. *No, no, no.*

Shit, shit, shit! Alec roared in his mind as we took in the thread that had unwoven below our feet. Panic swelled in his chest. *Adrastos?* he demanded.

I shook my head and threw myself down the rest of the stairs.

So much worse in real life than in the vision, the great beasts' maws were stained with crimson. Hairless and the size of horses, the great blood wolves had already drawn lifeblood from our ranks. There was no time to assess who wore their own blood and who wore another's. Fae clutched her arm around her ribs, a long dagger in her free hand, blood spattered against her face as she snarled at an oncoming monster. The creature dove, and Alec blasted a cannonball of a shield forward, knocking it backward.

These tormentors, at least, could be manipulated telekinetically. Marcus, Jason, and Damien moved together like a well-oiled machine to bring down a demon of their own. My eyes locked on August, whose daggers were both plunged into the chest of one beast as another lunged for him. I threw a shield forward to collide with the enormous, gaunt blood wolf. The wall was just enough to push him away from his mark, but not enough to bring him down. My canines slid into place as the wolf turned to me, and I ran my tongue over the tip of one before snarling at the hairless demon. It licked its maw, eyes locked on a new target. It lunged.

The great pony-sized wolf soared forward, onyx eyes fixed on me. I whirled, a new thread unraveling in my mind as I fought to stay present. I had to stay present, as the beast was above me, and my blade was plunging, angled up through its ribs to its heart. As the demon collapsed before my feet, another was upon me, gnashing its jagged teeth. A fierce wave of flames erupted from me, and the wolf yelped in pain as it skidded across the floor, engulfed in a bright orange inferno. The building began to fill with smoke, the screams of fire alarms shattering through the rooms above us. Charred flesh thickened in the air and washed horror over the fleeing onlookers. A wave of icy darkness pulsed through the room, and I knew he was close. His anger palpable as he marched toward the source of the chaos. New threads sliced through me, sucking the remaining air from my lungs in a gasp that caused August, Alec, and Marcus to whirl to face me. Three sets of wide eyes met my own. True terror written there. One. We had one thread left where all of us would leave that basement alive.

You've got this. I reassured them. Just to Jason and Damien, I added, *No matter what happens, you get your brother home to those babies. Do you understand me?* Their assent was wordless, but I heard it nonetheless.

The thoughts of the approaching monster reached my mind. Not Adrastos. But someone close to him. Demonic energy sizzled through the walls as the giant man of Renown lumbered down the hallway. He hadn't even emerged into the room when he threw his immense, dark power at August. So strong. Too strong. He knew exactly who was upon him.

Half a dozen visions flashed through my mind. Horror threatened to break my focus as I took the one path that would save us all. Holding my breath, I wrapped my shield around myself and leapt into the path of the fatal blow.

THIRTY-EIGHT
BROTHERS OF RENOWN
AUGUST

Agony rippled through my side and arm, and I roared. Alvara's horrible scream tore through me as she absorbed the impact of the giant's dark blow. But I felt it—each terrible inch of pain as her bones cracked under the sheer force. His abominable power shattered her shield as though it didn't exist. Through the bond that had formed between us, her pain became my own. That power was meant for me. Horror washed over me. My heart seemed frozen in my chest, bile rising in my throat.

Despite the pain tearing her apart, Alvara's mind remained calm as the enormous man emerged from the hallway, a taunting sneer etched across his cruel face and empty obsidian eyes. Cruelty was woven into his very essence. His inky hair fell to tattooed shoulders, and he wore only a gray tank and black denim pants—as if he were ordinary. He reeked of sin and blood, and... grief. His scent was a grotesque mix of pine and carrion. Desperation flared in my chest. Why wasn't she lashing out? Why not strike with those phantom talons and claw into his mind? Was she so badly injured she couldn't advance?

A humorless laugh, lower than even Marcus' or Aren's, rumbled through the room as the nearly gray-skinned man took in Alvara, who cradled her left arm against her body as she rose back to her feet in defiance. Her teeth were gritted with the effort. Still, her energy was calm, giving off only the scent of pain, but not of fear. It was a fight against every instinct not to rush to her and pull her out of harm's way.

Follow the plan. I would follow the goddamned plan.

Marcus and Alec did the same. Their bodies shook with the discipline of it, the latter straining against the pull of his wounded mate behind us.

As her vision had shown, the monster leaned down to grip Alvara's throat. She let the beast hoist her into the air, no more than a rag doll, onyx eyes meeting emerald ones ablaze. Her mind flashed in strobe-like bursts, and I realized she had allowed the assault to read him—every inch of his mind and soul, or at least as much as time allowed.

The great beast recoiled in recognition, dropping her back to the ground. But it was too late. She caught herself with a tiny whimper and smirked up at our enemy. Alvara pulled her shoulders back, chin raised defiantly, despite the arm cradled to her chest. Her smile grew—ferocious, all teeth and drawn fangs.

"Hello, Agamemnon," Alvara ground out through clenched jaws. Her bravado faltered as the inability to draw breath set in. The blow or the drop had broken her ribs. Alec filled the gap, swaggering forward on her opposite side, with a confidence I was sure he didn't feel.

"How kind of you to share your plan," Alec chuckled, a cold, mirthless sound. "We've been wondering why our healers were falling."

The briefest flash of surprise crossed the monster's face before it tightened into a scowl.

"It's already in play, half-breed. There's no stopping what's coming for you."

"Beg to differ, *Agamemnon*." Alec inched closer to Alvara's side, matching the monster's arrogance. The beast snarled at the sound of his name on Alec's lips. "Cool name, by the way. As in Menelaus and Agamemnon. Right?" Alec inclined his head as he touched Alvara's back, his hand glowing white. "So, you're... his brother. Adrastos' brother."

The answer was there in Alvara's mind, and Alec fished it right out as he healed her ribs—quickly, silently. Her chest slowly expanded, a little deeper with each breath. The monster's brows knitted together over those tight eyes. Anger flashed as he came face to face with his enemy, understanding dawning when his gaze flicked back to Alvara, who smiled sweetly through her pain.

"He said you were coming," Agamemnon snarled. "You really are the seer of the North, then." An emotion flickered across his eyes so fast I couldn't read it. He took a lumbering step forward, setting my hair on end.

"In the flesh, motherfucker," Alec snapped, stepping between Alvara and the beast, his arm around her shoulder, refusing to lift his healing touch from her spine. I moved to flank him, bolstering my shield around our group.

"Pathetic." The monster turned to deliver a backhanded blow, but his hand was glued to his ribs. Marcus and Alec pulsed shields forward. Alvara inclined her head, her smile twisting from sweet to cruel, and raised her good hand. She cupped it as if to strangle him, and as her fingers closed in, I realized that was exactly what she was doing. Slowly, she clenched her fist, and Agamemnon's eyes widened as the air was sucked from his lungs.

A collective roar erupted as the remaining three beasts sprang into action. The wind began to tear through the room as the monster staggered forward, forcing his way through the shield, like walking through waist-deep mud. Jason, Damien, and Fae engaged the blood wolves as I dove forward.

A scream from his mate had Alec whirling toward her, terror rippling off him as he dove for her. In that instant, the shield faltered, and Agamemnon lunged forward. He grabbed Alvara's throat and hoisted her back into the air. I hurled my shield against him again and again. He didn't so much as sway where he stood. Alvara's emerald eyes were unwavering as she stared him down in a race for the last ounce of air in their lungs. Marcus' shield battered against the monster, but he remained unaffected. I threw my body against it, not feeling the pain as I hammered it with my fist, lightning sparking. The storm flickered like a dying lightbulb, and panic sent my heart hammering in frantic staccato. I raised my own shield again, advancing with all the rage buried in my bones.

The lights around us flickered out, and I blinked frantically into the gloom. Alvara's storm ceased its assault. My shield guttered into nothing as an eerie melody began to creep down the hallway, lifting the hair on my neck. Bit by bit, my body drained of magic, the sensation like blood leaving veins.

Marcus stared at his hands, then threw himself forward, gripping his blade, but Agamemnon grinned, the expression entirely devoid of joy, and seized Marcus' throat. He hoisted the enormous Commander until his feet dangled just below Alvara's.

Marcus slammed his blade into the monster's arm, and Agamemnon bellowed, but barely yielded an inch to the blow. He just pulled back his lip like a snarling wolf. Marcus tried to kick, but that hand tightened around his neck, rendering him still. Both of their shields flicked out. A grunt of pain and a cry sounded behind us.

Slowly, her fractured arm trembling from effort or pain, Alvara reached her hand out to me. There was strength in the motion, expectation in her outstretched fingers. Terror coursed through my veins, ice and fire all at once, as the vision solidified. This was it. Our only shot. With a roar, I threw every ounce of myself forward. Like compacting the earth beneath bare hands, I shoved against the pressure on my magic, summoning it from the depths of my being. Alvara's wind softly whistled, gradually regaining its speed as our magic collided and merged, twisting into a hurricane of wind, rain, and lightning. A great crash of thunder rumbled through my ribcage.

An emotion that could only be described as shock skittered over Agamemnon's icy eyes. "Im-impossible," he breathed. In response, the room filled with the force of the mixing magic, a physical storm sleeting against our skin.

More, more, more! She demanded it all. Everything I had to give her. She sucked the magic from my body, and I bellowed, channeling all I had toward Alvara. Dark magic slashed against my shield, pressing in, but mine was stronger. *Ours* was stronger. Her eyes fluttered closed as the current rippled through her, muscles spasming under the force of the magic. When they opened again, her eyes glowed with that lethal green light. In the last seconds of air, her lips pulled up at the corners, and she slammed her good arm into the monster's face, palm across his eyes. He dropped Marcus to the floor, slamming his hand against her face in turn, covering her mouth and nose.

Jason! Her voice cracked in a roar of demand right as Marcus rolled to his feet, scrambling to reengage. An image flashed of empty cerulean eyes staring up at the ceiling, just as she sank her canines into his flesh. Black blood spurted, and the monster roared. Jason's body slammed into his now-lunging Commander, tackling him out of the way as the lightning exploded through her, arching down her arms into the monster. Agamemnon quaked in a terrible seizure.

A flash of light. A roar of outrage, and another man of Renown materialized in the hallway where Agamemnon had emerged.

"Fuck!" Marcus bellowed as he lunged at him, now fighting both of his brothers as they yanked him backward.

"I can't fucking shift!" Damien growled, a blade braced in his free hand. Behind us, Fae's cry was swallowed by a roar, and the brothers whirled as I threw myself toward Alvara. She fell to the floor just as Agamemnon collapsed.

The newcomer rushed forward as I did and hoisted the giant up, looping his arms under his comrade's and heaving him away from her. As he acknowledged who was struggling to her feet in front of them, his eyes flashed with recognition, followed by fleeting panic, and finally, outrage.

I stepped between them, covering her and bracing for the fight. Gasping, Alvara threw up her hand, and I did the same. Magic drained to the dregs; she trembled as she held her arm steady for one last blow. Keeping her safely tucked behind me, we hurled the remainder of our lightning toward the men of Renown, currents spiraling together in one lethal bolt.

But they were no longer there to strike.

THIRTY-NINE

PROPHECY

ALVARA

"That was Adrastos." The words were a hot rasp in my throat as the lights flickered back to life, our power returning with them.

Marcus appeared by August's side, his eyes wide as he stared down at me. "Ally," he rumbled, silver flashing in his remarkable blue eyes, his voice shaky with fear and grief.

"We're sorry," Jason breathed, his voice quavering, skin glistening with sweat. "So sorry. We—"

"I'll fucking deal with you later," Marcus snarled, leveling his brothers with a livid glare.

"We all fucked up, mate." Alec's tone was dry as he appeared at August's side. I didn't sense death in the room—nothing lurking in the smoky shadows, save for the dirty air and ash. "We knew the plan was balanced on a blade; it's not on you. Ally knew what she was getting into." He knelt beside me, glancing at August, whose hands trembled—with fear, or rage, or helplessness, I wasn't sure. "Fae just needs another nudge. Go finish her healing. I've got Ally." Panting, August met my eyes, and upon my nod, turned to help Aphaea.

Marcus knelt next to us, and as Alec reached for my ribs, Marcus gently placed his fingers on my fractured arm. I lifted the collar of my dress above my nose and breathed as deeply as I could, despite the crack in my ribs and the weight of the smoke. Sirens sang out in the distance. The two souls poured their own precious life force into my wounds, stitching them back together with glowing hands. The steady pulse of white behind us told me August was working on Aphaea too.

When the bones had fused, Alec looked to Marcus and urged we leave before the building collapsed.

Energy spent, the jump took the last of what I had to give. Every drop. When we landed at Marcus' loft, I collapsed to my knees. Curling over them, I gasped for clean air. A thick blanket was tossed over me, and then there was August, the sound of a metal kettle filling with water behind us. He wrapped the fabric around my exposed arms and legs and lifted me against his chest. I pressed my face against his warmth, breathing in the scent of sage and pine, the steady thump of his pulse lulling me to sleep. The feel of his toned muscles beneath me formed a wall between me and the world. When he laid me across the bed, sleep took me.

The soft glow of city lights filtered through sheer curtains, gently illuminating the cozy room—Marcus' guest room. I started awake, my eyes raking over the shadows in the corners. My hand instinctively traced the blade still sheathed between my breasts. A familiar pulse of energy and scent of home filled the room, steadying my heart. My mind reached out and found my friends mostly unconscious. I turned to August, who sat wide awake in the corner chair, watching me intently, his breathing shallow and steady.

"You knew."

It was a statement, not a question, and my heart sank at the subdued anger behind it. I patted the spot on the bed next to me, but August remained like a sculpture of stone.

"You knew more than one thread led to you being hurt or slaughtered. You knew we could fail. And still... you went."

"Come sit." When he didn't shift, my heart racing, I whispered, "Please."

The corner of his full lips quirked. "That's a hard word for you to say."

"Most people listen to me the first time."

"Don't start expecting that from me. Not when you pull this shit."

"Come here."

August took a heaving breath, then crossed to sit on the side opposite me. I fought the urge to reach out and take his hands, fought the warmth swelling in my chest. The shadows were heavy across his handsome, angled face, exhaustion evident.

"Yes." My voice was soft but unwavering. "Of course, I knew." His eyes guttered in response.

"Why?" August's buttery voice cracked.

"If I didn't go, Marcus would have fallen. There wasn't a single thread where he emerged."

"And you're worth less?" His demand was icy cold.

"Marcus has a family, August. A mate. A son and daughter. Yes. I would be less missed."

That tortured gaze fell on my face, guilt twisting in my gut.

"No, Ally." His voice was quiet but strong. "You wouldn't be."

I opened my mouth to argue, but the agony in his eyes took the breath from my lungs. Exhaustion weighed heavily, having long since burrowed into my marrow, so I only pursed my lips and bowed my head. Fatigue drew my body back against the mattress, and August startled a bit.

"Ally?"

"I'm fine... just... tired."

His energy steadied beside me. I pulled the sheet over my shoulder to cover my arm again, curling into a tight ball on my side. I heard the rustle of fabric across sheets, the shift of his weight on the mattress, and then the warmth of August's palm against my back nearly froze my heart in its cadence. He stroked soft, gentle patterns there, easing the tension from my body with a steady flow of energy.

"August?" My voice had faded to a hoarse whisper.

"Yes?"

"Stay with me."

When my eyes peeled open again, the soft gray of early dawn filled the room. August's breath was heavy against the back of my neck, his arm a warm, dense weight across my torso. The heat of his hard body cocooned me—muscled thighs tucked against mine, groin pressing against my ass. Christ, it felt good to be held. His steady exhales comforted me, even as they tore my soul into pieces. The reading he clearly no longer feared, so close to my skin. The delicious smell of him—*dear God.*

I tugged the sheet tighter around my face, and then the tears began streaming in heavy, salty trails across my nose and down my cheek. Guilt, sorrow, and longing danced together, tangling in a messy braid as my chest heaved with great breaths. Over time, I succumbed to the ache and the love of the soul wrapped around me, finally submitting to the way August called to me. I found sleep once more.

"COFFEE?" August's voice dragged me from the darkness. The room was warm with midday heat, despite a winter freeze nipping at its heels. I sat up, blinking sleep from my eyes, to find a soft smile on his face and a steaming mug outstretched. Gratefully, my headache was mild after the energy we'd expended last night. I accepted the mug and immediately sipped the bitter liquid, grateful for its warmth in my chest.

To his credit, August said nothing about the previous night or the promise he kept for me but sat at the foot of the bed. He sipped at his own mug, watching me as I did the same.

"How are your ribs?" he finally asked, doing his best to keep his expression neutral.

"Better." I stretched and twisted to test my claim, planting my hand in the warm linen sheets.

"Arm?"

"Better," I replied again, granting a tentative smile. His shields were up in full force, and I knew not to pry too much. I flexed my fingers, stretching my arm out and finding it, gratefully, at peace.

"Good. We need to talk." August's voice turned serious. My mind reached for his, only to find that incredible, infuriatingly impenetrable shield firmly locked in place. I wasn't sure how he knew what I'd seen in Agamemnon's mind, but it indeed needed to be discussed.

"I know," I sighed, sipping another gulp.

"Good. Look, Ally. I know I'm the rookie and all, but last night... can you, uh, not walk into situations that make my heart stop in my chest?"

I snorted, swallowing the laugh that followed. My power tapped at the barrier around his mind—a persistent psychic woodpecker—but that solid wall of August remained firmly in place.

"I'm serious," he chuckled despite himself.

"August... last night—"

"Sucked."

The corners of my lips pulled up. "Last night sucked. Yes. But there wasn't a single thread where you and Marcus walked away if I didn't take the hit. It had to be me."

He bowed his head forward, staring intently at his coffee. He wouldn't have done anything differently in my shoes. I knew it to my core—August would have taken the blow himself over letting any of us take it.

"Last night—me enduring a bit of pain—it was worth it. Worth the outcome. Obviously, I wish we'd killed Adrastos and Agamemnon. But I knew going in that was unlikely, and we took out a good handful of their allies. That makes it a win." I held August's smoldering gaze. "Damn, you make a good cup of coffee. Look. At the very least, they'll be grappling the next few days, which makes it the perfect time to dig into everything I pulled from those Renown. They know we're coming for them now. It should make them play closer to the vest."

He was quiet for a few moments, his eyes never leaving my face. Finally, he lifted his chin a bit, looking down his nose at me.

"How close?"

"How close... what?"

"How close were we to not bringing you home?"

I winced. "I came home, August. And so did Marcus. That's what matters in the end." I flashed him a playful wink. "I'm harder to kill than you might think."

August harrumphed and picked a fleck of lint off his black t-shirt. I couldn't help but notice how the cloth clung to him, the late morning light illuminating his eyes, bringing out flecks of hazel. Later. There would be time for thoughts like that later. But there were more pressing needs.

"There's something else, August." His eyes snapped back to mine, lint forgotten. "Agamemnon. Adrastos. You're their mark. You're not a random prize—you're the entire goal."

August blinked, his brows knitting together.

"I didn't get a full reading before Agamemnon realized what I was and dropped me. But you're their mark. He sensed it last night." I set my coffee on the bedside table and scooted forward to rest a hand on his thigh. Those piercing emeralds tracked my movements. "August," I breathed. "The healers are dropping, so at some point, humans and souls will be at the mercy of *their* control. They'll choose who lives and dies. You are an integral part of that plan. Your strength—they mean to wield it to rule them. I didn't see who betrayed us, who told them who you are. But they know. And they want you. Badly. The threads... are a mess. I need time to sort them out."

He was quiet for a moment, his eyes narrowed. "Why? I'm not half of what you are. Not half of Aren."

Without hesitation, I answered, "Maybe not *yet*. But you will be, August. You will be—more than I have ever been. The Great Commander will wield a call no soul will be able to avoid answering. That is what they want from you. To use that forced obedience to rule all clans."

I projected my mind, not for control, but to show him—a gentle nudge, an invitation. He answered immediately, opening for me. Commander of all armies, of all hierarchies, August at his strength, vivid and undeniable. The fall of the mortal world should they control him, and a long battle ahead if he successfully avoided it. Many scenarios, all of which led to him walking across that dark, bloodied killing field toward the monsters we had just escaped.

He blanched, his face going wan, then blinked as I pulled my mind away from his. Untangling our consciousness felt as intimate as pulling limbs apart, and my heart lurched at the ache, the desire to stay connected.

"Ally, I..." His mind swam with denial, and slowly, so slowly, that default shield closed the gap to guard him. "I'm not—" I didn't need access to his mind to know the fear of his inadequacy, so I cut him off.

"You are, August. And the sooner you embrace who you are, the sooner you can learn to wield it, and the sooner the threads will solidify, so I can figure out how in the hell to proceed with this mess. How to defend everything you love."

"They're going after—"

"Everyone. Yes. There is a thread for every person in your life. Everything, and everyone you care about enough to turn yourself over. To sacrifice yourself. Including me. Including your family. I can't see which thread they'll pull on because there are too many decisions yet to be made. Many are yours to make."

"And all end at the battlefield."

My body boiled with anxiety at that truth, my canines sliding into place in response to a threat not here to attack. I sucked on one and did my best not to recoil. "Yes. No matter what we do. Something. Someone. Will be enough to bring us to that killing field. And our warriors will fall."

FORTY

BATTLE CALL

AUGUST

A scream so agonizing that my blood curdled in my veins. They were breaking her. Breaking one bone at a time and forcing me to watch. I thrashed against my chains, against the cold, gray hands clamped around my throat, yanking my hair to force my eyes up. Forcing me to watch. To witness Alvara clawing towards me, sobbing, her face swollen, livid purple marring her cheeks, and bleeding lips. Those beautiful eyes were red-rimmed, the whites turned a horrifying ruby. The blood vessels had burst as they tortured her.

"Please!" she sobbed, pulling her broken body across the bloodied mud. A pale hand outstretched towards me. "Don't hurt him."

A strangled sob tore from my chest. Tears poured down my face. They had been for some time. The blood and salt were all that scented the air. They'd stripped our magic. Or we'd used it down to the dregs. But there wasn't an ember, a whisper of wind, or a spark of lightning between us. Not an ounce of magic left to heal her. If our friends were nearby, they had nothing left to give us. No aid was coming.

"Don't hurt him," she sobbed again, as a club crashed down onto her pleading, pale hand. She cried out, the sound barely audible as the air left her lungs, cradling the hand to her chest. Her fingers were bent wrong, red now painting her fair skin. Still, she inched forward. Still, she tried to come to me. Broken, bloodied, and dying. Agony tore cries from her chest as she came for me.

A thick, gray hand reached down and pulled her up by her hair. Her cry cracked through the world as he lifted her. Her body was... wrong. Broken.

There was blood—so much blood. Everywhere. It soaked what remained of her ribboned clothes, the torn skin beneath.

Those horrible gray hands set her on her knees, and she cried out. Broken. They'd broken her. Her legs buckled under the weight. Another set of hands heaved her upright, splaying her arms open as though she would be crucified there, in that rust-painted mud. Blood dribbled down her chin, leaked from her nostrils, rivulets running down her pale throat. Her slender, beautiful throat, now marred with bruises where hands had crushed her skin.

Mud squelched under heavy boots, and I looked up into the rain to see Agamemnon standing there, the drops splattering against his deathly skin. Those obsidian stones where eyes should be sneered down at me.

"Pathetic." He spat the word and then whirled on Alvara, backhanding her swollen face. She didn't cry this time. Didn't scream. Whether it was that iron will or she was simply out of screams to give, I wasn't sure.

She lifted her face to him and shot a mouthful of blood towards the demon beast. So, iron will, then. He pulled a knife from the baldric across his shoulders. She didn't waver, those agonized eyes staring down death incarnate.

Adrastos, coming up from the side, yanked what was left of her shirt away from her sticky body, and his brother plunged the knife down to free it from her skin. He tossed the strips of linen aside, leaving the bulk of her torso exposed to the pouring rain. She was covered in wounds. Everywhere. Her breasts, covered only by what remained of a thin elastic, heaved as she sucked in a breath. The surrounding demons cackled like satisfied hyenas. I roared my outrage, but the chains held me as I hurled toward her, biting into flesh and muscle. My body barely registered the pain as I bellowed her name.

She dragged down another breath, steadying herself against the agony. The agony she was already in. Against the torment she knew was coming. A great leather whip uncurled from Adrastos' fist. He lowered onto his haunches to look her in the eye, snarling. She just bared her teeth. For once, I wished she would concede. Stop this. Somehow. Why was she awake? Why didn't her mind carry her under with the agony coating every inch of her?

"Say it," Adrastos' low, smooth voice slithered along my bones like a serpent. "You can make it all stop. Either of you. Give me what he wants." Hidden in his eyes, I swore there was a plea.

Alvara's eyes narrowed, and I willed her to stop. To stop fighting. But she spat blood in Adrastos' brutish face instead. "Go to hell."

The words were meant to be a snarl. Meant to be one last act of defiance. But there was barely air left in her to lift the retort off her lips. And as Adrastos stood, wiping the blood from his face, her eyes guttered. She locked onto me, lips trembling. She began shaking. In fear, pain, or cold. It didn't matter.

No. Not like this. Not this goodbye. That's all I could see in her eyes, our minds reduced to no more than mortals. The whip cracked.

I roared, but Alvara bit her lip. Hard enough to draw blood. She wouldn't give him this. She wouldn't die cowering.

That horrible crack sliced through the air as it bit her flesh. Her eyes slammed shut, and she ground her teeth against the agony. Screams poured from me, my mind vaguely aware my own limbs were growing wet and warm below the shackles.

I couldn't. I couldn't. Not like this.

Not like this.

"ANYTHING!" I cried out, my voice hoarse. "Anything. Please. Please!" The chains and hands that had bound me released me, and I collapsed into the mud. I dragged the icy chains forward, towards her trembling body, now collapsed in on itself.

"Anything," I breathed, bloody hands reaching out for her.

Her eyes, barely conscious, flicked to mine, and her lips formed one word. My name...

"August!!" Clear as wind chimes, Alvara's voice pulled me into consciousness. Thunder clapped, too close. Much too close. And then my skin became aware of the dampness saturating each inch of the bed, colliding into me in droplets.

My eyes flew open, and I recoiled, flying upright. The storm was inside our room. Was inside... me. Breath ragged, I panted, gaze flying from one part of the room to the other. Alec came bursting through the door, eyes wild. Water coiled around his fingertips. Fae was on his heels, their hands raised, ready to fight, just as Alvara was, on her knees across from me.

The storm ceased. My body hurled forward to heave into the trash can below. I vomited again. And again. Until only bile burned in my throat, my stomach seizing. Footsteps padded across the room as our companions closed the distance. More from the hall.

They were coming for her. For Alvara. To get to me.

My stomach heaved violently, but there was nothing left to empty.

"August?" Alvara said again, her voice desperate. My shields were up. She hadn't seen. Hadn't read. I whirled to her, desperate to see her in one piece. Her hair was plastered to her face from the rain. *My* rain. The tendrils were nearly black in their dampened state. The clouds faded into mist, lightning crackling as the energy dissipated.

She hadn't wanted to be alone, and again, I'd foolishly curled up next to her. Listened to the steady cadence of her breath as I drifted to sleep. Felt her warmth through the sheets between us. A dangerous game, perhaps. But one I wanted to play. At least... one I'd wanted to play until this moment. Staring at her perfect, moon-pale skin reflecting the city lights, as she peered through the darkness.

How?

Alvara was the most powerful being I'd encountered. The most powerful calling to a sire who had outlived history itself. A soul that could raid or cripple minds without raising a hand. That struck fear even in Agamemnon. How would she have fallen captive? It didn't matter. The vision was crystal clear. Real and tangible. More vivid than the warnings I'd received before they came for Layla. My body trembled as I looked at her, eyes burning.

She had thrown herself in front of a lethal blow of dark power for me only one night earlier. They had seen. Known what she was to me—what I was to her—in a way we didn't yet have the courage to embrace. We had shown our cards in that pitiful basement. I would damn the world if it meant Alvara would live. If it meant I could stop her from suffering, the world could burn.

"I know what they're going to use."

The day before, the vision had been full of training. I had actually kept up with the coven; my weeks with Alvara had paid off. We drank copious amounts of coffee and planned, schemed each detail of our remaining sting in New York. Discussed the threads of the larger threat posed by the Men of Renown. We had gone to bed in high spirits. Spirits now lying in shreds after the most horrific thing my mind had ever seen.

Marcus paced from one side of the loft to the other. Jason, sitting on the coffee table, stared into the electric fireplace, his hand braced against his mouth. Damien had gone to the patio to summon Aren, while Alvara, for once, was rendered immobile—perhaps at her fate, perhaps scrambling to make sense of the threads as she tore them to shreds, searching for what led to the horror in my vision. Alec and Fae were stone-cold carvings in their chairs, their eyes unseeing, locked on the city beyond us. For once, no shred of humanity remained in their unblinking, unflinching bodies. Perhaps they were watching as Alvara's mind stripped apart the tapestry of what was to come and rewove it in different ways, looking for something—anything—to give us an advantage.

With a crack and a flash of light, Aren, Ansel, and Lana appeared on the patio. The dim light illuminated their forms on the balcony. Aren threw open the glass door, which only didn't shatter because Marcus conjured a shield to catch it.

"What the fucking hell happened?!" he boomed, rounding the corner to take us all in. I swore his pale eyes glowed with rage, emanating from him in tangible waves. Ansel, eyes full of lethal intent, followed closely, marking the exits and studying the loft, the shadows within it. His mate was right behind him, her gaze darting from detail to detail in the same manner.

"You all seem to be in one piece." His anger faltered, a muscle in his jaw feathering.

"For now," Alvara replied, her voice soft, eyes still seeing another world. Aren's intensity fell on me. I bowed my head, that terrible nightmare running back through my mind. I could have sworn the Commander's heart faltered—literally faltered. He recoiled from my thoughts, shaking his head. But silver lined those light blue eyes.

"Ally?" It was a demand. "Give me the threads. What is there?"

"Too damn many," she murmured.

"We're sure this wasn't... a nightmare?" Lana's bravado was mercifully absent this time. She studied me, her eyes wary of what she might find. I shook my head. Alvara mirrored the motion, still distant, unthreading and threading, weaving and unweaving.

"It's there, Aren. It's there, at the end of many. I can't see... can't see all the trigger points. But the mess of threads—several lead to the vision August had."

The Commander's brooding eyes fell on me, jaw set and narrowing. "Why Ally? Of everyone in your life, Mr. Porter, *she's* who they've decided holds the most leverage?" He motioned to Ally, her expression still blank with visions. "This goes beyond a soul bind."

"Ally wouldn't hesitate to come for you, Commander."

Aren hiked a brow, shifting on his feet as he scrubbed a hand over his jaw, clearly unconvinced. "And you're telling me that's all this is? Loyalty to your *sire?*"

Clearing my throat, I shifted forward uncomfortably, suddenly painfully aware that every set of eyes except hers was on me. It wasn't the time for heartfelt confessions, so I lowered my voice, correcting, "Loyalty to *her*, sir."

Ansel's brows quirked infinitesimally, his shoulders relaxing as he and Alec exchanged a glance. "Ahh," he breathed. "Acceptance?"

"Not quite. But we're getting there," Alec said, lips tugging up at the corner.

"What if..." Fae's voice was hoarse, just shy of a whisper trailing in on a phantom breeze as she interjected, drawing their scrutiny. God, I'd have to thank her for that later. "What if we separate you two? If there appears to be a divide in the coven?"

Alvara's green eyes returned to the present for a heartbeat, darting to Aphaea before vanishing into the beyond again. She shook her head softly. "We are weaker apart. They would never believe he would abandon me, divide or not. They saw. They saw him channel his power through me to attack Agamemnon when I was weak. That kind of bond... is rare. So rare. It doesn't just vanish over an argument."

"No. It doesn't," Aren rumbled, settling smoothly beside Alvara. "What else is there? How do we shift it?"

"Too many threads. I don't know. But it's not the only outcome. It's not... finalized."

"That's good, right? How long do we have to figure this out?" Fae encouraged.

"The rain has begun, but the snow has not yet melted." Alvara locked her gaze with her friend. Alec and Aren both swore, low and equally filthy. Weeks. We had weeks, at best, until the skies would hurl sleet down and the snow vanished.

"Okay, so let's break this down..." Aren, mercifully serious and not making light of the dream—or the fact that I now had to replace every item in Marcus' guest room after my storm—remained undaunted. That battlefield calm settled over him as he assessed the visions Alvara cast before us, the different ways this could unfold, the decisions that might or might not change it. But one certainty remained solid in every thread: war was coming.

And it was coming *for* me.

FORTY-ONE
RACE
ALVARA

August's training had paid off, and now I had to push my legs to keep ahead of him. His longer stride gobbled up the earth in powerful pulses of muscle and determination, as though we could outrun the visions, the fate we saw coming.

We had spent hours huddled together in Marcus' living room, the modern furnishings suddenly cold and unwelcoming. No matter which thread I spun down, no matter how many decisions we took turns making, each path led to that battlefield. Beyond that...

It was a mess. A giant, cosmic knot I could not for the life of me untangle. That battle would determine my ending. This Adrastos knew my capabilities—leaving all his options open so I couldn't stop him from coming. *Motherfucker.*

I would plead with Aren, with Alec, any of them, to make me a martyr before they allowed those monsters to take me and use me against him. To protect the greater good, to protect me from an end so much worse than the sword or bullet of a friend. A knowing settled in my gut. Looking up, I caught those stony silver eyes, shadowed and full of understanding. He crossed his arms, muscles taut. Ansel cocked his head, pleading eyes watering as his brow crumpled with grief, gaze dropping to his feet. His chest expanded deeply, and he ran his tongue over a canine before lancing me with that quicksilver intensity again. Two soft nods. That was all I got before he turned his attention to the cigarette he'd been turning over between his fingers, slipping it between his lips. It was enough. For me, he would make the hard choice.

Every scrap of air leaked from my lungs, relief washing through me.

August could not fall. Could not yield. His survival was the survival of humanity, of the world as we knew it. Every thread where he survived showed me the same thing—the same final stand for souls and humans alike. I couldn't see past my death but assumed it would only stoke his resolve to destroy them. My suffering...he could not endure my suffering, as our bond became suffocating. He would yield.

Perhaps August had sensed my resolve forming, as a chill enveloped that windowed room, so many floors above us now. Perhaps he also needed to feel some semblance of power, a way to escape the tension bottling inside each of us. Perhaps that's what drove him to request we run. We weren't the only ones needing to escape, and our little pack now barreled down the sidewalks together. The city noise had long since faded from my focus, only the soft, steady *thud, thud, thud* of our feet against the pavement keeping me anchored in real time.

The mortal realm nestled comfortably into their blankets and sweaters, gathering around their fireplaces and ovens that smelled of pastry and nutmeg. Thoughts of the holidays—both forlorn and overjoyed—barraged our minds like the steady plunk of raindrops on water.

It was only the two immense shields between us that seemed to keep the distant voices from escalating to a bellowing roar.

The winter air shredded my lungs, but I forced my muscles to keep moving. To keep running. Heart thundering against its cage, the demand went down the chain of command, requiring my body to comply. Perhaps there was a small piece of me that hoped I could outrun this fate, too.

Are we to freeze off our fingers, then? We won't likely win if we're crippled. Lana's mental voice grated on my nerves, but Ansel and Marcus both snorted. Indeed, my hands in their gloves had long since released the ache of cold for a terrifying numbness. I felt, rather than saw, Aren shoot her an amused glare. My shields locked up, and Lana huffed at being shut out entirely. She didn't make to leave, to jump back to the loft or cease her running—wouldn't, I realized, with me facing down potential torture and slaughter. Indeed, she and Ansel would likely grant me no semblance of privacy until we found a way around the battle.

Thud, thud, thud.

Our feet continued their steady assault on the pavement, quieter than any human could possibly be. Counting my breaths seemed a good place to focus until the cortisol in my body could return to normal.

But there, in the shield's corner, a white light seemed to press against it. August. I cracked a sliver open just for him.

Training has...become a release for me. Keeps my head clear.

I've always been the same. Keeps me sane—a bit of an addiction.

We all have our vices. I felt his attention searing my skin, and a genuine smile played on my lips as I flicked my gaze to him. August was, not surprisingly, watching me as we ran, his eyes scraping up and down my body like a physical caress. Heat flushed me, my cheeks burning.

We exchanged small, timid smiles, as though he also didn't want to allow himself to feel what this unavoidable future would do to us.

You know...if you don't start training with Aren again, I'm about to lap you...Sire.

I shook my head, eyes narrowing slightly as I glared at him. *In your dreams, Rookie.*

Amusement danced down that line to me, and my smile warmed over the heat of my own ragged breaths.

Big talk for someone dodging training these days. Too good for it, I suppose, in your old age.

I rolled my eyes. *You and Alec embarrass the twins plenty on your own.*

He shrugged. *But how much more satisfying for them to get schooled by a girl?*

They learned the hard way that my gender doesn't dictate the size of my brass. Trust me, we've fought our share.

True, was all he let me hear, his jaw ticking. He pushed into his run, and I felt the challenge in that long stride. Muscles singing, I leaned into my own. He pushed farther forward, and I did the same. Again, and again, and again. I knew he was baiting me, pushing me to keep me focused on the present. I didn't care. It was working. Muscles pumping waves of fire, lungs screaming, I shot to the front again, soaring with every ounce of strength I had.

That all you got, Coach? August gained speed, fists unclenching at his sides as he poured himself into the sprint.

Our coven and friends gradually fell further behind, unmotivated by our silent competition. I dropped my shield enough to feel them out. Aren and Marcus still trailed closely. Alec stayed by Fae's side, the rest of them huddled behind.

Still, we pushed, farther, harder, faster, our shoes slapping against the pavement now, as mortal as could be.

First one back wins? I could feel his smile, although I didn't dare glance his way as I focused my burning eyes on the front awning of the Westerlunds' building.

Wins...what exactly?

A round of truth or dare.

Child.

It's that or strip poker.

I snorted. *I wouldn't last long.*

Don't know how to play poker?

I met his cocky stare, trying to hide as I fought to keep my breathing even. *I'm just not wearing much under these clothes.*

August cleared his throat, the sound tight, making it impossible to fight back my smile. "Fuuuck," he growled.

I'd been fooling myself, thinking I stood a chance. August kicked it into gear, and I swore as I stretched to keep up. Full throttle, we both sprinted for that stretching red and green awning, for the miniature Christmas trees wrapped in colorful lights and garland, and a now wide-eyed bellman called Ray, blowing hot air into his cupped, mittened hands. He watched us now, and I swore a twinkle of amusement played in his eyes as we hurtled for him, maxing out our human speeds. There was no focus left to drop my shield to feel him out, but the twitch at the corner of his chapped lips said enough. *Fun*, we were bringing him some ounce of fun on this frozen tundra. A defiant shriek erupted from me as August's long legs gobbled up the sidewalk, and he got a step ahead of me. Two. Three.

Aren's booming laugh behind us told me enough, but still, I pushed. Tried. Tried, and failed, as August blew past Ray and stuttered to a stop a solid heartbeat before my own feet crossed the muted shadow of that awning.

"Not...fair." I panted, lacing my hands together to rest on the back of my head as we walked our heart rates back down. He huffed a great laugh.

"How?!" he demanded.

"Your legs are longer, dammit." I heaved in air.

August's laugh was breathless and ragged, but sincere, and he winked at me. Color swelled in his cheeks as his rare cocky grin plastered itself across them.

"Sore loser, Coach?"

"Maybe a little."

That smile, God, that smile. August beamed at me, his radiance nearly buckling my knees. Although I told him internally that was the shaky recoil from our frozen sprint down the sidewalk.

"Truth," I panted, still walking in a circle as our companions slowed their pace to a trot to bring their heart rates down.

"I didn't say when I'd cash in my prize, did I?"

"Oh, jeez."

"Yep. Gotta choose wisely." He gulped down air, grinning like the cat that ate the canary.

Aren, still thoroughly amused with my losing a race, loped up the sidewalk next to Marcus. Aren and Ray opened the door for us, and August motioned for me to go inside. The warm air hit like a battering ram, thick and stifling, but a shiver walked down my spine, joints seeming to sigh in relief as we stepped into the lobby. Marcus was on my six, as August had insisted, but that gentle tap, tap, tap brought my mental shield down again.

You know we'll figure it out, Ally. All of it. If anyone can solve this, it's you, and Alec, and Aren.

And you?

That internal satisfaction. *And me. Anything, Ally, I'll pay anything to make sure we both get out of that field alive.*

I nodded once, just once. Teeth chattering, skin stinging against the change in temperature, we all filed into the elevator.

AUGUST WORE a suit of midnight black that shimmered deep blue in the right lighting, like a star-flecked sky. His tie was a rich merlot purple to complement my dress. Tousled curls tucked behind his ears. A tentative grin spread across that handsome face as he saw me and accepted my outstretched hand. The gold gown he'd bought me fit as well as that black glove, clinging to each curve, the plunging neckline lined with sheer skin-toned fabric that shimmered a bit in the light. Just like the vision. He tucked my arm under his elbow, and the warmth of him through that beautiful suit came crashing into me, just as that familiar scent did.

"You are...breathtaking, Ally."

I smiled in thanks, inclining my head towards him. "You look quite dashing yourself, Mr. Porter."

Fae appeared at the top of the open stairs. Her scarlet chiffon gown rested around a plunging v neckline, bunching at her tiny waist before billowing away from her perfect little hourglass form. A slit came up to her mid-thigh, and I grinned, knowing she was still a walking armory, as I was, with the sheaths August had sewn into the slips under the flowing fabric. His attention to detail, the way he built our life into them, was amazing.

With three extra sets of eyes set to patrol and shield the exterior, I hoped the evening would unravel the easier of the threads before us. Would give August a victory that didn't bring our hearts near stopping. Fae leaned into the metal stair rail, gracefully hoisting her weight onto it so she could slide down the banister, full lips plumped into a smug smirk. Alec, in perfect timing, jumped to the bottom of the stairs, popping into the air before her with his hand out to grab her already outstretched fingers. She hopped off the rail with a sweeping motion, and Alec fanned his mate out for the room to admire, spinning her in a circle, then two. The red chiffon of her gown glimmered like stardust under the lights. He tucked her in tight to his side and placed gentle kisses along her cheekbone. She beamed, leaning into him. For a breath, arm in arm with August, I thought of what it would be like...to be human. To be normal. To be arm in arm with a handsome date, watching my best friends in their lighthearted preparation for a masquerade ball. To enjoy life without the weight of saving it all the time. I sighed.

August, sensing or hearing the movement, gave my silk-clad fingers a little squeeze. My eyes flicked to his, and there was a light in those emeralds as he stared back at me, warmth seeming to roll off him.

Aren cleared his throat as he entered the room—as though we couldn't sense his very essence radiating through our bones.

"Alright, guys, lay it out one last time." And so we did, step by step, player by player. We recited that we intended this for reconnaissance, but if we had a chance to liberate Jones' body or bring him to mortal justice, we would. We each tied our masks into place. Each of us locked in the decisions that were ours to make, as August had suggested, and after a heartbeat, Aren looked to me.

FORTY-TWO
THE GALA
AUGUST

"Alright, Ally. Give me the numbers." Aren crossed his arms, his gaze fixed on his calling.

Alvara met his stare, her eyes glazing over. Those full lips parted as she drew in a long breath. She blinked, and when those shimmering purple lids lifted, she was focused again. Her gaze flicked from Aren to Marcus and back again.

"Honestly? Fifty-fifty chance this all goes to shit. Fifty percent chance we're in, eat awful bougie chicken, dance, get our information, and leave undetected."

"And the other fifty?" Alec drawled from her other side.

"Fifty percent chance we land in one of three... more *eventful* threads that lead to combat, an exorcism, and the mortals believe there was a domestic terrorist attack at the ball." She pressed a slender finger to her lips, widening her eyes in a feigned display of innocence and indifference.

"Outcome?" Aren demanded.

She flashed a lethal grin, eyebrows lifting, light dancing in her eyes. "Always successful."

Aren rumbled a laugh. "Alright. Any injuries or fatalities?"

"Two of the threads have minor injuries. Shit gets scary for a minute. No fatalities."

"Worth the victory?"

"As long as nobody makes any dumbass, impulsive off-plan decisions... without a doubt."

Does that mean you're the one injured, then? I snapped at her, images of our last group outing fresh in my mind. She elbowed me in the ribs. Hard. Wincing theatrically, I managed a low laugh.

Never a wound that takes more than a healing hand, a cup of tea, and a nap. Get over it, August. Would you be happier if it was you?

Yes, actually, much happier. Thank you.

Well, I guess you'll be pleased. There are a few of those too. Cold. Calculated. Like a battle general assessing a soldier." She slipped her arm out from mine and strode over to Aren and Marcus. Flicking her gloves off, she raised her hands—both Commanders clasped her offered forearm, and she showed them the threads in her mind. Too fast and unfocused for me to make out. Perhaps it was intentional, or perhaps it was just the speed at which she could share a true reading.

They both gave her a small bow of their heads as she released them. Marcus straightened his suit jacket, and Aren crossed his arms again. It was then that Marcus' eyes sought mine.

"A word, young Commander?" Marcus inclined his head to me, and Alvara scowled as her phantom hands recoiled from the wall he'd placed around his mind. As solid as bricks and mortar. She wrinkled her nose in frustration. While I knew if she truly needed access to his mind, she would find a way, she turned her attention to Fae out of respect. I nodded in ascent.

Marcus led me out the glass door onto the narrow balcony overlooking Chicago. The night was thick with winter chill, no stars visible beyond the city's glare.

"I like you, Rookie." Marcus shot me a sideways grin. "You've certainly proved your loyalty these last few days. A word of advice?"

I wasn't so sure I was going to like what he was about to say, but nodded anyway.

"There's no point in trying to control the path of a hurricane, is there? Resisting its strength will land you face down in the cold water of a surge. Move with it. Move with it until you become the eye in the center. Survival is in the silence, not the roar of the wind." Without further explanation, the Commander turned and went back into the loft. I blinked. Once. Twice. Trying to clear the warning from my thoughts. And yet, something in my soul understood. So, I stared out at the gleaming city lights and began to pray.

Alvara had, unsurprisingly, been right. The gala hosted a cacophony of voices and pretentious hors d'oeuvres. They had, indeed, covered the chicken in a sauce that was trying too hard, and somehow still managed to be dry. The only perk was the way Alvara stayed glued to my side, breathing into my shield. Her eyes focused and unfocused, always probing the future to ensure she wasn't missing something.

Jones had a small entourage with him. Guests made a special effort to come and shake his hand, introducing themselves. Always begging for power at every corner, I supposed. Yet, Senator Jones's dark blue eyes continually flicked past the groveling guests to Alvara, regal and breathtaking in that gold gown at our table towards the back. After I'd seen him watch her a dozen times, I snorted when I caught him staring again.

"What?" Her voice was a smile. I looked back to see it across her face.

"You have an admirer."

"Or he's scented me and knows what I am."

I stared the man down again, and he held my gaze before flashing a cocky grin and glancing back to Alvara. My stomach roiled, and I shifted a bit closer to her. It didn't seem like a threat so much as a pure male challenge over a beautiful woman. Still, my very being clenched.

"I'd bet money he just wants you."

She raised her gaze to stare at the man we'd come here to learn about before rolling her eyes and saying, "Perhaps."

"Doesn't take a psychic to see that one."

"No, it doesn't."

Alec and Fae waltzed up to the table, drinks in hand, both a bit sweaty from their countless twirls on the dance floor. Recon, Alec called it, on the guests, of course. I bit back a laugh as he pulled his mate up and slid his hand down her backside before they moved into the dance. *Yes. Recon. Very good.* Alvara at least thought it was funny too. They each set their extra champagne flutes in front of us.

"Either there aren't very many of them tonight," Fae whispered, "or they are extraordinarily glamoured to the point where even I can't scent them."

"Have you counted how many *guests* there are?" Alec's words were only for Alvara. She rolled her eyes. "They *are* extraordinarily glamoured. About two dozen, if my estimate is correct. But I haven't dared a full drop either. August and you should take a stroll, get some air... and space to think." Alec gave her a wink that could have been encouraging or mischievous. I wasn't sure which. "They don't seem to intend any kind of conflict."

Alvara's eyes flashed up towards Jones again. She didn't seem entirely convinced. She surveyed the dance floor, rolling her eyes at the Westerlund twins, who had both asked particularly pretty women to dance. With a great sigh, Ally was on her feet. I rose with her.

"You're all a bit pitiful at this, you know."

"None of your projections included any results until fourth quarter anyway."

Alvara narrowed her eyes, brows dipping in the center. "Yeah. You all still suck for that. I would've gone."

"You were busy. And Sundays are for the boys."

"*Bullshit,*" Fae coughed, pinching Alec's bicep hard enough that he jumped, earning a round of laughs.

Ansel still owes me twenty for that game. Ally snipped down the line.

Clairvoyants don't get to make bets. That's just stupid, Ansel growled from the van.

"Besides," Alec cut in. "There's no rule that says we can't enjoy ourselves, is there?" He grinned, backing away with Fae in tow.

"I suppose not." But her words were stilted. I grinned at her and stretched out my hand. She flashed one of those heart-melting smiles and swiped her silk gloves from the table between now-empty plates. Once they were back in place, she accepted my hand and followed me along the edge of the dance floor. The venue's walls were draped in black fabric that seemed to absorb the light. Purple tablecloths adorned each surface, save the banquet tables, which were white. Alvara, in her dazzling gold gown, was the only thing that caught the light as the fabric scraped against the ground. But she glimmered. It even seemed she had thought to swipe sparkling cosmetics across her cheekbones.

If Alvara was usually breathtaking... tonight, she was resplendent beyond words. My heart seemed to gallop any time she moved, my chest tightening each time she flicked those dazzling eyes my way. Her gaze trailed over face after face, and I felt her shields open just a crack. Just enough to start probing the minds around her. But her heart began to race under the number of them, and I slid her fingers to my opposite hand, freeing my closest hand to stroke her low back. Calm her. Anchor her. Her ribs expanded beneath my fingertips as she took a breath.

You've got this, Ally.

A subtle nod, her slender chin dipping down as her eyes focused obediently. She tightened her grip on my other hand. After a long moment, she closed her eyes and blew out a breath.

"Twenty-two. Plan still intact."

"Good. Lock it up."

She smirked, and her shields snapped closed. I threw mine around her as well, buffering her from the event's undulating energy. The pulse of this thrumming city seemed to be alive on its own. Immediately, her breaths became graceful again, and she turned her eyes to me.

"You're a blessing for me, I hope you know. These events... with so many people. They were usually my breaking points before. Alec helps, but... thank you..." The long spindles of her power caressed my mind. I opened for her, *focusing on being my shield specifically.*

Warmth bled into my chest, my face. I smiled back at her and inclined my head. *It's an honor, Alvara.*

A blush colored her cheeks, and then she returned her gaze to the spinning dancers. The reading was set for the last hour of the event, when the crowd would disperse. It would be quick. She would feign the smitten kitten, too intimidated to say hello in the crowd.

As I watched her now... gliding through the throngs of milling guests and laughing reunions... there was nothing self-conscious about her. Towering over the bulk of the crowd, twinkling in that gown, head held high as she scanned each set of eyes, each face. There was nothing meek or mild about Alvara. She held a gravity to her, an undeniable presence. Like the moon in its graceful orbit. The crowd ebbed and flowed towards her and away like the sea. Perhaps that was just Alvara, or perhaps she sought to capture him wholly before she devoured his mind. Perhaps she meant to dangle herself out, irresistible and enthralling, so that when she at last deigned to acknowledge him, the man within would lean into her. For a goddess like her would bow to no one. She was both trap and hunter, all at once. My stomach churned at the very concept of allowing her to bait any man, mark or not.

Mate. Marcus had called her my mate. As in *soul mate.* As in the woman—the soul, the female—specifically crafted to be my match, my equal. Shit, that insinuated I was *her* equal. I thought for a moment of the power radiating from her...

The chaos of the last few days had swallowed the conversation. Swallowed the fact that the word clanged through my insides... and rang true. Resonated in the deepest part of me. I watched her moon-pale face, the glimmer in her eyes as she soaked in the humans simply enjoying themselves. The joy it brought her to watch them be happy.

Mate.

"Tell me about Jason."

Her eyes flicked to me, brows arching. "What about him?"

"It seems like there's... history there?" A blunt, bold question.

"Not a requited one, I'm afraid. He's a good man. But he's not my man. Never has been." A blunt, bold answer in return.

"He's... gifted, like you? I mean, not like you. But he's gifted?"

Lord have mercy, when the girl smiled, it about undid me.

"Yes. They all are. Like you." *Jason reads energy. Beyond what you and I do. Beyond scents and minds, he sees auras in vivid color. As clear as you see me, he sees energy. He sees if souls are connected, deeply or distantly. He sees if they've been frayed or darkened.*

As if our conversation had summoned him, Jason appeared by her side. "Alvara, you look marvelous, how nice to see you." He swept her into a hug like a long-lost friend.

"It's lovely to see you as well."

"August, I've found twenty-two of our classmates! Have you seen them all?"

"I have indeed." I accepted his outstretched hand and gave it a formal shake.

"I forgot how... nasty the politics get at these things." He rumbled a low laugh and sipped his champagne, but his eyes narrowed. Infinitesimally, and for only a flash. It was enough. Alvara turned her head to the side in that feline way she did when her nerves spiked. Sure enough, her heart sped up.

I need you to bend your shield to connect the ten of us mind to mind. No further.

I took a grounding breath and then pushed and pulled, sculpting my shield to accommodate her request. It flexed and buckled around the constant movement of the guests. But it did it. I did it. I gave her a nod.

Jason, what did you see?

Some of them are not possessed at all—not human at all.

Her eyes flicked to him. *Glamoured?*

Yes. Well glamoured.

I thought I caught a second hierarchy scent in the women's room. But it was so brief, and nothing since... I didn't think it lingered. Fae sent the thought to us. Everyone continued milling about, giving no sign that anything was amiss. Jason turned to join our reverie of the dancers and sipped on his drink.

Ahh... so it's the going to shit plan then? This should be fun. Alec tapped the blade within his sleeve. Alvara snorted and then sighed. I swore I could feel Aren's amusement in our minds.

Indeed.

As the clock hand made another full rotation, I thought perhaps we were wrong. Perhaps, as the elderly, sponsors, and poor saps with early flights meandered down the hall to exit, we would still play a good fourth quarter. That things were fine, and Ally was fine. But it was the way the Senator moved as she closed the distance between them, the hunger in his eyes as they devoured her, that told me how wrong I was.

Yes. Tonight was indeed another going to shit plan.

It was a predator's movement, the way he turned on her when she approached. The way his feet shifted into a fighting stance. The way his smile twisted into a cruel smirk, eyes zeroed in on his prey that made me shout one word down the mental line between us, shattering the shield so she might see.

Don't!

And when their skin touched, a wave of power burst from her with so much kick it rattled the glasses. It reverberated through my feet, my chest, through time itself. In statue-stillness, Alvara's face went utterly blank.

No major injuries. No fatalities. That was what she'd promised me.

But the moment her face slackened and her eyes glazed over, I knew it wasn't a reading that glued her to the spot. Wasn't the reading her visions had promised us. Darkness roiled in my mind—a cackling, cruel shadow within our mental bond. I slammed my shield up, but it didn't stop the sheer terror that seized me. Alvara's terror. She swayed, and the Senator's cruel smile stretched ear to ear as the remaining guests dropped their glamours, revealing the creatures that had worn human skins. There were *no* true humans left. But there were all twenty-two demons, now stalking towards each of us.

Alvara looked like she would topple, and I made to dash for her.

She knew, August. Ally knew what lurked beneath his skin, and would not have gone in if she could not win. Marcus' words down the line did little to soothe the panic devouring me. They did little as her eyes rolled, and that thing in the Senator's body laughed, a joyless sound. A sound that raked claws down my spine. It did little as she swayed again. I lunged as she fell towards the ground. And then I was there, an involuntary jump, as the thing in the skin suit flipped her pale, lifeless hand towards me. It flashed its teeth, and, arm around her waist, I jumped us back to Alec's side. Something hot and rancid burned in my nose. Carrion and ashes, I realized, as I set her down at Alec's feet.

In the split second since I'd moved us, the Westerlunds had engaged with the demons. Swords met talons, talons tore flesh. The hiss and cry of pain filled the air, and screams erupted on the sidewalks beyond the exit. Aphaea leapt from our side towards the Senator, and I could feel the others closing in. Heart hammering, I looked to Ally. Her eyes had closed, and her muscles were twitching as Alec brushed a strand of dark hair off her straight, slender nose. Still, her chest rose and fell evenly.

"What did you do?" I demanded, and the Senator huffed a laugh.

"Gave her some company," he purred. "Felix, my friend, say hello."

Alvara's eyes flashed open. But it was not that emerald green that locked onto me. Not the sparkling meadow lake I loved. But a thick, lifeless, inky black.

"Shit." Alec took a step back, hands raised to wield a shield. Her delicate, muscled body rose in a smooth motion. Different from the grace I knew.

"Ally!" I bellowed her name like a battle cry as two of the demons advanced on me. The black decor of the ballroom seemed suddenly horrifically ironic. "Ally!" I threw a hand out with so much force that the demons were thrown into the opposite wall. Bones crunched as drywall crumbled. They didn't rise. I threw my attention forward and startled. She was only inches from my face. Not *she*. Not Alvara. The thing called Felix. My stomach roiled. Rage and terror seared lances down my veins.

Alec snarled towards Jones. "Are you insane? Do you realize who you're dealing with? I would release her if I were you."

Jones sneered, "Why would I do that?"

I stared into those depthless black eyes, searching, pushing for the woman within. Alec crept up behind her, hands ready to seize either side of her. Somewhere to the side, I was aware the Westerlunds continued to fight, Fae doing the same, moving to take on the Senator herself. But I searched for her in those dark pools. A cruel smile flashed across her perfect features. With the snap of her fingers, Alec was flung backwards and pinned to the wall. He gasped for air, hands frantically clawing at his throat. But the thing turned back towards me. Slimy talons clawed at my shield, but it held.

Alec, through his gasps, laughed coldly. His words a rasp, "So she doesn't turn you to ash, you idiot."

His threat was undercut by the snarling inhuman voice coming from Ally's body. Directed at me.

"You. You we need to kill. To do so slowly. She will break... if we break *him*." The demon said over Alvara's shoulder to the leader. With that, the Senator flung his arm forward and telekinetically pinned Fae to the wall beside her mate. Both writhing against the binds. Marcus snarled, throwing his opponent to the ground. We both flung our shields forward, Ally's solid, trained body barely stumbling, but the human Senator lost ground. The other beasts lunged forward, and the Westerlunds were once again engaged.

I whirled and bellowed down the line. *Alvara, come back to us! You are better than this.*

Silence. Where confidence, skill, and knowledge usually sat... nothing. Just an empty void. The demon wielding her powers made to throw me backwards, but I was faster. I pinned my shield against hers. She bared her teeth, and the demon threw more force against me. It was then that I realized it didn't know who it inhabited. That it didn't see the truth of Alec's swaggering threat. Didn't see what she could do. She had hidden her fire, her storm, her strength. It didn't know it could incinerate us all in an instant.

It was a fool's hope to believe perhaps The Great Commander could draw her out of that inky pool.

Alvara, I command you to come back. You are still here. You are stronger than this.

Distant. A knocking. Like three clicks of high heels down a long hallway. And then, as though walls had been stuffed between us, her muffled voice trailed into my mind.

I know.

FORTY-THREE
DAUGHTER OF THE KING
ALVARA

The ice was everywhere. Everywhere...and nowhere. Just as I had been for these long months—or was it years? Time had long since ceased to exist, as the ice across my eyes felt as impenetrable as steel, biting into my skin. Again, I threw open my hands, slamming them against the chains that tethered me to what I assumed was the dais I had glimpsed before the helmet's face guard locked over my eyes, confining the world to thin slits of light and shadow. In those fleeting moments, I had seen the stark, towering onyx marble walls of the castle, as though the room had been carved from stone and midnight, rising above us as tall as Grayshell.

They didn't break me. Didn't hurt me. I kept waiting for the torture to begin, for the breaking and healing, for the whips and the bones that mended wrong. Waiting for them to draw screams from me until I caved and my very spirit shattered. But they never came.

They had left me in this vast, empty blackness. Left me chained to this dais. No one came—not to hurt me, save me, or feed me. But hunger did not come for me either. That hollowness in my belly was not for food, but rather for *them*. For my family, left behind. For home. For him.

I could see a man's terrorized face in a brief flash and shied away from the image. What had become of him? Was he alive? Had they made it out? What had been the point, again? What were we meant to do...August. I missed him. I missed the others too. But mostly, I missed August. His laugh, his smile, his knowing when his shield would bless me. The way he looked when he talked about his family. About...

Stop. Don't think of him. Don't think of any of us. Build your walls.

Shield your mind, Ally. The voice was hauntingly familiar. Devastatingly familiar. I should know that voice as well as my own. But his name... I couldn't remember it. Shouldn't remember it, I realized, as a set of light blue eyes and an eternal smile flashed in my memory.

The demon... The demon? The plan had... gone sideways, and the demon...

Fuck. I had forgotten where this started. Sweat pooled in my palms against the gauntlets. The demon...

I began to build my walls, thicker, taller, and deeper than they had ever been. I built them of the eternal light of Grayshell, forged from the unyielding will of my sire. The owner of the voice. The owner of the voice I wanted here, I realized. With me. Always. But not here—not really. This wasn't *here* to begin with. So, I built walls of sun and backroads, laughter and singing.

I took a deep breath and became the ice that bound me, and the walls transformed to embody that too. I inhaled the reek of carrion, brimstone, and cold steel to become that, as well.

Pain shot through me like a spear, radiating down my spine from my neck. An icy spider danced along my back, across rivulets of sweat, as my hands clasped around my windpipe—biting metal met the skin of my neck as the gauntlets stung. My muscles were shaking, terror having long since gripped them. With a tug, my mind yanked forward toward the pain, forward toward the coughing and choking, forward toward...my name. Someone was...

He was calling my name.

The unforgiving marble below my folded legs seemed to rumble, responding to that face and name. Seemed to purr in gratitude.

A flash of... Alec, his name was Alec... pinned against a wall, and then the unseeing blackness snapped into place. Panic spun a web within my gut —panic, and pain, and fear. Shame. I realized it was shame that made me feel as though I would soon vomit. I'd gotten them into this mess. Had they gotten out?

I tried to lift my hands the last few inches to peel off the damned guard over my eyes, but the chains cracked painfully against the movement, and I growled. Panic threatened to choke the life from me—the walls pressing in on all sides—as the air slowly seemed to leak from my lungs.

Think, Ally, think. Slowly, cautiously, I lay down, pulling myself as close to the base of those chains as I could. Finally, my fingers reached my face. They were as frozen as the rest of the world, more ice melting on my skin as they clawed and pulled at the helmet locked around my head. I sobbed as it refused to release, sobbed as I clawed beneath the metal over my eyes, but still, it didn't yield. Warm liquid trickled down my cheeks. Blood, or tears, I wasn't entirely sure.

Alvara, come back to us! You are stronger *than this.*

God, that voice. That buttery, beautiful voice—the voice of a thousand lullabies, of comfort, warmth, and home. So familiar. *His* voice. As though he were the only man—the only soul—that existed, he called to me.

But the stones. The helmet. The chains. How in the world was I supposed to reach him? Panic, slick and oily, seeped further into my body. I didn't dare say his name. He was more powerful than any of us, more powerful than—don't. *Don't say his name. Their names. Don't.*

Higher still, my walls solidified. A tower within a tower. The stones stacked side by side, with no gap for anything to slither between. An impenetrable fortress sealed in concrete and iron.

Hours passed. Perhaps days. Still, the blinder would not budge.

Still, no one came.

Not to ask questions, not to demand the truths be told. Not to hurt me...not to save me. Just unrelenting cold. The eternal ringing of that voice. The one that meant I was safe. That I was home. That voice was as much a part of me as my own hammering heart in my chest. Sleep. I needed to sleep. Exhaustion clawed at every inch of my mind. Perhaps here, lying on the bitter stone floor, was as good a place as any to finally... just... close my eyes.

Fuck. Don't you give up, Ally. Come on, baby. I command you to come back. You are still here. You are stronger than this.

The words—that voice—clanged through my body like steel on steel, rattling me to my very soul. Dammit. I *am* stronger than this. I am Alvara Goldman, second in command of the Grayshell Hierarchy. The most powerful seer *alive*. A wielder of all elements. I am stronger than stone. Stronger than ice...

And so, I became them.

Forged myself anew with the stone, turning crystalline and fiery all at once.

Embodied the strength, and will, and light buried deep.

I know! I cried out into the void. He was there. He wasn't leaving.

"Get off of me," I snarled, tearing at the metal plate. "Get. Off. Of. Me."

Somewhere above my tower of steel and stone rang out a cackling, cold, joyless laugh. The demon was with me. With me and...*not*. Preoccupied, perhaps.

The command rang through each muscle and bone, the summons of The Great Commander, calling me home. Ordering me to come back. I had to go back. Had to go back... had to go *back*. I gritted my teeth as I yanked on that goddamned face guard with all the strength I had, sobbing as it pulled on my skin.

Ally, baby, come home. Come back to me. His muffled voice wrapped around me, a scarf of warmth within the fortress. I had to go back...

A knowing settled in my ribs. "I am a daughter of the King. In Jesus' name, you will release me." The mask did. As though the name unlocked it.

Again, that command rang in my ears, as though it had reverberated off each stone I had built in my tower to defend my mind. To defend...*him.*

Fucking hell. Alvara, you come back. Come back to me, baby. Just me and you. Okay? We haven't even started. You're stronger than this. Be stronger than this. Again, and again, and again his voice echoed off the stones, smashing into my soul, my body.

I snarled again, "I am a daughter of the King. You cannot touch me. I am a daughter of the King. You are not welcome here."

A low, serpentine hiss. "Silence, pretty one. This is my body now."

"The fuck it is. *I am a daughter of The King.* You have no power here."

Another hiss, as those words again echoed through my very bones. That voice, like an iron anchor within a tempest sea, holding me to my center—to my very core. The storm battered against the ship, the world tilting as cold, ice, and ache beat against my very being.

Ally, I'm right here. I've got you—We've got this. We face this together. He growled. *Come on, baby, show them who you fucking are.*

"You have no power here. You WILL leave me, in the name of Christ —" The thing recoiled, the ice retreating from my skin. "Get the *fuck out!*" The roar exploded through the walls, through the black granite. It tore through the world, through all that I was. Searing pain, and yet...

"I am a daughter of the King," I gasped. "No harm will come to me."

FORTY-FOUR
FIRESTORM
AUGUST

"Fucking hell," I growled, casting a crackling wall of fire around us. "Alvara, you come back. Come back to me, baby." I gritted my teeth, holding my shield against the demons hurling themselves against it. My gaze flicked between her round obsidians where emeralds should be, searching, praying... "Just me and you, okay? We haven't even *started*. You're stronger than this. You have to be stronger than this."

Alvara brought shaking hands to her face, clawing at her eyes as if to expel the monster from her skin. She bared her teeth, her energy pulsing like that of a wild beast unleashed. Then she began screaming, a defiant roar as I lunged for her, but the powerful smash of metal against wood made me turn.

Aren, Lana, and Ansel rushed in, blades drawn, teeth bared. A roar erupted from the Commander as he charged, the others flanking him. I turned back to Alvara, who still screamed her outrage, and dove for her hands as her nails dug into her skin.

Leave her. Aren's command froze me to the floor. Anger rippled through me as I pushed against the magic locking my muscles in place. *Trust me.* The thought was a growl.

I whirled on him, but he was slicing down demons like stalks of wheat, a veritable wall of muscle and metal. With one glance back at Alvara, I obeyed, staggering away a step, but unwilling to leave her side.

"Ally, I'm right here. I've got you—we've got this. We face this *together*," I commanded, my voice hoarse from the effort of blocking the attacks.

Another assault slammed against the shield, but it didn't buckle. The air crackled with electricity. "Come on, baby, *show them* who you fucking are."

Her melodic voice cut through the din: "I am a daughter of the King," a haggard breath. But it was Alvara's voice, clear as day, "No harm will come to me."

The world seemed to freeze as it exploded.

From behind us, double doors burst open, and the bay and roar of great beasts filled the hallway. But beside me, Alvara erupted in light, fire, and wind. The blast sent me slamming to the ground, my knees singing as they hit the marble floor. Alec and Fae fell from the wall. Through the pounding in my skull, their gasping breaths cut across the roar of demons pouring into the ballroom. I threw my physical shield wide, and it shuddered as they battered the perimeter. Undiluted fear coursed through me, adrenaline sluicing through my veins. My heart hammered a staccato beat as I struggled to focus—on the herd of demonic, skeletal beasts barreling toward me, or on Alvara...

Alvara, whose every inch of skin glowed white-hot like starlight, eyes vibrant gold, her hair and gown floating and whipping in a phantom breeze. Her fingertips and the very air around her were engulfed in blue flame. Her arms stretched wide as water solidified out of the very air beyond her flames. Her rage felt like a tsunami racing down the horizon. One word barreled down the bond, clear as day.

Duck.

We did. All of us. Unquestioning and unified, we abandoned our positions—even Aren, who wielded two blades against three rabid blood wolves. Shields erupted from every side of me, and I swore I heard Alec laugh through his gasps.

The world rumbled and swelled with the power she demanded of it. Dark and light, rattling outrage mixed and roared forward as a crackling blue wave burst from Alvara, the epicenter of a nuclear explosion. The boom was deafening as the building shuddered. Every towering window in the ballroom shattered, the crystal chandeliers bursting into countless shards, now projectiles aimed at her enemies. They roared as the pieces embedded in their flesh. Water, fire, and ice surged forward, incinerating, drowning, freezing, and crushing every demon within the blast.

Save for Jones, now cowering in the corner, shielding his face.

Alec, still panting, huffed a low laugh. "I tried to warn you. You didn't know who you were dealing with."

A soft smile curved Alvara's ample lips as she turned to face Jones. I rose and took my place beside her, fingers itching to grasp hers as they flexed and curled by her side. Soothing her magic. I felt it retreat into her.

Jones's chin trembled, his dark blue eyes wide as he looked between us, breathless.

"Im-impossible."

Alvara cocked her head to the side, in that feline, predatory twitch. Her smile broadened as a growl rumbled in my chest, sparks popping between my fingers as lightning crept up my arm. My hand reached out for him, wanting to crush his throat myself. But she raised her elegant fingers, signaling me to halt. Her voice was a lover's caress, my blood chilling as she smiled at the demon.

"You had information we needed. It *was* personal. As you've provided nothing of use, I'm done with you."

"Adr—"

"Adrastos can't save you. Not from us."

"He is just the beginning. Adrastos will come for you—for his vengeance. But he is only the beginning. The terrors that rule him will make Adrastos' torture seem like—"

Jones's body snatcher was silenced with a flick of Alvara's wrist, her power unhinged by whatever had just transpired. I almost felt bad as I sensed her mental claws grasp the mind within the man.

"What are you?" the guttural thing within Jones hissed, the body shaking.

"I am a daughter of the King. And you are not welcome here." She knelt gracefully and flicked her fingers. Dancing light and fire took the form of butterflies, and the demon sneered, despite the whites of his eyes still showing. It was only once they flew into his body that his face contorted with panic and pain. Light shone through his eyes as black seeped from his flesh like blood. Her power crackled and sizzled within him, causing the inky creature to bubble and evaporate into steam.

A moment later, Jones took a gasping breath, those now-lighter sapphire eyes wild until they locked on Alvara. Her glow was fading back toward a human appearance.

"Thank you," he croaked, his voice a dry, hollow rasp as he collapsed onto the floor.

Her power retreated into her body, the room suddenly shadowed and hollow. She turned toward me, but her lips were bloodless, her cheeks just as wan. I wrapped my arms around her waist, and she leaned back into me, breathing a bit labored as she managed a soft smile.

"You brought me back," she whispered.

Safe. She was safe. The word repeated in my head like a metronome as she laid her head against my chest, her claims ringing in my bones as Marcus strode up to me, a smirk on his face—the eye in the storm. *Jesus.*

I looked around and summoned a glass that remained whole among the rubble. Alec filled it with water as it floated toward us, and I set it in her shaky fingers. Tremors rippled as she raised the glass to her lips, and I reached out to steady her. I fought down my outrage, my terror at the risk she had again assumed for herself, and instead pressed my face against her curls, breathing in the scent of honey and cinnamon, whispering into her ear.

"You did it. You're safe now. I've got you."

The sound that came from her was nearly a purr as she sipped her water and nestled into my chest. She was safe here. Safe *with me*.

But I couldn't shake the feeling this was just the eye of the storm.

FORTY-FIVE

SNOW

AUGUST

Marcus' safe house in Manhattan wasn't nearly as elaborate as Aren's homes had been, but it would work—warded and secure in the human sense. The ten souls and one mortal body seemed to press against its size; the cramped loft was meant for two. Alvara peeled herself out of my arms too soon. She was safe there, pressed against me like she'd been carved from my frame. Marcus tossed her an apple, and she swiped it out of the air and into her mouth in one swift motion. Alec and Fae both gratefully accepted their own. Livid rings of bruises lined their throats, but they were otherwise unscathed.

Jones was still unconscious, his breathing and heartbeat steady. Alvara, still struggling to form coherent words, had opened her memories to us, revealing all that she had seen within his mind. Perhaps, despite his flaws, the bastard was worth saving. Alvara certainly thought so.

She showed us what it had been like as the possession took over her mind—how memory distorted and her sense of self slipped away in that Middle Realm where time was non-existent. Aren and my voices pressed against the blackness, keeping her anchored.

A lesser woman—a lesser soul—might have succumbed entirely to that murky reality.

Jones' resistance had ensured that even in his position of power, the demons seldom mentioned names in his presence. They didn't give him the information we needed to summon those responsible for this mess. Because it was all one mess: the healers, the corruption—all linked back to whoever held the chains of the two Renown whose names we already knew—his handlers. Adrastos and Agamemnon answered to something beyond them.

The brothers of Renown seemed to have nominated themselves to clear the path to a dark utopia where humans were ruled and owned in exchange for a life without the struggle of being good or the ambitions that pushed them too far—a modern-day Sodom and Gomorrah.

In Adrastos' mind, The Great Commander would stand between them and that vision or join their ranks to rule the mortals—another blade in their arsenal.

Alvara folded in on herself in her chair, burying her face in her hands, elbows resting on her knees.

Having freed Jones, she would now manipulate his mind. She'd already planted the tale he'd spin to officials about the ballroom she'd left in ruins. Honestly, it was a miracle she'd had the restraint to leave the building standing at all.

Slowly, that telltale smirk stretched across Aren's face as he lifted his shoulders, reaching for Alvara. She scowled at him—or whatever he spoke between their minds.

"I didn't say it was my fault. But so many of their motivations are just... like my own."

"You want them to free themselves from their weakness, even if that takes a little tough love. They want to lord over them like gods. It's not the same thing." Ally's eyes flickered in response, and she rubbed them again. Aren continued, "You know, I've been fighting these bastards for nearly fifteen hundred years. You would think they'd be more creative than world domination by now."

Alec snorted, running his hands through his light hair for what was probably the dozenth time. "At least our opponents are predictable."

"In motive, perhaps. Just not in their plans," Lana countered. She too leaned forward, folding in on herself. It seemed most of us were daunted by the sheer numbers opposing us. We would need help—lots of it.

The Renown, while rare to spot, were not rare in number, as I'd been led to believe. Aren and Ansel had waged such a war on the grey demons that many believed their numbers were dwindling. But it seemed they had kept many of their kind hidden away for such a time as this. Brutal, muscled, and primarily male, their army appeared to be at least twice the size of Grayshell. We had no way to get an accurate count, short of drawing them out, which posed more risks than Alvara or Aren were willing to accept just yet. And even if we could, it wouldn't ensure they would unleash the full might of their host upon us.

Alec tossed his apple up into the air and watched it spin before palming it again. Again. Again. Finally, he leaned back in his chair.

"So. We draw out Adrastos or Agamemnon?"

"They're not the head of the serpent," Aren countered. Ansel, sitting across from the Commander, rubbed at his dark stubble. Those silver eyes glinted with the challenge approaching, but his lips remained sealed. "Killing them would likely only anger whoever holds the leash."

"But it would draw him out, wouldn't it?"

"Maybe. Maybe not." The Commander shrugged. "Our best bet is getting Ally's hands on one of them so we can grasp the scope of this mess, keeping August in the clear until we know what's going on."

"And what, exactly, would that entail?" I shifted in my seat, glancing between Alvara and Aren, who exchanged wary, anxious looks.

"August, you're not even fully trained. We haven't been able to trigger you to remember what you are—to remember how to become The Commander. It would make the most sense to keep you in Grayshell." My blood ran cold as Aren raised his palms, as if to tell me not to make this difficult.

"Like hell am I sitting this out while any of you are down here fighting."

"You have a choice, August." Alvara's eyes sparkled with an intensity that nearly took the wind out of me. "You're not our subject."

"Then you have it. I'm not standing down."

Aren, leaning against the wall by Marcus, opened his mouth, but Alvara spoke first, straightening her spine. "August just held steady and anchored me here. He is the key in the coming war. It's his right to decide for himself." She looked to her sire, who closed his mouth, lips quirking at the corners as he surveyed her. He narrowed his pale eyes, then with a sigh, gave her a single nod.

"I trust you both."

"So, we all fight then." Lana tossed her white hair over her shoulder. "We're going to need every sword we've got."

"And then some," Ansel grumbled, running his scarred hands over his hair.

"Allies shouldn't be too hard to come by. I have a few life debts that might need calling in." Aren rolled his neck, that grizzly grin on his face as he popped his knuckles.

"We are, of course, at your service." Marcus and Aren clasped forearms before pulling into a hug. Jason and Damien both bowed their heads.

"As we are at yours, brother. Always."

"Who else?" Ansel stood. "Who else have we got? I respect Marcus, but his coven is small. We're going to need twice what we have to even stand a fool's hope against *that*." The image Alvara had implanted in our minds flashed before me—thousands of Renown, clad in terrifying black metal armor, bearing an assortment of wicked-looking weapons. "As Grayshell is the largest hierarchy in Middle Realm, who else can we call on? Furthermore, who will answer?"

Fae stood as well, only rising to Ansel's shoulder. "Nathara, perhaps?"

Ally snorted. At the same time, Aren shook his head and ran his tongue over his teeth. "They have numbers, but they're no soldiers."

"Unless you need an exorbitant number of healers, or have a need for rune readers and crystals, they're no help to our kind." It was the first time I'd seen Alvara sneer about souls. I tucked away that kernel of information for later.

Marcus seemed to understand her and offered, "You lot have always been close with the Thornquist clan. They'd answer a call for aid, wouldn't they?"

"Most likely. If we can find them. Kingsley isn't exactly known for holding still."

"No, he's not. But his territory isn't that large, is it? How hard is it to find a coven within three states?" Marcus challenged.

Alec's eyebrow rose. Something in the way his jaw clenched left me feeling that perhaps allies would be harder to establish than Aren believed —and that Alec didn't care for those being proposed. He caught my glance and shook his head.

"When they don't want to be found? Very. Last I checked, Kingsley covers their scents. He's thorough when it comes to disappearing." Fae wrinkled her nose. A thought occurred to me.

"We can't travel between Middle Realms? Wouldn't the hierarchies be connected?"

Aren and Ally exchanged glances, some unspoken tension rising between them. It was Ally who answered. "In theory, yes. But Middle Realm is a frequency—each hierarchy its own within it. To be welcomed into another one, we have to merge with that frequency. It's...easier said than done. And that's if we can travel across the gaps between them."

"What's in the gap?"

"Wards. Like...a great desert full of snakes. That sort of thing."

I gaped at her, eyebrows raised. "*Why?*"

Amusement played across her lips. "So that if one of us is compromised, we're not all taken down with them."

"So, no one travels between Middle Realm hierarchies?"

"Few have ever tried. We just jump between our earthbound homes. It's faster...and...less treacherous."

"Shit. So, if we're to find *Kingsley*, we..."

"Head to the north."

"Oh."

Alec snorted and narrowed his eyes at the Commanders. "Marcus?"

"Yeah?"

"How's your relationship with—"

"Don't say what you're about to say." Alvara glared at him, her face drawn. My curiosity piqued as Alec snorted. She continued, "It's a useless question. Besides, we've already discussed too much where the walls have ears. Meet me back where this night started." She rose to her feet, that casual grace returning to her muscles as she reached for Jones' still-sleeping body. Without another word, she jumped with him.

When Alvara arrived back at Marcus', her exhaustion sagged her shoulders. Even her hair seemed to have lost a bit of its shine. She had jumped directly into our room—Marcus had altered his wards to let us all in and out freely—and began peeling the gown off her skin. *Fuuck.* Blood rushed to my groin, and I cleared my throat, setting my tea down on the table beside my armchair in the corner. She paused, flashing a quick smile that didn't quite reach her shadowed eyes.

"Thank you, August. For the respect..." She took a heavy breath. "After three hundred years of war...it's just a body." She shrugged. "Unzip me?"

I swallowed the lump in my throat. The book I'd been reading on the seat behind me, I cleared the space as she pulled her hair over a shoulder, exposing her slender, bare shoulder blades between the fabric. My cock stirred, heat welling up my spine as my eyes dared to soak in her shape—her subtle curves and hollows. Dangerous games. My body ignited as the scent of her enveloped me. *Just a body.* Christ. It became a fight to keep my breathing even as I swallowed down what her bare skin did to me. I was sure she could scent it as I carefully dropped the zipper to the low of her back, hesitating as my fingers grazed the curve of her tight, muscled ass. Lungs empty of air, body begging for one taste, I fought the urge to run a finger up her spine.

Dress loose around her lean frame, I jumped downstairs.

Holy shit. How much longer? How much longer could I be near her, watch her, see her...*want* her like this without doing *something*? Anything. The ache settled into my bones, a ruthless psychomachy threatening to split me in two. She knew—couldn't have missed my thoughts over these long months.

Movement caught my attention, and I turned toward the grand windows overlooking the city. Snow. Snow had settled into Chicago—presumably the same storm that had silently crept into New York when we left. How many fucking hours had I been sitting in that chair?

The city lights glowed against its shimmering surface as great swirling clumps fell to the earth. Everyone had long since fallen asleep, so it was a relief when the door opened silently beneath my fingers. The bitter chill bit into my skin with an invigorating hello. I welcomed it, breathing in the harshness of winter.

The rain has begun, but the snow has not yet melted. The thought peeled through me. How many weeks did I have to save her? To save us? As flakes melted against my bare skin and settled on my eyelashes, I focused on breathing. My mind went as stark and silent as the winter night.

FORTY-SIX
REAPERS
ALVARA

August jumped out of the room, granting me a privacy that my exhaustion deemed sweet but unnecessary. The dress slid to the floor with a rustle of fabric against skin. I eyed the bed, seriously contemplating collapsing into it clad in nothing but my undergarments, but instead strode to the corner where August had been sitting, reading one of Marcus' books. On the table between the two chairs sat two cups of tea. I stared at the gift for a moment, mesmerized by the swirl of steam, before shifting to pick up the fullest one.

The moment my skin touched the surface, I was thrust into a vision of August: first, his worried pacing, then his tea preparations, followed by him sitting in this very room, sipping his cup, staring out the window with hollow eyes. Finally, he cleared his throat, turned to the cup as though he could see me, smirked, and chuckled, "Hey. I'm glad you're okay. A cup of tea and a nap, as requested." The image faded, and my breath released, guilt swirling as my mind retraced the snappy words I'd thrown at him earlier. *Never a wound that takes more than a healing hand, a cup of tea, and a nap. Get over it, August. Would you be happier if it was you?*

The cup was warm to the touch, and a moan escaped my chest as the hot liquid poured down my aching throat. Steam caressed my face as if a hand were concealed within it. He cared about me. August. He cared about me, worried for me, and I snapped at him for it. Snapped out of impatience... and perhaps... out of ego. Ego that I would always find a way out, that I had it handled. But... I only had today handled because he waited for me, held his ground as he stared down a demon, and called me home.

. . .

ONE OF AUGUST'S hoodies and my favorite pair of sweatpants seemed like the perfect attire for the evening. His scent wrapped around me, reminding me of what he'd done tonight with every inhale. I downed the cup of tea he'd left, nestled down in bed, and called him back to join me. The bond between us went silent. I nudged again. Nothing. Anxiety coiled into a tight spring in my chest, and I peeled myself back out of bed, hurrying for the stairs. His name was on my lips as the door nearly collided with the wall under the force of my panic. But there, standing in the threshold at the top of the stairs, was a bare-chested August. Snow clung to his curls and lashes. But I had only a heartbeat to note the details before I realized there was fear in his eyes and his heart was pounding.

"August?" I inclined my head, raising my brows in question.

"Something is wrong. We need to go."

"Go? Go where? August, what—"

Two doors creaked open too quickly beside us, and I turned to see Aren in a fighting stance, fists clenched at his sides. Alec came hopping into the hallway, still yanking on his boots.

"What's wrong?" he said blearily. Alec wiped his hands over his eyes, and Aphaea appeared behind him, her platinum hair mussed, her porcelain face twisted into a grimace.

"What in Sam Hill is *that?*" Lana's irritation wafted up the stairs, and I furrowed my brows.

"Ally?" Aren's voice wasn't a question so much as a command.

"Nothing. I was about to go to sleep."

"But her magic is drained to the dregs. I could feel it the moment she landed. She could miss something." August ran a hand through his hair.

"My *energy* is low. Yes," I admitted. The energy around us began to swell, as though the air itself pressed down on us, pulling and yanking, as if it would have me see what lay outside the window. At once, we all turned toward the flurries of snow swirling outside the glass.

Well, I felt that.

Aren huffed a laugh but strained his eyes, as though he could peer across the city through the snow. We all mirrored the motion, scanning as many rooftops as we could see through the blizzard and towering structures. Aren's energy twisted into the closest vibration of fear I'd felt in some time, and I turned to find him with narrowed eyes, shoulders pulled back, arms loose, feet staggered. He flexed his hands.

I...I recognize the feel of him.

"That's a *person?*" August's voice was soft, his body so close I could feel his familiar warmth against my back. Aren gave a curt nod, his brow furrowed. As his eyes widened, I jerked back toward the window. The energy swelled again, only a few blocks away, and a subtle red shield glimmered along the edges, like a crimson aurora borealis. Within its center, a scintilla burst apart, like a tiny star imploding on the horizon.

"*Shields!*" Aren boomed, throwing both hands up and ushering us away from the window toward the wall. My feet felt heavy as I tried to follow, my eyes still glued to the horizon. August wrapped his arms around my waist and hoisted me over to the wall, turning me to face him.

I felt the Westerlunds stirring in their bedrooms downstairs as our shields opened. Shit. They'd been asleep through it. August's eyes widened, sensing them too. In the distance, there was a whirring noise, like we were huddling under a bridge as a train passed over. Or a tornado barreling down on us. August knelt beside me and slammed his hands into the floor, Alec only a heartbeat behind him. Their shields burst open in a blinding wave of white light, and August echoed Aren's command down the mental bond to our brothers. Their sleepy energies barely had time to comply before the attack collided with our building, the glass rumbling and rattling, the floor turning to liquid below our feet, and that distant whir became a roar in my ears. Our shields waved around us like molten lava, threatening to buckle. I poured my strength into mine, my arms trembling with the force of it. Nothing. I had nothing left to give. My eyes burned, tears threatening to fall as I forced my shield to hold. August, sensing my struggle, reached up a warm, broad hand and set it against my back.

Like jumper cables, his energy flowed through me, electric tingles racing up my spine as power surged from us, reinforcing my crackling shield. The tears poured freely then, exhaustion taking hold of my mind completely. Somewhere beyond the roaring in my ears, someone was screaming. Screaming in fear. Perhaps pain. I couldn't sense them, couldn't read them. It seemed every ounce of who I was had been drained.

As suddenly as it had burst open on the horizon, the power shuddered to a stop. The screaming went with it. Our shields remained for a moment, our eyes all turning in opposite directions.

"Is it... clear?" Aphaea whispered the words, as though she feared speaking it aloud would welcome it back. Aren, his shield nearly a solid barrier around the group, strode to the window to stare out at where that light had flashed on the horizon.

"It seems so."

"What was that?" Alec rose to his feet as our shields retreated into us. He scowled out at the city.

"I..." Aren hesitated. I hadn't seen him lost for words. Not once in three hundred years. Lana and Ansel came sprinting up the stairs, blades drawn and eyes wild. They surveyed our huddled group quickly before turning toward the window. Their eyes returned to Aren as he finally spoke. "I believe The Reapers have found us."

Despite the fur-lined coat pulled tight around my waist, the storm was brutally cold, my skin protesting against the bitter wind. It had only been a few blocks, but Aren insisted we walk rather than jump. Conserve our energy. Conceal our movements. It seemed The Reapers were legends from before my time. But Aren... Aren had encountered them many centuries ago.

The Reapers knew no powers aside from their ability to drain the strength from their prey. At least when Aren had encountered them, they wielded no elements, not even earth, as most of The Renown did. But Aren's first escape had been narrow without his elements. And in the centuries that had passed, the Reapers had plenty of time to learn additional skills, just as we did. They had been mere newborns when he'd fought them before. He was only a handful of decades older than them, and it had been the closest he'd come to death in his millennium... until his run-in with the crowned demon in the fall.

We had briefly discussed this possibility months ago, and yet the words still crashed across my mind as he said them. I'd never seen the Reapers or felt the lethal pull of their magic on my own until we encountered them with the Westerlunds. And even then, as August and I acted in the face of it, I hadn't believed that's whose mind I'd infiltrated. It would have been helpful for the visions to include that particular nugget of information...

My teeth began to chatter, and I fought down the instinct to summon a flame to warm us. If I was being honest with myself, I wasn't sure my energy had replenished enough to summon so much as an ember, anyway. Exhaustion filled my legs with sand, my shoulders curling in. Even breathing took more effort than I wanted to expend. August seemed to sense it and hovered by my side like a sentinel. He ran his gloved hand up and down my back, a silent reassurance that he was with me. For a moment, I wished his warmth could reach through the layers of down, fabric, and fur. But the touch was enough.

Twelve o'clock. Aren growled down the line.

I steadied myself with a long breath. Still, no visions came. Sure enough, straight ahead, too far to scent, three figures gathered at an intersection of alleys. We each straightened, hands poised on weapons, eyes straining. Ansel and Lana naturally turned to guard our backs, in case we were being herded here. In case we were walking into a trap without visions to guide us. They knew I was spent. August's hand solidified on my back, a steady presence across my spine. Was he still sending me his energy? Still trying to strengthen a battery that was drained to the dregs?

The figures turned, hoods concealing their faces, to watch our approach. The two on the sides summoned shields, and the man in the center drew one of the two gold swords strapped to his back. Like Aren. The buzz of power around us told me Aren, Alec, and August had done the same before my senses did. The scrape of metal on leather told me Ansel and Lana were not waiting to draw their blades. I made to peer into their minds but remembered to conserve energy, instead glancing behind me to ensure no enemies lurked there. None did. Returning my attention to the three ahead, I focused on breathing. We were steps from being close enough for me to cast my power ahead and touch their minds when they each turned and sprinted down opposite sides of the alley. As if they knew.

The one with swords headed straight ahead, the two with shields to either side.

"Do we divide to follow them?" Fae whispered.

"That's their intention," August and Alec countered simultaneously.

"We risk them herding us if we stick together." Lana kept her sword by her side, and I fingered my own dagger, still sheathed.

Aren glanced at me out of habit, huffed a breath, and directed, "Westerlunds hang back, be ready to shift, and wait for trouble to sound. Respond to who needs you. August and Ally will take the one wielding swords, Alec and Fae take the right flank, Lana and Ansel the left. I'll follow my intuition once you're moving."

We all nodded and sprinted after our marks on nearly silent feet. August and I barely made it two blocks before the hair on the back of my neck began to rise. I glanced over my shoulder to see Aren slowly beginning to follow us, one sword drawn. My breath hitched a bit. Not a good sign.

The Westerlund brothers were a vague shadowy outline through the onslaught of white, only a block behind him, still in their human forms. We slowed to a walk, gathering breath and strength as something in my core screamed that this was wrong. *Not right, not right, not right*, it seemed to chant. August set his gloved fingers against my own, and I curled around him. We both kept our heads on swivels, side to side. He bristled, and my attention turned toward him.

"Something is... wrong." The words were a whisper on his lips. I nodded my agreement, squeezing his fingers before dropping his touch to draw my dagger, flipping it and weighing its familiar balance in my hand. Aren was still following us, his energy palpable. He kept watching our six as we scanned from nine to three.

I scented him before I saw him—scented the spice, ice, fire, and night. The darkness around us somehow thickened. I whirled, blade drawn, fingers itching to unleash the last of my strength against whatever The Reaper had for us. So busy looking to the side and front, I'd never thought to look *up*.

Aren's bellow of warning came one heartbeat too late, as a colossal bird soared down toward us. Swords raised, we hissed together until the blinding light burst forth from the great winged beast. When the flash faded, the silhouette of a man stood before us. August beat me to him, sword swinging. The shadow parried through the snow, streetlamps the only light in the night. Again and again, they danced through the onslaught. I dove forward, but the man pulled his second sword and spun it in a circle, intending to engage us both. A snarl tore from August, and he slashed and swung with a vigor he'd yet to show. Again and again, they spun and parried, August trying to keep the man's focus. But beneath the shadowed hood, I sensed his stare circle back to my face.

Slowly, I raised my free hand to pull down the fur-lined hood, allowing the light to strike my features. The man hissed and staggered under August's brutal blow, and his scent flared as blood was drawn. Familiar. That smell of burning forest on a moonless night. Just as I meant to engage, I hesitated at the tang of his blood in the air.

Not right, not right, not right.

The vision flashed so violently into my weary mind that I gasped—so brief it barely made sense, but I knew in my gut it was the only warning I would get.

As the air was ripped from my lungs, I dove forward, rallying every last scrap of strength in my core. As the man's attention turned to me, I realized I was screaming. With a flick of my wrist, my dagger spiraled forward as I slammed my other hand into August's back. Every single ounce of energy left in my body was thrown forward, and August had time only to turn, panic in his wide eyes, before he vanished from the alley with a crack. Whether it was the forced jump or the last ember of power leaving my body, I wasn't sure.

The man whirled forward, having caught my blade. The earth tilted below me, nothing left to throw against him as he hurled his force at me. A flash of shield appeared and vanished between my hands, and the man laughed as he sketched a taunting bow.

Aren was close enough to sense, close enough to hear his warning bellow.

Again, the scent of rotting woods hit my senses, my final warning before a blast of dark power collided with me from the sky, pulling me into the blackness.

FORTY-SEVEN
BONES
AUGUST

The bellow of outrage didn't have time to leave me before she'd done it. One heartbeat, I heard her gasp, scented her fear. The next, she was colliding into me. And then the ground fell out from under my feet. It was a sloppy jump—fast, forced, frantic. I didn't even know we could do that to someone.

When I landed in Marcus' home, it was on my hands and knees. My palms barked with the impact.

God dammit, Ally! I hollered, my anger sending tremors down my legs as I rose. She had benched me mid-fight. Sent me here. *Why?!* I asked as much through the mental connection. My heart faltered as those angry words met silence. Nothing. Blackness stretched down the bond between me and my girl. *Ally?* Again, nothing returned. No apologetic nudge or cocky justification. No humor or reassurance. No view of the ongoing conflict. My heart became a roaring staccato in my ears. *Guys??* Only stunned silence responded.

Fuck.

I jumped back to the alley. Only heartbeats had passed, but I found Aren on his knees in the snow, rage radiating from him, hammering against my ribs. I whirled, scanning every corner. The Westerlunds were sprinting through the snow, their shouts inaudible as the shimmering white blanket absorbed the sounds.

No. Even my mental voice was a hoarse croak. I shook my head. *No.* Aren looked at me, eyes glistening, chest heaving. The images played out in my mind. Seconds. I had been gone only seconds, and they'd *taken* her.

Aren had tried to leap into the shadow of their jump, tried to follow the shadow magic... but collided with a ward. A wall. He had just fallen to his knees when I'd reappeared.

The others were closing in on us, and it was Alec's voice that broke the silence. Broken. Ragged. Raging. Calling her name. Just her name.

"Where?" he demanded, eyes on the Commander still kneeling in the snow. I thought he might strike him. Aren looked up, eyes hopeless, and shook his head. "God dammit!" Alec roared. He whirled, throwing his blade into the mortar of the brick wall across from him with a crack that reverberated like a gunshot. His fingers raked through his long curls as he fell to his haunches.

"Fuck." It was a whisper on Ansel's lips, dark eyes wide and stunned. "They knew. The masquerade. The exorcisms. They knew."

"The trap was for August." Aren's voice was breathless. "It was meant for August. Alvara... she was... a consolation prize." He'd seen the vision that led to her hurling me back to safety. Seen it as darkness descended.

Lana swore, low and filthy, sheathing her blade to rub at her face, then hold her head. Fear had given way to vicious retribution, and the need for vengeance pulsed in the surrounding air. One image danced between our minds—the image that had summoned them all to her side. The image of Alvara, battered and broken at the hands of monsters. Alvara. *My* Alvara. *Mate.* My soul mate.

I tapped down that connection, reaching toward her, begging her to respond.

We became statues in that alley, staring unseeingly at the spot where she had last been. Ansel moved to it, removing his glove to sense the energy where she had vanished. Perhaps read it as she would have. Nothing. There was no trace of her.

The cold eventually brought our minds back to the present, bodies demanding a reprieve. One by one, we vanished from that dusted alley. I was the last. The last one standing, staring, begging God, the Universe, any being that would listen, for mercy. For a miracle. For her to appear, panting and out of breath from her escape. From slaying them where they stood, cleaving them from the earth like weeds. For her to be here, where I might finally tell her all I felt, all I knew, all I wanted. Taste her lips. Feel our breath mingle.

Please.

I begged. For Alvara, I was not above such things.

There was no sense of time, sitting in that pool of grief. Begging. God. The Universe. The Goddess the witch clans allegedly worshiped. I didn't care who answered, as long as someone did.

My skin was stinging, limbs entirely numb, breath frozen in my beard, when I finally made the jump.

The scent of coffee greeted me. Coffee and adrenaline. The air was rotting with the latter. They'd been chugging the scalding, bitter liquid for a while, only a small cup left in the pot on the counter, all in fighting leathers and armor. All huddled around a map now taped to the great island in the kitchen. Aren's shoulder blades looked like they might burst through his shirt—might grow wings and fly after the great bird that had attacked us.

Marcus and his brothers were picking chicken legs clean, not bothering to eat the meat. They just tossed the remnants onto the counter beside them. I watched as they separated meat and tendon from the bones.

Aren, his knuckles white under his grip on the counter, growled. "We do not practice dark magic. We do not—"

"Aren." Ansel's voice cut into my consciousness. His tone a warning bell. "It's *Alvara*, Commander. There is a time and a place for restraint. This is not it." I somehow registered the small mercy in those words. Somehow knew that Aren's grinding teeth were in true discomfort, that Ansel was keeping his perspective. The stomach-turning image of Alvara's broken legs and defiant face flashed in my vision. I swallowed down the bile that followed. It wouldn't end that way. I would burn the world to the ground before it ended like that. Burn out each den of those monsters before I'd let it come to *that*.

Vaguely, I heard Aren swear and grant his consent to whatever plan they were hatching. A flicker of gratitude blinked in my chest.

A glass of water appeared in front of me, and somewhere in the distance, I heard Alec order me to drink. I did.

Someone patted me on the back. As if in condolence. I snarled my warning.

They shifted, debated, and argued.

Something was on fire.

"Nathara would nail my balls to the wall if she knew we were using chicken bones," Jason muttered to no one in particular.

"Well, it'll have to fucking work," Aren growled. "Because it's all we've got."

And then Marcus was there, staring at me, hand braced on my shoulder. He didn't heed my warning growl. Instead, his fingers gripped deeper into the muscle and bone until it hurt.

"Mate, I need you to focus." He snapped his other fingers, and I settled my gaze on his cerulean blue eyes. Pain. Agony and anger, mingling with a hidden shadow of alarm dwelled there. "Mate. Stick with us. We will find her. We will get her back. We need you to do the scrying."

"What?" My voice came out breathless. It didn't even sound like my own.

"Scrying. Your connection will be the most powerful."

"I—Alec or Aren will know—"

"Alec and Aren aren't her mate. You *are*. You will have the strongest connection. Jason says your braid is the most interwoven. It would be better if the mating had been made official. Even as it is, you will be our best chance."

"Scrying? I—"

"You can't screw it up, mate. We've cleared the bones, we've done the enchantment. You just toss them."

"Well, you think about Alvara. You think of her everything—her smell, her energy, the way she feels, the way she looks, the way her smile affects you. You think of *Ally*. And then you toss them." Jason held his fist out to me. I opened my palms, and a half dozen bones clattered into my outstretched hands, still warm from having the remaining tissue boiled off. I stared at them. Stared and stared.

"Find her, August." Aren set his hand on my shoulder. I turned to him, to find his tears had long since been spent. His pale blue eyes lined in red. Not really believing it, I nodded. And thought of Ally. Of all she was. To me. To the world. I thought of her mighty blade and keen mind. Of how badly the world needed her relentless courage. I thought of how badly I needed her. How much I loved her. How desperately I needed her to know that. To man up and say it, even just once. I thought of her scent, her feel, the way she moved like water over stones, the way her voice reminded me of chimes on the wind. With one last prayer, I tossed the bones onto the map.

FORTY-EIGHT
ULTIMATUM
ALVARA

Mother *fucking* birds?!

The sharp metallic tang of blood was thick in my mouth, and my head felt like death itself hung in the shadows within it. Throbbing pain arched down my spine like a death knell. Somewhere in the distance, soft music was barely audible. The warm canvas beneath me felt like the hammock curve of a cot, and I could smell smoke, sweat, and unwashed bodies.

I peeled my tongue from the roof of my mouth, hating the feel of cotton that was left in its place. My mind seethed with anger that I hadn't been looking up.

Birds. Fucking shifting shadow birds.

"Not like this," a guttural voice sliced through the air, tinged with an English accent.

"She will *break* him. She is the key in all of this." The second voice was even lower, laced with the same accent—a bass deeper than Marcus'. If I hadn't already schooled my muscles into stillness, that voice would have frozen me. I knew that voice. I'd heard it in a dozen visions, echoing from that dark basement hallway.

"She is the key in *more* than just this, or did you not see inside her mind as I have?"

"There is no binding a power like that. It's bullshit. Just some fucking wall to defend her mind."

"Horse shit, Ag. And you know it. Don't let your bloodlust get the better of you."

"Bloodlust?" A guttural growl. I tried to reach into their minds, but my thoughts couldn't budge against the pain thrumming through me. The only view I had was the darkness behind my eyelids. "They fucking deserve what's coming to them, and you know it. It's not bloodlust; it's fucking justice."

"She's an innocent in this." The other one snarled, but the first continued, "You didn't even bother to look through her memories, did you? To scent her? To see what she *is* to him? What use will he be if he's in splinters? I swear, you have the nuance of a brick and the profundity of a shot glass." In any other situation, I would have laughed. As it was, I kept my breathing as even as possible.

"Oh, fuck you. Why even bother—*how* can you possibly defend *her*? Do you realize how many of us have fallen at the hands of that *bitch*? Can't you feel their souls on her? Smell them? She has slaughtered our kind for sport."

"It's a war, Ag. She wouldn't be much of a second if she wasn't good at her job. She wouldn't offer *us* anything if she wasn't good at her job."

"Prick."

"Bloodthirsty bastard."

Another growl. "They're not even—"

"They *are*. Don't go there with me. If you destroy one, you destroy the other. Besides, her start wasn't much different than our own. But you're too goddamned blind to see that."

"Are you telling me you think you can *turn Alvara* of *Grayshell*?" A snort of distaste, and humorless rumble of laughter. "She's Aren Amadeus' pet, for God's sake." The second voice spat the words, dripping with disdain for my Commander. My sire.

"She sees everything. She's a better ally than an enemy." Something in their dynamic, in the snarl that followed, felt authentic enough that it was a struggle to keep my heart from racing. My breathing remained steady and slow, feigning sleep. Were these Renown? My abductors didn't seem to have harmed me beyond knocking me unconscious, but the headache pounding in my skull was ferocious—like someone had smashed an anvil atop my forehead.

Not much time could have passed, as my energy had not refilled in the slightest, and the blood in my mouth was still tangy.

The sudden rustle of leather—perhaps tent flaps—caught my attention, and the warm breeze that followed confirmed my suspicion.

"Adrastos, you're needed." My stomach twisted into a tight knot at the name, even if I'd known it, sensed it, heard it. The energy shifted as someone approached, icy fingers brushing my hair away from my face and the sweat from my brow. They were uncharacteristically gentle. It took all my training to contain the flinch. My stomach roiled at the touch, the scent of flame and pine.

When he spoke again, his voice was low, hushed, and untamed. "If you so much as threaten her, I'll cut your balls off myself. Do you understand me?"

Another snarl was the only response. Another flap of leather, and warm breeze over my damp skin. There was a gentle flicker of flame nearby, a brazier perhaps. And I felt no draft except for the one at my back. So, only one exit until my flames returned. Could I feign unconsciousness long enough to gain the strength I needed? Unlikely.

So, the growly one must have been Agamemnon. As if in response, the reek of carrion and pine filled my nostrils. How was one scent still so human, while the other had succumbed to the demons within?

There was a tug on my arm, an ache there, like my skin was tighter than it should have been. Healing a slice, perhaps. I tried to scent the room further without breathing too deeply, straining my senses for anything to give me an advantage. A quick mental count confirmed my weapons were missing from where I'd left them. A sliver of cold pressed between my breasts told me they had seized all but one. Not that a dirk would do me much good against an enemy like this, especially without elements behind it. The murmur and distant bellows of laughter were enough. The baying of beasts and scrape of steel. A war camp? But where? The constant hum and chirp of birds and clicking of insects confirmed I was somewhere in the south.

"So?" Agamemnon demanded.

"Reinforcing the wards. They're actually *scrying* for her." A dark chuckle. "Interesting. We don't have much time."

"Wake the bitch up."

"Watch your tongue. You're no better than they were."

"We need to see if it worked."

"I still think you should have waited."

"You'll shut your fucking mouth if I'm right."

"Our chances of getting her to ally go down tenfold."

"So what?"

"You're hasty and nearsighted."

"You're blind and fooling yourself."

"Perhaps. But that's not for you to say."

"Right. Let the bitch make her own decisions." There was a scuffle, then the sound of flesh on flesh. A growl. And then Agamemnon snarled, "You'll damn us all by the end of this."

"You didn't see it. Sense it. You didn't see her flare when I went in to fight him—didn't see the way she gave up everything to save him. We wield both, or none. Kill one, kill both. She is who and what I believe she is. Now get out."

"Draz—"

"Get out."

Agamemnon harrumphed, but his angry, bitter, rotting presence left the small space on silent feet. The flap of the tent was the only indication he had, in fact, heeded the order. A moment passed. Another. There was a creak of wood, a sip of liquid, and the thud of a glass on a table. A long, dramatic sigh.

"So, are you going to open your eyes, or keep pacing your breath until we're all dead?"

I flicked my eyes open, making sure to glare as I did. But before me was only the smooth leather surface of the war tent and several stacks of leather-bound books bearing Latin titles. I braced myself and sat up smoothly, summoning Alec's swagger and Fae's easy grace. With a roll of my neck and a crack of my fingers, I turned to face the man we'd been hunting for these long weeks. I noted the brazier two feet to my side and the weapons propped against a bag by the tent flaps behind him. My face sculpted into a cool, calm, serene mask of boredom as my eyes scoured over the man in front of me. It took all my restraint to keep my breathing even. Aside from August, the broad-shouldered being across the room was the most handsome male I'd ever laid eyes on.

Like his brother, Adrastos' chiseled face was framed by onyx sheets of shoulder-length hair. That's where the comparisons halted, however. While most of the Renown were pale to the point of corpse-like gray, his skin retained a kiss of sun—more than mine, certainly. He grinned broadly as I studied him, balancing precariously on the back two legs of the wooden chair he sat in, his feet propped atop an ancient desk, fingers laced behind his head. The picture of arrogant leisure. If I'd had my strength, a flick of my finger would have sent that chair tumbling, the man landing on his back. That would wipe the smirk off his face.

He grinned, seeming to think as much, jerking his feet off the table and planting all four chair legs back on the ground.

"Nice of you to join me." He snapped his fingers, and two gold plates and goblets appeared on the desk. He snapped again, and they filled with steaming food and drink. Nice trick. This soul had to be nearly as powerful as Aren. Nearly, I assured myself. The smell of garlic and herbs made my mouth water. How long had I been out to be so hungry? "Eat, Princess."

I snorted and scowled at him.

"Are you, or are you not, a *daughter of the King*? I do believe that's the title you assumed to vanquish the demon in Senator Martin Jones earlier this very night. And I suppose, though the fool would never claim the title of King, being the second to Aren of Grayshell makes you hierarchy-royalty too."

I loathed the sound of Aren's name on his tongue. But I had no strength to summon. No bravado could cover the fact that I had no way to vanquish the demon in front of me. Only, Adrastos didn't feel like a demon. He didn't reek of death, sin, and anger, as his brother did. And his eyes...

I held that gaze, unwavering, determined not to be the first to blink. Adrastos smiled, the expression a bit crooked, unsettlingly...human. He blinked first, sighing just as theatrically, then stood. He moved as quickly as Alec could, nothing human about the way he suddenly sat by my side.

"I'm sorry about my brother. He's...impulsive. And petty. And shortsighted." He reached toward my cheek with a lover's familiarity, and I bit back the vile words that danced across my mind. Stay alive. Just stay alive until my strength returned. I flinched away despite myself when those icy fingers touched my cheekbone. Nothing. No reading. No visions. Just the sting of his flesh against a scrape I hadn't realized I had. Panic roiled in my gut. Panic and nausea. There had never been a touch that didn't come with a story.

Adrastos' eyes narrowed slightly. He hummed. "Interesting."

I stared into those eyes, just as human as my own. The flicker of the brazier trickled through them, and I studied the light in those irises—deep brown, like freshly tilled soil or a dirt road after the rain.

"Are you saying my eyes look like mud?" Amusement twisted his handsome features.

The surprise flashed across my face before I could control my reaction, and he raised his eyebrows in response.

"I suppose I am. I didn't mean it that way, though. You're not...what I expected," I admitted.

"I know," was his only response. I narrowed my eyes, willing my mind to go blank, to divulge no new information. "Irritating for you, isn't it? To be wrong?"

"And what, exactly, am I wrong about?" I kept my voice a mask of boredom. Indifference.

"Me. Us. The side you stand on." He tucked a strand of hair behind my ear, the familiar touch eerie and unsettling. His eyes traced over my face, head cocking slightly as he braced his jaw.

"What?" I demanded.

Adrastos snorted, shaking his head as his hand fiddled with a gold, ruby-encrusted hilt on his hip. "You remind me of someone. Couldn't be, though. I'd know her anywhere." He waved away the topic. "Besides, that was a lifetime or two ago." He reached for my face again, and I leaned away.

"Hold still." The command in his voice made me bristle, but I held my ground. He pressed his finger to my face, and I jammed my eyes shut, flinching as light burst from him. The stinging stopped.

"You..."

"Healed you. Yes."

"But why?"

"You weren't to be harmed in the first place. Now, eat. Drink. Heal." He rose and crossed the short gap to the desk. I wanted to throttle him, leap across the distance, wrap my arms around his throat, and strangle him. He snorted another laugh. "You could try, Princess. But I wouldn't if I were you. You'll find your strength is...lacking." He plopped down on the wooden chair behind the desk, rubbing his temples, eyes closed in apparent frustration.

"Stop calling me that," I growled. He chuckled—actually chuckled. I should've incinerated him the moment he'd jumped into that hallway to save his brother. He gave me a dry smile that told me he was indeed reading every word that crossed my mind. And yet...mine remained...silent. "What did you do to me?"

He sighed loudly and pinched the bridge of his nose. "I didn't do anything. My bouncing baby brother, however, decided to take it upon himself to test a theory. Evidently, it's even more effective than I'd dreamed it would be."

I glanced down at the tightness on my arm, where a bandage was stuck to the skin. My glare would have brought lesser men to their knees, but Adrastos met my stare. "He *drugged* me?"

A curt, apologetic nod.

"I would have preferred you speak with us first. Would have preferred you had your tools at your disposal so you could, in fact, see that I speak truth."

"How convenient for you—to spin your webs however you like and claim I'd find them true if I stood in my power...rather than face it yourself."

"Oh, trust me, *Princess*, I have no intention of facing off against you in your full power. I'm ambitious, not suicidal."

"If you don't intend to duel, then what do you intend for me? You dared to bring me here. You know who and what I am. As it stands, I'm sitting here at your mercy. So, humor me."

"I intend for you to see the truth and join our cause toward a better world."

"A better world?" I huffed a laugh. "I've seen the visions of the future you cast. It's tyrannical, demonic, and delusional."

He grinned broadly. "The futures I cast to whom? Men who seek power?" His words were a drawl. He scoffed. "They see what they want to see."

"They might see what you tell them to Adrastos, but I see the truth."

"Well, truth seeker, tell me then. What is my grand plan, as you clearly know it so well?"

"You believe in our superiority to humans. In restoring a structure of nobility to *rule* over mortals."

"I believe in freeing mortals from expectations they cannot meet."

"If by 'free' you mean succumbing to their wickedness?"

"Can you deny that they are already doing so?"

I stared him down for a long moment, willing the walls into place—walls built using energy I no longer had. "No." The word was matter-of-fact.

"I didn't think so. So what's the point, Prin—"

"Don't finish that."

"Fine." A lupine smile carved into his cheeks. "So what's the point, Alvara of Grayshell? Why fight so hard to guard them when they won't even fight for themselves? Why fight for their light when they themselves want nothing but shadow? Why force them to be what they are not?"

"I believe in doing what's right. God intended them to *be* the light, not the shadow."

"And yet...they fall short. Daily. They're tormented by their imperfection—the very humanity they're promised redeems them. Why torment them with what they *cannot be*?"

"You'll damn them all."

"They damn themselves." He sneered, running an enormous hand through his long, straight hair. The worst part was that I couldn't argue with him; I couldn't fully disagree. "They spit in the face of the gift they were given, which is so cruelly withheld from our kind, due to no crime of our own."

"*Your* crimes will land you in Hell in no time."

His eyes guttered, shadows dancing within. "As will yours, Alvara of Grayshell."

"We don't know that. We are half human, half—"

"Redeemed? Loved? Wanted? Think again, *Princess*. Your aunts and uncles above us would smite you the moment they laid eyes on you. All but one."

My eyes narrowed, just a fraction, but I wasn't willing to say the name he was baiting from me. The corner of his lip twitched, reading my anger, my stubbornness, and loathing.

"The only one who believes we have a right to exist—that we are as much a product of love as our human counterparts. That we deserve to set our own fate. Lucifer sees how we were wronged."

"And you believe him? The great deceiver spins lies in your ears, and you obey—"

He slammed his hands into the table, rattling the metal plates as he stood. "The great deceiver paid no attention until I saw their evil for myself. You think the Creator's most beloved angel of music dared to question his creator for *nothing*? He saw the wickedness, the ungrateful wretches you serve so adamantly, and witnessed how his Creator stooped so low to become one, saw that he—that *we*—would be cast aside despite our superiority."

At some point, I had risen to my feet, teeth bared at him. "You're no better than the wickedest of men."

"You *are* better than the *greatest* of men. *We* are. That's the difference. While you and Aren spin webs of delusion, suffering from self-imposed kalopsia, you fail to become all that you are designed to be. Created to be. But you worship the ground these evanescent, ungrateful mortals piss upon."

"We *worship* one God."

"And yet your life is dedicated to becoming weapons of death. What would the Prince of Peace say about that?"

"Only death for evil creatures like you, who value no life but their own."

"The lives I valued were all snuffed out like chattel by those you are sworn to defend." I bit back the words on my tongue. Sensing my silence, perhaps my flicker of surprise, he continued, "They're a miserable lot. All of them. Save the scattered few with the courage to *be*. The grit to persevere, as you do. The tenacity to follow the light. And I assure you, cousin, they will be spared. Lights like that are not so easily snuffed out. Nor would I wish them to be. Lights...like *you*. I cannot promise they won't suffer in the transition. But I assure you, they will rise in any environment." Adrastos sighed again and sat back into his chair, scooping his ancient goblet to his mouth. "Like a phoenix from the ashes, born anew."

He continued as he set it back on the wooden table before us. I found my seat again. "You have spent more time with them than I have. I'm sure at this point we can agree, most would happily sign away their freedom should we offer to *provide*. They're weak, courage-less creatures, prone to laziness and self-absorption. They are cruel and selfish as a whole. They don't care to fight, let alone excel. They want this. Want *me*. Want to be handed the bare necessities, left to their own pleasures, and stripped of the burdens this world has thrust upon them. I will not torture or torment them, as you no doubt believe. I will free them. Free them of the expectations your lot have placed on them all these years. They're incapable of being any more than they have always been. They will not change. They will not better themselves. Surely you, of all people, see that."

Silence settled between us. For a moment, my focus wandered to the stacks of books placed sporadically throughout the space, most leather-bound and gilded. A stack of great black tomes caught my attention, and I tucked away the titles for later: *Radices Medicinales et Herbae, Audentes Fortuna Iuvat, Maledicta et Illusiones*. My Latin wasn't as polished as Aren's, but from what I could tell, he was studying medicine, herbs, and illusions. I flexed my fingers under the table, willing the embers back where they belonged. Willing any flicker of power to appear so I could get out of here. He sneered and rolled his eyes, leaning back in his chair.

"Try as you might, Alvara of Grayshell, there is no lifting what has been done to you unless Agamemnon wills it so, or the breath drains from his lungs. You are, as you say, at our mercy for the time being. Eat. Drink. Heal. I'm sorry the drug slowed that last bit down." Adrastos twirled a gold fork between his fingers and speared a vegetable from his plate.

I eyed the food before me, still steaming with warmth. Chicken in a cream sauce, steamed broccoli, and carrots. Despite the grumble in my belly, there was no way I was eating anything he had provided. He sneered, rolling his eyes before slamming his fork down on the table and reaching across for my plate. He snapped his fingers, and both our chicken breasts were finely diced. He dumped my portion onto his plate, mixed the food together with my fork, then scooped half the contents back onto the gold platter in front of me. He did the same with the wine in the goblets, pouring them back and forth between the two, swirling the ruby liquid as he set it in front of me. Adrastos stuffed his mouth with the now-mixed food, washing it down with a gulp of wine so quickly his eyes watered. He extended his hand as if to say, 'there you go.' I shoved the plate an inch away from me. He telekinetically shoved it back.

"If I wanted you dead, Princess, you would be. Now. Eat. *Please*." The last word came through clenched teeth.

"Why bother? With any of this?" I motioned to the food in front of us, then touched the place he had healed on my cheek. He continued chewing, eyes growing hazy as he did. He took another long mouthful of wine before swirling the liquid in circles in his goblet.

"I like you, Alvara of Grayshell. Aren chose his second well. The fact that you cut down my men like you're mowing your lawn..." Apparent amusement tugged at the corners of his lips as he raised his cup in salute. "I expected you to be...larger." He chuckled around the last word and then took another swig. "As it is, you would make a much better ally than an enemy. I have no quarrel with you, or your golden boy Commander for that matter. Not yet, at least. And I believe in the strength of The Great Commander. In what he represents. In why he's here."

"He's here to rid the world of evils like you."

"The Great Commander is, again, here, *Princess*, to make the world a better place."

"He only rises when there are threats to the peace..."

"Threats like me? Is that the tale you've spun for yourself?"

"That's the truth you've brought to light with your army. With our healers falling like fish in a barrel."

He grimaced and stuffed his mouth with chicken. After a long moment, he wiped his face. "Trying to control demons is a bit like herding cats."

"There's a coven to the west that would mock you for that."

"Ahh," he cracked a laugh—a real one that touched his dark eyes. "The witch clans and their *familiars*. Yes. I'm acquainted with them...Okay, trying to control demons is like...nailing Jell-O to the wall. Does that work?" He blinked pointedly.

"If your intentions are as you say they are, why work with them at all?"

"They are, in fact, in great need of leadership, vastly outnumber *our* uncle, and enjoy...certain simple pleasures."

"If by 'pleasures' you mean tormenting the mortals—"

"They only whisper and confirm what the mortals *want* to hear."

"And take their bodies, hold them captive."

"Oooh, that bit is dauntingly inconvenient. How did you get that bastard out of you?" He narrowed his eyes and smirked suggestively enough that I wanted to kick him. He shook his hair out. "Let me rephrase—how did you vanquish that second hierarchy underling?"

"Burned to ash," I said through gritted teeth.

"Spicy little thing, aren't you?"

"Give my gifts back, and I'll give you a demonstration." I flashed a smile that was all teeth, and he grinned before tossing a carrot into his mouth. He chewed for a moment before swallowing. I wished he'd just choke.

"I'm sure you would enjoy that. For now, however, you will eat, and I will tell you how you walk out of this camp alive, with your powers restored, and what is coming down the pipeline for your precious pets. Deal?"

I scowled, wetting my lips and inhaling deeply, scenting the food for anything. But could my enhanced senses be trusted if my other gifts were gone? His plate was almost empty, and he reached over the table to spear one of my pieces of chicken before popping it in his mouth with a swagger I had never quite mastered.

Adrastos gulped pointedly.

"Fine," I growled. One thing was true: if he'd wanted me dead, I would be. Long before I had awoken, he could have slit my throat. So, options weighed, I ate.

The food was somehow still warm on the plate and as heavenly as anything I had ever tasted in the mortal world. He grinned triumphantly, snatching his goblet off the table, swirling it, and inhaling the scent of the Malbec in the glass.

"So, you are going to tell anyone who asks—especially my bastard of a brother—that you will pass my message along to your Commander, and extend our offer of an alliance to your hierarchy." He held up a hand as he saw the protest across my face or mind. "And I will ensure your full strength is returned to you. I do apologize that the crawlers are aware of where you've been staying, so I would highly recommend you and your friends return to your respective Middle Realms...until you're ready to duke it out."

Adrastos took a long sip of wine before resuming his swirling of the goblet. He inclined his head expectantly, and I sighed before taking another bite. "Good girl." The words were like nails on a chalkboard. He continued, "You'll return to The Great Commander, share what happened here, and the depth of our devotion to him—I'll explain in a moment, don't get ahead of yourself—and resume your training. You will eat, you will train, you will have a very merry Christmas, and you will watch as what I'm about to warn you of comes to pass.

"The four horsemen of the apocalypse have been beating at their doors for some time now. The first will ride a white horse, equipped with a bow, set to conquer the human realms. Sound familiar?" I nearly choked on my wine as the image of August on a flying white horse flashed into my mind. "Ahh, good. Your...special friend, our mutual acquaintance, the soul with the longbow. He is set to rival the first horseman. The second, on the red horse, rivals your beloved sire, who I pray is not too big for his britches and does, in fact, have cattle to go with his enormous hat." His distaste nearly dripped from the words. "You have a tracker who is, in fact, a goddess when it comes to fertility—not just the bouncing bundle of joy kind, but the leafy green kind as well. She will push against the third. And I'm afraid, dear cousin, the reason your healers are falling is in preparation for the plans of the fourth. The fourth horseman will only be brought down by a combination of things: you, my beautiful angel of *death*; The Great Commander, whole and healed; the fertility goddess; the warrior; the witch; *and* The Wraith."

I blinked at him, staring for a long while before my voice came out like a growl, "The Wraith?"

"Oh yes, she's a gem. And will undoubtedly make her appearance at the worst possible time for me. It's...in her nature." He shrugged. "Past life drama, don't ask. And no—I don't know what form she's going to take in this one. She was long since glamoured and warded against me."

"So, you're just going to release me—so we can stop the four horsemen, do your dirty work for you, and you can come in to convince them you're their hero at the end?"

He simpered, his tone flat. "You will conquer the horsemen again, because it's the right thing to do for the wellbeing of your *pets*. Light against dark, all that good stuff." He waved his hand in a flourish. "But I will, in fact, benefit from you clearing my way. In return, none of mine will attack or interfere with any of yours. We get through this mess together—as tenuous of a peace as that may be—and go our separate ways." A quick swish of his wrist, as if waving smoke from the air, cleared the topic. "If my calculations are correct, the first horseman will arrive before Cupid turns the town pink, so I would highly suggest being prepared by January."

"Why are you telling me this?"

"Because I like you. Your fire. Your adept blade. Because The Great Commander can bring this dream of mine to pass if all souls unite behind it. And because he needs you, Alvara. The Great Commander cannot do his job without you by his side—a great queen for a great king."

"And that's why I'm alive? That's why you convinced your brother to spare me?"

"For now. Should you choose to reject our alliance, Agamemnon, I'm afraid, takes poorly to such things. And as for me..." He shrugged with a nonchalance I wasn't sure he felt. "Perhaps the horsemen will need hands to burn the humans to the ground, should it seem I won't get my chance to create a better world."

"So, I become your lackey, or you help bring about the apocalypse? That's seriously your bargain?"

"Be it what it may."

"You're delusional."

A smile that would have brought lesser women to their knees. "And you have more faith than they deserve. They're coming for you, with or without me. And it will be a hell of a lot easier to glue this world back together if we work as allies. Would it not?"

I stared into those earthy eyes. He meant it, what he said. He believed all of it. It was right there on the surface of those too-human pools of brown.

"Aren will never bow to another man."

"But he will kneel before The Great Commander." It wasn't a question but a knowing. I knew it too. Should August ascend to that depth of power, he would be able to wield all hierarchies together under one banner. He was here to stop the damned apocalypse. Revelations come to life. Goosebumps danced down my spine as I realized Aren was already preparing himself to step aside and make way for a prophesied leader. A flaw in Adrastos' plan popped into my mind.

"The Great Commander would, in fact, also have command of *you*."

"August Porter is young. I believe he will agree with my thoughts. My plans."

"August Porter is twice what you will ever be. And he believes in freedom."

Those shadows danced across his features, seeming to emanate from him. "Then he is a foolish child. And will fall as an infant."

"So, you'll kill him? Be rid of him should he not comply?"

"Should it come to that. Though it would pain me to waste such a tool."

"You're not a leader, Adrastos. You're a dictator."

"Perhaps. But I will dictate what is right for my people."

"And who, exactly, does that entail? It certainly doesn't include me, or Aren, or August."

"I'm growing bored of this. Perhaps Agamemnon was right. Think on it, Alvara, my sweet. Think on it, and watch. Watch as the world begins to fall before the first horseman has even arrived. I will expect you all to give me an answer by the time a warm snap melts the snow. Should you refuse our proposed alliance, we will see who the better soul is that day." A flash of that bloody field with August walking across it burned in my eyes. His mouth curled, "Ahh, that. An ugly, ugly day should you wish it on yourselves. So easily avoided." He clicked his tongue.

"You were to use me to get to him."

"I wish to ally with The Great Commander. Not destroy him."

"And killing me would destroy him?"

His face went solemn. "Yes. It would. One in the same, evidently."

"So, you spare me to get to him instead?"

"Tonight, dear cousin, I do."

"So, what do you have up your sleeve, Adrastos? What else to barter him out? To make him let you use his power?"

"That is something I hope you choose not to find out." He pinched the bridge of his nose again and sighed dramatically. "Our time is out, I'm afraid. Your companions are quite persistent beings, aren't they? They've already scried for your location and will come to get you if I don't return you promptly. It will be a shit show." He sighed dramatically, feigning fatigue. "Take my word for it." My mind whirled at the idea of Aren stooping to such a thing—witchcraft; they had taken to witchcraft to track me down. He raised his right hand, setting his left on his heart. "I solemnly swear your power shall return to you by midnight tomorrow. On my life." Adrastos stretched out his hand. I raised my own, thankful that it was steady, as he clasped my forearm. I nearly recoiled as it burned, but he grinned and tightened his grip. Tiny letters and numbers burned against my pale flesh in a tight cursive scrawl.

AA21.25

"So, you know how much time I have left to make good." He chuckled. "As do I." He turned his forearm up to reveal his own arm had my initials branded into his flesh, with the same numbers beside it. In sync, both markings clicked down to 21.24. A timer, I realized. I stared at him, and my awe must have been obvious because he chuckled. The expression touched his eyes with a vulnerability I did not expect. "Let's get you home."

FORTY-NINE
BROKEN WARD
AUGUST

If someone didn't make a God-damned game plan to end the bickering, I was going to explode—literally, burst into flames as violently as Alvara had only hours ago. My Alvara. Captive, in enemy territory. And the coven was dissolving over how best to liberate her. A good thirty minutes of arguing had passed since those bones circled perfectly around Florida. A piece resembling a cross settled over one of the southernmost islands. That would be our starting point. But the who, what, and how of the matter had both Commanders' neck veins bulging as they debated. Aren wanted to go in guns blazing, while Marcus insisted they guard her with the entire army; only a fool would go in without reinforcements.

I was leaning towards grabbing Alec and Ansel and spiriting her away ourselves. One look at the two men focusing solely on me, and I knew they'd join me in a heartbeat. Only, we didn't know exactly where the camp was or the size of the force concealed on the island. We had no idea where she would be within it or how they were ranked for infiltration. If I was honest, Aren's all-guns-blazing idea was starting to look appealing. Burn the whole God-damned place to ash, as Ally would for any of us.

They were shouting again, and my rage was nearing its melting point.

"Enough!" I slammed my hands on the counter, pausing when the island trembled beneath me. "Ally would already have a plan by now, goddammit. You don't have another seer? Someone who can tell us which route will work?"

"Well, boys, I must say, it is nice to feel useful." We all spun towards the drawling voice behind us. Goosebumps erupted as quickly as my shield did.

The man of Renown from the hallway. From the visions. Adrastos, I realized with no small kernel of horror. His imposing figure leaned casually against the balcony's doorframe.

A feral growl tore through my chest, echoed by each male beside me. Marcus, sandwiched between Aren and me, sprouted dark claws from his knuckles. I bared my teeth. Adrastos clicked his tongue loudly enough for us to hear his admonishment. "Leash your pet, Commander. I have something that belongs to you."

"Watch your tongue, Adrastos." Aren stepped forward, flames dancing between his fingers. Dual swords glowed against his back.

"I was talking to *him*." Adrastos jerked his chin in my direction, his eyes flashing with challenge.

"Where is she?" I growled.

"Safe. Sound. Waiting in between."

"In between *what*?"

"*Worlds*, princeling. Waiting between worlds."

"Bring her back," I snarled. The air began to stir; the pendants above the island swayed and clinked, papers rustled, and the bones on the map slid off the counter to clink onto the floor. "Unharmed would be in your best interest."

Adrastos tilted his head sideways, the movement eerily reminiscent of Alvara's feline assessment. But he knew that, judging by the chiding grin on his face.

"Now." Thunder clapped overhead, inside the loft. Adrastos' muddy eyes flicked upwards, his cocky grin unfazed.

"Interesting. Are you as spicy as your mate, princeling?"

"Don't you fucking touch her."

"Ooooh, I like you. Now don't go worrying your pretty head; Alvara is fine. I didn't touch her." He narrowed his eyes, bobbing his head as if weighing the truth in his statement. "Well," he added with a lover's smile, "not in the ways *you're* worried I would."

"Bring her back," Aren repeated the demand.

"Oh, I will. Once, and only once, you've agreed to the terms."

"What?"

"Alvara carries a message from me and mine. You are to hear it out in its entirety. You are to consider the proposal. In exchange, she will be returned *unharmed*."

"What's the catch?"

"No catch, Commander. Your word for my own. An alliance—a flimsy one, by the looks of it—can be struck."

"Go to Hell." Alec prowled forward, a blade in each hand, spitting towards the man. Ansel loomed behind him, motionless as marble.

"Interesting. A fiercely loyal group of males this woman has." A dagger soared toward Adrastos' face as he spoke, and he barely twisted away in time to avoid its full force. Still, red bloomed across his cheekbone. He wiped a finger down it, wincing as it healed instantly, then popped the bloody finger in his mouth. "And females, evidently."

Lana snarled a warning, wielding two new blades. Fae had palmed her knives, legs braced in a fighting stance. Unfazed, Adrastos continued, "As I said. Hear her out. That's all I ask."

"Fine," I gritted through clenched teeth.

And then she was there, appearing out of nowhere. Not as if she jumped, but as though Alvara had been standing in front of him glamoured, and the glamour had been lifted. He shoved her forward, and Aren and I lunged to catch her. The male vanished as I wrapped my arms around her, and Aren shielded us both. The others charged forward despite Adrastos' retreat.

Adrastos' voice lingered in the air. "Alvara, my sweet, do take note. The medicine you were given tonight is in no short supply. Should you reject our proposal, our next meeting will not be so civil."

Lana hissed, and a shield of air barreled forward. I could have sworn I heard a laugh ring out in the distance.

I pulled her away to look at her, scouring over her face. There was no blood where there had been, only the stains along the neck of her hoodie—my hoodie—proving she had been struck at all.

"Are you hurt?" I lowered my eyes to lock on hers. She blinked and shook her head.

"No, they didn't touch me. Didn't do anything."

"Anything?"

"We... talked. Well, Adrastos talked. He made me eat dinner."

I glanced at Aren, whose eyes were as wide as my own. "They want an *alliance?*"

She nodded, still looking dazed. "Yeah. There's... a lot. A lot to discuss. But I—I just want to *sleep.*"

"Of course, Ally. Let's go upstairs."

"Not here. Grayshell. It's not safe here—crawlers or something. Adrastos warned me they would come."

"Ally—"

"Grayshell."

I breathed in her scent, but it was different. Simpler. Not quite as sweet. More... human. "Ally... your magic?"

She held out her arm, where it looked like she'd been *branded. AA 21.19.* "Adrastos swore on his life it would be returned before the timer finishes."

"Can she—can she go to Grayshell like this?" I looked up at Aren, pleading silently.

His face was solemn, but he nodded. "She's still an ascended soul. Just empty of energy. We'll have to take her. Same with the Westerlunds, should they accompany us."

"Thank you for the invitation, brother." It looked painful for Marcus to peel his eyes away from Ally. "But I think we need to get to Westerlund. Hold my mate. Our families. Pray. Fill in the hierarchy about what happened. Send us word about what's to come?"

Aren gave a quick nod, and Marcus mimicked the motion to his brothers. They vanished.

I wrapped Ally in another hug, feeling her warmth against me. She nuzzled her head into my chest, pulling the hood up over her head. I laid my face on the top of her hair and breathed deeply.

"Are you ready?" A subtle nod. "Okay. Hang on tight." No giggle or nudge. She just wrapped her arms around me, gripping my back through the layers of our clothes.

The moment our feet landed in Grayshell, she released me, looking up to me. "I need Saraya."

"You said you weren't hurt?"

"To try to look at whatever is in my blood. They're going to weaponize it. The drug. The drug that took my gifts."

"Shit," Alec swore behind me and sprinted out of the hall. *I'll bring her to Ally's room. Go.*

Alvara's grand bedroom had somehow accumulated more books since I'd seen it last. How or when she'd found a moment to read any of them, I wasn't sure. Between our own missions and the dozens of callings she had vanished to, there hadn't been much time to relax. Or research, if that's what the leather-bound volumes were for. As we walked into the room, she waved a hand toward the bathroom. Nothing happened, and her lips parted in surprise before she shook her head, glaring down at her fingers as if they'd betrayed her. I suppose, in a way, it probably felt like they had.

"You want a bath?"

"I need to wash tonight off of me." Her voice broke a bit, and she pushed her hands away from her body, as if she could force-field it all away. She stripped my sweatshirt from her body, tossing it on the floor in one motion. A simple black tank top remained, paired with black sweatpants. She had never looked so vulnerable, her eyes closed, brow furrowed, as she yanked the hair tie out of her bun. Her long, soft waves fell in curtains on either side of her face.

"Get yourself a drink, Ally. I'll draw you a bath."

"I can do it."

"I know. But let me? Please." Anything. Anything to keep my hands busy and convince myself that I could help her. Somehow. Even if it was a small, trivial task, at least it could serve *her*. She met my stare and seemed to understand. Ally inclined her head, lips pressed thin, and turned toward the bronze bar cart full of crystal decanters and glasses.

I walked to the great wood door she had vanished behind the last time I'd been here. Sure enough, a magnificent bath chamber lay on the other side. A low whistle seemed the appropriate response. Most of the room was made of deep emerald and white Carrara marble, interwoven with shimmering golds and deepest blacks. I wasn't sure what kind of stone it was, but its regality was undeniable. Fit for a queen. She deserved all of it and more. She deserved peace and joy. More than what awaited us. I shook the thoughts away.

The vanity was backed in white marble, great curving gold mirrors above each sink. The bath in the center of the room was closer to a spa than a tub. Two could float side by side, with room to move and balance. The great white basin seemed to shimmer, even dry. Gold faucets surrounded it, and I flicked on the closest one. Each head released a pouring stream of steaming water. It crashed into the bottom with a roar that sounded too loud in the precarious silence of its owner, who had appeared on cat-soft steps in the doorway. She held two crystal glasses brimming with amber liquid. She extended one to me. *Sweet Lord, yes.*

Alvara smiled sweetly but didn't shift, and I realized her end of our connection was still silent. Not just *her* powers, but her very essence as an ascended soul of Grayshell had vanished. Her connection to us. I winced and stepped forward to accept the glass. Her lips curved softly, but the small smile never reached her eyes. An eccedentesiast, attempting to mask a raw wound.

"You don't have to hide. Pretend to be okay. Not for me, Ally."

It seemed to be all the permission she needed. Her face crumpled, shoulders curling as she retreated into herself. Tears began shimmering down that sculpted face. A shuddering sigh broke from her, the sound shattering a piece of my heart. Hopeless. Whatever had happened between the swaggering Adrastos and the divine woman in front of me had left her hopeless. The proposal couldn't be a good one. And by the look on her face, she couldn't see a way out of it, either. She took another shuddering breath and downed the contents of her glass. I followed suit, setting mine on the counter. A thought occurred to me, and I caught myself as I went to send it mind to mind.

"Your gifts... They're really gone?"

"Until Agamemnon releases them."

"You're sure? All of them?"

Her glare said enough, and I smiled at her. Emerald eyes, still beautiful even now, narrowed infinitesimally, as though she could still read my thoughts.

Bold, daring, potentially idiotic idea.

But as the swirling steam filled the room, and I surveyed her curled shoulders, dipped chin, and the heaviness in her silver-lined eyes, I knew what I would do for any other woman I had loved like this. Never like *this*. But loved...

Hesitantly, I stepped forward, my stomach flipping like a fast drop over a roller coaster's edge.

I gently removed the empty glass from her curled hand. She allowed it. I set it on the counter with a soft clink, never breaking our gaze. She blinked a few times as I closed the distance between our bodies. Her breath quickened, as did that metronome heartbeat. Gently, slowly, I wrapped around her, not bothering to avoid her bare arms or the skin of her waist peeking out from beneath the bunch of her tank top. The heat of her against my skin—God, it undid me. It seemed the same for her as she gave a broken, desperate breath.

I hesitated, but her eyes flashed to mine, the little spark I loved making an appearance, and she closed the rest of the distance. She collapsed against me, and I encompassed her entirely in my arms. I stroked her back, moving my hands to her biceps, making lazy, long patterns up the sides of her forearms. She slid her hands under my shirt, pulling it up, up, up, until it bunched between us. Her breathing grew more rapid as she slid her fingers up and down the planes of my back, skin to skin. I breathed in her scent, relishing the feel of her for a moment. Just her. Us. No powers or shields.

Just Alvara, the warmth of her, and supple velvety skin against my calloused fingers. For a moment, we were frozen there. When my heart steadied, I allowed my fingers to trace one of the ridged scars across her upper arm. Her breath was hot against my chest and neck, quicker as I retraced the scar.

"Renown blade," she whispered against me. She slid her hands over my pecs to my shoulders, then down, leaving a blazing trail in her wake. Her soft skin met another scar, by her elbow, and I stopped to finger its edges.

She chuckled softly, but it sounded sincere. "That one I deserved." I stifled a laugh, and before I could ask about it, she continued. "Alec and I have a Christmas tradition. And I got a bit over-competitive one year." I leaned back to look at her, brows raised mockingly. *Of course you did*, I meant to say, but she chuckled, "Oh, shush, you." She smiled fondly, soft crinkles appearing by her eyes. "And may have taken a dive off my sled across the ice."

I traced another scar, and another, and another. She told me about each of them, eliciting deep belly laughs more than once.

"Why keep them?" I finally asked. "Why not just heal them completely?"

She shrugged one shoulder, still tight against my arms. "Some of them, we do. But keeping them... it's like writing my story on my body. Preserving it." I nodded, thinking of the scars on my own body in the same light. "I've earned them. So many of them. Doing what I believe in. What's *right*." The emphasis on that last word seemed to tense her heart, and she laid her head against my chest again. The tears began anew, wetting the skin through my shirt. I continued lazy circles up her arm, moving my other hand to stroke her hair, pulling it away from her damp face. She breathed in deeply, and I knew she was scenting me too. I wondered if this feel of us, together, with nothing between us, would solidify in her mind as I knew it would in mine. Wondered if she was inhaling my scent for that very purpose, as I breathed in her sweet, summery cinnamon. I noted the hint of almond oil in her hair as I kissed her precious mussed curls, the top of her head. She shuddered into me, and I wrapped my arms tighter around her, as if I could protect her there. Shield her from the world.

The pain that monster had caused her, with whatever had been said or done, was inexcusable. He would not live for it. He had signed his own execution order when he shoved her toward us, a distraction for his own exit.

Fuck. I'd come so close to losing her. So close to never even getting this moment, holding her in my arms, where she belonged. I couldn't afford to be a coward. Not with her. Not again. Consequences be damned.

Gently, gingerly, I pulled our bodies apart to look at her face. I lingered for a moment, studying her full pink lips. Noted that there was life in those eyes, yes, but it was still dimmed. Rage threatened to boil within me. So, I pulled her face upwards with a finger under her delicately pointed chin. Cupping each of her slender cheeks, I leaned forward. Alvara closed her eyes, leaning into the touch. For a second, I wondered what it felt like to be touched and have her mind stay silent after all these years.

Slowly, I kissed each eyelid, so softly my lips barely registered the caress. I kissed away each salty tear that glimmered on her cheeks, willing the pain away. She whimpered, her hands sliding under my shirt up my back, making my cock twitch. Growing need demanded my attention, challenging my control. *You're not a damn animal, keep it together.*

A disciplined breath steadied me as I shifted, slowly, cautiously, deciding to test the waters.

Her lips yielded beneath mine—hot, soft, and deliciously tempting. It was supposed to be a chaste caress, supposed to be simple. But fucking hell,

Alvara moved with me as if we'd done this a thousand times. I breathed in her air like it was mine for the taking, my hands shifting into her hair, one sliding along her jaw to grip the back of her neck. I pulled her bottom lip between my teeth, desperate to taste her. The more our lips met, the more I craved. Starved for her, fire licked up my spine, as if her suppressed power had found a conduit, consuming me in the process. Fucking hell, this woman would be the death of me.

A little noise escaped her, somewhere between a whimper and a moan. I buried the desire to hear more of them. Tonight was for comfort, for finally touching and soothing, not claiming. With a groan, I peeled our lips apart, chuckling as she reached to follow. Our smiles hung in the air between us, and I swore under my breath. Slowly, deliberately, I pressed my lips to her forehead.

Alvara's breath hitched, and she hastily tried to pull off my shirt. I wrapped my fingers around her hands, and she paused. Most of my chest exposed, I leaned down and kissed her hair.

"I don't expect anything from you, Ally." I meant it. It wasn't the time. It wouldn't feel right, even if she offered, vulnerable as she was. I had only intended to comfort her, to feel her for a moment, to give her a touch she hadn't known in centuries, to show her how beautiful she was to me.

"August?"

"Yeah?"

"Stop talking," she breathed, pressing her lips against my now bare chest. She flicked the shirt the rest of the way off and dropped it to the ground.

FIFTY

SOUL BOUND

ALVARA

"I don't expect anything from you, Ally." I could tell he meant it. He didn't want me to assume anything. But I wanted him. More of him. All of him, if he was ready. I'd waited too damn long as it was. His touch, his kisses, his scent—every part of him was like a high I had no intention of coming down from. And to know him like that... Not just for a reading, or to use my gifts like the war tools they were. But to touch *me*. It had been nearly three hundred long, exhausting years without such a caress.

It was heaven, an aching kind of bliss.

My heart hammered against my ribcage, a violent assault, and I willed it to calm, closing my eyes, breathing him in. August. August Porter. The man who had so patiently waited these months. Who hadn't reprimanded me for shoving him aside when a gruesome death loomed in my path. Who had trusted me through fear, grief, and doubt, staring down a demon that hijacked my body, digging for me beneath it. Who made me laugh. Who wanted me. Evidently not for my strength. Not for my gifts. But for me.

This version—the pathetic, stripped-down, mortal version cradled in his broad, strong hands. At my lowest point, he still wanted me.

"Stop talking." It was supposed to be a demand, but the words came out breathless. More heat blossomed within me, as though the warmth of him flooded through my body. I tossed his shirt to the ground.

August's eyes scoured my face, as if he were really seeing me for the first time. Perhaps, with my power vanished, he *was* seeing the real me beneath all the energy, bravado, and fire. He bowed his forehead to mine, gently tapping my nose with his. Our breath mingled between us, his scent as much an embrace as his body. Again, he traced those calloused, gentle fingers up and down my arms, leaving goosebumps in his wake, heat trailing beneath my skin.

"I'm sorry," he whispered, his warm breath against my lips sending anticipation up my spine, my core winding tighter with every heartbeat. I pulled back a bit, inclining my head to the side in question. He made to explain, "For waiting so long. For not... not making the time to let you in. For not... opening up to your mind in that way. I wish that I had. I wish we'd had more moments like this. I wanted to so many times, but the timing always felt... wrong." The words tumbled from him, and he tucked a stray lock behind my ear, leaving his palm against my cheek. "I'm not afraid of you, Ally. I trust you. I... I want you. All of you. I—"

It was my lips that silenced the onslaught of August's thoughts—of guilt, wanting, and worry. Raised onto my tiptoes, I pressed our lips together, and that heat radiated through every inch of my body, settling in my low belly. "I said *stop talking*."

I brought our mouths back together, and it seemed to unlock him. August's hands were suddenly everywhere—stroking my shoulder, wrapping around the small of my back, pulling me against his warm, hard body. His fingers slid through my hair to cup the back of my head, urging me tighter into the kiss. My own roamed over the fire of him as it consumed me wholly, fingers scraping over the broad, unyielding muscles of his back. I slid one hand into his curls, pleasure coiling within me at the feel of them between my fingers, and the intimacy of his hand tangling in mine, wrapping it into a fist he locked at my nape.

He pressed his soft lips into mine again and again. Gently, he pulled on my lower lip before releasing it from his teeth, tracing its shape with his tongue. With a soft moan, I opened for him, and my breath caught as he pushed inside, exploring every inch of my mouth. I welcomed him, savored the feel of his tongue against my own, his heat lashing against every wall. I gently sucked him deeper, and a groan escaped him as he pulled me tighter still, his demanding tug on my hair adding a delicious hint of pain as he tilted my face to his. His body was just as hungry to devour me as I was him. He wrapped his palm around my hip, gripping me possessively and guiding me toward the vanity until my ass hit the granite. Lips still locked, tongues exploring, August dropped his second hand to my waist. My breath snagged and my eyes flew open as he lifted me onto the counter. My legs wrapped around his hips, pulling him tighter against me, hands racing to wrap around his back. I would never get enough of his mouth. Of his touch.

It was the sudden slap of water lapping onto the marble floor that pulled us apart. August swore under his breath and dove for the gold faucet. I laughed despite myself, then drew in a long, steadying breath. My hands trembled. So did his, I realized with no small bit of satisfaction. He plunged a bare arm into the deep pool of bubbles, the water rising above his shoulder to his neck, wetting his longest curls. He pulled the plug to let a bit of the water out, making space for me. He grinned over his shoulder, the expression equal parts amusement and exasperation, muscles rippling down his abdomen with the small twist. August was beautiful. I'd known that, seen him sparring and running shirtless. But seeing him like this, with the heat a living thing between us—a sentient sculpture in front of me. When the water had lowered an inch, he plugged the drain, rose fluidly to his feet, and shook off the water like a dog. I laughed as it splattered over me. He scowled at the soaked floor and twisted his hand with a flick of the wrist, summoning the water off the marble and channeling it into the sink.

"Show off," I grumbled. Amusement rumbled through him.

"It's good for you to get a taste of what being with you is like most of the time." August winked playfully, then grinned, his face flushing. "Where do you keep your towels?" I inclined my head toward the towering cabinet beside my vanity, littered with lotions, cosmetics, and countless brushes. He crossed the room and removed three. August laid one out like a rug at the base of the tub and set the other two on the now-dry marble beside it. One for my hair and one for me, I realized as he made for the door.

"August?"

He paused on the threshold, eyes bright on my face. He took one lingering step back toward me and closed the gap when I motioned him forward. August intertwined our fingers, pressing my palm against his in a movement that felt intensely intimate. He seemed to note the same thing as he smiled that crooked grin and gave my hand a little squeeze. His warm lips found my own again—once, twice, three times—still warm, still urgent. Just a fraction less so after the interruption. He pulled me against him, squeezing our bodies as tightly together as possible. Before I could pick up where we'd left off, August made to step away again, and every exhausted piece of my body whimpered in protest. He grinned sweetly, warming my cheeks.

"Stay." The word was a whisper, breathless and wanting. August's smile faltered, his eyes hesitant.

"Ally, I... I want to. Believe me. But... after all you've been through tonight, you deserve time to... rest. To think."

"I don't expect anything either, okay? I just... stay? Please." I did, in fact, want more from him. I wanted to give him everything, to devour every inch of him. But his honor—it was a part of what I loved about August Porter...

His eyes took turns on each of my own—careful, calculating, evaluating the sincerity in my request. Whatever he saw was evidently deemed satisfactory.

August inclined his head in acquiescence, his voice soft as he said, "Anything."

"Thank you." I squeezed his hand.

"I'll give you a moment of privacy. Tell me when you're properly under the bubbles?"

I snorted. "Are you always so damn noble?"

August winked, that crooked grin pulling at his features. "Would you like to find out?" He raised my hand to press it to his lips, then made to leave the room, chuckling when I gripped him tighter. "Ally." His tone was cautious, but the hunger in his eyes was as fierce as my own.

He sighed as I let go of his still trembling hand. I turned from him and began to lift my shirt over my head. August groaned, and I felt his eyes linger on my bare back before I heard him turn away. His breathing grew ragged. I could see the movement reflected in the mirror beside us, so I watched him there. He closed his eyes and pinched the bridge of his nose as if in deep concentration. I laughed and tossed the shirt onto him, earning a low chuckle. August tugged it off his head when it landed and wrapped it around his hand, breathing in my scent.

"Fuuuck, baby," he said, blowing out a hard breath. "Such a tease."

"It doesn't have to be teasing."

He groaned again. "*Oh*, but it does." My sweats and underwear hit the floor. "We have company." My exhausted muscles nearly made me cry out as they collapsed into the sloshing warm water. I shifted to listen and found, sure enough, the soft padding of footsteps down the hallway. We both inhaled deeply.

"Saraya," we said together. I slid down, dropping until the bubbles kissed my neck. "I'm all covered up. You can send her back."

I could hear the grin in his voice as he ran his hand through his hair. "Don't think for a minute we're done here."

SARAYA CAME AND WENT QUICKLY, three vials of crimson still warm in her hand. She vowed to do all she could, eyeing August slyly—no doubt scenting all that had just happened between us—and made for the exit. He walked her to the door, and I heard the bolt click into place behind her.

He hesitated, halfway back to the bathroom, his footsteps pausing before he appeared, a tentative smile pulling at the corners of his swollen lips. Without a word, he slid down onto the towel on the floor, his back pressed against the tub. I shook my head, but a smile grew despite myself.

The marble edge was like ice against my wrist as I set my hand there.

Without looking, August's fingers came up to tangle with my own. He leaned his head against the tub and breathed deeply. We sat that way in silent, easy companionship as the window above the spa lightened from black to navy. My eyes slipped closed, the lateness of the hour and the stress of the past days settling across my body. Softly, August finally spoke.

"I do believe...you owe me one truth."

The warm water splashed and lapped against the edges as I shifted my weight to lean over the rim of the pool. I stroked my wet fingers through his hair, and he leaned into the touch. "I believe I do," I whispered back. God above, had that race really been less than a day ago? A lifetime had passed since he'd beaten me back to the doorman. Exhaustion settled deeper into my bones, my eyelids growing heavy, as I continued to process everything that had occurred. I let them close, my head propped against the edge of the bath.

"Good. One truth. Do you have the energy?"

"Yes," I lied. He hummed and was quiet for a long while. Whether he believed me or not wasn't entirely clear.

"What...what are we...to each other, Ally?"

My breath came fast and sharp. What are we? Lovers...mates? The truest kind, perhaps. My heart skipped into a gallop. Nothing seemed adequate for what I felt for August—the loyalty and connection, the searing desire burning up my core like kindling. For the trust I had in him. He brushed his finger across the back of my hand, and I suppressed the shudder of desire that ran down my spine, becoming intensely aware that I was boldly, brashly naked below the rapidly vanishing cover of bubbles.

"Without a reading..."

August cut in with a huff, shaking his head. "I don't *care* about the reading, Ally. It will say whatever it says. What do you want? What am I, right now, to you, in *this* moment?"

Everything. My other half, my anchor, my home. Guilt twisted in my stomach as I realized I loved him as I had loved no one since Michael. I had never intended to love anyone as I had loved Michael. Then my heart began to hammer again, as I realized that perhaps...I loved August more...more than I had loved Michael. Or anyone, ever. More than I loved myself. I had known that the moment I realized I could never let an ounce of harm come to him—the first moment I'd pushed him out of harm's way, and each time after.

"You are...my home, August. You are...I believe when I can finally read you—which I want to do so badly. But I want the *time* to do it right. To soak up your story when I am rested, strong, and patient." I inhaled to steady myself, wiping the sweat from my brow. "When you are too. But...I believe you are mine. My *mate*. My match." He blew out a long breath. I didn't need to see his face to scent the salt in the air, the tears my words elicited. I squeezed his hand against the tub, supposing he had been waiting to ask the question for a long time, just as I had been yearning to tell him. "If you will have me, of course."

August huffed a broken laugh and turned to face me. We leaned our foreheads together, and it was my turn to wipe the warm tears from his face.

"You are more than I ever dared to want...everything I never knew I needed. And I believe—and have been told—that you are my mate, too."

"Did Jason...?"

He nodded. "Evidently the bond is obvious."

"That shithead. Holding out on me."

August smiled, mirroring my own, then pressed his lips to mine again. "You're cold," he whispered. I had indeed begun to shiver as the water chilled, my skin all pruny. I hadn't cared, as long as he was there. "Alec showed me how to warm the bed. I'll get it nice and toasty for you." I nodded in gratitude, our foreheads still connected.

I wore only August's discarded t-shirt and a lace pair of black underwear when his eyes found me crossing the threshold. Devoured me, actually, that gaze lingering on my bare legs and sending tension spinning in my belly. Only the sound of the suction in the tub broke the silence between us. The watery light of Grayshell's early dawn began to creep in around the border of my heavy red drapes.

August, perched atop my bed, threw back the resplendent burgundy and gold comforter and patted the spot next to him, his expression soft. I crossed the room on shaky legs and all but collapsed beside him. I curled onto my side, allowing my muscles to melt into the mattress. Allowing my mind to soak up...silence. It was so strange, that ringing hollowness. His breath hitched, and then warm fingers stroked the hair off my face, pulling it back from my neck. Somehow, it felt as though we had done this countless times before—his touch familiar, his scent like mountains wrapping around me. He hoisted the overturned blanket over us and slid down to spoon around my body. Heat raged through me, and I sighed, leaning into his warmth and hard muscles curved around my backside. Legs and arms skin to skin—a dream long since forgotten. He pressed kisses to my temple, my cheek, the hollow of my neck, and the sensitive skin where my neck and shoulder met, behind my ear. All the while, his hand trailed across my belly, squeezing my hip, wandering lazily up my torso. Teasingly, he softly stroked my nipple, peaked through the t-shirt, and I moaned. Torture, this waiting, this taunting.

"August," I breathed. "Please."

He chuckled against my neck, sending goosebumps down my flesh.

"You too, huh?" I wrapped my fingers in his, pressing him harder against my chest. "Ally, when I take you, you'll have seen every single part of me, and there won't be an inch of you I haven't explored myself. I want to let you see everything...before you give me...anything."

I nearly growled, and he laughed again. "That's...not fair," I breathed. "I want to devour you, to take my time when I *see* you. When I see all of you."

"The feeling is mutual, then." August slid our hands down across my belly. Lower. Need ate at me, my body arching into him, willing him to touch me, a tightness spiraling into torturous tension in my core.

"August, with everything going on, I don't know when—"

His fingers teased along the edge of my panty line, and my breath caught entirely. I felt him smile beside my neck, felt his breath hitch as my own did, before he whispered in my ear, "I can be patient." He nipped at my lobe, and I groaned but released his hand. August laughed softly against me again. His fingers lingered for a moment; he took a heaving breath against me and wrapped his arm around my chest, gripping my shoulder, pulling me against him. He nuzzled into my neck, kissing and breathing in deeply.

"Cruel man," I breathed, as sleep pulled at me. His amusement rumbled through my ribs. August covered my neck in kisses, leaving a trail of summer in his wake.

"I love you, Alvara."

My eyes burned, and I pulled his hand up to my lips, covering his warm, calloused palm in kisses.

"I love you, August."

His breathy sigh and the flex of muscles around me was the last thing I registered.

FIFTY-ONE

LEMONS

ALVARA

When consciousness found me again, the bed was anticlimactically cold, and mid-day light streamed in through the open windows. I inhaled the lingering scent of August against my sheets, stretching out for a body that was no longer there. Paper crinkled beneath my fingers, and it took me a moment to realize my mind was still silent.

Shit.

I sat up, wincing against the headache pounding like war drums against my skull. Blinking, my fingers trembled around the note left in bed beside me.

Gone to get breakfast. I'll be back soon. Merry Christmas Eve, my love.

Shit, shit, shit. I pulled up my arm to examine the brand there: 11.04.

The bastard had *branded* me. Like cattle. *The lives I valued were all snuffed out like chattel by those you are sworn to defend.* I recoiled from the memory of those words—sincere, sharp, meant to sting. And they did. What had Adrastos lost? What had he endured to crave power so violently?

I swore, my breath coming in a forced gasp. *Ten hours* had passed since that surreal meal, powerless, with an enemy in his war tent. Nevertheless, no ember kindled in my veins. What had they given me? What would we do against such a thing, if they weaponized it properly? That had to be the plan. What advantage was Adrastos surely giving himself while my strength lay in the balance—while my gifts remained disabled and our defenses were down? I growled and slammed my palms against my eyes, as if I could rub the pain away. And God, that complete silence...

How many times had I wished for a reprieve from the voices, from the connection to the hierarchy, from the chatter of minds and prayers? And yet... it left me feeling intensely naked. Hollow.

I rose and dressed in jeans and a t-shirt. It was a battle of wills between me and my combat boots, perched at the edge of the bed, that August bore witness to. I finally finished yanking the damn thing on when he chuckled from the doorway, snapping my attention to him.

"Need a hand?" He grinned at me over a tray of steaming food—scrambled eggs, roast potatoes, pastries—and two cups of hot coffee. Lord, I loved Grayshell. The smell made my mouth water. I supposed one quiet meal wouldn't hurt. Another moment pretending August and I could be normal—an everyday man and an ordinary woman finally admitting their love for each other. I did my best to return his smile, but when his eyes narrowed, I knew it hadn't reached my own. Hadn't convinced him.

"What is it?"

"Still nothing." I tapped my finger against my temple.

"Ahh... that. Perhaps... we'll make the most of it?" He set the tray down beside me, grazing my cheek with the back of his hand, trailing a finger down my neck as he leaned in to steal a kiss. My heart quickened, breath hitching, but August peeled us apart before I could lose my mind. "Your visions might be AWOL, but I promise I have plenty of thoughts I'm dying to make reality," he said coyly, running his tongue over his lower lip. I laughed, thighs squeezing together, even as he pulled away to retrieve the coffees.

"If I have the time to enjoy you when this comes back online"—another tap of my temple—"believe me, I will dive right in."

"Why does it sound like you're jinxing us?"

I sighed. "Because Murphy is a bastard."

"Perhaps," he said, grinning. "But I don't need anything spectacular to happen. I just want you. Just as you are. I want us, as we are. Whatever is revealed, I'll take it." He leaned in close, and my eyes fell closed. August brushed his lips across my eyelids with a heart-wrenching tenderness that melted my mind. His hands clasped either side of my cheeks, and I leaned into his touch, savoring the simplicity of it. The natural feel of him against me. Another part of that need I had buried deep last night stirred, a great beast awakening after a *long* hibernation. He seemed to sense it, perhaps scent it, as he pulled back, grinning.

"Shush, you."

He raised his hands in defense.

"Don't be so smug." I winked at him.

August snorted and shook his head, pressing a kiss to my forehead before handing me my cup.

We ate and discussed trivial, lighthearted things between stolen kisses—

our personal stories, mostly. Sharing details we somehow hadn't in the long months we'd spent in each other's company. We relayed all the conversations about our relationship—Alec, Aren, Marcus, even the insinuations Adrastos had thrown my way about what we were to each other. That my life had been spared under the pretense that it would destroy him if they claimed it.

"Now that," August said, eyes solemn, "I believe."

"I certainly don't intend to exist without you." I shook my head. A few topics back, we'd wound up horizontal on the bed, my boots now a heap on the floor. He sprawled out on his side, propping his head on a fist as I finished breakfast, leaving the perfect spot to cuddle against his chest, my arm wrapped around his ribs, hand caressing patterns across his back. Our legs were happily tangled together, August's fingers alternating between stroking long lines down my arm and brushing through my hair. I studied the hard line of his stubbled jaw, his eyes half-hooded with sleepy, contented desire, before succumbing to the urge to trace his cheekbones and the tiny crook in his nose.

Nerves made it hard to swallow, my voice softer than I'd like as I asked, "When did you know?"

August's head tilted as he gently tucked a strand of hair behind my ear, a soft smile curling his lips. "That you were supposed to be mine?"

I nodded, smiling as his throat worked. He hummed thoughtfully, blinking as he pinched the end of a curl between his thumb and forefinger, studying it determinedly. Something like pride glimmered in his emeralds when they again met mine.

"I no longer remember a time when I didn't."

AREN WAS WAITING FOR US, expectantly poised at the edge of the island when we entered the common room. So was everyone else, it seemed. I surveyed the coven, sprawled in chairs and loveseats, books and maps spread everywhere. Steaming cups of tea and coffee were set on every surface. Heat flushed my face as I took in the knowing smiles on Fae and Lana's faces, the cozy grin on Alec's, and the eternally prying eyes of Ansel. Oh, they scented it alright, or sensed it, or read it in what looked like August's wide-open mind.

"Alright, lovebirds." Aren smirked at our joined hands. "About damn time." He clapped August on the back, earning a wince twisted by glowing male satisfaction, followed by a chorus of laughter from the group. "Now, let's get down to it. Ally, tell us everything."

So, I did.

After I finished the long and short of my encounter with the brash, infuriatingly articulate Adrastos, I met six pairs of wide eyes. They exchanged long glances, and I realized their minds were whirring. Only, I still couldn't hear them.

"Okay, so the mind-to-mind connection is annoying when you're not a part of it," I grumbled.

"Shit. Sorry!" Alec's eyes widened, and he shook his head as if he could clear it. "We... uh... we're a bit lost for words."

"That would be a first."

He chuckled, but his expression remained solemn as he clarified, "So... uh... Adrastos is the dark side of your coin? He has the same... abilities?" Alec ran a hand through his tawny hair.

"As best as I can tell. If I get my gifts back and can get near him, I guess I'll know for sure. But he read my mind like it was spelled out in front of him. Certainly seems to have played with multiple threads of how all this plays out."

"Which is why you're alive." Aren rubbed his hand over his stubbled jaw. "Because tearing August's mate away wouldn't have gotten him what he wanted."

"Evidently, he believes we are so intensely intertwined that killing one is to kill the other."

Everyone was quiet as the clock tick-tick-ticked away the minutes, and I just stared, unsure if they were still chatting between minds. Finally, I turned, searching for an answer from my sire.

"I've seen it before," he said with a grimace. "Rare. So rare, that kind of Soul Bond." Aren's brow furrowed.

"But... possible?" August's feet collapsed from their perch on the ottoman, landing with a heavy thud. He leaned forward, glancing at me before schooling his expression back into neutrality.

Aren nodded grimly. "Yes. Should one of you be injured in battle, we must guard both of you. It's a tether, if he's telling the truth, to one world or the next. Your life cycles would be synchronized. I've only ever seen it once —only ever heard of it in two mutually ascended souls. Kingsley and Rosaleigh are Soul Bound."

Ansel let out a long whistle and leaned back in his seat, crossing an ankle over a knee. He scrubbed his hand along his jaw, mirroring Aren's motion. "Well, that... complicates things."

"Lucky for us, Alvara is a fucking badass, and August is more than capable." Alec shrugged. "More power to you—if you don't have to... face surviving that." He stared at Fae, his eyes filled with pain. He shook his head. "I couldn't ever... couldn't endure... that."

Each head in the room nodded, even Aren. Ansel leaned forward. "I have. Have had to outlive her—never for long, but... the agony is... devastating."

Lana's face had gone pallid, and she nodded slowly, lips pursed and eyes fierce.

"So. You two are mates. Adrastos won't hurt you because he intends to use you. Agamemnon is the loose cannon we have to watch." Fae mercifully spoke up, changing the subject. I hoped she could sense my gratitude, my relief. Ansel narrowed his eyes a fraction, the movement barely detectable, but it was to him that I looked.

"Sometimes it's not the bloodthirsty ones you have to watch." He dropped his leg down and leaned his elbows onto his knees. "Adrastos might be playing nice now—cousin, *my sweet*, and all that bullshit—but... when we don't comply... his lethal side will inevitably come out. I say we take him out before he can do the same. And go after Agamemnon with the full force of our host. Did you get a number on theirs, by the way? You didn't mention."

"Not exact, but it's in the thousands. I didn't get a good look at the war camp or read him. Enough to concern me."

"What are the pros and cons if we... if we accept the alliance?" If hearts could stop beating, they would have when those words left August's lips. Every pair of eyes landed on us.

"Are you mad? He means to—"

"Enslave the humans. Yeah, I get it. But what if we accept the alliance and survive... the *horsemen*?" His voice dripped with skepticism. "Deal with Adrastos and Agamemnon later, when the timeline isn't as... severe."

"Deals between celestial power wielders are *binding*, August." I held out my arm, exposing the brand. "I hate not knowing what they're up to today, but I'm only as calm as I am because he placed the wager of his life on his promise. Branded it on his skin too. Breaking a bargain like that... I don't know if it can be survived."

"Besides," Aren interjected, shaking his head forlornly. "If he's as clairvoyant as Alvara... there would be no way to hide that kind of treachery. He'd sniff it out years before we could pull one over on him."

"So... if Agamemnon doesn't release your power tonight, what happens?" August raised his brows.

"Adrastos dies. To pay the debt. Beyond that..." I bit my lip.

"The rest of us bring the full force of the hierarchy down on Agamemnon personally. His death would also satisfy the debt, evidently, and your power would return then as well." Aren rubbed the back of his neck.

"Is it wrong that's how I'm hoping it goes?" Alec grimaced. "Let the brothers self-destruct. Bring an end to the crazy one. We already fought the angry one—he's nothing special."

"The crazy one. Is he... though? Crazy, I mean?" Fae spoke up, voice soft, expression wary.

"Let's be real," Lana cut in. "All the hot ones are."

Four sets of male eyes jerked to her. Ansel and Alec wore matching scowls, August's mouth hung open in shock, and Aren's face furrowed like she'd announced a weekly orgy, earning a snort of amusement.

"*What?*" She shrugged, unapologetic. "We were all thinking it."

"*No,*" August said indignantly as Aren barked a laugh. He looked to Alec and Ansel for backup. "We certainly *were not.*"

Shaking their heads, brows furrowed, Ansel and Alec echoed the sentiment with a chorus of, "Hell no."

When August's attention snapped to me, I laughed, nodding as my face flushed. "Yeah... we totally were."

"Jesus," Aren muttered, chuckling as he shook his head.

"Anyway," Fae interjected, as Lana gave her mate a smug, satisfied smile. "He doesn't seem crazy. Convicted. Poor moral compass. But... by the sounds of it, he's oddly civil and well-spoken for a Renown."

I nodded. "He's... convicted, certainly. I didn't need my gifts to see that he truly believes what he speaks."

"Can we reason with him?" Lana stroked the pommel of her sword, the Celtic knot upon it.

"I... I don't know. He... was quite confident we would come to his side of things. I don't see him... wavering, faltering, or fleeing. Adrastos will be an enemy to contend with."

"Why don't we go in hot—now—guns blazing, while they expect us to be complacent?" Alec turned to Aren.

"Inevitably, there's another trap waiting. Without Ally... I don't feel like we should pull trigger on anything." Aren crossed his arms and sighed. "Which is, of course, the reaction they're expecting after the stunts they pulled. Counting on it, I'm sure." Ansel nodded his agreement, and Aren bit his lip. "It's Christmas. It's... the wrong week for bloodshed. We should be celebrating!"

"Our complacency could get us killed," Ansel countered. "Letting them keep her gifts, letting them implement whatever they have up their sleeves. It's what they expect. But... I don't like the idea of going in blind, either."

"So, we let Ally recoup. We enjoy the holiday," Alec said with an airy shrug. "We unleash her when her power is back and see what to do from there."

"It's going to be like a clairvoyant volley, you realize? Impossible to stay ahead if he's as gifted as Ally. Now that he knows we're parrying." August squeezed my hand. "She'll pull threads, but the moment we decide, Adrastos will see it. He'll evaluate his options and adjust accordingly. When his choices are made, she'll see them, and so on and so forth. Unless you keep her on an IV, watching twenty-four-seven..."

Understanding settled in the group. We were fighting fire with fire on that route. Aren pressed his lips together.

"It will be a clairvoyant volley," Aren repeated, blowing out a heavy breath.

FIFTY-TWO

TRADITIONS

AUGUST

If there was anything I loved about the surreal Grayshell grounds, it was the eternal spring—the warmth that seeped between my bones and loosened my muscles. Alec, it seemed, liked to poke raw wounds and had asked the group who would kick Ally's ass first now that the playing field was even. She had snorted, a sound that was both a laugh and a challenge. Somehow, that translated to us stepping outside onto the bizarre grass that wasn't really grass for sparring—no powers, no elements. Just true hand-to-hand combat.

"You have the benefit of having been inside minds for so long that you understand how they work." I tucked a strand of hair behind her ear. "You can still anticipate their moves. Just remember their eyes, their center of gravity. Their decision-making doesn't change just because you're not in their heads anymore." I wrapped tape around her wrist, and she gave me an obedient nod, though nerves flickered in her eyes, unease evident in the tension of her shoulders and ramrod-straight spine. I wrapped my arms around her waist and kissed her cheek. It was a marvel how natural it felt, as though it had always been that way, and she leaned into the touch.

Alec bounced on the balls of his feet, grinning at us from his spot in the "ring." Aren boomed with laughter from the other side at something Ansel had said. They both sat on their haunches, fingers laced together. Wagers had been placed on these first rounds as Ally acclimated. Aren would always bet on Ally—always. But despite her lost clairvoyance, it seemed Ansel would, too. It was Alec and Lana who thought her skills would be hindered.

I kissed her again, then leaned down to whisper in her ear, "You are the bravest, most intuitive person I know— with or without foresight." Alvara grinned at my words and turned to face me. She pressed her soft lips to mine, gave me a nod, and strolled into the ring. I raised my voice a bit so Alec could hear, "Now. Go kick his ass."

And so she did.

It seemed my *mate* did, in fact, have a natural inclination for violence. Aren had told me that what seemed like a lifetime ago. When I'd first arrived at Grayshell, he had chuckled about it. He was still chuckling now as she pinned Alec for the second time. Aren and Ansel both roared with laughter as he tapped out. The Commander rolled onto his back, clutching a stitch in his side. Alec won the round in between, so it was no surprise when he begged for best of five after she released him again.

"I'll even heal your scrapes and bruises for you," he grinned at her, but she shook her head.

"Honestly, Alec, I'm not sure why you crave the humiliation." She flashed him that feline grin I loved and raised her brows. Fae choked on what might have been a laugh, lacing her fingers together and pressing them to her lips as if in prayer, her brows raised with amusement as she stared at her mate in the ring. Her shoulders shook with suppressed giggles. She relaxed and grinned when Alvara and Alec embraced in a great bear hug. As they pulled apart, he set his hands on her cheek and wrist, healing two small scrapes. Some territorial instinct within me flared, but I silenced it. Alec playfully mussed her hair as Aren often did, and I swore at myself for the reaction.

Alvara made a beeline for me, wrapping her arms around my waist and settling against my chest as if she always had. Then she ran her fingers over my arm, my neck, feeling every inch she could reach. She seemed just as desperate to feel me as I was for her. I kissed the top of her head.

"Good girl." I'd barely whispered the words when she pinched the skin on my arm. I yelped. Alvara smirked before kissing me again. In a twirl of restored confidence, she looked back at our coven, swinging her arms to stretch them out. I crossed my arm under the opposite elbow, resting my face against my fist.

"So. Who's next?" She stepped back toward the ring. Aren and Ansel exchanged glances, clearly debating mind to mind who would challenge her. I cleared my throat.

"Uh...what about me?"

She whirled on me, eyes narrowing. "Interesting." She ran her tongue along her teeth, surveying me like a predator sizing up its prey.

I shrugged a shoulder, feigning a nonchalance I didn't feel.

"I accept your challenge, August Porter."

The coven erupted with shouts, bets, and taunts, but my eyes didn't leave hers as that coy grin stretched across her face, her eyes alight anew. Not a spirit easily broken. If anything, she was relishing the challenge. I inclined my head to accept, and Aren boomed his amusement.

He clapped his hands together. "Well, this should be fun."

Alvara was a machine, through and through. The woman didn't tire. From the moment she rolled her neck side to side, her energy shifted. She shot me one last coy wink, then schooled her face into indifference, chin raised tall. Game on.

From that point on, her strikes were fast, her movements fluid as water. In what felt like mere seconds, she had me on my back, her knee in my chest and a fist against my throat, miming a blade. She grinned and dipped down to kiss me. With her breath hot against my face, I accepted. Then, with the little leverage she'd given me, I shoved her over my head. She tucked and rolled just as Aren and Alec erupted with taunts from the sidelines.

"Don't get cocky now, love."

Alvara gave me a playful hiss and crouched like a cat ready to spring, but I was faster. I lunged for her, but she rolled backward, flipping out of my path and back to her feet.

Our grins mirrored each other as the others caused one hell of a ruckus. She lunged for me, throwing her body around mine and flipping her legs up. That girl was going to *Black Widow* me.

I snatched her out of midair, and she shouted before righting herself. Legs wrapped around my waist like a boa constrictor, she threw her slender arms around my throat. I wedged my fingers between her arms, and she trembled to keep her lock on me. Stars popped into my vision as she squeezed tighter still. My knees gave out, and instantly she released me, planting her feet to steady us.

She raised her brows in silent question. I nodded, panting for breath. She wrapped her arms around me, and I huffed a laugh.

The Commander's voice carried to us as Alec passed him a wad of cash. "I will *always* bet on my little shadow."

"Damn, Ally," my words whooshed out in a breath.

"She's second for a reason," Ansel drawled from the sidelines, shaking his head in silent awe. Lana rose from Fae's side across the yard, her movements lithe. She narrowed her eyes on her mate as she slowly leaned over the old general with the swagger of a courtesan, making a show of plucking a twenty-dollar bill from between her breasts before dropping it in his lap. Ansel's throat bobbed before he cleared it, sketching a bow to Ally as we passed. She grinned, inclining her head to accept the show of respect.

"Need a cigarette after that handoff?" Fae teased as Lana resumed her place beside her. Laughter echoed off the courtyard walls. Aren also dipped his head, a proud smile on his face. Their thoughts were sincere when I pried forward. Nobody had pulled punches. She was who she was, with or without her magic.

A human with her capabilities would have made one hell of an assassin.

SHINING snow came up to my thighs, pressing against the suit I'd found lying across Alvara's bed when I made it upstairs. Her and Alec's little tradition, it seemed, had infected the entire coven over the years. So here we stood, balls deep in fluffy frozen water.

It was worth it, though, watching her climb into her sled, beanie pulled tight over her brow and scarf up to her nose. Nearly as pale as the snow around us, a small strip of skin and Ally's eyes were all that were visible. Alec was already propped in his own sled beside her, with Aren on the other side. Fae stood ready to count them down, bouncing in her boots to try to warm herself.

All that stands between humanity and hell...are three warriors on sleds. The irony drew a chuckle from me, and Aren echoed it with his own rumbling laugh.

Just you wait, Rookie.

I shook my head.

"On your mark! Get set! Go!" Fae waved her outstretched red scarf, and the three of them took off.

The two males began to lead, and I heard that wind-chime voice cry out, "No powers!" Aren boomed a laugh but slowed, and Alec zoomed away in a defiant flash down the mountain. "Cheater, cheater!" she hollered after him.

My cheeks hurt from laughing.

"They usually use wind to win," Fae explained as she appeared by my side, tossing her platinum braid over her shoulder. "And to cheat." She winked. "It usually turns into a full-blown snowball fight."

"I can imagine." I laughed as Ally pegged a now-returning Alec square in the jaw. She cackled and made a break for it, but only made it a few feet before he tackled her into the snow. They came up, scarves fallen, faces Rudolf-red with cold, but laughing so hard they shook, and I couldn't help but do the same.

The three of them hauled the sleds back up the hill and offered them to those of us standing. I accepted Aren's, sat down, and patted the snow beside me. Ally grinned, holding the sled out toward Fae and Lana, now glued hip to hip for warmth. They exchanged a knowing smile and nodded toward me. She didn't hesitate, and we didn't wait for a third to take their place but shifted in unison. As we soared across the snow, Ally threw her head back and laughed to the sky just beginning to glimmer with stars, laughed to the pines above us. I couldn't help but join her.

Her joy was...an unexpected treasure. Her rosy face cracked in that mile-wide smile, something I hadn't realized I needed until this moment. My heart ached for her, for this happiness. But a bitter voice in my mind reminded me this bliss was on borrowed time. The brand on her wrist ticking down until reality would collide like a freight train. My face must have betrayed my trepidation as we skidded to a halt because she shook her head as if to say, *Don't ruin it. Just let it be.* I nodded.

And then waylaid her with a snowball.

She fell off her sled, squawked indignantly, then pulled herself to her knees. She kept her face hidden as she packed the snow between her hands. I dove for her, and together, we tumbled into the snowbank. I shielded her head with my arm as we collided with the bank against the tree. The impact against the towering pine sent a blanket of white down upon us. It buried us entirely, and I fought not to panic as we clawed our way back to the top.

I had never been so frozen in my life as I was when we cleared that fallen drift. But she was smiling, still so light. Free.

She hit me with another snowball, and I growled, lunging. She shrieked as I tackled her, smacking my back with her mittened hands as she roared and screeched with manic giggles. And then we froze—bodies pressed together in the snow, heavy exhales mingling between us, our eyes burned over every inch of each other. I kissed each of her frozen cheeks and then her cherry-red nose, which she wrinkled in response. Perhaps that smile was indeed frozen on her fair face.

I buried myself in her neck, kissing and nipping at the sensitive flesh. "Let me get something straight," I growled into her. Ally made a breathy little sound in her throat and pressed into my touch, her body pinned beneath my hips. Leaning in to nip at her ear, I asked, "The guy who had you tied up last night was *hot?*" I reared back for a view of her face just as her eyes rounded, earning a dark chuckle that rumbled in my chest. "Yeaaaah, baby, we'll be discussing that later."

Hands outstretched, I seized her arms to hoist her upright. But we were pelted by snowballs, and both dashed for cover as the others descended the hill. They hollered the entire way. We both bent to pack snow, but they just snatched our sleds and sprinted for the top. I flashed her a wide-eyed grin, and she mirrored it before we both lunged out from behind the tree. Battle cries erupted from us as we ran after them, slinging snowball after snowball. The grizzly laughed until I thought he'd lose his voice, then dove belly-first onto the sled like a seal.

It could have been hours out there by Aren's safe house—hours of sled races and hot cocoa, of endless whitewash and snowball fights. I wasn't sure how much time had passed, but my cheeks and belly ached with the hysterics. We all noted the numbness in our bodies when we entered the cabin to thaw out. We clomped our boots on the front porch, freeing them of snow, then filed into the cozy little space to get warm. We stripped our soaked clothes and left them in front of the fire, and then the party wordlessly split into two. Another tradition, I assumed, by the routine way they did it.

Aren, Alec, and Ansel waved me over to his bar cabinet, but my eyes stayed locked on the girls as they crossed into the tight kitchen. Aren furrowed his brow as he inspected his stash, then hoisted up an antique-looking bottle of bourbon and grinned. He spun it in his hands and handed it off to Alec to open. He pinched a half dozen glasses between his fingers and walked them to the kitchen, where the girls were still pulling bowls and ingredients from the cabinets.

Glasses lined up and filled, the beginnings of cookie dough seemed to form in the glass bowl as Alvara beat butter and sugar. Already, I could feel the heat from the oven warming the space.

Behind us, Ansel and Lana turned on Bing Crosby's music, and the crackling fire flickered light across the walls. Laughter reverberated through the small space, and we all drank our drams deeply. Happy, I realized with a start. I was happy. Here, with them. With our little family—soul group, whatever we might be. To whichever end this war would serve us, it would all be worth it for having found *this*.

I stayed to myself for a long while. The men continued raiding Aren's liquor collection while the women whipped up treats. I watched the numbers tick down on the brand on Alvara's arm—her rolled-up, flour-coated sleeve tucked just above it. He would die for that too—for marring her body.

My eyes wandered upwards, quickly forgetting all violence as I soaked in Alvara's jubilation. Flour dusted her arms nearly to her elbows, a streak across her cheekbone as though she'd shoved her hair back. Alvara was forming balls of dough between her hands, continuing to laugh and talk, exchanging endless stories with Fae and Lana, the three of them sharing smiles over long-lost memories—victories won and friends lost.

She emptied the last scoop of dough from the bowl and scraped a bit off with her finger to pop it in her mouth. When her gaze fell on mine, firelight flickering across her emerald eyes, lips firmly wrapped around her finger, my heart tightened. *Mine.* And now she knew it all...I studied the way the skin around her eyes wrinkled when she smiled, the way her full lips parted, the way she moved.

You are the most beautiful thing I have ever seen. You're all I've ever wanted. I love you, Alvara of Grayshell.

Without breaking her gaze from the bowl she was cleaning, she grinned and said, "I love you too, August of Grayshell."

Her head snapped up, eyes wide with realization. Something like panic slithered into her expression, and I lunged forward, wrapping her tiny waist in my arm and pulling her against me. I brought my other hand up to cup her face and kissed her—passionately, urgently. I poured everything I wanted to say into that kiss. She parted her lips for me, and I breathed her in as quickly as I could. But as her mind began to connect with mine, I peeled our lips apart and stepped back.

"I'm ready when you are." It was all I could think to say.

Then she was there, that fiery presence flickering back to life in the depth of my mind—a light in the darkness. Stronger and more present than the others. Stronger, I realized, because Marcus was right. She was mine, and I was hers. That's why her absence was physically hard. Why I *felt* when she was injured...

The entire room held its breath as the energy ebbed and swelled around Alvara. Eddies of power seemed to pour into her, and her eyes fluttered as her hands stretched out and flexed, accepting the swell. I realized she was egging it on, willing it back into place.

When she opened her eyes, the gold in her deep emerald irises began to glimmer. Alvara's power, I realized, was reunited with its wielder as well. Like a living entity, it too seemed to celebrate.

Alvara glanced down at her arm as the branding mark vanished—a debt made good. She rolled her neck and popped her knuckles. Simultaneously, the scrapes and bruises across her skin vanished as her healing restored as well. My breath came in a desperate whoosh of relief. And yet. And yet, I wanted to reach for her immediately, to keep the connection we had formed. To deepen it.

It was a different sentiment than the one in her mind as she focused on Aren and flashed that feline smile. "Let's go get this son of a bitch."

The Commander grinned.

FIFTY-THREE
WORKING THEORY
ALVARA

It seemed Adrastos *was* as sharp a seer as I was, and tracking the son of a bitch down indeed turned into a clairvoyant volley. Just as August had anticipated, for each thread I pulled, a new one spooled out. For every choice any of us made, five new directions emerged, and then ten as Adrastos adjusted.

We had interrupted our Christmas Eve tradition of cozying up at Aren's cabin after sledding, baking cookies, and watching movies, to get our asses back to Grayshell and devise a game plan that would take control back. My primary concern was what Saraya had found in my blood—ideally, so we could create an antidote, but at the very least, to duplicate it and keep the battlefield even. Even if Adrastos would inevitably know about it.

Cookies were still, naturally, essential on Christmas Eve, so Fae and Lana continued the project in the common room kitchen while the rest of us marked maps and sketched visions and plans. The timer chirped, and Fae jumped up from her perch on the side of Alec's armchair, heading for the kitchen as I drifted away from the present.

I felt as though my body had frozen, unresponsive to my prompts—concrete limbs for a mind working in overdrive. My visions didn't include the past, so I couldn't discern the kind of bullshit the brothers had pulled while my gifts were out of commission. But whatever they'd done, the visions of their future were brighter. In neutralizing Aren's weapon, they had given themselves a significant advantage.

August sat on the floor below me, and I was vaguely aware of his warmth and pressure as he leaned against my knees. I couldn't help wishing we'd had even an hour more to hold each other—to really hold each other. But a connection as strong as ours would take days to revisit if we weren't interrupted. Weeks, perhaps, if there were depths to sort through, and given the binding on our memories, I assumed there would be. August sighed through his nose, reading my thoughts, and laid his head back on my thighs. He closed his eyes and hummed, seemingly oblivious to Aren and Ansel's current debate, just as I was.

More and more conflicts flashed through my head, all ending at the same damned bloody killing field, with August walking across it. And that was as far as I could get; there were too many threads after it. But the vision of me, bloodied and broken, had indeed vanished.

So, that much of Adrastos' taunting was true. He could not kill one of us to use the other. *Soul-bound.* Interesting. I should have known—August was the only soul I had ever feared failing so much that I'd become prone to panic attacks, the only calling that brought that kind of desperation to my search. And uniquely, intensely, perfectly my counterpart regarding our gifts. Gifts and elements that could braid, connect, and lend strength to one another when needed. Soul-bound, indeed.

A soft smile tugged at his full lips at that. *Once I ascended, I nearly forgot about everything—my old life. I thought I loved Layla, but it was like she was a distant dream as soon as we were together. I couldn't explain it. Didn't understand any of this soul group, soul-bound, soul mate stuff.*

I thought about that for a long moment, giving myself space to process the flicker of guilt I'd felt over Michael. I allowed myself to acknowledge that love long lost. Allowed myself to breathe and know that I was not dishonoring him in finding my true soul mate in August, and that he would want me to be happy, all these years later.

Three hundred *years later, Ally. Trust me. If he loved you half as much as I do, he would want this for you too.* I blinked back the burning in my eyes.

I love you, August Porter. If all of this was necessary to get to you, I would do it all again. Even now, with this storm bearing down on everything. I would do it all again.

"Ugh. You two are going to make me sick. Can you focus, *please?*" Lana pinched the bridge of her nose, blinking dramatically. But there was mirth in her eyes, tugging at the corners of her lips. I shook my head. Ansel flashed that rare smile at his mate and rolled his eyes before turning his attention back to Aren.

"No promises," August muttered under his breath, opening his eyes to look up at me, amusement flashing there.

"Honestly though, Al. I kind of need your nose to the ground. You know I'm *Team Allgust*, but can it wait until this shit show is over?" Aren smirked as he spoke, and Alec shot water out of his nose at *"Team Allgust."* Spluttering and coughing, he set his hand on his chest, trying to choke down his laughter. I snorted and raised my hands in surrender. August rolled his eyes but turned over, kissed each of my knees, and walked to sit at the bar to rehydrate after our festivities.

An hour went by—maybe more, maybe less—but the fire dwindled to flickering embers when I came out of the tunnel of visions, volleying between me and Adrastos. I might have been kidding myself, but there seemed to be amusement outlining them now, as though he knew. Knew we were in this volley and took pleasure in the game. I gritted my teeth and hadn't realized I was growling until I noticed everyone's eyes on me.

"Useless," I barked. "I have my gifts back, and they're freaking useless. Especially when every choice you all make is blocked before we could even begin to implement it. We're playing cat and mouse, and Adrastos is the damn cat."

A collective sigh rippled through the group; Aren and August both rubbed at their temples, as if they could feel the pounding in my own.

"As long as you can adjust as he does, though, doesn't that put us in an odd clairvoyant stalemate?" Alec ran his hand along the back of his neck. "Perhaps you can't give us a path, but he knows the gifts among us exceed those of the average Renown. You haven't seen anything spectacular in your visions of them, outside of sheer numbers. Perhaps Adrastos is as much the mouse as you are. It's why he approached you at all. He can't beat us—join us?"

I shook my head. "I can't describe it, but I can feel him in the visions now. Like he's *enjoying* this. Playing a game."

"The Reapers are nearly as old as I am," Aren said, his expression soft as he leaned forward to brace his elbows on his knees. "Maybe you are the first challenge he's had in a millennium. Of course he'll enjoy toying with you. He's never had an equal. I didn't know *you* had an equal."

"How does one conceal a power like that for a thousand years?" Ansel's eyes had lost any sign of amusement as he contemplated it. Aren only shook his head. "There's laying low, and then there's...this. Even Alvara is known in most circles."

"We haven't attempted to conceal her, though," Aren argued. "When her gifts emerged, I wanted them to know she was coming for them. Wanted them to know what they'd face if they fucked around."

"So, what are we going to do? Sit here and play mental tennis, or *do* something?" Lana rang her hands together in frustration. Idle hands did not suit her well. Silence settled over us for a long while. At some point, Aren rose and added logs to the fire, stoking it back to life. August was again planted by my feet when I emerged from my visions. No progress. None. Stalemate, indeed.

Our indecision began to wear me down, my willpower faltering, and despite ten hours of it last night, I wanted to sleep. Exhaustion had burrowed its way into every inch of me. In fact, I wasn't sure when I had last felt rested. We were quiet again for a while, contemplative. I didn't bother casting visions—they weren't gaining us anything anyway.

"There are a few things I can't figure out." August sat up a bit, propping against an arm and running his other hand through his hair.

"Welcome to the club," Ansel sighed, forlornly biting into the cookie Lana held up to him from her spot on the floor.

"No, but really. They've caught us—caught Ally—off guard a few times now. *How?*"

"Always a last-minute, impulsive decision," the words came out like a sigh. "Something out of character. Something I couldn't see coming until we were in the middle of it. The threads were likely there to pull on, but I certainly didn't see them as viable enough to pay attention to." I rubbed at my eyes.

"Right. So we don't form a plan. Each of us decides, prepares, and implements our own plan. We do so thoroughly. Ally will make a last-minute decision. Giving Adrastos too many threads to choose from...it's our best bet."

"Perhaps," I conceded. August continued.

"And then we have two gaps in our timeline, where we had premonitions—knew something was going sideways but didn't know what."

"Samhain and last night."

"Exactly. We have no answers about what occurred in either gap." The flicker of the now-roaring fire caught my attention, and I studied it for a long while, thinking, probing, wishing my visions could rewind too. When nobody seemed to have any ideas, August continued. "We were being tested? Ally might have been tested." He rubbed his hand over his mouth, his jaw tight, eyes narrowing as he thought through it. "And what did we do? Both times."

"We froze. Yielded." Alec scowled at him. "What are you getting at?"

"We don't act unless we're certain," Aren answered, understanding settling across his features. "Does Adrastos believe we'll stand down if we can't see a thread we're confident in?" His eyes flicked up to me. It made sense that he would have been studying our response if I couldn't see clearly. If he could strip our gifts through some curse of Agamemnon's power, he would believe we would stand down.

The group nodded as my thoughts untangled themselves.

"Then we neutralize Adrastos. We level the field. How do we fare against the Renown in hand-to-hand combat?"

"Pure hand-to-hand?" Aren grinned broadly, widely, confidently. He nodded. "We kick their ass. They might be bigger; many are stronger..."

"But we're faster, more skilled," I interjected, finally catching on and smiling. "So we *let* them weaponize Agamemnon? Let them strip the energy—but we do it on our terms. We do it *on* the battlefield, so they're affected too. Or we weaponize it ourselves."

"You think it will work that way? We can be selective with our shields." Alec pulled his power back, and I felt it leave my body, then expand again to wrap me up.

"I think either we find a way to strip their strength or let them utilize theirs. Agamemnon injected me with whatever power he wields as Reaper. I think contact must be direct. Either way, we figure out how to fight without sight."

"It will come down to our wits in the moment, then, if we can neutralize Adrastos."

I nodded. "We need to see what Saraya has figured out."

HER FACE SAID ENOUGH when we walked into the empty infirmary. Not good. Saraya sat at her steel workstation, microscopes, samples, and enlargements neatly lined out in front of her. Stress lined her brow, which seemed permanently furrowed.

"Nothing?" The breath left my body as her eyes widened desperately.

"Well...not nothing. But not...anything workable." She flashed me an apologetic wince. "The good news or the bad news?"

"Bad."

"I don't see how we can weaponize it." Saraya had shifted into doctor voice, her face schooled into calculative neutrality. Aren swore under his breath.

"Okay. And the good news?"

"I know how to neutralize it." She took a breath, and I stared at her expectantly. "It's him, Alvara." When I blinked, she opened her mind, and like the shattering of a small dam, I saw it all.

FIFTY-FOUR
SANCTUARY
AUGUST

We both slept fitfully that night, still sharing a bed but banished to opposite sides, tucked between different layers of sheets. Alvara was right; the energy needed for a soul-bound reading would be immense. She sincerely felt we'd need days to do it right—to see it all.

Alvara was usually right...

So I let it be. Let it be, despite every instinct urging me to soothe her restless sleep. To stroke her hair, her face, her neck; to pull her from those nightmares with my lips. To worship her—body and soul—and claim her pleasure as I brought her release. To do it again and again until her limbs went numb and she could finally rest. Instead of easing the tension, our stolen kisses had ignited a goddamned inferno that I knew couldn't be sated with anything short of connecting in the most primal way. We needed to give each other everything.

Instead, I just lay there, glaring at the dark canopy of her four-poster bed.

My heart had been racing since Saraya had revealed what she knew. The drug in Alvara's blood wasn't a drug at all—but a separate strand of DNA. Nephilim DNA. Agamemnon's, as far as we could tell.

Aren said The Reapers had only been able to strip powers when they were in close proximity to their victims. It seemed Agamemnon was learning how to strip them at a distance. And Alvara had been his guinea pig. Saraya feared that she was too far behind to understand how they intended to weaponize him against our souls. She hadn't a clue and showed no sign of sleeping until she could solve it.

Evidently, I would have been better off working beside her than tossing all night. We had to solve this. Had to outmaneuver this bastard, no matter what it took. The air crushed my lungs under the weight of it.

Resigned to torturing myself, I reclaimed the gap between me and Ally, curling my body around hers, wrapping my arms around her ribs, relishing the way she leaned into me and inhaling her scent. Alvara arched her tight little ass back into my groin, and my cock jerked as every drop of blood rushed to it. *Goddamn.* But then Alvara moaned, the sound breathless and throaty, even in sleep.

"*August.*" It was just a breath. But every muscle in my body went rigid. Another slow, heady groan slipped from her lips, and my blood began pounding. I fucking needed this woman more than the air in my frantic lungs, my cock so hard it was painful.

Fuuuck. In two swift motions, I was off the bed, and in another, I'd cleared the doorway.

They'd left the Christmas decorations scattered throughout the temple after midnight mass. With glowing candles everywhere, flickering off each gold surface, the sacred space soothed my frayed nerves incrementally. Even the incense smelled familiar—like home, vaguely of pine and cinnamon. I'd attempted to dump my baggage here during the service, but the weight had only grown heavier as the evening wore on.

I'd never been a religious man, never cared for the structure or the rules. But as my knees met the marble, breath still coming in ragged little pants, I turned my face up to the looming altar and prayed. Something cool tingled through my veins, sending chills across my skin, as if peace had washed me clean. I breathed it in—that peace, that rare moment of solitude.

The weight of this reality was suffocating, even as I tried to bleed it into the stone floor. "*Please,*" I mumbled, my voice cracking. "Don't take her from me. Not when we just found each other." My voice was rough as I swallowed thickly. "Tell me how to save us."

Someone cleared their throat, and when I turned over my shoulder, I found Ansel watching me from the back pew, his elbows braced on his knees, eyes shadowed in the candlelight. A muscle in his jaw feathered, brow furrowed in understanding. He gave me a nod of acknowledgment and rose on a heel to leave the room.

It was long after four in the morning when I finally found sleep.

HER WHISPER TICKLED MY EAR. "Merry Christmas, August Porter."

Slowly, begrudgingly, my eyes opened. She was glowing—not just literally, as the sun streamed in behind her, illuminating her in a halo of light—but she was smiling radiantly, her entire body doing the same. The smell of baked goods and coffee caught me next. Seeing the observation in my mind, she turned behind her and summoned a plateful: donuts, puffed pastries, and hand pies, all as beautiful as the ritziest magazine.

I straightened up, stretching and yawning. She giggled softly and bit into one of the donuts. "Morning, sleepyhead. No rest?" She inclined her head to the side. I shook mine. "Well, we have stimulants and an ungodly amount of sugar. Hopefully, it will make up for it."

The coffee was, as usual, nearly scalding and bitter in the best way. I sighed and accepted a hand pie from her tray of goodies.

"You seem...chipper? Any progress on Adrastos?"

She sighed and bit into her pastry, her throat bobbing as she swallowed. "Screw Adrastos." She flashed me a cheeky, crooked grin, and I snorted a laugh. "Today is my first Christmas with my soulmate. I'll solve the world's problems later." She licked the sugar off her fingers one at a time, and I groaned as heat flooded my body. Alvara flashed me a coy smile.

You're a brat, you know that?

Maybe a bit. You like it. She raised a solitary brow.

Maybe a bit.

She perused the plate of pastries and plucked up a Danish—cherry, by the smell of it. I sipped another scalding mouthful of coffee. When I was fully alert, I surveyed the room and widened my eyes at the pile of gifts in front of the mantle. Alvara was already striding for them.

"You all still exchange presents?"

"Why wouldn't we? Immortality is boring if you don't enjoy the little things." She picked up a box and rattled it as relief washed over me. It would have been awkward if I was the only enthusiast.

"But...you already know what they are, don't you?"

She tried hard to look insulted, setting her hand over her heart. "August Porter, are you suggesting I would do such a thing?"

I arched my brows and stated flatly, "You know what each and every one of those boxes is."

She grinned. "Down to the price tag."

"Well, that takes the fun out of it."

"It really does. But it's the *thought* that counts, right?" She smiled sweetly, flourishing her hand to emphasize her words.

I sighed and rolled over to the bedside table, reaching for my gift for her. It wasn't there—just her usual collection of pens, papers, and books. I turned back and scowled at her. There, in her slender ivory fingers, was the long, skinny box I had tucked into the drawer only the night before.

"I love it, August, really! I'll never take it off." She tore into the silver paper I'd so meticulously folded, having the box open and necklace free in a heartbeat. I laughed as she clipped it around her neck, the small pink ward stone settling between her breasts. "It's almost as effective as you are. Almost." She threw me a wink, tapping her new amulet. "Thank you, August."

"But I suppose you still get to surprise all of us?"

"Surprising anyone is a bit of a challenge with the mental connection, but I do my best." She tossed me a small box wrapped in green, nearly the same color as her eyes. Then she thought very, very hard about a giant pink elephant. I shook my head, cheeks aching with the smile on my face, still sore from all our laughter on the mountain. I made to tear off the paper, but my heart felt heavy despite her merriment. Heavy with the lack of answers, with the lack of a plan.

Alvara gave me a knowing smile. "We're just in a stalemate, love. I intend to keep it that way for the time being. It will break. Just...for today... we'll let it be Christmas?"

I pursed my lips and forced a smile. She sat beside me as I stripped the paper and folded it into a pile between us. The rattle of metal on cardboard shifted and slid, and I narrowed my eyes at her.

"A necklace for me too, Coach?" She kept her face schooled into indifference, but her lips tugged at the corners. Her mind stayed firmly fixed on that pink elephant. I picked at a piece of shipping tape she had used to seal the box and sighed when I peeled my eyes from her face, realizing she had taped most of the box shut. "Cruel woman," I chuckled, and she grinned mischievously.

"That's half the fun, though."

"Torturing the recipient?"

"Gotta make it worth it." I chuckled as she sprawled out on the bed before me, inclining her head with that effortless grace of hers. She summoned one of her Scottish dirks from her desk, and it floated directly to me. I snatched it from the air, slicing along the seams, trying not to let her radiant amusement distract me. Her heart picked up pace as I peeled open the box and pulled out the flimsy white tissue.

At the bottom of that cardboard box, metal glinted—a sheathed silver blade and a once-gold antique pocket watch. I lifted the watch from the box, and something heavy settled into my chest. A story, I realized, as I weighed the small circle in my hands, running my thumb along the ancient chain.

Open it.

My gaze flicked up to her nervous eyes and blushing cheeks before returning to the delicate pattern on the face. I turned it in my hands once, then twice. Finally, I clicked the top button. Surprise washed over me as the spring easily clicked the face open. The old paper was aged with time, the numerals still visible in faded gray. On the opposite side, sealed against the glass, was the shadow of a black-and-white portrait. A portrait of a girl, perhaps just past her childhood.

I lifted the watch, eyes straining, heart heavy with the familiar pull of the object between my fingers. The faded outline of full lips, a defined jaw, high cheekbones, and large, dark eyes. Hair, midnight dark in the old ink, tucked into curls, and a black dress nearly concealed her neckline. A bewildered grin pulled at my mouth as I looked up at Alvara, who smiled sweetly at me. I narrowed my eyes. Her face was so familiar that my heart became a weight in my chest, sinking lower, deeper, to my core. It tugged at my mind—a memory, buried deep. A glinting gem at the bottom of a frozen lake, tucked between shadows.

The strain was enough to make my breath come heavier.

"This is...you? Younger, but you." She nodded, quietly, hesitantly. "I... I feel like I should... remember you. This way, I mean. Did you—did you trigger something?"

"Not specifically." She gave a timid shrug. "It was... an intuitive tug, I suppose. The watch was my father's." She let out a long, low breath. "During the railroad boom, they became common. I don't really have anything from this life—my human life, I mean. But that, I've held onto. My father kept it in the last years of his life and promised it to my future... betrothed."

"Michael."

A nervous nod. "And I know we've only just... finally acknowledged our feelings, but—I thought you should have it. Before... everything happens. I think reunited, soul-bound mates would supersede betrothed." She smiled broadly around the words.

I let out a long breath, steadying my hand as I turned it over in my fingers again, studying where it was worn, where the design had been rubbed shiny, versus where it had aged. The heaviness within such a tiny object was striking.

"Ally, this is—"

"Yours, if you'll have it. I've meant to have the watch restored, to get it working. Lana is good with trinkets and bobbles. I just hadn't prioritized it."

"Thank you." I exhaled again, wanting to kiss her, to hold her as she offered up a piece of herself. She just grinned at me.

"Soon, love. But I will take my time with you, August Porter. You're a story I will not rush reading." I rolled my eyes, but then she pointed back to the box—the blade within it lay forgotten. Gently, as if it could dissolve into dust and memory, I set the watch aside before picking up the blade.

The sheath was thin—supple black leather. The small pommel was round, engraved with a Celtic knot that braided down into the blade itself. I slid the blade free and weighed it—surprisingly heavy for a knife this size. It seemed to sing in my hand, as though the steel longed to be held. Clean and oiled, there was no need to feel it to know she kept it precisely sharpened.

"A throwing knife?"

"My favorite one. Alec teases that the Celtic witches must have enchanted it to always meet its mark."

"Couldn't have just given you credit for being proficient?"

She smirked. "Of course not. But it seems to strike true no matter who wields it. A piece of a past life, perfectly preserved. Ansel gave it to me a few centuries back. Wouldn't tell me why, or who I had been to him. But he... remembers me. Swore he'd fill in the gaps at the right time."

I knew the old general kept secrets, kept his thoughts close to the vest, but this...

"He knows who you were and hasn't found the right time to tell you in a few *hundred* years?"

"Evidently not. Frustrating as it may be... I trust him. He's earned that much."

Evasive, arrogant bastard. We were going to have words; his secrecy be damned. She grinned even wider at the protective blade I balanced.

"Snoop." I nudged her foot.

"I call her Heart Tracker. For... obvious, morbid reasons." She grimaced but continued, "And I hope she serves you well in the coming weeks."

"You really think it will still come to a battle? Still no way around it?"

"Adrastos wants you. And it seems if we don't agree to an alliance, he will find some way to make you agree to serve him. Evidently, I am no longer his bait. It will come to a fight if I can't think of something cleverer to get us out of it. Trust your blades."

"You will. Think of something clever, I mean. And trust your blades." I playfully nudged her through the blanket, and she jabbed me back. "Thank you, Alvara, for the gifts. I—I don't know what to say."

"I wanted you to have a piece of me with you, no matter what happens."

"I will have all of you with me, no matter what happens."

She grinned, but the shadows in her eyes twisted my stomach into a molten knot.

"What did you see, Ally?"

"Nothing I won't try to work my way out of. He's... good, August. At what he does. At this game of his. As good as me, certainly. Maybe better."

"You'll figure him out, Ally. We will. Together."

She granted me a small, thin-lipped smile. "Do you trust me, August?"

There was no hesitation in my answer. "With my life."

"Thank you for that. For believing in me. Things might get... intense. And I need you to trust me. Please don't let that go."

My throat felt swollen as I swallowed down the fear rising there. Images of the injuries she had already subjected herself to in the name of victory flashed through my mind. Selfless, masochistic soul. I could have sworn the corner of her mouth quivered, just a bit.

I managed a small nod. With focus, my lungs dragged down a long, steadying breath. Loving Alvara was, indeed, like loving a force of nature. But she was the cleverest, most calculated, level-headed being I had ever known. Down to those injuries. Those courageous sacrifices. And I loved her more than life itself, so I was allowed to speak my heart.

"I will follow you to the end of this life and into the next, my love."

Her throat bobbed, eyes welling. I leaned forward and carefully tucked her hair behind her ear. I wasn't sure if she was breathing as I pulled back.

"I was hoping you would say that."

The fireside had grown quiet at last, all of us resting our hands on full bellies. If there was one thing Grayshell did exceptionally well, it was holiday feasts. Despite gorging myself to the brink of nausea, the saccharine smells still filling the room kept me wishing for more space for the sweets, pies, and tarts now stacked tall in the grand hall. Alvara, book in hand, lay across my lap, humming to herself as she read. My fingers meandered through her endless curls, occasionally braiding thin lines of chocolate strands together—something I had learned from and for Freya, what felt like many lifetimes ago.

A part of me still ached with homesickness after hearing her voice on the phone. My mother had been less than amused at my flimsy excuse, demanding that the next holiday season be spent with them. Only fair, she said, for this new *infatuation* to trade off years, obviously. I laughed and assured her she'd get to meet Ally soon. But it was of Freya and James that I was thinking as the fire popped, drawing me back to the room.

Fae, after kissing my cheek in thanks for the new silver bandolier, had settled in, curling up like a cat beside us and falling asleep. Alec and Aren were lazily playing a game of chess, sprawled in their armchairs, flicking their pieces along the board in a half-hearted manner, too overindulged to grumble when the other bested them. Alec had bestowed meticulously balanced, custom-engraved daggers on each member of the coven, while Aren proudly revealed new body armor he'd commissioned for us—fierce-looking skintight suits that resembled golden dragon scales, allegedly just as difficult to pierce. The Commander had grinned as he gave us the tutorial, pointing out all the hidden sheaths and blades. More pride swelled within him as he showed Ansel how to turn them black, in case we needed to conceal ourselves in the shadows. Lana was the most pleased of our group, literally squealing as she tested a mechanism in the sleeve that slid her favorite blades directly into her palms. Running her fingers over the Grayshell crest on the chest plate, she formally dubbed them our battle blacks. She and her mate would, of course, be using the recon side most often.

Now, she and Ansel were perched in the window seat, feet touching as they scoured through books of their own.

"Research," the evasive warrior had told me when I inquired, not bothering to look up from the page in front of him. "On clairvoyance—on Alvara and Adrastos. We need to figure out how to stand a fool's chance against the coming host."

I looked around the warm room, trying to breathe in the sight of that flickering fire and the soft croons of Bing Crosby—Aren's favorite—turning on the record player.

Despite the apparent bliss of our little cadre, my stomach turned in uneasy circles, my heart never quite reaching its usual unperturbed beat. My focus remained on the ivory curves of Alvara's soft skin, her rosy cheeks warm with brandy and fire. The way her eyes shifted as she read line after line, page after page of the book clasped in her long fingers. Her chest subtly rose and fell in easy, drowsy breaths. Breaths that suddenly hitched, her brow furrowing, eyes narrowing with amusement. She snorted. No one seemed to notice but me.

"What?" I asked casually.

"Adrastos just stuck his tongue out at me. He's just toying with us now." She stated the observation with no urgency, but every head snapped in her direction, save for Fae, who still slumbered.

"He...what?" Aren demanded, sitting up in his chair. She set her book on her chest and replayed the vision in her mind.

Knowing it would soon be taken anyway, I unleashed every ember of power on the first line of foot soldiers, leaving only ash in their wake.

It was odd, watching directly through her eyes. But I could feel the steady beat of her heart, the unfaltering strength within her, and somehow, it soothed me, despite the host bearing down on her.

Panting, sucking down breath as viciously as I could, Ansel whispered in my mind, "Twenty-five hundred."

Aren rumbled a morbid laugh. "That might be a record." I nodded, still panting, hands braced on my hips. *It wasn't enough. Still wasn't enough. Their numbers were staggering. I began to burrow, to dig deep into my strength, rallying another blow before the energy was stripped from us.*

August was engaged with the pony-sized wolves, his blade slicing through them with unmet precision. Too easily. Something wasn't right.

As their bodies fell, they shifted—souls, shifting souls, trapped within their beast forms as a distraction. I whirled but found Aren's hulking form between me and Adrastos, his blade tipped against Aren's throat. Ansel snarled a warning growl...and the entirety of my gifts drained from me. A cruel smile twisted on our enemy's thin lips, and then he grinned—a real one —and stuck his tongue out at me like a child.

Aren rumbled a laugh despite the taunting clairvoyant slap. Alvara seemed entirely unperturbed.

"For each plan I hatch," she sighed, "he crafts his own counterattack. This is only a game to him. One of many, no doubt."

"Perhaps if you spent less time reading smut, and more time playing chess, you would have beaten him by now." Alec flashed a teasing smile, wiggling his queen under a nonchalant finger.

"Perhaps if you stopped talking shit, you might actually win," she snapped back. Alec furrowed his brow and returned his eyes to the board just as Aren claimed the game. That grizzly bear grin stretched across the Commander's face, unruffled by the opponent toying with his second.

I tried to embrace their blasé demeanors, to mimic the ease of Aren's movement as he relaxed into his chair, to absorb a bit of my mate's composure as she flipped her novel back up, staring down her nose. But it was Ansel, those startling silver eyes locked on me, who seemed to understand. He jerked his head toward the door, folded his book under his arm, and left the room without saying a word. Movements lithe and predatory, even in the Christmas facade we all seemed to cling to.

Peeling myself away from Alvara went against every instinct in my body, but I forced myself to follow. When I found the warrior, he leaned against the marble balcony overlooking the hall below. Book casually folded in one hand, his forearms braced against the banister. If I didn't know better, it seemed as though shadows emanated from him, his very being weighing down the hallway like the marble beneath him. The dark heaviness of his presence halted my steps.

"You're going to give yourself up." It wasn't a question or a command, but something between the two. He rubbed a scar-flecked hand over his jaw before setting it against his book again.

"If that's what it takes, yes."

"Ally has yet to crack a thread where you don't. Why?"

I hesitated, staring at that face, which seemed carved from granite.

"I'm not sure, to be honest."

"If not Ally, then what—who—would be worth dying for?"

"He doesn't seek to kill me."

"Enslavement isn't better."

"No," I acquiesced. "It's not."

"It wouldn't be the first time you sacrificed yourself for the greater good."

I scowled at him. "If you know something that might help us, Ansel, now would be the time to reveal it."

He ran his tongue over the front of his teeth, sucking on one. "I'm going to ask you for something your instincts are not going to like." He pointed his book my way, emphasizing his intent as he said, "I need you to grant me your trust, August. When the timing is right, everything will come to light, but I must wait for the moment to present itself. And this isn't it. Aren and Alvara trust me to make the hard calls—including honoring this one. Can you?"

Cold steel locked on me as I ground my teeth. With a frustrated huff, I nodded, and he released the air he'd been holding.

"I don't care for delving into past lives. They're vivid enough without a mind carver digging them up." He cleared his throat. "I'm not entirely certain—the way Alvara can be certain—but your energy is...familiar. Someone I served a very long time ago. He sacrificed himself for our kingdom."

"Seems to be a common thread."

If I didn't know better, I'd say the corner of his lip twitched, just for a split second. "Indeed." He sucked on his teeth again, seeming to grapple with something. "The shadows don't tempt you." It wasn't a question. "You're sent here to light the way when the world goes black." When it was clear I had nothing to say to that, Ansel continued. "Being soul-bound doesn't change that. You'll likely re-circulate together, and now that it's easier to survive childhood, find each other relatively quickly when we talk in terms of mortal life. Since the mortals have...sanitized...finding each other has gotten easier. That being said...soul shock is real. And I would be prepared for it, if I were you."

"You speak as though there is no chance of victory."

"I don't sugarcoat bullshit."

"You know, I believe that." I snorted as he chuckled—the sound so rare it was startling.

"I've been watching Ally. Closely. Watching her interactions with Adrastos. He's *taunting* her. Like a cat playing with its food. I think he already knows his plan and is making decisions for fun to keep her off his trail. I think she knows it." He sighed deeply before continuing, "He's played this game before—perhaps with the two of you, with the way he behaves around her. Speaks to her. Ally is...the best of us. The strongest—next to you, I suppose, whenever your power actualizes." Ansel became quiet for a long while, and I just allowed him to think. Something in my gut said whatever he had summoned me for was worth waiting to hear. Worth the tug toward Alvara as her chiming laugh carried over the rumble of Alec and Aren in the room behind us.

"Have you studied astronomy much?"

"Not beyond high school."

"Lana and I love space. You've inevitably noticed we're not...great team players." Amusement narrowed those silver eyes. "But we've always liked to study the stars. When things are calm...on the soul front, we like to take to a desert and stay up all night together." I raised my brows suggestively, and he sniggered—a one-shoulder shrug. "Aside from very needed alone time, learning about the stars—the constellations. It's become a favorite pastime. When decades blend into centuries, you'll get it." Ansel sighed deeply through his nose. "Has Aren ever told you about a soul nova?"

"Like a supernova?"

He nodded, and I shook my head in response. "It's not very common. Even fewer are willing to...talk about it. You see, we're all granted a certain...level of power in our souls. Some of us are red dwarf stars—like me, Alana, or Aphaea—we're skilled, but not exactly overpowered by our gifts. We can last an eternity if left alone. Nobody really bothers with us because we don't draw much attention. But our lifespan is long enough that we become quite...proficient in certain areas." He bobbed his head, shrugging a shoulder. "I mean, Fae can wield all the elements with a decent amount of strength, so she might be a bit more than that. But not by much. There are main sequence stars—yellow stars, like our sun, for example—that are powerful enough to affect and nourish life, to affect seasons and elements, like Alec, like Brody and Marcus, and their brothers." Ansel ran a palm over his beard. "Souls like Aren, like Nathara, Ragen, and Reyna, perhaps this... Adrastos..." Ansel narrowed his eyes, jaw set, selecting his words carefully. "They fall somewhere in the realm of the giants. Not always the most prominent, but often dense with power. So immense, they affect everything around them. Everything in proximity. Nothing is untouched before they burn out—and it seems they're given the skill sets to write history. But Alvara—and I believe you—you're super giants."

I choked on a laugh as he raised his eyebrows.

"Do you know what a supernova is?"

The violent death of a star—the explosion or implosion of a sun that had burned through its resources—flashed through my mind. An old lesson, buried in the files of random, useless information in my brain. Ansel gave a small smile as the information darted through my thoughts.

"Good. Your mate, I believe, is like a supergiant...*masquerading* as a dwarf star. Trying to convince herself she isn't what she is. A lot like you."

A wry smile. "She *contains* herself. Holds back, while the others nearly burn themselves out with simpler tasks. I've sensed it since we met. Her lives are brief but immense. She's young in this life—a baby, at this point—and barely has begun to burn through her resources...still burning hydrogen, if we keep up our star analogy. I am concerned that Adrastos will be...a *violent* accelerant. In her effort to protect what she loves, she might enter such a state of fusion that her power...unleashes itself upon us all. And, like a supergiant...the effect would be—"

"Catastrophic."

A solemn nod. "The way she eviscerated those demons and didn't even try. Came back from her possession stronger, rather than depleted. It's like... challenges just burn through one layer of her—like they release something new each time. Hydrogen to helium, and so on. Has she told you much about her mortal...existence?"

"Not a ton. She doesn't like to remember..."

"Michael."

I nodded. "Or the end of all of it. It seems that's what's most vivid."

"It usually is. Alvara was gifted—or cursed, perhaps—as a human, too. Her visions came before she ascended. Not as powerful as they are now, of course, but she could read snippets of people's futures through body or blood. Like a psychic. Her body would've been burned again, or at least ostracized, if they'd found her. She's probably faced the executioner more than we know, as her mortal bodies haven't even contained what she is."

"Did Michael know...that she was...different?"

"He loved her despite it. Or so I've gathered."

"Why are you...sharing all of this with me?"

"Aren knows she's changing—can feel it—and has confided in me that he's unsure of what to expect, or how to...control that unleashing of power. Harness it, so it doesn't decimate anything she doesn't mean to."

"Should you be sharing this with me, or was it discussed in confidence?"

A genuine smile barely touched the shadows in his eyes. "He says you're a good man. I really want to believe him." He rubbed his hand over his jaw again, then dragged his fingers through his hair before continuing. "Aren will come to you if he feels it's necessary. I...*I* feel it's necessary. I've led many armies, August. Death has been my...friend...my gift and my curse. And I have a knack for moving soldiers where we need them, when we need them. My gut says we need you. Aren trusts me to...place our pieces on the board, per se. And I need you by Alvara's side." He sighed, straightening so he could sit against the railing. "Whenever you can be. Be her...anchor in this. Because I've never once seen two souls toss their powers through each other the way you do. I've seen Aren command people through an exorcism. But you anchored her here, and you're a fucking newborn. Perhaps—and there's no way to know until we have to try it—the two of you can pull each other through the coming…implosion…too. Maybe, if you keep her preoccupied channeling your power like a conduit, she won't unleash her own."

We both watched the hall below, bustling with souls coming and going. Retrieving cakes, cookies, and pies, busying themselves with returning the treats to loved ones. The Greek Brothers emerged, each holding a different pie, happily embracing a group of women who joined them as they left the hall.

"You believe I will somehow protect Ally when I turn myself over to Adrastos?"

"I don't know. She hasn't seen why you do what you do, just that you do it. But I believe we will come upon an event that will require you to keep Alvara anchored to this world so she does not destroy the very thing she intends to protect."

He patted me on the back and turned for the common room.

"Ansel?"

He paused his long stride and turned halfway back toward me.

"Help me understand when to move."

A flash of a grin crossed his stone face before it vanished just as quickly. "My pleasure, Commander."

FIFTY-SIX
OUTMATCHED

ALVARA

He was late. Arrogant prick.

I sat in silence, filling the void with the scrape of my blade against stone. The days following Christmas dragged on endlessly, and sleep felt elusive. August carried a weight with him since that evening—something from his conversation with Ansel in the hallway.

Both men kept their walls around me as thick as stone, yet August's eyes often traced my face as if he feared he might never see it again. Guilt pushed me to do the same. After Adrastos had stuck his tongue out at me, I resolved to stop playing his games. The visions were brief and ghostly—uncommitted, I realized. He would make no true decisions. But the ideas that rattled in my mind day and night might help me understand our enemy. So, I allowed it.

Soft as a mountain cat, I barely heard the shoes crunching on gravel in the asphalt alley. The subtle clink of a stone rolling into a pothole was the only detectable sound. I schooled my face into the cold boredom Ansel and Aren had taught me.

"I've grown tired of your games."

"Is that why you've stopped playing with me, cousin? You've grown bored of me already?" His drawling accent scraped along my spine, but I didn't turn, wouldn't grant him the satisfaction. Adrastos' smoky mountain scent filled the alley as he gracefully sat beside me. His proximity turned my stomach to lead, and his too-familiar, sprawled position made my teeth grind. "Why, Alvara of Grayshell, have you stopped bothering to block my plans... yet that blood-soaked battlefield remains—more gruesome than ever? I don't care for the number of men we'll both lose when they would better serve us standing together."

I didn't respond, focusing instead on scraping steel across stone. He rumbled a low laugh.

"Testy, testy little thing, are you? Don't appreciate a challenge?"

"Don't appreciate playing cat and mouse when lives are on the line."

"Oh, come now, little cousin. It's been a millennium since I've met a mind like mine."

"I'm nothing like you." My voice dripped with boredom as I gave him a pointed glare that had made lesser men cower. He only smiled, a twisted, predatory thing glinting in his brown eyes.

Smile turning sly and crooked, he crooned, "Why else would you be here, answering my summons?"

Again, I focused on the blade in my hands. His walls were as thick as my own, leaving nowhere for my talons to reach within that concrete mind. I sighed dramatically.

"I actually have things to do today. You called this meeting, *cousin*. So, talk."

"Well, you're no fun at all."

"I don't find bloodshed to be a game or a joke. My friends fell in those visions. I won't play your games, Adrastos. Get to the point."

"Why don't you read me yourself? Perhaps we can come to an agreement when you've seen the truth of it."

"As I said, I have somewhere to be." A lie. I had nowhere to go until we figured out how to circumnavigate the man to my left. But with my gifts thoroughly intact, his mind tapped impatiently against the obstinate walls of Grayshell granite. Slowly, he retracted his energy back into himself, but he seemed to sense it, narrowing his eyes and inclining his head toward me.

"You make me sound archaic," he sighed, stretching out on the pavement beside me.

"Aren't you?" I snapped back.

That predator's grin flashed across his face again. "Not as old as your oaf of a Commander."

"Oh, go fuck yourself," I glared at him. "Aren is the greatest of us."

Adrastos snorted, eyes narrowing in accusation. "Aren *fears you*. He seeks to keep you on his leash."

"How sanctimonious of you." His mind scraped over my walls, and I suppressed the shiver that followed.

"What are you implying—exactly?" His voice turned taunting.

"You only seek to use me to control August."

"I seek to free you. To make you the queen you are. Contrary to your belief, I would serve *you* in the world I'm creating."

I scoffed, flashing him a glare, letting a bit of my energy slip from its restraints, knowing it would show in my eyes, in the aura around me. The bastard just grinned.

"What a prison you've built for yourself. Don't you want to be free? Haven't you proven you can control what's inside you? You've contained it long enough this time."

I refused the bait, instead asking, "Don't the humans deserve to be free?"

"They will be. Free of the burden of endless choices. They will serve our kind and have all that they need. The exchange will be even, scouts' honor." He raised his right hand. "They will get what they desire. Surely you see that."

"They deserve to choose that for themselves, don't they?"

"Their choices bring only bloodshed and death. Fuck, we could do that for them."

"You know, a few humans decided tyranny was good too. See how well that worked out for them?"

"Humans can't get anything right. Perhaps it's time we give it a try." Adrastos let out a prolonged sigh, sitting up to brush pebbles off his scarred hands. His inky hair was braided back from his face, and he wore a plain black turtleneck, matching pants, and leather loafers. Surely his weapons were stashed somewhere beneath, but I couldn't see them. He didn't come here to fight. When another minute passed in silence between us, I rose and began walking away.

"You mean to decline my invitation for an alliance." It wasn't a question.

"I will decline any proposal that involves enslaving another being to my will. Should you wish to join the family, *cousin*, and stand for freedom, there is a place for you at our table." I turned away but could have sworn a dark chuckle echoed behind me. A moment later, he stood in my path.

"Move." My tone left no room for inflection.

"Or what?" He flashed a cocky grin. "You'll turn me to ash, like you did those demons?"

"Don't tempt me with a good time, Adrastos." Perhaps it would be better—easier—if we settled this one-on-one. Handled this rivalry here and now.

"Spicy little thing."

"Sick coward."

The humor left his face, and for the first time, I saw the Commander of The Renown standing before me. His voice turned icy.

"I am many things, Alvara of Grayshell. But you will find that a coward, I am not."

"Prove it. You know—somewhere in you—you know this isn't right. You could save them. We could save them together—all the power players in one place. Set aside your ego and stand for what's *right*."

"Set aside yours and see what's inevitable." I scoffed, but he continued, "They will bow to us, or they will bow to another ruler. At least we will be benevolent. Let me show you—"

Before Adrastos' outstretched hand could reach mine, I spun away, my arms surrounded by a flickering barrier of white-hot flames. I knew the power surged from me in waves, evident in the longing on his face. He could sense it, buried in my eyes.

"Careful, Adrastos. It will be hard to rule as ash and cinder."

"Do it, then. Cousin. You know you can. So, why not? Why bother speaking to me at all?"

I stared at him for a long moment, then raised my hand between us. The flames grew to an inferno, and I flashed him a slow smile. "Because there's humanity in you, Adrastos of the Renown. Not yet drowned out by the company you keep. I believe any brother—even the most tarnished—can be redeemed. Until you prove otherwise, I will not give up on you."

He snorted and made to reach for me, but the flames erupted into a wide barrier between us, a wall of fire raging and licking at the brick on either side.

"Amazing," he murmured. I scowled at him. "What does your mate say about all of this?" A wicked grin spread across his face. Rage boiled in my blood, pressing against the surface, yearning to reach him. "Congratulations, by the way," he drawled, dripping in sarcasm.

"Touch him and find out how brightly your *little* cousin can burn."

"Even if he comes willingly?"

"He would never."

"I don't think you know him as well as you believe. I've seen him, luv. Seen him cross that battlefield to join me."

"Always under duress, you piece of shit."

"Such language." He tsked and shrugged his shoulders nonchalantly. "Perhaps I haven't given the two of you the proper motivation. Perhaps the love of your pets isn't enough perspective for you."

"I only came tonight to see if you could be reasoned with. It seems a pity to incinerate a gift like yours." I shrugged. "Aren was right. He usually is. I'll see you on the battlefield, Adrastos." I reduced my flames to embers and turned to leave the alley, but Adrastos burst into flames of his own. Tall black flames, like shadow, but hot enough to singe my skin if I moved closer. Fascination tugged at my mind. Shadow walkers weren't uncommon; we had a dozen or so in the hierarchy. The gift had been commonly bestowed within a far-off bloodline that had long since fallen from grace, but shadow *fire...*

A wicked grin spread across his face, as if he could sense my confusion. His features, once so handsome, twisted with cruelty. I studied the flames surrounding him, the way they moved, so similarly to my own. The dark to my light.

"We are two sides of the same coin, Alvara of Grayshell." Adrastos' honeyed voice turned sharp as he growled through tight teeth, "Don't think for a moment I haven't considered what it would be like to burn you to dust." He shrugged, and his words slowed back to a drawl. "Not a very familial thing to do to a cousin, is it?"

"And blackmailing them is?"

"Would you have considered it if I'd just called you up and asked you to coffee?"

"Certainly would've been the more *familial* thing to do."

"But would you have considered?"

"I'm not considering now. I've met your kind. Killed your kind." My teeth ground together. "Painted the earth with evil just like you, and not for a moment have I regretted it. Don't think, *cousin*, I won't do the same to you." He flared his flames, but I was faster. My shield burst into a great wall between us, fire erupting and licking at the edges of it, the buildings beside us. Rivulets of water began to swirl in from every edge of the alley, suspended in the air like glittering glass beads, a storm raging from the earth rather than the sky. I inclined my head, grinning. "If you want to play, we play one-on-one. Leave my family out of it. My friends out of it. And I won't wipe your kind from the face of the planet in one burst. Guard your mind all you want; I can still see the longing in your eyes when you watch me. Can still see the fear there. Just like the others." He whipped his shadow flame forward, but it sizzled against my shield. I gave him a look that suggested how pitiful his attempt was. He sneered at me but I continued. "You know, should you challenge me directly, you *will* fall. It's why you proposed this flimsy alliance, why you've built that dark host. I know it. You know it. It's why we've been playing vision tennis these last weeks. You don't want to face me."

"No. I don't. It would be a shame to waste your talent, to send you back to recirculate, hopefully to a smarter host next time. Despite your arrogance, I like you, cousin—"

"Stop calling me that." My voice remained steady, bored, mimicking his cool drawl. "You are no family of mine."

"Fine. I like you, Alvara. Your spunk, your flames. And I need your mate to stand a fool's chance in this world shortly."

"He would never build the world you envision. He'll fight against it to his last breath."

"Let's hope it doesn't come to that."

"Let it go. Let us go."

"Now, I'm afraid I just can't do that."

I pulled all my elements back within me. "Then you will lose... everything you've ever wanted." It was a promise, and Adrastos reduced his flames to dark shadow embers. He took a long breath.

"Perhaps...we will agree to disagree, *Princess*, until you see reason. Until...we can properly motivate you to see reason."

I strode for the alley's end, but his enormous hand came down on my shoulder, yanking me back to face him. "Take your hands off me before I burn them away."

"This isn't how tonight was supposed to go. Not how you and I were meant to go." A muscle in his jaw twitched as he ground out the words.

"And how did it play out in that delusional head of yours?"

"You actually heard me out. You listened to all we could accomplish— for our kind *and* theirs—and then you went home, deliberated with that mate of yours, swayed your Commander to see sense. Together, we stop the horsemen from destroying this place. This is my home, Alvara. I won't lose it to an ancient prophecy."

"Then take it up with your beloved uncle."

"Lucifer has done all he can to keep them sealed away. His tricks are spent."

"Then there is nothing more for us to say. August and I will sooner burn with the mortals than serve you. Remove your hand, or I'll do it for you." I raised an eyebrow over a saccharine smile, dripping with a promise of death. He took his hand from my shoulder and stuffed it into his pocket, but something like pain flashed in his eyes. He meant every word he said, the reality he'd spun for himself. I almost pitied him. Almost.

"I'll give you another chance. One more chance to make sense of this mess for yourself. You'll see—you'll both see—that I am your way out of this. Go home to your mate, Alvara. Talk it over. Cast your visions of the future, feel out what's coming. Call me when you're ready to serve the alliance."

"Go to hell."

He shrugged. "The offer stands. For now. I'll have to get...more creative if, like a petulant child, you can't be reasoned with."

I backed a few paces away, refusing to drop that dark gaze, and jumped home to Grayshell.

FIFTY-SEVEN
MELTING
ALVARA

When I arrived, August lay sprawled on the grand table, one hand lazily supporting his head while the other extended in front of him, wiggling as though he were playing invisible keys. He wore a long-sleeved white shirt and grey sweatpants, his chiseled abdomen peeking between the two. I bit my lip, admiring how sexy he looked when relaxed. Watery dawn light trickled down from the towering windows behind him.

Above his outstretched hand glittered a spiraling tower of sparkling snowflakes. I couldn't sense his energy or his thoughts through the shield he'd built around himself, but he turned his gaze to me. The flakes melted together, forming a horse made of water. With a flick of his wrist, the great stallion galloped away, making a loop around the room before misting into a flurry of snow against the stone wall.

"Beautiful, this magic...this place." His words were quiet but not weak. He propped himself on his elbows, a muscle feathering in his jaw as he took a prolonged breath and blew it out through his nose. "Did you get anywhere? With Adrastos?"

I let out a long breath of my own. "How did you know?"

A wry smile tugged at his lips as he tapped his chest with a wide palm, right over his heart. "It was like...a tug in my core. Like you needed me, somehow. I used to get milder tugs like that—but I thought it was just a sire-offspring thing. Didn't realize it was some supernal soulmate bond. But it was there again, pulling me toward you. Only, I didn't know where you'd gone. I hoped I was wrong. But of course, I wasn't. You're...well...you." He sighed deeply. "I'm glad you're home safe."

"I'm sorry if I startled you."

"You can wake me up, you know? If you need to challenge our enemies, I'd like to be there."

"I'm afraid...to hand you to him on a platter, when you're all he wants."

August's expression softened. "You know you can't run off into danger and expect me to sit on my hands, right?"

It was true; if this dynamic was going to work, I couldn't be more protective of my male mate than I allowed him to be of me. I nodded.

"So...you get anywhere?"

I shook my head. "I don't think there's anywhere to get. I'm afraid he's... convicted. In what he believes. He offered to let me read him—he's that confident in his cause."

"And...did you?"

I shook my head again, closing the gap to sit beside him on the table. Immediately, August's warm hand began stroking lazy circles down my back. Leaning into the touch, I nearly purred before a sigh escaped me. "He's a condescending, arrogant prick."

August snorted. "Are you surprised?"

My breath came out in a long sigh. "No. A fool's hope, I guess, that perhaps he could be reasoned with. I just...God, I hate war. Hate blood and death and pain. This battle, August..."

"I know," he breathed, laying back down on the table and motioning for me to join him. I did, curling into his side, resting my head against the soft spot between his shoulder and chest.

"Can you show me again—your water *magic*?" I giggled at the word. It was cute how he viewed our ability to wield elements. He wrapped his arm tighter around my torso and shifted his fingers, freeing a towering lioness from the water in a ferocious leap. She prowled across the air in front of us, stalking and gnashing her teeth. "When did you practice *that*?"

"All the times you were out saving the world. Saving callings. I decided to use that time for something fun. If we weren't training and you were off fighting demons, I needed to distract my anxiety, so...I did this." The smile in his voice brought a grin to my face. I nuzzled into his chest again.

"You were nervous for me?"

"Don't smile so big when you say that. Of course I was nervous for you."

"I've been doing this—"

"For three hundred years. I know, I know. But I...you know...cared for you. Despite myself."

"Despite yourself," I mocked, pinching his side. The energy of his smile filled the very air I breathed.

"Yes. Despite myself. I tried so hard to convince myself it was something else. Some other attachment. I didn't think you would...return the sentiment."

How I wanted to ask.

I kissed his chest and set my hand over his heart, feeling it thrum against me through the thin fabric. The scent of him sent heat spiraling through my core, and I hummed. "I'm sorry. If you didn't realize what you are to me. I can be a bit...preoccupied." I watched his lioness transform into an enormous flock of birds that dove toward us before spiraling away.

"Your focus, my love, is unparalleled. Confusing as hell...but incredible."

For a long few minutes, August played with his water creatures, freezing and unfreezing them, turning them into snow flurries, and melting them back into beasts, dolphins, wolves, and mice. It was beautiful magic.

SOMEWHERE BETWEEN OUR morning run through the grounds of Grayshell and breakfast with the hierarchy in the hall, my mind turned molten hot. Anxiety rippled down my body, filling my bones with deep-seated dread that I couldn't shake. It didn't matter that the coven was present, that the visions hadn't changed. It didn't seem to matter that August kept that grin on his face, or that Alec swaggered about, joking about me slicing down Adrastos. That swirling lava just tightened in my gut, threatening to bring breakfast back up.

Perhaps it had been a mistake, thinking the clever, handsome Commander might be swayed—might see reason or value life. Maybe even value me, as he claimed to. The Renown were notorious for their ruthlessness. I'd sliced down enough of them to know their cruelty. Now my mind reeled with his words, his taunts, his flaunting of his powers, however reserved he'd kept them. I hadn't even begun to show mine, hoping the flicker of them would be enough to keep his ambition at bay. Hoping, and allowing that hope to die all in the same heartbeats. He'd already seen the magnitude in his visions, of course. But I'd seen much of his as well.

August didn't ask questions when I slipped back into my battle-black skintight suit. He didn't question me as I laced up my boots. He just mimicked my motions and followed my lead. He stayed close as I ran, and ran, and ran, as if I could sprint my way away from the visions assaulting my mind.

You'll see—you'll both see—that I am your way out of this.

According to the visions, Adrastos told the truth. Lucifer, damn him, was about to either lose control or free the horsemen. Our coven was at the heart of the thin line of resistance—the thin line of defense for mortality—the thin barrier of hope and redemption for a people determined to damn themselves. But there were those still fighting, trying to be and do good. Trying to be worthy of a sacrifice no one could ever repay. They would suffer when the horsemen came too. It was all there. In the visions. And so, his words echoed within my skull.

We are two sides of the same coin, Alvara of Grayshell. Don't think for a moment I haven't considered what it would be like to burn you to dust.

For all intents and purposes, it seemed we were, indeed, equals. I couldn't outmaneuver him. Couldn't outsmart him. Even his gifts seemed a rival for my own—the dark shadow to my light.

Anger, white hot and unchecked, boiled against my skin as my mind replayed both interactions. Over the visions he cast of our kind ruling over mortals, degrading them as servants and slaves *in exchange* for meager survival.

Suffocating pressure pressed against my skull, my skin, aching in my bones. I wanted to scream, wanted to thrash that beautiful, arrogant face. Breath hot and ragged, my legs obediently kept firing, kept moving, propelling my body forward. Round and round, my mind began to spin. The ground beneath me seemed to tilt, ribs crushing the last of the air from my lungs, while the sky itself began to press down on me. Somehow, the ever-spring of Grayshell became sweltering hot, flush rushing through my body, sweat soaking the small of my back and the gap between my breasts. My feet skittered to a stop, spraying tiny gravel pebbles in a wave as my momentum abruptly halted. August slid to a standstill beside me.

"Ally?"

"I can't—I can't beat him. I...I don't know how to beat him."

"Breathe, Ally."

"I—I can't beat him—I—" I gasped for air, flexing my fingers, fighting down the anger, the energy, the nausea—everything threatening to burst through me.

"Breathe, Ally." The dominance in August's tone, the sheer depth of his calm command, seemed to snap something in me. Tears poured down my face, but I forced my muscles and bones to obey. Inhale. Exhale.

Slowly, eyes trained on mine, August reached forward and wrapped his warm arm around my waist, pulling me to him. The sky still seemed to threaten a crushing embrace, panic seizing my mind like it held me in a fist. He slid a sleeve over his hand and cradled the back of my head, leading me toward his chest. I complied, focusing on my breathing. I felt his shield slide over me as he stroked a gentle pattern up my back. Like a spiritual Novocain, that calm steadiness of August washed through me.

Inhale. Exhale. Inhale. Exhale.

August's heart thundered beneath my face when I could finally find it through the roaring in my ears. That steady pulse, warm against me, settled something within.

"Breathe," he said again, voice gentler as my panic simmered. "Just breathe." His fingers settled over my spine, pulling me tighter against him. A cool wave pulsed from where his fingers rested, washing down over my chest, my stomach, my core, eventually trickling into my legs. Cool and steady, his calm washed over me.

Inhale, exhale, inhale, exhale.

"Good, Ally. Just breathe." The cold continued to creep up my neck, easing the physical tension there before washing down through my arms to my fingertips. I closed my eyes, blocking out the ever-bright Middle Realm. His heart gradually steadied, his fingers still stroking cooling patterns down my back. After a long while, I lifted my head. The world still seemed to spin around me, but it was no longer so crushing. I stared up into his emerald eyes, locking onto the bottomless pool within them.

Inhale, exhale.

"Hey," his voice was soft again, the cool command gone. "What was that?"

I shook my head. "I've tried it hundreds of ways, August. There's no way to win. I can't see past the knot, and only a few threads seem to lead to our emergence *free*. He will come for us. For you. For me. The others...are collateral. It doesn't matter how many ways I twist it. It's always the same."

"So, we have to go through it."

"We have to...go through it." Inhale, exhale. Breathe. Breathe. *Breathe.* Slowly, gradually, the spinning began to cease. "Ansel, Lana, Fae. I think... we will lose one of them. I keep seeing them dead—Ansel most often. There's...an unknown at play that might come into it. But they must be bound too because I can't...see..." I rubbed at my temples as they throbbed. "But the only threads we stand a chance in—the Renown fight without elements."

"They don't have their magic?"

I shook my head. "No. They don't. But Adrastos will know their odds diminish without it. How do we strip them when they strip us?"

"I don't know." An honest answer. I buried myself against his chest again.

"An unknown?"

"Sometimes, my visions can't manifest who makes the decision that changes things. Especially if it's a stranger. Familiar beings, souls, are easier to read." August nodded as though that made perfect sense.

"If we don't take his offer, Adrastos will come for me...for us? In all the threads?"

I nodded.

"Then let's get ready for him."

Every blade, large or small, in the hierarchy's arsenal was sharpened, cleaned, and oiled. Bows were re-strung, guns cleaned, and magazines loaded. I stared at the hall, full of our warriors as they inventoried and prepared for a battle we knew was coming. A warm snap was due to hit Colorado in three days' time. Where everything started, so it would finish. I'd known the location of the low-lying clearing, known that snow would blanket the ground, save for large patches that melted with the rain. I'd known it would come to that, although we still didn't know what brought us to him. What the trigger was. It was always different—usually an innocent from August's past or a soul in the hierarchy. Noble as he was, August would never stand for innocent blood being spilled in his stead.

The risks were explained, the odds, death tally, and numbers presented in the great hall by the rarely serious-faced Aren. Catastrophic odds—a force thrice our size. The souls wouldn't leave the burden upon August alone, or even upon the coven alone. Word was sent to Marcus and the Westerlunds, although no reply had been received. Few details could be provided anyway. So how were they to reply? *Yep, heard everything's going to shit—hit us up, we'll be there?*

The healers were busy preparing every medicine for infection and wound care; endless piles of bandages were delivered to Saraya, her healers brushing up on every form of field care they could think of.

An icy, merciless, and unrelenting guilt filled my veins. I had failed them. Failed my family, my friends, my hierarchy. We came up against a clairvoyant enemy, and their strongest clairvoyant couldn't compete. Couldn't outmaneuver the bloody mess barreling down on us. They rallied for an enemy with impossible odds, for a cause we didn't yet know. We just knew we would answer the call for aid. Whomever it may come from.

FIFTY-EIGHT
LITTLE NOVA
AUGUST

Ally was eating herself alive. Like a volcano brewing to burst, her energy seemed to wind tighter and tighter as the days dragged on. Whether she got any sleep at all, she gave no indication. The bed was empty when I rose, as she was always already down helping the warriors train, stretch, and pack on muscle. It was also empty when I went to bed, too exhausted to stand, as she was assisting Saraya and the healers stock poultices, tinctures, bandages, and teas—so many little concoctions they would wait in the wings with, so our wounded would stand some chance at mending. There would be many. That thought soured my meals and my sleep.

The sunlight had long since faded into moonless black, and the subtle blink of starlight, and sleep still evaded me. The room, eerily silent in the face of the looming battle, seemed to nudge me out the door. As quietly as possible, I padded down the abandoned hallways. According to Ally, the warm snap would begin tonight back in the lowlands near my lake house. All the souls that would answer our call had long since retired, sleeping, if their bodies were smarter than our own. The image of that meadow soaked in blood was a permanent resident behind my eyes, taunting me with its inevitability.

I found her in the hall, huddled over the long table of arrows.

"You've already counted them, love."

"I know I just—"

"Come sleep, Ally. We need your strength." Careful, specific words, because it couldn't be about her wellbeing—not for Ally. It had to be for us.

For her family. She eyed me, too smart for those reassurances anyway. Desperation, vibrating and palpable, seemed to roll off her as those eyes devoured me. "You know Aren would tear you a new one if he knew you were still down here, love."

"I just... I need to do something." She braced her hands on her hips. The knot within her seemed to contract, like a gravitational pull. Supernova indeed. My nerves hitched, reliving the words Ansel had shared with me.

She could, I realized, break in such a way that she could bring the entire world down with the implosion. The power resting in her was literally a force of nature. I took a step into the room, and she tensed but held her ground.

"My little nova," the words slipped out on a sigh, and she quirked her head as I continued, "you need your sleep, Ally. You know as well as I do that, with or without your magic, you are our most lethal weapon. We need you rested, fed, and ready to go whenever the shoe drops." Her eyes flicked back to the arrows piled on the table. She ran her leather-wrapped finger over the black fletching of the nearest one and then looked up at me with a gentle nod. I held my hand out. Mercifully, she accepted. As her gloved fingers intertwined with mine, we squeezed each other reassuringly. Okay. We were okay. And we would figure out a way to walk away from this.

ALVARA CURLED herself tighter against me in bed, risking only inches between the skin of her neck and my chin. Such a ridiculous, stupid thing— to be so close and not be able to touch each other. To comfort each other. To find some damned release when the world was winding us both so tightly. Perhaps we could transmute that into power, strength, and magic. But not without the ungodly agitation it gave me to have her so close, to soak in her scent and the warmth of her body pressed so tightly against mine. Selfish, stupid need.

"It's not selfish," she whispered. "Me too. Deeply regretting not getting inside you months ago."

I laughed, breathing in the almond oil in her hair, the sweet summer scent of her. "I think you have that backwards, love."

She chuckled. "Tell me that once I've been in your mind fully."

I shrugged, knowing she'd feel it even if she couldn't see me. "I love you, Alvara."

"I love you too. To the end of this life, and into the next."

Blinking back the burning in my eyes, I admitted, "It's not fair. Facing down death when we just finally found each other."

"It's not. Not at all. I waited three hundred years for you, August

Porter." She took a long breath. "But I'd do it all again, just to see you smile. To feel you for the one night I got to. It would all be worth it."

"You're not allowed to talk like we're not coming back from this."

"The odds—"

"Fuck the odds, Ally. Damn them back to Hell where they belong." I pulled her long locks over her shoulder as she turned to face me. "We do this together, and we fight like hell."

"Until the very end," she whispered. The salt of her tears stained the air as they streaked down her fair face. I thought of that night, already so long ago, where I'd kissed each drop off her cheek. She seemed to think of it too as she wiped them away, the smallest smile tugging at her lips.

"Baby, I'll be waiting in our encore."

AS WEAPONS now lined all the long tables, the souls of Grayshell were gathered around them, wolfing down scrambled eggs, bacon, and porridge. We all stood together, talking, laughing, and keeping each other distracted. We didn't talk about the numbers or the fact that our sources on the ground found the snow near my home melted. I didn't tell them I'd dreamt of an enormous bird made entirely of fire. We just soaked up the presence of too many souls packed into a too-small great hall. We soaked up the shoulders we rubbed and the laughter that filled the bright walls.

Something Fae said across the hall elicited an eruption from the men gathered around her. Even Ajax, the lightest in complexion of The Greek Brothers and darkest in spirit—threw his head back and howled. She tossed her long platinum hair back over a shoulder and beamed at them, her laughter shaking her curvy frame. Even Lana was grinning, shaking her head at her sister.

Her mate, ever the war general, had found Aren the instant he'd finished breakfast. The two of them were making the rounds among warriors, Aren cracking jokes, and both soldiers handing down words of encouragement. Strategy for our larger opponents—passing along every nugget of information Alvara had gathered from all the renditions of what could come. We might not know when the battle was coming, but we knew it was soon.

It had been the first thing Alvara said when she woke—that she could feel it, even if she couldn't see it.

My mate, mercifully, had cleared a plate and gone back for seconds before stepping into Aren's shadow to encourage the front lines that would follow her into almost certain death. Everywhere The Commander and his second went, they were met with that Grayshell Salute—a fist across the heart, brought to the lips, and extended in greeting. The most seasoned among the warriors made jokes that they would welcome a re-circuit, sick of this life, and ready to feel mortality again. She'd sock them in the arm and demand they come home, and they'd grin and nod obediently.

Alec was uncharacteristically quiet, contemplative, sprawled across two chairs in the back corner so his feet could be up. He'd eaten without saying much, his usual humor seeming to be stifled. Perhaps it was how riled up Alvara was. Perhaps it was the fact that Aphaea arrived with her hair in Viking braids, the voluminous pony in the back. She'd chosen the modern, slick suit that looked like black dragon skin, forgoing her usual silver armor. Alvara was in the same uniform, down to the braids through her endless hair and the thick band of charcoal war paint across their eyes—the painted white skin and red lips.

Most likely, though, it was that he, like Ansel, had been watching Alvara's mind like a hawk these last weeks, knowing that Aphaea might not return home with us. The ungodly agony of that kind of loss roiled in my stomach. Breathing became difficult. If it wasn't Alec, it was likely Ansel or Lana who would return to a cold bed and a broken heart.

He'd tried and failed to convince Aphaea to stay with the healers when the time came, to stay out of the fray. She simply said she was born for this and had seen battle more times than he had. They'd kissed, deeply, desperately, and she'd promised she would find him in the next life, as they always did, if it came down to it.

My stomach had been tied in knots since. Brody, towering as tall as Aren, his gold hair in its usual Greek twists, sauntered over to me. He'd opted for his traditional Greek fighting leathers. He patted me on the back, those dark brown eyes surveying me.

"You seem oddly steady for a first battle, Commander."

"I'm not Commander yet," I reminded him, but grinned nonetheless, fighting the ache solidifying in my chest. "And I'm afraid this isn't my first battle, either."

"Good man. Glad to know you're steady as your mate."

"She's a fearsome thing, isn't she?"

"The fiercest." He grinned in a boastful way. An Olympian surveying a gold medal teammate. "I'd be so lucky if my mate has half her valor."

It wasn't the sound of the mug shattering or the way the entire room clattered into silence behind it. It wasn't the way the air swelled and flexed around her like gravity around the sun. But the way her breath hitched in her chest so violently had me moving for her, and every soul in the hall kneeling before their second, awaiting orders.

Alvara's long, delicate, scar-flecked hand pressed against her mouth.

"No," she said, voice strangled. Tears swelled in her eyes as she lifted them from the place of other. She found me, still on my feet and wading around our kneeling host, and shook her head as the tears streaked down her cheeks. Aren and Alec were beside her as quickly as I was.

"Alvara?" Aren set his hand against her arm, locked against her throat. Rage and horror flashed across his features, his dark brow furrowing, and pale eyes flicking to me. Dread turned to grief, a near hopeless apology.

I wet my lips with my tongue, watching the tremble in her chin as she raised it in defiance.

"They took her," her voice broke. "They took *them*."

"Who, Ally?"

Her lips quavered, tears pouring freely down her cheeks as she closed her eyes and whispered, "All of them." She struggled to breathe, and unable to speak, she opened her mind and shattered me entirely.

Agamemnon had Freya. Adrastos must have seen—seen that she was my Freya, seen our loyalty to each other. They had stolen away James, Layla, and Sam for good measure. *Taken.* Captives to the brute and his swaggering brother.

Ransom, in exchange for my servitude. Four in exchange for two.

"August," Alvara's voice cracked on my name, but she kept her chin raised high. "I'll get them back."

Her idea played out in her mind, and I studied it as intensely as I could. There could be no gap—none—between making the decision and taking action. No lag where Adrastos could intercept the plan and make his adjustments. She continued offering scenarios, one by one, knowing she could not allow one to settle into her heart. I looked to Aren, desperate rage pounding against my ears. It could work.

Insane, masochistic, hell of a fucking gamble. But it could work. And she had been winding her power so tightly that she needed the release, the outlet, before it burst from her skin.

"The first one was most effective," I muttered, trying to track her fragmented thoughts as rapidly as she let them play out.

"Bullshit. The first one will get you killed," Aren countered gruffly. Ally's resolute eyes found mine.

"But it opens their defenses for the rest of us," Alec stated matter-of-factly, studying the pattern in her thoughts, his eyes tortured with understanding. There were very few threads where she and I made a reappearance. Dread, heavy and molten, settled in my gut.

Chest rising and falling in rapid succession, Aren growled, "We both know there are always other fucking threads, Ally." His eyes went razor sharp. *"Everyone start making decisions. He can't know how we're coming. Fucking mean it."* The coven immediately complied.

"Aren," her voice cracked with a plea as visions spun out, her eyes zeroed in on his face. "August is my mate, Aren. Mine. I will follow you to the ends of the earth, but do not ask me to stand this one down. You guys are my family, but he is my *everything*. I should have been there myself. All those sentinels..." She jammed her eyes closed, the threads pouring out like silk into a web. "She's in this position *because of me.*"

I didn't have to clarify which *she*—my Freya.

"She's *my* mate's *baby sister,* Aren. Captive among demons and creatures more beast than man. What would *you* do in my position?"

"Fucking hell!" Aren raked his fingers through his short hair as Alvara's eyes flicked between Alec and Ansel. The former's jaw clenched while the latter sucked on a tooth, but both of their eyes fell to the floor when Aren drew in a sharp breath, gaze burning with fury as it rotated between the three. "Over my dead body." Scrubbing a palm over his face, Aren turned to pace as I shifted on my feet.

Alec mumbled something that sounded a lot like *"That's what we're trying to avoid.*

When Aren rounded on us again, his voice was low and steely. "You get the fuck in, you find them, and you get the fuck out. We fight another day." Ally's jerky nod was amputated by a collision with The Commander. Aren crushed her against him in a bear hug, and she buried her face against his shoulder for a beat before peeling away.

Ansel set his hand on my shoulder as Alvara slid her gloves on, already armed to the teeth. She continued rattling ideas through her mind with the rest of them. No decisions. We all followed her from one plan to the next— each crazier and more explosive, not allowing our minds to settle.

"August," Ansel said in that gravelly voice of his. I jerked my eyes from my mate to the warrior. "Now would be a good time to move." I gave him a blunt nod of understanding and took Alvara's now-gloved, outstretched hand. He inclined his head as he said, "Godspeed, both of you."

WHEN SHE JUMPED, she dropped us directly in the center of Adrastos' host. Dropped us in the center of a sea of leather and canvas tents, and an enormous fire pit. Right in the place he had taken her himself. Foolish move.

We were surrounded by Renown finishing their breakfasts. They startled back from us as the dust plumed around the impact. One fell over a stool. Another poured coffee down his front. Shouts began—she hadn't bothered to be quiet or subtle as we landed. She *wanted* them to know who was coming for them.

When she opened her eyes, Alvara's gaze glowed a terrifying gold and green, and she snarled a warning growl as the soldiers fell over themselves, stumbling from the shock of our appearance. She lifted her chin.

"Fuck the odds," she growled.

Then she wholly unleashed herself upon the war camp.

FIFTY-NINE

RETRIBUTION

ALVARA

If Adrastos wanted to make this bargain personal, then I would *make it* personal. I'd spent days burning through the surface of my elements, burrowing into the depths of my power through my fear, anxiety, and rage. The drowsy camp of Renown, wielding mostly earth on their best days, didn't stand a chance.

It took only four steady heartbeats to draw up that strength—power and anger—after my feet hit the dirt in the center of the war camp. My mind exploded as our boots struck the dirt—searching, shredding, clawing through what little I had left of the wards, scanning for any sign of them. There was none. The brothers hadn't returned either.

Flames, white-hot and searing pale blue, burst forward in a colossal wave—a terrible, awe-inspiring wall of fire, even as I wielded it. Row after row of tents vanished, leaving only drifting clouds of ash.

August, his back pressed against mine, was only a heartbeat behind, blotting out the watery sunlight with livid thunderclouds. The horizon flashed, and the ground shook under the ensuing clap. No rain came to spare them, only the livid bolts of August's fury, unleashed on any foolhardy enough to run toward us instead of joining the waves of shouting, fleeing men.

Is she here? Are they here? August asked, realizing the advantage we had in a surprise attack. I pressed my mind through the camp again, stretching far and wide. Plenty of concerned confusion filled the air at the sound of our arrival, but no mortal minds were present. Each fragment of terrorized consciousness was laced in shadow and death.

No. Not yet. We'll beat them back.

Anger rumbled in his chest. "Burn it all."

"My pleasure." I roared, plunging deeper into my strength, through layer after layer of livid outrage. The camp became an inferno.

Realizing the source of the attack, looming figures began racing through the smoke toward us from all directions. I could see them through August's eyes as much as my own. My flames licked and devoured; his lightning struck with lethal precision.

Christ above, Ally. Aren's voice was nearly a whisper in my mind.

At least twenty-five hundred of them, Ansel warned, his voice gravelly and weighted with concern. August bristled behind me.

I'd seen what a blast of my temper could do—seen it again and again on different fields, in vision after vision. I knew its reach precisely. That didn't stop the sick oil from twisting in my stomach, sliding up the walls of my ribs. Chest heaving, I surveyed the damage. *Jesus Christ.*

Don't you dare, baby. August's command was soft, but my eyes burned anyway. I furrowed my brow, remembering their faces—Freya, James, Sam, and Layla—at this motherfucker's mercy, and why this had to be done.

They brought this on themselves, Aren muttered.

It was easy for him to say when he wasn't the one who had incinerated an enormous crater in the center of the camp, leaving no trace—no bones to prove they'd ever been here at all. My temper quelled, my mind pressing out, searching for Adrastos or Agamemnon, for Sam or James, whose minds would be most familiar. Nothing. My rage began to simmer in my blood.

He won't be stupid enough to put them where you'll easily find them. But you can make him pay until he begs for forgiveness. Ansel nudged us forward. I nodded, though he couldn't see. More for myself, if I was being honest. This was war. This was war, and I was a weapon.

Reluctantly, cautiously, energy swirling around us, wind tearing at the intricate ponytail I'd swept my hair into, August and I peeled our backs apart. We stalked a few paces forward toward the approaching shadows.

They have magic, August thought from behind me. Itching for a fight, I flashed a grin that was all teeth at the tight group closest to me. He sensed the power welling in them, just as I did.

I could do this. For Freya, for James and Sam, I would do this. *Fuck, get it together, Ally.* With a flick of my wrist, I whipped a long line of flame toward them, which licked the invisible shield between us with a deafening crack. Sparks sizzled up its side.

Hang in there, kid; the cavalry is coming, Aren assured, but the words sent a chill down my spine. They couldn't be here. Not for this.

Ar, please. I have a plan. Trust me.

Ally. I could hear the growl in his tone, and panic sliced through me.

Be ready to move if we get back.

When. When *you get back.*

I grimaced, trying to keep my internal voice steady as I sucked in breaths.

Eyes up. On your two, kid. Focus.

Jerking my head up to the right, I surveyed the men in question. I stretched my arms wide, loosening my joints as I grinned at the opponents advancing on us.

Six of them were on my side, all as broad as Aren, hidden beneath dark hoods, faces shadowed under August's storm, which crashed a warning. I didn't care—*couldn't* care—who they were or what they looked like, or even what gifts they possessed. They were on the wrong side of a battle that could not be waged.

When they were within about twenty yards, I slammed my feet to a halt, burying my boots into the loamy earth with the force of it. My hands tucked by my ribs, I pressed against the invisible wall, shoving my own shield against theirs. Sparks and smoke sizzled in a roar that split the air, and the advancing Renown began shouting as my wall of white-hot light steadily crushed their collective shield back toward them. Like a soda can in my hand, I squeezed, and it began to crumple. Tighter. I smiled as they bellowed, struggling to hold it upright.

Wind whipped past me in a violent rage, and their hoods fell. I fought the urge to look behind me to check on my mate. August could handle himself.

The men in front of me were all Renown—dark eyes, but none of obsidian. No sign of demons. I inclined my head as one of them made a break for it, sprinting behind them. For escape, or to seek aid, I didn't care. He'd signed his death warrant when he bowed to Adrastos and Agamemnon.

One hand pressed against the shield, I reached the other skyward. Curling it into a fist, I plunged it down, and those white flames erupted along the line of the shield. My hand burst into a flurry of flames, and I opened my palm, flicking my fingers until they formed a great lioness. There was nowhere to run when they turned in an attempt to escape. My shields were steady, trapping them for her. The fire beast sprinted forward in great leaping bounds and devoured them whole. Ash began to rain down around us as my flames continued their assault, unrestrained. Screams pierced the air, mingling with the cracking of wood as it scorched, and the rolling thunder of August filled the chaos, the reek of burnt flesh, urine, and singed earth making my eyes water.

The next wave of advancing resistance hesitated, outstretching their beefy arms. The ground shook, and I flashed a smile Aren had affectionately dubbed "*death dealer*." I wiped the sweat from my brow, knowing every ounce of my loathing was visible in my eyes. I steadied my breathing, stilled my heart and mind.

We could play with earth, then.

A great wave curled over the singed field below us. I rode it and sprinted forward, preparing to leap over the next one. My footing was mercifully steady as I jumped over the second roll of earth. I had only a heartbeat to pray August was just as stable behind me. A great shard shot forward, earth and stone screaming as they split in two. I threw my hands forward, shattering the attack. The dirt shuddered as I yanked it forward—a great stone spear spiraling out of the ground. It impaled two of the men advancing, a third rolling out of range. I felt Alec's silent approval in the back of my mind. The third—the one who was lightest on his feet—snarled.

Panting, I braced my hands on my hips and flashed him a saccharine smile. "Earth is fine, but I prefer fire." I dropped my hands to my sides, and in a sweeping arc, brought them above my head in an air-shattering clap. A screaming flame erupted with the movement, and its shattering noise startled August enough that he glanced back at me. From his place on the field, I looked toward a twelve-foot phoenix of flame. Fitting, perhaps. He jerked his gaze back to his opponents and the fallen in his gifts' wake. I did the same, sending my wings of fire crashing forward.

Somewhere in the distance, creeping over the screams and the roar of fire devouring the field, a melody played. Something in the short pattern sizzled my rage. Quiet and steady, it played on the wind. Haunting, I realized, something in me that I couldn't place. I shook my head as if I could shake the sweet melody away, feeding more of my rage into the flames. No more Renown advanced. None were suicidal enough to.

Sweeping surveys confirmed it. No more would fight. They were fleeing before us. As my mind lashed forward, I realized, perhaps for the first time, what August and I looked like as we bore down upon the camp of sin and greed.

Judgment Day.

I lifted my face to the wind to roar, "Is that all you've got?"

Behind me, August, his anger visceral and voice guttural, bellowed, "Adrastos!" The power in that summoning raised goosebumps along my body. I began retreating to his side, unwilling to put any more distance between us. "Adrastos!" It was a threat, a challenge, and it sent a thrill down my veins. He was ready. He had to be. "Adrastos!" August continued calling out to the Commander behind these cowering forces. Still, my fire lapped up tents like fuel.

But God above, that *was* a music box, I realized—a music box somehow carried on the wind over the carnage. Something deep in me stirred, the sensation wetting my anger, cooling it down. Goosebumps lined my arms as I pressed my back against August. His fingers found mine by our sides and intertwined. Unease settled into my bones as I drew my blade, thumb sliding over the Celtic knot in the hilt.

"Adrastos!" August bellowed, and that same primal thrill shot through me. He would put an end to this himself. We would, side by side.

I'll be waiting for our encore, my love, he whispered in my mind.

Still, that eerie melody filled the wind, louder now. This time I felt them before their scents filled the air—like shadow and death, their power rippled through the camp. August felt it too, though it did nothing to dampen the rage coursing through him.

I pressed my mind forward again—still no sign of Freya or the others. They weren't here. That dark power ebbed forward, and my stomach twisted with the sheer strength of it.

You've proven your point, Ally. Get the fuck out, Aren growled, pressing against my mind as if he could physically scoop us out of the camp now sitting in cinders. As if I could leave without them. But that chiming music sent a spider of ice down my veins, drawing me in as my body shuddered.

SIXTY

DANCING WITH DEVILS

ALVARA

The invisible wall of shadows crept closer, a steady wave of anger, sin, and death crawling down my bones. August's command faded, leaving only the sound of his panting breaths as he kicked over a singed tent support with his blood-spattered boot.

Do you...do you know what that is?

No. But I—I feel like I should.

Same.

Slowly, a wave from the back of the field extinguished my flames under the shadow that wasn't a shadow.

Alvara, enough. Aren's voice was icy, full Commander mode, ringing over the sound of the music box. *What the fuck are you doing? They're not there. Get your asses—*

And just like the flames in the field before me, Aren vanished. Darkness, deep beyond the grey of the still-rolling storm, pressed down upon us.

I'm sorry, I sent one final thought to my sire.

I took a long, steadying breath as every ember within me extinguished, sizzling as if a bucket of water had been thrown against it. August's storm clouds dissolved as quickly as the flames ceased their rampage. But that omnipresent shadow remained. I looked up at the now-black sky. Midnight, devoid of stars. And still, that music box ticked along with its taunting, haunting melody. August palmed his heart tracker in his left hand, his right still wrapped around mine. I pushed against the earth, but there was no escaping now. Either I was just crazy enough for this to work, or this would indeed be our grand finale.

Seeming to read my mind despite the silence, August pressed a kiss to my gloved hand.

The chiming melody grew louder as we advanced. Chills rippled down my arms and spine. Men of Renown were returning to the outskirts of the tents. Whether due to the ceasefire of our strength or the dark shadows somehow calling them home as their master returned—perhaps both. They believed they were protected now. But the brothers of shadow could not protect all of them. Not against Grayshell's best. If I was being sent to recirculate, I would damn well make a dent in their forces first.

The smell of charred carrion and the reek of released bowels thickened the air. Nausea roiled in my gut, but still, we advanced. August squeezed my fingers, then released them to my side, drawing his sword as the returning Renown drew their blades and barreled forward. We inhaled a thorough, steadying breath in sync as they began their charge.

I took one last, long glance at August. His chiseled face, those vivid eyes, the way his loose curls fell over them. Scouring every detail, I committed them to memory. I'd meant what I'd told him—that it was all worth it, that I would do it all again if it meant finding him—but I prayed the next life wouldn't take so painfully long to reunite us.

And then I made my decision. I committed to it, allowing it to settle in my bones as something concrete and unwavering. The wind began to stir, and I lifted my eyes, listening to the beating of feet against the earth, and flickers of flames extinguishing, leaving crackling embers and spirals of smoke around us.

As the first group of assailants came roaring forward, weapons swinging, I twirled and began. We both dropped three. Three more came for each of us. They fell. More—so many more—came barreling down, and I heard August bellow his indignation beside me. Nothing floated down the telepathic line between us; there was just the relentless smash of steel on steel. He was fine. I palmed one of the throwing knives from the black bandolier and flicked it through the eye of one.

But where he fell, another took his place, skilled and raging.

I dodged below the steel of his comrade and aimed to slice my dagger across his knees. He was too quick. In a smooth motion, I advanced, my focus razor-sharp as he curved his blow down toward my head. I leaned back just enough for his strike to miss, hissing as it scraped through the dragon-scale armor on my bicep, hot blood spurting. The clack of my teeth rang through my skull as pain lanced up to my shoulder and through my elbow. *Son of a bitch.*

Suddenly, August was moving with me, in unison, as if we had choreographed our dance of blades and blood. He sensed the intuition still speaking in my ears, guiding my movements as challenger after challenger fell. Some served as shields, others I shoved aside as my own weapons. His movements mirrored mine, tossing me limp bodies as assailants lunged forward. I turned to shield him from blades I *sensed* coming for him.

Breath hot, it scraped down my throat. Dodge, weave, advance. Again and again, I blocked their blows. My focus remained set on the quickest one. Preoccupied dodging his rapid-fire advances, I barely registered the enormous man as he swung forward—my muscles acting on memory, rotating as he took me to the ground. It came hard and fast, and no amount of training could prepare my ribs for the agonizing collision with the earth or the crack of his fist as it slammed into my face. He rolled away with our momentum. Breathless, I shifted, but my attempt to crawl was short-lived as his hands yanked me beneath him.

August. I couldn't go down. Not here. Not now. Not like this.

Gasping, my fingers fumbled for the knife tucked into the sheath on my hip. I hissed as he lunged for me, blood splashing my face when the blade sliced through his jugular. The glint of silver in the moonlight caught my eye as his body fell forward, and I threw him across my chest, arms shaking as the sword sank in with a meaty *thunk*. I kicked him off into the next piece of swinging steel. Too many. There were too many emerging from the remains of the camp. Still, I hurled my dagger at the quick one.

He dodged, and I growled, even as the blade embedded in the throat of one behind him.

August roared in pain, sending every muscle in my body taut. It took every century of my training to keep moving. One of them feigned left, and I struck to his right. My sword sunk between his ribs, and hot, rancid blood poured down my hand. I jerked it free and sliced across the throat of the next. I just needed a second to breathe—needed to *breathe*—

The smell of August's blood assaulted my senses, igniting my fury into an inferno. My *mate's* blood. I kept moving. Kept killing. Even as a slice seared like fire across my arm, scarlet spilling across my suit again. Even as one smashed a burly fist into the side of my face, my teeth ringing with the impact, my feet fighting to stay under me. *Cocksucker.* Panting for air, I smirked as that one bit the dirt.

There, not twenty yards away, was Agamemnon. His dark power billowed around him as he tilted his head, surveying me.

"Mine," I growled, the word for no one in particular. In that solitary breath, I drew and hurled one of my favorite throwing knives. Agamemnon barely dodged it, whirling. His snarl when he turned back to me was all animal, onyx eyes alight with rage, and my blood ignited with fury.

Those between us fell like dominoes under the speed of my assaults, and then I was upon Agamemnon. The hulking brute snarled, a cruel smile playing on his lips as he drew the enormous, jagged sword from the sheath down his spine. My heart thundered, breath coming in hot, ragged pants as I circled the beast that had caused all this pain. He circled back. Indeed, those charging August and me seemed to freeze as their master raised his blade on a long arm and pointed it at me. An arrogant challenge. His shadows billowed. The power palpable as he contained our own.

August roared, and I realized they had disarmed him. *Shit, shit, shit.*

Agamemnon raised his brows behind that extended sword. Fear skittered down my spine, needles pricking against my ribs, but I suffocated it.

Shock flashed across those obsidian eyes when I bared my teeth at him. Shock as he realized I would not turn for my mate. Not anymore. We weren't walking out of here, anyway. That was what I had decided—that it was a good day to die. And it would be a warrior's death that finally claimed me.

I would at least take him with us.

We continued to circle, and the others held their expectant line as more soldiers arrived on the scene, waiting for blood to spill... *my* blood to spill.

Stepping over slain soldiers and piles of ash, we rounded on each other. I begged my lungs to catch a scrap of breath as sweat dripped down my back, my face, my chest. I didn't waste my strength on a threat of an execution promise. No, I would save it for his death blow. But ice still balled in my gut as my eyes spotted August at sword tip. Veins freezing over, I noted the gash across his ribs. I marked the three Renown who held him in place, arms behind his back. I marked them for death if I managed to step away from this. Fear guttered in their eyes at my expression, and I sneered.

They didn't strike the lethal blow. Still under orders to bring him in, then.

I had no such reservations.

My long blade slid from its sheath down my spine, and I advanced. Again and again, Agamemnon feigned right. But when I struck for his exposed left side, he parried and swung. His sword—*God have mercy*—was as mammoth as its wielder. I nearly bent over backward to dodge it. The air was crushed from me as his knee collided with my belly, a rib cracking. August bellowed my name. My knees screamed when they met the earth, but I rolled, finding my feet. The Renown roared in anticipation. But I gulped down a breath and twirled, barely evading his chopping assault that would have taken my head.

Just keep moving, Ally. Don't stop. Take this sick bastard with you.

My muscles obeyed. Kind of. The shaking had begun, exhaustion threatening to turn them to rubber. *Not yet. Keep moving.*

I did. Again and again, I twirled and parried. Jumped, ducked, and dodged as he hacked toward me relentlessly. A manic lumberjack, his sword swung like an axe. No precision, just lethal rage.

August bellowed my name. But he was too little, too late, as the blade from behind sliced across my thigh. An involuntary scream tore from my throat as agony seared through muscle, and I collapsed to my knees in the sloshing mud. As I scrambled to right myself, Agamemnon roared the word I had taunted him with.

"Mine!" The warrior instantly backed up. Heat poured down my leg, soaking through my skin-tight suit. I didn't look down, didn't allow my mind to register it as I kept my weight over the protesting bones and torn muscle, stifling the scream clawing up my throat. Fuck, I was slower... too much slower.

Still, I shifted just as Agamemnon's attack met my own. Blow for blow, our steel clashed. Every inch of my body trembled with effort and shock as the wound gushed onto the earth. This was it, then. My last stand. Worst case, Adrastos would free our family when they were no longer leverage. Aren would see to the rest. We would not become the enemy's weapon.

The beast barked a laugh as my leg buckled beneath my weight, body vibrating with the effort of staying upright. Someone kicked me from behind, and a sob tore up my throat as I fell into the puddle of ash, blood, and mud. I was even with August, still held by the steel pressed against his throat.

August's desperate eyes met mine, and I willed him to remember. To remember all I'd said. To remember that I loved him. For his soul to somehow remember to find me next time. Faster. I willed him to trust me in this desperate move, too.

Agamemnon whirled, a cruel smile stretching across his face as he threw his sword down with all his might. Too fast. I braced for the impact, for the blow that would end this, and for the agony to register before the black. I heard August's desperate howl as it descended.

But no impact came. Distantly, as if through someone else's mind, I heard the steel collide against ringing metal. When I peeled my eyes open, a combination of shock and twisted satisfaction reeled in my chest. Because my gamble had paid off. It wasn't Aren bracing the enormous gold shield against the brutal assault. It wasn't miraculously August, or even Alec, or surefooted Ansel.

But Adrastos.

SIXTY-ONE

BARGAIN

AUGUST

I'd promised Alvara—sworn I would trust her to the very end, and into the next life. I had broken that promise.

Not as I lost my sword. Not as the enormous, rancid beasts yanked my arms behind my back or kicked me to my knees. Not even when the one with a scar down his face, where an eye should be, pressed the icy tip of my sword against my neck...It was the look in her eyes, as she stared me down, so many words left unsaid. The last look in her eyes, as she closed them instead of raising her sword...

I shattered.

Shattered into pieces as her arm fell, and that sword thudded to the earth beneath her, her fingers loose and limp. Shattered as she turned her face away to *accept* the death blow.

The world—the roar of the Renown, the pulse in my ears, the haunting melody—all went silent as time stood still. As everything froze, save for the sword descending on Alvara. It vaguely registered that I was screaming her name while I fought against the cleaver at my throat and wrenched at the hands on my arms.

Should I have blinked or flinched in that moment, I would have missed it.

Would have missed the way Adrastos materialized from the shadows between Agamemnon and Alvara. The way he threw the full force of his strength into blocking that executioner's blow. Would have missed the way the reverberation sang up the steel so violently that Agamemnon staggered back several steps, his weapon falling to the earth beside Alvara's.

"Enough." Adrastos' voice was calm, quiet, steady. Lethal. He stared down a seething Agamemnon, who opened his mouth, but thought wiser of it as Adrastos' anger flared in palpable shadows. No. Shadow *flames*. Fire made of the darkness he came from.

The soldiers fell to their knees around us, kneeling, I realized, to the *King* of Renown. Not Commander. They bowed their heads. Deeply.

"General, I gave you very specific orders. I will deal with you later." With a snap of his fingers, Adrastos banished his brother. The brute vanished as quickly as Adrastos had appeared. To Lord knew where.

"And you!" He whirled on Alvara, who knelt in the mud, her expression smug. There wasn't a part of her, save for her black-painted eyes, not spattered in blood. Most of it, mercifully, was not her own. Even the deep black of her suit did nothing to conceal the dark stains. Gore was caked in thick globs through her dark hair. She lifted her chin, defiant, as the King turned on her, rage seeping through him. Real, true, and unchecked anger poured from him in a flood of power. I barely saw him raise his arm, but the smack that met Alvara's face startled through me. My snarl broke the air, and I didn't care that the steel bit into my skin, didn't care that more hot liquid welled and slid down my neck.

Adrastos crouched down, knees bent as he cocked his head to the side. A red welt was already burgeoning across her cheekbone. She raised her face to him, unflinching. But he wrapped his long fingers around her bloody jaw. His eyes went distant for only a heartbeat before snapping back... like he could control his reading.

"You know, little cousin," he growled the words. "I gave you *very* specific instructions. All of which explicitly require that you *not die*." The last words came through clenched teeth.

"Get your hands off her!" I growled at him. He rumbled a low laugh but tossed her face to the side, and to my surprise, did. He whirled on me, that cruel smile playing across his lips.

"Ahh, Mr. Porter. Glad to *formally* meet you. Wish it were under... more tasteful circumstances. But alas, your mate opted for a *theatrical* reintroduction." I just glared up at him. He flicked his wrist, as though swatting away a fly, and the beasts holding me released my arms, but not without shoving me forward toward the gore-splattered earth. I caught myself and rose to my feet. "I can see the sentiment is not shared." He gave a long, dramatic sigh and tossed aside his shield, which met the earth with a metallic clang that split the air.

Adrastos closed his eyes and pinched the bridge of his nose, sighing a long breath through it. He didn't see as Alvara wobbled to her feet. Didn't see as she drew one of her countless blades and twirled it between her fingers. Didn't see as she turned the precise point... towards her own ribcage, angled up, perfectly poised to claim her own heart.

"*Ally.*" My voice cracked as I stared her down. She didn't look up from the silver dagger in her hands, didn't look up as her lip quivered and her fingers began trembling. It was the tone in my voice that caused Adrastos to raise his head and survey her. Undiluted fear filled those muddy eyes as he slowly lowered his hand.

"You wouldn't," he breathed, eyes narrowing. As shock filled the shadows in them, Alvara said nothing but tightened her grip on the dagger and raised her face to him. Chin held high, her lips pulled up at the corners as her eyes filled with righteous defiance. Victory, cool and calculated, flashed across her face. "According to *your* texts, there's no coming back from that particular sin."

She took a deep breath, and the silver tip pierced through the first layer of that dragon-scale armor with a soft *chink*. My breath caught. So did Adrastos'.

"I'd wager my God will understand the circumstances."

"I would be *very* sure of that before you take that bet, *Ally.*" Adrastos stepped toward her, but she pressed the poniard into the scales, a tiny groan of pain escaping her as it reached her pale skin. He froze, dark eyes wide and shadowed in what could only be described as betrayal, fingers twitching. Even his breath seemed to freeze.

"Ally," I cautioned, my voice steadier. But my hands trembled as I shook my head. Adrastos' eyes didn't leave her. I could almost see the debate raging in his mind, could almost see the way he calculated which of them was faster. "I love you," the words were a desperate whisper, and I allowed the plea there to break through. Adrastos whipped his gaze to me, inky hair fanning out around his shoulders. Sizing me up. Searching my mind for any sign she was bluffing. When he found none, his eyes glazed over into the other world, as Alvara's so often did. When they focused again, he whirled on Alvara.

"You would abandon your coven? Your pets? To this mess?"

A gentle, one-shouldered shrug. "You tell me."

He heaved a long, heavy sigh before muttering, "Jesus Christ. I suppose it was time *someone* managed to surprise me." He pinched the bridge of his nose again, took a long breath, and then, with a flourish, sketched a pointed bow. "Well, cousin, you certainly know how to prove a point in ten minutes or less." He gestured to the smoldering crater in the earth, the ash where there had once been tents. "Your terms." The steely command in the growled words threw me, caught me off guard. And I realized the two clairvoyants had indeed, at last, outplayed their volley. In her own selfless, masochistic way, she had outmaneuvered him. Dark as her path might be, she had won.

"Return August's family, unharmed."

"I'm afraid I can't do that until you both agree. My brother will only trade his prizes for your fealty." She dug the honed tip into the delicate ivory skin between her ribs, and red blossomed, leaking down the shaft of it as her teeth clicked together audibly. Adrastos sucked in a sharp intake of air.

"Ally." It seemed to be the only word my mouth remembered how to say.

"Leave us," the King demanded. At once, his soldiers obeyed, marching away, leaving the three of us standing alone on the blood-soaked dirt. A long minute passed as the dozens of men retreated. As the ground stilled beneath my feet, I dared to edge closer to Alvara. Adrastos' eyes flashed as he took her in, read her resolve, perhaps in her eyes, perhaps her mind had opened to him. Or perhaps whatever he saw in the other world they vanished to was enough to prove she wasn't bluffing.

Adrastos sighed, long and pointed. "He'll never agree to a one-on-one duel, Alvara. There's no point in asking. And if I honored your request, and you won, Agamemnon *wouldn't* honor it. Besides, the hostages aren't even here. I can assure you, if you kill me now, he'll never see them again." He jerked his chin my direction. "What's the other option?" She raised her brows, and he rolled his eyes as they went hazy again. When they focused, he narrowed his gaze on her. "The bloody skirmish?" The corner of her full lips tugged upwards as she surveyed him. "On my terms."

"Ally," my warning barely seemed to register with her.

"Which are...?" Adrastos narrowed his eyes, as they again glazed into the otherworld between them. "You've lost your damn mind. A level playing field?" he demanded through a joyless, hollow laugh. She gave him a cold nod. And I remembered. Remembered her saying the only threads in which we were victorious, we fought without magic. Because the Reaper would steal ours away anyways, while leaving theirs intact. Adrastos raised a solitary brow before drawling, "Agamemnon will never agree."

"Then we keep our gifts. But... given my little demonstration this morning, I'm sure we can agree it will be in your best interest if you sacrifice yours too." A cold, calculating smile stretched over her features, matching her icy tone.

Adrastos shook his head, but I could have sworn admiration shone in his eyes. Through the anger. Through the fear. He liked her, cared for her, perhaps, in his own sadistic way. She had counted on it. He pried his eyes away to survey the smoldering killing field. Alvara's temper... so briefly unleashed.

"The victor wields The Great Commander." His eyes flashed to me but steadied on Alvara. I recoiled. I would die before I served this monster.

She considered for a moment before saying, "Level field. August's family and friends will not be harmed. They will be freed immediately, regardless of the victor."

"Should you show up for our battle of wills and your hierarchy fights, August's family will be released unharmed, regardless of the victor. They will be released immediately upon your victory. Or when I deem it safe, in the case of mine."

I snarled, but Adrastos kept his eyes on Alvara, flicking between the poniard in her fingers and her cold eyes. He inclined his head, gaze unfocused.

"No guns," he scoffed. It must have been a detail in her mind. "Blunt and tasteless request, *Your Majesty*. If we're dueling for dominance over a weapon..." Adrastos looked me from head to toe, sneering. "We do it as we used to. Blades, archers, fists, and feet."

"If we're fighting with archaic weapons, so too shall we take the form of battle lines." At first, the request struck as odd, but with a pang, the faces of Grayshell flashed in my vision. Every single Grayshellian warrior had once fought in them—knew them well. But were the Renown so different? I reached for that connection, cursing when it remained silent.

The Renown King's lips pulled upwards. "Ahhh—it's been too long. So, we go back, little cousin, to fighting as we first did, side by side those many lifetimes ago."

Whether she understood the life he referred to or not, she didn't let on. Alvara's face stayed a serene mask, and she took a long breath. "August and I walk away from this meeting, unharmed. And we want proof of life for the hostages."

Adrastos considered, one arm crossed over his torso, the other resting upon it to rub his jaw.

"You and August walk away today, unharmed. I'll even heal you since we're leveling the field. You gather your team. Five hundred, max—"

"Your host is twice that size."

"So, you do occasionally pay attention to the visions hurled at you."

"You don't get to choose how many we bring." As she jerked her chin up at him defiantly, I wondered how many we had on hand.

"But you'll bring five hundred. I've already seen it. Stop being difficult."

"We want to see August's family."

"As I said, the hostages are not here, as I'm sure you sensed before my brother arrived. But proof will be provided tonight, at the time and location of my choosing. And should I win, you will *both* serve *me*—no murder by suicide." He glanced between us. I kept my mouth closed. *Trust her. Trust her until the very end.*

She repeated the first few terms back to him, adding, "Should you win, and we are both alive and functioning, we will both serve you in stopping the horsemen—"

Adrastos caught her wording and cut her off with another sneer, "Should I win, you will both serve me indefinitely, for whatever my bidding may be."

Alvara shrugged as if to say, 'it was worth a try', before continuing, "Should we win, you can choose between death or serving *us*. If Aren leaves any piece of your host alive, they will be at our disposal as well." Madness, this game of hers. Absolute madness. A dark smile spread across Adrastos' face.

"I'll never get Agamemnon to agree. These were his men you executed so swiftly."

"Funny," she grinned, and in that moment, I saw Alec's cold swagger and Aren's amusement wash over her. It was a striking, strategic mask. "That sounds like it's not my Goddamned problem."

Adrastos narrowed his eyes but stared her down. "If either of you has been dealt a lethal blow, the duel will cease, and your lives will be forfeit." When she said nothing, he continued, "Fine. You've struck your bargain. Now get that thing away from your chest."

She didn't smile, didn't change her expression, but kept it schooled in cool indifference. Arrogance settled in the subtle arch of her brows. Her dagger found its sheath. Adrastos let out a sigh of relief. He stepped closer to her, and I bit my tongue to keep from speaking as he closed the gap and set his hand on her face. She didn't flinch as the light glowed around her. As the wound sealed, and the welt, bruises, and swelling vanished. Had seen this coming, I realized, as our basest gifts trickled back into our veins. Still as a cat, Alvara didn't shift as he healed her arm, her leg. He bade me forward. I didn't move, and with a roll of his eyes, Adrastos crossed the gap and healed the wounds across my ribs, neck, and leg. I recoiled from the closeness, this strange alliance between the monster and my mate. Recoiled from the way he smiled as he did it. He turned to walk across the field, but the thing brewing in my gut could no longer be contained. A way out. I had to give her—*them*—a way out.

"Adrastos." He paused, and Alvara's sharp eyes flicked to me, seething with warning. "This is between you and me. It should have been fought that way."

Adrastos' dark eyes landed on Ally as he pressed his tongue to his cheek, his hands sliding casually into his pockets. "You know little of your mate if you truly believe she would have stood down and watched you get dragged away half dead. Besides, as I told your defective magic eight ball, my brother would honor no such arrangement should it—by some highly unlikely turn of fate—fall your direction."

"You could have just taken us now—"

A cruel leer twisted his features before he purred, "But where's the fun in that?"

"Do you not care about the men you'll lose? You know Ally will cut them down—magic or no. Aren will crush their bones to dust for threatening his callings. Why duel?"

Adrastos ran his tongue over his teeth as anger roiled in his eyes. Suddenly, he vanished into the shadows, reappearing inches from my face. "Honor," he ground out. "Because I'm a man of honor—and your family deserves the *chance* of returning home." Adrastos smirked at my repulsed scoff. He turned to leave, and anger boiled in my veins. I lunged forward, grabbing his arm. He whirled as my fist flew, but before it could strike, he vanished into smoke. His corporeal form reappeared a few feet away.

"Time for that later, princeling."

As his form again became nebulous, I hurled the words at him, "A caveat—should I choose to come willingly, the battle will end. My family— all of them, and the hierarchy—will go free and unharmed."

A humorless laugh. "You could save us all a bucket of time and blood by just coming along now." When I didn't move, he shrugged his shoulder. "Should your stomach be unable to handle the bloodshed, Mr. Porter, you know where to find me. You have my word, once your allegiance is sworn, the duel will end." His features twisted into a wry smile. "Last chance to do so peacefully, little princeling." When I said nothing, he gave a small shrug and pointed sigh.

Alvara, anger rolling off her, made to speak, but he was gone.

SIXTY-TWO

JUMP

ALVARA

Oxygen slammed into my lungs as the light of Grayshell showered over my skin. It had been a gamble to bet on Adrastos, but as that warmth caressed my senses, I inhaled as deeply as I could. It had worked. The relief was cut short by raised voices upstairs. My eyes flicked to August, who jerked his chin forward, prompting me to sprint past the lines of warriors strapped in their weapons and packs, each granting me wide-eyed Grayshell salutes.

"*Who* is your *fucking* Commander?"

"You, sir." Alec. *Ohhhh, fuck.* I'd known before I asked that Alec and Ansel would have my back in this. It was a calculated risk, albeit also a desperate Hail Mary, and they had both sworn to buy me time when Aren inevitably wanted to come down guns blazing. But he shouldn't be the one paying for it.

Panting, we slid to a halt outside the war room, August snatching my hand and intertwining our fingers.

"Aren." I kept my chin high as we walked in. Aren had gathered the leaders—the souls who would have been our generals in a human army. I wet my lips, soothing my nerves as I took in the shattered mirror on the wall, Alec's bleeding cheekbone, and Ansel's split lip. *Fuckfuckfuck.*

Aren leaned against his desk, every muscle in his jaw and neck taut as his razor-blue eyes met mine. A muscle feathered across his cheek, and I forced a swallow. In all our years together, I'd never directly gone rogue—certainly hadn't kept a thread from him that was so crucial. He wouldn't have let me go...

"He took it really well," Ansel drawled dryly, his gaze roaming over us for injuries.

Alec closed the gap, throwing his arms around my neck. I breathed him in, anchoring myself in that familiar hold. "Jesus, Ally, what the fuck."

"I know. I'm sorry; it had to be done."

"Oh, I know." He peeled himself away, moving to grasp August. "I meant you could have fucking warned me about that left hook. *Christ.*" Fae, pale beneath her war paint and battle blacks, shook her head with a sigh.

"I held back, asshole." Aren growled, glowering at him as he rubbed the back of his neck. That gaze landed on me. "Any more *surprises*, Alvara?" I shook my head, words evading me as we stared each other down. "Anyone else would be on the fucking bench."

"I know."

"Do you?" He challenged, crossing his arms. "Because I think you forget we can help you pull threads. Sometimes I think you forget we do this shit as a team, Ally."

"I know."

"Bullshit." The entire room froze, my stomach solidifying as we all turned toward Lana, who'd melted into the shadowy corner, an arm crossed beneath her elbow to survey her nails. "You're not the only one with something to lose here, Alvara." My eyes burned, and August squeezed my fingers.

"She's right." Fae slid off her stool, crossing the room to wrap around Alec. "You went dark, and we lost our shit up here."

"I'm—I—"

"You're not sorry," Ansel cut in. "Just don't, Ally. We know you meant what you did. And it fucking worked, so let's get down to brass tacks and talk sentimental shit once we bury these fuckers."

Alec snorted at the same time I did, and when I turned back to Aren, he was smiling softly, shaking his head in that knowing way of his.

"You and I will have words when we get back." He knocked twice on the desk. "Brass tacks. Lay it out, Alvara. And this time, I do expect to see all the damning details—am I clear?"

WE QUICKLY TORE through the most solidified visions and hashed out the little strategy we could all agree on as long as Agamemnon's power remained intact. It felt like going in entirely blind.

Too soon, we had to begin assembling our host, as Adrastos had very intentionally given us no time to recover. Warriors and healers with families huddled together, wrapped in embraces. Aren sought me out, a deep crease between his eyes. Wordlessly, he grabbed my shoulder and yanked me into him, crushing me in his arms and burying his face against my hair.

"Thought I lost you again," he rumbled quietly.

"I know, Ar. I—"

"Will always do what needs to be done." His arms released me as I swallowed and gave him a curt nod.

Aren knelt, and with a clatter of metal and leather, the legion followed suit. He bowed his head and led the prayer—the only battle ritual any of us knew.

We all moved in sync with our Commander as he rose, gave the Grayshell salute, and said, "Free our family. Then, let's get this son of a bitch."

Something was off. The instant the energy began to pull, the moment the window to Grayshell opened for us to move through, we all felt it. That dark shift, like shadows brought to life, and a slow, chiming music box seemed to sing against the walls. But the momentum of the jump was already in motion. My eyes snapped up to Aren's, fighting the pull of the jump, as the whipping shadow fire of Adrastos appeared between us.

The last thing I saw was that sneer across his cruelly beautiful face, and then screaming split the air as Grayshell vanished.

The moment our feet touched the earth, the connection to the Middle Realm shattered like a vase off a countertop. Our connection, mind to mind, vaporized. The fire in my veins was suddenly trapped within them, unable to flicker. A chill snaked through me as Aren roared, the sound unlike any I'd ever heard, as agony and rage overtook him. He tried again and again to jump back, to go home, to take us with him, to go alone. None of it worked.

I didn't bother looking at the stunned, horrified faces surrounding me as my knees buckled, leaving me crouched with my face buried against my hands. My heart hammered a violent drum against my ears. We had them all—every available, able-bodied, trained warrior of Grayshell, save for a handful left behind to update the souls on the battle below. They were good warriors—good students—but none had the strength to battle Adrastos and live to tell the tale. Babies. We had left them with babies. I had failed.

I had failed to protect Grayshell. Our home. I had never seen it coming.

I'd never thought in a million years that it *could* be breached. That that was going to be Adrastos' angle. But we had been warned. Warned it was poised to fall.

And still... I had failed them.

SIXTY-THREE
PROOF OF LIFE
AUGUST

Slowly, much too slowly, we walked through the damned forest to the coordinates. In a few long months, I had grown so dependent on my magic that approaching this field without it felt agonizing—empty, as if someone had hollowed out my gut. There was no going back now. No jumping to safety. With that psychopath, potentially no safety to go home to. Horror had settled over us at that thought, at our helplessness for our family back home.

There was only battle to be had.

Alvara kept her hand in mine, grasping me like a life raft after her ship sank at sea, as if we could avoid what we were fated for. I focused on the warmth of her battle-worn palm against my clammy skin. The wind chilled the sweat on my brow, carrying the scent of burning timber and the stench of demons that made my eyes burn.

Close. She didn't have to say anything for my instincts to know we were finally near, marching forward along the edge of an immense ravine—a gaping canyon that seemed to have devoured the mountain and trees along with it. Of course Adrastos would choose this ominous place to battle, where the earth could swallow us as easily as our enemies. Creatures in the distance bayed and howled.

Only Aren, Alvara, and I stood before the brigade, leading them into violence, into bloodshed, and into damnation. For me. For my weakness. As if she could still read my mind, Alvara squeezed my hand reassuringly and shook her head gently.

Not your fault, she seemed to say. *Don't let go.*

My mind reeled from the precise brutality of her power before Agamemnon drained it. Despite Alvara unleashing the *Angel of Death* upon the enemy, decimating their numbers in minutes, my family remained captive... Free only if we fought. Truly freed only if we won. And in their place, how many souls would fall?

Rage brewed in my chest, a wild animal roaring to escape its cage of bone and muscle. The hours between had done nothing to dampen my anger.

The hair on my arms stood on end, goosebumps racing down my flesh. That rancid, icy chill wrapped creeping tendrils around my legs. Death—heavy, dark, and unavoidable—scented the air. I shook the nerves from my bones and demanded my body make its stand. There were other endings. There were threads to pull, even if we couldn't untangle them. Even if they were few and far between.

Knowing my soul as well as their own, Ally nodded, while Aren's anticipatory grin stretched across his face in my periphery.

"You will die a different day, Commander. That's an order," he growled. Even without magic, my body straightened. Die. A. Different. Goddamned day. I nodded. His grin was more a flash of teeth, and somehow it rallied my courage.

There, in the stormy shadows, stirred the icy crawlers, lurking at the base of every tree along the clearing's edge. Why was it always a clearing in the damned woods?

We marched past them, snarling as they hissed at us. *Come and get us, motherfuckers.* But my own snarling reminded me that crawlers clung to darker beasts. They served them.

"Twenty bucks says they brought tormentors," Alec growled behind me, his leather armor crackling as he shifted.

"Make it fifty," I spat back. He made a manic noise, close to laughter. Aren knelt, running a bare hand over the ground as he whispered one last prayer. Together, Alvara and I released our hands and drew our weapons. The rustle of wood and leather told me the archers did the same behind us.

And then I saw it—beyond the clearing. They had burned the forest, leaving jagged, toothy black stumps. Like the teeth of the canyon, they formed a perimeter at the edge of the clearing before that daunting drop. Smoke hovered eerily over the charred earth. Slowly, meticulously, they rose from the embers—a planned entrance, meant to strike fear in the hearts of our host. Towering bodies emerged between the singed trees. Ally hissed; it was a message for her, a taunt of the power now bound within her blood and bones.

Despite Alvara's nuclear death blow, they still had at least twice our numbers. And that was before the chained beasts staggered forward, hackles raised, growls rumbling the earth. My ribs cemented into place.

Adrastos, head and shoulders taller than the rest, stepped to the forefront of the burned earth, the clearing an eerie stretch between our forces. His dark hair flipped in the wind as he sneered at us.

"It can all be over, Commander Amadeus." His swaggering drawl was all mockery. "We will have The Great Commander by this night's end. I've seen it. Your *second* has seen it. Save yourself the heartache."

"Eh. We've faced worse odds." He shrugged, the nonchalance chilling in the face of the looming bloodletting. Low, anxious laughter rumbled through our lines.

"We were promised proof of life." Alvara's eyes seemed to burn like embers as she spoke directly to Adrastos, her magic just below the surface of those emerald irises, ready to burn them all alive the moment she broke the Reaper's negotiated spell. Carved of stone and hellfire, she stood unyielding.

The Renown broke into howls, and their beasts bayed in her presence.

Alvara didn't flinch when Adrastos snarled at her demand. Gone was the swaggering *cousin*, gone was the negotiator. In his place stood a furious, bloodthirsty King. What had he sacrificed to force Agamemnon to accept the terms of the bargain?

Even as Alvara studied the change in him, she didn't waver. Eyes resolute, she stared him down. "Now."

Adrastos sneered, but Agamemnon met her steadfast gaze, his tan clothes still stained with the splatter of her blood, and turned behind them. He disappeared behind the row of bodies and smoking tree stumps. A ripple went down their line, and slowly, they began crashing their swords against their shields—a war drum meant to intimidate us. The souls didn't waver.

Somewhere behind their line, someone was screaming. First a woman, then two muffled male voices, followed by a chorus of jeers. My stomach twisted.

When Agamemnon returned, only a few heartbeats later, Layla dangled in the air, suspended by his brute hand on her throat. Her feeble nails clawed at his arm, and her feet thrashed.

"No!" I roared, lunging forward. "You agreed they'd be unharmed!"

The giant gave a bone-chilling laugh as he threw her to the ground. The sickening crack of skin and bone colliding with earth cut through the dead world. She clung to the charred grass, heaving for air. And still, the war drum thundered against their shields. Again. Again. Again.

One slender hand came to her throat, as if she could urge the air back through her touch. Coughing, she spat blood at the monster's feet. He kicked her slight waist, and she heaved over with the blow. Something within me broke. I had done this. Brought this upon her.

"Enough!" Aren boomed.

But the souls were done watching.

SIXTY-FOUR
DEATH DANCE
ALVARA

A great metallic crash split the world in two as the forces collided. The Renown roared as our arrows rained down, so thick they blotted out the sunlight filtering through the storm clouds. In a blur, Agamemnon threw Layla over his shoulder and heaved her across their line. Her hoarse scream reverberated in my skull, shattering my resolve.

Line after line of giants crumbled under our arrows as our swordsmen charged forward in a tight, ancient formation of muscle and shields, led by Aren, August, and Ansel. The tightly woven advance rendered the opposing archers nearly obsolete, our leaders swiftly dispatching any who broke through the wall, with Lana quick to jump in their wake, even faster to slice down the few men who made it past them.

Again and again, I loosed my arrows, praying for each to fly true. They did. Even as our warriors rushed by us, fierce as a river over rapids in the belly of the ravine behind us.

Instinct pulled me to the earth, twisting, as an arrow barely scraped past my face. The warm bead of blood across my cheekbone was a jolt, the sour, metallic tang filling the air around us.

—

THE LEFT FLANK CRUMBLED. Within an hour of that initial volley, it broke. Like the canyon edge eroding into the water below, it fell to pieces under the unending assault of the Renown. Aren, a moving boulder of muscle and fury, barreled down on the gap as the warriors forced through it.

Even over the roar of battle, the crash of steel, his bellows to get back in line rang over us.

Ansel, the living shadow he was, was only heartbeats behind him, echoing his barked commands to hold the line, to get in formation, as though no time had passed since he commanded legions. Where he arrived, dark soldiers fell. Like smoke on the wind, Ansel moved with awe-inspiring precision. Beside me, Alec and I freed arrow after arrow, pushing back against the Renown poised to breach the left wing. It had been so long— centuries, at least, and lifetimes for many—since any of us had battled like this, without elements or firearms, locked in tight formations, line after line.

The Renown spotted Ansel, unaware of the little phantom quietly cleaning up the mess in his wake. They spotted him as he cut down his enemies in a dance of death, and they charged. He didn't slow, didn't yield. From this distance, I couldn't tell if any of the blood across his scaled suit was his own.

Arrow after arrow, we rained down our reinforcements. One by one, we picked off those in the breach. Aren, like a boulder in the river, filled the gap in the dam. His death dance was less graceful than Ansel's, but even more devastating as he claimed two or three at a time, using their bodies like shields and weapons.

Agamemnon prowled along the rear of the host, conserving his energy, unleashing his lethal brutality only when unavoidable. To my horror, his gaze seemed fixed on Aren as he cut down row after row of challengers. Waiting. Biding his time for when Aren finally fatigued. I didn't need my gifts to see that much.

The left flank switched from panicked yelps from our side to the agonized screams of the Renown. A victorious battle chant broke out below, stirring something within me at the reprieve as Aren battered the line back, and Ansel, August, and Lana sliced down those who breached. A small mercy, I supposed, if we could just hold the line. If Aren and Ansel could hold it.

The earth rumbled, and every drop of blood in my body turned glacier cold and scalding hot at once. The roars cut through every ounce of courage reinforcing the left flank, as agonized screams filled the cold air.

The tormentors had been freed.

SIXTY-FIVE
BLOOD WOLVES
AUGUST

Blood. So much fucking blood. The only comfort was that, from my tally, each soul seemed to claim three before a single blow could be struck against them. Speed and anger propelled them relentlessly forward in waves.

The snap of bone jerked my attention. Panting and soaked in blood, Aren dropped the limp gatekeeper—a demon ranking just above a crawler—to the ground, its skeletal head slamming into the dirt a second later.

His eyes locked on mine as he flexed his hand, rotating his wrist. Aren sucked in a breath and jerked his head toward the chaos. "Be certain, Commander Porter." Another lesson. Possibly our last.

A slow smile slid across his features when I nodded my assent, and we dove forward together.

The crawlers still fell with mortal ease. The crunch of spine against my blades brought a sickening satisfaction.

A deep roar shook the earth, and I swore.

Tormentors.

Not just tormentors. Blood wolves.

Screams ripped the night into pieces, and my feet charged forward, toward the agony of my family. Toward the blackness of certain death. Aren barked orders behind me, spouting out instructions to souls he trusted.

The screams were my guide, and I felt Aren, Lana, and Ansel close rank on my heels, their energy still immense in mortal form.

Icy numbness, a deep battle calm, crept through my mind like ice to a burn. My eyes ceased to see the faces of those cut down by my blades. I lost count. They just fell—sometimes before I registered the break of flesh and bone. Centuries of war led each movement, and the power locked in my chest rumbled. Magic, swollen and angry, pressed into my limbs for escape, guiding instead the fatal blows of my blades.

It felt like a lifetime of blood and blows before we made it.

We reached an opening in the killing field. Not an opening. The earth was painted rusty red with fallen souls. Their mutilated bodies lined the ground. Healers. *Slain healers.* Slain soldiers below them. A mangled mash of blood and flesh.

Two enormous tormentors in wolf form tore their corpses to pieces, snarling as they did. I bared my teeth, and Aren's growl rumbled through me. Two more crept up behind their bloodied comrades.

Inhuman eyes gave no quarter. They would receive none from the coven.

"Come and get us, motherfuckers," I spat through bared teeth.

Ansel and Lana spun forward first, a twin tornado of glinting gold and silver. Ansel was a blur of black, Lana's whipping silver braid her only signature. Blades hacked through not one, but two of the monsters before the others registered the attack. Great snarls tore from them as they dove forward. My hatchet met the face of one, while Aren's now-black sword swung down to behead the fourth.

But there were more.

More in their wake, having sensed the death of their own. All muscled, hairless wolves, six, seven, eight feet tall even on all fours. Gnashing their impossibly long teeth. Muzzles already drenched in red. They growled, and we hissed, bracing ourselves. The monsters tried to split our ranks, to herd us like sheep, to move us where they could pick us off easily. We held the line, and for a heartbeat, the small assault was motionless.

Carved of stone as darkness crept in.

The Renown were closing in on us. Their ranking warriors spotted the savage path of bodies.

No time.

The advance was fluid, the fraction of our coven shifting like a whip as we struck forward. Again, and again, and again.

One. Two. Three down.

I roared as one dove for my sword hand, fangs just scraping enough flesh to draw streams of red to the surface. Baring my teeth, I lunged forward. Aren bellowed. Lana gave a yelp. I focused on beheading the beast bent on disarming me. Aren's blade swung down as my own did, and it fell. Pain registered somewhere in the back of my mind, in the wrist it had struck.

No time. Keep moving.

My stomach roiled as, somewhere in the distance, someone yelled to get back in line. If those lines failed, if they buckled, we were all as good as dead. The sheer size of them... But Ansel had all but held the breaking segment himself. If I could just get him back to the front...

Lana and Ansel, both bloodied, drove twin blades up into the ribs of one of the blood wolves with lethal, synchronized precision. With immortal speed, Ansel dropped the beast and loosed two throwing knives into the throats of advancing Renown already within a body's length from us. His bandolier was looking thin.

Aware of the same observation, Ansel dove forward, tearing his knives from their flesh as they drowned in their blood.

He spun, extraordinary grace rippling through his muscles, and threw them again. Again, and again, they met their mark. I held his back, deflecting the attackers that came for the old general.

He drew two more blades, eyes on the last of the Renown advancing toward us. Just as a blood wolf collided with him.

The outraged roar in my chest broke into the night, and I dove forward, sword raised.

But the two grappling bodies moved with such speed I couldn't swing. Not without risking Ansel.

Ansel's agonizing scream shredded apart the very fabric of the air. He roared as the beast tore great gouges of flesh from his belly, somehow still throwing the creature from his frame with just enough force for me to lunge forward and deliver the fatal blow.

The beast's enormous head fell to the earth, maw still open with murderous rage.

Numbly, I turned back as Lana collapsed to her knees by his side. Her beautiful face contorted in a scream I could not hear, her braid swinging down to shield her mate, who writhed in agony against the earth. Her blade clattered against the stone by her knees. She pressed her pale, spindly hands into the impossible wound. Fingers spread wide, as though she could will the flesh to seal back together.

I whirled, just as another beast lunged for the back of my neck. Sword instinctively raised, we collided. The force of the thing took us both to the ground. Wind rushed out of me. Pain rippled. Muscles trembled as I forced air back into my body. Blade pressed against the wolf's great, fleshy neck, we roared at each other, saliva and hot blood spattering from its maw onto my face.

Then it went limp.

The blood wolf collapsed into me with the bright green fletching of an arrow barely protruding through its eye. It took all my strength to roll the great beast off me. I staggered to my feet, gasping and rasping for air, stumbling to retrieve my sword. When I was back on two legs, I spotted that eternal pale face and familiar eyes, just long enough for her to know she'd succeeded.

And she was gone. Back into the battle.

I moved toward Aren, but it was redundant. He snapped the beast's neck with a crack. Its limp body dropped to the ground.

Lana was sobbing, unspeakable agony filling her wails, the sound more horrific than any I had ever heard. She was pulling Ansel's limp body against her own as she staggered back, out of the fray, retreating toward the wooded wall. Aren was bellowing for a healer, but his voice trailed into the chaos. There would be no healer. I stared down at the bold warrior, and horror settled in my stomach. Blood. Too much blood.

St. Michael, send help.

Alvara was coming; I could feel it in my bones as she sprinted forward. Alec too—his energy just as familiar. Only... urgent. No trace of that constant calm.

"Hold the line!" I barked at Aren. He gave a quick nod and swung his sword through the air. The motion would be menacing to the enemy, but I knew he was testing his wounded shoulder, blood pouring from the gash inflicted by one of the wolves. The bone-chilling screams of great cats tore through the air, and my heart sank. More beasts.

Still, I advanced.

SIXTY-SIX
PRAYERS
ALVARA

The killing field had long since descended into a melee, the left flank crumbling entirely after the wolves were released. Hands sticky with drying blood, I knocked an arrow, trying to keep a tally of the precious few I had left while keeping an eye on the ground for strays.

The twang of Alec's bow, followed by a low, "Fuck," drew my attention. He'd stayed planted by my side, his face twisted in a snarl, amber eyes dark with rage. I hadn't realized just how long we'd been on that field until his fingers fell away from his empty quiver. He'd rained down hell for us—every last arrow with lethal precision.

"To the bitter end." His voice was hoarse from barking commands, but he threw his arms around me.

"Until we meet again." I pressed a kiss to his cheek and then leapt aside to block a blade, gutting the man wielding it. Alec brought his sword down to sever the head as the man fell beneath my blow.

He pulled me against him one more time, clapping my back, then dove into the fray, Fae a phantom on his heels, her white ponytail billowing in the wind. I leapt onto a nearby rock, gaining a vantage point.

The sky fractured with lightning, and thunder roared so close and immense that the boom reverberated through my body. Not lightning. Not lightning at all. But a portal. Blinding white flashes—three in a row—and three equally blinding rays of light shone on the ground between August and me. I staggered back, swore under my breath, and thanked all that was holy.

Standing before me in full spirit armor were Brody, Ajax, and Alastair, surrounded by a dozen unfamiliar faces. Out of the light, they emerged like Greek gods summoned to a killing field, weapons already drawn. Grayshell... later, I'd think of it later.

Perhaps those prayers we were all muttering were working after all.

Feral joy filled my heart, and I knew it showed in the grin I flashed them before diving back into the brawl. The three brothers were death incarnate—Saraya's rivals to Ansel and Aren in the sparring ring, and they brought reinforcements. Not many, but it was something. With that small comfort, I hurled myself toward our coven.

What I wouldn't have given to still have both of my blades.

The tormentors were tearing us to pieces, and it was with horror that I reached back to realize my quiver was finally hollow. My small stash of throwing knives would do no good against the beasts—their rippling muscles would only be aggravated. Hurriedly, I slung my bow across my body and dove into the chaos. There would be arrows to collect. Obediently, my legs sprinted full force across the field of battle, over bodies and sprays of blood.

They were converging on Aren and August, now guarding our Ansel. *Ansel.* I stuffed down the wave of nausea at the sight of that lethal soul soaked in crimson—his own blood. *Jesus Christ.* My hand shook as it covered my mouth.

My axe spun across the gap, meeting its mark and drawing their ire.

One lunged, and my parry allowed me to see the hatchet embedded in its comrade. I dove forward, summersaulting across the ground, and heaved the thing free, spraying that inky blood everywhere.

August was engaged with another blood wolf, Renown rapidly closing in. He advanced—relentless. Ares, made flesh.

The rest of our force seemed to be retreating, returning intuitively toward our Commander. Our numbers were dwindling at a terrifying rate. If something didn't shift, this battle would leave us enslaved by sunset. *Dead,* I corrected.

Still, I refused to yield.

I whirled to see the tormentor hadn't been aiming for me—but for Aren. My feet moved over bodies, but it felt as slow as sand as I ran for him. Three of the beasts were converging from all sides—the last standing defender between them and Ansel. His powerful blood called them like a siren's song.

Aren, a wall of ancient power and rage, did not yield.

One dove, and I hurled the hatchet with all I had. It found its mark, embedding in the neck of the first as it tumbled earthbound.

The scream tore from my chest as Aren spun with the attack, the second tormentor's gnashing teeth embedded in his side. Aren roared as he staggered under the force of the assault, barely keeping his footing as he raised his weapon. I sprinted the distance between us and heaved my blade down through the creature's spine with a crunch that reverberated up to my palm.

Aren's sword and my own both withdrew with a sick, meaty slide as he kicked the tormentor's corporeal form to the ground. Darkness oozed around it, that rancid, tar-like blood soaking into the earth.

Too many. There were still too many of them.

We whirled and both raised our swords to slice through the underbelly of one that had lunged for his head. As it slid down our blades, the weight ripped them from our grasps. The wild thing still flipped its head, gnashing its teeth and striking out with those fatal, taloned paws. One sliced a thick line across my shoulder, but I'd lost all sensation ages ago. A black and silver bolt shot through its eye, and I found Alec on his knees by Ansel, crossbow now held in his steady, bloody hands. I didn't think of where he'd gotten it.

One nod of thanks, and I was moving, kicking the thing over to seize our blades.

Aren gave a disgusted, pained grunt and wrapped his hand over the blossoming crimson on his side. "Go!" he barked. I didn't let myself think. Didn't stare too hard at the gaping wound in his side. I just whirled, eyes scouring for where to go. Horrible dread twisted oily tendrils around my heart and throat, slithering around my body.

August. Where was August?

SIXTY-SEVEN
LAMB
AUGUST

Eyes burning, I surveyed the killing field, tamping down the grief in my heart. The Renown were advancing. The tormentors. Hell, the tormentors. Teeth as long as my thumb, canines even longer, their maws tore into still more souls. Horror consumed my body as I watched them fall under coordinated strikes. Their staggering numbers were still too vast—at least as long as the tormentors stood. With no SOS to our neighboring hierarchies, we would indeed fall.

The world seemed to slow around me, my body numb as reality soaked my muscles with the blood seeping through each scrap of fabric. So fast had the chaos erupted. Too fast. We'd lost our lines the moment the blood wolves tore a hole through the center.

Aren and Alvara were a good hundred yards away, their backs to each other as they defended the healers, who were now miraculously kneeling over Ansel. Aren... God dammit, *Aren* was bleeding, an arm wrapped around a wound in his side. Alvara was so blood-soaked there was no way to know if any belonged to her.

Hours. I realized it had indeed been hours.

Thunder shattered the skies, the sound reverberating through the earth. Then Adrastos, his voice magically amplified, called for silence. He demanded they cease fire. The world froze, and I felt his eyes on me before I saw him.

His amplified voice boomed, "Serve me, Porter. In exchange for the mortals. Simple. Easy. As discussed. Personally, I'd let them burn—they'll die anyway." A sickening smile. I gripped the hilt of my sword tighter. There was nothing human in his face. No soul behind the dark gaze as he stepped away from his core of ruthless fighters. "But you won't do that, will you?" A cruel smile twisted his features.

Agamemnon stepped forward with Layla again. This time she dangled in front of him, her slight form spinning slowly in a magically suspended circle. The sheer jumper she'd been taken in had long since soaked through in the rain, streaks of blood marring the neckline, and every detail of her body—wracked with sobs—was visible through it. Red clouded my vision, my pulse roaring in my ears as a snarl clawed from my throat. Her eyes were tight with tears, her mouth sealed shut under a filthy gag. Something inside me broke irrevocably at the sight of her so broken and objectified as the legion of Renown heckled and laughed.

"Lying filth!" I roared, raising my sword as my body began trembling with rage. "They have bro—"

"Have we? Broken the bargain, little Commander?" Adrastos interjected.

"Or did we agree to return your *family*, unharmed?" Agamemnon's eyes were fixed on me as the vile words left his lips. "We said nothing of your human whore. Perhaps we start with her. We'll resort to the man if her life doesn't hold enough weight."

My stomach became a writhing, molten snake. Holy fuck. When Adrastos had repeated his side of the bargain, he had said family. *Family.* Not friends. My eyes widened, fire burning against them as though my power was working to push its way out. The brothers laughed as I hesitated, realizing our mistake.

"She is family!" I roared. "She's James' mate!"

Adrastos tossed his head back and laughed. "Humans don't possess enough resilience to have *mates*," he spat the word. "Besides, we still have the stowaway—what's his name?"

"Didn't care to ask," Agamemnon sneered. "Didn't matter, once his jaw cracked."

"Regardless. I suppose he'll die just as well."

"Fuck you!" I roared, trying to see through the line of giants to their other captives. My family. Sam. When their bodies didn't part enough to reveal anything more, I glanced back at the line of souls, still holding steady despite being nearly weaponless, many clutching wounds or dragging the injured behind them.

Ansel was unspeakably broken. Fae was drenched in scarlet, her lips an eerie pale, chest heaving. They would fight to the bitter end by my side. Returning my gaze to the giants, my voice hoarse, I barked back. "My hierarchy is allowed to leave. Unharmed. You let them go home. My friends *and* my family—they are free, now." Layla's eyes widened, and she began shaking her head, frantically trying to dissuade me. That broken piece of me fractured into countless, unrecoverable shards.

The Renown snarled, and the crawlers stirred around them. But my eyes were only for their leader...

Adrastos gave one jerked nod, his eyes unwavering.

One step forward.

"Your deal has been struck, demon."

Alvara's howl tore through me, and I breathed against the agony there, louder than Adrastos' sneer of victory or roar for silence. I held my hand up, a silent plea for her to stop. To surrender... to surrender *me*. There was no coming back from *this*. And it was the only way. She knew it. I knew it. The visions knew it.

We had entered the knot.

It was all for nothing—the agony of the morning. The bloodshed. It wasn't enough. Perhaps it spared us some semblance of loss here on the field, showed them what her wrath would bring them. But it wasn't enough.

One last glance—it was all I could grant myself. To gather the courage to do what needed to be done. It all but undid me. Seeing her frantic face twisted in panic. Seeing the emerald-green eyes I loved so much, so distorted with agony. Aren dove to keep her from dashing to me. Wincing in pain, he dragged her lithe body against his own. She kicked and screamed her defiance. The blood wolves snapped and snarled at her, ready to block her should she charge.

Never had I wished so badly that she could see inside my mind. Wished she could see *everything*. Wished she could have known what she meant to me—really meant to me, beyond mate, beyond love, beyond all the trivial bullshit titles.

She stilled for a heartbeat, eyes wild. Everything in me shattered at the betrayal that could not be avoided. Alvara had tried. *We all* had tried— again and again. But the visions remained the same. Our fate unchanged. This was the only way.

I love you. I knew she couldn't hear me. Couldn't feel the thought press into her mind like a lover's caress. But I thought it, nonetheless.

Slowly, pain rippling through my very soul, I turned back to Adrastos. His curled lip was sickening, twisting my stomach into an icy knot as he demanded I kneel and drop my weapons. Never in my life had I thought to kneel, and yet, on that killing field, for my family, I did.

Gingerly, I placed my sword on the earth below my feet, blood dripping onto the field. The demons heckled like raging hyenas, and Adrastos and his brother roared with satisfied laughter.

"Come along, princeling." There was nothing human left in the eyes that stared me down, but I would not yield. Would not flinch at the fate dealt to me. Wouldn't grant him the satisfaction of showing my fear. My body honored the commands, heart steady.

And then the first blow struck.

SIXTY-EIGHT
THE WRAITH
ALVARA

The sadistic laugh ripped through my body almost as violently as the blow to August's face had. The world moved like molasses through an hourglass, and every muscle in my body seized, my knees buckling as he fell to his. Aren's steel arms locked around my chest, trapping me against his immense body as a scream tore the tender flesh from the inside of my throat.

Again and again, I screamed August's name, the anger swelling in my chest like a wildfire ready to consume the mountainside. In a desperate attempt to free myself, I threw my legs into the air and swung my weight forward. But Aren's strength was so far beyond mine that he barely shifted under my frantic leverage, his unwavering grip crushing the air from my lungs.

"Ally," he hissed through gritted teeth, the heat of his breath against my ear. "Please!" Never, in three hundred years, had I heard Aren beg. Not for anything. But he begged me now. "Please, Ally. You know this *has* to be. This moment is *fixed. Remember.*"

Fae's desperate eyes caught mine, and for the briefest flash of a second, I surveyed her. Her delicate fingers pressed against the wound in her side, her beautiful face marred with crimson and a livid bruise. Still gasping for breath, she shook her head slowly. There was no escaping this fate. We had tried countless times to unravel the knot of this battle, and there was no escaping it. Every thread spun into, and away from it. She pursed her lips and pulled her shoulders up in a pitiful surrender.

Sensing my resignation, Aren loosened his hold just enough for air to return to my lungs. I looked around at what remained of our family.

Lana, gold scales mostly torn from her bloody body, hair matted with blood, cradled Ansel's limp hand against her chest, her sobs nearly silent as the healer beside her frantically packed the wounds in his abdomen, hands miraculously steady.

"Stay with me, stay with *me*," Lana's voice cracked before she sucked in air. Her teeth dug into her lip as she stroked his face in frantic patterns. "Mo grá. Stay."

"Milseáin," Ansel's rasp was barely audible, and I jammed my eyes closed.

Numbness had long settled into my bones, and I felt a swell of power welling in my chest, white-hot and rapidly expanding. The world around me grew numb as I opened my eyes to Alec's trembling hands applying pressure to the deep wound in Ansel's chest, trying to staunch the flow until the healer could get to it. From navel to the top of his sternum, the ancient General bled. My throat thickened with dread as I tried to swallow down that suffocating fear.

August and Adrastos were halfway across the field now, the latter gripping August's elbow as though escorting a troublesome child. Agamemnon unceremoniously plopped Layla in the mud, and the soldiers shoved her roughly behind the line again. He turned back to acquire his prize.

My legs began to tremble—with fear or the rage pulsing through my body, I wasn't sure. Someone was wailing, others crying the names of the fallen, many wincing as wounds were tended to by the healers remaining on the field.

Slow and steady, August marched toward his end—either enslavement or execution if we couldn't free him here. His honor was his death. As though fear miraculously couldn't touch him, he took his mark in the center of the field, as Agamemnon lumbered toward him.

His towering figure moved forward with an arrogant sway. His battle had been won, his target finally acquired. A booming, mocking, merciless noise came from deep within his chest. A laugh, I realized. Lifeless and bloody, the sound brought ice to the air.

Hurling myself against Aren's arms, I screamed, "Don't touch him! Don't fucking touch him!"

Another sickening laugh escaped the monster as his obsidian eyes turned to me. He cocked his head to the side, a vile smile playing on his bloodied lips.

"You know," he growled, "I'm not sure what would be more fun. Watching her as you bleed out, or making you watch as we take turns bedding your bitch." Our legion of souls recoiled with hisses and cries of outrage. Lana's head snapped up from her mate, her lip curling back. Even Adrastos looked affronted by the words. His prize, I reminded myself. August was to be Adrastos' prize. He wouldn't let them kill him.

August let out a low growl as he drew his fangs, "Fucking so much as *look* her way, and I'll tear your throat out with my teeth!"

The same menacing growl rumbled through the coven, and I felt Aren's grip loosen, felt the icy chill of his own fangs bearing down. He tried to pull me behind him, but I held my ground and bared my teeth. A snarl erupted from my chest as our surviving warriors rose to their feet, an eerie, formidable silence settling over them. Ansel, still in the capable hands of the healers, hissed.

Adrastos flashed a feral smile. "Slow down, Commander." Another icy laugh followed. He was reveling in the challenge before him, relishing the silenced hierarchy bound by the word of a Commander ascending out of order. He growled something to the skeletal, cloaked demons holding the line behind him. There was a chorus of jeers and taunts, and they flung the hostages to the muddy earth with dangerous force, all bloodied and bruised. They'd broken our bargain. If we could reach them in time, August could be free.

"Leave them alone!" August roared, his voice fierce. I could feel his heart splintering as he took in James, Layla, Sam, and Freya, all bound and battered. Layla huddled into James, while Sam rose to his knees, bearing a ferocious black eye, blood dried across his mouth, his nose purple and crooked, obviously broken.

"Go!" August barked at his family. "Now. Get to Alvara."

None of them moved. Their eyes locked on August with savage love. Sam and James both shook their heads, and Freya rose to her feet, chin raised in defiance. She wrinkled her nose in disgust as she glared back at her captors.

Alec stepped into my peripheral vision, and for the first time in our long lives together, his energy was anything but calm. A volatile pool of fury and loathing, he reached down to hold on to me. The blood dripping from his fingers onto my trembling hand was still warm, and he stared at me with intensity.

"Ansel?" I demanded.

"Will heal. As soon as the shield is gone, Fae and Lana will get him to Grayshell," he whispered as quietly as he could.

I nodded, returning my attention to the field. But Ansel's blood smelled like lightning and soil, and *magic*. It smelled like raw power. The kind of power that only came with the strongest of emotions. It tingled against my skin. Was it possible to read his thoughts through the Reaper's spell?

Ansel, who had mastered that battlefield calm of an unshakable General many lives ago. Who knew my story as well as I did. Who studied our capabilities and weaknesses...

Eyes narrowed, I risked another glance at Alec, who side-eyed me before turning his gaze back to August. He gave me one nearly imperceptible nod, and I felt my heart quicken. A flash of a story from long ago...

A panicked glance back at Ansel found pained silver eyes waiting for me. Another tiny nod. I bowed my head and closed my eyes in gratitude for whatever message he had sent me. In centuries together in this life, Ansel had never invited me to read his history. I began to pray—pray this would work. Prayed whatever he was desperate to tell me would come to fruition.

Fingers trembling, I brought my hand to my mouth, willing my swollen lips to part enough to drag the blood across my teeth and tongue.

The world spun into darkness as millions of visions enveloped my mind, and I fully submitted to them. My legs tried to quit, but Aren held me upright, still pinned against his chest, the warmth from his blood seeping deeper into the clothes on my back. He was my anchor as not one, not two, but all of Ansel's long lives swirled through my mind. The overwhelm was immense, and I slammed my head back into Aren's chest as though I could silence the pounding pain there.

Ansel had always been a formidable warrior, every life lived on the hilt of a blade and the back of a mount. His intuitive knowing that Lana was in the world was parallel to none, and he would stop at nothing to find her. And God, Lana—she was everywhere, her rare smile, her rarer laugh, the way she moved so elegantly behind her blades. Her body. I did my best to turn from those memories—the ones he no doubt had kept guarded all this time.

Ansel's loyalty to us was more than I could even imagine. His love for me, for Aren, and even for August was shockingly palpable. His wounds only a small token of his affection for his coven. His family.

And then...

The edges began to fade into something nebulous as the vision turned blinding, like staring into the sun. I brought my hand to my mouth again and sucked the blood clean off, ignoring the metallic tang in my mouth, not allowing myself to register what I had done as the vision slammed against me like a tsunami.

Lana and Ansel had a *daughter* in one of their cycles. A real daughter, in both biology and soul. A brash, brazen girl, fierce as a lion. Her energy was unmistakably warrior, unrelenting, like a black flag always hung at her door.

She was skilled beyond even my abilities in combat. And she had died a martyr in her last life with her parents...died for...her King. Her country. Her kingdom. She'd made a vow to her best friend, the Queen, as the unnervingly familiar soul bled out against her lap. The Queen had called the young assassin "The Wraith" for her ability to infiltrate enemy lines unnoticed and unleash her deadly fury. Some thread to reality pulled and pulled, but I slammed it out, focused on this piece of Ansel he had shared.

The Wraith had loved her Queen, and the Queen loved her. In the Queen's dying breaths, the Wraith vowed to protect the King at all costs. A King she served to the last fatal slash of her nearly invincible blade, and desperate breath on her lips.

Tears poured from my eyes as I gasped for air, the vision fading into stardust. The energy was unmistakable. The soul impossible to *not* recognize. Lana's sobs grew more desperate, and I didn't need her thoughts to know their warrior daughter had completed her urgent ascension. It had been her rise that had incapacitated Ansel, leading to his injury.

...The weapon we had been praying for. The weapon neither the Renown nor August could know sat right under their noses.

The vision brought victory into my bones. A fool's chance, perhaps, but it's all we needed. All I could ask for.

I eyed Ansel and realized his silver eyes were pouring tears. While he would have been justified to cry in pain, in fear as death beckoned, the man was no mere mortal, and his pain would only fuel him. Those tears were odes to his long-lost daughter.

A daughter he was telling me to *use*. A Hail Mary pass to a second-in-command he loved like a sister.

I nodded my assent. It could work.

It had to work.

Agamemnon and August were within swinging distance of each other, Adrastos still glued to August's side, when I returned my gaze. Both were screaming epithets through bared teeth, and the sight of August—feral and menacing—sent a jolt of electricity down my spine. We could do this. We had to be able to. Because I could not lose him. Not to those monsters. It would kill me in a far more gruesome way than the Renown would.

"Aren," I whispered. "You have to let me go."

"Ally—" his growl was a warning.

"I cannot show you, under their shield. But you have to trust me. Ansel has a plan."

I felt the energy as Alec and Aren exchanged silent approval.

"Don't let me go. Not yet. You'll know when. Make it look real, and then you'll know the sign to attack."

He exhaled a pointed sigh, but I felt his body rock forward just slightly, anchoring my feet firmly against the ground.

"August!!" I screamed, letting all the pain of the battle consume me. Embracing every inch of agony and ire, I let the scent and energy fill the clearing as fire within my chest grew to a precarious inferno. Perhaps it was magic, after all—that ferocious energy slammed against my ribs like a prison. Like it could break out if it hit hard enough.

August's panicked eyes met mine for a moment, and then Agamemnon's colossal fist slammed into his face. I roared at him and thrashed against Aren. August staggered back but steadied himself, baring his teeth. Hisses and growls erupted from our warriors, and the metallic clang of blades filled the air.

I cried out for him as the monster's evil smile turned to me, ready to devour my suffering. He would enjoy every sadistic moment of tearing us apart. We wouldn't let him.

August spat blood into Agamemnon's face. "Do we have a deal? Or are you a coward behind all that muscle?"

"The deal stands!" He kicked Sam in the back and laughed as he fell, the noise shrill and icy. Adrastos snarled something to his brother. His General.

"Get them out of here!" August bellowed toward us. Alec cleared the space between us in a handful of heartbeats. He scooped up Layla and James, leading them back to drop them at our feet. He returned and pulled Sam's larger frame up from the ground, wiping the blood from his face before bringing him back, freeing them from their binds, but I shifted my attention back to the center of the valley.

"Don't," the word was barely a whisper on my lips. Alec glanced at me but kept his attention on Sam, as if tending to a wound, explaining the delay.

My eyes locked on tiny Freya, still standing tall, defiant. Short auburn hair whipped in the breeze like a flag; she stood toe to toe with the giants around them. August strode forward and untied the ropes binding her trembling hands. She finally freed herself from her gag, scrunching her face up in relief, then threw her slender arms around his neck, sobbing as they embraced. Freya's wrists were an angry purple, and she buried herself against her big brother for a moment, ignoring the monsters' commands to move.

All my anger, all that fire slamming against my skin, funneled into the roar that erupted from me—feral and promising death. The souls echoed Aren's own snarl as it rumbled through me. My smile grew savage as the demons and blood wolves hurtled toward me, and Adrastos' eyes followed. Aren knew. Sensed it or scented it, I didn't care. He released me, and I unleashed myself into our enemies, knowing Alec and the Commander were on my heels.

But the demons and wolves were easy work. My eyes circled back to August and Freya. Freya, as her hands steadied, planted a kiss on his cheek. Freya, as she whispered something in his ear. Freya, as she slowly stepped away from her brother and turned her attention to the giant.

And then the world went still as she flashed a coy smile at Agamemnon and drew her glorious fangs.

Anger spasmed in my gut as I took in the livid bruise along her cheekbone, the blood and bruises lining her slender arms, and the filthy fabric they'd used to gag her.

Freya stood, raising her chin in a glorious fuck-you kind of defiance toward the commands of the giants. A torturous mixture of pride and fear gripped me—pride that my baby sister possessed a pool of courage so abundant she dared to defy monsters. She dared to wrinkle her face in disgust as they spoke and yank her arm from their gargantuan hands. Her energy was enormous and electric, somehow bottled within her slight frame. Jesus, she was still just a kid.

But they had shown her no more mercy than an animal led to slaughter.

My blood boiled furiously against my skin as I stared down into the depthless black eyes of our most brutal enemy and reached forward to free her hands from the ropes that bound them.

The rope fell to the bloody earth, and my stomach turned at the furious color of the welts left on her wrists. She tore the filthy gag from her mouth, chucked it aside, and then threw herself against me. Wrapping her arms around my neck, she shuddered into me. But once she settled, her body stilled. She didn't tremble, as I'd expected. Steady. Breath easy. Each inhale felt oddly intentional, strength emanating from her as though she were drawing in power before she acted. Fear roiled in my gut for what they'd do to her if she made to resist this bargain.

She nearly growled when Adrastos barked for us to separate, then turned her face to mine, planting a quick kiss against my cheek. In the same terrifying moment, I heard Alvara's curdling scream for me, louder than ever. When I looked up, I found her heaving against Aren, seeming to burn his hand around her as he recoiled, and she yanked free from his grasp. In a blur of fury and metal, she threw herself into the demonic line of defense in front of them, and the four cloaked demons fell to their knees as their skeletal heads toppled to the ground, as if she had sliced through them all in one brutal swing.

Fighting erupted anew. The wolves lunged for Alvara, and Adrastos dove into the chaos toward her, the cloaked demons flanking him. Aren and Alec rushed into the demons before them. An outburst of screams, snarls, bays, and shouts filled the air, and Agamemnon turned his attention to their greatest threat.

But Freya held my focus as she whispered in my ear, her words setting the hair on my arms on edge. "It's been too long, Your Majesty. Move when I do. Deal?" Something hard and chilled pressed into my hands, and I realized Freya had slipped the hilt of a blade into my palm. The eerie resonance of her words made my brain recoil, but in a heartbeat, I decided not to question her as she effortlessly pulled herself from my death grip. In the next, Freya flashed a mischievous smile at the monster, and my breath caught. The fact that she had drawn fangs—that she was *one of us*—barely registered before she dove toward Agamemnon, a blur in the night.

He staggered backward in shock, but he was too slow. In one motion, Freya had thrown her tiny body around his back and pierced his meaty neck with her long teeth.

Protective instincts propelled me toward Agamemnon and Freya. They were still grappling as the monster roared his indignation and made to flip her off his back. She had him in a near chokehold, legs wrapped tightly around his torso, fangs sunk deep in his flesh. His cruel face twisted in outrage, pain, and shock as I lunged forward with the blade she had slipped me. He parried the attack and brought his sword down against my dagger. It took all my strength and both hands to force back his wallop. He threw his body forward in a violent lurch, tossing Freya from his back. The motion yanked a bellow of agony from him as she tore muscle clean from his shoulder. The wound poured a wave of dark blood down his body, reeking of decay.

I couldn't help but stare, bewildered, as the young woman I thought was my gentle baby sister pulled another knife from under her blood-spattered blouse. When in the hell had she managed to take them? She turned her face to spit his filthy blood to the ground and wiped her arm across her face. Snarling a feral, horrifying noise, Freya bared her teeth at the monster. Her eyes darted to me, and she jerked her head behind me before lunging for Agamemnon.

I whirled just in time to dodge the blade of one of his soldiers. Lightning fast, I slid downward and sliced the dagger across his knees before stabbing the blade through his Achilles. He roared as he fell, and the sound cut off with a sickening gurgle as I sliced his throat. In a frantic attempt to stop the bleeding, the monster dropped his sword, which clanged against rock. He held his enormous hand to the wound as he fell to the ground. I swiped the weapon and then whirled back to Freya and Agamemnon, still engaged in a bloody duel as the battle raged around them.

Freya was merciless in her assault on the monster, and he returned the fury, bringing the full weight of his arm down relentlessly, leaving her the briefest seconds of respite between each blow. She snarled defiantly, her arms trembling under the effort of blocking his attacks. I quickly weighed the dagger in my hand, studying its balance. These were Renown blades, likely poisoned or enchanted. Freya saw my movement and dropped to her knees. A flash of victory twisted Agamemnon's cruel features until my blade sunk into his chest with a meaty thud.

He staggered.

Yanking the blade from his chest, Agamemnon roared in anger. The sound was echoed by his soldiers, and my eyes had only a second to assess the chaos before he advanced. I couldn't tell where Alvara was or spot Aren or Alec. Then we were dancing, swords clashing. Freya lowered into a crouch, head cocked to the side, analyzing the giant. Teeth bared like an animal, dagger clutched defensively in her right hand.

I circled the giant, assessing him. He was losing blood from the two wounds at an encouraging rate, his teeth bared in either anger or pain. The wound from the blade shouldn't seal if we kept him on his feet, if Alvara and Aren's dire injuries were any indication.

"Once I've gutted you," Agamemnon growled, "the bitch is next."

I knew he meant Alvara. The growl in my chest was low but enough to spark light in his eyes. He anticipated the fight, lived for it—a sadistic warrior to his core.

I wouldn't grant him the satisfaction.

Agamemnon was larger than me, already out of breath from the battle, his conflict with Freya, and the deep wounds in his chest and shoulder. It was now or never. I clicked my tongue, a sound I'd used to encourage my mounts in past lives, and Freya's courage grew palpable. She dove forward, somersaulting, while I dove in the opposite direction. Split his attention. It was our best bet.

Freya threw her knife with expert precision, thudding into the giant's thigh. He roared and made to kick her. I slid forward on my knees, swiping for his Achilles, but he anticipated the attack and whirled, so my knife met his ankle instead.

He bellowed, but it didn't have the impact I needed. I found my feet and wheeled back to face him, teeth still bared. The monster narrowed his eyes, darting between Freya and me before surveying above our heads, looking for backup.

There was no one coming to help. It was down to the three of us.

Agamemnon flashed a vicious smile and dove for Freya. She spun to avoid his advance, slamming her fists into his back. His steps barely faltered, but she danced away, unfazed. I dove forward, sword raised, and slashed. Dodging his counterattack, I retreated toward our line. Again and again, he struck his blows. I focused on keeping him mobile, committed to the plan of using my endurance to wear him out. Whirling sideways, I made way for Freya to take her swings. She dodged his blow by dropping low again, creating a window for me to barrel forward.

A guttural cry somewhere to my right tore through the air, and it was just enough. Eyes wide in terror, Agamemnon turned his attention to the sound, and a shudder of energy rippled through us. Agamemnon roared in agony at what he saw, and that second cost him.

I plunged my sword through his soulless heart.

As he staggered backward, sliding off my blade into a heap at my feet, an animal scream split the battlefield. Ears ringing, I whirled to see Freya crouched, readying herself, terror saturating her scent. An enormous sleek black jaguar bounded toward us. She raised a sword from the muddy earth, her hands bloodied. But the great cat looked at me, and I threw myself forward to stop Freya's sword. Because against that sleek black fur sat two sharp, cerulean blue eyes. Beyond it, two more identical cats shredded enemy lines.

"Fuck, it's good to see you, brother." I grinned, and for an instant, it seemed the great beast mirrored my expression before diving for the heap that was Agamemnon and tearing him to pieces.

Energy shifted violently, a tremor rising from the ground through my bones. Tangible hope flared in my soul, and I snapped my head up.

Alvara. She was braced against Adrastos' full weight, and with an agile spin away from him, I saw her slide the blade from his ribs—the same attack I had used to claim his brother. He fell to his knees, clutching the wound in his chest. She snarled as she spun to face a rush of combatants. Power flooded back into my veins, blood roaring as it reunited.

The shield was broken.

With a crackle, I turned and hurled electric energy into the wall of Renown advancing on Aren. His booming laugh filled the clearing as the wall crumpled to the ground. The field erupted with a torrent of wind, and I heard fire igniting from multiple sides. The sound of rushing water roared in my ears as the elements returned to their weavers.

The earth trembled beneath my feet, energy quaking within it. The quake grew more violent, and I looked up. A boulder of horror settled in my stomach when I realized Alvara was no longer standing over Adrastos' body. The rumble intensified to a roar, the ground becoming waves of liquid beneath me. I stumbled forward, eyes scouring the chaos.

"Alvara!" I yelled, my gaze skimming over mutilated corpses and moaning bodies that teetered on the brink. Familiar faces with glazed-over eyes tore at my chest, but I kept hunting for her as the world became deafening. The trembling earth broke, an enormous wall jutting up in front of me.

Up, up, up it soared. A colossal divider sliced through the field.

I pulled magic from my soul and hurled a ball of fire toward the towering wall, but the burst of flame only sent shards of muck showering down on us.

"Alvara!"

Desperately clawing for more strength, I summoned an electric burst and directed the power into the wall of clay. It trembled, great bricks of earth crashing to the ground, but it ceased stretching skyward. I scrambled up the wall, vaguely aware that a silent Freya was tight on my heels. I climbed with every ounce of strength left in my body. My nails filled with dirt, muscles screamed, and my fingers threatened to break with every violent claw into the muck as we scaled the side of it.

Freya was only feet below me, a knife clenched between her teeth. Laying on my stomach across the narrow, rocky top, I threw out a hand for her. She clasped it and hoisted herself the last few feet. She swept her hair back into a tight bun at the nape of her neck, tucking drenched red strands behind her ears. I stared at her for a moment, reconciling the girl who had cried when I'd accidentally run over a toad with the lawnmower with the cutthroat assassin I'd seen tear Renown flesh from bone with her magnificent teeth.

Reading my mind, Freya shook her head.

Later. Her desperate voice echoed in my head.

In my *head.*

Alvara!

Thunder boomed above us, the sound of the sky splitting open reverberating through my muscles. Within moments, my clothes were soaked through with torrential rain.

"Alvara!" My voice twisted with grief, likely inaudible over the roar of shaking earth, pelting rain, and battle. My muscles obediently threw me to my feet. The abrupt hilltop offered an unexpected vantage point, and I used it to search the remaining skirmishes below. It took only seconds from that perspective to spot the rapid flash of bright orange fire bursts on the far side of the field. Orange, not white.

A rapid-fire flash of her power lit the horizon beside the looming canyon. Alvara was engaged with *five* Renown, surrounded by crawlers, nothing but a blur of flame and shining steel against the black backdrop of charred wood, smoke, and the canyon just beyond it.

"Go!" Freya spat through the ceaseless downpour. "I'll be right behind you."

And somehow, I knew she would be. I grabbed the back of her neck and pressed our foreheads together for a heartbeat before kissing the crown of her head.

With one last breath, I leapt off the wall.

SEVENTY
LAST STAND
ALVARA

All I could feel, all I could see, was fire. It seeped into my bones, my blood, my soul. The rain turned to sizzling steam in my wake, even the storm incapable of suffocating the blaze.

I screamed the curse as another giant bore down on me, throwing out a wall of flame, the gravel in my voice betraying the desperation in my bones. It was a suffocating feeling, being unable to stop when every muscle and organ begged for reprieve. The flame engulfed the front runner, and he fled, screaming and frantically batting at himself, racing toward the river. The earth groaned and shuddered again, and I looked at the other three who had surrounded me, wolves on the prowl. Their obsidian eyes were red-rimmed, grimaces stretching across their ashen faces. Loss left them nowhere to turn. If they left one of us breathing, we would come for them, and they knew it. That kind of motivation made them even more savage than their fear of Adrastos and Agamemnon ever had.

Slowly, I stalked in a tight crescent, eyeing them with all the abhorrence I could muster, while judging the distance to the cliff behind them. We had reduced the Renown to wounded, cornered animals. I cocked my head, using the heartbeats of rest to refill my screaming lungs. Again, I circled slowly, hands splayed open toward the earth, ready to summon my power. The one with the scar across his neck flinched, and my eyes rested on his marred face. He had likely been beautiful once, now tarnished by corruption and a life of blades. He pulled his lips back in a grin that was all teeth. I hissed and summoned fire in my palms, the roar engulfing my arms.

"Bring. It. On." I growled through my teeth. Skinhead chuckled, the sound sick and contemptuous. But he held steady.

Eye Scar dove first, and I dodged sideways to avoid the thrust of his outstretched blade, pulling on the steel telekinetically. He held it with all his might, and I released my hold, causing him to jerk the hilt back into his own gut. As Skinhead charged forward, I ducked low, swinging my leg to pull Eye Scar's feet out from under him. I used all my strength to throw his body weight over my own, shoving him toward Skinhead just as his blade thrust for my chest. He impaled his comrade, and a furious shriek tore through the thunderous rain.

The earth swelled in waves reserved for the raging sea, and I swore, staggering for my balance as Skinhead launched himself at me, his steps just as off-kilter as my own. An arctic chill ran goosebumps up my flesh, and my heart wrenched. Crawlers. Drastically outnumbered, there was no help coming for me. Nobody left to hold my six.

Skinhead steadied himself as the earth solidified again. He didn't hesitate as he swung a great clenched fist for my face. I dodged, but received a knee to the gut, knocking the wind from me. My ribs felt on the edge of shattering as I collided with the ground, the giant's weight collapsing on top of me. The clamp on my ribs slowly eased, and I gasped for air, but Skinhead settled his weight over my hips. I bucked against him, but his weight was too much for my worn muscles, and he sneered as his power was confirmed. Neck Scar was advancing too, his face terrifyingly drawn into a toothy grin as he spun his blade between his fingers.

His heavy fists pounded down, and I caught one in both my outstretched hands. The other collided with my mouth. My teeth sang. Blood filled the wells beneath my tongue and down the line of my gums. I blinked away the rolling tears and growled at him.

I forced a breath into my breaking ribs, just enough to spit blood into his face. Skinhead lunged for my throat, but my palms slammed into his face. I braced against the earth, not about to topple into the chasm looming beyond. His arms were longer than mine, and he wrapped his enormous hands around my throat.

"Not...today...Satan—" My voice was hoarse and barely audible. I gasped for oxygen and finally loosed the word, "Ignus."

His eyes widened as my power surged through my hands. He flew back, but I followed his retreat, pressing my hands deeper into the meat of his cheeks, simultaneously mesmerized and horrified as he screamed in agony. He clawed at his chest as orange light illuminated his flesh until the flames engulfed him completely. The flailing fireball rolled off the cliff with a scream.

"Fuck!" I sputtered, inhaling as deeply as I could. Struggling to my shaking feet, I looked up, resting my hands on my legs for a moment as Neck Scar surveyed me. "Your funeral, fucker!"

Between gasps, I spat a mouthful of blood onto the ground at my feet and grinned at him, daring him to advance. Neck Scar sneered and lunged forward. I parried and tore his sword from his hand with the power still tingling in my fingers. Telekinetically thrown, the blade twanged into the earth with a harsh sting, and the metal reverberated into stillness.

I forced myself upright and winked at him, taunting. My hands were nearly limp at my sides, my legs long since turned to jelly, but Neck Scar was dragging too. He shrugged his shoulders as if to say, 'here goes nothing' and dove forward. The shield I summoned wasn't quite strong enough, and he collided with me, low and forceful, and we plummeted to the ground, fighting for dominance in a sputtering tumble. Blow for blow, we brawled against the dirt. He was stronger than I was, but I was faster and nearly dodged all his attacks. His fist smashed against my face again, and somewhere in my mind, the agony registered. But I wrapped my arms around his neck and head-butted him with all the strength my bones possessed. Blood poured from his nose and mouth, and he spat in my face.

"Bitch!" he panted. My breaths became hot daggers in my throat.

I pulled water from the earth and flooded him, but his outstretched hand brought a wall of clay straight into my side, knocking me on my ass. My trembling arms shoved through the blanket of earth, and my battered body fought to its feet again. He was gasping as he rose, and we circled each other for a moment before he glanced at his sword, still planted in the ground before the cliff face, merely a dozen yards away.

We dove.

SEVENTY-ONE
CATCH
AUGUST

Alvara had sprinted forward in a race for the sword, and judging by the agony in that scream, the giant had won the brawl. I leaned into my run, my eyes trained on the shapes only a hundred yards away. Vaguely aware of people in pursuit, my gaze demanded a glance.

Freya. In step with Aren and Alec. Thank God.

I sprinted toward the circle of bodies left in Alvara's wake and saw her on her knees, the monster's bloody hand wrapped around her throat.

"No!" I bellowed, throwing my hands out. *Hold on!*

Sending every ounce of energy left in my body, I hurled my power forward. She opened her eyes and reached out for me, her pale fingers dripping red and trembling in the air. Her eyes flashed a luminescent green as she splayed her fingers open, reaching out in desperation.

Power surged from my center, a great wave of anger and strength, my body and soul willing it toward her as I fell to my knees. Someone shouted my name, but I couldn't tell who. The world had grown muffled, like being submerged underwater, with all the sounds suspended outside it. A white-hot pain tore through my chest and drilled into my mind as my energy transferred to my queen.

ALVARA

Iron hands were strangling me. My legs trembled as the metallic warmth of fresh blood seeped down my pant leg, my muscles howling with the agony of the slice from his blade. My breath came in shallow, desperate gasps, and my vision blurred just as August yelled my name. Energy surged through my fingertips, tearing up my arm like fire and ice. Air forced its way through my lungs, and I cried out in unison with the giant, bringing my hands together on either side of his mammoth head.

The electric shock ricocheted through every fiber of my being, channeling down my bones like a great lightning rod, surging into the enormous body attacking me.

August.

The arc between us strengthened, and a tormented sob escaped my lips as the energy radiated through me. I dropped my hold, and we both collapsed onto the earth, heaving for breath. My arm reached out toward him, and another electric surge channeled through me—the giant writhed in agony, his body convulsing around the alien energy coursing through his bones.

The hair on the back of my neck stood up, and the energy behind me swelled to such overwhelming strength that my heart hitched.

The familiar whoosh of a blade slicing through the ether. I twirled and snatched the dagger from the air before my eyes found August, on his knees not fifty yards away, panting with exhaustion, his glinting green eyes locked on mine. He nodded. Alec and Aren were running toward us, another fifty yards behind August, who was getting to his feet. And...Freya was between the men and August, her small fingers outstretched toward me, her eyes wide.

She yelled my name, and I whirled just in time to slice the blade across the giant's too-close chest as he collided with me like a train. We rolled, mud coating my skin as I struggled to scramble to my feet. But he was too fast, diving for me, leaving barely enough time to think, let alone move. With a grunt of pain, I managed to tuck my knees between our bodies and threw him off me. He rolled toward the cliff face as I righted myself.

Hurling the blade into the ground between us, I siphoned away more of August's power.

SEVENTY-TWO
CHASM
AUGUST

Alvara's bloody hand was nearly limp as she reached for me, a crackling stream of ice tearing through the air between us, an electric current spiraling in a blue braid of energy. Flames burst from her hands, three elements swirling in a torrent through her body as she dove forward to grasp the hilt of the dagger embedded in the Earth.

I was running towards her at full tilt when the ground buckled, and a massive slab broke away in front of her, splitting into a long arc around the outskirts of the battlefield.

In the minds of our comrades, I saw the great flames licking at the sides of the canyon, hell coming to claim its souls. The fire danced up the canyon walls, long whips snapping forward to wrap around the ankles of demons and Renown alike. *Holy shit.*

The souls staggered back from the edge in terror as the enemy fell into the expanding crack. Rain streamed down Alvara's face in rivulets. The scarred monster she'd battled clung to the edge of the gorge, bellowing for aid that wouldn't come.

As fire coiled around his legs and torso, he screamed in agony before succumbing to the flames and vanishing into the abyss.

Shouts permeated the air, but all I could hear were the souls.

"Is it over?"

"Are there any left?"

The onslaught of names reverberated in my ears, and I heaved a breath as Alvara collapsed, folding in on herself, the glow of her power fading from her body. She turned her bloody face back to me, her eyes desperate, her hoarse voice barely escaping across cracked lips.

"August—"

A deafening crack and rumble of the Earth followed. Horror struck her eyes in the split second she realized what was coming as the ground beneath her crumbled into the fissure.

ALVARA

A TSUNAMI of exhaustion slammed through me, the air in my lungs coming in desperate, short gasps as I fell onto my hands, struggling to keep my composure and stay vertical at all. They were close—so close. I just wanted to see him. Just one more time before retribution claimed its prize. August. Because, dammit, I loved him. More than the fate of my soul or the world beneath my knees. I loved *him*. Our eyes met, and somehow, it seemed he knew. Knew all he meant to me and how badly I wanted to pour my heart out to him. When I opened my lips, the faintest breath escaped, and my voice cracked.

"August—" It was one breath. That's all I had. One last wave of terror tore through my body in agonizing clarity, and the earth surrendered. The shuddering chasm swallowed me whole, and I slammed my eyes shut. I didn't want to know. Didn't want to see.

Except...I didn't fall. Instead, I levitated, hovering just below the edge of the cliff. I looked up to my hand to see what bound it to the mortal world. August was laying down, one forlorn arm outstretched into the gulch. In a reckless heartbeat of courage, he dove further forward, his other hand grasping my forearm, long fingers digging into the flesh of my elbow, while mine desperately clung to the strong muscles that lined his bones. Air surged into my lungs in an excruciating wave, and the world—with all its pain and fire—vanished.

I dug my fingers into Alvara's elbow, the skin slick with blood. The metal scales had long since burned or sliced away.

The reading took her. Her eyes rolled back in her head, and my grip tightened desperately. "Alvara!"

Her eyes twitched in a frantic seizure. She didn't have the strength left for this. Not now. Not after everything. A cry tore from her, piercing my heart, and her arm went limp against mine.

"No!" I roared as she slipped inches away, deeper into the chasm. Aren's weight landed on my legs, his arms wrapping around them. I threw my other arm over the edge, digging my fingers into her limp arm, feeling her wrist threaten to dislocate under the weight of her slack body. Her head lolled back in an unnatural way, and something deep within me cleaved in two.

With a great heaving pull, I hoisted her body up over the edge of the crevice. Like a rag doll, she draped over mine, and great hands grabbed our clothing, rolling our bodies further from the brink. As gingerly as I could manage, I placed her on the ground and tore my arms away from her skin. She stilled, slowly turning onto her side. A gush of blood escaped her lips as she collapsed onto the cold ground beneath her.

Aren was bellowing for the healers, barking commands at the warriors who had finally arrived to aid the last of their standing hierarchy.

I pushed myself back, away from any exposed skin. Alec dove forward, attending to her wounds. He pulled a small blade from its sheath and stabbed through her battered pant leg to free the injured flesh. It wasn't as bad as I had expected—the image of Aren's poisoned wound still vivid in my mind—but she had lost a lot of blood. Alec freed a stab wound on her chest, tearing through the suit and laying the scraps aside. There was another on her ribs, and several across her shoulders, stained dark red, which had scabbed on their own.

Saraya appeared, her face grave and marred by the carnage of battle. Blood soaked her trembling hands, and by the smell, it was not from any one individual, but from the many wounded behind us. She took in the sight of Alvara and fell to her knees, hurrying between each injury, swabbing magic healing balm along them one at a time. The injury in her leg was the deepest, by some miracle. Saraya stitched it up with expert motions, with Alec acting as her assistant.

"It's her magic. After all that exertion, her visions drained her." I didn't say it as a question, but as a knowing. Four sets of narrowed eyes set on me, but they all nodded, lips pressed thin.

"Anybody got anything left to give?" Aren looked between us. My hands were still shaking from pouring my force into her. I closed my eyes, searching the hollow well inside me, but it felt bone dry.

Alvara *needed* me. There had to be something.

A flash of light drew my attention, and when my eyes opened, Alec's hands shook above her, glowing with white magic. Saraya joined him. Aren slowly knelt beside her, placing his expert hands over her heart. I noticed the wound in his own side had already been roughly stitched together when his power returned. His face was pinched with effort as he closed his eyes, pulling his strength forth for her.

I took a heaving breath and stretched forward just as Freya knelt, too. Together, we placed our hands over her wounds and breathed our energy into her.

In unison, our magic fluttered out like an old light bulb. Aren loosed a heavy breath and rocked back to sit in the mud, bowing his head into his hands. The rise and fall of Alvara's battered chest steadied detectably as the rain slowed while we attended her wounds. I turned my face to it, welcoming its icy pelts to wash away the death clinging to my skin. Alec did the same, his jaw still clenched. Only Freya kept her eyes trained on Alvara, unblinking. Unyielding as a lady-in-waiting before her queen. The thought resonated in my heart and swelled with a truth within my soul. So many questions. The answers would come. Just not yet.

It was Alec who finally found the courage to ask the question we were all petrified to voice. A single word was all he could muster, his voice cracking in the middle of it.

"*Grayshell?*"

Aren's eyes were consumed by shadows, his lips a tight line, and he shook his head bleakly. Ice curled tightly within my chest. "No one was able to make it back. I have no idea what's come of it."

"The injured?" I asked.

"Are being attended to," Saraya whispered. But there wasn't the confidence in her voice my heart craved.

Grayshell. So many souls left behind—healers and sentinels—leaving those souls nearly defenseless. Sarah had warned us that the hierarchy was poised to fall, and still, it crumbled right below our noses. Shame and anger flared in my chest, but no more power ebbed there. There was nothing left to draw forth; the last glimmering sparks had been surrendered to Alvara. As the rain finally ceased, I focused on the rise and fall of her exposed ribs, marred by livid purple bruises. As the air returned and left in soft sighs, I allowed my muscles to relax.

I peeled what was left of the linen tunic—the thin layer beneath her armor—from my body to wrap it around hers. She felt too exposed, lying there vulnerable and half-naked before us. Aren and Alec bowed their heads, guilt twisting their minds for not having guarded her sooner.

"Even if," my voice was husky, and the burning returned to my throat when I spoke, "the dimension fell, it lives on in all of us who have survived. We will not let it fall in vain. In the meantime, we must assume it still stands. That the wardings held. That the spell closed us off from it, and nothing more." Raking my nails through my hair against my scalp, I willed it to be true.

Something like pride flickered in The Commander's gaze as he nodded. "Well put, Commander Porter. As for our fallen, they deserve the honor of a soldier's funeral, and we will give it to them. Until we meet again."

"Until we meet again," we all murmured our assent. "May it be soon."

Weighted silence settled over us, a fog on the water. My eyes never left her. They traced her features, memorizing the outline of her body within the thin rain-soaked linen. Her still rising and falling chest. Alive. She was alive. After a long while, her breathing and heart began to quicken, and all my muscles went taut. Aren wiped the strands of hair from her face, and she gave a soft whine before licking her chapped lips.

It was only a whisper. Just my name. My body lunged forward of its own volition, and Aren helped her sit up, cradling her against his frame.

She gulped and then coughed, and Alec summoned a stream of water to her lips. She drank gratefully, then blinked open her eyes. They immediately found mine, and emotion welled there. My own eyes stung with the ache, but as her tears poured down her cheeks, my face grew wet, too.

too.

"August—" the sob broke her voice. "Michael?"

Aren and I exchanged glances, confusion mirrored in his expression.

"Ally, you're okay. We have you."

"I know. August, you...we—" She shook her head as though to clear it. Instead of trying to explain, she reached her long, stained fingers out to me. I shot my eyes to Aren, then closed the distance between us. I knelt by her hand, our faces so close our breaths mingled.

It was impossible to hide the tremor in my fingers or the racing of my heart. This wasn't how this was supposed to happen. Not how it was meant to go. But she had what we'd been waiting for. I swallowed my nerves and reached out to accept her outstretched hand.

SEVENTY-FOUR
REGRESSION
ALVARA

Michael stood looking out the window of our little apartment. The moon illuminated the tiny dwelling with a silvery glow, far greater than the faint orange flicker from the hearth. Most nights, he'd wake, terror plaguing his dreams and stripping his warm body from our bed. As I approached, he turned, his eyes softening. He reached out a long hand and stroked his calloused fingers down my face. I leaned into his touch, soaking in his warmth. He turned me away from him, pulling my back against his firm chest. Wrapping his long arms around me, Michael set his hands gently on my belly and kissed the length of my neck.

His breath warmed my cheek, and I felt blood rush there as he whispered, "I love you. And we will figure this out."

I nodded, leaning further into his warm embrace, desire stirring in my core—a longing to be touched and kissed, to feel entirely full.

After a long while, he kissed my cheek again and whispered, "Walk with me?"

I rushed through the rest of the memory that had haunted me for three eternal centuries: the way we pleaded for mercy that was never granted, how he fought them off as long as he could before they murdered him in cold blood on the icy Boston streets...

...Shrieks of agony filled my ears as I stared down the man in front of me. My stomach heaved at the terrifying reek of charred flesh, my eyes pouring with pain radiating through my muscles and the blistering of my skin from the long hours in the stocks. Jacob would save me—I didn't know how, but I knew he had to. It was the only way. I raised my head, my neck screaming

with the effort, squinting through the well of tears pouring down my cheeks to search for him.

No.

They had him; his limp body hung between two monsters pretending to be men. I screamed his name again and again. The villagers hurled more rancid remains at me, and I cried out as a liquid burned against my eyes. The smell of kindling. A blinding flash of light and panicked screams...and my name on the air.

The familiar voice screamed my name, brittle with agony, "Mary!!!"

He was coming for me. He would.

But the pain was blinding. The world was on fire.

That memory wasn't new to me, but *it* had never been *so* vivid. I'd never *known* the name of who I searched for in the crowd of people calling for my death. *Jacob...*

...*"Carlyle?" I called over my shoulder coyly. He had already stripped the heavy armor from his tight-muscled chest, weapons safely stashed under the shrubs to his side. His skin nearly glowed under the moon, and his smile was heart-shattering. I slowly stepped into the steaming spring, skin smarting as my toes inched into the rocky bed of clay and stone...*

...*"Saoirse, to you," I smiled softly at the young woman we called The Wraith. Her dark cloak matched the midnight shade of her ebony hair, which hung in a long braid down her back. Warm tawny skin, speckled with freckles, crinkled around a sly smile as the young woman rose from her bow.*

"With all due respect, Your Majesty, you have more than earned your title."

"With all due respect, your Queen believes you've earned a less formal tone. Aren't we friends yet, Niamh?"

"Friends, My Lady?"

"I would quite like to have one friend in the world, Niamh. And I would like it to be you."

"As you wish, Your Maj—" She grinned as I narrowed my eyes. "Saoirse."

Conn entered the room, his cloak billowing behind him, hair frosted with the kisses of winter. He closed the distance between us and set his palm against my face. I leaned into the embrace, inhaling his scent.

"My love, it's time to go..."

"...Frida? Frida, did you hear me?"

I shook my head frantically, tears soaking my face. My very soul was shredding in two as I begged, "Don't!" The demand fell short. "Stop talking like this." I raised my trembling hands, breath coming faster—too much faster—as I wiped his blood on my dress. Bjorn lifted his crimson palms, wrapping his rough, slick fingers around either side of my face. He raked his hands *through my hair, and a sob broke through my lips. I reached to set my hand across his sharp jaw, his tears soaking my palms. He kissed each eyelid, then my cheeks, breath coming in wet, haggard gasps.*

"Frida. With me and my father gone, the city will not hold. You must run. Promise me. Promise me you'll run."

"Stop!"

My agonized cry cut the vision off. There were more—so many more lives to dig through, but my energy was entirely spent. I opened my eyes to find four stunned faces in front of me. Aren's tight expression twisted in grief; Alec's eyes were wide. Young, beautiful, blood-spattered Freya was the only one with confirmation in her eyes, so like her brother's that they took me back. The Wraith—my *friend*.

August's hands trembled, his eyes wide, wild, and watering. His lower lip quivered as his gaze scoured mine, as though he could dive deeper into my soul.

Voice hoarse, he whispered, "Saoirse?"

His visible flood of emotion triggered my own, tears pouring freely in warm waves down my face. A wince escaped with the effort it took to rise off Aren's chest, sitting up as August shook his head softly.

"Yes. And Frida, Ceana—"

My explanation was cut short as August threw himself forward, his hands cupping both sides of my face with familiar gentleness.

Emerald eyes, red-rimmed, frantically searched back and forth between each of mine as memories bubbled to the surface at his touch. They were cut short as his shield slammed into me. I knew it only worked because my power was so spent, but I didn't care. His breath filled the space between us with his tantalizing scent as he leaned forward and silenced my words.

His lips were warm and urgent against mine, and it completely undid me. The world vanished. All the pain, fear, the ache of wounds, worn muscles, and drained power vanished into the abyss of August's kiss. Air no longer felt cold; it simply...was. My hands moved of their own accord, raising to tangle in his tousled hair, invigorated by the rain-saturated tendrils. He leaned back for the briefest moment, only to wrap his arms around me and hoist me onto my knees, guiding me to straddle over him. His arm remained, an iron anchor, wrapped around the small of my back. August's free hand returned to the side of my face, cupping my cheek and neck as his lips pressed down again on mine. Heat swelled from my core through my limbs, and I breathed it in. I reveled in it. Soaked in every ounce of desire, of longing, and of the tension that had built between us during those long months. Everything about his embrace felt like home—familiar and safe—and as vital as the air in my aching lungs. He pulled my bottom lip between his teeth, and my breath came faster, more urgent.

Again and again, he brought our lips together, the feel of our breath mingling, of his hand against my back, made my core coil like a spring begging to release. I brought my hand to his face and felt the tears still pouring from him—felt the many lifetimes of love and loss within them. Felt the pulse of his emotion through my chest as his heart hammered, just as rapidly as my own. All the grief I'd held for Michael through this life spilled forward, and a sob broke us apart. He kept my body pressed against his, the bulge against my thigh more enticing than I could articulate. I wanted him —all of him. To be his, forever. To connect after centuries apart.

August kept our foreheads pressed together, his calloused hands tracing my face, warm palms wiping the tears from my cheeks before stroking along the line of my neck. The heat of him caressed the sides of my breasts, then gripped my ribcage before squeezing my waist, as though he feared I'd vanish if he stopped touching me.

Perhaps one of us would. It certainly felt that way to me, too. When I finally opened my eyes, he did the same, and a frantic kind of laughter danced between us. We had survived the battle of the Renown. Survived August using himself as bait. We had found each other all over again. How many times had his soul tried to reach me?

After a long while, foreheads resting together, our breathing slowed. We peeled ourselves apart and looked around. Our companions had granted us a private reunion, and I saw them scattered through the clearing, levitating the injured to Saraya's improvised med tent and praying over the dead.

August cursed under his breath, and with a sigh, pushed himself away from me. He stood, looking every bit the Commander he was forged to be. He reached his hands for me, a cheeky grin on his face, and pulled me to my feet. I winced when the wound tugged on my leg, but looked down, relieved to see it had webbed itself back together. Gratitude swept over me. I caught August examining my injuries before he gave me an approving nod.

"Our people need us."

SEVENTY-FIVE
AFTERMATH
AUGUST

The rustle of tent flaps caught my attention as I stitched up a wound no one had the magic left to heal. I turned just as James and Sam stepped into the med tent, their eyes immediately snapping to me. Shoulders relaxing, I exhaled in a whoosh as they both closed the distance and threw their arms around me. None of us had many words to share, but we clung tightly to one another for a moment, apologies pouring from my lips as they muttered reassurances. I would find a way to protect them—somehow, someway, I would shield them for the rest of their too-short mortal lives.

We broke apart only when a small, timid voice croaked, "August?"

I whipped my head up, finding Layla, the neck of her ruined pajamas peeking out from beneath a familiar denim jacket that skimmed her thighs. I'd have to thank Alec for that later. Her face bore no evidence of what they had done to her, those wide eyes trained on me. James and Sam stepped back as Layla closed the gap, throwing her body against mine. I tentatively locked my arms around her, my heart aching as her sobs shook against me, weeping into my chest. I wrapped a hand around the back of James's neck, pulling him in as Sam looped his arms around the opposite side of us. We all bowed our heads together as Alvara appeared, offering me a small smile meant to comfort.

Westerlunds will take them for now. Keep them safe.

I pursed my lips, disliking the idea of splitting up one bit. But I nodded. Alvara would know—she would have looked for the best option before bothering me with it. She gave a pained smile and then nodded back before disappearing onto the field.

Freya and a handful of warriors from other covens were to accompany us to August's lake house, already guarded by wardings. It felt nearly treasonous to leave the twenty healing souls with so little protection—especially with Ansel among them. Had it not been the dead of winter, we all would have camped outside the cramped little cabin.

Marcus made his way over to us, his brothers flanking both sides, guards still high as they surveyed the meadow. He inclined his head in a respectful bow to Aren, who mirrored the motion.

"Grateful you're in one piece," August clasped Jason's shoulder, earning a wry smile.

"Glad you kept your sister from slicing my head off."

August chuckled, and my curiosity peaked. I laughed when I saw the memory, beyond grateful my mate had recognized those cerulean eyes.

"Will Ansel—" Marcus nearly choked on the words, and Aren finished for him.

"Heal? Yes. I'm praying it continues to go that way."

"What now?" Damien, his arm still slung around Alec's shoulders, turned to August, then to Aren. It was Aren who spoke.

"Find a way back to the Middle Realm. I'll walk the damned white desert if I have to. But we need a way in."

"Westerlund is at your disposal, Commander. We have room for more survivors. Call us should you need it."

"Thank you," we spoke as one unit, and Marcus flashed that grin I'd come to love. He inclined his head in a bow, and the brothers vanished.

Saraya's soldiers and the mortals between them followed only a heartbeat behind.

Dividing our forces felt so counterintuitive, but half a dozen large pods seemed the best option under the circumstances. Smaller groups would leave us too vulnerable until we could learn how Adrastos had broken our connection to Grayshell. Until we found our way back and could ascertain what demon they had been serving and how many more like them were waiting to strike.

Struggling to keep my eyes open, we begrudgingly formed our tight circle, joined hands, and made our way to the lake house. The moment we were satisfied we were not about to be attacked, we made up beds consisting entirely of blankets, too small for the soldiers' long frames. August's hand hadn't left mine since we landed, and he guided me to the kitchen, where he'd sent someone to prepare hot toddies. It felt as though I could truly inhale for the first time in many hours, and I took a moment just to breathe in his scent and listen to the steady thump of his heart. One gentle smile later, he led me to the small bedroom in the back of the cabin.

The floor was the same warm hardwood that stretched through the kitchen. Three walls were painted a mellow grey, trimmed in white, with one emerald-green accent wall across from us, adorned with a bold geometric design of wood trim. An industrial-looking platform bed took up the center, constructed of rustic dark wood and metal. It was a humble but tasteful master suite—luxurious but not extravagant or over-furnished. I smiled at the humility he'd shown even in one of his most successful lives. From what I'd seen of the visions, the soul we called August remained humble, even as a petty king.

Wordlessly, he led me to the white barn door beside the bed, gently pushed it open, and flicked on the light to reveal a small but stunning bathroom. Black granite counters and a matching slab glittered across the floor, which stretched into a meticulously organized closet. Great glass and metal doors framed a shower built of the same stone. The copper claw-foot tub was also quite alluring, despite the depth of my exhaustion.

He kissed my fingers before releasing them, my hand immediately aware of the absence. August pulled out two deep green towels and turned on the shower, which had a glorious array of modern jets spraying water from all heights on the wall, a skinny showerhead that could be removed, and a lovely rain fixture on the ceiling.

August turned to look at me, his expression clearly satisfied with my reaction as the corners of his beautiful lips quirked upwards.

"We have two tankless heaters—more than necessary, if I'm honest. So even if the others wash up, you'll have hot water if you want it. I'll give you some privacy." He bowed his head and turned to leave. I snatched his free hand and gave it a gentle tug. There was no way in hell I was letting him walk away—not after everything we'd survived.

Eyes locked on mine, he pulled me against his body, wrapping our tangled hands behind him to guide me closer. His lips were gentle as he kissed me, soft, heated, and yielding. His warm scent filled my mouth, nearly making my knees buckle. August smiled against me, feeling the weight I leaned into him.

My fingers found the hem of his shirt, and he raised his arms so I could peel it off him. Carefully, August stripped the hoodie from my body, his movements minutely aware of each healing injury. He kissed the wound on my shoulder and gingerly fingered the line of my bra. I exhaled softly and shrugged off one of the straps.

August chuckled when I tossed it aside and then pressed his body against mine, pushing me toward the glass wall. His warm skin, crushed against my breasts, felt akin to breathing air after drowning, filling my desperate body with tingling heat. The glass was still chilled, and I felt my breath catch as it pressed against my backside. In a quick movement, he dropped my underwear down my legs and leisurely traced a soft pattern up the backs of them, around the outside of my hips and waist. I rested my head against the shower door as the tickle worked its way up my body. He pressed his lips against my neck, my jaw, my lips, and suddenly he had both my wrists pinned above my head, the air escaping my lungs as my heart galloped. I didn't even mind the painful tug on the wound on my chest.

Bucking my hips, I could feel the hard length of him through the layer of pants between us. That heat, that intoxicating, addicting warmth swelled in my core, twisting and tightening. I raised my head as he kissed down my jawline, gulping in as much of the now-steamy air as my lungs could manage. Telekinetically, I pulled on the belt around his waist. When his lips reached my ear, he chuckled again and nipped at the lobe with his teeth.

"Not yet," he growled darkly, and a shudder ran down my body. He released my hands and stepped back. As he loosened his belt, his eyes scraped over my body from head to toe. He dropped his hold, and I took in the full length of him, my mouth going dry.

Chest heaving, August blew a controlled breath out and opened the shower door for me. His eyes again worked their way down my body, bringing a wave of heat to my cheeks as my mind and body contested for control.

"*Fuck*, Ally," his voice nearly rumbled. Guttural and teeming with want, he rasped, "You're so damn beautiful."

"Come here," I panted, stepping inside without hesitation. As he followed me into the shower, his fingers traced up the length of my spine. I pulled my hair around my right shoulder, turning my gaze to the left to see his face as heat licked up my flesh. August studied my back, and his rough fingers gingerly traced the patchwork of scars across my skin. With a soft click, the shower door sealed, and August closed the small gap between us, pulling me into him.

The near-scalding water was absolute bliss as it poured from so many sides down the length of our embrace and cleansed our skin. August wrapped his arm around my stomach, pulling our slick bodies together. Strong fingers traced the line of my collarbone, then he brought the removable showerhead against my chest. Warmth blossomed across my sternum as he danced the water across each of my breasts, using his free hand to gently caress my skin. With so much care, it brought tears to my eyes. August washed each wound and kissed every new mark and healing scar, all the while whispering that he loved me.

When the blood had all been washed down the drain, he took the time to wash my long hair. Delicately, I returned the favor, taking time to clean the wounds across his ribs and chest. Full lips upturned in the timidest of smiles, August turned off the water and swept my legs out from under me, lifting my body as though it weighed nothing.

August laid me down with breathtaking reverence, deliberately propping his weight on his arm. My heart stuttered as he cupped my breast, his lips pressing against my jawline. August grazed the skin across my neck with his elongated canines, and I arched into him, a whimper crossing my lips, pulse racing.

"Ally," he purred my name against my neck, between kisses. His warm hands traced tickling patterns across my belly, down the crease of my hip, and along my thigh before he slowly, so slowly, inched back up. I wrapped my hands through his hair to lock him to me, bucking my hips against his, wanting more.

He panted again, my name like a chant on his tongue, "Ally."

I wrapped my injured leg around his waist, ignoring the tug of barely healed skin, and pulled his body over onto mine. Bucking my hips again, he nearly growled, his desire evident as the hard length of him slid across my entrance.

"Mine," August growled, pressing his forehead to mine as he slid one hand down to the inside of my leg, this time more firmly, steadily caressing his way to the apex of my thighs.

"Prove it," I panted back, my voice breathless. His hunger took over then, and everything ignited; my power licked against my skin, craving to merge with his as much as my body did. August's movements turned feral as he dug his fingers into my ribs, encompassing my cage, while the pad of his other palm ran over my needy clit. My breath caught as a wave of pleasure shook through me, his fingers working expertly against that bundle of nerves.

The insatiable need for him became so overwhelming that it wouldn't take long for him to bring a peak crashing over me. I gasped as the wet tip of him slipped between my thighs again, the teasing anticipation torturous.

With a bit of effort, I squeezed my hand between us to wrap my fingers around his hard, smooth shaft. Two could play that game, and he responded with a low groan. The heat that had been building exploded when I touched him, burning through every inch of me as my core wound so tight I felt likely to burst if his fingers continued their movements.

"August, *please*," I panted, and a breathless chuckle rumbled in his chest. He moaned as his fingers pressed against my center, coming away soaked with my need for him. He rested his head on my shoulder, breath hot against my chest, as he slipped a finger into my entrance. A curse slipped through his lips just as my spine arched off the mattress in a spasm of pleasure. He growled, the vibration shimmering across my neck where his lips rested.

"Never thought I'd get to feel you again," he whispered before dragging himself out of me. August brought his fingers to his mouth, sucking on two before sliding one back inside me. "Fuuck, baby, you taste even better than I remember." He pumped his digit again, this time growling, "Fucking *mine*." My muscles rippled around him, pleasure coiling to an unbearable level as I nodded incoherently. Just when I thought I'd come apart around him, he slid out, only to put two fingers back in, his palm demanding against that bundle of nerves as he curled his fingers against my walls, my body writhing under his touch.

"God," I gasped. "August!" He continued his steady, leisurely rhythm as my body stretched around him. A dull ache formed as he worked in steady motions, his lips pressing kisses to my neck.

"Open up for me, little nova." August curled his fingers, hitting nerves so heightened that I lost control entirely, my eyes rolling back as my head fell to the mattress.

"August," I cried out on a desperate exhale.

August slid his fingers out, quickly wrapping both arms around me, locking our bodies together as he hoisted us upright. He sat on his knees, holding me over his lap, his body still wrapped around me like a vice. He reared back, eyes sweeping over my bare skin.

"You're so fucking perfect... beautiful," he breathed against my skin, trailing kisses around my breast until his tongue lashed out against my already pebbled nipple. The air hitched in my throat, goosebumps erupting down my body.

Gently, he nipped at my flesh, the teasing pain heightening my anticipation even more before he soothed the skin with a kiss. "Soaked," he said quietly, rumbling deep in his throat. Slowly, August slid his grip down to my waist, eyes locked on mine as he gently lowered me onto the length of him, pausing every few seconds to let my body stretch.

A moan of pleasure escaped me as my insides convulsed around him, ignoring the slight twinge of pain and reveling in the fullness. I closed my eyes, head falling back as I breathed him in.

August panted against my throat, his teeth tracing along my skin as he allowed me time to adjust to him. "And all fucking mine." I could feel the smile across his warm lips as we rocked together. He brought his mouth to the tender skin where my neck and shoulder met, kissing and sucking, sending waves of heat down my body.

My arms wrapped around him, fingers digging into his muscled back of their own accord, and then I pulled him forward, urging us back to the bed, needing his solid body over mine. He followed, mouth firmly planted against my own as we collapsed onto the mattress. Something between us stirred, like fire and sparks colliding. With agonizing slowness, he dragged himself out of me and then thrust back in. Again and again, he gradually sped up his movements, knowing how my body ached for release.

My heart hammered relentlessly against my ribs, and I knew he could hear it, just as I could hear his thundering away. August rose on one arm as he slid out again, stealing one last glance with my own as he stroked his fingers across my cheek and jaw before burying his face in the damp hair against my neck and pushing inside me again, sheathing himself fully. I cried out in pleasure, bucking my hips to meet his movement, my mouth falling open as he reached his free hand around to cup my ass and pull me tighter against him.

I couldn't remember—who I was, where we were, or why we hadn't been devouring each other the whole time. I couldn't recall my *name* as he thrust into me again, his kisses growing bruising with desperation as release barreled toward us both. That coil wound tighter and tighter within me. A gasp tore through me as that Soul Bond burned hotter, as though we were being welded together with each thrust, claw against flesh, and wild kiss.

August's movements were fluid as he drove himself in and out of me, panting against my neck until sweet, desperate release finally tore from my body, my eyes fluttering shut as I trembled with the force of it. He groaned as my body spasmed around him, and my waves of pleasure pushed him right over the edge. He thrust harder and faster until he stilled, buried to the hilt, as his own release pulsed, spilling himself inside me.

As he pulled out, August shifted his weight back onto the bed before guiding me onto his chest, his arm around my shoulders. I laid against him, my leg wrapped across his hips, careful not to lay my face over the clotted slice in his pectoral muscle.

Gradually, our breathing slowed and our hearts steadied as August traced feather-light patterns on my arm with his wonderfully calloused fingers. When our flesh had cooled considerably, he lifted the crisp sheet over us, and I nuzzled tighter against him, wordlessly kissing his chest. I could feel his smile before he chuckled and pressed his lips to the crown of my head. My eyes fell closed.

So softly I could barely detect it, August said, "Goodnight, Mrs. Porter."

I managed a small smile against the heat of his chest before sleep whisked me away.

SEVENTY-SEVEN

FAMILY

ALVARA

I closed the curtains tighter to buy August some extra rest, then tiptoed to the door, careful to close it with the softest click possible. The internal chatter of the warriors began to rush into my mind as I put distance between my body and my favorite shield. I winced, my blood turning hot as I realized with absolute certainty that there was no way their immortal ears had not heard our lovemaking. My dread was confirmed as I stepped into the bright kitchen, the reflection of snow bouncing light everywhere.

Ajax and Alastair were sprawled on the bar stools at the small kitchen island, scrambled eggs steaming on their plates. Both men looked enormous in those thin modern stools, their broad shoulders spread wide over the low backs. The brothers were almost naked, wearing only undershorts, their confidence oozing in waves as they occupied the space, coffees in their large hands. Ajax had the shoulder-length honey locks that adorned Brody's head, tucked into Greek beads as they had worn it in their first life. Alastair was the literal black sheep of the brothers, his dark brunette waves contrasting sharply.

Both brothers raised their eyebrows suggestively, lips twisted into teasing smirks as they sipped their steaming coffee in unison. Alastair's dimples popped into place, the true proof of his amusement. My blood flooded to my face, and I scrunched up my expression before burying it in my palms. There was a gentle clink of ceramic on stone as they began to slow clap, stoking the fire in my cheeks.

"Oh, shush, both of you!" I barked, raising my head and scowling at them. Alastair, a feral grin on his beautiful face, stood and moved silently to stand only feet from me. His eyes were still teasing, but he cocked his head to the side and stretched his arms wide.

"It's about time, second!" he boomed in that signature accent, not bothering to lower his voice. I felt the flush spread down my neck but accepted his hug.

"We've all been waiting," Ajax added, clapping me on the back.

"Lost a good bit of money, you know."

"We'd bet this would happen months ago."

"You're both so damn stubborn."

"That *reading*, though. Pretty God damned magnificent."

"Worth the wait, by the sounds of it."

I smacked the back of Alastair's arm as we separated. He was all smiles, an enormous cat that had eaten the canary.

"Shussssh!" My scowl returned, and they both roared with amusement, laughter shaking through my flushed body.

"*Now* she calls for quiet!" Alastair chortled.

"My dear, a *mortal* two doors down could have heard that consummation."

"Look at her blush. Do you think we can get her to a thirteenth shade of red?"

"Perhaps a reenactment for Ms. Goldman?"

"It's Mrs. Porter now," August's amused voice cut through the clatter of dishes and the men's teasing. They both grinned before falling silent, bowing their heads and taking their food upstairs to the loft. He pressed against me in an instant, his arm around my stomach, my body squeezed between his hips and the counter. August kissed my cheek, tucked my hair behind my shoulder, and trailed kisses down the back of my neck. My eyes fluttered shut as I leaned into him.

"You know," I breathed, "Aren will demand something more formal. A celebration, perhaps."

He laughed, the shudder of his ribs against my own as welcome as his embrace. Someone upstairs—likely Alastair—turned on *Days Like This* by Van Morrison.

"Fine by me. You will be a goddess in white."

"I think her chance to wear white ended last night," Freya laughed, slinking to the counter with the graceful prowl of a mountain lion. *The Wraith* was about right.

I grinned and slipped from August's grasp. She strode to meet me, and we wrapped our arms around each other, our hearts beating against one another.

"Hello, old friend." The words were a smile, and I pulled back to tuck a strand of short chestnut hair behind her ear. She wore it in a tight A-frame bob in this life, and it was strikingly fitting for her fierce energy. The bruises and cuts across her face had almost vanished entirely overnight, leaving only a thin white line and a bar of blush. She had been not only my assassin but also my lady-in-waiting and best friend in my brief life as Queen Saoirse. It had been lifetimes without each other, but it felt as though no time had passed. Her soul had followed August's. *Conn's*. And my gratitude was eternal for that.

"The others say you're a reader in this life. The best they've ever seen. Makes sense, given what you could do in mortal bones. I'll book a time for you to take a deep dive someday soon." She turned to August. "Brother," she said as she threw her arms around his neck. "I have to say, I prefer King to brother, you obnoxious twit."

August chuckled and crushed her in a bear hug that had her squealing in laughter. "Funny," his voice was a growl in their embrace, "I prefer *you* as an assassin."

I turned to the fridge as they continued their reunion and began pulling out what I needed. Someone had gone to the grocer while we slept: eggs, milk, bread, vanilla, and cinnamon. I was whipping together my batter when August returned to my side, a smile in his voice as he brewed a pod of coffee.

"Making French toast seems a little domestic for a queen, doesn't it?"

I flashed him a cheeky smile, and he grinned, tucking my hair behind my ear again. "Not more so than a king brewing his own coffee."

"That was a good life."

"Yes," I agreed. "It was."

"But I think finding each other post-ascension is better."

"I wholeheartedly concur."

August pulled aside the oversized t-shirt, exposing my shoulder, and trailed fiery kisses down my neckline.

We gobbled down our breakfasts while frying four loaves of whole wheat bread for our team, laughing and reminiscing over our coffee. It was when he slid me the third mug of steaming, bitter liquid that I finally sighed, reality settling in over me.

"We need to get clothes for everyone. We're a bit of a motley crew at the moment." I glanced at the gathered warriors in the living room and laughed at what appeared to be an enormous game of strip poker. So casually, they all settled in nothing but undergarments. A soldier's life, I supposed.

"I've already sent the *Oddessy* brothers into town to fetch clothes for everyone. I assumed August was fine with me dipping cash from the safe," Freya said nonchalantly from the couch, her nose in a book she'd swiped from the shelves. "They were eager to escape your nauseating reunion."

We exchanged smirks before bursting into laughter again. And then, wordlessly, August seized my hands and began to lead me in a dance to the guitar melody on the radio. We swayed shamelessly from side to side, and I breathed in his musk, fingers touching every piece of skin they could find, devouring the constant strobe of visions that came from a soul with so much shared history. He was mine. My husband. My soulmate. Everything. August was my everything. And good God, nothing in the world had ever felt so divine beneath my skin.

SEVENTY-EIGHT
LOST
AUGUST

Aren's hulking form was heavy with a sobering defeat, his forearms resting on his knees. His pale eyes were fixed on the snow below his boots. He wore only a long-sleeve t-shirt, jeans, and combat boots, unshaken by the chill of the mountain. The man *was* the mountain.

Alvara didn't drop my hand as she strode ahead, pulling me toward the little cabin. As she settled us on the porch next to her sire, I caught sight of Brody reuniting with his brothers in a wincing collision at the edge of my vision, his wounds still aching. The wood of the porch was cold and damp, even through the insulated jeans the brothers had bought for all of us. The smell of pine, smoking meat, and garlic hung heavy in the air, making my mouth water despite having gorged myself on the best French toast of my life.

Wordlessly, Alvara rubbed Aren's back, then pursed her lips into a tight line. When Aren raised his eyes to hers, they were rimmed with red.

"Aren?"

I needed my mind to be present, but she made me so God damned happy that I didn't really care if the world fell around us. But a defeated man had somehow replaced the hulking sixteen-hundred-year-old sage who had led our armies to brutal victory on the strength of his blade. He held out his great hand, and she took it in her own. Her eyes went distant for a moment, then snapped back to the present. The shadows flickering in her eyes were enough to decapitate my lightheartedness, leaving only fear in their wake. Alvara swore under her breath.

"The wounded?" I asked, dread gnawing at my stomach for those we had abandoned at the safe house. She shook her head, her brunette waves shifting with the movement.

"Grayshell. We still can't access Grayshell."

My stomach twisted.

"All those souls," his voice came out like gravel, rough and clipped. Pain rippled in those ancient eyes.

"We don't know that, Aren. Brody and his brothers came to us when we needed them. We couldn't get to Grayshell, but they could still escape Westerlund as planned. For all we know, nothing is wrong there, except for the number of missing warriors and healers."

"But I don't understand. That was Adrastos' spell. It should have broken when he fell." As the words left my mouth, I caught the anxious glance exchanged between Commander and second. "What?"

"Adrastos' body was not among the dead. Saraya's souls double-checked every corpse. Agamemnon was where you left him. Adrastos was not found." Anger, rather than fear, filled her eyes. Anger...and what looked like shame. She shook her head, brow furrowed, then her gaze settled on her hands, glaring as though they had failed her. Alvara's throat bobbed as she flexed her fingers before balling them into tight fists and lowering them to her sides. "What now?" Her voice was a husky whisper as she peered up at her sire, knuckles white and jaw tight.

Aren shook his head softly. "Adrastos is a problem for another day. He has no army. His general fell. You drove that blade in yourself. If he's alive, he was gravely wounded. He poses no threat compared to getting into Grayshell."

"He *is* the threat behind Grayshell. He must be alive, or we could go home."

Aren rubbed his temples, then his eyes flicked back to hers. "Will you call?"

It wasn't a command to a second; it was a plea to a confidant. A plea to a sister. A friend. She nodded, once. Alvara stood and pulled her fur hood over her head. Then she kissed his forehead, pecked my cheek, and walked away from us into the pines.

The living room had transformed into a crowded command center. Aren's luxurious leather furniture had been shoved and stacked against the wall in a haphazard tower of couches and chairs. Whiteboards had been pulled from somewhere and hastily nailed into the log walls. Stretching lists of names covered one board, while the other had a crudely sketched map of the globe, marking the locations of the Renown's attacks and known armies in red. Crawler attacks were in black.

Freya had marched inside like a commander on the warpath, barking orders and tossing out clothes. Graciously, the souls accepted the garments, tossing about shirts and jeans to ensure the right sizes got to the right people. They didn't pause to question the woman yapping directions—most exchanged amused glances behind the little newcomer's head—and a similar amusement filled me. She was just eighteen in this life and even slighter in stature than Fae. Her small body was still filling out with the strength of ascension, and I realized that she was the first soul I'd witnessed rise amid battle. But the soul within was far too large for the vessel that held it. How had I never felt that before? Never sensed her raw power? Been blind to the way her energy overflowed around her?

EMERGING INTO THE HALLWAY, a familiar scent and energy slammed into me before I saw them. Even Ansel, leaning his weight on Lana, smiled in greeting as our little coven entered from the back door. Alec, grinning like the Cheshire Cat, made straight for me. His hug was a blend of embrace and tackle. I laughed and returned his firm pat on the back.

"Miss me already?"

He mirrored the playful smile I shot him. "Always, brother." Alec narrowed his light brown eyes. "Your energy is...different."

Fae, smiling coyly as she appeared at his side, chimed in, "He's a mated man now. Or can't you tell?"

Alec's grin spread from ear to ear as he clasped my shoulder, squeezing it almost painfully in congratulations. "About damn time, you two. Sweet Jesus, it took you long enough."

"Only in this life, by the looks of it."

He snorted. "I'll admit, I don't understand how I didn't recognize her as Anna. That bit confuses the hell out of me. Alvara and I have read each other's souls to the depths until we scraped bottom. Or thought we did."

"It seems there's a lot of confusion going on for a coven of omniscient beings."

"Only in our egos, mate. We've never truly achieved such a thing."

"Evidently not."

His grin turned teasing as he raised his brows. "Worth the wait, I assume?"

Fae smacked his arm in scolding, but her eyes locked on mine curiously. My answering smile was all he needed to know.

A gust of icy air slammed into us, and I lifted my eyes as Alec turned. Aren had come in through the back door to the hallway, a soft smile on his face. The door clapped shut behind him. He cleared his throat, and amusement replaced some of the shadow in his eyes.

"So, congratulations are in order then."

I gave him a gentle smile. "Thanks for keeping her safe for me all these years."

He nodded. "You damn well better do the same for the next ones."

"Of course, Commander."

He grinned and crossed the hall to wrap me in a crushing bear hug, his shirt like ice and smelling of pine and snow.

"You two lovebirds get any more answers about The Great Commander?" He pulled away but left his hand on my shoulder.

"Weird snippets. We talked about everything over breakfast, and Alvara says we'll need a much deeper reading to go back so far."

Aren nodded knowingly and stuffed his hands in his pockets. "A man can hope, I guess."

"She'll get there; she always does." Ansel's voice was low but stronger than it had been when we left him last. I turned to him, and gratitude swelled in my chest. Gratitude that needed to be spoken.

"Alvara told me what you did last night—sharing your blood so she could see Freya for what she was. Opening yourself up, after all these years, so she could prepare herself. Thank you."

"She readied all of us, knowing August had an ally close enough to do something. You saved our lives, Ansel," Aren added. "Showing Alvara what needed to be done, allowing her to become the distraction and draw out Adrastos—it changed the tide."

Ansel's lips pressed tight, and he lowered his head in a tentative nod of acknowledgment. Freya stalked into the too-crowded hallway, weaving around us with inhuman speed, her stealthy movements powerfully feline. She wrapped her arm around Ansel, taking some of his weight on her little shoulders. Ansel's eyes gleamed with silver, and he kissed her temple. She and Lana led him out of the hall and into the living room. I nudged Aren gently in the ribs.

"How does she remember? So much, I mean? My memories came trickling back through triggers, but it seems like Freya remembers everything."

"Some souls do. It's not an exact science. She has died in both mortal and ascended past lives defending you or Alvara. It would make sense that she would remember what her task had been when she awoke to you in mortal peril again. That was her trigger. And soul parents that breed an ascended soul—that's a hard connection to lose."

The explanation didn't diminish the strangeness of it all, but I nodded nonetheless.

"You and Alvara haven't ascended together?" I shrugged. Aren frowned as he spoke. "Odd. Those memories are generally the first to return."

"Something to do with the binding?" I guessed.

"Must be."

I felt for her then, sending my energy out to find her focused on a flame in her palm, her thoughts hazy as she continued to cast them toward Grayshell. Relentless.

"Doesn't feel like she's had much success," I said grimly. Aren's lips pressed into a tight line, and his throat bobbed again.

"I know."

"She'll keep trying, though."

He nodded, took a heaving breath, and patted me on the shoulder before turning to leave.

In breaking our connection, Adrastos knew exactly what he was doing.

SEVENTY-NINE

ALLIES

ALVARA

Aren vowed that as soon as all our souls were whole, we would jump to a beach somewhere, where August and I could be formally wed. While neither August nor I cared much for formalities, Aren beamed a mischievous, toothy grin that left no room for negotiations.

"It's not actually about you, Ally. The least we can do, after all this hell, is give everybody something to celebrate."

We acquiesced, and his answering grin was so bear-like that I nearly shot coffee out of my nose. My mug made a soft ceramic clink as it met the hard table in the cabin's kitchen.

If I was honest with myself, I wanted to be formally married to August, in front of our coven and our friends. I wanted to be pronounced Mrs. Porter, for him to see me as his bride, and to kiss me as his newlywed wife, as mortals did. Our last wedding had been more than three hundred years ago, with no money and no family left to attend. Reading my mind, August beamed and leaned his forehead against mine.

"A beach wedding sounds lovely," he whispered, our breaths mingling between us as I smiled. "Well, an ocean-view wedding," he corrected, always thinking of me. I nodded softly, our foreheads bobbing together. Slowly, he pressed his warm lips against mine, and that agonizing heat spread through my core. August swiped his tongue over mine, and I welcomed his deepened kiss. Torturously, we pulled apart but kept our faces glued together.

"We still have a safe house in Naples, don't we?" I managed, my wide smile making the question lighter.

Aren didn't have to be visible for me to feel his enthusiasm. "A few, actually."

"The oceanside monster, with that giant balcony?"

"I could never part with that one."

"Naples is just lovely this time of year."

"It is, and I'm thinking yellow, for your sunny disposition," Aren teased, and I snorted.

"I'm thinking cerulean blue, like the ocean." The words came out breathy, almost foolishly mortal, as I allowed myself to dream for a moment.

August interjected, "White and blue, like the dress you wore to the All-Saints Day feast."

We locked eyes, and even with Aren's gaze on us, even with the winter wind creeping through the open kitchen window and the weight of Grayshell on my shoulders, it felt like the world vanished in those green irises. It was as if my life began and ended right there, in August. The moment was amputated by reality.

"The first group is ready to head south, Commander." Brody stood, body taut, hands formally placed behind his back at attention. Ever the soldier, with his two beautiful, lethal brothers flanking him on either side. There had been no visions, no leads on Adrastos since his body vanished, but the sinking sensation that he lurked in the shadows had left all of us on pins and needles. The search would begin by finding our allies within the hierarchies.

"Reyna should expect you, but proceed with caution. Our last battle beside the Bellatons didn't end the *most* amicably. Ally and I have discussed it at length. Take The Wraith. She'll prove useful. But wait for my command. We have a wedding to plan. It's near her territory anyway."

The three warriors lowered their heads in unison and left the room. A handful of our fighters followed in their wake, and I noticed August had stiffened. "You're sending Freya? She hasn't trained."

My fingers slid between his, and I gave him a gentle, reassuring squeeze as visions flashed.

"She has a divine memory," Aren explained. "In times like these, that will have to be enough. Her particular skill set could be... useful if Reyna needs convincing to join forces again."

"Reyna prizes cleverness," I added. "If Freya can best her and her defenses, it will command a certain level of respect."

"Freya is also *untarnished*," Aren continued, not hiding his distaste for the word. "That will be valued as well." Aren's face went solemn and thoughtful. "Reyna likes rules. Traditions."

"Staunch old bitch, and you know it," Ansel spat from across the room.

Aren's lips twisted into a smirk, but he stifled his laughter. Others did not, and I chuckled despite myself.

"Even so," Aren conceded, "your heir will be more welcome than I am."

Ansel gave a quick nod of approval and then relaxed back into his cushion. Being sedentary exhausted him far more than battle ever had. Fae and Lana were on either side of him, noses glued to their books. The fire popped and skittered as an ember burst, the pieces settling.

"You two will track down our cousins in the North—find Thornquist and his clan of shifters. Alec and Fae will connect with Marcus—I'll send word for them to prepare. When the rest are healed, Ansel and Lana will head west to find Nathara and her coven."

"Aren. Are you sure about bringing her into the fold? It's Nathara. Her coven believes they're witches."

"What we can do is not all that different from magic, is it?" Aren countered, brows raised.

"No, it's not," August agreed, perhaps too quickly.

"It's our best plan to start. Nat might not be... orthodox, but she will ally with the light if and when the time comes."

"I will choose to trust your intuition." A concession from a second to my Commander. Nathara and her witches brewed potions and tinctures, whipping up life-saving poultices like the best in Grayshell. But they also burned sage to cleanse the energy—why not dispatch the fuckers?—and charged crystals in the sun and moon, engaging in most forms of new-age sorcery. The fact that they proudly claimed the title of *witch* over Nephilim had always rubbed me the wrong way, as had their dedication to staying earth-side rather than existing in the Middle Realms with the rest of us. They had a shadowed counterpart fighting for territory in the South, and that fact stuck like an arrow in my chest.

I hesitated but still asked, "Are you going to the *Paladins*?" I tried to suppress the mocking tone, but it slipped out involuntarily. Aren's smirk, laced with equal amusement and shadow, made it worth it.

"We will sooner have a snowball fight in Hell than get Reyna to stand with the Paladins."

We would sooner have a snowball fight in Hell than have the Paladins stand with *us*.

Something stirred within me. A thread, I realized, faint and shadowed, pulling on... Aren. I narrowed my eyes at him, prompting the vision forward, receiving a flash of the bluest eyes I'd ever seen, framed by onyx hair, but the image dissolved. Whether it had not solidified yet or I simply wasn't meant to receive it, I wasn't sure.

"Aren, *you're* supposed to be the one to go west, if I'm reading this right."

Aren had always found the witch clans amusing, if nothing else. He honored Nathara as their Commander—their "high priestess"—and she had always been well-tempered and hospitable towards us. Even so, the idea of Aren marching into crawler territory on the west coast alone didn't settle well with me. So I added, "I would prefer Ansel and Lana accompany you. But it seems to be you who needs to go west. No one elsc." He asked no questions, pried no further; he could see in my mind that I had no details to give him. Aren simply nodded.

"Looks like I'm heading west then."

EIGHTY

SISTERS

AUGUST

There was nothing routine or ordinary about the beachfront mansion the coven had acquired years back. According to Ally, the grand estate had cost an absurd amount of money for any mortal to acquire and an equally absurd sum to furnish the damn thing. But I'd hand it to Aren; it was magnificent.

A gargantuan Spanish villa—built of stone, stucco, and ceramic tiles—stretched across a manicured lawn. It bore a guest house, a pool, and a mind-boggling wrap-around deck, poised like a jewel at the southernmost tip of Port Royal.

"Holy hell," I breathed as we pulled into the driveway. I couldn't conceal the awe in my voice. It was the same breathless phrase I'd mumbled when Ally tore the cover from her McLaren in the private hangar we'd jumped into. If I was honest with myself, I should have guessed that an immortal lifespan had collected immortal luxuries, but I'd never seen them do something so flashy. But the estate...

The stretching palm leaves rustled and hissed in the calm breeze, and the steady crash of waves immediately slowed my heart and eased my muscles. Even so, we paused and raised our hands toward the estate, stuffing my shield entirely within the box I'd carved for it so she could get a full read on the house.

She led me from one extravagant room to the next, in between kisses and caresses. The heat of her skin against mine, the thrill of past life memories, the slide of her palm along my back and down my neck had my blood roaring. I didn't hear a damn thing she said about the artwork or architecture.

"Jesus," I growled as she stroked her fingers along my cock through the denim. I grabbed her waist, yanking her against me, earning a trill of laughter as I forced her back against the nearest door, caging her in with my body. My mouth came down hard and demanding, and her lips fell open. With a flick of her tongue, I was lost in the taste of her.

Radiant face full of mirth, she pulled me into the bedroom. *Her* bedroom, I realized, as the collection of books became obvious, even here. They were stuffed everywhere. The white plaster walls climbed to a curved, vaulted ceiling, and I was vaguely aware of a chandelier hanging in the center, a million-dollar turquoise view stretching beyond.

But Ally was yanking my shirt free, hot breath raising goosebumps on my chest. I raked my fingers through her hair, sucking and pulling at her lower lip as she backed up until she bumped into one of four tall, arched windows. I traced my fingers up the line of her leg as she hitched it around my hip and palmed against the apex of her thighs. A groan tumbled from me as I found her absolutely soaked for me. Alvara moaned as I sucked at the skin of her neck, and her back arched as she pressed into my groin. That sound—God, that sound. I would devour her whole if she let me.

"You're mine," I whispered against her ear, and she shuddered within my arms. She nodded and then claimed a kiss, warm and urgent.

"And you're mine," she whispered.

"I'm yours." The words ignited my soul.

ALVARA

SOMEONE WAS SITTING ON ME. My hip ached, but the excitement in the air made up for any discomfort, as did the already familiar scent.

"Good morning, sleepyhead!" Freya slid off my hip and onto the bed, cradling herself against my torso. She tucked her auburn hair behind an ear and grinned at me. I blinked as my eyes adjusted to the blinding light around me.

"August?"

"No, silly, it's me. Frey-ah," she smirked. "I've banished your betrothed to the pool house with the other brooding warrior types, as per tradition." She rose, and, lithe as an incarnate shadow, strode to the window, throwing back the last of the curtains and pushing the blinding glow to an unbearable level. "The last time I watched you two get married, it was in a castle on the Irish moors, heavily guarded by knights. And while I suppose celestial warriors aren't that different from knights, I think this one will be much more fun."

"I certainly hope so," I yawned as I sat up, stretching my arms and rolling my neck. The familiar scent caught my attention, and I grabbed the coffee off the bedside table, sipping it down gratefully.

"He said you're basically useless without it, so I decided we'd get a jump on things." She clapped her hands twice—so loudly I flinched—and startled to see Fae and Lana dancing into the room, their broad, beaming grins brighter than the sun, arms full of fabric, curling irons, and an intimidating box of cosmetics. My stomach flopped backward like a pancake, and I snapped my eyes up to my soul sister, who merely grinned in response. Eyes stinging, I blinked, frantically trying to force the tears back down.

"You alright there, Ally?" Fae turned one armchair toward the window, rather than away from it, and tapped the back expectantly. I obliged her request, my heart a thunderclap in my chest.

"I just—I didn't think... After I lost Michael, I never thought I'd..." Their joy as they surveyed me knocked me right over the edge, tears pouring freely down my cheeks.

"Ooooh! Ally, sweetie!" Fae squealed, diving forward to sit on my lap. She wrapped her arms around my neck as Freya stepped forward to wipe the tears from my cheeks.

Together, we all wept, even Lana, her hand pressed to her lips as if she could contain the sobs while jerking her gaze away. I didn't bother. I let them rock through me as I thought about every life, each moment, and the thin threads that finally wove our paths back together. I thought about every detail of my mate: the way he smiled, studied, fought, loved; the way he followed me to death's door, unflinchingly; his unwavering honesty and loyalty.

And I knew what I had to do.

AUGUST

FREYA AND LANA had banished me and the boys before the coffee had even brewed. Alec had taken to firing up our own pot in the pool house's kitchen, while Aren tackled breakfast. Ansel was stretching by the window, his eyes on the vendors decorating the pristine lawn below. He was still a bit stiff but miraculously healed, save for the cruel purple scar stretching the entire length of his torso.

Aren had a chipper wedding playlist playing over the speakers, currently blaring *Gotta Good Feelin'* by Pigeon John. Some of the vendors, clearly fond of their client, sang along as they lined up chairs, draped nearly everything sedentary in white gauzy fabric, and positioned endless clusters of extravagant flower arrangements across every surface.

Alec laughed behind me, drawing my attention from the flurry of activity. Ansel, too, turned around to see our friends at the kitchen island. Alec was pouring us each a mug of coffee, and Aren was just behind him, sloshing a few ounces of Baileys into each cup.

"As the last time the two of you tied the knot *with* an audience was in Ireland, I figured we should make our coffee Irish today!" Aren raised his eyebrows along with his mug before taking a sip. "God, that's the stuff. Why don't we make all our mornings Irish?"

Alec snorted before taking a sip of his own. Ansel strode over, his long steps a bit stiffer after his injuries. He held a hardback book-sized gift wrapped in silver and white paper. Alec and Aren both beamed.

"A human tradition we decided to keep for ourselves," he explained, setting the rectangular box down on the counter with a heavy clunk. With a few quick motions, the ribbon unraveled, and I peeled away the precisely wrapped paper. Inside was a beautiful cherrywood humidor with a glass inlaid lid, revealing rows of wrapped cigars.

"You know, those are a bit of a collector's item."

"I would expect nothing less, gentlemen. Thank you."

"But... we're going to smoke 'em, right?" Alec grinned, and the Commander mirrored it.

"Hell yeah, we are. August and Alvara are getting married. There isn't a *more* special occasion than that."

"Hear, hear!" I wheeled toward that familiar voice, my cheeks aching as I spotted Sam and James standing in the doorway.

Sam closed the distance first, and we wrapped each other in a great bear hug. He laughed and pulled back to look at me. I grabbed his chin, turning him roughly this way and that. No sign of the black eye, broken nose, or bloodied mouth. Saraya's healers had done beautifully.

"All good, buddy! Your friends saw to that. You're good now, too, right?"

"Yeah, man. I'm alright. Ally, too, thank God." I turned to James, whose expression softened as he gave me a grin that didn't quite meet his eyes. "You okay, kid?"

"Yeah, I'm alright. Layla and I are both a little... shaken up. But we're alright."

The song ended and immediately transitioned to *Alive* by Tyrone Briggs.

"No more talk of war," Ansel, of all people, cut in, raising his mug. Aren slid two fresh cups across the counter, and Sam and James accepted them without question. Together, we toasted to Alvara.

THE STRETCHING green lawn had transformed into something magical. Twinkle lights glittered everywhere, and people were still buzzing about, getting the last of the details in order. The boys had decided we should take a break to catch a wave. Water still ran in rivulets down my body as I crossed back over the grass toward the pool house.

August? Alvara's mental voice halted my walk, and I grinned.

Hey, beautiful. How are you?

Better now that I can see you. I covered my eyes, and her laughter shimmered through the mental bond between us. My heart swelled against its cage. *It's just me in the dress you're not supposed to see. I, uh...*

A moment passed before I pressed back. *Ally? You okay?*

It was quiet for a bit before she responded. *I'm... feeling humbled.*

Humbled?

I just can't believe you're mine. You're here.

I chuckled, feeling her warmth between our minds, somehow even stronger now that we'd solidified our soulmate bond. *Same, beautiful. Same.*

August, I need to tell you something.

That doesn't sound good.

Well, it's... not. It's not good.

Ahh shit, you changed your mind.

A soft laugh. *Never. But August, I've made so many mistakes. I...*

Mrs. Alvara Goldman-Porter. There is no mistake you could make that would eclipse my love for you. Our love is not something fragile. It can handle missteps. At least, I hope you feel the same, because to be frank, I am a hot mess.

Nothing. No giggle or tug. Just quiet.

Ally? A shudder traveled down the line. *Sweetheart, are you crying?*

Maybe.

Relief washed over me, mingling with the desire to soothe, comfort, and protect. *Can I hold you?*

Freya would kill us.

She can try.

You should know, though, August...

Alvara, there is nothing you could do to change my mind. You are my soulmate. There's nothing you can say to change that—and whatever you're worried about, we will face it together.

Until the very end?

Baby, even then, I'll see you in our encore.

She was quiet for another moment, and I walked back toward the pool house, back toward the laughter of my now sea-drenched companions.

I love you. She finally answered.

Love you too.

See you at the ceremony.
I'll be the one in the tux.
A mock purr came down the line.
I threw my head back and laughed.

THE MURMUR of the crowd rising to stand sent a chill down my spine, despite the warmth of the day. Alec tapped my shoulder, and I turned around, my heart hammering in my ears. I didn't bother to hide the tears rolling down my cheeks as our eyes found each other down that flower-covered, shell-lined aisle. Those eyes, first seen in dreams a lifetime ago, were my home, my salvation, my anchor to this world.

Wordlessly, Aren slid his arm out from under hers and offered me her hand. I nearly choked, and a tear streamed down her cheek as I accepted it. The Commander stepped up to his place on the podium.

But it was to Ally that my eyes remained glued.

EIGHTY-ONE
SURPRISES
ALVARA

I stared off the balcony at the rumbling waves, glancing between them and the sky, a glimmering blanket of infinite darkness that kissed the distant, glistening waters. The bliss of the day faded with the sun, leaving in its place a dark expanse of the unknown. The same horrible memory played on a loop in my mind. My visions were still absent as August stepped up beside me.

His expression was gentle as he said, "I have an idea—don't *look*—just play along." When he noticed my narrowed eyes, he laughed. "Do you trust me?" I nodded. "Want to do something crazy?"

"Crazier than getting married?" I retorted.

He snorted, removing his shirt to reveal that spectacular, chiseled frame. "God, I think so."

"Damn." My lips quirked, but I studied him for a moment before offering a small nod. "Okay, Mr. Porter. I trust you." The moment the words left my mouth, the sight of his grin made my trust flee. But there was no time to adjust or defend myself, as August lunged forward, scooping my legs out from under me, and we jumped.

My spine went ramrod straight against him as we landed on the beach. Only the reflection of moonlight illuminated the undulating surface. August stood *in* the sand, and every muscle in my body seized.

"August, I—"

"Have not felt sand beneath your toes or the ocean on your feet in nearly three hundred years." I stared at him, and he gave me a gentle smile. "So, God sent you...me."

August slowly, gingerly knelt in the sand, propping my body on his lap, and filled a hand with the soft grains. He held it up within reach, and I eyed him for a moment, earning a wink. A deep, steadying breath later, I reached a tentative finger forward and caressed the warm, supple surface. My eyes rounded, and August grinned.

"I've been thinking a lot about the bond and how we connected after the battle." He let the sand slide through his fingers and scooped up a palm of water. I closed my eyes, flinching despite myself, but dipped my fingers into the cool cup of the sea. Nothing. August grinned, triumph in his eyes, as he set me on my feet and pulled me toward the tide, wading in backward himself. The waves gently broke against our legs, and I closed my eyes, allowing my skin to absorb the sensation of the warm saltwater, to savor every inch of the immense presence still detectable through the shield. I narrowed my eyes as he gently slid his hands back down my arms, lingering on the very tips of my fingers. And then he released me. I flinched, but the might of the ocean's memories left me unscathed. Nothing. Just internal silence and the external rumble of the waves greeting the shore.

"How did you...piece all this together?"

"Call it a gut instinct."

I wanted to smile, wanted to revel in the feel of this moment. But the heaviness I had wrestled with for days could be contained no longer. It pressed against my mind, a slithering snake made of guilt and grief, shoving its way free.

"August?" The word was hardly a whisper.

"Yeah?"

"I still need to talk to you...about...what's been bothering me." Shame washed over me, and I wondered if he could see the blood flush my face in the moonlight. He squeezed my hand in silent encouragement.

My lip trembled, and I sucked in a breath, trying to anchor myself in August, in the ocean against my feet...but the salt in the air became the taste of *his* sweat, and the warm splash of a wave drenched my fingers in too-familiar blood.

"I...couldn't put down Adrastos." The hand at my side flexed, and my breathing turned harsh in a futile attempt to push away the ghost of his dark eyes and the sticky coat on my trembling fingers.

I dove for the golden dagger, my throat raw with the cry tearing from it as his superior reach granted him the advantage. But as his fingers grazed the intricate hilt, the blade rattled against the earth, and in the next beat, the warm metal slid across the dirt into my hand. I rolled to my feet, barely noticing the ruby that glowed like embers against my skin. As I twirled forward in that fateful strike, shock burned in his eyes—a petrified recognition—and the blade showed me a single shattered image...

A wave collided with my thighs, rocking my balance and snapping me back to the present. I sucked down a breath. "I couldn't finish it."

I expected August to curse, recoil, or lecture me about my foolishness in not gutting him like the swine he was.

But when I opened my eyes, August's were glued to my face, studying my reaction, a soft, sad smirk carving his lips.

Gaping, I breathed, "When did you know?"

"The cabin."

And he'd said nothing. The real question was...

"*How?*"

He chuckled darkly, no trace of humor in the tilt of his mouth as he said, "You don't miss. And his heart is still beating."

Air leaked from my lungs like a punctured balloon, my shoulders falling as I flexed my fingers again. In that one pivotal moment, my hesitation had destroyed everything.

"I lost us Grayshell." The confession alone threatened to split me in two, the weight of it crippling.

August moved toward me as I took a shuddering breath, his strong hands wrapping around my biceps and pulling me against him, letting me bury myself against his bare chest. "I had one fucking shot. *One shot* to take him out, and—" A dry sob cracked my words as I fought the burning in my eyes. The words went breathless and began to string together as my ribs constricted. "And I lost my chance, and I'm messing everything up—the visions are a *mess*, and the horsemen are still coming, and *Adrastos...*"

"Ally." His tone dripped reproach, but I couldn't stop the words from tumbling out.

"I failed, August. Now the entire hierarchy is paying for it. Aren, you, Ansel. You're all paying because *I failed*." I raised a hand to wipe at the hot tear escaping, but August seized my wrist, wiping it away himself. "Adrastos will stand with them, and August, he's my—"

"I know," he interrupted. "Look at me."

When I didn't comply, another shuddering breath cracked through me. His fingers wrapped around my jaw, tilting my face until I slid my eyes shut. "I failed."

"I said *look* at me."

Heart racing like a murderous staccato, I did. The steady determination in his gaze stilled the panic running laps in my veins.

"Alvara Marie Porter. One damn hesitation in centuries of discipline does not make you a failure. You think Aren wouldn't have pulled that strike if he'd been in your shoes? You think any of us wouldn't have? Bullshit, baby. There's still some humanity in all of us." I turned my chin to the side, but August tightened his grip, dragging my eyes back to his and pulling my waist into his body with the other arm. "Listen to me. You couldn't have known. We handle this threat like we always have. Together."

On a shaky breath, I made to protest. "August, I'm—"

"Still the second in command of Grayshell. You will soldier the fuck up and figure this out. We all will." When I nodded against him, he continued, "Does knowing who he was change anything?"

I shook my head as much as I could, and when it was obvious my intention was no longer to hide, he released me, sliding his hand to the back of my neck to bring our foreheads together.

"No."

"Good. Then you won't miss twice."

I closed my eyes, anchoring myself there in the surf. August shifted around my body until his chest pressed against my back, his arms wrapped around me, as though he could protect me if I was concealed in their cage. We stared toward the future barreling down on us.

They were coming, whether we were ready or not. We had only one month before Adrastos predicted the first horsemen would arrive to wreak havoc on the world. One month, and Aren was trusting me to put all the pieces on the board, exactly where we needed them.

August was right. No matter the price...I wouldn't—*couldn't*—miss twice.

I turned to meet his gaze, which was teeming with challenge. "It looks like I have a heart to claim."

EPILOGUE

THE KING

Adrastos knelt on the black marble floor, his dark locks matted with blood. The tiles devoured the crimson as it pooled, indicating how quickly his body was losing its lifeforce.

The whip cracked.

His entire body jolted with agony; every muscle in his jaw and neck tensed as his arms strained against their binds.

With a flick of a hand, the soldiers released his deficient second, who collapsed into the gathering pool of blood, scarlet splatters painting his arms and face.

The King quirked a brow. This fucker refused to scream. Refused to show any indication that his wounds caused him pain, save for the brief grimace and the clench of his jaw.

A servant rushed to hand the King Adrastos' own sword when he held out a hand, the metal hissing as he pulled it from the sheath. "Pity," he drawled, "to waste such a useful skill set."

"I just need more time," Adrastos gritted through clenched teeth. He forced himself upright, his face contorting with pain as he balanced on his heels. "She will come to see our way, and he will follow."

"You failed. We'll be doing this my way now." The King slammed the sword back into place before addressing his newly appointed second, standing at attention, and jerked his head towards Adrastos. "Get this filth off my floor." She tucked a long silver strand behind her ear and raised her hands to summon him from his pathetic knees on the marble. There was no turning Alvara of Grayshell, right hand of Commander Amadeus. If the Porters wouldn't kneel, it was time to make them bleed.

TO BE CONTINUED...

READ COMMANDING EARTH AND SHADOW ON AMAZON.

WANT MORE ALLY & AUGUST?
READ THEIR BONUS CHAPTER HERE.

PREVIEW OF COMMANDING EARTH AND SHADOW

AREN

Night fell with the finality of an arena's roar of approval. The incessant sensation of Adrastos somehow watching us had my eyes peeled wide, staring at the undulating shadows of palm trees between stripes of light on the wood floor of my Florida bedroom.

Every life lost haunted those shadows. Haunted _every_ shadow. Every face, every name seemed to whisper within them, making sleep an evasive bastard. I swore, rising to rub at my eyes.

Of all the gifts to not be granted, I was barred from the one element my enemy excelled in the most. Between Adrastos' abilities and the fact that at least two of his reapers were still in play, I was battling a sense of dread that seemed to permeate every bone in my body, bleeding into the thread of my clothes.

Yet, those waving palms seemed to beckon me outside.

_My_ people. All I could think about was the way they voluntarily traded their lives to protect innocents. There wasn't a more Grayshellian way to go, and yet guilt had been omnipresent since we walked off the field. There should have been another play. Should have been a thread with a less catastrophic outcome. Jesus, the relentless mental acrobatics were exhausting.

Fresh air couldn't hurt...

With a huff, I abandoned my room, throwing open the door to the back yard and sucking down a lungful of warm air as I surveyed the thick layer of fog. It was as though the sea had breathed out the moisture it no longer wanted and given it to the land. In offering, perhaps.

And yet, as I walked across the manicured grass of my sanctuary, I couldn't shake the feeling that the fog and darkness were co-conspirators, watching me with those ever-present, unseen eyes. *His* omnipresent, unseen eyes. I had never faced a victory that felt so devastatingly like a loss. Never encountered an enemy that cost me so much. Adrastos would pay. But for that to happen, we had to get ahead of the sick bastard.

The sprawling property settled into complete silence, save for the hushed roar and hiss of the wake breaking on the sand before me, and the occasional bubble in the pool as the filters worked tirelessly. I focused into the darkness, willing my eyes to prod and poke, searching for the enemy I knew would inevitably come knocking. I just wished he'd get it over with already—was ready for the fight. For motherfucking retribution.

Ally had come so god-damned close. But his head belonged to me at this point, and I craved nothing as much as ending this with my own two hands. I owed it to my lost souls. The problem was, he was only the beginning.

It was knowing that, that drew my attention over a shoulder, not even the silent general able to outmaneuver trusty old intuition.

"Couldn't sleep," I stated, though Ansel had said nothing, aloud or otherwise. Ansel Callahan was the kind of man Commanders would fight to the death to possess, and he'd served as my right hand for centuries.

Christ, I'd almost lost him. The thought had my stomach threatening to wretch on an hourly basis. In a wordless show of solidarity, my advisor came to stand beside me, crossing one arm under the other to brace a hand under his jaw. He sucked on a canine before averting his gaze to the crashing ocean.

"Anything?" I slipped my hands into my pockets, keeping my focus on the fog as it threatened the perimeter. Ansel's long-suffering sigh said enough.

"He's in the wind, Ar. The order went out without room for negotiation. Adrastos' head on a platter, along with whoever he's serving. It's just a matter of time before something turns up."

"Yeah," I agreed, although the word sounded empty. We needed answers and we needed them now. Adrastos had outmaneuvered us at every turn, giving my second a run for her money. Which was fucking saying something. Even when she'd served us the upper hand, Adrastos still walked away after claiming three times as many souls as any opponent had in the near-millennia under my command. Nearly including the man to my right, who stretched his healing torso, jaw tightening with the motion, and making me straighten with concern.

"You alright?"

Ansel was still moving a little stiffer than I'd like to see, our disconnect from The Middle leaving his healing slow and blatantly painful.

One dark brow arched, daring me to challenge him as he drawled, "You worried about me, or something?"

"That was pretty fucking close, Callahan."

"Eh," Ansel said, shrugging a shoulder. "Just a love bite. Takes a hell of a lot more than that to kill me. We've had worse."

No, we hadn't. The two of us had never come closer to death than we had in the last four months. Hell, I'd never seen a soul come back from what The General had without getting them to The Middle.

"Damn straight," I agreed anyway. "You feel good about the plan? Where we're splitting ranks?"

"What's Ally say?"

"She's...off her game. Something happened out there. She's shutting me out. Doesn't wanna talk about it."

That got his attention. Ansel turned; a *v* carved between his eyes. The last time Alvara had shut me out was when we first found her in this life—after she'd unknowingly lost her mate.

Unwavering faith was sown into Ansel's reply. "She'll talk when she's ready."

"Always does."

"You think she blames herself for Adrastos getting away." When I just raised a brow, Ansel's lips quirked, as though the answer was self-explanatory. "It's Ally."

"It's Ally," I echoed. In a long, synchronized sigh, we looked back out toward the gulf as the waves collided into sand. Christ have mercy, if my calling ever truly lost her shit. It took a lot to push her that far, her determination to carry the burden of the world on her shoulders accompanied by a fierce conscience. We'd gotten our first taste of her wrath when Agamemnon took Freya. But if they ever pushed Alvara past her breaking point, the power welled within her would devastate the world.

"I still don't care for us being so divided without an anchor back in The Middle," I admitted, blowing out a heavy breath. "We're relying on fucking mortal tech to keep us connected."

"Do we have an alternative?" Ansel shifted a hand to his back pocket, a familiar tin click making me smile. The man rarely smoked, and when he did, the habit was as disciplined as the rest of him. *Just one.* "She's got it all laid out, Ar. Are we executing or deviating?"

"Fuck," I muttered, kicking off my shoes to ground in the sand. "I'm still betting on Ally."

"You know where my money stands."

"Alright. So, we execute."

"Porters round up the allies. We let her put all the players on the board. Alec and Fae head north to work with the Westerlunds. Freya, and the boys go lock in Reyna's allegiance. Marcus heads up connecting back with his contacts across the pond."

I sighed, adding, "We go round up the healers before Nat loses her entire team. Jesus. *Healers*. What the fuck is the angle there?"

"We'll figure it out. Just gotta find him."

"Put him down, find a damn door, and get our asses back to Grayshell. Not necessarily in that order." Never in Grayshell history had we needed an alternate route home. Every Commander in my lifeline simply jumped in and out, every soul utilizing the portal in the gathering hall where the wards made space for our movements. Still, any good soldier had a backup plan. Like Hazleharbor, Grayshell had back doors in. But when I'd gone to use the one in the mountains by my safehouse, it was gone, the link to The Middle along with it.

"Well, Ally thinks Nathara can help?"

"Ally thinks *my time in California* can help. That's all she's given me. Maybe Nat has a portal we can rig to get home? She said it has something to do with a book and some kind of a crown." When Ansel's lips slanted, I chuckled. "I know, man. It's vague as hell. We don't know how; we just know it works. We've done more with less. Speaking of, who all do we have working on tracking this fucker down? Fae has her ear to the ground. Westerlunds too."

"If anybody can find him, it's Aphaea Carter, or Damien Westerlund." Ansel's confidence forced a long breath into my lungs as I sensed the approach of still more company.

Damien Westerlund was a profound fighter, a phenomenal shifter, and upstanding father, but the skill set we were most indebted to was the one nobody cared to talk about. In all honesty, my eyes always glazed over before the man could get past 'a language of digits that allows me to exploit vulnerabilities.'

I'd never understood how he did it, but the shifter could work his way into and out of any database we had ever thrown at him undetected. The moment they'd gotten back to Chicago, D kissed his daughter, and took to the internet to set up his own web to drag the fucker into. His focus was so severe that his brothers, Marcus and Jason, stayed with him like sentinels. Bought him days to work.

There wasn't a camera in the country not plugged into his network now, facial recognition scanning for the sketch they had of Adrastos. The global network wouldn't be far behind.

"The Lord of the Dark Web will find answers." Alec's lilting voice made me smile despite myself as the shield sidled up on Ansel's other side.

Russet waves nearly long enough to pull back into a tie. Those amber eyes glinted, his omnipresent humor laced with the predatory strength he kept hidden beneath it. Alec was to Alvara what Ansel was to me. His loyalty was just as unflinching. That her team now possessed both of the hierarchy's best shields didn't feel coincidental. "There's nowhere to hide anymore. Between Ally, Fae, and Damien, we'll get him."

"We'll be ready this time," August said as he stepped up to my side, his jaw set in determination. I nodded, but pushed for a smile, pushed to relax for a beat. There was nothing about this victory that felt like a win, but we could damn well rally.

"Dammit, you guys couldn't give a man just a moment to think?" I ribbed, knocking elbows with the future Commander.

Ansel answered sardonically, the corner of his mouth twitching. "Have we *ever?*"

Alec chuckled before adding, "It's like you still don't know us, or something."

"Yeah, well...thanks." I huffed a breath, pulling a hand over the back of my aching neck. Exhaustion was filling my muscles with an ache that made it painful to keep my head up. My shoulder and side both still smarted where livid scars now stretched. Fuck, I missed The Middle.

"Hey," August said, tone steady as he clasped my shoulder, giving me a quick, reassuring squeeze. "Ball's in our court, Commander. We've got your back. It's your play. You'll make it count."

My play. Hell, I'd always known exactly what plays to call, exactly what strategy to implement. But I couldn't shake the feeling that we were already ten steps behind. What I needed was to hash this shit out.

"Pool house?"

"Pool house," Ansel agreed, running his fingers through dark waves before stiffly shifting that direction.

I glanced to August, asking, "You get anything from your girl?"

His mouth slanted, eyes sparking. "Fuck, I still love the sound of that."

"Never *stop* loving the sound of that," I ordered, side eyeing him. I liked the man. Really liked him, actually. They just...fit. And despite it violating every rule in the parent/guardian's handbook, I trusted him with my little shadow. Regardless... "Mate or not, my prior sentiment still stands."

August chuckled, sliding his hands in his pockets as the sand shifted beneath our feet. "We've chased each other for millennia. If she's not sick of me yet, I think we're in the clear, Commander."

"So. Learn anything?"

"Mmm, not so much. She's processing, I think. Something went... sideways out there."

In explanation, I stated the obvious conclusion. "He's breathing."

Ally took failure as a personal reflection of her value. Not just on our team, but as a living, breathing being. Something as vital as not finishing an enemy as formidable as Adrastos? That would eat her alive. The idea of her in that big house on the eve of the best day of this life, laden with guilt...made me sick. Of all people, she'd earned a moment of happiness.

"It's...personal," August clarified, his jaw ticking, brow furrowing.

"It's always personal," I countered. "If we're spilling blood, it's *fucking personal.*"

August nodded solemnly before looking up to survey the silent estate, the crash of waves fading behind us. "Give her time. She'll see her opportunity."

Ansel opened the door to the pool house, attempting to hold it for us as Alec scoffed, jumping forward to take the weight from him as he barked, "Like hell, gimpy, get the fuck inside."

"Piss off," Ansel growled. It took all my control not to laugh at his disgruntled expression.

"You, piss off. *Get inside.*"

"God dammit, Alec, I'm not an invalid," Ansel barked, earning mirroring smirks between me and my newest protégé as we flicked our attention to our squabbling companions. Well, at least his pride was still intact. That had to be a good sign.

"My mistake, didn't realize that purple stripe down your entire torso was a fucking fashion statement."

"You want one?" Ansel threatened, arching a brow, but stepping inside as Alec propped the door open for the rest of us. Despite his grumbling, I was almost certain The General's shoulders relaxed with relief as he moved toward a seat. Stubborn old bastard.

"Alright. One last time before shit hits the fan," I instructed. "Let's lay it out."

August looked to the clock on the stove as Alec moved for a bottle of brandy and I fetched the crystal glasses. "Alright," he agreed, but there was a warning lacing his tone. "One hour. And then we're all going to bed because my bride gets one motherfucking opportunity to just be selfish. And I'll be damned if we let yet another war take that away from her. Understood?"

"Yeah, yeah, understood," Alec said, mischief on his face as he slipped into his seat and reclined until he could kick his feet up.

Ansel and I responded simultaneously. Scoffing, I said, "I've been waiting to see her happy for *centuries*, kid. Get in line."

"She'll get her vacation, rookie."

"Five bucks says Freya has her ass up by sunrise." Nobody was dumb enough to take Alec's bet, because frankly, each of our lifelines interwoven with The Wraith promised the claim as fact.

"Alright," August grumbled, sliding a now full glass over to me.

I accepted, took a swig, and began spinning it, prompting the ice to click against the edges. "Ansel, give us the roster."

The Old General laid out the plan again, the players already on the board, and those we needed to move into position. He detailed the countries Ally was going to bring into the fold first when it came to human awareness of the conflict to come. When most the glasses were empty and we'd covered the map between us in pins and tokens representing our leaders and the covens still earthbound, I at last leaned back and filled my lungs to capacity.

"What do we have as far as known associates?" August asked, elbows braced on the table, curled fists resting against his lips.

"Not enough," Ansel answered succinctly. No need to clarify who we were talking about. There was only one target whose blood we'd race to spill. "You and Freya took out the first Reaper. The rest seemed like pawns."

"When the demon was still using Jones like a flesh puppet, it promised us that Adrastos was just the beginning. But...his men treated him like a King." August and Ally had replayed their experience on that muddy field for the group of us on more than one occasion, and as the young Commander remembered the way the Renown kneeled before the enemy, I shook my head, leaning back to cross my arms over my chest. This was the part that had me most confused.

"That bit still trips me up, too. But I know the Kings, Commanders, and Priestesses of the North American hierarchies. Not well. But I'd recognize the face." I always recognized the face. It's what made me good at being... well, *me*. "Most of them in Europe, certainly the majority when we add Marcus' network to the mix. I've never seen the fucker before."

"One thing at a time, boys," Alec cautioned. "We're working on a hell of a timeline here. Eight weeks to the first portals opening ain't shit. We need to make a move."

"Agreed," Ansel said simply. "Take the offensive. Well," his lip curled in amusement, turning pointedly to me. "Except for you. You get to go babysit some hippies."

I laughed, reaching out to squeeze my friend's shoulder. "You abandoning me, then?"

"Lana's still pissed at Ally about it, but no. We'll be there."

"That's what I thought."

"Just let me get inside Westerlund, catch this body back up. Make sure Freya gets settled."

"Good. So the real men will go lock in our alliances, while the two of you learn to make homemade soap and smell like patchouli," Alec said, but his smile was short lived as Ansel kicked the hind leg of his stool forward. It was only the shield's love of bending air that kept him upright. I bit back a laugh, but didn't bother concealing my smile.

"I mean, Ar's gotta track down where the fuck Adrastos put our portal," Alec said, steadying himself without missing a beat.

"Yeah," Ansel agreed flatly.

Alec kicked back on his hind legs again, shooting Ansel a glare that dared him to mess around twice. "What the fuck kind of enchantment locks us out and moves a fucking portal that's been in one spot for centuries?"

"The kind we need a magical mystery book to put right." I palmed my face, mind finally stilling enough to rest.

"You sure you don't want us on that, Commander?" August asked, balancing his glass on its edge, the amber liquid holding his attention captive.

"Nah," I said, scooting my chair back as our hour came to a close. "No point. Only a Commander can unlock it anyway."

All three of them nodded sagely, a precarious kind of silence settling between us as we all mulled over everything we'd gone over. Finally, August lifted his chin, expression twisted with something akin to sadness.

"I know I'm still the rookie, but I'm gonna miss you guys," he admitted at the tail end of a forlorn sigh, rubbing a thumb over the condensation on his glass.

"Me too, kid," I lamented. "Me too."

"Hey, Commander?" Alec asked, eyes flashing in a promise of something stupid weighing heavily in his mouth as he shifted his empty glass between his hands. "Once you've found Nathara's witch hunter, do us all a favor, and don't get eaten by a beast in The Middle."

I chuckled, shaking my head. "I'll do my best. Now. Our hour is up, and the lovebirds have more than earned our attention. Let's get some shuteye."

THANK YOU

To my readers: Thank you for taking a chance on a debut author, for betting on Ally, and making it to the final page. You guys are my freaking heroes.

Joel: Thank you for leaving me wild, for fanning my flames and pouring love, life and belief into me when I saw none. Thank you for making this possible, for fighting so hard so we could be free birds, for the endless cups of coffee served up how I like, and magically-materialized food and water (while I hyper focused for twelve hours at a time). Thank you for reminding me that Ally and August were still worth writing, all these years later. Love you baby.

Daddy: Thank you for taking a chance on an art school with a barefoot founder, an actual fiddler on the roof, and a group of misfit creatives. Your leap of faith saved my life, and now you can say your girls both did what we set out to do. Thank you for believing in me. For countless hours babysitting. For your ceaseless—and I do mean *ceaseless*—reminders that I was born to be a writer, and that I just needed to make my way back home. For teaching me to face my fears, that only I could spread my wings, and that the best things in life are worth fighting for with relentless ferocity.

Liddy Bug: For more than two decades, you have been the bright spot in all the darkness. Thank you for your unwavering loyalty, and endless encouragement. For countless cups of coffee, lofi beats and twinkle lights, for showing me how to make beauty out of the unexpected. Your drive to win, and inexhaustible ability to create something spectacular out of nothing is why this book exists.

My kiddos: If you're reading this, it better be circa 2036. Thank you for always making me smile. For sacrificing a year of our 'us time' so mommy could live her dream. Love you to the moon and back. Xoxo

Lili and Halaia: Dear baby Jesus, where do I start? My *two* Anam Cara. Thank you for believing in Grayshell. For speaking life into me. For straightening my endless mess of sauce-soaked noodles, for 3 am pots of coffee while we wrote and solved plot holes. For reading through the skeleton of this book until it began to form flesh. Thank you for talking me down on the countless panicked phone calls and 2am brainstorming explosions. I could never have gotten this to a first draft without you, let alone to the finish line. Thank you for loving me even though I perpetually over-caffeinated you, and am as easy to love as a tornado, wearing glitter and a hot pink feather boa.

Shay-la: FROM DAY ONE, BABY!! We're doing the damn thing. Thank you for being the goth to my glitter, for pushing boundaries, for bopping to tunes, for believing in me and being my ride or die. For being my safe space to ask all the stupid questions, and for believing in Grayshell from the moment I arrived, babbling about this crazy dream I had of this stupid-pretty, badass, half-angel psychic in an antique store. You're the real deal.

Darian, of M3zzamorphic Arts: Thank you for taking clips and descriptions, and my Grayshell playlist, and bringing them to life with art that made me cry.

Stef, at Seventhstar Art: For taking my incoherent babbling and curating the book cover and brand of my dreams! I still can't get over how beautiful your work is.

Heather: For taking over the things I suck at, and being my constant sounding board so I can get back to the good stuff haha 50% PA, 50% life raft.

Sam: In Sam we trust! Thank you for giving my babies such a beautiful refresher!! You are a badass.

ALSO BY S.J. BARNETT

ROMANTIC HIGH/URBAN FANTASY AS S.J. BARNETT

Commanding Flame And Shield (Grayshell Rising, book one)

Commanding Earth And Shadow (Grayshell Rising, book two)

CONTEMPORARY ROMANCE AS SYDNE BARNETT

Nomadic Rhodes

South of The Skyway (book 1)

Brewing Temptation (book 2)

Finding A Way Back Home (book 3)

The Hearts of Emerald Bay

(Rhodes universe continued, billionaire edition)

Salvaged Hearts

Mended Hearts (Coming Spring 2025, now available for pre-order)

Winning Hearts (Coming Summer 2025, now available for pre-order)

Catching Hearts (Coming Fall 2025, now available for pre-order)

ABOUT THE AUTHOR

Sydne Barnett is a lover of spunky, badass heroines, and heroes that embrace their wild. She's an avid reader, never turns down a good cup of coffee, loves hiking with her hubby, and lives for finding their next adventure.

If she's not writing, you can probably find her behind her camera, swimming, or curled up with a homemade pastry, watching Friends, HIMYM, or Gilmore Girls.

facebook.com/barnettbooktalk

instagram.com/barnettbooktalk

tiktok.com/@barnettbooktalk

amazon.com/author/sjbarnett